THE PAPER DRAGON

by EVAN HUNTER

THE PAPER

DELACORTE PRESS / NEW YORK

DRAGON

a novel by **EVAN HUNTER**

TO
ANITA

MONDAY

1

HE FELT GIDDY and foolish and awkward, and he also felt like a thief. He was fearful and elated and apprehensive and uncertain, but beneath it all he felt like a thief and this was confusing because it was he who had been wronged. And yet, he felt much the same as he had that day when he was eight years old and stole a box of crayons from the school supply closet.

Just that way, with the same sort of trembling nervousness, the same heady swiftness of triumph—he had stolen the crayons, he had got away without anyone having seen him, he had tucked them under his sweater with no one the wiser—coupled with guilt, the overriding shamefaced embarrassment sitting just behind his eyes, the sickly somewhat pale smile on his mouth, he could not understand this feeling of guilt. It was almost as if he were identifying fully with the real thief, experiencing the thief's own reaction to capture and exposure, that's the goddamn trouble with me, he thought, I empathize too easily.

He was a man of medium build, with black hair and brows, brown eyes darting nervously as he climbed the courthouse steps. There was an awesome scale to the architecture of the building, ten monstrous, white, Corinthian columns rising to support a windowed entablature, wide white steps flowing in a long horizontal swell toward brass revolving entrance doors, more windows ornately decorated with curvilinear bars. The solemn majesty of the law's trappings added to his nervousness, and yet he wanted to yell aloud as he entered the building, wanted to shatter the serenity of these hallowed marbled halls, but the nervousness persisted, the feeling that *he,* and not James Driscoll, was the thief.

He walked into one of the waiting elevators, and then stood in the far corner of the car, worrying his lower lip, staring at the floor indicator as the car climbed, come on, come on. It was December, and the car was briskly cool, but he could feel the sweat trickling from under his arms in a slow, sliding descent over his ribs. The car doors opened at last. He stepped uncertainly into the seventh-floor corridor. A bank of gray elevator doors, six in all, were ranged on either side of the windowless corridor, interspersed with wooden doors along its length and on either end. The corridor was rather like a badly designed room, too long for its width, dimly lighted, divided at its halfway point by the double doors to 705 and 706, which were the courtrooms. The doors were constructed of what seemed like heavy oak, panels repeating the low paneled ceiling, bronze studs shaped like daisies punctuating the wood, a brass knob set on each right-hand door. He saw the numerals 705 in bronze on the door opposite him, and was walking across the corridor toward it when Sidney Brackman looked up from the water fountain. He was forty-eight years old, a short undistinguished-looking person wearing a brown suit and shoes, a striped brown tie on his white shirt. His hair was prematurely gray, as was his closely cropped mustache. He turned as Arthur approached, and then extended his hand quickly and said, "Good morning, Arthur, how do you feel?"

"I'm worried," Arthur said.

"You have nothing to worry about. You'll make a good witness. Do you remember all the points we covered?"

"Yes, I remember."

"Good. We'll go over those points in court, you'll tell everything in your own words. It's the truth that will win this case for us."

"I hope so."

"I *know* so. I have no doubt. It's been a long road, Arthur, but the end is in sight, and the end will be victorious."

"How long will the trial last?"

"I imagine it will be over by Wednesday. Thursday at the very latest."

"That's what I thought. It seems like such a short time."

"A short time? For what?"

"To present everything. I mean, so the judge'll understand."

"McIntyre's a smart judge, Arthur. *And* a fair one. I know him from when he was first out of law school. He was a brilliant lawyer even then. Brilliant. He'll give you a fair hearing, and he'll make a fair decision."

"I hope so."

"Try to appear a little more confident on the stand, eh?" Brackman said, and smiled.

"I'll try," Arthur said. "But I'd be much happier with a jury."

"Juries are unpredictable. Besides, you'll remember that I *did* ask for a jury. But Willow made a motion to strike the demand because we were asking for an accounting of every dollar. Willow's point was that historically . . ."

"You know all this law talk goes completely over my head."

"Yes, I know that, but I wouldn't want you to think I'd made a mistake. I haven't made any mistakes so far, Arthur, not that I know of. We *did* ask for a jury. But it was ruled that an equity action, such as this is, has always been tried in a chancery court rather than a law court. The historical precedent goes all the way back to England."

"I don't know anything about historical precedent," Arthur said. "It just seems to me that our chances would have been better with a jury."

"Our chances are excellent just the way they are, Arthur. Now please don't start getting despondent. I know you get into these despondent moods every now and then that are difficult to—"

"I'm not despondent."

"Good. Leave everything to me. Please. Just answer the questions I put to you as truthfully as you can, and everything will be all right."

"Is that a guarantee?"

Brackman smiled again. "No, Arthur. Nothing in the law is a guarantee, justice is not infallible. That's what makes practicing law so interesting. Let's go inside, shall we?"

The courtroom seemed too large for the scant handful of people it contained. Wood-paneled walls endlessly echoed themselves, like flecked mirrors repeating the same dull theme, a pattern broken only by the windowed wall facing the entrance. The windows were open just a crack to the winter street below. The sounds of traffic rose indolently, entering the courtroom in muted tones. A fierce December wind eddied in the right angle of wall-against-wall just outside the windows, and then fanned over the sills to riffle the papers on the long leather-topped tables. Jonah Willow and his assistant were at one of those tables, talking in normal speaking voices that somehow seemed like whispers. At the other end of the same table, Samuel Genitori, the attorney for API, leaned over to say something to his associate. As Arthur followed Brackman to the plaintiff's table, he heard Willow's assistant burst into laughter, and the sound infuriated him.

Seated in the otherwise empty jury box to the right of the judge's bench were James Driscoll and his wife. Arthur studiously avoided looking at either of them. The lone spectator, on one of the six benches at the rear of the room, was a thin boy carrying a spiral notebook imprinted with Columbia University's seal. There was an air of quiet displacement in the room, as though everyone were waiting for an event that would most certainly be canceled. When Judge McIntyre entered from his chambers at ten o'clock sharp, and the clerk called "All rise!" Arthur felt a new rush of panic, an urgent need to bolt from this arena with its alien trappings and its professional cold-eyed combatants. Quickly, he glanced toward Brackman to see if his fear had communicated itself, and then immediately dried the palms of his hands on his trouser legs.

"The United States District Court, Southern District of New York, is now in session," the clerk intoned, "the Honorable Frank H. McIntyre presiding. Take your seats, please. Arthur Nelson Constantine versus James Driscoll et al. Are all sides ready?"

Almost in a chorus, Brackman and the defense attorneys said, "Ready, your Honor."

"All ready, your Honor," the clerk repeated.

"Are you representing the plaintiff, Mr. Brackman?" McIntyre asked.

"Yes, your Honor."

"Are you ready to proceed?"

"Yes, your Honor."

"Then let's proceed."

"I would like Mr. Constantine to take the stand, please," Brackman said.

Arthur rose and walked toward the witness chair. He was having difficulty breathing, and he was certain he would stumble and fall before he reached the front of the courtroom. The clerk held out the Bible. Arthur put his left hand on it, and then raised his right hand.

"Arthur Nelson Constantine, you do solemnly swear that the testimony you shall give to the Court in this issue shall be the truth, the whole truth, and nothing but the truth, so help you God?"

"I do," Arthur said.

The clerk nodded briefly and then moved to a small table adjacent to and below the judge's bench. He put the Bible on one corner of the table and then moved his stenotab into place, fingers poised over the keys. Arthur climbed the two steps to the witness chair, glanced up briefly at the judge, whose swivel chair was parallel to his and a step higher, and then looked away. Sidney Brackman walked slowly toward Arthur, smiled encouragingly, and then said, "Mr. Constantine, what do you do for a living?"

"I'm a writer," Arthur answered. His voice was too low, he

knew he could not be heard. "A writer," he repeated more loudly.

"Do you write under your own name?"

"Yes, sir. Yes."

"How long have you been employed as a writer?"

"Since 1946."

"Can you tell us what works you've written, Mr. Constantine?"

"Since 1946?"

"Yes, since 1946," Brackman said.

"Yes, well . . ." He hesitated. For a moment, he had forgotten the question. He looked hopefully at Brackman who seemed completely unaware of his discomfort. They had been talking about 1946, hadn't they? Should he ask what the question was, something about, oh yes, "Yes," he said, "the first thing I wrote after my release from the United States Army was a play called *Catchpole*."

"Mr. Constantine, are you familiar with this manuscript?"

"Yes, I'm familiar with it," he said, scarcely looking at it.

"Is this your name on the title page of the manuscript?"

"It is."

"Are you the sole author of this manuscript?"

"I am."

"Is this the play titled *Catchpole* which you wrote after your release from the United States Army in 1946?"

"Yes," he said, and wondered if he were supposed to say anything more about it at this point.

"I offer the manuscript in evidence," Brackman said, and handed it to the clerk.

"No objection," Willow said.

"No objection," Genitori repeated.

"I also offer in evidence the copyright registration certificate of the play."

Willow rose from his chair behind the defense table. "Your Honor," he said, "before trial, we conceded that the play was registered with the Copyright Office and a certificate granted in August of 1947. In fact, we conceded that it wouldn't be necessary to do anything more than offer the manuscript in evidence."

"Mr. Genitori, do you so concede for API?" McIntyre asked.

"I do."

Brackman nodded and approached the witness chair again. "Mr. Constantine," he said, "you have testified that you've been a writer since 1946. What else have you written besides this play?"

"Well," Arthur said, "I've been involved mostly with motion pictures and television."

"What films or television plays have you written?"

"Do you want me to go all the way back?"

"Please."

"Well, in 1948 I worked for Columbia under contract—Columbia Pictures. I wrote two films for them. Do you want the titles?"

"Please."

He was beginning to feel a bit more at ease. This wasn't going too badly after all. They were simply restating for the judge all the points they had gone over time and again in Brackman's office. He found himself relaxing. He crossed his legs and glanced at the judge, and then turned to Brackman and said, "The first was an adaptation of a *Collier's* story, a Western. I don't remember the title of the original story, but the movie was called *Brother to the Sun,* and was a very successful film. I then worked on an adaptation—or really a translation, I suppose you might say—of *King Lear*. I worked for several months with another writer on this, trying to get it into suitable form for the screen, and then the project was abandoned." He felt more and more relaxed. He looked at the judge once again, tempted to smile but restraining the urge, and then said, conversationally, "Olivier had already done *Hamlet,* you see, and I think Orson Welles was getting ready to release his *Macbeth,* and the feeling was that the trend had already peaked. Besides, it was proving very difficult to get a good screenplay from something as complex as *Lear*."

"Now this film *Brother to the Sun* for which you wrote the screenplay . . ."

"Yes," he said.

". . . you mentioned that it was a very successful film. Just what does that mean?"

"It grossed nine million dollars."

"I see. Go on, Mr. Constantine. What did you do after you worked on *King Lear?*"

"I left Columbia early in 1949, and did several films for Metro-Goldwyn-Mayer. The first of these was—"

"Excuse me," Willow said, rising. "Your Honor, I hesitate to interrupt the witness's testimony, but it seems to me that his career subsequent to the writing of *Catchpole* is not relevant at this point."

"I'd like to see where counsel is heading," McIntyre answered. "I hope this won't go on forever, though, Mr. Brackman."

"No, your Honor, it won't. As a matter of fact, Mr. Constantine, in order to save time, perhaps you could simply tell us how long you were employed by Metro as a writer?"

"From March of 1949 to February of 1952."

"For three years, is that correct?"

"Yes, almost three years to the day."

"And how many films did you write for them during that period of employment?"

"Eight films. A total of eight films."

"And you left Metro in February of 1952, is that correct?"

"Yes, sir."

"What did you do then?"

"In March of 1952, I was employed by API under contract to write and direct four films for them."

"By API, are you referring to one of the defendants in this action, Artists-Producers-International, also referred to as Kessler, Inc.?"

"I am."

"And you have testified that in 1952 you were hired to write and direct four motion pictures for API, otherwise known as Kessler, Inc.?"

"I was. I did so testify."

Genitori rose suddenly and said, "Your Honor, may the record show that the title of the defendant, Kessler, Inc., was changed by court order to Artists-Producers-International in January of this year?"

"Let the record show it."

Brackman seemed annoyed by the interruption. He looked at Arthur sympathetically, cleared his throat, and asked, *"Did* you, in fact, write and direct those four films for API?"

"I worked on one of them which was later produced and directed by someone else," Arthur said.

"What was the title of that film?"

"Area Seven."

"And you say it was produced?"

"Yes, sir."

"When was it shown?"

"Released, do you mean?"

"Yes, released."

"In May of 1953. It was nominated for an Academy Award that year."

"Did it receive the Academy Award?"

"No, sir. *From Here to Eternity* did."

"Your Honor," Willow said, "I must repeat my objection to the plaintiff's going into what happened after the writing of *Catchpole."*

"If your Honor please," Brackman answered, "I think this is relevant in two respects: one, principally, is to indicate that Mr. Constantine was actively employed by API from March of 1952 until April of—"

"Your Honor, witness has not yet testified as to the length of his employment."

"Nevertheless, Mr. Willow," McIntyre said, "the witness's employment by API would certainly seem to be relevant."

"And also, your Honor," Brackman said, "defendants might wish to create the impression that *Catchpole,* which was admittedly a failure, was Mr. Constantine's one and only creative endeavor. I want to indicate that Mr. Constantine is a man of recognized talents. I will certainly afford Mr.

Willow the same opportunity to enumerate James Driscoll's writing credits when—"

"Objection overruled, Mr. Willow."

Brackman smiled thinly. "Mr. Constantine," he said, "can you tell me when your employment at API terminated?"

"I was there for more than two years. I left in April of 1954."

"After having worked on the screenplay for *Area Seven* which—"

"Yes, that's right."

"—was later nominated for an Academy Award."

"Correct."

"Why did you leave API?"

"There was a difference of opinion about the movies I was being asked to write and direct."

"To make this brief then, Mr. Constantine, would it be accurate to say that from 1946 to 1954 your sole employment was as a writer and/or director?"

"That is entirely accurate."

"And without going into laborious detail, would it be equally accurate to state that since you left API in April of 1954, you have continued to work as a writer and/or director of screenplays and television plays, sometimes under contract and sometimes on a freelance basis?"

"That is equally true, yes."

"Are you actively engaged on a project now, Mr. Constantine?"

"Yes, I am."

"Could you tell us—"

"Your Honor, haven't we already indicated that Mr. Constantine is a man of recognized talents?" Willow asked.

"Let's try to make this brief, Mr. Brackman," McIntyre said.

Brackman nodded. To Arthur he said, "Can you tell us what that project is?"

"We are currently casting my new play for Broadway production," Arthur answered.

"Who is producing the play?"

"Stuart Selig and Oscar Stern."

"And are you the sole author of the play?"

"I am."

"Mr. Constantine, I would now like to take you back to your other play, the play called *Catchpole*, which you testified you wrote in 1946."

"That's correct," Arthur said.

"Was this play *Catchpole* ever produced?"

"Yes, sir, it was."

"Where was it produced?"

"It opened at the Fulton Theatre here in New York and it ran for twelve days."

"When was that?"

"In October of 1947. October 14th, I believe the date was. And it ran until the 25th, through the 25th."

"Had it been seen anywhere else prior to its Broadway opening?"

"Yes, sir. There were a series of previews held while we were still rehearsing the play in a loft on Second Avenue."

"Previews? For whom?"

"For college students."

"Of which colleges?"

"C.C.N.Y., Hunter, Brooklyn College, L.I.U., Pratt Institute, and several others."

"Was there a charge for these performances?"

"No, sir. We were still in rehearsal and we wanted the reaction of college students, since this was a play about young men in a time of intense personal strife."

Brackman paused, moved away from the witness stand, glanced at Willow, and then slowly walked back to confront Arthur again. His voice lowering to a solemn pitch, he asked, "Have you read the novel *The Paper Dragon?*"

"Yes, sir."

"Have you seen the movie *The Paper Dragon?*"

"Yes, sir."

"Can you tell us when you read the book?"

"I saw the movie in September of 1964, and I read the book shortly after that. A week or so afterwards."

"What course of action did you pursue after seeing the movie?"

"Well, I had been out of town working on a television pilot for MCA, Music Corporation of America. The pilot dealt with a team of construction workers who move around from one part of the country to the other—"

"Your Honor," Willow said, "the answer is not responsive."

"Please answer the question," McIntyre said.

"What was the question?"

The clerk consulted his notes. "What course of action did you pursue after seeing the movie?" he repeated.

Arthur nodded. "I was trying to explain that I had been out of town for several months because we were visiting the site of a dam in construction . . ."

"Yes, what did you do when you came back?" Brackman prodded.

". . . which is why I missed the opening of the movie, and all the hullabaloo around New York at that time. In any case, when I got back to the city, I went out with a young lady one night, and she said, 'Have you seen *The Paper Dragon?*' I didn't know what *The Paper Dragon* was, and I said so. She then told me that it was a direct steal from my play, and that I had better make sure I saw it."

"And did you then go to see it?"

"Yes, I did."

"And after seeing it, did you take the matter to an attorney?"

"Yes, I did."

Brackman nodded, walked back to the plaintiff's table, and returned with his hands full. "I would like to offer in evidence," he said, "this book which is the hard-cover edition of *The Paper Dragon,* as written by James Driscoll and published by Mitchell-Campbell Books, Inc."

"Any objection?"

"No."

"Mr. Genitori, any objection?"

"None."

"I also offer in evidence the reprint edition of *The Paper*

Dragon, published by Camelot Books, Inc., New York, a subsidiary of Mitchell-Campbell, Inc."

"No objection."

"No objection."

"I offer in evidence the shooting script of the film *The Paper Dragon,* as written by Ralph Knowles, and produced by Kessler, Inc."

"Is this being offered as against the defendant API only?" Willow asked. "Or is it offered as against the defendant Mitchell-Campbell?"

"It is being offered against API."

"No objection."

"No objection."

"Your Honor, the defendants have previously conceded publication of *The Paper Dragon,*" Brackman said, "and also of the motion picture."

"Conceded."

"Conceded."

Brackman returned to the witness stand. "Mr. Constantine," he said, "you have stated that between March of 1952 and April of 1954 you were employed by API as a writer-director, and that you worked on one film while you were so employed, a motion picture titled *Area Seven,* which was later nominated for an Academy Award."

"Yes, sir."

"Did you at any time during your period of employment at API have opportunity to submit . . . I'll rephrase that, your Honor. Did you ever submit the manuscript of *Catchpole* to anyone at API while you were employed there?"

"I did."

"To whom did you submit the manuscript? Can you remember the names?"

"I can."

"Would you tell us, please?"

"I first showed the manuscript to a man named Matthew Jackson, with whom I was working on *Area Seven.*"

"What were Mr. Jackson's duties?"

"He was under contract as a writer at API, and was sort of

overseeing the *Area Seven* project, since I was a new writer there and had never directed anything before. He was working very closely with me on the screenplay. We got to know each other rather well, and I thought I would show him a copy of *Catchpole* in the hope he could see movie possibilities in it."

"Did he indeed see movie possibilities in it?"

"No."

"Did you not, in fact, later have a conversation with Mr. Jackson wherein he definitely stated that Kessler's did not wish . . ."

"That's right."

". . . to buy the motion picture rights to *Catchpole?*"

"We had a conversation about it, yes."

"Your Honor, that was a leading question," Willow said.

"I am refreshing his memory on a point that is already in the record," Brackman replied.

"You were leading the witness, Mr. Brackman," McIntyre said, and Brackman shrugged in resignation.

"Did you have a conversation with Mr. Jackson?" he asked.

"I did," Arthur answered.

"Would you repeat the content of that conversation?"

"Jackson said, 'This is tremendous, but you know as well as I that this company is still back in the thirties with its musicals and silly romances. I think they'd be leery of an Army theme that tries to show the stupidity and foolish waste of war, especially since we've had this Korean thing since World War II. But I'd like to hold onto it, because I really like it immensely and if I can do anything for it, I will.' "

"Did Mr. Jackson ever return the manuscript to you?"

"No."

"To whom else at API did you show the manuscript?"

"Well, there was Joe Edelson, who was at that time head of API's story department. And Rudy Herdt, who was a producer, and Iris Blake, who was also in the story department."

"Were there any others?"

"Yes, I also showed it to Betty Alweiss, who was Mr. Kessler's personal secretary."

"What were the reactions of these various people to whom you showed the manuscript?"

"Their reactions—their collective reaction, I should say—was basically the same. They all liked the play, they thought it had some important things to say about a situation that needed comment. But they felt API wasn't ready to do anything as strong as this was, not right then, anyway. The collective reaction, I would say, was that the play was too outspoken, that the United States wasn't ready to take criticism of its armed forces, not when we had just come through a major conflict and also a minor one in Korea, which happens to be the setting of *The Paper Dragon*. To my mind, there was no question that everyone who read the script thought—"

"Your Honor, I regret having to interrupt the witness again," Willow said, "but he has just now made a statement as to the operation of his mind, and I think you'll agree that is clearly inadmissible."

"Sustained."

"Mr. Constantine," Brackman said, with a sigh directed at Willow, "would you please tell us what was said about the script, and not what you surmised or thought?"

"That's all that was said about it. They all liked the script, but they felt it was too strong for API to do."

"Were any of these scripts ever returned to you?"

"No."

"As I understand it then, Mr. Constantine—and please correct me if I'm wrong—during the period of time between March 1952 and April 1954, you showed a copy of your previously produced play *Catchpole* to five people at API?"

"Five people, that's correct."

"Were these five people all executives?"

"Not all of them. But they all had the power to recommend a story for purchase."

"And your story was not recommended."

"My play."

"Your play."

"No, it was not recommended for purchase."

"Nor were any of the copies returned."

"No, they were not returned."

"Mr. Constantine, have you examined your work *Catchpole* and also the book and movie versions of *The Paper Dragon?*"

"I have."

"What did your examination reveal?"

"That there are close similarities between *Catchpole* and *The Paper Dragon.*"

"Similarities to both the book *and* the film?"

"Both the book and the film, yes."

The courtroom was silent. Brackman took a deep breath. "What similarities did your examination reveal?" he asked.

"Your Honor, if I may . . ."

"Yes, Mr. Willow?"

"I think we might be able to save a little time here, if the plantiff is willing."

"How might we do that, Mr. Willow?"

"The plaintiff and his attorneys were good enough to prepare—for the pretrial examinations—several charts containing the alleged similarities between the works in question. These are rather detailed as to specific language, plot structure, and character. I would have no objection to the offer of these charts at this point."

Brackman shook his head. "I wish the witness to testify to the similarities in his own words."

"His own words are already on the record," Willow said.

"Your Honor," Genitori said, rising, "we have reams and reams of charts prepared by the witness and his attorneys. The entire matter is before us ad infinitum."

"If his Honor will allow," Brackman answered, "I would like to bring the matter before us once again—*from* the witness, *in* person, *before* this Court."

"I will allow it. Let him proceed."

Arthur looked at the judge, and then at Brackman. Brackman nodded.

"I would like to start with the thematic similarity of my play and the other works," Arthur said.

"Go ahead, Mr. Constantine."

As Arthur began speaking, he could feel the alert presence of James Driscoll sitting in the jury box on his left, patiently watching with the cold blue guileless eyes of a thief. He could feel the judge erect and attentive beside him at the raised bench on his right, someone only vaguely defined, someone who had the power to rule on what could and could not be said, someone who would in the final analysis make the sole decision as to whether he, Arthur Constantine, had been wronged. He could feel, too, and it added to his sense of security, the enormous paneled dignity of the courtroom, a federal court, copyright offenses were tried in federal courts, the American flag to the right of the bench, the wan December sunlight outside. He was completely at ease now, confident that the truth would be heard and justice would be done. His earlier panic, in fact, now seemed inexplicable, like the terror of a very young child waking in the dark.

"In my play," he said, "I was attempting to illustrate—"

"Your Honor," Willow said at once, "I move to strike that from the record. Whatever Mr. Constantine *attempted* to illustrate is not relevant to the issue before this Court."

"He is trying to be responsive," McIntyre said. "I will allow it."

"I maintain, your Honor, that any similarities must be solely between the works in question."

"I would agree to that."

"And that therefore the author's intent is irrelevant."

"I believe I will allow him to tell it in his own words, Mr. Willow. I think this will take us where we want to go."

"Does your Honor mean the end of the trial?"

"No, I'm referring to the testimony relating to similarities. The end of the trial, however, is another consummation devoutly to be wished. Please go on, Mr. Constantine."

"Thematically, my play deals with the lunacy of war," Arthur said. "My hero is a new lieutenant who feels that human life is more important than the quarrels of nations, and this theme is stated in Act I, Scene 4, pages 21 and 22 of *Catchpole*. This is also the theme of *The Paper Dragon*, where the hero is the same new lieutenant who feels exactly the same way, and who voices his feelings on pages 121, 122, 123, and 124 of the book."

"Do you consider this theme unique?" Brackman asked.

"I do not, sir."

"Do you consider it original?"

"I do not, sir."

"Do you consider it your exclusive property?"

"No, sir. But this suit is not based on a similarity of theme alone. In fact, if my play had developed its theme along certain lines and the novel had developed the very *same* theme along different lines, I would never have brought suit at all."

"How *are* these themes developed?"

"They are developed along *identical* lines," Arthur said. "To begin with, the hero of my play is shipped to the Pacific to wage war against the Japanese on Eniwetok. The hero of *The Paper Dragon* is also shipped to the Pacific to wage war, this time against the enemy forces in Korea. Now the men in the platoon to which the lieutenant is assigned, and specifically the men who are in one squad of that platoon—"

"Excuse me," Brackman said, "but are we discussing plot or character?"

"This is plot," Arthur said.

"Very well, go on."

"The men in the squad are described in Act I, Scene 1, page 3 of my play as 'battle-weary and battle-hardened.' In the book, the men in the squad are described with the words—may I have a copy of the book, please?"

"Certainly," Brackman said. The clerk handed him the exhibit copy, which he in turn handed to Arthur. Arthur quickly found the page.

"These are the words Driscoll uses to describe *his* squad. This is on page 42. 'Weary-eyed and cynical, they studied their new lieutenant in his college boy crewcut and freshly issued fatigues, and wondered how he could possibly lead them into hell.' In short, the men in both combat squads are hardened veterans in juxtaposition to inexperienced commanding officers—and the word 'weary' is used to describe them in both works."

"Go on, please."

"The first time Lieutenant Mason—who is the hero of my play—leads his platoon into battle, this particular squad is ambushed and a young private is killed by a sniper. In the book, this basic situation has been altered only slightly. The lieutenant's name has been changed, of course—to Cooper— and the incident of the sniper takes place *before* his arrival in Korea. It is a major this time who is killed by a sniper who has infiltrated the lines. That's on page 18. But the plot development is essentially the same, and it continues along parallel lines.

"In my play, for example, the men come to resent Mason enormously because they hold him responsible for the private's death. This is stated in Act I, Scene 3, pages 14 and 15. And whereas Mason tries to reach them in various ways, they remain resentful. In the book, the men resent Cooper because he is taking the dead major's place. That's page 51. The same attempts to reach the men are present, and the same continuing resentment is there. Moreover, the biggest troublemaker in Cooper's platoon is a man named Private Colman, and it is implied on page 56 that he has had homosexual relations with the dead major."

"You mean when he was alive, of course," Brackman said, and McIntyre burst into laughter. "I was trying to clarify," Brackman said quickly, "the relationship between—"

"Yes, of course," McIntyre said, still laughing. "Go ahead, Mr. Constantine."

"I mention this homosexual attachment," Arthur said, "only because in my play, a senior officer is also suspected of homosexuality and is sent back from the front to a hospital unit. This is in Act II, Scene 2, pages 6 and 7. It is there that he becomes the patient of an Army nurse who later falls in love with my hero. I think it is significant that an Army nurse appears in *The Paper Dragon* on page 124, and that a love affair between her and Lieutenant Cooper develops along lines parallel to my play."

"Your Honor," Willow said, rising, "I wonder if I might interrupt to ask Mr. Brackman how long this will take. I think we all agree that the final test in a case of this sort is a comparison of the works themselves. Mr. Constantine's opinion as to similarities is not in my judgment competent testimony. Couldn't we shorten this by putting in a paper calling your Honor's attention to the alleged similarities? I would certainly have no objection to that. But if Mr. Constantine intends to go on interminably, I must raise an objection."

"Mr. Brackman?" McIntyre asked. "What do you say to that?"

"I quite agree with Mr. Willow that a comparison of the works themselves is the heart of the issue involved here. But that is exactly what we *are* doing, your Honor, comparing the works themselves. As for the second objection, Mr. Constantine's testimony is *definitely* competent, and I believe precedent will so indicate."

"How much longer do you suppose he will be testifying, Mr. Brackman? Concerning these similarities?"

"The similarities of plot, do you mean?"

"I mean *all* the similarities."

"There are several more similarities of plot, your Honor, and then we had hoped to go into character and specific language."

"Won't there be an overlap between plot and character?"

"Only to a limited extent."

"How long will it take to outline the plot similarities?"

"Mr. Constantine?"

"Only five or ten minutes, your Honor," Arthur answered.

"And the others?"

"At least forty-five minutes, your Honor," Brackman said. "Perhaps longer."

"Well, I notice that Mr. Constantine has been making frequent reference to the prepared charts. Couldn't we simply submit those, as Mr. Willow suggested? I know you want the Court to form an impression of your witness, but I feel we've already done that sufficiently. I do think any means of saving time would be appreciated."

"Your Honor, I would prefer to do it this way," Brackman said. "If it will help, perhaps the witness can leave out the specific page references wherever possible."

"I stand on my objection," Willow said. "I do not see why Mr. Constantine cannot testify that he prepared these charts, and then offer them in evidence as an aid to the Court. *Solely* as an aid to the Court, your Honor, and *not* as expert testimony. To that, I would have no objection."

"Mr. Willow, I don't like to limit an attorney's latitude," McIntyre said. "If Mr. Brackman wishes to present his case in this manner, I think it only fair to allow him to proceed. But if he can think of another way to shorten the testimony, in addition to eliminating page numbers, I think we would all be enormously grateful."

"If he's going to eliminate page references," Willow said, "can he supply a list of them so—"

"I assumed . . ."

"Yes, of course."

". . . that he planned to do that, Mr. Willow."

"So that we may have them for reference during the cross, your Honor."

"Certainly. Please proceed, Mr. Constantine."

"In order to save time," Arthur said, "it might be possible to combine plot *and* character in explaining these three soldiers. Would you want me to do that?"

"Which three soldiers?" McIntyre asked.

"Private Colman in the novel, and Corporal Janus and Colonel Peterson in my play."

"Yes, please do," McIntyre said. "We would appreciate any means of saving time."

"Just so we can keep this straight," Arthur said, "let me again say that Private Colman is the prime troublemaker in the novel, and is also suspected of having had homosexual relations with the major. In fact, there is a stream-of-consciousness passage beginning on page 212—"

"We want to leave out the page references," Brackman reminded.

"Yes, I'm sorry. I was going to say that this interior monologue clearly indicates, *beyond* mere suspicion, that Private Colman *did* have homosexual relations with the major. In my play, the prime troublemaker is a man named Corporal Janus, but in addition there is the homosexual colonel who is sent up for observation—he later goes psycho, but that's beside the point. The point is the *two* characters in my play, Corporal Janus and Colonel Peterson, are *combined* in Driscoll's book to form the single character named Private Colman. In other words, Driscoll has taken a troublemaker and a homosexual and put them together to form a homosexual troublemaker."

"Did you find any other evidence of this merger?"

"Yes. The private's first name in Driscoll's book is Peter. His full name is Peter Colman. If we put this alongside the name of the character in my play, Colonel Peterson, we see that one name is an anagram of the other."

"Your Honor," Willow said, rising, "an anagram transposes the exact letters of a word or sentence to form a *new* word or sentence. There is no such transposition here, and I object to the misleading use of the word."

"May I amend that?" Arthur asked.

"Please do," McIntyre said.

"May I simply say that the names, when reversed, are very similar?"

"Shall I strike the anagram reference?" the clerk asked.

"Strike it," McIntyre replied.

"Please go on," Brackman said.

"Where was I?" Arthur asked.

"You were explaining . . ."

"Oh, yes, the combining of two characters to form a single character. The final evidence of this is what happened in the film based on the novel. For some unexplainable reason, the character named Peter Colman in the book has once more become two *separate* characters in the film. One of them is still Colman the troublemaker, but he is no longer homosexual. The other is a corporal who does not appear in the book, and who is very *definitely* homosexual. In other words, the screenwriter reversed Driscoll's copying process, and went back to the original play to recreate a character who was in the play but not in the book."

"Are these characters important to the play?"

"They are important to the play, the book, *and* the movie. Without them, the plot would stand still. In fact, it is Janus in my play and Colman in the book who suggest that the lieutenant be murdered."

"How do they plan to murder him?"

"In my play, a Sergeant D'Agostino volunteers to shoot the lieutenant from ambush. In the book, the men plan to lead the lieutenant into a Chinese stronghold where he will be killed. The motive is identical in both works, only the means differ slightly."

"Does the lieutenant actually get killed?" Brackman asked.

"Again, there is only a very slight difference in story line," Arthur said. "In my play, the psychopathic colonel steals a bayonet and escapes his guard on the night of the planned murder. He accidentally stumbles on Sergeant D'Agostino where he is waiting to ambush Lieutenant Mason. There is a struggle during which D'Agostino is stabbed and killed by the ranting colonel. And there is speculation later as to whether D'Agostino actually sacrificed himself in order to avoid having to murder the lieutenant."

"And how has this been changed in the book?"

"Your Honor," Willow said, "I have let one such allegation pass, but I must object to . . ."

"Sustained. Please rephrase the question, Mr. Brackman."

"Can you tell us the plot sequence in the book?" Brackman said.

"In the book, Lieutenant Cooper realizes at the last moment that the men are leading him into a death trap. But he also recognizes that his scout, Sergeant Morley, is in danger of losing *his* life as well. He takes the point from Morley, and sacrifices himself to the Chinese guns."

"How does your play end, Mr. Constantine?"

"It ends when the men in the squad, shaken by the turn of events, come to realize the idiocy of war, and gain a new respect for their lieutenant. The troublemaker, Corporal Janus, is exposed and court-martialed."

"And how does the book end?"

"The book ends when the men in the squad, touched by the lieutenant's sacrifice, come to realize the idiocy of war, and gain a new respect for him. The troublemaker, Private Colman, is exposed and court-martialed."

The courtroom was silent. Brackman looked up at the judge, and then turned away from him, nodding his head as though in silent agreement with an evident truth.

"Does that conclude your testimony concerning similarities of plot?" he asked Arthur.

"Yes, sir, it does."

"Would you tell us now—"

"Forgive me for interrupting, Mr. Brackman," McIntyre said, "but as I indicated earlier in chambers, I have an appointment this afternoon which necessitates my leaving at two-thirty. I was hoping we could take a very short recess now—aren't you tired, Mr. Constantine?"

"Thank you, your Honor, I'm fine," Arthur said.

"Well, I thought we might take a ten-minute recess now, and then perhaps continue without a lunch recess, adjourning at two, or a little after if we have to. Would anyone have any objection to that?"

"We would have no objection," Willow said. "But Mr. Constantine and his attorney may be exceedingly hungry."

"We would have no objection to continuing through the lunch recess," Brackman said dryly. "And we will try to conclude the direct by two o'clock, your Honor."

"I have no objection," Genitori said.

2

HE HAD RECEIVED what he supposed were stock words of encouragement from Brackman—You're doing fine, Arthur, you're coming across very well, I think the judge is considerably impressed—and then had left him in the courtroom with his partner. Now, standing near a door marked STAIRWAY at one end of the gray corridor, he lighted a second cigarette and glanced briefly at the closed courtroom doors. He honestly did not know how he was coming across, he had never been very sure of himself as a speaker. He felt that Willow was objecting too much and too energetically, and he suspected that Brackman was losing more points than he was winning, but he was completely ignorant of his own performance, grateful only that his earlier nervousness had miraculously dissipated.

Willow and his assistant came out of the courtroom and walked toward Arthur, heading for the men's room, he supposed. Willow was a tall ungainly man, and he moved with the uncertain awkwardness of a large water bird, neck craned forward, head bobbing, hair uncombed and hanging on his forehead, black-rimmed spectacles reflecting the pale light of the ceiling fixtures. Arthur supposed he was in his late thirties, but there was about him a boyish vitality that made him seem even younger. Neither he nor his assistant, a squat, very dark Negro wearing a gray tweed suit, even glanced at

Arthur in passing. They were in animated discussion as they walked by, but all Arthur could hear was a reference to "the evidentiary question." He watched as they pushed open the door to the men's room, and then he looked at his watch.

It was twenty minutes past twelve.

He felt alone, utterly and completely alone, he had never felt so isolated in his entire life. He thought it odd that he should have come through thirty-nine years of family to-getherness, surrounded by aunts and uncles and cousins and *compares* to find himself here and now, at what was possibly the most important juncture of his life, entirely alone. How do you come through it all, he wondered, and suddenly find yourself standing on the edge of the universe waiting for the waves to crash in, maybe to get washed out to sea, without Aunt Louise telling you every other week that you were "her baby," meaning she had served as midwife when you were delivered to your mother in a coldwater flat on East 118th Street? I could use Aunt Louise now, he thought, silly Aunt Louise who accompanied Italian immigrants when they went for their first papers, who was an active member of the Republican Club, who wrote songs in her spare time and claimed that they were all later stolen by the big band leaders —a family trait?—and who sent Queen Elizabeth a hand-tatted bonnet for young Prince Charles when he was born. "Look, Sonny," she had said, "I got a thank-you note from the Queen's secretary, a *personal* thank-you note," and Arthur had thought to himself it was probably a mimeo-graphed note sent to all the Aunt Louises of the world who tatted bonnets for infant princes. And yet he could use Aunt Louise now, he could use her quiet strength and penetrating eye, God but that woman was a dynamo of energy, what the hell was it she concocted—Aunt Louise's Ointment, did she call it? And wasn't it really and truly sold in drugstores all over Harlem, the indefatigable Louise running around sell-ing her product the way she plugged her terrible songs, she'd have made a great rumrunner, or in recent times an excellent dope pusher.

They called him Sonny when he lived in Harlem. I grew

up in Harlem, he always told people, and they looked at him as if wondering whether or not he had traces of Negro blood flowing in his veins, whereupon he always felt compelled to explain that there were *three* Harlems. You see, there is Negro Harlem and there is Italian Harlem and there is Puerto Rican Harlem. They are all very different and they are all identical, they are all bug-ridden and rat-infested, those are the three Harlems. But that of course was a mature judgment, a qualified appraisal by a man who was now thirty-nine years old, and not the way he had seen it as a boy. There were no rats in Harlem for Sonny Constantine—he still did not know why they had called him Sonny, he supposed there was a Sonny in every Italian-American family that ever existed. Or perhaps Al Jolson was hot at the time of his boyhood, perhaps any kid became a Sonny Boy and then a Sonny all because of Al Jolson singing through his goddamn nose like a Harvard man, perhaps that was it. But there were no rats in Harlem—well, once a mouse was in the toilet bowl, but only a mouse. It scared hell out of his mother, she came running out of the bathroom with her dress raised and her bloomers down, her behind showing, he wanted to look, but didn't dare, yelling to his father that there was a mouse in the bowl. So his father just flushed the toilet, naturally, goodbye mouse, out to sea where all good mice eventually go. His sister was terrified. He had called her a baby and a dope and a silly jerk, and then had listened to her crying in her room, really in his parents' bedroom because that was where she slept on a little cot against the wall near the window that looked down on 118th Street four stories below.

There were no rats in Harlem for him, there were no street gangs, there were no rumbles, there was only a placid ghetto —terrible word—a *neighborhood*, a haven surrounded by relatives, you could not throw a stone without hitting a relative. If your mother wasn't home, you dropped in on Aunt Tessie, and she gave you cookies and milk, or you went around to see Grandpa in the grocery store where he worked for a man he had known in Naples, or maybe you ran into Uncle Mike driving his truck for the furniture company. It

was said that Uncle Mike knew gangsters, and that the time
the social club was held up and they stole Uncle Danny's ring
and Uncle Sal's watch, it was Mike who got on his Neapolitan
high horse and went off some place into the mysterious
underworld where they talked of Petie Red Shirt and Legs
Diamond and got the goddamn jewelry back the very next
morning; he was a tough guy Uncle Mike, he could break
your head with a glance. His sister loved Uncle Mike, she
would almost wet her pants every time he stopped by. There
was an argument once, Arthur couldn't even remember what
it was all about, Mike taking out some girl from the bakery,
and Tessie getting all upset and coming to see her sister,
Arthur's mother, and her having a big argument with Mike
and calling him everything under the sun while his father
stood by and listened patiently and Arthur remembered how
simply he had flushed the mouse down the toilet, so very
simply, pull, flush, and out to sea without a whimper.

Christmases, they all got together, Christmases *then*, but
not anymore, blame it on urban renewal, blame it on the
decentralization of the family, the speedier means of communication and transportation, there were no more Christmases once his grandparents died. The family died when they
died, it shriveled outward from the center, everybody just
disappeared, where the hell were they all now? Dead or living
in California, which is the same as being dead. He had
dropped in to see Aunt Tessie and Uncle Mike when he was
out in Hollywood, and Mike who had known gangsters, Mike
who had threatened to break heads unless his brothers'-in-
law jewelry was returned at once, immediately if not sooner,
Mike was a tired old man, bald, his muscles turned to flab,
this was the man who used to move furniture and mountains
and fearsome gangs. They sat in the living room of the
Tarzana development house and had nothing much to say to
each other, how is your mother, tell her to write, did you go
to Aunt Louise's funeral, and Arthur had wanted to say,
"Don't you remember Christmas at Grandpa's house, don't
you remember?" But Uncle Mike was an old man, you see,
and Aunt Tessie limped, and there was nothing to say to

either of them, there was only strong Italian coffee to sip and Italian pastry to nibble, he had not remembered it as being so sweet. Boy, what his grandfather used to buy for Christmas, boy the way that house sang, that crumby apartment on First Avenue, it *must* have been a crumby apartment and there probably *were* rats in the walls. He certainly could remember cockroaches in his own house whenever they turned on the kitchen light, an army in hurried retreat. "Step on them, Sonny," his mother would yell, "get them, get them!" a game each night, the scurrying mob, and then they would all disappear into cracks and crannies, gone like the mouse flushed out to sea, except they would return again. "Where do they go?" he once asked his father, and his father replied, "Home."

Home.

There was everybody there on Christmas and his grandfather welcomed one and all, not only the family but also everybody he knew from the grocery store, the nice old man who wore thick glasses, Alonzo, Alfonso, something like that, who had the idiot son who would come in alongside his father like a ghost and sit there quietly and perhaps sip a little red wine his grandfather poured. And the men would talk about the old country and about Mussolini and about how beautiful Rome was at Christmastime, and Arthur would listen, standing between his grandfather's knees, with his grandfather's strong hands on his shoulders, and the women would be bustling about in the kitchen, Grandma fretting and fussing, and the girls—her two daughters and later Danny's wife, and then Sal's wife—all would be busy with the preparations in the kitchen, and the Christmas gifts would be piled to the ceiling under the Christmas tree, and Grandpa would keep pouring wine for all the relatives and friends who kept dropping in from all over Harlem, all over the world it seemed, *Buon Natale, Buon Natale,* the wine being poured and the smell of tomato sauce in the kitchen. God, there were things to eat, things Grandpa used to get in the grocery store, all imported, great provolone and salami, and fresh macaroni and bread, and Aunt Louise would make the pimientos, she would roast the peppers over the gas jet until they turned black, he always thought she was burning them, but no then she would scrap off all the black part and reveal the sweet orange-red meat, and then she fixed them with oil and garlic, oh God. She sent him pimientos in a jar every month, once a month like clockwork, the last day of the month, until she finally died, always the pimientos in a jar because once he helped her with the grammar in one of her song lyrics, just helped her put it in order, that was all, pimientos for life, a great title.

The meal went on for hours, they would sit at the table and dip cling peaches in wine, allowing the thick golden fruit to soak there for a bit, and then bringing it dripping red to the mouth on a toothpick. His grandfather would say "Sonny, here, have some," and hold out the red-stained toothpick with the rich juicy slice of fruit on its end, tart, strong, sweet, everything. The kids would run through the length of the railroad flat, chasing each other, and his grandmother would yell for them to stop before the people downstairs banged on the ceiling with a broom handle, and they would stop for a little while, collapsing on the big bed in the front room, his head close to his sister's, all of them sweating, all the kids in the family, more kids all the time, all of them giggling and sweating on the bed with the picture of Jesus Christ over it holding his hand above his exposed heart and sunshine spikes radiating from his head. "That's God," his cousin Joey once said. "The Jews killed him." He asked his grandmother about it one time, and she said, "That's right, Sonny, the Jews killed him," and then she told a story about a Jew who went to church one day and received holy communion and then ran out of the church and took the wafer out of his mouth immediately and went home and nailed it to the wall. "And do you know what happened to that holy bread, Sonny? It began to bleed. And it never stopped bleeding. It just kept bleeding all over that Jew's floor."

"What did he do?" Arthur asked.

"What did *who* do?" his grandmother said.

"The Jew. What did he do about all that blood?"

His grandmother had shrugged and gone back to cooking
something on the big wood stove in the kitchen, black and
monstrous, always pouring heat and steam. "Wiped it up, I
guess," she said. "How do *I* know what he did?"

But every time he looked at that picture of Jesus with the
heart stuck on his chest as if he had just had surgery and they
were showing how easy it was to expose a human heart these
days, the drops of blood dripping down from it, and Jesus'
hand just a little above it, and his head tilted back with his
eyes sort of rolled up in his head like a character in an Eisen-
stein movie, he always thought of the Jew who nailed the
communion wafer to the wall, and he always wondered first
why the Jew would want to nail the thing to the wall to
begin with, and second what he had done about all the blood.
In high school, after he had moved to the Bronx and met
Rubin, he realized his grandmother was full of shit, and he
never trusted her very much after that, her and her communion nailed to the wall.

His sister Julia broke his head one time, this was about the
time he fell in love with Virginia Kelly. Irish girls after that
were all premised on Virginia, the sixth grade Virginia with
long black hair and green eyes fringed with black lashes and
budding little breasts—he hadn't been too aware of those at
the time—and a way of tilting her head back to laugh, at *him*
most of the time, which was the unfortunate part of it all.
But oh how he loved that girl! He would watch her and
watch her and notice everything she did or said, and then
come home and tell his sister about it, which is why she broke
his head one day. She broke his head with a stupid little kid's
pocketbook by swinging it at him on its chain and clobbering
him with the clasp, and all because he told her she would
never be as beautiful as Virginia Kelly, no one in the world
would ever be as beautiful as Virginia Kelly, she had clobbered him, wham! Even then she had a lot of spunk, you had
to have spunk to live in the same house with a man like his
father, boy, what a battle *that* had turned out to be years
later. Where the hell are you now, Julie, living with your
engineer husband and your two Norwegian kids in where the

hell, Minnesota? There's no such place as Minnesota, don't kid me, sis. Do you remember breaking my head, and then crying when Mama took me to the druggist, and he examined it—who went to doctors in those days?—and wiped the blood away and said, "You've broken his head, young lady," and then put a strip of plaster on it? It was okay in a week or so, but boy did you cry, I really loved you Julie. You were a really nice sister to have, I hope your Norwegian loves you half as much as I did.

He met Virginia Kelly in the hall one day, he was coming back from the boys' room and he had the wooden pass in his hand, and Virginia stopped him. He was nine years old, and she was ten and big for her age, and she stopped him and said, "Don't look at me anymore, Stupid."

"Who's looking at you?" he said, but his heart was pounding, and he wanted to kiss her, wanted to kiss this quintessence of everything alien to him, the sparkling green eyes and the wild Irish way of tossing her head, all, everything. Years later, when he read *Ulysses,* he knew every barmaid in the book because they were all Virginia Kelly who told him once to stop looking at her, Stupid, and whom he never looked at again from that day forward though it broke his heart.

When he moved to the Bronx, the only person he thought he missed was Virginia Kelly. He would lie awake in bed at night and think of Virginia, and when he learned how to masturbate, he would conjure visions of this laughing Irish girl and ravage her repeatedly until one morning Julie said to him, "Hey, *I* have to make the beds around here, you know," and he pretended he didn't know what she meant, but after that he masturbated secretly in the bathroom and carefully wiped up after him with toilet paper. Somewhere along the line, he switched from raping Virginia Kelly to raping Hedy Lamarr, and he never thought of her again except once or twice when he remembered that there were people in this world who drove in red convertibles with their long black hair blowing in the wind, laughing, wearing silk stockings and loafers, the idealization of everything that seemed to him American, everything that seemed to him non-

Harlem and non-Italian. Once, in high school, Rubin said to him in the boys' room, jokingly, "Where else but in America could an Italian and a Jew piss side by side in the same bowl?" and he had laughed because he laughed at everything Rubin said, Rubin was so much smarter and better informed than he, but he didn't really get the joke. He did not by that time see anything funny about being Italian, nor could he understand what Rubin thought was so funny about being Jewish. It never once occurred to him, not then, and not later when he was hobnobbing it around Hollywood with stars and starlets and all that crap, nor even when he laid a famous movie queen who kept calling him Artie, for which he almost busted her in the mouth, except she really was as passionate as she came over on the screen, not in all those years, not ever in his life until perhaps this moment when he felt so terribly alone enmeshed in a law system created by Englishmen, not once did he ever realize how dearly he had loved Harlem, or how much it had meant to him to be Italian.

There was in his world a cluttered brimming external existence, and an interior solitude that balanced each other perfectly and resulted in, he realized, a serene childhood, *even* in the midst of a depression, even though his father was a mysterious government employee known as "a substitute" instead of "a regular," which he gathered was highly more desirable. There was an immutable pattern in his household, the same foods were eaten on the identical night each week, Monday was soup which his mother made herself, he hated soup meat, it was stringy and tasteless. Tuesday night was spaghetti with either meatballs or *braciòla,* Wednesday night was breaded veal cutlets with spinach and mashed potatoes, his mother once dumped a whole bowl of mashed potatoes on his head because he was trying to catch a fly as a specimen for the microscope he had got for Christmas. He threw a dissecting needle at the fly on the wall and, uncanny luck, pierced the fly, even Errol Flynn couldn't have done better. ("You *got* 'im, Sonny!" Julie shrieked in delight.) But a lot of gooey white glop came out of the fly and he refused to eat his mashed potatoes after that. So his mother, naturally, having inherited a few Neapolitan traits from Grandpa, even though she herself had been born and raised in the garden spot called Harlem, picked up the bowl of potatoes and dumped the whole thing on his head. His father laughed. He hated his father for two months after that. Couldn't he have at least said it wasn't nice to dump a bowl of mashed potatoes all over a kid who was maybe a budding scientist and certainly the best dissecting needle thrower in the United States?

Thursday night was some kind of macaroni, either *rigatoni* or *mostaccioli* or *fusilli,* again with meatballs, or maybe sausage, and Friday night was fish, of course. Oh, how he hated fish. There were three kinds of fish his mother made, and he hated each and every one of them. The first was breaded filet of flounder, dry and white and tasteless. The second was breaded shrimp, she sure had a mania for breading stuff, equally as tasteless, except they seemed to come in bite size. The third was a white halibut which she made with a tomato sauce, fresh tomatoes he remembered because the sauce was always pulpy and sometimes had seeds. This was the best of the lot because it was a little juicier than the two breaded concoctions, but he hated each with a passion and deplored the approach of Friday each week. He did not learn how to eat lobster until he went to Maine with a girl from Barnard one weekend, and had not discovered until just recently that his mother hated fish as much as he did and had only made it every Friday because she was a sort of half-ass Catholic who never went to church or confession, but who nonetheless made fish every Friday night. Breaded.

Saturday was either lambchops or steak. Sunday was Grandpa's house, the biggest feast of the week, the family represented in smaller groups except on the holidays, antipasto, spaghetti, meatballs, roast beef or chicken or turkey, fruit, nuts, pastry—his grandfather always went out to buy *cannoli* and *cassatini, sfogliatelli* and *baba* on his name day, a sort of pilgrimage every year. He would come back flushed with the cold (his name day was in November) carrying two white cartons of Italian pastry, tied with white string, "Did you get them, Papa?" his mother would ask. And Grandpa would nod and smile and then grab Arthur playfully and say, "Sonny, help me cut the string, the string is too strong for me."

Structured, everything structured and ordered, the activity in the streets as patterned as the regularity of meals and holidays, each season bringing its own pursuit, its own hysterical joy to the slum. (Slum? What's that? What's a slum?) Roller skates, and stickball, and pea shooters, and pushos, and hi-li paddles, and baseball cards, and roasting mickeys, and black leather aviator hats with goggles, and rubberband guns, one kid had six of them mounted in tandem like a machine gun, and pigeons on the roof, and stoopball, and boxball, and Skullies (I love you, Virginia Kelly) and Statues, and Johnny-on-a-Pony and Ring-a-Leavio, and little girls skipping rope, or playing that game where they lift their leg over a bouncing ball, skirts flying, "One-two-three-a-nation, I received my confirmation," Virginia Kelly had a plaid skirt, blue plaid, she wore white socks, she once beat up Concetta Esposito for calling her a lousy Irish mick, which after all she was. Patterned, structured, safe, secure, there were no rats in Harlem, there was only a street that was a city, a dozen playmates who populated the world, a million relatives who hugged and kissed and teased and loved him and called him Sonny, a busy universe for a small boy.

And juxtaposed to this, the inner reality of Arthur Constantine, the quiet, thoughtful, solitary child who played with his soldiers on the dining room floor, the big oaken table serving as suicide cliff or soaring skyscraper, the intricacy of its hidden structure becoming a bridge to be blown or a gangplank to be walked, each separate lead soldier—the heads were always breaking off, when that happened, you fixed them with a matchstick, but they never lasted long—each separate soldier or cowboy or Indian assuming an identity of its own. Shorty was the one with the bow legs, he had a lariat in his hand when Arthur bought him for a nickel at the Woolworth's on Third Avenue, but later the lariat got lost. Magua was the Indian, he was made of cast iron rather than lead, and he never broke, he outlasted all the others. Naked to the waist, wearing a breechclout, he was Arthur's favorite, and Arthur always put words of wisdom into his mouth, carefully thought-out Indian sayings that helped the white man in his plight. Magua never turned on anybody, Magua was a good Indian. Red Dance was the bad Indian, he had a bonnet full of feathers. When his head finally broke off because Arthur caused Magua to give him a good punch one day, Arthur never bothered to repair him. Instead, he bought an identical piece and named him Blue Dance, who he supposed was Son of Red Dance, and when Magua knocked *his* head off, too, Arthur switched to a villain named El Mustachio who was a soldier carrying a pack, and who didn't have a mustache at all. He would talk aloud to himself while he played with the tiny metal men, he would construct elaborate conflicts and then put everything to rights with either a wise word from Magua or a sweep of his hand, scattering the pieces all over the floor. If his sister ever tried to enter one of these games, he shrieked at her in fury, and once he shoved her against the wall and made her cry and then went to her afterwards and hugged her and kissed her and said he was very sorry, but he still would not let her into any of the solitary games he played with the metal men. He wondered once, alone in his bed and listening to the sounds of sleep in the room next door, whether he would even have allowed Virginia Kelly to play soldiers with him—and he decided not.

Where do they go, he wondered, all those black-haired girls with the green eyes and the wonderful laugh, when the hell have I ever loved anyone as deeply or as hopelessly as I loved Virginia Kelly? Where does it all go, and how does it happen that I'm alone on this day, with Christmas coming and no Grandpa to ask me to help him break the string on the white carton of pastries, this day, when God knows I could at least use Aunt Louise to tell me she has a friend who knows a magistrate, "Don't worry, Sonny, I'll speak to them at the Club," the Republican Club would set it all straight, or if not, then certainly a dab of Aunt Louise's Ointment would. Where? he thought. Where? I've been invited to orgies in Hollywood (and refused)—"The ideah is to have a few

drinks ontil ever'one get on-in-hib-ited, you know whut I
mean?"—I've seen my name on motion picture screens and
television screens and once on a theater program, Arthur
Nelson Constantine, the "Nelson" added by yours truly as a
bow to our cousins across the big water, an acknowledgment
of my veddy British heritage, Arthur *Nelson* Constantine
("What?" Aunt Louise would have said. "Don't worry, I
know somebody in the Republican Club.") I have gone to
bed with young girls, and some not so young, and once I
went to bed with *two* girls, and another time I went to bed
with a girl and another guy and I think we sent that poor
little girl straight from there to an insane asylum, but that
was in Malibu where such things happen often, I am told. I
have sat at the same table with John Wayne, who offered to
buy me a drink and then told a story about shooting *The
Quiet Man* in Ireland, and I have been blasted across the sky
at five hundred miles an hour while drinking martinis and
watching a movie written and directed by a man I knew. And
it seems to me now, it seems to me alone in this cold corridor
that the most important thing I've ever done in my life was
skewer a fly with a dissecting needle from a distance of five
feet, shooting from the hip, did I ever tell you *that* story,
Duke? And my mother rewarded me by dumping a bowl of
lukewarm mashed potatoes on my head. And my father
laughed. And the fly dripped its white glop all over the wall.

Where else but in America could a little Italian boy from
the slums of Harlem (Well, you see, there are *three* Harlems) sit at the same table with John Wayne and listen to a
very inside story about the shooting of *The Quiet Man* in
Ireland? Where else, I ask you, indeed. Oh man, I played the
Slum Kid bit to the hilt, everybody likes to hear how you can
make it in the face of adversity. The mouse that almost bit
my mother became over the years a foraging bloodthirsty sea
monster with matted hair dripping seaweed and coming up
out of the water with its jaws wide ready to swallow her
bottom and everything else besides. That apartment on
118th Street became the Black Hole of Calcutta, it's a wonder
the swarms of flies did not eat the eyes out of my head as I lay

helpless and squirming in the squalor of my pitiful crib, it's a wonder the rats did not tear the flesh from my bones and leave me whimpering helplessly for an undernourished mother to hobble into the room and flail at them ineffectually. I was born and raised in Harlem, you hear that, Duke? Not only was I born and raised in Harlem, but I managed to get out of Harlem, which is no small feat in itself. Moreover, I was educated at Columbia University, which is a pretty snazzy school you will admit, and I managed to become an officer in the Army, came out as a captain don't forget, and then went on to become a very highly paid screen and television writer who this very minute is negotiating, or at least *hoping* to negotiate, with one Hester Miers, you've *got* it, mister, the very same, for the starring role in my new play which will be coming to Broadway shortly. (I'll stand in that lobby on opening night, Virginia Kelly, and when you walk in and recognize me and come over to wish me luck, I'll tell you to go bounce a ball on the sidewalk, one-two-three-a-nation. I'll tell you I've got an apartment of my own now in a very fancy building on East 54th Street, with a doorman *and* an elevator operator, and I'll tell you I date the prettiest girls in New York almost every night of the week and I've been sucked off by more black-haired Irish girls than there are in your entire family or perhaps in the entire city of Dublin. And then I'll ask the usher or perhaps the porter to please show you out of the goddamn theater as you are disturbing my equilibrium.) I was born and raised in Harlem, so look at me. Something, huh? You don't have to be colored to be underprivileged, you know. Look at me, and have pity on the poor skinny slum kid, man, did I play that into the ground.

So here stands the poor skinny slum kid (not so poor, not so skinny, never having come from a slum anyway because it sure as hell wasn't a slum to me, it was the happiest place I've ever known in my life) standing alone in an Anglo-Saxon world being represented by a Jew (Where else but in America can a wop, etc.) and going up against a man named Jonah Willow, who sounds like a Eurasian philosopher, and

I'm scared. I'm scared not because there were rats in Harlem, I'm scared not because there were pushers lurking on every street corner, I'm scared not because teenage hoods came at me with tire chains and switch blades, I'm scared because I'm alone.

I'm scared because I've been making it alone ever since I was eighteen and got drafted into the United States Army, I'm scared and I'm tired, and I would like to rest.

He took a last drag on his cigarette, searched for an ash tray in the corridor, and found four of them fastened to the wall. He glanced over his shoulder to see if Willow and his assistant were coming back—the *hell* with them, let them be late—and then walked swiftly toward the courtroom. He pulled open one of the bronze-flowered doors and immediately saw Brackman and his partner at one of the long tables, Genitori and his assistant at the other. He saw Driscoll and his wife sitting in the empty jury box, just as before. He saw the court clerk hovering near the door to the judge's chamber, waiting to call, "All rise!" No one seemed to realize that beyond that paneled door the judge might be reading his newspaper or blowing his nose or laughing on the telephone or tying his shoelaces—or perhaps pondering the decision that would mean the difference between a sweet, staggering success and . . . what?

What you have now, Arthur thought.

Exactly what you have now.

Unnoticed, he took his seat at the plaintiff's table, and waited for the trial to resume.

"Mr. Constantine, would you please continue where you left off before the recess?" Brackman said.

"I was just about to begin with specific character similarities," Arthur said. "I was going to start with the character of Lieutenant Roger Mason in my play *Catchpole* and the character called Alex Cooper in *The Paper Dragon*. There are similarities there that go beyond the realm of coincidence, and I'd like to enumerate them."

"Please do."

"To begin with, the hero of my play is twenty-one years old, and fresh out of college. He goes into the Army as a private, is sent to O.C.S., and is shipped to the Pacific to fight the enemy. The man who played him on the New York stage was at least six feet tall, and he had dark hair and blue eyes—did I say he was a second lieutenant?"

"Your Honor, could the clerk—"

"Yes, certainly."

"Witness has referred to him only as 'a new lieutenant,' " the clerk said.

"Would you like to amend that in some way?" McIntyre asked.

"Yes, your Honor, if I may. I'd like to say that he was a *second* lieutenant. That's very important. Especially since the hero of *The Paper Dragon* is a second lieutenant, too. He is described in the book, in fact, as being twenty-one years old, fresh out of Pratt Institute, and drafted into the Army. He goes to O.C.S. and then is shipped off to the Pacific to fight the enemy. The enemy is a different one this time, admittedly, and the setting is Korea, not Eniwetok—but the similarity stands. In addition, the hero of the book is described as being six feet tall, and having dark hair and blue eyes. Physically, these two different men in two so-called separate works look exactly alike. You could almost say they were twins.

"Now the second similarity of character is the fact that there is a nurse in my play, and also a nurse in the book. In my play she is called Diane Foster, and in the book she is called Jan Reardon. Both girls are blond, both are young, both are from New York City. In fairness, I must say that the girl in the book is *not* a native New Yorker, whereas the girl in my play is. But in both the play and the book, there's a romantic attachment formed between the hero and the nurse."

"You're getting into plot again, aren't you?" Brackman asked.

"Only as it illuminates character."

"Go on, please."

"There is in my play a sergeant who is a member of a minority group, his name is Sergeant D'Agostino and he is an Italian. In the book there is also a sergeant who is a member of a minority group. His name is Sergeant Morley, and he is a Negro. Both these men play important parts in plot development, as I explained earlier."

"Yes, let's just stick to character similarities right now."

"There is a man killed in my play, right at the outset. His name is Private Hapsberg. There is also a man killed in *The Paper Dragon,* even before the hero arrives on the scene. *His* name is Major Randolph. I don't think the rank makes much difference, it's the idea of a sniper killing each of these men that—"

"Your Honor," Willow said, "it would appear to me that we are simply going over ground already covered. Unless this testimony regarding character similarities can demonstrably add to what we earlier heard, I must object to the witness continuing along these lines."

"It would seem, Mr. Brackman," McIntyre said, "that there *is* an overlap here."

"May I explain, your Honor?" Arthur asked.

"Yes, please."

"In developing a work of fiction," Arthur said, "the interplay between plot and character—"

"Your Honor," Willow said, "I do not believe this Court is interested in fiction techniques. We are here to determine whether or not an act of plagiarism took place. It is hardly to the point—"

"Please let him finish, Mr. Willow," McIntyre said.

"I was going to say," Arthur said, with a sharp glance at Willow, "that character and plot are inseparable in a good work of fiction. Character determines plot, and in turn plot shapes character. In other words, it would be practically impossible to discuss either without referring to the other."

"Yes, I understand that," McIntyre said. "But it *would*

seem that the character similarities you are now listing were adequately covered when you testified about plot. In that respect, I would agree with Mr. Willow."

"This is merely an amplification, your Honor," Brackman said.

"Well, I will allow the witness to continue," McIntyre said, "but I think we would all appreciate the elimination of material already covered."

"This is simply backing and filling, your Honor," Willow said.

"Whatever it may be, Mr. Willow, the witness may continue—with the reservation I have already mentioned."

"Well," Arthur said, and hesitated. "I'm not sure I understand, but . . ."

"We would like you to continue with character similarities," McIntyre said, "but we ask you to limit—"

"I understand *that*," Arthur said, "but it seems to me . . ."

"Yes?"

"I don't know if I'm allowed to say this," Arthur said, and looked at Brackman.

"Allowed to say what, Mr. Constantine?" McIntyre asked.

"Well, it seems to me that the only opportunity I'll get to present my case . . ."

"The Court has asked you to continue with your testimony," Brackman said, a note of warning in his voice. "If you have a question concerning—"

"I will hear the witness," McIntyre said.

"No, nothing," Arthur said, and shook his head.

"We're not trying to give you a fast shuffle here, if that's what you think," McIntyre said, and Arthur turned to look at him, and saw him as a person for the first time. He was close to fifty years of age, Arthur supposed, partially bald, with mild blue eyes and a pink face. He was frowning now, and his hands, delicate and small, were folded on the bench before him as he looked down at Arthur and waited for an answer.

"I didn't mean to imply that, your Honor," Arthur said.

"We have, I believe, allowed you every opportunity thus

far to present your case fairly and adequately. I assure you
that we have already studied the play and the novel and that
we saw a screening of the film on Friday. We have read the
pretrial examination transcripts, and we have carefully
studied the charts prepared by you and your counsel. You
will remember that we yielded to your counsel's request to
have you elaborate on these similarities in your own words,
despite defendants' objection. We are now asking, in the
hope of saving time, only that you limit your testimony to
similarities not already covered by your previous testimony.
We believe this is a reasonable request, Mr. Constantine."

"Yes, it's reasonable," Arthur said.

"Very well, then."

"But . . ."

"Mr. Constantine," Brackman said sharply, "are you ready
to continue?"

"Is something still troubling you?" McIntyre asked.

"Yes, your Honor."

"Then please say what's on your mind."

"Your Honor, this case is very important to me."

"I realize that. I'm sure it's equally important to Mr.
Driscoll."

"I'm sure it is, sir, but . . . well, Mr. Driscoll doesn't
happen to be on the stand right now, and I am."

"Your Honor," Willow said, "I must object to the witness
engaging this Court in argument. We are trying—"

"I will hear the witness," McIntyre said flatly. "Go on, Mr.
Constantine."

"Your Honor, tomorrow morning Mr. Willow will begin
his cross-examination and *that,* I'm afraid, is *that.* If there's
anything I left out or forgot today, it'll be just too bad. I
know the charts are a help, but . . ."

"*That,* I'm afraid, is *not* that," McIntyre said, "nor will it
be just too bad, either. Your attorney will have ample opportunity to conduct a redirect. I'm sorry, Mr. Constantine, but
I must now agree with Mr. Willow. This is a court of law and
not a first semester course on evidence or tactics. You will

please continue with your testimony, and you will limit it to similarities not previously covered."

"I apologize for the witness, your Honor," Brackman said. "Please continue, Mr. Constantine."

"Yes, sir," Arthur said, and swallowed. He was embarrassed and angry. Alone on the witness chair, feeling abandoned even by his own lawyer, he searched in his mind for character similarities, every eye in the room upon him, foolish and stupid, struck dumb by the judge's reprimand, his anger building, eyes smarting, hands trembling in his lap.

"If the witness could care to examine the charts to refresh his memory . . ." Willow said.

"I don't need the charts, thank you," Arthur snapped, and looked at Willow in anger, and then at Brackman in anger, and then glanced up at the judge in anger, the son of a bitch, shutting him up that way, humiliating him, Brackman allowing the humiliation and adding to the indignity by apologizing. The anger and embarrassment were identical to what he had felt the night the critics killed his play, those rotten egotistical bastards sitting in exalted judgment on something about which they possessed no real knowledge. How could McIntyre or Willow or even Brackman hope to understand the intricacies of a work of fiction? Oh yes, they would nod their heads in accord as they had this morning, Willow and McIntyre, two legal masterminds agreeing that an author's intent had no place in a court of law, no place in the judgment of a plagiarism suit, casually eliminating the inexplicable beginning of creation, snuffing out the spark of *idea,* eliminating conscious direction from the work—"I maintain, your Honor, that any similarities must be solely between the works in question."

"I would agree to that."

"And that therefore the author's *intent* is irrelevant."

Oh yes, irrelevant, and why hadn't Brackman objected, or had he secretly agreed with his colleagues? Perhaps he had only wanted to apologize at that point, perhaps that was it, apologize for Arthur ever having conceived and written *Catchpole* at all. How could one possibly hope to explain anything to them if they had already ruled out intent, already decided that only words were on trial here, words and nothing more? Never mind the act itself, the intent or its realization, hadn't he been a little bit insane when he created the psychopathic colonel, hadn't he hated with Janus and suffered with the lieutenant, loved the nurse and died with D'Agostino, never mind, never mind, it is all cut and dried. There are only one hundred and twenty mimeographed pages of a play called *Catchpole,* there are only four hundred and twelve pages of a pirated novel called *The Paper Dragon,* there is only an hour and fifty minutes of a film supposedly based on the novel, that is our concern here, the comparison of the works. The author's intent is irrelevant, the author is irrelevant, the *self* is irrelevant, the *man* is irrelevant. That almighty God son of a bitch McIntyre will sit there with his watery blue eyes and his pink puffed face and humiliate him the way the critics had humiliated him in October of 1947, the shame and embarrassment of meeting people you knew, the goddamn solicitous smiles as though a stranger had passed away, but not a stranger, something very real and intimate called *Catchpole* which had taken four months to write and five months to sell, and two months to rehearse, not a stranger at all. The guarded knives, the secret delight behind the words of condolence. You have dared, my friend, you have dared to expose yourself, and they have killed you, and I am glad, I am secretly and enormously delighted, how sorry to hear that your play closed last night, but after all what do the critics know? Yes, after all, what do the critics know, or the lawyers or the judges, Arthur thought. He had tried to explain how important this trial was to him, and McIntyre had countered by saying it was important to Driscoll as well, yes. Yes, assuredly, oh certainly but not in the same way. There was more on trial here than words, more than the comparison of two similar works of fiction, more even than the enormous amount of money that would go to the victor. There was an identity on trial, there was this very self McIntyre refused to allow, there was a *man.* And if Arthur allowed Driscoll to steal the work of fiction, then he also allowed him to steal the intent and the realization, the self and the person, the man. And then there would be nothing left, nothing at all.

"We are waiting," Brackman said.

"I'm thinking," Arthur answered.

"Take your time," McIntyre said.

"Thank you," Arthur answered, and he hoped the sarcasm was evident in his voice. "There are," he said, "in addition to those character similarities already mentioned, just a few others. In both my play and in the book, for example, there is a soldier who comes from Brooklyn, a soldier who comes from the South, and a soldier who is Jewish. They are all in the squad that becomes the focus of both the play and the book, the one the lieutenant has all the trouble with in the platoon he commands. Also, in the play and in the book, there is an elderly nurse who is a sort of friend and mother-confessor to the heroine. In the play, she has recently lost her husband—which is why she joins the Medical Corps. In the book, she has also lost her husband and become a nurse." Arthur paused. "I think those are the rest of the specific character similarities, those not already mentioned."

"Your Honor," Brackman said, "should any others occur to the witness . . ."

"Yes, of course, you may bring them out in the redirect."

"Thank you, your Honor. Would you now tell us please what specific similarities of language you found in the play and the novel, Mr. Constantine?"

"Yes, certainly," Arthur said. He turned to McIntyre. "I thought I might quote from the respective works, if that wouldn't take up too much time, your Honor."

"We have time," McIntyre said. "If you don't finish before two o'clock, there's always tomorrow."

"I'd like to quote then."

"Go right ahead, please."

"In my play, when Lieutenant Mason first arrives on Eniwetok, I have Corporal Janus, the troublemaker, say, 'Another ninety-day wonder. *I* wonder how long he'll last.' In *The Paper Dragon*, Private Colman looks at the lieutenant right after he first addresses the men, watches him as he's walking away and says, 'Straight out of college. They sent him here for his master's degree,' and Sergeant Morley says, 'Cheer up, Pete, maybe he'll flunk out.' That's his first name, Pete. Peter Colman."

"Mr. Constantine, we're all interested in saving time, but it's not necessary to speak this rapidly," Brackman said.

"I didn't realize I was."

"Just take as much time as you need."

"All right. I guess we are all familiar by now with what has been called the 'female rifle' scene in *The Paper Dragon*, where the men are disassembling their rifles. The lieutenant is going through the authorized method, straight from the book, and every time he comes to a word like 'rod' or 'butt' or 'trigger,' it breaks the men up. They're handling pieces, you see, which is Army terminology for a gun, and they keep making sexual allusions, and getting hysterical when the lieutenant says things like 'now twist the rod toward your body with your right hand and then exert a slight pull to the right,' I'm not quoting exactly, but the scene is intended sexually, and the men are doing all this to infuriate the lieutenant, who is running the session according to the book and trying to get a little order into what is a pretty bedraggled band of fighting men."

"This is in *The Paper Dragon?*"

"Yes, but its counterpart is in *Catchpole*. In my play I have the men discussing, within earshot of the lieutenant, the attempt of one of the men to capture a wild pig. Their references to the pig are purely sexual, and they are engaging in this kind of talk because the lieutenant had warned them he was going to try to 'clean up' the outfit before the final assault on Parry Island, those are his exact words. The pig is referred to as 'a juicy morsel,' and 'something to sink your teeth into,' and also at one point one of the men says, 'We almost *had* that sweet little piece of meat.' A piece of meat, of course, is a girl. I see there's a lady in the courtroom, and I hate to talk this way, but I'm referring to actual words in the works that are being questioned."

"You may say what you want to say, Mr. Constantine."

"In the motion picture, of course, this entire so-called 'female rifle' scene was eliminated. Now, in *Catchpole,* there are a great many references to Glenn Miller who was, as you know, a well-known bandleader during the thirties and forties and who was reported missing at about the time of the Eniwetok campaign, and I have the men speculating on what might have happened to him. In *The Paper Dragon,* which takes place in Korea in 1950, the Army men begin discussing Glenn Miller and how he could play trombone, whereas this is a new generation of men who actually would have very little knowledge of Glenn Miller or how he played trombone. The same references apply to the movie, and are mostly given to Sergeant Morley, the Negro."

"The same references to Glenn Miller, do you mean?"

"Yes. Now regarding the love story, the nurse in my play is a first lieutenant and of course the hero is a second lieutenant. There is a great deal of playful love-making where she constantly kids him about rank, and about reporting him to the company commander if he doesn't kiss her right that minute, all jokingly of course, but very important to the development of their affair. In the book, there is an extremely erotic sex scene where the couple are alone together for the first time, and she suddenly says, 'You'd better kiss me now,' and he says, 'Do you think it's safe?' and she replies, 'Do as I say, Coop. I outrank you.' The identical line is used in the motion picture. I'd like to say something here about the names of these characters, by the way."

"Go right ahead."

"This has to do again with specific language. My lieutenant's name is Roger Mason, and he is familiarly called 'Mase' by the nurse and by his fellow officers. The lieutenant's name in *The Paper Dragon* is Alex Cooper, and he is called 'Coop' by the nurse and by his friends. Which leads me to another startling similarity between—"

"Your Honor," Jonah said, "might we not do without the editorializing adjectives?"

"If you will simply state the similarities, Mr. Constantine," McIntyre said, "that will be sufficient."

"Yes, sir, I was only going to say that in my play the men keep calling the lieutenant 'Loot,' that's all. At one point in my play, the lieutenant says, 'How about lengthening that to Lieutenant Mason?' and Janus replies, 'Isn't that what I said, *Loot*?' stressing the word. Well, in *The Paper Dragon,* there's a scene where the lieutenant says to the men, 'A *lieutenant* is an officer in the United States Army. A *lute* is a Chinese stringed instrument.' And Colman, the troublemaker, answers, 'Maybe those Mongolian bastards would prefer lutes to bugles, Loot.' This same line is used in the motion picture, though of course the word 'bastards' is deleted. But the reference is the same in all three versions of my play."

"Objection, your Honor," Willow said. "There is only *one* version of the play, as I understand it."

"Sustained. Strike that."

"From where, your Honor?" the clerk asked.

"The reference to all three versions. There has been, as Mr. Willow pointed out, only one version of *Catchpole* submitted to this Court."

Brackman glanced at Willow ruefully, and then turned again to Arthur. "Would you tell us what other specific similarities of language you found?" he said.

Arthur cleared his throat. "In the stage play," he said, "we obviously could not use profanity in the New York theater, or at least the kind of profanity a combat squad would be apt to use in the midst of one of the bitterest campaigns in the Pacific war. But I had one man in the squad addicted to the use of a word which was easily understood by the audience as a substitute—an acceptable substitute, I should say—for a more obscene word. I had this one character, one of the minor characters in the squad constantly using variations of the word 'bug,' so that he would be saying 'This bugging Army food,' or 'This bugging war,' or 'Bug off, Mac,' expressions like that, which made it absolutely clear which word I really meant. In *The Paper Dragon,* because such language is allowed in novels, one of the characters in the squad is addicted to the use of the actual word, I think we all know the word I mean, in all of its various forms, the same way my character uses the word 'bug.' I don't remember this character's name. I think—"

"Is it Kenworthy?"

"That's right, his name in the book is Kenworthy. And every other word out of his mouth is an obscenity, identical to the character in my play."

"Go on, Mr. Constantine."

Arthur paused. Brackman studied him for a moment and then said, "Yes?"

"I beg your pardon?"

"You seemed to be hesitating."

"Oh. I was only trying to remember if I'd left anything out, before I come to the most amazing similarity of all."

"Your Honor . . ." Willow started, rising.

"I do think we might get along better without the descriptive adjectives, Mr. Constantine," McIntyre said.

"I'm sorry, your Honor. To my mind, this next similarity *is* amazing, and—"

"Objection, your Honor."

"Please, Mr. Constantine."

"I'm sorry. May I tell this last specific similarity of language?"

"Yes, certainly," McIntyre said.

"Well, in the actual campaign for Eniwetok, the 106th was the United States Infantry Regiment that made the assault, and the other forces involved were the 22nd Marine Regimental Combat Team, and a temporary command echelon called Tactical Group One—this was all in February of 1944 when I was there on the island. I was attached to C Company, and I guess you know that Army companies are broken down into platoons and then squads, as was the Army company in my play. A squad consists of twelve men, and that's the number of soldiers I focus attention on in my play—this was done because of technical reasons, I wanted to get a microcosm of the Army into this relatively small group of men. When I started writing the play, however, I thought it would be best to use a *fictitious* infantry division, so I—"

"Why did you want to do that, Mr. Constantine?"

"I didn't want to run into any possible trouble with the Army, or with the inadvertent use of names that might possibly belong to real men who had been in the 106th Regiment during the Eniwetok campaign."

"You were afraid of possible lawsuits, is that it?"

"Yes, I didn't want to libel anyone who might be an actual living person. So I invented a division, and I called it the 105th, the digits one-oh-five, and I almost changed the name of the atoll to a fictitious one. That is, I almost changed it from Eniwetok, but I decided that would be taking too much historic license. So I didn't, after all. But I would like to say that there were only sixty-seven infantry divisions in the United States Army at that time, and that there was not then during 1944, nor was there during the Korean conflict, nor is there today at present an Army infantry division called the 105th. That's important when we come to compare this with *The Paper Dragon*."

"Would you explain that, please?"

"Well, the actual Army divisions involved in the battle for Korea when the Chinese began their Ch'ongch'on River offensive were the 2nd, the 24th, and the 25th. There was no 105th Division involved because there is no such division in the United States Army. The novel *The Paper Dragon* is set in Korea during October and November of 1950, prior to and during the Chinese offensive across the Ch'ongch'on. It is significant to me that James Driscoll chose to call *his* division in *his* novel the 105th, the identical number I chose for the division in my play. I think it's safe to say that the possibility of coincidence involving those three digits, one-oh-five—the odds against hitting on those same three digits accidentally and in sequence would be staggering. Yet those same three digits are used to label a division in my play and in the novel." Arthur paused, and then looked up at the judge. "That's all I have to say about the similarities between the two works, the three works when we include the movie."

"Your Honor, may I now offer copies of the various charts?" Brackman asked.

"Does anyone object?"

"No objection," Willow said, "if Mr. Brackman will tell us which chart is which."

"I offer this chart titled Plot Similarities."

"Do we understand that these charts represent Mr. Constantine's *complete* list of similarities?" Willow asked.

"These four charts include each and every similarity Mr. Constantine found between the works in question. We have one additional chart listing the similarities between the play and the movie, and I would like to offer that as well."

"I would like to have it understood that these charts were prepared by Mr. Constantine, and are being offered to show James Driscoll's access to the play *The Catchpole*," Willow said.

"It's *Catchpole*," Arthur said.

"What?"

"It's *Catchpole*. There's no article. It's not '*The*' *Catchpole*."

"Oh. I'm sorry," Willow said. "But are we clear as to their offer?"

"We are clear, Mr. Willow," McIntyre said.

"The second chart is labeled Character Similarities."

"Mr. Brackman, we did not get the number designation of the first chart."

"Plot Similarities is—do you have the number?"

The clerk consulted his notes. "Plaintiff's Exhibit 5 is Plot Similarities," he said. "Character Similarities is Plaintiff's Exhibit 6."

"Then this chart," Brackman said, "Language Similarities, would be number 7. The last chart, Play and Movie Similarities, is number 8."

"That's correct."

"No objection."

"No objection."

"Does that conclude the direct, Mr. Brackman?" McIntyre asked.

"It does. Defendants may examine."

"In that case, I would like to recess until ten A.M. tomorrow morning, at which time you may begin the cross-examination, Mr. Willow."

"This court is recessed until ten tomorrow morning," the clerk said.

"I don't know why you let him do that to me," Arthur said outside the courthouse. He was watching the oncoming traffic for a taxicab, his eyes squinted against the strong wind, his back to Brackman, who stood with his gloved hands in his coat pockets, homburg tilted down, muffler tight about his throat, heavy briefcase resting beside him on the sidewalk.

"*You* let him do it," Brackman said. "You walked right into it."

"You should have stopped him. You're my attorney."

"You were your *own* attorney at that point."

"I was getting angry."

"Yes. So you attempted to argue your own case. That was a brilliant move, Arthur, absolutely brilliant."

"*Someone* had to argue it. *You* certainly weren't."

"Thank you, Arthur."

"Don't get petulant, Sidney. Petulance is unbecoming on a middle-aged man."

"Yes, and ingratitude is unbecoming on a man of any age."

"If we win this case . . ."

"If we win this case, I'll be amply rewarded, yes. *If* we win it. In the meantime, it's cost me a considerable amount of time and money, and I would appreciate your letting *me* handle it from now on."

"I didn't think McIntyre was being fair. He can't—"

"He can do whatever he wants in his own courtroom."

"But he has to be fair."

"No, he only has to be judicious."

"I still think he was rushing us," Arthur said, and raised his hand to signal an empty cab.

"Let it go by," Brackman said. "I want to talk to you."

"I have to get to the theater."

"The theater can wait. Let it go by."

Arthur waved the taxi away and turned wearily to Brackman. "What is it?" he asked.

"Arthur, do you want to lose this case?"

"You know I don't."

"You can lose it if you're not careful."

"I thought you said . . ."

"Yes, that we had an airtight case. But believe me, Arthur, you can lose it. And one sure way of losing it is to antagonize the man who'll be making the decision. That's one sure way of slitting your own throat."

"I'm sorry."

"Tomorrow's going to be a rough day, Arthur. Willow—"

"I said I was sorry."

"Willow is *not* on our side, you know, and he'll do everything he can to rattle you and confuse you and make you lose your temper. I want your promise that under no circumstances will you again address the judge personally, not to ask him any questions, not to offer any explanations, not for any conceivable reason. I don't even want you to *look* at him, Arthur, I want your promise on that."

"I promise," Arthur said. "I have to get to the theater."

"Can you be here at nine-thirty tomorrow?"

"I guess so. Why?"

"There are a few matters I want to discuss when you're not in such a hurry."

"All right, I'll be here."

"Nine-thirty," Brackman said. "There's another empty one, grab him."

"Can I drop you off?"

"No, I'm going east."

The taxicab pulled to the curb. Arthur opened the door, and then said, "Judicious *is* fair."

"Look it up," Brackman said, and Arthur climbed in and closed the door behind him. "The Helen Hayes Theatre," he said to the cabbie, "Forty-sixth and Broadway."

It had turned into a bleak, forbidding day, the sun all but gone, dank heavy clouds hanging low in the sky and threatening snow. Through the taxi windows, he could see pedestrians rushing past on the sidewalks, hurrying to cross the streets, their heads ducked, their hands clutching coat collars. Behind them and beyond them, the store windows beckoned warmly with holiday tinsel and mistletoe, colored lights and ornaments, wreaths and sprigs of holly. This was only the twelfth of December, with Christmas still almost two weeks away, but the stores had begun preparing for the season long before Thanksgiving, and the city wore a festive look that unified it now as it did each year. He could remember the long walks to the library from his home on 217th Street, the store windows decorated as they were here but with a shabby Bronx look. They had moved to the Bronx when he was twelve years old, the decentralization was beginning, the second generation was starting its exodus to what then passed for the suburbs. The trip to Grandpa's house each Sunday would be longer and more difficult to make, discouraging frequency, trickling away at last to family gatherings only on holidays or occasional Sundays, disappearing entirely when his grandfather died. The street they moved into was another ghetto, smaller, cleaner, with a rustic country look (or so it seemed after Harlem) trees planted in small rectangular plots of earth dug out of the sidewalk, mostly two-family brick houses, Olinville Junior High School across the street, its fence stretching halfway up the block from Barnes Avenue, they used to play handball in the schoolyard. He tried out for the handball team when he entered high school, but did not make it. He was a good student, though, his marks always up in the eighties and nineties, and an omnivorous reader. He would go to the library on 229th Street and Lowerre Place maybe two or three times a week, even before it got to be a gathering place for the high school crowd.

There was a feeling of prosperity to the new apartment (he recognized now that it was hardly less shabby than the four rooms they'd had in Harlem) with its new furniture and its new linoleum, the three-piece maple set his mother bought for him, with the dresser that had a hidden dropleaf desk full of cubbyholes, and the pink curtains in Julie's room. She was nine at the time, and had already begun to hang all kinds of crazy signs on her door, GENIUS AT WORK and BEWARE VICIOUS DOG, he got such a kick out of her, she was really a great kid. His father had become a "regular" by then, and was working out of the Williamsbridge Post Office on Gun Hill Road. He would set the alarm for four-thirty every morning, waking up the whole damn house, and clamoring for his breakfast, a real ginzo with ginzo ideas about the woman's place and so on. He could have let Mama sleep, instead of making such a big deal about breakfast, racing around the apartment in his long johns. "There he goes," Julie would yell, "they're off and running at Jamaica," and Arthur would lie in his bed under the quilt Aunt Louise had made for him, and quietly snicker, he sure was a nut, that old man of his.

There was, too, the same feeling of belonging in this new ghetto, though now there weren't aunts and uncles to meet on the street or to drop in on during the afternoon. But there were Italians all up and down the block, half of them barely able to speak English, and there was a funny kind of intimacy, a feeling of safety, an instant understanding that was not present out there in the White Protestant world, though at the time he was not aware such a world even existed. He knew only that he felt comfortable on his own block, with people who were easily recognizable, like the business with all the women named Anna, for example. His mother's name was Anna, but there were also four other women named Anna on the block. So instead of using their last names, which is what any decent New Canaan lady would have done, instead of referring to them as Anna Constantine or Anna Ruggiero or Anna Di Nobili, the women had a shorthand all their own, Naples-inspired he was sure, instant ginzo communication. His mother was Anna the Postman, and the other women were respectively Anna the Plumber, and Anna the Butcher, and Anna the Bricklayer and also Anna From Wall Street, he smiled even now, thinking of it. But he was comfortable then, comfortable in his growing body, and comfortable in his new home, where in the silence of his bedroom (unless Julie was practicing her flute in her own room next door) he would take the little maple lamp from the dresser top, the lamp shaped like a candlestick with a little shade on it, and he would put the lamp on the floor and play with his soldiers in the circle of light it cast. The dining room table had been sold before they left Harlem, they now had a three-piece living room suite and a big floor radio that looked like a juke box, but there were worlds to discover on his bedroom floor and he searched them out with his faithful Magua and his intrepid Shorty, his imagination looser now, fed by the books he withdrew from the library each week.

Every now and then he would take Julie to the library with him, leaving her in the children's section while he roamed in his mature twelve-year-old masculinity through the adult section, taking a book from a shelf, scanning it, deciding whether or not he wanted to read it. He never bought any books then, and he did not know there was such a thing as the bestseller list of the *New York Times Book Review*. He had not ever, in fact, even *read* the *New York Times,* although kids used to come around to the classrooms selling the *Times* and also the *Trib*. He grew up with the *News* and the *Mirror* and the *Journal-American* (he later felt betrayed when even these friendly and well-known newspapers killed his play). He wondered now when he had last gone to see a play that had not received rave notices, when he had last read a book that was not on the bestseller list. It had been much simpler then, the long walk to the library along White Plains Avenue, the library snug and warm, the aroma of books, the feel of them in his hands. And at Christmas, the tree opposite the main desk, decorated with popcorn, the Dickens novels bound in burnished red leather, tooled in gold, spread on the floor beneath the tree, more appropriate at Christmas than at any other time. The librarian was a nice German lady named Miss Goldschmidt. "Merry Christmas, Arthur," she would say. "What are you reading *this* week?"— the cherished copy of *The Talisman* with the jacket picture of the knight on horseback, he slid the book across the desk and Miss Goldschmidt beamed approval.

"You sure that's on Forty-sixth?" the cabbie asked.

"I'm sure," Arthur said. There were not too many things he was sure of, but he was dead certain that the Helen Hayes was on Forty-sixth Street because *Catchpole* had opened at that identical theater when it was still known as the Fulton in 1947, to be mercilessly clobbered by all ten gentlemen of the press the next day—back then, *PM,* the *Mirror,* the *Sun,* and the *Brooklyn Eagle* also had a say about what would be permitted to survive. He thought it supremely ironic that his new play was holding readings at the same theater, but he fervently wished it would open someplace else, *anyplace* else, where he would be safe from the evil eye. Evil eye, my ass, he thought, but hadn't his grandfather come to America from an impoverished mountain village called Ruvo del Monte, and wasn't there still enough of this heritage in Arthur to cause suspicion and doubt? In fact, hadn't his Aunt Filomena been hit by the iceman's runaway horse on First Avenue the very night after his mother had dreamt it? Any place but the Fulton, he thought. You can change the name, but the jinx remains. And yet he knew his fears were idiotic, God, look at what the wind was doing out there, papers blowing in the gutter, hats skimming off heads, look at that woman trying to control her skirts, God this was a city, what a city this was.

He wanted to own this city.

But more than that, or perhaps a part of it, an extension of it, he wanted to know that this was where he belonged, this city into which he had been born, this city whose streets and gutters he knew from the time he had felt for immies in deep puddles along the curb, this city whose rooftops held secret fluttering pigeons to watch, hot, sticky tar to mold into huge, strange shapes, chimney pots behind which you could pee, this city that had grown to include the Bronx and a two-family house opposite the junior high school, hide and seek behind hydrangea bushes, fig trees wrapped in tarpaper against the winter's cold, a two-cent Hooton with nuts every afternoon on the walk home from Evander, Bronx Park and the winding river path, Laura in the woods behind the

Botanical Gardens, they'd been eaten alive by mosquitoes, this city, this.

He wanted to claim it, but more than that he wished to be claimed by it.

Those solitary walks to the library alone, when alone his thoughts would spiral and somersault, when alone he would build magic castles bright with minarets and floating golden banners, when alone he was master of a world in which he walked proud and unafraid and people knew his name and dreaded it, hands thrust deep into the pockets of his mackinaw, the library books dangling at the end of a long leather strap except when it was raining and his mother made him put them in a shopping bag from the A&P, those solitary walks when he knew without question who he was and what he would become.

He wanted the city to tell him who he was again.

He paid the driver and got out of the taxi, walking directly to the stage entrance and opening the door onto the long alley that led to the rear of the theater. Selig and Stern were standing at the end of the alley, in whispered consultation just outside the metal stage door. Selig was wearing a black overcoat with black velveteen collar and cuffs, puffing on a cigar and standing alongside the iron steps that ran to the upper stories of the theater. The alleyway was gray, capped by an ominous piece of gray sky that hung high above it like a canopy. Selig stood in black against the rusting iron steps, surrounded by gray walls and gray smoke. His face appeared gray, too, as though someone very close had passed away during the night.

Stern was wearing a blue plaid sports jacket with a navy blue sweater under it. He was rubbing his big hands together as though chiding himself for having anticipated spring in December, his shoulders hunched, shivering with each swirling gust of alley wind. He looked up in surprise as Arthur approached, and then said, "Is the trial finished already?"

"No, we broke early," Arthur replied. "Is Kent here?"

"Not yet," Selig said.

Kent Mercer was their director, a faggot whose nocturnal revels ("I'm a *night* person," he would protest, "that's why I'm *in* the theater, really") often terminated along about dawn when less talented citizens were rising and banging on the radiators for heat. No one expected him to be on time because he never was, and no one ever mentioned his tardy appearances—except Selig, who would invariably remark, each time Mercer arrived late and pantingly out of breath, "Have a good night's sleep, Kent?"

"Where is it?" Stern asked, shivering. "The trial, I mean."

"All the way downtown. Foley Square."

"Is that near the traffic court down there?" Stern asked.

"I think so."

"I was down there once on a speeding ticket," Stern said.

"Mmm," Arthur said, and wondered how Stern could possibly equate a traffic ticket with something as important as a plagiarism suit. Of the two men, he liked Stern least, which in itself was no recommendation for Selig. "Have you heard from Mitzi?" he asked.

"Not yet," Selig said.

"Well, what's happening with Hester's contract?"

"You know as much about it as we do," Selig said mildly, and then puffed on his cigar and looked at the wet end as though suddenly displeased with its taste.

"Last Wednesday—"

"That's right," Stern said. Stern had an annoying habit of agreeing with a statement before it was finished. Arthur was tempted to say, "Last Wednesday someone told me you were a son of a bitch." Instead, he glanced at Stern in brief anger, and then said, "Last Wednesday you told me Hester liked the play."

"That's right," Stern said.

"That's what her agent told us," Selig agreed.

"Aren't you fellows cold out here?" Stern asked.

"No," Arthur said. "And on Friday, you told me she wanted to do it, and it was now a matter of negotiation."

"That's right."

"This is Monday," Arthur said.

"You know Hester."

"No, I don't know Hester."

"She's not sure now."

"If she was sure Friday . . ."

"We don't even know if she was sure Friday. We only know what her agent told us."

"Her agent said she wanted to do the play, isn't that right?"

"That's right."

"And that she was ready to negotiate."

"That's right."

"Well, has an offer been made?"

"She's getting a thousand a week at Lincoln Center, that's whether she's in any of the plays or not. If we even *hope* to spring her, we've got to offer at least fifteen hundred."

"Well, how much *did* you offer?"

"It hasn't come to that yet."

"Look, would someone please talk straight?" Arthur said.

"We've always talked straight with you, Arthur," Selig answered.

"*Was* an offer made?"

"No."

"Why not?"

"Because she still has to talk to the people at Lincoln Center about getting sprung."

"Won't they let her go?"

"We think they will, but it's a matter of sitting down with these people and discussing it."

"Well, when is she going to do that?"

"As soon as she's sure she wants to do your play."

"That's right," Stern said.

"Let me try to get this straight," Arthur said. "*Does* she want to do my play?"

"It would seem so."

"When will we know?"

"I'll call her agent again, if you want me to," Selig said. "Is that what you'd like?"

"Yes."

"I don't think we should push this," Stern said.

"Why not?"

"Because if we can get Hester Miers to take this part, we'll raise all the money for the play immediately. That's why."

"I thought we *had* all the money already," Arthur said.

"This show will cost eighty thousand dollars," Stern said.

"Have we got all the money, or haven't we?"

"No, Arthur," Selig said. "We have *not* got all the money."

"You told me . . ."

"That's right," Stern said.

"You told me all the money was in. You said . . ."

"That's right, but a few of our people have dropped out."

"Well, even if a few of them have dropped out, that doesn't mean . . ."

"One of our people was a man who'd promised us a very large sum of money. He'd decided to put it into a musical instead."

"How much do we still need?"

"We still need sixty thousand dollars," Selig said flatly.

"That means we've hardly got *any* of it," Arthur said.

"If we sign Hester, we'll get all of it," Stern said.

"Then for God's sake sign her!"

"She's not sure she wants to do it."

"Call her agent. I want to know."

"Mitzi will say what she said over the weekend," Stern said. "Hester's not sure."

"If you want me to call her, I will," Selig said. "I'll do whatever you want me to do, Arthur. After all, this is *your* play."

"That's right," Stern said, "but calling Mitzi won't do a bit of good."

"If Arthur wants me to call her, I will."

"Is that what you want, Arthur?"

"I want this play to go on," Arthur said fiercely.

"We all do."

"That's right. But calling Mitzi isn't going to help. She'll say she hasn't been able to reach Hester."

"Look . . ."

"This is the theater, Arthur. These people are sensitive individuals who—"

"Sensitive, my ass!" Arthur said. "My play is in danger of collapsing, and you're telling me some twenty-two-year-old kid has the power . . ."

"She's twenty-five, and she's very talented, and your play is *not* in danger of collapsing."

"I won't let this happen," Arthur said, and there was such an ominous note in his voice that the alley went immediately still. "Call Mitzi. Tell her we have to know, and we have to know right away."

"Don't push this," Stern warned.

"Oscar, if *I* don't push this, perhaps you'd like to tell me just who will."

"We all want the play to go on. We love this play."

"You've loved it for eleven months now, your option expires in January."

"That's right."

"Yes, that's right, and January is next month."

"We can always talk about an extension," Stern said. *"If* we get Hester."

"If we get Hester," Arthur repeated.

"That's right, *if* we get Hester. If we get Hester, we get the money, it's as simple as that. Once we get the money, we can talk extension. If you're willing to grant it, we can go into rehearsal as soon as we finish casting these minor parts. Probably in time for a spring opening."

Arthur nodded. "And if we *don't* get Hester?"

"Let's see what she has to say, okay?"

"Okay, call Mitzi," Arthur said.

"It'll have to wait till tomorrow."

"Why?"

"Because she's in Philadelphia," Selig said. "One of her clients, Boris Whatsisname, opens in Philadelphia tonight. She's got to be there to hold his hand."

"Well, can't you call her there? Philadelphia's only—"

"I don't want to bother her with something like this when she's got an opening. Be sensible, Arthur. It's not going to pay to get impatient here."

"All right."

"All right, Arthur?"

"I said all right."

"I'll call her in the morning, first thing."

"All right."

"And then I'll get to you."

"I'll be in court. The cross starts tomorrow."

"You call me when you're free then, all right?"

"All right," Arthur said.

3

SIDNEY LOOKED AT HIS WATCH the moment he entered
the vestibule of her building. It was a quarter to four, and
she had promised to wait until at least five, but he was afraid
now that she had grown impatient and left earlier. The
nameplate over her bell was lettered in delicate black script,
Charlotte Brown, and it annoyed him just as it always did.
He knew her as Chickie Brown, and the formal black script—
especially since it had been clipped from her business card—
conjured an image of a person about whom he knew very
little, Charlotte Brown, who was part owner of a travel
agency on Madison Avenue, where she arranged vacations
to Haiti or Istanbul for fat matrons. Scowling at the nameplate, he pressed the button below it, and hoped there would
be an answering buzz. He gripped the knob on the inner
vestibule door with his right hand, put his briefcase down
on the floor, patted his hair into place with his free left hand,
and waited. Sighing, he walked back to the row of mailboxes,
rang the bell a second time, returned to grip the doorknob
again, waited, went back to the bell a third time, waited
again, and had to ring yet another time before she answered.
Her buzz sparked an intense and immediate anger within
him, how *dare* she keep him waiting so long? The anger
mounted as he pushed open the frosted-glass door and stepped
into the hallway. Did a man have to ring a bell four times

before he was admitted to a building? An attorney? Angrily, he climbed the steps to her third-floor apartment. Angrily, he knocked on the door.

"Sidney?" she called.

"Yes," he said. "It's me." For a moment, he thought his anger had caused him to forget his briefcase in the vestibule below, and then he realized that he was holding it tightly in his sweating left hand. The door opened.

"Hello," he said brusquely.

"Hello, luv," she answered warmly.

She was wearing dark green slacks and a white silk blouse. A string of green beads circled her throat. Her long hair was piled carelessly on top of her head, held there haphazardly with a green ribbon, bright russet strands falling onto her cheek and forehead, trailing down the back of her neck.

"Come in," she said, "come in," and walked barefooted toward the plush-covered chair near the window, where her cat lay supine on the arm, his tail switching nervously. She passed her extended forefinger along the length of the cat's back, and then lowered the shade against the gathering dusk. The cat's name was Shah, and Sidney despised him.

Chickie turned from the window with a pleased smile on her face, as though she had been contemplating his arrival all day, and was now enormously satisfied by his presence. She touched the cat again in passing. He lifted his head to accept her hand, and then the tail switched again, and he turned to look at Sidney with a malevolent jungle stare.

One day, you little son of a bitch, Sidney thought, I will be in this apartment alone with you, and I will drown you in the tub.

"What kind of a cat is he?" he asked Chickie.

"A nice cat," she answered.

"I meant the breed."

"Persian."

"Is that why you call him Shah?"

"No."

"Then why?"

"Because he's a nice cat. Aren't you a nice cat, Shah

sweetie?" she asked, and she dropped to her knees before the chair and put her face close to the animal's. "Aren't you a lovey-cat, Shah honey?"

"Please, you'll make me vomit," Sidney said.

"I think Sidney has had a hard day in the mines," she said to the cat, and then rose and grinned and said, "Would you like a drink, Sidney? Would that help?"

"I had a very easy day," Sidney said, glaring at the cat. "I just don't happen to like your cat."

"Sidney!" she said. "I thought you *loved* Shah."

"No, I *don't* love Shah."

"I thought you did."

"No, I do not. Point of fact, I do not love *any* cat in the world, *least* of all Shah. Don't ever leave me alone in the apartment with him, or I'll drown him in the tub."

"Do you hear that, Shah?" she said playfully. "Watch out for Sidney because he'll drown you in the tub."

The cat made an ominous sound from somewhere back in his throat. "That's right, you heard her," Sidney said, and Shah made the same ominous sound again.

"He understands you," Chickie said.

"I hope he does. Why do you keep him around?"

"He was a gift."

"From whom?"

"A man."

"Who?"

"Before I knew you."

"I didn't ask you *when,* I asked you *who.*"

"An Indian."

"From India?"

"Yes, of course. Did you think I meant a Mohican or something?"

"I never know what you mean, exactly," he said, and sighed.

"Don't you want to know *why* he gave me the cat?"

"No."

"All right, then I won't tell you."

"Why did he give you the cat?" Sidney asked.

"Why do you think he gave me the cat?"

"Because he knew you loved cats."

"No. That is, he knew I loved cats, yes, but that's not why he gave me a present. The cat was a present, Sidney."

"Why did he give you a present?" Sidney asked, and sighed again.

"You think it's because I went to bed with him, don't you?" Chickie said.

"Did you go to bed with him?" he asked wearily.

"Sidney, what a question to ask!"

"Well, then why *did* he give you the filthy little animal?"

"You're angry now."

"No, I'm not angry now. But sometimes I get awfully goddamn tired of these Burns and Allen routines."

"I didn't mean to make you angry," she said, "I'm sorry." She rose quickly, lowered her eyes, and padded to the bar. "I'll make you that drink," she said.

"Thank you."

The room was silent. It could have been a shuttered room in Panama, there was that kind of afternoon hush to it, the waning light against a drawn shade, the silk-tasseled lower edge, a contained lushness, the green plush chair with the gray cat purring on its arm, the moss green of the velvet curtains and the burnt sienna walls, the scent of snuffed-out candles and perfume.

He had felt in Panama a centuries-old decadence that clung to every archway and twisted street, a miasma of evil, a certain knowledge that anything ever devised by humans had been done in this city, and he had been excited by it. Now, watching Chickie as she moved barefooted over the rug, the drink in one hand, he felt the beginning of that same kind of excitement, a welcome loss of control that he experienced whenever he was near her, a heady confusion that threatened to submerge him.

She handed him the drink. "What is it?" she asked.

"I had to ring four times," he said.

"What?"

"Downstairs."

"Is that what's bothering you?"

"Yes," he said, and accepted the drink.

"I'm sorry, Sidney, but you'll remember—"

"It's all right."

"You'll remember that I advised you not to come in the first place. I have to leave in a very few minutes. . . ."

"Where are you going?"

"To the agency. I told you that on the phone, Sidney, and I told you I'd be very rushed."

"Why are you going to the agency?"

"I have work to do."

"I thought . . ."

"I have work to do, Sidney."

"All right, I'll pick you up later for dinner," he said.

"No, I can't have dinner with you tonight."

"Why not?"

"I'm having dinner with Ruth. We have a trip to work out. I told you all about it."

"No, you didn't."

"A very important trip that may materialize," she said, nodding.

"That *may* materialize?" he said. "I don't understand."

"Ruth and I have to work out this trip together," she explained very slowly, "that may be materializing."

"A trip to where?"

"Europe."

"For whom?"

"For a client, of course."

"But what do you mean it *may* be materializing?"

"Well, it isn't certain yet."

"When will it be certain?"

"Very soon, I would imagine. Your hair sticks up in the back, did you know that?"

"Yes. Can't Ruth handle it alone? There's something I wanted to—"

"No, she can't. Do you want a refill, Sidney?"

"No. Why can't she?"

"Because it would be a very long trip, Sidney. *If* it materializes. It would be for the entire winter, you see."

"I see."

"Until the fifteenth of June."

"I see."

"Which is why it's so terribly complicated. Are you sure you don't want a refill?"

"No, thanks. Maybe I can see you later then. There's something—"

"I'll be busy all night."

He stared at her for a moment, and then said, "Chickie, are you lying to me?"

"What?"

"Are you lying?"

"About what, for God's sake?"

"About this trip, about tonight, about . . ."

"Sidney, I'm a very bad liar. I wouldn't even attempt lying to you."

"I think you're lying to me right this minute," he said.

"Now stop it, Sidney," she warned. "You may have had a difficult day, but let's not start hurling silly accusations around, shall we not?"

"I'm sorry," he said. "I h-h-have had a d-d-difficult day, I'm sorry."

"That's all right, Sidney, and don't start stammering."

"I'm sorry."

"What you need is another drink," she said, and took his glass. "And then I've got to get dressed." She put two ice cubes into his glass and poured more bourbon over them. She handed the glass to Sidney and then said, "Shall I take Shah out of the room? Would you like me to do that?"

"Yes, I'd appreciate it."

"I will then. Come, Shah," she said, "come, pussycat. Sidney doesn't like you because of the Indian, isn't that true, Sidney? Come, Shah, sweetie."

She lifted the cat into her arms, cradling him against her breasts. "Drink," she said to Sidney, and then suddenly stopped alongside his chair. "Drink," she repeated in a whisper. A strange little smile twisted her mouth. She stared at him another moment, smiling, and then turned her back to him abruptly and went down the hall to her bedroom.

He sat alone in the darkening room, sipping his drink.

He supposed he would ask her when she returned, though he would have much preferred doing it over dinner. He did not relish the thought of postponing it again, however. He had been on the verge of asking her for the past week, and each time he had lost his courage, or become angry with her, and each time he had postponed it. He had the feeling he could put it off indefinitely if he allowed himself to, and he did not want that to happen. No, he would ask her when she returned, even though he was still a little angry with her.

He had to watch the anger, that was the important thing. Oh yes, there were other things as well—he talked with his hands a lot, he had got that from his father; and the stammering, of course, but that was only when he got excited; and his inability to extricate himself sometimes from a very complicated sentence, three years of Latin at Harvard, a lot of good it had done him. But the anger was the most important thing, that was the thing he had to control most of all because he knew that if he ever really let loose the way his mother . . . well.

Well, she was dead, poor soul, nor had it been very pleasant the way she went, lingering, lingering, he had gone to that hospital room every day of the week for six months, at a time when he had just begun the partnership with Carl and really should have been devoting all of his energies to building the practice. Well, what are you supposed to do when your mother is dying of cancer, not visit her? leave her to the vultures? God forbid. And the anger, her immense and enormous anger persisting to the very end, the imperious gestures to the special nurses day and night, oh the drain on his father, the shouted epithets, thank God most of them were in Yiddish and the nurses didn't understand them, except that one Miss Leventhal who said to him in all seriousness and with an injured look on her very Jewish face,

"Your mother is a nasty old lady, Mr. Brackman"—with the poor woman ready to die any minute, ahhh.

The anger.

He had never understood the anger. He only knew that it terrified him whenever it exploded, and he suspected it terrified his father as well, who always seemed equally as helpless to cope with it. His mother had been a tall slender woman with a straight back and wide shoulders, dark green eyes, masses of brown hair piled onto the top of her head, a pretty woman he supposed in retrospect, though he had never considered her such as a child. They lived on East Houston Street, and his father sold shoes for a living, shoes that were either factory seconds or returns to retail stores. He did a lot of business with Bowery bums when they were sober enough to worry about winter coming and bare feet instead of their next drink of smoke. He had always admired the way his father handled the bums, with a sort of gentleness that did not deny their humanity, the one and only thing left to them. Except once when a drunken wino came into the store and insulted Sidney's mother, and his father took the man out onto the sidewalk and punched him twice in the face, very quickly, sock, sock, and the man fell down bleeding from his nose, Sidney remembered how strong his father had been that day. The wino came back with a breadknife later, God knows where he had got it, probably from the soup kitchen near Delancey, and his father met him in the doorway of the store, holding a length of lead pipe in his right hand and saying, "All right, so come on, brave one, use your knife." His mother called the police, and it all ended pretty routinely, except for his mother's later anger.

The anger exploded suddenly, the way it always did, they were sitting in the kitchen upstairs, the second floor over the store, and his mother began berating Sidney's father for what Sidney thought had been his really courageous behavior and suddenly she went off, click, it was always like that, click, as though a switch were thrown somewhere inside her head, short-circuiting all the machinery, click, and the anger exploded. She got very red in the face, she looked Irish when she did, and her green eyes got darker, and she would bunch her slender hands into tight compact fists and stalk the kitchen, back and forth, the torrent of words spilling from her mouth in steady fury, not even making sense sometimes, repeating over and over again events long past, building a paranoid case, well, no not paranoid, building a case against the world, reliving each injustice she had ever suffered at the hands of the goyim, at the hands of childhood friends, at the hands of his father's family, at the hands of her ungrateful whelp of a son, nothing whatever to do with the drunken wino (or whoever or whatever it happened to be), the supposed original cause of her anger. "No justice," she would scream, "there's no justice," and the flow of words would continue as she paced the kitchen before the old washtub, and Sidney's father would go to her and try to console her, "Come, Sarah, come, darling," and she would throw off his imploring hands while Sidney sat at the oilcloth-covered table in terror, thinking his mother was crazy or worse, well not crazy, "She's excited," his father would say, "she's just excited."

Those were not happy times. The war had ended long ago, but the Depression was on its way, and there would come a day when even Bowery bums no longer cared whether or not they were wearing almost-new shoes, or *any* shoes for that matter, when the best defense against a nation sliding steadily downhill was indeed a bottle of hair tonic in a dim hallway stinking of piss. He came to look upon those Bowery ghosts as a symbol of what America had become, and he dreaded growing up, becoming a man in a world where there were no jobs, and no justice, especially for Jews. He was very conscious of his Jewishness, not because anyone called him Jew-boy—hardly anyone ever did since he hung around mostly with other Jewish kids, and since all of his relatives were Jews, and every function he attended was either a Jewish wedding or a bar mitzvah or a funeral, well, yes, there was that one incident, but even that was not so terribly bad, his mother's anger afterwards had been worse than the actual attack—he was conscious of his Jewishness mostly in a religious way, strange for a young boy, almost a holy way, everybody in the family said that Sidney would grow up to be a rabbi. In fact, his Uncle Heshie from Red Bank used to jokingly call him Reb Shiloach, and this always pleased him enormously because he thought of the town rabbi, the old rabbi in the Polish town from which his mother and father had come, as a very learned man who dispensed justice, who read from the Holy Book and dispensed justice to Jews, the one thing that had somehow been denied his mother only because she *was* Jewish. He sometimes visualized himself in the role of the Talmudic scholar, searching for the holy word that would put an end to his mother's anger, "Look, Mama," he would say, "it is written here thus and so, so do not be angry." And all the while, he feared the anger was buried deep within himself as well. He had seen murder in his mother's eyes, he had heard hatred in her voice, had the seed really fallen too terribly far from the tree? Was it not possible that he too could explode, click, the switch would be thrown in his head, click, and being a man he would kill someone? Later, when it happened with the Irish kids, when they surrounded him that day and pulled down his pants and beat him with Hallowe'en sticks and he did not fight back, he wondered whether he was really a person in whom there lay this secret terrible wrath, or whether he was simply a coward. He only knew for certain there had been no justice for him that day, that he had done nothing to warrant such terrible punishment, such embarrassment, the girls standing around and looking at his naked smarting behind, and later crossing their fingers as he walked home, "Shame, shame, we saw Sidney's *tushe,* shame, shame," chanting it all the way home like a litany, there was no justice that day, but neither had they called him Jewboy. Maybe they just wanted to take down my pants, Sidney reasoned later, who the hell knows?

The wrath exploded that night, he was certain it would, and it did. He did not at the time connect any of his mother's explosions with sex—if you had asked anyone on the Lower East Side who Sigmund Freud was, they'd have recalled the man who peddled used china from a pushcart on Hester

Street and whose name was Siggie Freid—but in later years it seemed to him that the justice she so avidly sought was somehow connected with events that invariably concerned sex, and he began wondering what could possibly have happened to his mother back in Europe. But no, he never really consciously thought that, no one ever consciously thinks that about his own mother, it only came to him on the gray folds of semirecognition—the wino had said, "You've got some tits there, lady," the Irish boys had taken down Sidney's pants, the sewing machine salesman had asked if he could step into the parlor for a moment, the argument with Hannah Berkowitz had involved the use of too much rouge, the girl his mother found him with on the roof was Adele Rosenberg who was sixteen years old and wore no bloomers in the summer, but *everybody* knew that, not only Sidney, and besides they weren't even *doing* anything. All these events returned to him grayly, darkly, as though on a swelling ocean crest that dissipated and dissolved before it quite reached the shore, leaving behind only vanishing bubbles of foam absorbed by the sand. The black and towering fact remained his mother's anger, which was to him inexplicable at the time. It was simply *there*. Uncontrollable, raging, murderous. He would dream of bureau drawers full of women's hair, brown and tangled. He would dream of hags sitting next to him in movie theaters, opening their mouths to expose rotten teeth and foul breath. He would dream of running through castles where dead bodies were stacked end upon end, decomposing as he raced through them, filling his nostrils with suffocating dust.

He feared his mother, and he pitied his mother, and he despised his mother. And he loved her as well.

Because of her, he never lied about being a Jew. A lot of the kids in the neighborhood and on the block were lying in order to get jobs, this was 1934, 1935, the NRA had already come in, the blue eagles clutching lightning were showing in all the shop windows all over the city, things were a little better, but it was still difficult to get a job, especially a part-time job, and especially if you were a Jew. He never lied about being a Jew, and he never told himself later that the reason he didn't get the job was because he was Jewish. He blamed his inability to find work on a lot of things—his looks, his height, the stammer he had somehow developed and which always seemed to crop up when he was being interviewed for a position, the somewhat high whininess of his adolescent voice, all of these things—but never his Jewishness. His Jewishness was something separate and apart, something of which he could be uncommonly proud, the old rabbi quietly studying the Holy Book in the sunset of his mother's town, the townspeople standing apart and waiting for him to dispense justice.

He was able to enter Harvard only because Uncle Heshie from Red Bank died and left his favorite nephew a small sum of money, sizable enough in those days, certainly enough to pay for Sidney's undergraduate education. He left for Boston in the fall of 1936. He was eighteen years old, and five feet eight inches tall (he assumed he had grown to his full height, and he was correct). He had black hair parted close to the middle and combed into a flamboyant pompadour that scarcely compensated for the cowlick at the back of his head. He came directly from Townsend Harris High School, where his grades had averaged 91 per cent, and from which he had graduated with honors.

At Harvard, in his freshman year, they called him Lard Ass, and he once drank fourteen bottles of beer and passed out cold. At Harvard, in his sophomore year, he joined the Dramatic Club and became reasonably famous for his clubhouse imitation of Eddie Cantor singing "If You Knew Susie." At Harvard, in September of 1939, when the Germans were overrunning the Polish town where his mother had been born and perhaps putting to death forever the image of the village rabbi studying the Holy Book by the light of the setting sun, Sidney met a student nurse named Rebecca Strauss—"Watch out for those nurses, Sid," his roommate told him. "They can give it a flick with their finger, and whap! it'll go right down, quick as that"—and began dating her regularly. Rebecca lived in West Newton and worked at Massachusetts General where her father was a resident surgeon. She had dark green eyes and masses of brown hair, and she was the most beautiful girl Sidney had ever met in his life, prettier even than Adele Rosenberg who wore no bloomers in the summer. He grew a mustache for Rebecca because he always felt he looked silly and immature beside her, even though he was two months her senior. She said she loved the mustache and that it didn't tickle at all when they kissed. When he finally told her in confidence about his mother's raging fits—he had by that time begun to think of them as "fits," similar to epileptic seizures or paranoid delusions—she said they did seem very much like hysterical symptoms, collaborating his own feelings that something dreadful had happened to his mother when she was still a girl in Poland.

"She may have been raped or something," Rebecca said.

"Do you think so?"

They were lying in the grass bordering the Charles, she was in his arms. It was the spring of 1940, he could hear crickets chirping in the night, and the gentle flow of the river, and in the distance the highway traffic.

"Yes," Rebecca said. "Sometimes a man can't control himself, you know. And he'll do things. To a girl."

"Maybe," Sidney said, thinking of the time with the sewing machine salesman, had the man been unable to control himself?

"And sometimes a girl can even *want* a man to. Do things, you know."

"I g-g-guess you're right," Sidney said. Had his mother *wanted* the salesman to do things?

"Do you ever feel . . ." Rebecca moved closer in his arms. He could smell her hair, the crickets seemed suddenly louder.

"What?" he said.

"That you can't control yourself?"

"I'm always afraid of that," he said.

"Of not being able to control yourself?"

"Of losing my temper. Of g-g-getting angry the way my m-m-mother does."

"I meant . . ."

She was silent again. Her hand was resting on the side of his face, she was curled in his arms, he could feel the swell of her breasts against him, the crisp starched white of her nurse's uniform.

"What I meant," Rebecca said, and again fell silent.

"I know, you mean people sometimes . . ."

"Yes," she said, nodding.

"Sure, which is . . ."

"That it's understandable," she said, nodding. "If a man and a woman."

"Yes, it's possible," nodding.

"Yes."

"If they're close to each other."

"Yes."

She moved. Her starched skirt edged back over one knee and she took her hand from his face to lower the skirt again, long legs sheathed in white stockings, she moved closer.

"I myself, I know," Rebecca said.

"Sure," Sidney said.

"Get hot sometimes," she said, and quickly added, "I've never told this to anyone in my life."

"Reb-b-becca . . ."

"So hot I can't stand it," Rebecca said. "I've never talked this way to anyone in my life."

"You . . . you ought to be careful," he said, "t-t-talking that way."

"I know, I know," she said, moaning the words. In the silence, she moved again. The starched uniform made tiny crisp sounds as she adjusted her body to the length of his, moving minutely in against him, her arms tight around his neck, trembling.

"Do *you* get hot?" she whispered.

"Yes."

"So hot you can't *stand* it?"

"Yes."

"Are you now?" Her voice so small.

"Yes."

"I can feel you." A whisper.

"Are . . . *you?*" he asked.

"Yes, oh yes."

It all happened, it was too, he didn't plan, hands under starched, and her white thighs, she turned, white stockings, and it happened and he, she moved beneath him, silk, all opening, the slip and, in a tangle of, and white garters, hands under, wet, and she said, oh she said, oh she said, wide, and was all, he didn't, held and clawed and, legs spread, and he was, she moaned, wet and garters, wet and, oh she said, oh love she moaned, oh, her head was, she was, he could feel, tossing, it happened, it was happening, he was, baby, he was, honey, lips and wet and hard and hard, I love you, I love you, I love you.

Ahhh me, he thought back with a sigh, it has never been like that again, not the way it was with Rebecca in Boston, two dumb young kids discovering what humping was all about, and going at it with a secret eagerness that, God we couldn't wait to see each other each time. Three, four times a week, sometimes more, going at it with a secret soaring joy that shouted to the world, *we* knew what it was all about, *we* had discovered it, *we* had patented it, we were the only two people humping in Boston—by the river, and in the back seat of the '36 Plymouth I bought, and in a Providence hotel one weekend, and once in Dr. Strauss's Oldsmobile parked behind the hospital, and then day and night in the apartment I took on Massachusetts Avenue in Cambridge, when I entered law school. Day and night, it's a wonder I learned any law at all, the only law I knew was whatever sweetly called to me from between Rebecca's legs. And then, I don't know, I don't know what happens, war happens, I guess. You get put into 1-A when you're in your second year of law school, and I guess you figure you'd better get into the Navy where the beds are always clean, so the legend goes, and there're always three square meals a day, so the legend goes, before they draft you into the infantry and you get your ass blown off invading the fortress of Europe. And besides, by that time Rebecca had met a young captain who was stationed at the Air Corps base on Jeffries Point. It was wartime—I saw him once, he was very tall and blond, he had blue eyes, he looked a little like Terry in *Terry and the Pirates* which Papa brought home every Sunday when he bought bagels on Rivington Street—it was wartime, so who could blame anyone? Who could blame the captain for succumbing to Rebecca's Law, and who could blame Rebecca, blossoming wild and willful Rebecca, young, sweet Rebecca, for wanting to go to bed with Terry, or even Pat Ryan, for that matter? I'd certainly have done it with the Dragon Lady if she had come along. Or Burma.

My ship was commissioned in Boston, I guess it was 1943, and I called Rebecca Strauss, or at least I called her number in West Newton, and her father got on the phone, Dr. Strauss, and he said, "Hello, there, Sidney, how have you been, fellow?" sounding like a goy, I could visualize him in Bermuda shorts, holding a five iron. I told him I'd been down to fire control school in Fort Lauderdale—"Oh, learning how to put out fires, huh, Sidney?"—(I didn't bother to correct him)—and that I'd been assigned to a destroyer and we were here in Boston before heading down to Gitmo (I used the Navy slang for Guantanamo just to show him how salty I was, and also to imply to him somehow that I had been humping his daughter for three years, put *that* in your scalpel case, Dr. Strauss) on shakedown cruise and I was wondering if I could talk to Rebecca, say hello and all that. Well, gee, Sidney, Dr. Strauss said, sounding more and more like the president of the local Grange, I'd be very happy to let you talk to Rebecca, but she doesn't live here anymore. You see, Sidney, she was married in October, perhaps you know the fellow (*fellow* again), perhaps you know him, a very nice fellow from Detroit, Michigan, his name is Lonnie Scott, S-C-O-T-T. No, I said, I'm sorry, Dr. Strauss, I don't think I ever met any friend of Rebecca's named Lonnie Scott, S-C-O-T-T. Oh, he's a *very* nice fellow, Dr. Strauss said, very very nice, they're living in California now, he's stationed out there, he's a major in the Air Corps, a very *nice* fellow, Sidney. Well, Dr. Strauss, I said, if you should have the opportunity to write to Becks (I used this pet name in an attempt once more to inform Dr. Strauss that his daughter *Becks* and I had been intimate for three years, get it, Dr. Strauss? Intimate. I-N-T-I-M-A-T-E) if you should happen to write to old Becks, why you just tell her Sidney called on his way through Boston to say hello and remind her of old times (in your Oldsmobile behind the hospital, for instance, Dr. Strauss, which I thought but didn't say). Why, sure, Sidney, Dr. Strauss said, sounding more and more like an Ohio preacher every minute, sure, fellow, I'll tell her you called— and say, good luck with that fire fighting, it's a dangerous business especially aboard ship. It sure is, I told him (do you get hot, Sidney, so hot you can't stand it?). Goodbye, Dr. Strauss.

Goodbye, fellow.

The war meant nothing to Sidney. He never saw any action, and the only danger to which he was exposed was that of tedium, even though he was aboard a destroyer. (Once they shot at a floating Japanese mine, and exploded it. Everyone cheered.) He was honorably discharged in September of 1946, and spent the summer with his parents who had moved from Houston Street to Walton Avenue near Yankee Stadium. His mother had one of her "fits" in August, shortly before he left for school again, it had to do with the doctor she had begun visiting, something about his nurse, Sidney couldn't follow it, nor did he try. He simply sat in terrified patience while the raving and ranting ran its course, his father fluttering about her like a broken butterfly, trying to calm her, Sarah's green eyes flashing, brown hair streaked with gray now, back straight and stiff, pacing, pacing (he remembered the soft embraces of Rebecca Strauss, they *do* sound to me like hysterical symptoms, she may have been raped or something, Rebecca's Law. Only once did they ever exchange harsh words, the time she was ten days late and they were frantic, no, twice actually, because she was also late after that long weekend in Providence, she almost climbed the ceiling that time, Rebecca, Becks, my love).

His mother died in 1953, after he had been practicing law for five years and had already started the partnership with

Carl. He was so enormously relieved by her passing that for several weeks afterward he walked around in a gloomy cloud of guilt, questioning his love for her, had he wanted her dead? blaming himself for not having insisted on chest X-rays earlier, and yet delighted, but had it been his fault? had he wished it once too often? and yet deliriously happy that she was dead and finally in the ground where nothing but the worms could tremble if she took a supernatural fit. He began to question, too, his own monumental anger, was it really such? Or had he simply built an elaborate defense against his own fear, constructing an image of a violently dangerous human being (inside every skinny Jew there is a fat Nazi) whom you had better not fool around with, Mama, because he is as equally capable of murderous rage as you are. He didn't know. Even now, he still thought of himself as a person with a low boiling point, a violent man who easily lost his temper—and yet he knew he hardly ever raised his voice to anyone.

Well, Chickie made him angry, yes, but that was different because with her it was a teasing sort of thing, and more like, well—when he was with her, and she began to tease him that way, began to coax him into anger almost, he would feel an odd quaking inside him, something like what he had known on Houston Street, sitting at the oilcloth-covered kitchen table, which was odd because he certainly wasn't *afraid* of Chickie. And yet, the way she came at him, the way she approached everything they did together, the sex so different from what it had been with Rebecca, she created a, a turmoil in him, yes, that was both exciting and confusing and, he supposed, well, yes, he supposed so, yes, frightening sometimes. He could never understand, for example, why she constantly made oblique references, and sometimes not such oblique ones, to the men she had known. Surely she knew the habit infuriated him—or was that why she persisted? He could not understand. Point of fact, there were a great *many* things that baffled him about Chickie Brown, nor was his confusion something recent. It had been present six months ago when she first walked into his Wall Street office, and if anything it had assumed greater dimensions since.

"Mr. Brackman," she had said, "I'm Charlotte Brown," and he took her extended hand. He had known a great many women since Rebecca Strauss, both casually and intimately, but he had never felt for any of them an iota of what he had felt in Boston. And now, shaking hands with this tall and magnificently proportioned young lady, his heart began to pound foolishly and he found himself staring into her eyes, offering her a seat, barely knowing what he was saying to her. There was a fullness to her palm, a moistness to her flesh that he found intensely exciting, as though her handshake had inadvertently revealed a guarded secret and become a shared intimacy.

She sat opposite his desk, and he found he could not take his eyes from her, found that he was openly coveting her, and wondered that she was not embarrassed by his lavish attention. There was about her, he supposed, a look of easy availability that brought her youthful beauty dangerously close to the edge of cheapness, a look he found wildly stimulating. Her hands were in constant motion, now moving to touch her throat, now absently toying with a button on her blouse, now drifting toward her thigh to rest there a moment, now brushing at her cheek or her eye. She crossed and uncrossed her legs constantly and a shade too carelessly, but completely without guile. She kept jiggling her foot, and she had a habit of giggling unexpectedly. As she related her legal problems to him—she was part owner of a travel agency, and they were having trouble collecting from a client the monies advanced for airline tickets, hotel deposits, and so on—he barely heard a word of what she said, so intense were the lewd fantasies he built around this innocent young girl. It was not until toward the end of their interview, after he had agreed to take her case, that he began to suspect she was enjoying his insistent scrutiny, if not actively encouraging it. Surprising himself, he asked if she would like to discuss the case more extensively over a drink, and she surprised him even further by accepting his invitation.

He had not understood her then, six months ago, and he did not understand her now. He was proud of her beauty, flattered by her youth, but embarrassed by the tawdry look she narrowly escaped. He was wildly excited by her readiness and her intense passion, but frightened sometimes by her sexual knowledge. He was amazed by her shrewdness and appalled by her stupidity. She could doggedly argue a subject until he flew into a rage, and then instantly calm him with a subjugating kiss. She could bring him to the very edge of climax and then infuriatingly declare she was not in the mood for sex. She could cause him to roar with laughter, or weep in supplication. The first time they had gone to bed together, she had whispered, "Come, Sidney, I am going to take you where you've never been," and she had kept her promise.

He heard the bedroom door closing. To the closed door, she said, "Now you be a good pussycat, you be a good little Shah, do you hear me?" Her heels clattered along the corridor. She came into the living room buttoning her suit jacket. She smoothed her skirt over her hips, turned a small pirouette, and asked, "Do I look all right? I feel as though I dressed in a hurricane. I *hate* to rush."

"You look beautiful," he said.

"You dear man," she answered, "how can you even *see* without the light on?" She turned on a table lamp, and then stooped to kiss him on the cheek. "I really have to run, Sidney. You can sit here and finish your drink, if you like. Just pull the door shut behind you when you leave, it'll lock automatically."

"When will you be back?" he asked.

"Not until late."

"Maybe I'll stay here and wait for you."

"No, I'd rather you didn't."

"Why not?"

"Because I'll be exhausted, Sidney dear."

"All right." He paused. "Have you got at least a minute?"

"Yes, but barely."

"There's something I want to ask you."

"Not about the Indian."

"No, not about the Indian."

"Good." She smiled and sat on the arm of his chair. "What is it?"

"I don't know if I've ever explained my situation to you."

"What situation?"

"With the firm."

"No, I don't think you have. But Sidney . . ."

"It's not a very big firm, Chickie, not a very big firm at all. There's myself and my partner, and we each earn somewhere between ten and fifteen thousand dollars a year, I want you to know that."

"Sidney, I never asked you what—"

"I know, and I appreciate it, but I want you to understand the full picture. I'm not what you would call a very successful lawyer."

"Sidney, you're a very *good* lawyer."

"Well, I hope so, but I'm not a very successful one. There are lawyers in this city who can count on a hundred thousand dollars even in a bad year. I'm not one of them, Chickie."

"Why are you telling me this?"

"Because I want you to know."

She looked at him curiously, and then frowned. "You're not going to cry or anything, are you, Sidney?"

"No."

"Because I really haven't got time for that."

"No, I'm not going to cry," he said.

"Good. What is it then?"

"If I win this case, Chickie, I will be a very big lawyer."

"Will you?"

"We're suing for an accounting of profits, Chickie. It's our estimate that the movie earned in the vicinity of ten million dollars. We can't tell for certain because API isn't required to produce its books unless we win, or unless they're necessary to show we *are* entitled to an accounting. But ten million dollars is our guess."

"Sidney . . ." she started, and frowned, and glanced at her watch.

"I'll tell you the truth, neither Carl nor I wanted to take it on at first, my partner. We weren't sure there was a case, we knew very little about plagiarism. But you'd be surprised, Chickie, you'd really be surprised at how many plagiarism cases have been won on evidence that seems silly at first, similarities that seem ridiculous. The ones Constantine pointed out seemed just that way to us in the beginning, until we had a chance to examine them in the light of other cases. There *was* copying, Chickie, I sincerely believe that now. Driscoll was clever, yes, he altered, yes, disguised, yes, but he copied. I believe that, Chickie, I'd *better* believe it— the case has already cost the firm close to ten thousand dollars, not to mention time, but it'll be worth it if we win." Sidney paused. "The fee we agreed to is forty per cent of whatever we recover. Do you understand me, Chickie?"

"I think so," she said. She was still frowning, but she was listening intently now.

"Forty per cent of ten million dollars is four million dollars, Chickie. If we win this case, my partner will get two million dollars and *I* will get two million dollars. I will be a very r-r-rich man, Chickie, and v-v-very well-known." Sidney paused. "I will be a successful lawyer, Chickie."

"You're a successful lawyer now," she said.

"Not like J-J-Jonah Willow."

"You're every bit as smart as Willow," she said. "Don't stammer."

"Yes, but not as successful." He paused. "Maybe not as s-s-smart, either, I don't know."

"You're just as smart, Sidney."

"Maybe," he said. He paused again. "Chickie, as you know, I have a widower father to support, he has a garden apart- ment in Queens, he's a very old man, and no trouble at all. I pay the rent each month, and I give him money to live on, that's about the extent of it."

"Yes, Sidney."

"Chickie, I've been wanting to ask you this for a long time now, but I never felt I had the right. I'm forty-eight years old, going on forty-nine, and I know you're only twenty-seven and, to be quite truthful, I've never been able to understand what you see in me."

"Let *me* worry about that," she said, and began stroking the back of his neck.

"B-b-but, I feel certain I'm going to win this case and that would ch-change things considerably. That's why I f-f-feel I now have the right."

"What right, Sidney?"

"I guess you know I l-l-love you, Chickie. I suppose that's been made abundantly apparent to you over the past several months. I am very much in love with you, Chickie, and I would consider it an honor if you were to accept my p-p-proposal of matrimony."

Chickie was silent.

"Will you marry me, Chickie?"

"This is pretty unexpected," she said. Her voice was very low. He could barely hear her.

"I figured it would come as a surprise to you."

"I'll have to think about it, Sidney. This isn't something a girl can rush into."

"I realize that."

"I'll have to think about it."

"I'll be a very rich man when I win this c-c-case," Sidney said.

"You dear man, do you think that matters to me?" Chickie asked.

He lay full length on the bed opposite the window, his hands behind his head, staring up at the ceiling. He had been lying that way for close to an hour now, ever since their return to the hotel room. He had not closed his eyes in all that time, nor could Ebie fool herself into believing he was actually resting. There was a tautness in his very posture, an unseen nervous vibration that she could feel across the length of the room. His silence was magnified by the rush-hour babble from below. In the echoing midst of headlong life, he lay as still as a dead man and stared sightlessly at the ceiling.

"Are you all right?" she asked.

"I'm fine," he said.

"Dris?"

"Yes?"

"I'm afraid."

"Don't be afraid, Edna Belle."

"Can't we talk?" she asked.

"What would you like to talk about?"

"Can't . . . can't you reassure me? Can't you tell me we're not going to lose?"

"I'm not sure of that, Edna Belle."

"Please don't call me Edna Belle."

"That's your name, isn't it?"

"My name's been Ebie for the past God knows how long, please don't call me Edna Belle. I hate the name Edna Belle. You know I hate the name."

"Ebie is an affectation," he said.

"It's not an affectation, it's my *name*. It's an important part of me."

"Yes, I'm sure it is."

"Yes, it is."

"I said yes."

"Then please don't call me Edna Belle."

"I won't."

"And if you feel like getting angry, please . . ."

"I'm not getting angry."

". . . don't get angry with me. You have no reason to get angry with me."

"That's true. No reason at all."

"Get angry with Constantine, if you want to get angry. Or his lawyer. *They're* the ones who are trying to ruin us."

"If you ask me," he said, *"you're* the one who's getting angry, not me."

"Because you're not giving me the assurance I need."

"False assurance is a beggar's—"

"Don't try to get literary," Ebie said.

"Was I getting literary?"

"You were trying to, there's a difference. I can't stand it when you try to sound like a goddamn novelist."

"Have no fear. I am not a goddamn novelist."

"What are you then?"

"A Vermont farmer."

"You were a novelist before you were a farmer."

"I have never been a novelist," he said.

"No? What do you call *The Paper Dragon?*"

"Luck," he said, and closed his eyes.

The room was silent. From the street below, she could hear someone shouting directions to a truck driver at the *Times* depot. In the distance, Sardi's neon sign stained the dusk a luminous green, and the surrounding gray and shadowy buildings began to show lights in isolated window slits. She stared at him without speaking, and then pressed her face to the glass and watched the truck as it backed into the depot. How simple it is, she thought. How simple they make everything. When she turned to him again, her voice was very low. "They can take it all away from us," she said. "We can lose everything, Dris."

"We lost everything a long time ago," he answered. His eyes were still closed.

"No."

"Ebie. We lost everything."

"Thank you," she said, and sighed. "That's the reassurance I wanted, thank you." She glanced through the window. "That's the encouraging word I wanted, all right," she said, and pressed her forehead to the glass.

At home they called her Edna Belle, and they called her brother George Benjamin, always using their full Christian names. In the center of the town, there was an enormous statue of Andrew Jackson, said to have been razed by the Yankees during the War between the States and left there as a grim reminder to the people of the South, never repaired or rebuilt, standing in ruinous splendor. She and George Benjamin would go down to the monument and play at its base with the other children. Once she cut herself falling on a piece of broken glass there; she still had a crescent-shaped scar on her thigh as a reminder of the accident. Sometimes she would wander down to the center of town alone, and she would sit and sketch the monument in charcoal, the way the general's broken sword ended abruptly against the sky, with the bell tower of the church beyond, and down the street the white clapboard courthouse. She loved to work in charcoal, smearing the black onto the page with her index and middle fingers, rubbing it, shading it, smoothing it into the paper. It was very hard to draw niggers, even in charcoal.

She found the bird one day at the base of the monument, a sparrow who had broken his leg, probably by flying into the general's broad bronzed back or the shell-torn rim of his campaign hat. The bird lay on his back with his beak open, his throat pulsing, no sound coming from him, but his tongue or whatever it was leaping into his throat, beating there, as though he were mutely begging for assistance. She reached down for the bird, and he tried to regain his feet, the broken leg hanging crookedly and, still dazed, flopped over onto his side. No eyes were showing, his eyes were rolled back into his head, only an opaque white showed. She cradled him in her hands, and then couldn't pick up her sketching pad or her box of charcoals, so she left them at the base of the monument and walked slowly home holding the bird gently in her hands, his throat working. She was terrified lest he try again to fly away and fall from her hands to the pavement—she knew that would kill him. They all said the bird would die, anyway, even George Benjamin said so. But she took care of him until he got better, just as she knew he would, and one day he flew off before she had a chance to take him back to the monument where she had found him. She used to look for him at the monument after that, thinking he would maybe come back, like in picture books, but he never did.

Her father owned the dairy in town, the name of it was Clover Crest Farms, which she had helped him pick. He had wanted to call it *Dearborn* Farms, but even George Benjamin thought *that* was pretty corny, and a bit egotistical, naming the thing after yourself. Her father was a very tall man, with blond hair like her own. Her mother had blond hair, too, well everybody in the family did, except George Benjamin. His was a sort of reddish color, like Aunt Serena's and Grandmother Winkler's. Edna Belle looked a lot like her mother, leastwise that's what everybody was always telling her, and she was proud to believe it because her mother was a very beautiful and elegant woman. They had two niggers working for them, Lucy who was the kitchen help, and Aurora who did the cleaning, and who was always pregnant. They both adored Mother, you could just see they thought she was beautiful and very elegant, which she was. But it was surprising the two niggers thought so, there never was no love lost in that town.

Edna Belle especially loved the way her mother talked, she could sit and listen to her talk all day. She had a voice, well, there was just nothing like it, that was all, deep and warm, and breaking into a marvelous laugh when you least expected it. She always made Edna Belle feel very grown up, because she talked to her about real things and not the usual dopey stuff grownups say to children. Whenever they talked together, Edna Belle felt as though she were talking to an older and much smarter friend who was beautiful and wise and very elegant besides; well, she was a wonderful person, the niggers were right. And her father, he was simply the happiest person she knew, always joking, always making mother and everybody laugh. One time he filled the refrigerator with milk for her, just filled it from top to bottom with milk, and when Mother came home from marketing that afternoon and opened the refrigerator door, why there they were! maybe thirty or forty bottles of *milk!* "Oh, that nut!" she said, laughing, she used to laugh a lot, Mother.

George Benjamin was the least talented person she had ever met in her life, he couldn't even draw a straight line. He would always come up to her and say, "Edna Belle, show me how to draw a damn horse," or "Edna Belle, how do you make it look like it's getting smaller in the distance?" but he was just hopeless, no talent at all, she sometimes used to feel sorry for him. He had a chemistry set, and once he burned his hand, and she took care of him the way she had the bird. Well, not *exactly* the same because it was Aurora who changed his bandages and all, but she made sure there were

always fresh-picked flowers in his room, and she would leave
little drawings on his pillow for him to find when he woke up
in the morning. The hand business only lasted maybe two
weeks, but she took very good care of him in those weeks, she
really loved him a lot, even though he begrudged Daddy a
few laughs at his jokes. He kept one of her pictures, the one
she made of the pond on the old Barrow place near the mill.
He said he liked that one best because it reminded him of
fishing there. She knew, of course, that he fished there when
she'd *made* the drawing, of course, that's why she'd made it in
the *first* place.

Her best friend was a girl named Cissie Butterfoster, whose
name broke her up, but who was a nice girl, anyway. Cissie
wore pigtails, and Daddy used to kid with her, saying, "Why
do you wear your hair like the niggers, Cissie?" and Cissie
always would blush. Until much later, when she was in high
school, and then one day she just said to Daddy, almost
making *him* blush, "You sure do take a deep concern over my
hair, Mr. Dearborn," which was sort of snippy even though
she *had* developed a very good pair of boobs by then, but to
imply Daddy was flirting with her or something! But when
they were small together, they did have some very good times
together, Edna Belle and Cissie, even when they teased about
her last name, Butterfoster, what a last name. Edna Belle
once said to her father that they ought to start a division of
the dairy called Butterfoster Farms, and that broke him up,
with George Benjamin sitting there smiling and watching
Daddy, and Cissie laughing, too—she was a pretty good sport.
She was the first girl in the crowd to start menstruating, and
she always bled a fearful lot, and had the most dire cramps.
She made Edna Belle cry in pity one day, writhing the way
she was on her bed and saying, "Oh, Edna Belle, you don't
know how lucky you are! You don't know what it *is* to be a
grown woman," which Edna Belle learned soon enough, and
without half as much hysterics. But still and all she *had* felt
genuine pity for Cissie that day, and she had no doubt the
cramps were real. Cissie told her Tampax could break your
cherry, what a lie. She also said horseback riding could break

it, and doing pushups could break it. According to Cissie
anything could break it, a girl had to be careful just getting
out of *bed* in the morning, otherwise Goodbye, Charlie. She
stopped hanging around with Cissie in their sophomore year
at high school because everybody was saying things about her
by then, and besides Daddy warned Edna Belle about her
reputation in a small town, and about chumming with Cissie
who had taken to wearing such tight sweaters. Edna Belle
figured if Cissie *had* them, why not? though she never said
this to anyone, least of all Daddy, and anyway her own were
so small, like Mother's.

Besides, she was very much interested in art by this time,
and was being encouraged to undertake all sorts of school art
projects by Miss Benson, who was her teacher. It was Miss
Benson who helped her to overcome her fear of working in
pen and ink, which she had always had trouble with before,
being left-handed and smearing the ink every time her hand
moved across the page. Miss Benson also taught her there was
a freedom to art, that once you knew what you were about,
why then you were entitled to this freedom, but that first you
had to earn the right to it by learning what you were about.
That until you knew how to draw something in its right
proportions, why then you had to draw it correctly and
properly each and every time, and then, only then could you
afford to go off and make an arm longer or a leg shorter or
give a face three eyes or whatever. Well, she had Picasso in
mind, you see, or someone like that, though Edna Belle never
thought of herself as having *that* kind of talent, still Miss
Benson was terribly encouraging.

There was no question that most of the two hundred
students who attended the high school liked to hear Miss
Benson's stories about Rembrandt (Charles Laughton) and
Gauguin (George Sanders). Miss Benson made these men
come to life somehow, as though she were adding personal
information even Hollywood had missed. Besides, for students like George Benjamin *anything* was better than having
to draw. True, it got to be something of a drag when Miss
Benson went on and on about sculpture in Mesopotamia

during the fourth and third millennia before the Christian
era (like, man, who *gave* a damn?) or when she showed slides
of all those broken Greek statues, but for the most part, the
kids thought she was less painful than many of the biddies
around. None of them, however, thought quite as highly of
her as did Edna Belle.

She was, Clotilde Benson, a fluttery old woman who indeed
spoke of Van Gogh as if she had personally been the recipient
of his severed ear, an uncompromising, old-fashioned instructor who insisted on certain artistic verities and some artistic
conceits, an unkempt and sometimes slovenly person who
habitually wore a loose paint-smeared smock and who stuck
colored pencils haphazardly into her gray and frizzled hair, a
vain and foolish woman whose students laughed behind her
back each time she sneaked a look at herself in the reflecting
windows of the supply cabinet, an inadequately trained art
teacher working in a scholastically poor high school in a town
that had gone dead a hundred years ago. It was rumored, too,
and this only by Cissie Butterfoster who was given to lurid
sexual fantasies, that Clotilde Benson had once conducted a
scandalous love affair with a nigger lawyer in Atlanta. The
romance had supposedly begun when she was twenty years
old and going to art school there, and it had ended when six
righteous Georgians rode the attorney off the highway one
night and proceeded to educate him (they were all carrying
knives) as to why it was highly improper for a colored man to
pluck a Southern flower, you dig, boy? They then casually
dropped in on Clotilde that same night at about three A.M.,
and while she stood shivering in a flannel robe over girlish
cotton pajamas with delicate primrose pattern, told her she
had better get the hell out of Atlanta before somebody cut
her similar to how they had cut that nigger lawyer, or hadn't
she heard about that yet? Clotilde admitted as to how she
hadn't heard a word, trembling in the night and holding her
flannel robe closed at the neck over her primrose-patterned
girlish cotton pajamas. The six gentlemen all took off their
hats and murmured good night to her in the dark, and she
heard one of them laugh softly as they went out of the drive-

way and into the waiting car and—according to Cissie—that
very same morning Miss Benson caught an early train out of
Atlanta and back home, apparently having decided she'd had
enough of all this Gauguin-type reveling, and convinced that
such living only led to shame and degradation. That was
Cissie's story, and it sounded good, and there were plenty of
kids who were willing to believe it, although none of them
ever had the courage to repeat it. The only one who neither
repeated it nor believed it was Edna Belle. Oh yes, she
believed that *maybe* Miss Benson might have *possibly* been
in love with a nigger (although the idea was pretty repulsive) but she would never in a million years believe Miss
Benson had turned tail and run like that, even if the man
had've been a nigger like Cissie said, though Cissie was a big
liar, anyway.

One afternoon—autumn came late to Edna Belle's town
that year, the leaves were just beginning to fall, they trickled
past the long high school windows in the waning afternoon
light—Edna Belle stayed behind to work with Miss Benson on
the layout for the school magazine, which was called *Whispers,* and which Edna Belle hoped to serve as art editor next
term. The art editor this term was a senior named Phillip
Armstrong Tillis, who was very talented and who had drawn
both the cover of the magazine as well as the end papers, and
who Edna Belle had dated once or twice and who, frankly,
she was really crazy about. He was not a very good-looking
boy, his nose was too large for his face, and he wore eyeglasses, but he had a wonderful sense of humor and a crazy
way of looking at things, very offbeat and cool ("I used to
have this little turned-up button nose," he once said, "but I
had an operation done to make it long and ugly") and she
loved being with him because he was always thinking up
nutty things to do, like pulling into Mr. Overmeyer's driveway to neck one night, instead of going over to the hill near
the old burned Baptist church that had been struck by
lightning. When Mr. Overmeyer came out to see what was
going on, Phillip Armstrong got out of the car and bowed
from the waist and said, "Good evening, sir, we were wonder-

ing if we might park here for a few moments to discuss a
matter that's of great importance."

"With *me,* do you mean?" Mr. Overmeyer asked.

"No, sir, the young lady and I wished to discuss it pri-
vately."

Mr. Overmeyer looked so relieved that (*A*) it wasn't some
hoods from Connors who were looking for trouble, that (*B*)
it wasn't some crippled war veterans selling magazine sub-
scriptions, and that (*C*) he *personally* would not have to get
involved in this discussion, whatever it was, that he
mumbled, "Sure, certainly, go right ahead," and then went
back into the house and drew the blinds to assure Phillip
Armstrong of the privacy he wanted. They had necked up a
storm that night, and she had let Phillip Armstrong touch
her breast right there in the driveway, but only twice.

The reason Phillip Armstrong wasn't there that November
afternoon to help with the layout was that he had come down
with the mumps, of all things ("You know what *that* does to
a grown boy, I suppose," Cissie said) and was home in bed. It
was just as well because if Phillip Armstrong *had've* been
there, then Edna Belle and Miss Benson wouldn't have
talked, and Edna Belle's whole life wouldn't have changed.
In looking back on the conversation, Edna Belle couldn't
remember exactly what they'd said that was so terribly important, what they had discussed in such personal terms, this
woman and her sixteen-year-old student there in the gathering gloom of a high school classroom, the light fading against
the long windows, the empty desks stretching behind them,
and the smell of paste on their fingers, and snippets of
shining proofs clinging to their hands, the drawn pencil lines
on the blank pulp pages, the long galleys from the editorial
staff, and the careful selection of a rooster drawn by Anna-
belle Currier Farr and something called Monsoon by a freshman named Hiram Horn, the proofs spread out on Miss
Benson's desk top, "There, Edna Belle," and "There," and
"How's that?" completely absorbed in the work they were
doing, Miss Benson finally snapping on the desk lamp, and
the warm circle of light flooding the dummy as the magazine

began to take shape and form, the colored pencils sticking out of Miss Benson's hair and reflecting light. Whispers, they whispered now, the school was empty, but what did they say, after all, that had not been said a thousand times before? What was there in Miss Benson's impromptu and heartfelt talk that was not clichéd and hackneyed and shopworn and, yes, even trivial? It had all been said before, there was the tinny ring of half-truth to it, and whatever importance it seemed to possess at the time surely came only from the dramatic setting, the classroom succumbing to dusk, the desk lamp being turned on, the young girl listening while the older woman earnestly and sympathetically talked to her about life and living, about pity and understanding, about art, and about love. All of it said before. And better, surely, so very much better than old Miss Benson could ever have said it even if she were skilled with words, which she was not, even if she were half the gifted artist Edna Belle supposed she was, which she was not. All of it said before.

But never before to Edna Belle.

And so she listened, nodding her head as they worked at the desk, fingers thick with paste, and she smiled, and once she giggled and covered her mouth, and tilted her head again in fascination, and brushed a golden spray of hair from her cheek and said, "Yes, oh yes, I know, I *know*."

They walked as far as the monument together. Edna Belle watched Miss Benson as she turned left at the corner near the courthouse, walking with the peculiar waddle that made the other kids laugh, but walking with her head very high, and she suddenly knew it had been true about the nigger.

She sat at the base of the monument.

She could remember only snatches of what Miss Benson had said, something about honesty, about always being true to whatever it was she believed, and of not being afraid, something about talent and its use, and something about a larger talent which she called, Edna Belle was not sure, a *capacity* for giving, yes, for loving, "Yes, oh yes," Edna Belle had said, thinking of Phillip Armstrong. And then Miss Benson said how it was important to get out of this town, go to New York or Chicago, study there, or Rhode Island, there was a fine art school in Rhode Island, but get out of this town, Edna Belle, get out of the South before they cut a piece out of your life and leave you to shrivel and die. It is not shameful to love, she said earnestly, it is never shameful to love, almost on the edge of tears.

The leaves swirled about Edna Belle's feet, the lights were on in the square, a sharp wind swept from the north around the corner of the church. She nodded quietly and to herself because she had made up her mind that she was a woman now, and then she rose and walked home, occasionally nodding, and then tilting her head in wonder because everything seemed so suddenly clear. And yet she knew Miss Benson had not told her anything she did not already know.

In September of 1946, when she was eighteen years old, she followed Miss Benson's advice and left for Pratt Institute in New York City. She rarely thought of the old woman anymore, except to wonder if she was still alive, still living in the South. But whenever she remembered her, as she was remembering her now in a seventh-floor room at the Hotel Astor, staring through a window at the traffic below, the lingering image was always of Miss Benson turning the corner near the courthouse, her head held high.

Without moving from the window, Ebie said to her husband, "In Alabama, when I was a little girl . . ."

"Spare us the magnolia blossoms and white linen suits," he said.

". . . before I even knew there were such things as witty novelists who . . ."

"I'm not a novelist."

". . . who could make clever remarks about magnolia blossoms and linen suits, when I was still a little girl in Alabama . . ."

Her voice trailed. She kept staring through the window.

"They loved me," she said at last.

4

THE CAR PULLED IN AHEAD UNEXPECTEDLY, entering
the highway after barely braking at the full stop sign on the
approach ramp. Sally Kirsch had opened her eyes not a
moment before, seeing the other car, hearing the squeal of
tires as Jonah applied his brakes, and bracing herself for
what she knew would be an accident. Across the river on the
New Jersey shore, she could see the Spry sign blinking idiotically as the automobile swerved, parkway lights ahead in a
winding curve downtown, the glare of northbound traffic
on the left, and then a splash of sudden brighter yellow as
Jonah's headlights illuminated the other car.

"You dumb bastard!" Jonah shouted, and these seemed to
Sally the first human words he had uttered all day long. He
yanked sharply on the wheel, trying to avoid the crash,
braking desperately, tires whining. The other car was a
yellow Buick, vintage 1953, and the man driving it glanced
to his left an instant before the cars collided, noticing Jonah's
car for the first time, it seemed, and opening his eyes wide
and then wrenching the wheel over to the right too late. Left
fender hit right fender with terrible crunching impact. The
cars ricocheted one from the other like billiard balls veering
in opposite directions. Sally felt herself being hurled forward,
perversely grateful for the break in the monotony, pushed
her hands out in front of her, and then pulled them back

instantly when she remembered she could fracture both wrists that way. Her head collided with the padded dash, there was the further squeal of tires behind them, and then silence. She shook her head. She could taste blood in her mouth. One of her teeth felt loose.

"Are you all right?" Jonah asked, and she nodded, and he got out of the car. She heard other car doors slamming, and she sat up tentatively, surprised that nothing was broken. "Didn't you see that stop sign?" Jonah was yelling.

She glanced through the windshield which was miraculously intact, she was certain everything would have been shattered by the collision, including herself. The man getting out of the other car was a short dark man in a short green coat and baggy slacks, a black fedora pushed onto the back of his head. He had apparently cut himself when the cars collided, and a thin line of blood was trickling down the right side of his face. Jonah was holding his left hand in his right and Sally wondered whether he had broken any bones. Dazed, she watched the two men as they approached each other.

"Are you talking to me?" the little man said. "To me, are you calling a bastard?"

"What's your name?" Jonah said. "Damn you, I'm going to . . ."

"To me, are you asking the name?" the little man said. "I will throw you in the river, you stringbean! I will pick you up and throw you in the river."

"I'd like to see you try that," Jonah said, and took off his glasses and moved closer to the little man, as though he would step on him and squash him flat into the pavement.

"You hit me, and I die," the little man warned. "I bleed from the head now, you murderer. Hit me, and I die. Get away from me!"

"You're a maniac," Jonah said. "How dare you drive a car without looking where—"

"To me, are you calling a maniac? A *fink* is what you are, to call a decent man a maniac. Get away, get away, do you see him?" he asked the gathering crowd. "He is making obscene and threatening gestures!"

"Let me see your license," Jonah said.

"Let me see *your* license, fink!" the little man answered. "Do you hear?" he said to the crowd. "Do you hear his threatening?"

"There's the police," someone said, and Sally heard the sound of a siren and turned her head to see a police car approaching in the distance, its red dome light revolving and blinking.

"Good," the little man said. "The police, you hear, fink? Now we'll see who threatens, fink."

"Did anyone here see this accident?" Jonah asked.

"I, the maniac," the little man said. "I, the maniac saw it! I saw *all* of it, a hundred miles an hour this fink comes swooping down a public highway!"

"You're a lying little bastard," Jonah said, "and you're making me very angry."

"*You,* I am making angry, you?" the little man asked incredulously. "I am here bleeding in a hundred places, and *you* are standing angry? Where are the police, those finks? Where are they, I ask!"

"All right, what's the trouble here?" the patrolman said, coming out of the squad car. His partner stepped into the highway and began waving traffic around the wrecked autos.

Sally, dazed and certain she was in shock, began giggling. She had not, until the moment the two cars struck, enjoyed either the drive to Poughkeepsie, their brief stay at the college, or any part of their return trip. Jonah had left her to wander the campus that afternoon while he chatted with his world history professor, and she had been unexpectedly depressed by the sight of all those young girls in candy-striped stockings and short suede skirts, God, had it really all been *that* long ago? Nor could she honestly say that Jonah Willow was exactly an exciting conversationalist. There was a tenseness about him that made her want to scream aloud, a social unease that seemed to translate itself into a physical deformity as he drove the convertible, knuckles white, body hunched, long legs cramped. All the way up to the college, his conversation had consisted of a series of ominous grunts designed to stifle discussion. Not once did he mention the trial, and this puzzled her. She was a lawyer, certainly not as experienced or as well known as he, but a lawyer nonetheless; she had thought he would welcome her opinions, or at least her thoughts. But even on the return trip, when she tentatively asked whether his meeting with the professor had been profitable, he replied only, "Not very," and once again fell silent. Weary and discouraged, she retreated to her corner of the car, closing her eyes and listening to the lulling hum of the tires against the road.

"Are you asleep?" he asked at last.

"What?" she said, startled.

"Are you asleep?"

"No. Where are we?"

"On the West Side Highway. We just went through the Spuyten Duyvil toll booths."

"No, I'm not asleep," she said, suspecting she had been. "I just have to close my eyes every now and then. Otherwise, I read everything."

"Oh," he said, and she looked at him a moment, expecting more, and then closed her eyes again when she realized nothing was forthcoming. He did not speak again until shortly before the accident. She must have dozed off a second time because she sat up in alarm when she heard his voice.

"What do you mean?" he asked.

"What?"

"About reading everything."

"I'm a compulsive reader," she said.

"Oh," he answered.

End of conversation, Sally thought.

"Yes," she said, persisting in spite of better judgment, "I can reel off word for word every sign and billboard we passed on the road today. My mind's like a hall closet."

She waited for him to make some comment, hardly expecting that he would. When he did not, she sighed, and closed her eyes again. The accident occurred not two minutes later. Now, watching the police officer as he examined both men's licenses, watching him turn solicitous and then obsequious as Jonah casually mentioned the name of a circuit judge, watching the little man go pale and almost faint when he realized he had rammed into someone with high legal connections, Sally still felt giddy and numb, and her front tooth hurt like hell, what a damn silly thing to get involved in, an accident when she was so close to home.

Still, Jonah's profanity had exploded into that dreary automobile ride like a mortar shell, and she was grateful for the careless little man who was now explaining to Jonah and the policeman and anyone who would listen that he was a poor but honest bricklayer coming home late from a job in Harlem, anxious to be reunited once more with his wife and six kids—she was sure he had said *five* kids the first time around—and therefore perhaps a bit unheedful of traffic signs, but he *had* stopped at the sign, he had come to a full if brief stop. What *was* he, did the attorney think, some kind of maniac who would endanger the life and limb of innocent people on a public highway? Did the attorney, did these honorable law enforcement officers, did these good citizens believe for a moment that he would do a fink thing like that, crashing into innocent people—arguing his case right there on the highway without benefit of counsel while Jonah kept holding his left hand in his right, and Sally could see now that he was wincing in pain.

She got out of the car suddenly and walked to where the small man was still pleading his case, turning to a fat smiling bleached blonde now, and advising her that he had been a citizen for fifteen years, having come from Cairo, and that he had never been in any kind of trouble with the law before this, nor ever in an automobile accident though he had been driving since 1956, did he look like a fink, he asked the bleached blonde. The blonde smiled and then clucked her tongue sympathetically, but remained noncommittal as to whether he was or was not a fink.

"I think he's hurt his hand," Sally said to the nearest

patrolman. "Are we going to be much longer here, or can we get him to a hospital?"

"You're bleeding, miss," the patrolman said.

"I'm all right," Sally said.

"Can you drive?" the patrolman asked Jonah.

"Yes, I can."

"Maybe we'd better do as the young lady suggests. We can run you right over to Harlem Hospital, right on Lenox."

"No, it's nothing," Jonah said. "I just wrenched it when we collided, that's all."

"Something might be broken in there," the patrolman said.

"Why is nobody here to worry about *my* head?" the man from Cairo asked. "I'm sorry, your worship, but my head is bleeding, too, don't forget."

"You'd better get him to the hospital," Jonah said.

"You come along, too, Mr. Willow. No offense meant, but I think we'd better take a look at that hand."

"It's beginning to swell," Sally said.

"Miss, do you know your lip is cut?"

"What?"

"Your lip, miss. It's bleeding pretty bad."

"I think we'd *all* better take a little ride over to the hospital," the other patrolman said.

"I don't see any need for that," Jonah said.

"Begging your pardon, Mr. Willow," the patrolman said, "but I don't think Judge Santesson would like it if we let a friend of his go home with a broken hand or something."

"All right," Jonah said, "let's get it over with."

They did not get it over with until eleven o'clock that night. By that time Jonah was in a surly, cantankerous mood. He told the frightened little man from Cairo that he was going to do his damndest to have his driver's license revoked, and then got into an argument with the policemen about the advisability of doing any further driving that night.

"Let's take a taxi," Sally said.

"How can I lay bricks without the license to drive?" the Egyptian said.

"Why don't you take a taxi, Mr. Willow?" the cops said.

Jonah took Sally's arm and led her out of the hospital and then got into a further argument the moment they entered the automobile, simply because Sally suggested that *she* ought to do the driving, a swollen lip seeming to her less restricting than a sprained and taped wrist. Jonah testily informed her that he was in perfect physical condition, and then proceeded to prove his point by racing down to the Village (*your* license ought to be revoked, she thought, but did not say), scaring her half to death, and parking the car in a clearly marked No Parking zone in front of her building.

The hallway was silent. They climbed the steps to her fourth-floor apartment, Sally leading, Jonah following. He did not say a word to her as they walked up, radiating only what seemed to be sullen anger. Outside her apartment, she opened her bag and searched for her key in silence.

"I'm sorry about the accident," he said abruptly.

"It wasn't your fault."

"Your eyes were closed, I thought perhaps . . ."

"No, I saw what happened."

"In any case, I'm sorry." His manner was still brusque and scarcely civil. She found her key and inserted it in the lock. "And I'm also sorry you had such a terrible time," he said, "but you see . . ."

"I didn't, don't be silly."

". . . I'm not very good at small talk."

The hallway was silent again.

"I have a great many things on my mind," Jonah said. "I'm sorry."

"That's all right," Sally said. She twisted the key. The tumblers fell with a small oiled click.

"I'm sorry about the profanity, too," he said.

"That's all right," she said again. She listened as he continued to apologize for his swearing in the car and on the highway, his voice lowering, listened as he told her how sorry he was for having argued with the policemen and for having threatened the little Egyptian, "I know this is the first time we've been alone together, without a lot of people chattering away, and I wish I could have been more entertaining. But you see . . ."

"That's all right, Jonah," she said.

". . . I had hoped this friend of mine could help me, he's an expert on military engagements, that's his forte, Sally. He's written several really good books, and I thought he could help me. I thought he could come up with something more than he did."

"I know it was a disappointing day for you."

"Yes, it was."

"But I *did* enjoy the accident. The accident was fun," she said, and smiled.

"May I see you again?"

"Yes," she said.

"I'll call. The trial should be over by the end of the week, perhaps we can get together Friday or Saturday."

"Well, call," she said.

"I'd give anything to possess your trick," Jonah said suddenly.

"What trick?"

"Of closing your eyes to shut out the print, to shut out the noise of the world."

"I do it in defense," she said, watching his face.

"That's just it," he answered. "I *have* no defense."

"What do you mean?"

"Nothing," he said, and smiled. "Good night, Sally. I'll call you soon."

"Good night, Jonah," she said, and went into the apartment.

He went down the steps rapidly, keeping his left hand off the banister because the wrist was throbbing and each time he tried to flex his fingers a sharp pain shot up the length of his arm, damn stupid little man. It was bitter cold in the street outside; he feared they would have sleet or hail rather than snow—nor gloom of night can stay these couriers from the swift completion, would they tear down the post office now that they had demolished Penn Station? There was nothing permanent in this city, it was a city determined to obliterate its past. If there is one thing all Americans share in common, he thought, it's this lack of an historical sense, a tendency to want to change the recent past as well as the nation's ancient heritage. Oh certainly, destroy the jail where they kept the accused in the Salem witchcraft trials, cover the shame of hysteria, but Penn Station? That noble structure razed to the ground to make way for a sports arena? Heinous crime, I sound like my father, he thought.

He walked quickly to the car, his ears tingling, and then fumbled with the key in the lock, it's foolish to lock a convertible, he thought, they only slit the canvas top. He closed the door behind him rapidly, started the car, and then sat in silence for several moments while the engine warmed and the heater began to operate. He took a pair of fur-lined gloves from his coat pocket, put them on, pulled the tails of his coat out from under him, twisted himself into a comfortable position, turned on the radio, and then eased the car away from the curb. There was an order to everything he did, he was certain he performed the same operations in sequence each time he entered his automobile. He was equally certain that his father, Zachary Willow, drove in an identical manner, and that his grandfather and *his* father before him had undoubtedly performed similarly in a horse and buggy on the cobbled streets of Danvers, Massachusetts. He had gone back there once to trace the heritage, a tribute to Zachary, who insisted that a man should know his roots, though Jonah had been born in Stamford, Connecticut, and could not have been less interested in a pilgrimage to the home of his forebears. But he had found there in the library records the history of a family, the cursive script difficult to read, embellished with curlicues and substituting *f*'s for *s*'s, words capitalized for no apparent reason, the ink brown and fading on yellowed brittle pages—Benjamin Willow married to Margaret, and before him Nathan married to Elizabeth Anne, and somewhere back in the almost illegible record, a Jonah Willow, apprentice seaman on a whaling ship out of New Bedford. He had made the drive back along the turnpike, the road markers showing peaked Pilgrim hats and witches on

broomsticks, possessed if not with a sense of self, then at least
with a better understanding of his father.

Zachary Willow was a lawyer, and his father and grandfather had been lawyers before him. There was in him a sense
of order that was firmly rooted in a judicial system evolved
from the English, and based in part on the Roman Corpus
Juris Civilis, derived in turn from such early systems as the
Code of Hammurabi and the Laws of Manu. In the law,
there was stability and certainty, precedent and continuity.
Zachary ran his Stamford house as though it were a courtroom, meting out justice to Jonah and his brother Lucas as
though they were prisoners before the bar, firmly imbuing in
them the knowledge that there was right and there was
wrong and there was nothing in between. The law, to Zachary Willow, was inflexible and clearly defined: it prescribed
social behavior as surely as the Bible prescribed moral behavior. The law was the law, and you did not fiddle around
with it, and you did not try for fancy interpretations because
it had not been designed for that. It was simply and inde-
structibly created by men, to instruct them in, and to enforce
for them, the rules of civilized behavior. "Where law ends
there tyranny begins," read one of the inscriptions chiseled in
marble on the Criminal Courts Building, and Zachary Willow might have chiseled it there himself.

That the behavior in the old Stamford house was sometimes less than civilized could not be blamed on Zachary. His
eldest son, Lucas, must have been a trial to him from the very
beginning, although Jonah only became aware of the conflict
much later, when his brother entered high school and began
playing football. Until that time, frightened of his father and
simultaneously respecting him, almost venerating him, Jonah
did not once suspect that his brother's opinion of the old man
could be any different than his own. Surely there was serenity
in the Shippan house, its green shutters facing Long Island
Sound, the lawn sloping down to a seawall from which you
could see sailing ships and pleasure boats, a view that never
tired Jonah; there was, perhaps, still a trace of the original
Jonah Willow in him, the man who'd sailed for whale out of

New Bedford. "Call me Ishmael," he had once dreamily said to his brother while they sat side by side on white wooden lawn chairs on the green grass sloping to the Sound, and watched a double-masted sailboat cleaving the water. Lucas had replied, "Call *me* Shlemiel," but this, of course, was after he had joined the football team and was playing offensive back and feeling his oats. "I like physical contact," Lucas always said, "I like knocking guys around."

Jonah's mother was a slender woman with a flawless English complexion and magnificent brown eyes. Her family had come to Massachusetts in 1734, from a town in Wales—she always pronounced it quickly and melodically for him, slurring her *l*'s and *m*'s, but he could never pronounce it himself and had only seen it written out once. Watching her as she stepped surely and lightly over the sparkling grass to the seawall, he often visualized her ancestors walking in just such a manner, the hands delicately clasped, the head expectantly tilted as though listening for a hidden sound, before the splendid ruins of a castle overlooking the valley. She was soft-spoken and spoke rarely, but her silence could fall upon a room like a thunderclap in recrimination never voiced against one or another of his father's stern pronouncements. Her smile was sometimes like a knife; he had often seen his father's bluster grow larger and therefore less meaningful as he rushed suicidally against that naked blade of a smile, her brown eyes solemn and unamused above it. His mother was not an affectionate woman, or at least not a demonstrative one. He could only remember her truly embracing him once, holding him close to her breast and frantically stroking his face, and that was the time Lucas pushed him off the seawall and he cut his hand on a sharp rock.

There was never any doubt that Jonah would one day become a lawyer like his father, nor ever any doubt that he would eventually marry Christine Dunseath. Looking back, he supposed now that the divorce was also inevitable. But he never had an inkling of *that* until it was fully upon him, and he certainly didn't anticipate it when he was courting her as a boy or when they were newly married and trying to make their way in New York. His courtship (the word was his father's and not his) was a natural development encouraged by proximity; the Dunseath family lived next door to them on Shippan Point. Albert Dunseath was Stamford's water commissioner, a ruddy-faced man with a hearty laugh, sparse blond hair covering his tanned pate, combed sideways to disguise the encroaching baldness. His wife was a dark-haired beauty from whom, fortunately, Christie had inherited her looks. She was an avid horsewoman, and was always stamping in and out of her house in jodhpurs and riding boots, flicking a riding crop against her legs, Lady Fitz-Ashton returning from an outing on the moors, Some tea, Lady Fitz? She scared hell out of Jonah with her imperious air and her startling beauty, the black hair cut in severe bangs across her forehead, the proud nose and generous mouth, blue eyes flashing, the riding crop flicking against her thigh, terrifying. Christie was hardly less terrifying as a child, a hellcat who gave Lucas a bloody nose once when he tried to take off her pants behind the tool shed near the big dying maple. Lucas was eleven at the time, and Jonah was ten, and Christie was perhaps eight, yes just eight. Lucas had got her pants halfway down over her knees when she suddenly decided she didn't like the game they were playing. She twisted away from him, her small white bottom flashing in the dappled shade, and hit him with her bunched fist. Jonah was terrified that she would tell her mother what had happened and cause her to descend upon their household like the mounted fury she most certainly was. But Christie was as frightened as he, and never said a word about it. She studiously avoided Lucas from that day on, though, and maintained a cool and barely polite attitude toward him to the end.

Jonah began seriously dating her when they were still in high school—boat rides up the Connecticut River, and long drives to New Haven where they went to see out-of-town tryouts of incoming Broadway plays, and into New York to see the stage shows at Radio City and the Roxy, or the big-name bands at the Paramount and Strand. He once waited in line with her for three hours outside the Paramount on a freezing day in February, to see Frank Sinatra, whom he hated the moment Christie began shrieking; he thought she would faint dead away right there in the balcony, many of the girls actually did. Or just being together, walking home together from school on a bright spring day, or sitting on the lawn at night, fingers barely touching, a farewell kiss behind the shed where Lucas had tried to take off her pants, the sight of her as she walked between the forsythia bushes that separated the two properties, a curious walk, so unlike her mother's, almost as though she were gliding, a model's walk, with pelvis thrust forward and head erect.

She wore a blue gown to his high school prom, she had taken to wearing her hair like her mother's by then, sharp bangs across the forehead, blue eyes twinkling beneath them in secret amusement (secret *contempt,* he later came to realize), the pale blue of the gown emphasizing her eyes and clinging to her childish body. She was almost seventeen, but her figure seemed to resist all womanly transformation. Narrow-hipped and small-breasted, slender and slouched, she achieved a look that only years later would become fashionably chic. Her face was undeniably beautiful, though, her eyes sometimes flashed at older men who stopped dead in their tracks and then quickly surveyed the slender body and shook their heads in wonder, dazed by their obvious mistake. When he danced with her, he could feel every inch of her body pressed against him, the small budding breasts that would never really develop into an abundant bosom, the protruding bones of her hips, the mound of her pubis, the curve of her back where his hand rested, his fingers sometimes spread to touch the tight firm buttocks, he had seen her almost naked once, white and dappled with maple-shadow as she twisted away from his brother's hands, the blue eyes angry and not at all amused that day.

He asked her to marry him on that graduation night, resplendent in his white dinner jacket, holding her cool and slender in his arms. The senior class had rented the country club and hired the best young band in the area, a fourteen-piece orchestra with monogramed stands and identical blue jackets, white shirts, blue bow ties. The trumpet section rose to take their chorus of "Summertime," straight mutes protruding from the golden glowing bells of their horns, ceiling lights glistening with blues and reds and greens that shimmered in brass-bound reflection, he danced with Christine Dunseath and asked her to be his wife. He was eighteen years old, and a languid June breeze blew in fresh over the dewmisted golf course and through the open French doors of the ballroom. She nodded when he asked her, and he said, "You will?" in surprise, and when she answered, "Of course," he whispered a kiss into her hair.

He had thought at the time, being eighteen, the United States involved in another great war for democracy, that he would naturally be called into the Army, that he would naturally serve his country, become a hero perhaps, though not a dead one. When he registered for the draft, however, he was afraid he might be rejected because of his eyesight, and even debated memorizing an eyechart before going down for his physical. But he decided against it, sweated through the examination instead, and immediately afterwards asked the doctor how he had done. The doctor told him his eyes were okay as far as the Army was concerned, proving once again the old military adage about healthy seeing-eye dogs. The military, however, did not yet possess either an adage or a deterrent for poison gas seeping into a man's system through a hole in his eardrum. Jonah was surprised to discover that he possessed just such a punctured eardrum and that the Army did not want him, better luck next war, Mac. Poison gas at the time was the ultimate weapon, the dread weapon each nation hoped would never be used again. In later years, Jonah would come to appreciate the irony of having been rejected because of the fear of poison gas, only to have the war finally decided by the use of a weapon a million times more heinous. He would also come to appreciate (and this only very much later) the supreme irony of fighting wars under the guise of preventing them, and would come to the conclusion (never admitted to a soul) that all men, *including* Americans, were warlike and that the invention and use of "The Bomb" was restraining them from doing what they really loved doing most: killing each other. ("I like physical contact," Lucas had said, "I like knocking guys around.") Lucas himself had enlisted in the Marine Corps when he was just eighteen, against Zachary's wishes, but what could the old man do? He was a hero, his captain later wrote, who managed to kill sixteen Japanese soldiers before being killed himself by a mortar explosion. "I am sending you a small carton of his effects, please know that we respected your son highly and share your loss deeply," kind captain sitting out there in the Pacific with jungle rot on his balls and dead youngsters on his hands. The small carton of effects included the maroon-and-white letter Lucas had received in high school for being the team's star halfback, a hero even then. Jonah's keenest memories of his brother would always be of those crisp October days, the sky above the high school field, the handoff to Lucas and the plunge, God, how he could run! Even at Yale years later, even as a law student there (his father and grandfather had of course studied law at Yale) he would experience a strange, odd sensation whenever the team came out onto the field, a shudder would run up his spine, and he would once again see Lucas charging into the opposing line, would remember once when Lucas got up and limped away from a pile-on and then waved to Jonah where he was sitting in the stands, his grin cracking white and sharp across his mud-stained face. *I like physical contact, I like knocking guys around.* He had knocked around sixteen of them before they'd brought him down, you do not get up and wipe mud from your jersey after a mortar explosion, you do not smile into the stands at your kid brother.

He married Christine Dunseath in the First Presbyterian Church on Stamford's Bedford Street in the summer of 1952, after he received his law degree from Yale. The reception was held at her parents' home on Shippan Point, outdoors in the garden. The forsythias were still in bloom, spilling their petals onto the ground, he remembered fleetingly the image of a younger Christie threading her way through those bushes on too many nights too long ago. She had not changed that much perhaps, there was still the look of a very young and vulnerable creature about her, except for the snapping eyes that flicked as surely as a riding crop against a jodhpured thigh. At twenty-four, she was still wearing her hair in bangs, continued to wear it that way even to the time of the divorce when she was thirty-four and a mother, and when her eyes betrayed the fact that she was no longer a high school girl. Across the lawn, moving from guest to guest, her champagne glass in one delicately poised hand, while Jonah's mother sat unsmiling with a fan spread on her lap, dark eyes solemn as she watched her son's bride—did she ever think of Lucas in his jungle grave, or had there even been a grave? Christie Dunseath, radiant in white, black shoulder-length hair, swooping black brows over blue eyes, laughing. And water commissioner Dunseath, almost entirely bald now, ruddy-faced and a trifle drunk, embracing her as she came across the lawn, Mrs. Dunseath uncomfortable in a yellow diaphanous gown, no riding crop in her hand, no horse between her legs, older now, but her face still clinging to its girlish mold, the way Christie's would for years to come, except for the eyes.

Their first apartment was a three-room flat in a tenement on East 73rd Street, a street teeming with children during the summer, swarming with traffic that headed west from the East River Drive exit, noisy and smelly and wretchedly hot. Christie had never been able to stand heat, she ran from the sun the way albinos do, always seeking the comforting shade of an umbrella or a tree, her white skin turning lobster red if she were exposed for as long as five minutes. The apartment was an inferno, and the secondhand fan he bought on Canal Street did little to dispel the fetid air. He would come home from work each day to find her limp and haggard on the bed, her eyes silently accusing, and he would remember his mother's mute disapproval of Zachary, the cutting edge of her smile. He later wondered if their marriage did not really suffocate forever in those first terrible months in that grubby apartment. But at the time, he was too involved in coping with the profession he had chosen, hurling himself against an indifferent city swarming with talented young lawyers like

himself, expecting Christie to cheer his efforts, applaud his
small triumphs, urge him on to greater heights. She did this
unfailingly until, almost a year to the day after her marriage,
she became pregnant. Then, frightened by the changes in her
body and the impending responsibility of motherhood, wishing for the Shippan house and the easy life she once had
known, she turned to Jonah—childishly perhaps, unrealisti-
cally perhaps—wanting him to take care of her, wanting him
to tell her that everything would be all right, that there was
nothing to worry about, that this was all a part of it, all a
vital part of it. And he might have provided her with the assurance she desperately needed and sought, had not a very
important change taken place in his own life at exactly the
same time.

Raymond Gauthier was a bald-headed New Yorker of
French descent who had lost his right eye in Italy, and who
wore a black patch over the empty socket. He resembled a
motion picture pirate, with powerful shoulders and chest,
pepper-and-salt hair curling over the open collar of his shirt,
the dangling arms of a gorilla, thick thighs and enormous
hands. Jonah always visualized him with a belaying pin in his
fist, following Burt Lancaster over the side of a burning
Spanish vessel. His wife was a Brooklyn girl named Helen,
whom he openly and frankly described as an ex-junkie who
had married and later divorced a saxophone player. Jonah
surmised that Raymond was kidding about this, at least about
the junkie part, but he nonetheless watched Helen very
carefully, and every time the poor girl scratched at an itch, he
assumed she was overdue for her next fix. Helen had dark
black curly hair which she wore cut very close to her head.
She had slightly bucked teeth, and her eyes were green and
faintly Oriental; sometimes when Jonah looked straight into
them, he could believe she had once been an addict. He was
tempted on several occasions to ask her about it directly, but
then of course he knew it was just another of Raymond's
jokes.

Raymond had been practicing law in New York since
1951, and felt it was time he took a partner, an idea Jonah

clutched at immediately; Raymond had a going practice, Jonah was still chasing ambulances. Neither of them knew that the treason case would come their way so soon, or that it would catapult their newly formed partnership into that rarefied upper atmosphere of the legal profession, where clients were abundant and fees were outrageous, and fame was suddenly upon them like a sunburst. They knew only that they liked each other, and respected each other, and could possibly put their separate talents to fruitful use in a partnership. The treason case was still six months away. The plot itself was at that very moment, in fact, taking definite shape and form in a Jersey City basement, the plans being drawn, the bombs manufactured; the execution and subsequent capture were still in the offing. But the formation of the partnership meant that he and Christie could move instantly from their shabby East 73rd Street townhouse (Mr. and Mrs. Jonah Willow of New York and Shippan Point) into a better apartment on Central Park West, large and airy, and not terribly expensive because the neighborhood was supposedly succumbing to the Puerto Rican influx.

The new apartment did little to lift Christie's spirits. She had begun to show in her second month, and she now tried to conceal the pregnancy as though she were the victim of a back-alley rape. She incessantly blamed Jonah for what she called his "animal impetuosity," and one night delivered a five-minute kitchen diatribe on "the primitive and unreliable birth control methods available to American women." She then developed a theory relating her pregnancy to Jonah's work, claiming he was always too busy to do anything but make love, and further claiming they had used sex that summer as a substitute for other forms of entertainment (*"What!"* Jonah said) which would not have been necessary if he'd taken her to dinner or the theater every now and then (*"What!"* he said again). Besides, she said, this new partnership of his was all craparoo, and he knew it, the same as everything else in this stupid world, "craparoo" being one of Mrs. Dunseath's more choice expressions, passed on to her daughter the way some families pass on the Limoges or the

Sheffield plate, an expression Jonah hated, and one which Christie used with increasing frequency to describe almost anything.

Stalin's succession by Malenkov that year was craparoo, as was Salk's development of a trial polio vaccine. Hillary's and Tenzing's conquest of Everest was likewise craparoo, and even the first test explosion of a hydrogen bomb by the Soviet Union was so classified by Christie. The exchange of ideas in those last few months of 1953 became virtually impossible. Coupled with Christie's craparoo concept was an almost biblical attitude that found voice in her second most favored expression, undoubtedly inherited from the water commissioner himself: *This too shall pass.* Why bother wondering whether Dag Hammarskjöld would make a good secretary general of the UN? His term would only last five years anyway. Why concern oneself with Senator McCarthy's belief that a Communist Party cell was in operation at the Lynn, Massachusetts, plant of General Electric? Wouldn't this eventually blow over? The theory applied to everything, all human endeavor fell before it and was trampled: the latest world event, the newest novel, the most recent motion picture, the goddamn Pillsbury bakeoff. All was either trivial at worst or transient at best, and who really gave a damn?

I really give a damn, Jonah thought, and began wondering whether or not anything at *all* mattered to Christie. Well, she's pregnant, he thought, she's going through a difficult time, she's only twenty-five years old, been married a year and a little more, this is difficult for her. She's really a very sensitive and vulnerable person, it's easy to see how things in this neurotic world of ours can confuse her and force her to build defenses against involvement, she's only exhibiting the symptoms of our times, she's a sweet confused kid, and I've got to help her. But where do you start when someone doesn't even realize that "craparoo" is as phony as whatever it purports to define? Crap is crap, and shit is shit, and craparoo is neither, no matter what Mrs. Albert Dunseath astride her Arabian stallion may believe or have caused her daughter to believe. So where do you begin, and what do you say?

He said nothing, he did not begin. Instead, the marriage began to die in that second year while Amy grew inside her belly and Jonah fell into Christie's own trap: it was all trivial and inconsequential, the normal difficult adjustment newlyweds have to make, it would pass, it would pass. It did not pass, and eight years later he would wonder whether he could have said or done anything to change the situation, whether there was still time then before the treason trial began, before everything else became terribly more urgent and important than the woman who was his wife.

The treason case broke in July of 1954, two months after Amy was born. His daughter weighed nine pounds two ounces, huge for a girl, causing Christie to go into shock shortly after the delivery, throwing up all over the floor of her room while the night nurse ran to fetch a mop instead of a doctor. He cornered the nurse in the hospital corridor, a big red-faced mean bitch with gray hair and a nose like a cleaver, and he told her she had better get the doctor immediately before he strangled her. Her red face went very white, two glacial spots showing one on each cheek and then spreading to the rest of her features as she struggled with indignation and anger, and then swallowed both and went trotting off down the corridor, white skirts flying, crepe soles padding, you're goddamn *right,* Jonah thought. His daughter had the Dunseath look, passed directly from Lady Fitz to Christie, each lineal reproduction slightly less perfect, as though the mold were losing its firmness: Mrs. Dunseath had been breathtakingly lovely; Christie was merely beautiful; and Amy, his daughter, was only pretty. But oh what a true loveliness about her, something Mrs. Dunseath could not have acquired in a thousand years of breeding, the black hair and the light eyes, yes, the finely turned profile and the generous mouth, yes, all these though less classically stated, but her manner as well. Ahh, her gentle, shy, and inquiring manner, the delicate grace of her, *this* was the Willow legacy. *This* was his mother gently walking toward the seawall, her head tilted in anticipation, his Amy, his darling girl.

In July of 1954, a young man named Kaneji Yoro, accompanied by another young man named Peter Koenig, set a series of homemade bombs against the walls of Gracie Mansion, detonated them, and began running downtown in the direction of Wall Street, hoping to lose themselves in the lunch hour crowds. They were picked up before they had traveled three blocks, and were immediately charged with attempted murder, the mayor and the governor having been in executive conference within when the bombs went off. The charges were later expanded in the indictment to include arson (because the building caught fire), anarchy (because they found in a Jersey City basement several documents in the defendants' handwriting which outlined an escalating scheme of methodical destruction that would eventually lead to chaos and insurrection), conspiracy (because the two men had been out of state when they conspired to commit their act against the peace of New York), and, finally, treason. Treason, of course, was the most serious of all the charges and was a crime punishable by death. Since Article 212 of the New York State Penal Law defined treason as consisting of "a combination of two or more persons by force to usurp the government of the state, or to overturn the same, shown by a forcible attempt made within the state, to accomplish that purpose," Jonah could not see how the district attorney hoped to prove there had been an attempt at overthrowing the government, notwithstanding the timely presence in Gracie Mansion of the state's highest executive. The documents in the Jersey City basement indeed supported a charge of anarchy, bolstered as they were by copies of books by Engels and Marx, issues of the *Daily Worker*, and even one or two party directives. Attempted murder was also well within the bounds of realistic possibility, and a conviction on that charge alone would have netted the perpetrators twenty-five years each in prison, a long enough span for any young bomber. The enormity of the crime, however, this attempt on the lives of two important officials (by Communist anarchists, no less) undoubtedly called for more severe punishment than the law allowed, so the district attorney had gratuitously tacked to his indictment the charges of arson, conspiracy, and treason. The arson charge amused Johah. The conspiracy and treason charges incensed him. He could not believe that Yoro's and Koenig's respective Japanese and German ancestry had anything whatever to do with the indictment ("Of course not," Christie said. "The war's already forgotten. It's all craparoo") but he nonetheless detected in the public reaction an attitude of outraged piety and righteousness. Hadn't we been reconstructing and regenerating those dirty Nazi bastards and sneaky Jap finks ever since the war ended, a war *we* had won, mind you? So now two snotnosed red Communist Fascist punks try to blow up Gracie Mansion with our beloved mayor and governor inside, dirty red subversive Jap rat bastard Nazis—notwithstanding the fact that Yoro was born and raised in San Francisco or that Koenig's father was a respected employee of the *Reader's Digest* in Chappaqua, where he had been born and where he had sired his anarchist son.

Jonah wanted to take the case because he felt the treason charge was unjustified and unjustifiable. Raymond wanted to take the case because he was shrewd enough in his ancestral French way to realize that whoever defended these two young Communists would become famous overnight. Their initial separate motives were later ironically reversed: it was Raymond who wrote a paper explaining the principles involved in the case, which he read at the annual meeting of the American Bar Association; it was Jonah who conducted the court trial, Jonah whose name and picture appeared in all the newspapers, Jonah who came out of the proceedings a well-known legal figure and a champion of the rights of the individual in a free society.

The district attorney eventually dropped the absurd arson charge, but Jonah permitted his clients to plead guilty only to attempted murder and anarchy, fighting the treason charge as well as the linked charge of conspiracy (if there had been no treason, how could anyone have conspired to commit an act against the peace?) on the grounds that whatever eventual overthrow may have been contemplated by the pair, its execution had certainly not begun with the bombing of the mayor's residence. Youthful ego and exuberance aside, even these misguided twenty-year-old boys could not possibly have intended their deed (he almost said "childish prank") as the beginning of a bona fide uprising. The jury was out for six hours. It convicted Yoro and Koenig of the first two crimes, and the judge sentenced them to consecutive prison terms of twenty-five years for attempted murder and ten years for anarchy. The case was won, and a style was set. The style was not immediately manifest, though. Like the dissolution of Jonah's marriage, it resisted definition until it was fully recognizable. By the time the tone of the partnership was realized, the tone of the marriage was also realized, and it was curious that both marriage and partnership dissolved in the same year, only several months apart, though neither had anything to do with the other. Or was that true?

He pulled the car to the curb outside his building. The doorman standing just inside the glass entrance doors immediately put on his gloves and came out to greet him.

"Put her away for the night, Mr. Willow?" he asked.

"Please, Dave."

"What happened to your fender here, Mr. Willow?"

"I had a little accident."

"Really got mangled, didn't it?"

"Mmm."

"There's a good body man over at the garage, if you want to . . ."

"I'll talk to him about it in the morning, Dave."

"Will you be using her tomorrow, or . . ."

"No, I'll need a taxi."

"Right, Mr. Willow. G'night now."

"Good night, Dave."

He walked quickly into the lobby, stopping at the long table with the mirror over it, picking up his mail. There was nothing from Amy. He scanned the envelopes rapidly, and then walked back to the elevator bank.

"Good evening, Fred," he said.

"Evening, Mr. Willow." The elevator doors closed. "Getting pretty cold out there, isn't it?"

"Bitter," Jonah said.

He got off on the sixth floor, and walked to his apartment at the end of the hall. Bessie had left a light burning for him in the entry alcove; the apartment was otherwise dark. He went into the kitchen, turning on lights ahead of him, and found a note from Bessie scotch-taped to the refrigerator door. *Your daughter called,* she had written in pencil, *says you should called her back at school tonight or Wesday noon.* He nodded briefly, took off his coat, and then went through the apartment to the master bedroom overlooking Park Avenue. He was about to place his call to Pennsylvania when he realized it was past midnight. He would have to call on Wednesday.

His wrist hurt like hell. He undressed slowly and carefully, cursing the Egyptian under his breath—that was another call he'd have to make, to Judge Santesson, see what he could do about that crazy son of a bitch.

The cross begins tomorrow, he thought.

Wearily, he pulled back the covers, the blue and violet flower-patterned sheets Christie had brought home from Lord & Taylor, traces of her lingering in the bedroom even though the divorce had become final in August of 1962, the painting they had bought in Rome, St. Peter's in sunlight, the crayoned drawing Amy had given them as a Christmas gift when she was only four, traces, traces.

The cross begins tomorrow, he thought.

In a little while, he fell asleep.

TUESDAY

5

IT BEGAN SNOWING early in the morning, but by nine-thirty there was scarcely any cover at all on the sidewalk outside the courthouse. The snow was fine, a sharp powder that sifted from the sky only to be blown off the streets and sidewalks, patches of gathered white suddenly in motion, rearranging to reveal black asphalt and gray concrete, moving again like mist on a bog, to form yet another pattern directed by the wind. Arthur stood with Brackman just inside one of the barred windows fronting the street, looking past the thick white columns to the shifting snow beyond. He had not been able to sleep last night, and his eyes felt heavy and puffed.

"I want to give you some tips about Jonah Willow," Brackman said.

"I feel like hell," Arthur said.

"You'll wash your face before we go in. That'll make you feel better."

"That'll make me feel worse."

"Arthur, do you want me to tell you about Willow, or do you want to make wisecracks? If you want to make wisecracks . . ."

"You have no sense of humor, Sidney," Arthur said.

"That's right. Not when ten million dollars is at stake."

"All right, tell me about Willow. What should I know about him?"

"He's very smart," Brackman said. "That's the first thing you should know."

"I'm smart, too," Arthur said.

"Yes, but you're not a lawyer. Willow is smart, and he knows the law, and you can bet he's researched this case from top to bottom and can quote you precedent in Sanskrit. Don't underestimate him at any time during the cross. That's my first word of advice."

"All right, I won't underestimate him."

"Especially if he seems to be fumbling for words. That's an old trick of Jonah's, he does it to give the witness a false sense of confidence. Then he springs like an animal."

"I'll watch for it."

"He has a habit, too, of shooting questions at you from every corner of the universe, seemingly without logical order. *He* knows where he's going, but very often the witness can't connect the line of progression because the questions aren't in sequence. Watch out for that, Arthur. He can have you admitting your mother is a whore, and then ten minutes later contradicting it."

"You *do* have a sense of humor," Arthur said.

"So watch for that," Brackman said, ignoring him, "questions out of sequence. I'll help you all I can from the table, but there'll be times when I can't object, and I won't. You're up there alone, and you've got to watch yourself."

"I'll be very careful."

"Take your time with him. If he asks a question that sounds at all tricky, hesitate before you answer. If he pushes for an answer, ask him to repeat the question, even though you heard it the first time around."

"That'll fool him, I'll bet."

"It won't fool him for a minute, but it'll gain time for you while you think. And if you need more time, even *after* the question has been repeated, simply say you did not understand the question. While he explains it to you, you keep thinking. And then you answer it."

"Okay," Arthur said.

"If he asks a question that requires a 'yes' or 'no' answer, and you feel that such an answer will hurt you, I want you to say—and please memorize this, Arthur—I want you to say, 'I can answer that with a yes or no, but the answer will be misleading.' Have you got that?"

"I can answer it with a yes or no, but the answer will be misleading, right, I've got it."

"Good. Don't lose your temper."

"I won't."

"Don't raise your voice to Willow."

"I won't."

"Don't argue with him. Just answer . . ."

"I won't."

". . . the questions."

"Okay."

"And don't let him trick you into saying anything you don't want to say."

"I doubt if he can do that."

"I'm telling you he can."

"Words are my business, Sidney."

"They're Willow's, too, and you're playing in his ball park."

"I'll remember."

"Be especially careful of the negative question—where if you answer yes, you're really saying no."

"I'll be careful."

"This is the cross-examination, Arthur, and during the cross he's going to try to get you to contradict everything you said in the direct. Failing that, he'll try to make you appear foolish or ridiculous. He can be a ruthless man when he wants to, I've seen him in action, and he can make you feel like a child or a stuttering moron. If that happens, just take your time, regain your composure, and continue answering the questions truthfully. Don't lie, Arthur. Not about anything. I can guarantee that if you lie, Willow will pick up the lie later, and then your credibility will be questioned and that could very well lose the case for us. Am I making you nervous?"

"Yes, you damn well are."

"Good. I want you to be nervous because that'll make you careful. Don't forget, Arthur, this is where they got Jesus."

"What?"

"By the cross," Brackman said, and grinned.

"Mr. Constantine, had you ever met James Driscoll before the publication of *The Paper Dragon?*" Willow asked. "Just a moment, and I'll set a date for that."

"October of 1963," Brackman said.

"Thank you, Mr. Brackman," Willow replied. "Yes, Plaintiff's Exhibit 2 does indeed show that the copyright was in 1963. Thank you very much." He turned again to the witness chair. Arthur studied Willow's face and wished he could see through the reflecting lenses of his glasses.

"Had you met Mr. Driscoll at any time before October of 1963?"

"No, I had not," Arthur replied.

"Had you in fact ever set eyes on him before the beginning of this trial yesterday morning?"

"No, I had not."

"Is it correct to say that you never gave a copy of your play to Mr. Driscoll?"

"That is correct. I did not."

"Did you ever submit copies of your play to Mitchell-Campbell Books?"

"I don't think so."

"Well, surely you must *know*, Mr. Constantine."

"I have an agent, Mr. Willow, and he takes care of such matters for me. If you want to know whether I myself ever sent a copy to Mitchell-Campbell, no, sir, I did not. Nor to Camelot Books, nor to Mr. Driscoll, either."

"Did you ever ask your agent to send copies of your play to *any* publishing house?"

"I did not."

"Before this action began, Mr. Constantine, had you ever met Mr. Chester Danton of Mitchell-Campbell Books?"

"I had not."

"Had you ever met any other person employed by Mitchell-Campbell Books?"

"No, sir."

"Had you possessed any personal knowledge of James Driscoll's writing habits or procedure?"

"No personal knowledge, no."

"Had you possessed any personal knowledge of the editorial work done on *The Paper Dragon?*"

"No."

"Had you possessed any knowledge whatever of the author-editor relationship between James Driscoll and Chester Danton?"

"No knowledge whatever."

"Are you aware of the complaint in this action?"

"I am," Arthur said, and glanced quickly at Brackman.

"Is it based upon information you supplied to your attorneys?"

"Yes."

"Did you read the complaint after it was drawn?"

"I did."

"Did you swear to its truth?"

"I did."

Willow walked to the defense table. His assistant handed him a document, and he carried it back with him to the witness chair. "This is from paragraph 12 of your complaint, Mr. Constantine." He adjusted the glasses on the bridge of his nose, flipped through the document—which Arthur now recognized—and began reading: " 'On information and belief, James Driscoll and Mitchell-Campbell Books conspired to deprive plaintiff of his rights in the copyrighted composition.' " Willow looked up from the document. "Did you swear to that statement, Mr. Constantine?"

"I did."

"Did you then possess any knowledge or information concerning a conspiracy to plagiarize your work?"

"Oh, I see," Arthur said.

"Yes, what do you see?"

"Mr. Willow, I can only repeat what I said at the pretrial examination. I do *not* know how the plagiarism was effected, I do *not* know of any confidential meetings, or secret correspondence, I did *not* wiretap anyone's telephone. But I do know that there are similarities between my play and *The Paper Dragon* that far exceed the possibility of . . ."

"Please answer the question," Willow said. "Did you in fact possess any knowledge or information of such a conspiracy?"

"I had no such knowledge or information, no, sir."

"You have testified that you swore to the truth of your complaint."

"Yes."

"Did you swear to the truth of a similar complaint against API?"

"Yes, but . . ."

"Even though you then possessed no knowledge or . . ."

". . . these complaints are only legal terminology for . . ."

". . . information as to its truth. Thank you. Mr. Constantine, can you tell me if any other play of yours was ever produced? In addition to *The Catchpole*, I mean."

"It's *Catchpole*, not '*The*' *Catchpole*. I think I pointed that out to you before."

"Yes, *Catchpole*, forgive me."

"The code name for the invasion of Eniwetok Atoll was 'Operation Catchpole.' That's where I got the title."

"Isn't there another meaning of the word 'catchpole'?" Willow asked conversationally.

"Not that I know of. I believe it was coined for military purposes, a coined word."

"I think there's another meaning, Mr. Constantine."

"I wouldn't know it."

"It's archaic, of course," Willow said, "but a catchpole was a petty officer of justice, especially a man who made arrests for debt."

"Is that so?"

"Yes."

"I didn't know that."

"You were not aware of this other meaning when you wrote your play?"

"No."

"In any case, I will try to remember the correct title from now on. *Catchpole*."

"I'd appreciate it."

"*Have* you had any other plays produced?"

"I have a play in production now," Arthur said.

"Do you mean you have a play in rehearsal?"

"No, we're not in rehearsal yet. We're still casting it."

"When do you plan to open?"

"We haven't set a date as yet."

"In what theater will you open, Mr. Constantine?"

"That hasn't been decided yet."

"Has the play been fully capitalized?"

Arthur hesitated.

"Mr. Constantine? Has the play . . . ?"

"Not yet."

"Then this 'play in production,' as you refer to it, is really in a very *early* stage of production, isn't that so?"

"That's so, yes."

"In fact, we might say that until it is capitalized . . ."

"The play is under option," Arthur said. "It's our intention to produce it as soon as possible."

"Your *intention*, yes."

"Yes."

"But in fact, you have not had a play actually produced, actually presented since *The Catchpole*, forgive me, *Catchpole*. I'll try to remember."

"I've had movies and television plays produced."

"Yes, but not a stage play."

"No. Not until this play, which is in production now."

"Which is 'under option' now, isn't that what you mean?"

"No, I mean 'in production' now. We are actively casting it."

"But we may say, may we not, that since October of 1947, which is when *Catchpole* was produced—a period of more than nineteen years—you have not had a play produced on Broadway or off-Broadway or, in fact, anywhere in the world. Isn't that true?"

"That's true."

"Thank you. Mr. Constantine, you testified that you were sent to the Pacific as a new lieutenant, a *second* lieutenant I believe you said, after a short period of training as an officer."

"I did not say that."

"I beg your pardon?"

"I said that Roger Mason, my character in *Catchpole,* was sent overseas after a short period of training."

"Would you say that your character bears any resemblance to you?"

"Some."

"Were *you* also sent overseas after a short period of training?"

"I was."

"Do you feel this experience was unique?"

"Unique?"

"Yes, sir, unique. You know the meaning of the word 'unique.' "

"Yes, but I don't understand the question."

"I am asking you, Mr. Constantine, if during World War II, during the period of time before and during the Eniwetok landings, I am asking if it was unique to send an officer overseas after only a short period of training?"

"I don't know if it was unique or not."

"Have you ever heard the expression 'ninety-day wonder,' Mr. Constantine?"

"I have."

"It was a common expression, was it not?"

"It was a derogatory expression."

"But common. You did, in fact, use this very expression in your play. One of the enlisted men refers to Lieutenant Mason as a ninety-day wonder, doesn't he?"

"Yes, I suppose so. I don't recall exactly."

"Let me refresh your memory then," Willow said, and turned again toward the defense table.

"I'll take your word . . ."

"Here we are," Willow said, leafing through the manuscript. "Act I, Scene 1, page 4. This is Corporal Janus speaking. He says, 'Another ninety-day wonder. *I* wonder how long he'll last.' Do you recall the speech now?"

"If it's there, I recall it."

"It is here, Mr. Constantine. As a matter of fact, you cited it only yesterday in referring to one of your specific character similarities."

"Yes, I remember now."

"When you wrote your play, you were undoubtedly fully aware of what the Army called 'ninety-day wonders,' weren't you?"

"I suppose I was."

"And therefore you must have also been aware that so-called ninety-day wonders were not unique, Mr. Constantine."

"Yes."

"You know they were not unique?"

"I know that."

"Do you think they were unique at the time of the Korean conflict?"

"I have no knowledge of the Korean conflict."

"Then you are possibly not aware that the average training time for an officer in October and November of 1950—which is the time span covered by the novel *The Paper Dragon*—the average training period for an officer was ninety days. Did you know that, Mr. Constantine?"

"I did not know that."

"Will you accept my word for it? Or need I produce a letter received from the Office of the Chief of Information, United States Army, stating it as a fact?"

"I will accept your word for it."

"And will you further agree that ninety-day wonders were not unique during World War II, nor were they unique during the Korean conflict?"

"I would agree to that."

"That Roger Mason being a ninety-day wonder was not unique?"

"Yes."

"And that Alex Cooper, the lieutenant in *The Paper Dragon* was not unique, either."

"Yes."

"That both characters in fact are commonplace characters who might be found in any war at any time in the world's history?"

"I don't know about that."

"But you *do* agree, Mr. Constantine, that wherever there are wars, there are also officers hastily trained to fight them?"

"Yes, I would agree to that."

"Thank you. You are a writer, Mr. Constantine . . ."

"Yes, I am."

". . . so surely you must know that the basis of all drama is conflict."

"Yes, I know that."

"If a man were writing about an Army combat squad, wouldn't it be natural to have the conflict take place between an officer and his men?"

"No, it would not."

"It would *not* be natural?"

"I can imagine any number of conflicts taking place in a combat squad, and they need not all be between an officer and his men."

"The question was whether this would be a natural development."

"And the answer is that this would be only *one* of the possible developments."

"Would you say that one of the developments in *The Naked and the Dead* is a conflict between a man or men in command, and those who are not?"

"I have not made a study of *The Naked and the Dead*."

"Would you say that one of the developments in *From Here to Eternity* is a conflict between a man or men in command, and those who are not?"

"I haven't studied that one, either."

"You testified that the film based on that book won the Academy Award in 1953."

"Yes."

"Did you see the film?"

"No."

"Did you read the book?"

"No."

"Did you read *The Caine Mutiny?*"

"Yes."

"Do you agree that one of the developments in *The Caine Mutiny* is a conflict between a man in command and men who are not?"

"*All* the men in *The Caine Mutiny* are in command."

"You mean that the leading characters are officers, don't you?"

"Yes."

"But Captain Queeg is in command."

"Yes."

"And Maryk and Keefer and the others are all subordinate officers."

"Yes."

"And the conflict is between them."

"Yes."

"The conflict is between the man in command and those below him in rank."

"If you wish to put it that way, yes."

"Is there another way to put it, Mr. Constantine?"

"I am merely saying that this is only *one* of the paths a war story can take."

"But this is a very natural development that has been utilized time and again by a great many writers producing works about men in war."

"Yes, I would say so."

"Would you also say that another possible development would be a conflict between an officer and a *specific* enlisted man?"

"That's one of the possible developments, yes."

"Such as the conflict between Roger Mason and Corporal Janus in your play, and the conflict between Alex Cooper and Private Colman in *The Paper Dragon*."

"Is that a question?"

"The question is would you consider this conflict a natural development in a work dealing with an Army combat squad?"

"I don't know if it is a natural development or not. It was a development of *mine* when I was writing the play."

"Do you claim it as a *unique* development?"

"I claim it as an integral part of my play. In that respect—"

"But not unique."

"Not unique, but—"

"Thank you, Mr. Constantine. Would you also—"

"I would like to finish what I—"

"You have sufficiently answered the question."

"I'd like to hear what he has to say, Mr. Willow," Mc-Intyre said. "Go on, please."

"I was going to say that simply because a line of development is a natural one doesn't mean that two separate writers would automatically choose it as their approach. If we pick apart the play and the novel, piece by piece . . ."

"I am prepared to do *exactly* that," Willow said.

". . . the isolated pieces and fragments would *seem* to be coincidental, I mean the similarities between them would seem coincidental. But when we put them all together, we're presented with overwhelming evidence of . . ." Arthur hesitated.

"Yes, Mr. Constantine?"

"Of copying," Arthur said.

"You seemed reluctant to use the word."

"I don't like to call a man a thief."

"But that's exactly what you've done in your complaint," Willow said and paused. "*Do* you or do you *not* believe Mr. Driscoll copied your play?"

"Actually sat down and copied it, I don't know. I mean, I don't know if he actually had a copy of my play on his desk while he was writing his novel."

"You are aware, are you not, Mr. Constantine, that access must be proved in a plagiarism case?"

"I have been so informed by my attorneys."

"But you don't know whether or not James Driscoll actually *possessed* a copy of your play when he was writing his novel?"

"I was not there when he was writing his novel."

"Please answer the question, Mr. Constantine."

"No, I don't know if he had a copy." Arthur paused. "But if he didn't have one, then he must have seen the play."

"When it was performed in New York, do you mean?"

"I don't know when. The similarities are too astonishing for someone who did not have prior knowledge—"

"We are here to decide whether there *are* similarities, Mr. Constantine, astonishing or otherwise. In the meantime, do you believe that James Driscoll saw your play during its brief twelve-day run at the Fulton Theatre in October of 1947?"

"I don't know."

"But you testified that he must have seen it."

"Yes."

"Well, *when* do you think he saw it?"

Arthur glanced at Brackman, and Brackman nodded. "There was also a series of previews," Arthur said.

"Are these the previews you testified to during the direct examination yesterday?"

"Yes."

"Did you personally distribute the tickets to those previews?"

"I did not."

"Who was responsible for the distribution?"

"Our press agent."

"How do you know they were distributed?"

"I was told."

"Then all you know about the distribution is what you were told."

"Well, we were concerned with getting a representative college audience."

"Yes, but all you actually *know* about the distribution is what you were told, is that true?"

"Yes. But I know the tickets were sent out to various colleges and universities."

"Do you know *which* colleges and universities?"

"Yes."

"Of your *own* knowledge?"

"No. The names of the schools were given to me."

"By whom?"

"We had a meeting and decided we wanted this play to be seen by representative college kids, and we decided to distribute a limited amount of free tickets."

"*Who* gave you the names of the colleges to which the tickets were actually sent, Mr. Constantine?"

"I don't remember exactly who. It could have been anybody involved with the show, though it was most likely the man who was handling our press for us, I'm not sure."

"All you know is that somebody said something about having sent these tickets out."

"That's right."

"Which schools, to your recollection, were these mysterious tickets sent to?"

"Objection," Brackman said.

"Sustained."

"Which schools received these tickets, Mr. Constantine? Would you name them, please?"

"I named them yesterday."

"Please do it again, would you?"

"They were sent to City College, Hunter, Brooklyn College, L.I.U., Pratt Institute, and Fordham, I believe."

"You *believe?*"

"I believe they were sent to Fordham. I'm not sure about Fordham."

"But you *are* sure about Pratt Institute?"

"Yes, I am."

"Are you aware, Mr. Constantine, that in 1947 Pratt Institute was a highly specialized school teaching art, engineering, library, and home economics?"

"Architecture, I thought," Arthur said.

"Yes, as part of its art program. Were you aware of that?"

"I thought it was primarily an architectural school."

"In any case, more than half the students there at the time were taking courses like Industrial Design, or Illustration, or Food and Clothing. Would you agree that it was a highly specialized school?"

"Yes."

"And yet, in your search for 'a representative college audience'—I believe that was your exact language—you included Pratt among these other schools?"

"Yes."

"Did you know that James Driscoll was a student at Pratt Institute in 1947?"

"I didn't know that."

"You've never heard that before, Mr. Constantine?"

"I knew he was a student at Pratt Institute, but not that he was there in 1947."

"In other words, when you testified that free tickets were sent to Pratt Institute in 1947—a highly specialized school, even though you were looking for a representative college audience—when you so testified, you were not aware that James Driscoll had been a student there at the time?"

"I was aware that Mr. Driscoll went to Pratt Institute, but I had no knowledge as to the date, I just told you that. If you want to know whether I think Mr. Driscoll could have seen my play in performance, yes, I think he could have seen it."

"That was not my question."

"It seemed to be your question."

"It was not. I'll rephrase it so that it will be perfectly clear to you. Do you not feel, Mr. Constantine, that your having sent free tickets to Pratt Institute at the very time James Driscoll was a student there is a remarkable coincidence?"

"I do not. To the best of my knowledge, we sent the tickets to Pratt. If Driscoll happened to be a student there at the time, that's a plain fact, and there's nothing coincidental about it."

"Thank you." Willow sighed and walked toward the defense table. He leafed through a batch of papers his assistant handed to him, his back to Arthur all the while. Apprehensively, Arthur waited for Willow to turn toward him again. Brackman caught his eye and nodded encouragingly.

"Mr. Constantine," Willow said, walking slowly toward him, "you have testified that you served in the United States Army during World War II."

"I did."

"Were you an officer?"

"I was a second lieutenant."

"Like the character in your play?"

"In that he was a second lieutenant also, yes."

"Were you in command of a platoon?"

"I was."

"How many men were in the platoon?"

"Forty-one."

"As in your play?"

"As in *any* Army platoon during World War II."

"What was the composition of this platoon?"

"What do you mean?"

"What sort of men were in it?"

"I still don't understand you."

"Where were they from, what was their education, their racial or religious background, and so on?"

"I don't remember. There were all types of men in the platoon. And there were replacements from time to time. I can't remember all the background details of each man."

"Was there a man from New York City in your platoon? Besides yourself, I mean."

"I think so."

"Was there a Southerner?"

"There might have been."

"And possibly someone from the Middle West? Or California?"

"Possibly."

"Men of high school or college education perhaps?"

"Perhaps."

"Was there a Catholic?"

"Yes."

"And a Protestant, and a Jew?"

"There could have been. I don't remember."

"Was there a Negro?"

"No."

"The Army was not integrated at that time, was it?"

"No."

"Was there an Italian in your platoon?"

"Yes."

"Was this the only platoon you ever commanded, Mr. Constantine?"

"I commanded several other platoons later on. And when I made captain, I was given command of a company. This was shortly before I was discharged."

"Would you say that the composition of these other platoons you commanded was roughly the same as that of the first one? In terms of background?"

"Roughly, yes."

"There were New Yorkers possibly, or Southerners, or men from California or the Middle West. There were Catholics and Protestants and Jews. There were men of Irish descent or Italian descent. There was, if you will, a cross-section of America."

"I would say so."

"Do you suppose this was true of *any* platoon in the United States Army during World War II?"

"I would suppose so."

"Do you suppose it was also true of any platoon in the United States Army during the *Korean* conflict?"

"Possibly. But that doesn't necessarily . . ."

"If a man sat down to write a play or a novel about the Army, would he not be likely to include men of various backgrounds, such as those who might be found in a *real* platoon?"

"Yes, but . . ."

"Would he not be likely to include a member of a minority group?"

Arthur hesitated, and then looked out at Brackman.

"Mr. Constantine," Willow said, "would you answer the question, please?"

"I could answer that with a yes or no," Arthur said, "but the answer would be misleading."

Willow looked up in what seemed like genuine surprise. He stared at Arthur for a moment, and then said, "Please answer it any way you wish."

"A writer would include a member of a minority group only if it served a purpose," Arthur said.

"What purpose does Sergeant D'Agostino serve in your play?"

"He is a catalyst."

"For what?"

"For everything that happens on the island. He's the man who sacrifices himself for the lieutenant. He's the man who—"

"What does this have to do with his being Italian?"

"It adds to the conflict. Corporal Janus harps on this. It causes further conflict between the lieutenant and the squad."

"The fact that D'Agostino is Italian?"

"Yes. Driscoll does the same thing in his novel. Only the character is Negro."

"You mean that Mr. Driscoll uses a Negro character to further the conflict between the lieutenant and the squad, is that true?"

"That's it, yes."

"By having a scene in which the lieutenant is suspected of bigotry, is that what you're referring to? Where Sergeant Morley believes the lieutenant is a bigot?"

"Yes, that's the scene."

"And you had earlier used this same device in *Catchpole*, is that right? This is why you chose to put an Italian in your fictitious squad. To point up a conflict with the lieutenant along lines of possible prejudice."

"Yes."

Willow walked to the defense table. "Here's a copy of your play," he said. "Would you kindly show me the scene or scenes wherein Lieutenant Mason and Sergeant D'Agostino confront each other in such a manner?"

"What manner do you mean?"

"Show me a scene where the lieutenant is suspected of prejudice."

"It isn't a scene, there are only references."

"Show me the references."

"I'll have to look for them."

"Please take all the time you need."

Arthur accepted the manuscript. He began leafing through it. He could feel sweat running down the sides of his chest. He wiped a hand across his lip. "I don't know if this is what you're looking for . . ."

"I'm looking for any lines in your play that would indicate Sergeant D'Agostino suspects the lieutenant of being prejudiced against Italians. Or rather, Mr. Constantine, *you* are looking for them."

"May I read this?"

"Certainly."

"This is in Act II, it's Corporal Janus speaking to Sergeant D'Agostino. He says, 'I understand you, Mike. You're a Wop and I'm a Pole, and we just don't fit.' "

"And this—"

"There's more."

"Please read it."

"He answers—"

"D'Agostino answers?"

"Yes. He answers, 'We're just poor little orphans, huh, Danny?' and Janus says, 'We're misfits. They'll never understand us as long as we live.' That's the reference."

"The reference to what?"

"Prejudice."

"As I understand it, Mr. Constantine, this series of speeches you have just read to us constitute the sole reference to prejudice . . ."

"There are others."

"Find them, please."

"Perhaps more specific," Arthur said.

"Yes, please find them."

He wiped his lip again. He knew *exactly* why he had made

D'Agostino Italian. He had done it to point up the conflict, the very conflict Willow was harping on, and which Driscoll had stolen and amplified in his book, making the character a Negro to cash in on the burgeoning civil rights movement, where *were* those other scenes? "Well, here," he said, "on page 2–16, there's another short encounter between Janus and D'Agostino that I think points up this business of racial prejudice between the lieutenant—"

"*Racial* prejudice?"

"No, I mean his prejudice against Italians."

"Please read it, Mr. Constantine."

"D'Agostino is talking about the feast of La Madonna di Carmela which they have every year on 115th Street in Harlem. I don't know whether or not you're familiar with it."

"No, I'm not."

"Well, he's talking about the feast—he refers to it as 'the *festa*,' that's the Italian word for it—and he says, 'Whenever I went to the *festa*, Danny, I felt as if I was stepping into a world I knew inside out and backwards, you know what I mean? All the sounds and all the smells and all the people. It was where I belonged.' And Janus replies, 'Yeah, not on a goddamn island in the middle of the Pacific with a lieutenant trying to get us all killed.' "

"This is the specific reference?" Willow said.

"Yes, it links D'Agostino's Italian background with the lieutenant."

"In what way?"

"D'Agostino is talking about where he belongs, and Janus subtly implies that he does not belong here with the lieutenant."

"Are there any other references, Mr. Constantine?"

"There are several more, I'm sure. This was a thread I put into the play, a constant nagging by Janus, a constant reminder that the lieutenant is aware of D'Agostino as an Italian."

"If you can find any more references, we would be grateful," Willow said.

"Well, if you'll give me a few moments . . ."

"Certainly."

"Oh, yes," Arthur said, "that's right. The scene with the Jap, when they capture the Jap. Just a second now." He began turning pages. "Yes," he said, "no, wait a minute, yes, here it is, the end of Act II, just before the end of the act. They've captured a Japanese soldier, and they're trying to interrogate him, but they can't find anyone who speaks Japanese. So Meredith, he's one of the men in the squad, says, 'Do you think the Loot speaks Japanese?' and Janus says, 'Don't be silly, the Loot speaks white American Protestant.' Then he turns to D'Agostino and says, 'How about you, Mike? Japanese is just like Italian, ain't it?' That's the thread being picked up again, of course, the constant juxtaposition of D'Agostino being Italian and the lieutenant being aware of it, that's the reference here."

"I see," Willow said. "Are there any others?"

"I'm sure there must be, but those are all that I can think of at the moment." He leaned forward to hand the manuscript back to Willow.

"No, please hold on to it," Willow said. "There are several other things I'd like you to find."

"If I knew you were going to ask me for specific references . . ."

"That's what we're dealing with here, Mr. Constantine. Specifics."

"I thought we were dealing with plagiarism."

"That is *your* allegation."

"Wouldn't it be more to the point to compare the two works instead of—?"

"Mr. Constantine, it would be more to the point to allow me to conduct my own cross-examination, if that's all right with you."

"Certainly."

"Thank you. You said yesterday in testifying about thematic similarities that your hero, and I am reading from the record now, 'is a new lieutenant who feels that human life is more important than the quarrels of nations, and this theme is stated in Act I, Scene 4, pages 21 and 22 of *Catch-pole.*' Would you please turn to those pages now?"

"Pages 21 and 22?"

"That's right."

"I have them."

"Would you read to me the line or lines that indicate the lieutenant felt human life was more important than the quarrels of nations?"

"May I look this over?" Arthur asked.

"Certainly."

Arthur slowly and carefully read the two pages, and then read them again. "I believe this is the reference," he said.

"Yes, which?"

"Lieutenant Mason is talking to the men, it's this one speech beginning on the bottom of page 21, and carrying over onto page 22. 'I know you men are wondering what we're doing on this godforsaken island,' he says, 'I know that's foremost in your minds especially when intelligence tells us there are thirty-five hundred Japs dug in on this atoll. You're all experienced soldiers and you know that even if we blast them out of their holes here, we've got the next island to take and the next one after that, so what's the use, what are we doing here? I know you're thinking that some of us may die, *all* of us may die, and for what? For a barren stretch of Japanese real estate in the middle of the Pacific? No. We're here because there's a job to do. It's as simple as that.'" Arthur looked up. "I believe that's the reference," he said.

"To human life being more important than the quarrels of nations?"

"Not in that specific language. I never claimed that identical language was used in the statement of this particular theme. But there are the springboard references here, the touchstones Driscoll used in shaping his theme, the references to death and dying, the references to empires and their holdings, the references to the grim realities of war, the thirty-five hundred Japs holed up on the atoll, and having to be blasted out. All of these add up to a specific similarity of theme, though not of language."

"Thank you. You also testified yesterday, and this too relates to the theme of your play, you testified that Mr. Matthew Jackson at API, in expressing his reaction to *Catchpole,* said—and again I quote from the record—'I think they'd be leery of an Army theme that tries to show the stupidity and foolish waste of war.' Mr. Constantine, do you agree with Mr. Jackson's statement? Would you say that your play tries to show the stupidity and foolish waste of war?"

"Yes, it does."

"Would you say that this is also the theme of Mr. Driscoll's novel?"

"It is very definitely his theme. The themes are identical."

"Now would you mind showing me where in your play, which scene or which speech or even which line illustrates this theme, the stupidity and foolish waste of war?"

"The entire play illustrates the theme."

"In what way?"

"The antagonism of the men is stupid, the plot to kill Mason is stupid, the accidental killing of D'Agostino by the psychopathic colonel is stupid, everything that happens from the moment the lieutenant *arrives* is stupid. And the men finally realize this at the end."

"Where do they realize it?"

"At the very end of the play."

"Find the place for me."

"Certainly. They realize just what we've been talking about, that war is stupid and a foolish waste."

"Please show me where this realization takes place."

"It's here at the end of the play," Arthur said. "Here, it's on page 3–4–36, shortly after D'Agostino is killed and Janus is exposed. The speech is given to one of the minor characters, his name is Franklin. This is what he says: 'Lieutenant, we didn't know what we were doing. You get out here in the middle of nowhere, and you forget what reality is. You're surrounded by so much bugging killing, so much bugging blood, that you forget what's right or wrong. Now Mike is dead, and for what? The *real* enemy is still out there. We were wrong, lieutenant. We apologize.' This was a very moving scene, as it was done, and it clearly stated the theme of the play."

"Which was what?"

"That war is idiotic."

"Where does it say that?"

"A writer doesn't state his theme that obviously, Mr. Willow. If he did, it would become tract writing, it would become transparent and condescending. I tried to state the theme in human terms, one human expressing himself to another, one human apologizing to another. The man who apologizes for the rest of the squad is a grizzled combat veteran who kills Japanese soldiers the way you or I would brush our teeth in the morning. He comes to the lieutenant and he says in effect that war changes men, makes them lose their sense of reality, wastes their minds and their bodies. He says this in very human and believable terms, but he is nonetheless stating the theme of the play."

"You also testified that the collective reaction of those who had read the play at API was, and I quote, 'that the play was too outspoken, that the United States wasn't ready to take criticism of its armed forces, not when we had just come through a major conflict and also a minor one in Korea.' Do you feel this was a legitimate reason for the rejection of the play?"

"I don't know if it was legitimate or not. I *do* know that's why the play was rejected."

"Because—and again I quote—'it was too strong for API to do.' Is that correct?"

"That's what I was told."

"This was when, Mr. Constantine?"

"What do you mean?"

"When were these reactions to the play given to you?"

"In 1952 sometime."

"Mr. Constantine, would you say that *From Here to Eternity*, which won the Academy Award in 1953, was a strong movie that dealt harshly with the United States Army?"

"I couldn't say. I neither saw the picture nor read the book."

"From what you know of it, Mr. Constantine, would you—?"

"Objection," Brackman said, rising. "Witness has already stated he has no personal knowledge of either the film or the book in question."

"Sustained."

"If I told you that the book and the film were both highly uncomplimentary to the United States Army, would you accept my word for it?" Willow asked.

"Yes, I would."

"Thank you. Why then do you suppose these people at API said the United States wasn't ready to take criticism of its armed forces?"

"I cannot account for the actions of API."

"Is it true, Mr. Constantine, that your play was submitted to API in September of 1947, a month before it was produced on Broadway?"

"That's true."

"Why was it submitted?"

"To try for a preproduction deal."

"Was it rejected at that time?"

"Yes."

"Is it also true that the head of API's story department in New York was invited to the opening night performance of *Catchpole* on October 14, 1947?"

"I think so, yes."

"Why was he invited?"

"*All* the movie people were invited. We were trying for a movie sale, of course. That's standard procedure."

"Was an offer made after opening night?"

"No."

"Did you see the reviews of your play *Catchpole* after it opened?"

"I did."

"I ask you to look at this review from the *New York Times* of October 15, 1947, and tell me whether it is the one that appeared after the opening of your play." Willow turned to McIntyre. "Your Honor, Mr. Brackman has already agreed that we would not have to prove publication, which would be a simple matter."

"Do you concede publication, Mr. Brackman?" McIntyre asked.

"Yes, of any material that appeared in a magazine or newspaper."

"Please answer the question then, Mr. Constantine."

"Yes, that's the *New York Times* review of my play," Arthur said.

"I would like to offer it in evidence," Willow said.

"I object to it as irrelevant, your Honor. Whether it praises or faults Mr. Constantine's play, it hardly pertains to the matter of plagiarism."

"Why are you offering it, Mr. Willow?"

"Your Honor, the critical appraisal of *Catchpole* is of enormous relevance to this case. Mr. Driscoll is said to have plagiarized the play, but the only support for this allegation is a purported similarity between the two works. I ask now why anyone would *wish* to steal a play that had already been rejected by each and every major motion picture studio, that had been greeted with universally bad notices, and that ran for only twelve days on Broadway."

"Your Honor," Brackman said, "the law books already show that it is the relatively unknown work which most often becomes the target of the plagiarist."

"We could argue that all day, your Honor . . ."

"Yes, I'm sure we could," McIntyre said.

". . . and still not come to an agreement," Willow continued. *"Abie's Irish Rose* was certainly highly successful, and I'm sure my opponent recognizes it as one of the most prominent plagiarism cases. And whereas there are examples of plagiarism from more obscure properties, I still feel that critical and popular acceptance of a work is relevant to the issue here."

"Mr. Constantine has already testified that the play ran only twelve days," McIntyre said. "This does not indicate, to me at any rate, that it was a hit. Why you would wish to offer

additional evidence to that point is beyond me, Mr. Willow.
I will not admit it."

"Will you allow it to be marked for identification, your
Honor?"

"I will."

"Mark it 'Defendants' Exhibit A for identification,' " the
clerk said.

"May we also mark for identification the review that appeared in the New York *Herald Tribune* on October 15,
1947?"

"Is this another review of *Catchpole?*"

"Yes, your Honor. Your objection is only to relevance, is it
not?"

"It is not admissable."

"I made the offer first in evidence, so that the record will
be clear."

"The record will note your exception."

"Mark it 'Defendants' Exhibit B for identification,' " the
clerk said.

"Thank you," Willow said. "Mr. Constantine, when did
you begin work on your play *Catchpole?*"

"When I got out of the Army. That was July of 1946."

"And when was the play completed?"

"About three or four months later. Toward the end of the
year."

"November or December, would you say?"

"Yes. November, I think it was."

"When did you begin attempting to find a producer for
it?"

"In January of 1947. There was no sense trying to do
anything during the holidays. I had the play mimeographed
shortly before Christmas, and I began sending it around after
New Year's."

"Is this customary procedure?"

"Sending the play to producers, do you mean?"

"No. Having copies mimeographed."

"Some authors do, others don't. It depends on how many

people you want to reach. And also whether you can afford to have the work done."

"How many people did you want to reach, Mr. Constantine?"

"As many as possible. I wanted my play to be produced."

"How many copies were mimeographed?"

"A hundred, a hundred and fifty, I don't remember the exact amount."

"And I take it the result of all this was that you succeeded in getting a producer?"

"That's right."

"So it would seem to have been a good procedure," Willow said.

"It worked for me."

"To get back, you say you began work on *Catchpole* shortly after you were discharged from the United States Army. Would you say that your Army experience was still fresh in your mind when you began writing?"

"I would say so, yes."

"Army routine, Army terminology, Army regulations?"

"Yes, all of it."

"As well as the language used by soldiers, of course."

"Of course."

"In your military experience, Mr. Constantine, did you meet many men who used obscene language?"

"I met some."

"Who used obscene language such as Mr. Driscoll uses in his novel, and such as you more discreetly use in your play?"

"Yes, I met some. Mostly uneducated men."

"There *were* some of these in the Army."

"Is that a question?"

"Yes, it's a question."

"Yes, there were uneducated men who used obscene language."

"Do you think they were rarities?"

"No."

"They were commonplace?"

"They were to be found everywhere in the Army."

"During World War II?"

"Yes, and during the Korean War also, I would imagine. That's where you're leading, isn't it?"

"Do you feel, Mr. Constantine, that the character named Franklin in your play—the man who is addicted to the use of obscene language—do you feel he is a unique creation?"

"I do."

"You feel that a soldier addicted to the use of obscene language is unique?"

"Franklin swears in a specific manner. He uses a specific word as verb, noun, adjective, adverb. I think we know the word I mean."

"Yes, I'm sure we do."

"I changed it to the word *bug* in my play."

"And you feel that a character who uses this word as verb, noun, adjective, and so on is a unique creation of your own, is that correct?"

"That's correct."

"And not simply a valid fictional representation of a commonplace individual who is to be found wherever there are armies or Army posts or barracks?"

"I consider him unique."

"Would it surprise you, Mr. Constantine, to learn that in a play titled *The Eve of St. Mark* . . . do you know the play?"

"Yes, I know it."

"It's by Maxwell Anderson, he's won several awards for playwriting, including the Drama Critics Circle Award and the Pulitzer Prize. I think you may know of him."

"Yes, I know of Maxwell Anderson."

"In his play *The Eve of St. Mark* there is a sergeant named Ruby, who is addicted to the use of the word *ruttin'* . . ."

"Rotten?"

"No, *ruttin'*. R-U-T-T-I-N-apostrophe, very similar to your use of the words *bug* or *bugging*. Does that surprise you, Mr. Constantine?"

"I'm not that familiar with the play."

"It opened at the Cort Theater in New York on October 7, 1942, five years before *Catchpole*. It ran until June 26th of the following year, and was later made into a motion picture. Do you still maintain that your character Franklin is a unique creation?"

"I do. He is unique in my play."

"But not in someone else's play? He is unique only in *your* play?"

"I had not seen Mr. Anderson's play, nor was I aware of the sergeant in it. Besides, the word *bugging* is not the word *ruttin'*."

"Nor are either of them the actual word Mr. Driscoll uses, isn't that so?"

"It's so, but the intent is the same."

"The same as what?"

"The same as using the word *bug,* which I had to use for the stage."

"But not the same as the word *ruttin',* which Mr. Anderson had to use for the stage?"

"I merely said the words *bugging* and *ruttin'* were not identical."

"But they are similar?"

"Yes, they are similar."

"In intent?"

"Yes, in intent, too, I suppose. But . . ."

"Yet you still maintain that your character's use of obscenity is unique?"

"It is unique, yes."

"Thank you. Mr. Constantine, what procedure did you follow in submitting your play for production?"

"I usually mailed it out."

"To whom?"

"To anyone I thought might be interested. This was my first play, and I was new at this sort of thing. I didn't have an agent at the time. I sent it to anyone I thought might help me in getting it produced."

"And that included?"

"What?"

"To whom exactly did you send it, Mr. Constantine?"

"Producers, agents, investors, anyone interested in the the-

ater . . ." Arthur's voice trailed. It had occurred to him that
this was the second time Willow had brought up the matter
of submission, and he wondered now where he was leading.
He sensed a trap. Every intuitive power he possessed told him
that Willow had picked up the scent of something the first
time around, and was now tracking it down. But Arthur did
not know what. He found himself suddenly alert, staring
intently at Willow, leaning forward in the witness chair,
waiting for the trap to make itself more evident so that he
could avoid it.

"Did you send a copy to Mr. Hollis Marks?"

"I don't know any Hollis Marks."

"He is an agent. Did you send the play to him?"

"No. Oh, is he Driscoll's agent?" Arthur asked suddenly.

"Yes, that's right."

"No. I did not send a copy of the play to Driscoll's agent.
But there were enough copies around the city. Driscoll could
have easily seen one."

"Yes, you testified that there had been a hundred or a
hundred and fifty copies mimeographed, didn't you?"

"That's right."

"Who mimeographed these copies, Mr. Constantine?"

"York Duplicating."

"Here in Manhattan?"

"Yes."

"Was the number a hundred? Or a hundred and fifty?
Which?"

"A hundred and fifty, I believe."

"And you began mailing these out in January of 1947?"

"Yes."

"To producers, agents, investors, and anyone interested in
the theater?"

"Yes."

"Did you deliver any of these manuscripts personally?"

"Some of them. Most of them were sent through the mail."

"With covering letters?"

"Yes, of course."

"Did you ask for their return?"

"I don't remember."

"Did you enclose a stamped, self-addressed envelope for their return?"

"No."

"Do you know of anyone at Mitchell-Campbell who saw a copy of the play at the time you were distributing it?"

"No, I do not."

"But there were hundreds of copies distributed, weren't there?"

"A hundred and fifty."

"*All* of the mimeographed copies were distributed?"

"I don't know. I assume most of them were. Let's say somewhere over a hundred copies were being sent around to various people."

"And yet you have no knowledge that either James Driscoll or anyone at Mitchell-Campbell saw a copy of your play at that time."

"No direct knowledge, no."

"Your entire allegation is based on the fact that you believe the works are similar?"

"They're virtually parallel."

"Since you have the script in your hand, Mr. Constantine, I wonder if you would mind pointing out to me the line or lines that label the Army division as the 105th."

"It was not labeled in a line."

"Then how exactly was it labeled?"

"In a stage direction."

"Would you point this out to me, please?"

"Certainly." Arthur began leafing through the manuscript. He was beginning to think he had been wrong, that no trap had been conceived or intended.

"Here it is," he said. "The top of the second act, page 2–1–1. It describes the command post, and it says, 'A battered jeep is parked just outside the headquarters shack. The division insignia hangs over the door to the shack, the number 105 in yellow on a black field.' That's the reference."

"Thank you. Did you see this play in performance, Mr. Constantine?"

"I did."

"Did you see every performance?"

"Every performance."

"Was the insignia a part of the scenery for the play?"

"It was part of the set dressing."

"By which you mean it was affixed to the wall of the headquarters shack."

"The *outside* wall of the shack, yes."

"The number 105 in yellow on a black field."

"Yes."

"Was this your own description of the set?"

"It was."

"Did this description appear in the mimeographed version of the play? The one you sent around for people to read?"

"It did."

"It was not later added? I mean, Mr. Constantine, was the description of the set and its dressing added *after* the play was actually produced?"

"No, it was in the original copies I distributed."

"And the insignia *did* actually appear in the play as it was produced on the New York stage?"

"Yes, it did. If you want to call our set designer as a witness . . ."

"I don't think that will be necessary. When you held your preview performances in the Second Avenue loft, Mr. Constantine, the ones to which the college audiences were invited —was the play performed with scenery?"

Arthur hesitated.

"Mr. Constantine, would you answer the question?"

"No. The play was not performed with scenery."

"Is it my understanding, then, that the division insignia was *not* hanging on the wall of the headquarters shack during the preview performances in the Second Avenue loft?"

"It was not."

"Was there indeed a headquarters shack at *all* in the Second Avenue loft?"

"There was not."

"The play was presented on a bare stage?"

"With furniture."

"Then anyone who had been present at those preview performances could not possibly have seen the number 105 in yellow on a black field."

"That's right," Arthur said.

"In other words, in order for Mr. Driscoll to have seen the number 105, he either had to be present at one of the Broadway performances, or else he had to have a copy of your manuscript. Those are the only two ways in which he could conceivably have known about the number, is that right?"

"Unless someone told him about it."

"Someone who had seen the play on Broadway or read the manuscript?"

"Yes."

"But you have testified that you did not send a copy of the manuscript to Mitchell-Campbell Books?"

"That's right."

"It would have been someone else then, is that it? Someone *not* connected with Mr. Driscoll's publishers?"

"I don't know who it might have been. Copies of the manuscript were floating all over the city. It could have been anyone who read the play, or anyone who saw it. It ran for twelve days. There were matinee performances on some of those days, so we can add . . ."

"Whoever saw or read the play undoubtedly attached great significance to the number 105."

"I did not say that."

"Do *you* attach great significance to that number, Mr. Constantine?"

"I do."

"Do you feel it is an integral part of your play?"

"I do."

"Even though it appears only briefly in one scene of the play, and then only as part of a background insignia hung to the wall of a shack?"

"It was clearly visible to the audience. Yellow on black is a particularly vibrant color combination."

"But do you feel the number added to the value of your play?"

"It was a part of the play."

"Was it of value?"

"To me it was."

"In what way?"

"It designated the division."

"Was this designation significant?"

"To me it was."

"Would it be significant to anyone else?"

"Apparently it was also significant to Mr. Driscoll."

"Was the number of any significance to the audience?"

"It told the audience what division was involved in the invasion."

"Was this of great importance?"

"I think so."

"How?"

"It was a part of *my* play. It came from *my* mind. It was a numerical designation for a division *I* invented. *That* is its significance and its importance and its value. It is *mine,* and not another man's."

"You began working on this play of yours in July of 1946 . . ."

"Possibly August."

". . . and completed it in November sometime, is that what you said?"

"Yes."

"You then had a hundred and fifty copies mimeographed, and in January of 1947 you began distributing those copies."

"That's right."

"And you distributed well over a hundred of them?"

"A hundred and ten, a hundred and twenty, something like that."

"Mimeographed copies?"

"Yes." Willow had returned again to the mimeographed copies, and now Arthur was certain a trap was being baited. He wondered why Brackman did not object, wondered why

Brackman did not rise to give him some clue as to the nature of the trap. He looked at Brackman hopefully, but the man seemed completely unaware that Willow had again returned to the same topic. Couldn't he see that this was a persistent and recurring thread, similar to the thread in *Catchpole,* where Janus is constantly badgering D'Agostino about . . .

". . . to different people?" Willow said.

"I beg your pardon?"

"The question was, Mr. Constantine: Were these hundred and twenty mimeographed copies distributed to different people?"

"Yes, they were."

"Beginning in January of 1947?"

"Yes."

"And ending when?"

"When I found a producer."

"Which was when?"

"May of 1947. May 11th, to be exact, I won't forget that date. That's when the play was optioned by Mr. Frederick Gerard, who eventually produced it later that year."

"You personally arranged for or actually made delivery of one hundred and twenty mimeographed copies of your play between January and May of 1947?"

"Yes, I did."

"Do you believe Mr. Driscoll somehow came across one of these copies at that time?"

"You'll have to ask *him* about that."

"I am asking *you.*"

"How would I know whether or not he saw a copy at that time?"

"Mr. Constantine, instead of engaging me in argument, would you please answer my question: Do you believe that Mr. Driscoll saw a copy of your play at that time?"

"He could have, yes."

"Do you think he *did?*"

"It's possible that he did."

"In addition to having seen a performance of your play?"

"Yes, in addition."

"Do you feel he could have successfully plagiarized your work after having seen only one performance of the play?"

"Yes."

"That would have been sufficient?"

"Yes. Besides, it ran for twelve days. He could have seen it any number of times."

"He could have been so impressed by it the first time that he ran back to see it again and again, is that it?"

"Ignoring the sarcasm, that is *not* it. I don't know what goes on in Mr. Driscoll's head, either now or in 1947."

"Do you know how old Mr. Driscoll was in 1947?"

"No, I do not."

"He was eighteen."

"I was eighteen when I got drafted into the Army to fight a war," Arthur said.

"Which is commendable, but hardly to the point. Did you go into the Army as an officer, Mr. Constantine?"

"No. I was sent to O.C.S. after my basic training."

"And emerged as a second lieutenant."

"Yes."

"And you were sent to the Pacific in time for the Marshall Islands landings."

"Yes."

"Did your men ever call you 'Loot'?"

"Yes, they did."

"The way they call Mason 'Loot' in your play?"

"No. In my play, they use the word in a derogatory manner. If we're going to get into this again . . ."

"Into *what* again?"

"Into hastily trained officers, and platoons composed of cross-sections of America, and the prevalence of minority group members, and ninety-day wonders and soldiers who use obscenity, all in an attempt to show that Mr. Driscoll was only following his natural bent, he was only creating a wholly original work of fiction out of common everyday experience, I'm sorry, Mr. Willow, but I don't agree with you, and I see exactly what you're trying to do."

"I am *trying* to ask some questions," Willow said, "if I may be permitted, your Honor."

"Please go on, Mr. Willow. I find nothing objectionable in your line of questioning."

"Your Honor," Brackman said, rising, "Mr. Constantine is not an attorney, though perhaps he did feel Mr. Willow was badgering him."

"I am not aware of any badgering," McIntyre said. "Please go on, Mr. Willow."

"Would you not agree, Mr. Constantine, that the word 'Loot' is a common expression in the United States Army, whether it be used affectionately *or* derogatively?"

"I would agree," Arthur said tightly.

"Your claim, however, is that both in your play and in *The Paper Dragon,* the men use this expression in order to annoy the lieutenant. They use it derogatively. In fact, you pointed out an example of its use in your play, and an example of its use in the novel. Your claim is that they constitute *specific* similarity of language, isn't that so?"

"That's right. And they do."

"The language you referred to in your play was, and I quote, 'How about lengthening that to Lieutenant Mason?' to which Corporal Janus replies, 'Isn't that what I said, *Loot?*' You indicated in your testimony yesterday that the word 'Loot' was stressed, isn't that so?"

"That's absolutely correct."

"Now would you please show me the page in your play where those lines appear."

"They're in the second act," Arthur said.

"Please find the page."

Arthur was angry, and worried, and not a little confused, and very disappointed in Brackman who, he felt, had apologized again rather than objecting, and who had completely missed the point of what was happening, missed the trap that Arthur was sure Willow had baited and somehow sprung, though he still did not know what the trap was. That was supposed to be *Brackman's* job, goddamnit, to see a closing trap and to prevent its jaws from clamping down, what the hell kind of a lawyer *was* he? Angrily, he flipped through the pages, and then suddenly stopped.

"Have you found it?" Willow asked.

"It wouldn't be in this version," Arthur said.

"I beg your pardon?"

"Those two lines were not in the original mimeographed version of the play."

"Am I to understand that there is yet *another* version of *Catchpole?*"

"Not another *version*, actually. But certain line changes were made in rehearsal and appeared in the play as it was produced. These would not be in any of the original mimeographed copies."

"In what copy *can* these line changes be found?"

"I imagine in the actors' scripts, or the stage manager's. The ones that were used during the actual rehearsal of the play."

"Do you *have* any of these copies, Mr. Constantine?"

"No, I haven't."

"Does *anyone?*"

"Not to my knowledge. The members of the company may have retained them, I wouldn't know about that. This was almost twenty years ago."

"In other words, these two lines to which you refer are not to be found in the copy of the play now before this Court."

"That's correct. But the lines *were* spoken on the stage."

"And you heard them spoken?"

"I did. At every performance."

"Am I to understand, then, Mr. Constantine, that with respect to these two lines—which you claim have their counterpart in the book titled *The Paper Dragon* and also the film of the same name—with respect to these particular lines, unless James Driscoll actually saw a *rehearsal* script of the play, he could not possibly possess any knowledge of these lines, is that correct?"

"No. He could have seen the play in performance."

"We have got down to the point, have we not, where in order to show access, we must also show that Mr. Driscoll saw the play during its twelve-day Broadway run. Otherwise he would not have known of these lines inserted during rehearsal, nor would he have known of the division insignia bearing the number 105. Isn't that correct?"

"Your Honor," Brackman said, "I would like to remind Mr. Willow that it is not our burden to prove that James Driscoll actually *attended* a performance of the play, no more than it is the burden of a plaintiff to prove, for example, that a defendant actually *read* a novel he is said to have plagiarized. It is sufficient to show that the opportunity for copying existed. The play *Catchpole* was there to be seen in New York City, and I think we are very very safe in assuming James Driscoll was *also* here in New York City at the time and perfectly capable of visiting the Fulton Theatre to take a look at the play. I would not like Mr. Willow to lead us into believing it is our burden to supply witnesses who actually *saw* James Driscoll entering the theater and taking notes on the play."

"I believe Mr. Willow is sufficiently aware of the meaning of access," McIntyre said. "Please go on, Mr. Willow."

"I have no further questions," Willow said.

"Thank you," McIntyre said. "Mr. Genitori, I know you would like to begin your cross, but I see it's ten minutes to twelve, and I think we had better take a recess for lunch."

"Certainly," Genitori said.

"This Court is recessed until two P.M.," the clerk said.

6

THE SNOW ON THE GROUND before the federal courthouse seemed an extension of the white steps themselves,
blanketing sidewalk and street, blurring the defining lines
of the five concrete islands that formed Foley Square. The
largest of these islands was directly opposite the courthouse,
across a narrow stretch of pavement that seemed more like
an expanded footpath. Duane Street on the left of the courthouse, and Pearl Street on its right bracketed the building
and pierced the square which was not a square, Duane continuing west toward Broadway, Pearl abruptly ending against
a long green fence behind which construction was in progress, the fence surrounding a barren lot where pile drivers,
tractors, and trucks were inactive during the lunch hour. The
benches on the island opposite the courthouse were lightly
dusted with snow, as were the green shrubs backing them.
The steps leading down to the BMT subway were similarly
covered with snow, and a man coming up from underground
looked skyward as though surprised to find it was still
snowing, and then hesitated at the top of the steps to adjust
his muffler and to put on his gloves. The area from Reade
Street north was dismally gray except for the bright orange
sign of the Nedick's on the corner of Duane. There was another touch of color looking south, where a tall building on
Centre Street rose out of the swirling snow, its red brick

and green trim lending a festive holiday look to the area.

There were two good restaurants on Duane near Broadway, both of which were habitually frequented by the men whose business was the law—Gasner's, and slightly further west, Calate's. In addition, there were dozens of small coffee shops and cafeterias, delicatessens and hamburger joints, a Schrafft's on Park Place, and a Longchamps on Murray Street across from the statue of Nathan Hale. The restaurant Sidney chose was on Reade Street, closer to the courthouse but not as popular as Gasner's. Mother Sauce's featured an authentic Jewish cuisine and a proprietress named Martha Schwartz, who had earned her nickname, or so the legend went, the afternoon she drank three off-duty detectives from the D.A.'s office clear under the table and almost through the floor. Sidney could not vouch for the authenticity of the legend but he recounted it nonetheless to Arthur as they entered the place and waited for Mother Sauce to seat them.

She was a woman in her late sixties, silver-haired and sharp-eyed, wearing a white apron over a severe black dress, and moving around her small crowded restaurant with uncanny speed. The place had been designed with total architectural disregard, its low ceiling supported by a myriad of wood-paneled columns and partitions, tables and booths shoved into niches and nooks or built around posts and into crannies and cul-de-sacs, jutting from behind paneled walls, angled against sealed doors, nestled against windows. In the midst of this monumental disorder, Mother Sauce moved swiftly from table to table, around column and post, into paneled alley and byway, along a labyrinthine route to the kitchen, haranguing and harassing her waiters, circuitously back to the cash register, carrying a menu to a hidden booth, rushing toward the paneled bar, coming again to the door, where she greeted Sidney by name, beaming a smile, and then leading them to a booth at the rear of the restaurant, partitioned on each side to conceal the booths flanking it. Sidney excused himself at once—"A courtroom is bad on a man's kidneys," he explained—and left Arthur alone at the table. A waiter appeared immediately and took his order for a Dewar's on the rocks. Mother Sauce handed him a menu and then hurried away. The booth was small and cozy, upholstered in rich green leather like the tabletops in the courtroom. A pair of small shaded lamps hung on the wall over the booth. The tablecloth was spotlessly white, and the drink when it came was more than generous. Arthur felt himself relaxing for the first time that day. Grateful for Sidney's absence, he studied the menu in silence and with increasing appetite, only vaguely aware at first of the voices coming from behind the paneled partition on his left.

". . . in command of the situation, I would say," a man's voice said.

"Are we?" a woman asked.

"Yes, I would say so."

Arthur glanced at the partition, and then studied the menu again. He was ravenously hungry, and everything looked good, the consommé with noodles and matzoh balls, the borscht . . .

"I don't think we have anything to worry about," another man's voice said. "We're not going to let them get away with anything."

"Except maybe Dris's reputation," the woman said.

"No, not that either," the first man answered, and Arthur suddenly recognized the voice as belonging to Jonah Willow.

"We won't let them get his reputation, either, don't worry," the other man said. "Only a miracle could convince McIntyre there was any plagiarism here."

"That's right," Willow agreed. "In fact, this case should never have come to trial."

"Then why did it?" the woman asked. She had been speaking with a Southern inflection that suddenly disappeared, leaving behind a voice honed razor-sharp.

"An offer to settle would have been an admission of guilt," Willow said.

"Even a token settlement?" the woman asked.

"*Any* settlement. Besides, these people aren't looking for tokens. They've asked for damages and an accounting of profits."

"Will they get it?"

"I've never met a Harvard lawyer I couldn't beat," Willow said.

"I'm a Harvard lawyer," the other man said.

"Yes, but unfortunately you're on my side."

Arthur started to rise. He knew for certain now that one of the men in the adjacent booth was Jonah Willow, and he was fairly confident that the other man was his assistant. In which case, the woman was undoubtedly Mrs. James Driscoll, and Arthur had no right sitting there listening to them talk about the trial. As he rose he wondered whether Driscoll himself was at the table, maintaining a discreet silence, and he suddenly wanted to hear whatever Driscoll might say. Abruptly, he sat, telling himself again that he really should leave, he really should move out of the booth and away from this conversation, but remaining where he was, fascinated, compelled to listen, and actively hoping they would reveal a piece of information that would prove helpful to his case.

"What if they win?" the woman asked. She had to be Driscoll's wife, she couldn't be anyone else. Her Southern inflection had returned, her tone was again calm and reasonable, her voice softly resonant.

"They won't," Willow said.

"But if they do."

"We appeal."

"And if we lose the appeal?"

"We pay the two dollars."

"Yes, and then API and Mitchell-Campbell will turn right around and sue my husband for their losses. Isn't that so, Mr. Willow?"

"Your husband made certain warranties and indemnities in the contracts he signed, Mrs. Driscoll. One of those was that the work was entirely original with him and did not infringe on the rights of any other individual. If we lose this case, yes, API and Mitchell-Campbell would have the right to counterclaim over and to recover against him, yes."

"Whom would you represent in such a case, Mr. Willow?"

"I'm not sure I understand you."

"My husband? Or Mitchell-Campbell Books?"

"Such a case is an impossibility," the other man said. "We're going to win this suit, Mrs. Driscoll."

"I'm only asking Mr. Willow *suppose*. Whom would you represent, Mr. Willow?"

"I would have to represent Mitchell-Campbell," Willow said. "My firm works for them on a retainer basis."

"And would you then claim, for Mitchell-Campbell, that my husband did indeed steal Mr. Constantine's play?"

"If this court decides . . ."

"Would you?"

"Mrs. Driscoll, if this court decides against us, we would most certainly appeal to a higher court."

"You're evading my question, Mr. Willow."

"I think I've got *another* Harvard lawyer on my hands," Willow said, and laughed.

"What I want to know, Mr. Willow, is whether you really believe my husband is an honest man."

There was a slight hesitation.

"Yes," Willow said. "I do."

"You don't think he stole that play?"

"I do not," Willow said. "Do *you?*"

"What?"

"Do *you* think he stole it?"

There was another hesitation. Then Mrs. Driscoll said, "Of course he didn't steal it."

"Then we have no problem," Willow said.

Arthur rose suddenly and left the booth, his back to the partitioning wall, his heart pounding. He should not have eavesdropped, he should have warned them, he should have said Stop, I don't want to hear this, his father and mother in the room next to his, the wind outside and the sound of an occasional automobile in the street below, his father whispering in Italian, whispering, don't let me hear, he thought, don't you know Julie's in the room with you? I do not want to hear. Blankly, he moved away from the booth and into the restaurant, circling the columns, moving between the tables, trapped in a forest of furniture and glistening white tablecloths, the hum of conversation, the brittle sound of laughter and the clink of silverware, where should he go, should he find Mother Sauce and ask her to change their table, where was Sidney, where the hell was the men's room, where behind these columns and walls had Mother Sauce hidden the men's room? He saw the telephone booth and hurried toward it, entering it and swiftly closing the door behind him, hiding, I should not have listened. He dried the palms of his hands on his trousers. His face was flushed and he felt feverish and weak. He sat silently expectant, certain that the phone would ring and expose his hiding place. He caught his breath and looked at the dial. Selig, he thought. He dried his palms again, and searched for a dime, and then he dialed Selig's office number slowly and carefully. Selig answered on the fourth ring.

"Did you reach Mitzi?" Arthur asked. His heart was still pounding. He looked through the glass door of the booth furtively, fearful he would be discovered by Willow, exposed by Willow who would reconstruct the eavesdropping and berate him for it, scold him the way McIntyre had yesterday, make him feel foolish and guilty and afraid.

"Not only did I reach Mitzi," Selig said, "but I also asked her to ask Hester to call me at the office, which Hester did not ten minutes ago. I've been on the phone with her all this time."

"What did she say?"

"She likes the play."

"Good, will she—"

"But she has some questions about it."

"About the play?"

"Well, about the character."

"About Carol?"

"Yes, that's the part we want her to play, isn't it?"

"Yes, of course."

"Well, that's the part she's got questions about."

"What kind of questions?"

"I don't know, she wants to talk to you," Selig said. "She won't talk to anyone but you."

"When?"

"Tonight?"

"Where?"

"It'll have to be late, Arthur. She has a perform . . ."

"I don't care how late . . ."

". . . ance at Lincoln Center, you know. She probably won't be free until eleven-thirty or thereabouts."

"Fine. What shall I do, pick her up at the theater?"

"No, she said she'd rather meet . . ."

"Where?"

"The Brasserie. She doesn't eat until after performance, so she can grab a bite there, if that's all right with you."

"That's fine."

"Eleven-thirty at the Brasserie."

"Right," Arthur said.

"You know what she looks like, don't you?"

"Yes." Arthur paused. "She didn't tell you what's bothering her, huh?"

"She didn't say anything was bothering her, Arthur. She said it was a charming play, and she loved the character, she loved the girl Carol, but before she did anything or said anything or instructed her agent to do anything, there were some things in the character she wanted to clarify, so that she would understand the character more fully and be able to approach it more intelligently."

"Did she say that? That she wanted to approach it more intelligently?"

"I'm repeating word for word what she told me, Arthur."

"Well, that sounds pretty encouraging, doesn't it to you?"

"Actresses are strange people," Selig said.

"Granted, but—"

"She may simply want to have an intelligent approach for the next time she *reads* it, Arthur. It could mean nothing more than that."

"Still, she wouldn't—"

"She's a very talented and high-strung girl who is afraid of her own shadow because she's so lovely, and talented, and insecure," Selig said. "She likes the play, she likes the part, but she's afraid to make a move from Lincoln Center where she's got only a little role in a Restoration comedy, but at least she's got respect and she's working steady and she doesn't have to rely on her own judgment, God forbid your play should be a flop. So she says she wants to talk to you about the character. What she really wants, Arthur, is for you to convince her she'll be doing the right thing by kissing off Lincoln Center and taking a chance on an unknown quantity. That's what this is all about."

"Okay," Arthur said.

"So explain the character to her."

"I will."

"You're a good talker."

"I'm not so sure about that."

"How's the trial going?"

"Okay."

"Call me tonight no matter how late it is," Selig said. "I want to know what she says."

"All right, I will. The Brasserie at eleven-thirty, right?"

"Right. Good luck, Arthur."

"Thank you," Arthur said, and hung up.

He sat in the booth for several moments, silent. Then he opened the door and looked for Mother Sauce. When he found her, he said, "I wonder if you could change our table."

"Something's wrong?" she asked.

"No, but I think Mr. Brackman and I would prefer another table."

"You're in litigation?"

"Yes."

"I understand," she said knowingly, and led him swiftly to the other side of the room.

European posters covered the walls of the small travel agency, brightly printed in yellows and whites and tans and greens, blatantly selling sunshine and sand while outside the plate-glass window the snow continued to fall. From where Chickie sat behind one of the two desks in the office, she could look out at street level onto Madison Avenue where lunch-hour pedestrians were battling the strong wind and wildly swirling flakes. She shivered involuntarily and looked up at the wall clock. It was ten minutes to one, and Ruth was not due back until the hour, but Chickie was very hungry and hoped the snow would drive her back sooner. She sat with her legs crossed, her skirt above the knee, amused whenever a male passerby stopped to peer through the front window of the agency, and then embarrassed and flushed if the scrutiny persisted, wanting to giggle.

The poster to the left of her desk, cluttered with travel folders and carbon copies of letters to hotels and auto-rental establishments, advertised Positano, the white and pastel houses climbing the hillside, the beach below, the rowboats hovering on the water. She glanced at it idly and then reread a letter from the Dorchester in London, confirming a room for Mr. and Mrs. Bernard Jannings, beginning January 10th. She wondered why anyone would want to go to England in January, and then immediately thought of Italy and Greece, and then of course remembered Sidney's proposal.

As she saw it, life was merely a matter of making the right decision at the right time; she should have known that long ago, when she was seventeen, but she hadn't. Well, she knew it now. Sidney had asked her to marry him, this is so unexpected, she had said, I'll have to think it over, meanwhile thinking that two million dollars was a lot of money, if he won his case he would get two million dollars. *If* he won, but how could he *possibly* win, a jerk like Sidney? Still, the possibility had to be considered. She could manage to live with *anyone* for two million dollars, and besides, Sidney wasn't all that bad, even though she didn't love him. There was a lot to be said for Sidney, but at the moment she couldn't think of a thing.

The decision, anyway, had nothing to do with Sidney. It had only to do with two million dollars, which he might or might not get, that was the trouble, too uncertain. Decisions were never easy for a girl to make even if she knew all the facts, but sometimes the damn facts came in too late or not at all, that was it. How could she possibly second-guess this

idiotic trial? No jury, isn't that what he'd said? Two million
dollars riding on an Irishman's heartburn. Or lack of it. How
could you decide? Better to take the bird in the hand. Still,
two million dollars.

(*Take it, no, take it, no, no,* and then his hand under her
skirt, and she slapped him without wanting to, without
thinking, forgetting for the moment, completely forgetting
he was from the college. "Go out with the college boys,
Duck," her mother advised. "Get yourself a rich boy from
New York who'll be a doctor or a lawyer one day.")

Well, here he was, a rich (if he won the case) New York
boy (forty-eight years old) who was a lawyer (but not a very
good one) and he had made an honest old-fashioned proposal: I am forty-eight years old, harumph, harumph, and I
know that you are only twenty-seven, but I think you know I
love you, I think you truly know that. Yes, I *know* you love
me, baby, I can wrap you around my finger, I can make you
jump through hoops, I can get you to run naked in the snow
on Madison Avenue, you little *shmuck,* of course I know you
love me. Come sing for me, baby, sing your little heart out
and then come on down on Northeast Airlines, brother *do* I
know you love me!

But what to do?

Use your instinct, sweetie, use that famous woman's intuition they're always talking about, where was it in the winter
of 1957? Or maybe it was operating full blast, maybe I knew
exactly what would happen if I slapped him, who knows?
And maybe the flushed, no, the, the almost I don't know, that
tight hot embarrassed feeling (I always see myself as a frightened young girl standing alone on a station platform, a
suitcase in my hand) that feeling of, heavy eyes, and almost
smarting, tears about to come if something doesn't happen,
frightened for two weeks after that night in his car when I
slapped him, was it really fear? Or was I waiting for what was
about to come, not knowing what, the way I feel embarrassed
and hot and try not to giggle when a man stops at the front
window to look at my legs, and want to touch myself, who the
hell knows?

So he asks last night, naturally. Knows me six months but asks last night when I'm on my way to Ruth's apartment to meet Jerry Courtlandt and his brother there, to go over the European trip with them. I should have said no immediately (*Take it, no, I don't want to!*) I should have said Look Sidney, this is a lot of fun and all, you know, I mean I kind of enjoy having you around, you dear man, to play with, you know, you're a very nice playmate to kick around the block, but marry you? Now, really, Sidney, let's not get ridiculous. I'm twenty-seven years old, I am a *beautiful* young girl! Please don't make me laugh, Sidney.

Touching, though.

Really touching that he should ask.

Really.

And two million dollars, *if* he gets it, well, with two million dollars, who knows, Sidney? Maybe I could learn to love you, who knows, baby? Italy and Greece. Hot sand under me. Stretch, mmmm, relax.

Come on, Chickie, just relax, will you? No, I want to go home.

Home was a two-family clapboard house in a town called Ramsey, four miles from the university. The houses were semidetached, each with a small backyard and a peaked attic, identical except for the paint jobs. Their own house was further distinguished by the aspidistra her mother kept in the window, even the college boys had to ask what aspidistra meant. Her grandmother had kept one in the window of their tenement flat in London, when Agnes Brown nee Mercer was a child. And so now Agnes kept one in the window of the small house in Ramsey, Pennsylvania; it was important to maintain one's heritage, keep the bloody aspidistra flying, the man had written. Pennsylvania was Fourth Street in Ramsey, and an occasional trip into Philadelphia, and it was also the high school on Buchanan Street, and later on—even before it happened—trips to the college, the road straight as an arrow along the railroad tracks and past the power plant and then out into the beautiful rolling Pennsylvania countryside.

Her father owned the drugstore in Ramsey, an aging pharmacist who had also come from London in his youth (the sign outside his shop read "Chemist"). His name was Edwin Brown, but Mother called him Luv or Duck and Chickie called him Dads, and all of his customers called him Mr. Brown. She doubted if he even *knew* his first name, for all the use it got. For that matter, she herself had been called Chickie ever since a cousin from Philadelphia spent the summer with them (coming out of the slums on the city's south side to breathe a little country air) and had trouble pronouncing the name Charlotte, being only three years old and barely able to pronounce her own name, which was Mary. She liked the name Chickie because her mother made it sound like a synonym for Duck, which was her favorite term of affection, and also because when she got to be thirteen and developed a good bosom, the name seemed to apply somehow, seemed to impart a mysterious sort of womanly glamor to her, or so she thought. Chickie Brown, Chickie Brown, Chickie Brown, she would practice writing it in a broad developing hand, using a thick pen point, heavily capitalizing the C and the B.

She was kissed for the first time at her sixteenth birthday party by a boy named Frank Simms, whose father worked out at the gun factory. She blushed furiously, and then quickly raised her eyes to where her father stood in the doorway gently smiling, and hastily lowered them again. The university boys discovered her when she was seventeen, as inevitably they had to, but her mother approved of her dating, and in fact encouraged it. She knew that Chickie was a good clean girl who would probably marry young and raise a houseful of kids, so why not someone with a college education? Chickie, in her seventeenth year, was proud of her appearance, not a little annoyed whenever she asked her father how old she looked, and he smilingly replied, "Why, seventeen, luv," when she knew damn well she looked much older. She was taller than most of the girls at school, with very good breasts she had had from thirteen, and wide hips that everyone said were excellent for the bearing of children, and a narrow

waist, and shapely legs—you were supposed to have good legs
if the ankles were slender, which hers were. Agnes had taught
her to carry herself as tall as she was, and not to slouch the
way some big girls do, so she wore high heels with authority
even when dating shorter boys. Her walk was rapid and
direct; she never pranced or paraded the way a lot of the
other kids did, as if they practiced wiggling their behinds
when they were home in their own rooms. Chickie thought of
herself almost as her mother did; she was good and clean and
wholesome, and she was sure her innocence accounted for her
fresh good looks, the shining green eyes and fine complexion,
the full mouth touched with just a bit of lipstick, the red-gold
hair trailing halfway down her back because it had never
been cut, or sometimes swinging across her mounded sweater
front in twin braids, tiny green bows picking up the color of
her eyes. She thought of herself as an English girl or something. A healthy English country girl. She did not know she
was just a townie.

They taught her that in the first six months of 1957, after
she had dated the president of one of the most powerful
fraternities on campus, or so she had been told. In fact, one of
the reasons she began dating Buddy was because she *knew* he
was the president of a big fraternity, and *knew* it was powerful. She could not imagine what *kind* of power a fraternity
could wield, but the notion was intriguing nonetheless, and a
little frightening. Perhaps nothing would have happened
were she not both frightened and intrigued, perhaps that was
all a part of it. Even now, when she thought back upon it, she
could feel a tremor of fear, and she quickly pulled her skirt
down over her knees, very flustered all at once—the image of
a frightened girl on a station platform, that girl on the empty
platform.

They had parked after the movie, and Buddy was kissing
her—she let most of the boys kiss her, but never on the first
date—when he gently tugged her hand toward him, and she
realized he had opened his zipper, and he said, "Take it, go
ahead." She said no, she didn't want to, but he kept insisting
and pulling her hand toward him while she kept saying No,

No, and suddenly he let her go and thrust his own hand up under her skirt, and she slapped him. The automobile was very still for perhaps a minute, it seemed like a year, and then Buddy said, very softly, "You shouldn't have done that, miss," and started the car and took her home.

She did not know why she was so frightened in the two weeks that followed, unless it was remembering the tone of his voice and the word "miss," which seemed to be promising something terrible. She had no idea that they were carefully mapping out their campaign in those two weeks, or that she would assume the importance of a military target in the patient months that followed. She did not know that men could be that way, or would want to be that way. She only knew that she was frightened. And yet, oddly, she kept waiting for the phone to ring, waiting for Buddy to call.

The campaign started on a Saturday afternoon two weeks after she had slapped Buddy. It started in her father's drugstore, and it started with an apology from Buddy, who was all smiles and embarrassment and who told her he had behaved very badly and wished she would forgive him. He was with another boy, a good-looking blond boy named Paul, whom Buddy introduced as a brother and one of his closest friends. Paul nodded shyly, and they all chatted for a few more minutes, and then left Chickie. She felt very happy about the chance encounter with Buddy, and not a little relieved that she had misread the tone of his voice that night two weeks ago. The next morning her telephone rang, and she was surprised when her caller identified himself as Paul, "You know, we met yesterday in the drugstore."

"Oh, sure, Paul," she said. "Hi."

"Hi. Listen, I hope this isn't out of line."

"What do you mean?" she said.

"Well, Buddy is a fraternity brother, you know, and . . ."

"Yes, I know that."

"I didn't want to ask *him* whether you were, you know, whether you had any kind of an understanding or not. But if you *have* . . ."

"No, we haven't," Chickie said.

"Well, in that case," Paul said, and he sighed in relief, "I was wondering if you'd like to go see a movie tonight. I know this is sort of short notice, and tomorrow's school and all, but I promise I'll get you home early, that is if you'd like to."

"Well, it *is* short notice," Chickie said.

"Yeah, I know that."

"And I'd have to ask my mother."

"Well, would you *want* to?"

"Well, if she says it's all right, I guess I would."

"Well, fine." He paused. "Would you ask her?"

"Sure, can you hang on?"

She asked her mother, who said it was all right, as long as they didn't get home too late. Paul picked her up at seven that night, and they went to a movie in town and then stopped for hamburgers, where they met a few other fellows from the frat, all of whom were formally introduced by Paul, who seemed very proud of her, and who watched with a sort of quiet glow while they offered their hands and very gentlemenly said, "Pleased to meet you, Chickie." He took her home early, as he had promised, and did not even try to kiss her good night. She learned later, only much later when they told her all about it, that the meeting in the drugstore had been no accident, that Paul had made his first call from the frat house, with the other fellows standing around him, and that the subsequent introduction to the boys in the hamburger joint had all been carefully planned and synchronized because they were out to get her. But she did not know it at the time, and she felt only flattered and not at all suspicious when Paul called again on Monday to ask if she'd like to have a soda or something Wednesday night, and she said Yes, she'd love to. He took her home at ten-thirty, and again did not try to kiss her good night. She wondered about that a little, somewhat puzzled, but figured he was just a shy boy. On Thursday, a boy named John called to say he had met her Sunday in the hamburger joint, "Remember me, I'm one of Paul's brothers, I've got straight brown hair?"

"Oh sure," she said.

"I know this might seem a little forward," he said, "calling when we hardly know each other, but there's going to be a party at the house tomorrow night and look, I'll be honest with you. A girl who was supposed to be coming down from Bryn Mawr for the weekend got a bad cold and she can't make it, and I'm really up the creek. I thought maybe, well . . . I know I'm not putting this right, and I wouldn't blame you for saying no. But it's just that I really *am* hung up, and I honestly would like to take you to the party. If you think you'd like to come with me. Though I know this is all very sudden."

Chickie agreed that it was very sudden, but she saw nothing wrong in helping out a fellow whose girl had come down with a cold, especially since he was one of Paul's brothers. The party that Friday night was a nice gathering with some girls from town and some girls from colleges in Pennsylvania and here and there. Everyone was very nice to her, even Buddy and Paul who were with other girls but who each danced with her once and told her what a really nice person she was. John, the fellow who was her date, was a very good-looking boy who resembled Tony Perkins and who had cultivated the same sort of shy smile. He drove her home to Ramsey at two o'clock in the morning in a red MG convertible, and thanked her profusely at the door, telling her she had saved his life and wondering if he could see her again maybe next weekend. She said she would love to, and they made a date for the coming Saturday. But before then, she received calls from two other frat boys she had danced with, and before she knew it the weekend was booked solid. Then Paul called and asked if she'd like to hack around with him again this Wednesday the way they had last, have a soda or something, and she said yes, she'd love to. Buddy called that same day to tell her they were showing some old monster movies over at the school gym on Tuesday, and would she like to go with him?

The scheme had been devised in the reading room at the frat house, Buddy telling the others what had happened and then enlisting their aid in teaching this kid a lesson she would never forget, that you don't go around slapping the president of their frat, or *anybody* in their frat for that matter. The boys all agreed that this was a horrible offense and if permitted to gain circulation, if permitted to spread to all the other townies, could lessen their stature and their ability to get into townie pants every now and then.

These were all nice boys, Chickie was later made to understand, who really had nothing against her and who perhaps, for all any of them knew, simply wanted an activity to carry them through the long winter months and into the spring. Chickie was unfortunate to have been chosen as their extracurricular project for that semester, but then she shouldn't have slapped old Buddy, nor should she have been so obviously intrigued nor so obviously frightened. The boys knew she was frightened, and they also knew she was intrigued. In addition, they were all much older than she, being nineteen or twenty or thereabouts, worldly-wise in the ways of townie maids, and bolstered by the solidarity of brotherhood and the knowledge that they would not have to score *this* one alone. *This* one was to be a joint effort without a chance of failure, a little cooperative project which, if they played their cards right, could provide something steady for the rest of their college days.

The plan was rather clever, if they said so themselves, and once it proved effective against Chickie, they tried it often and with varying results against several other girls—until a supposed virgin named Violet Plimpton discouraged any further joint efforts by causing twelve boys in the frat to come down with cases of the clap. Chickie, though, was a clean girl, and a nice girl, and in fact a very sweet girl against whom they harbored no ill feelings, if only she hadn't slapped a fraternity brother. They modestly admitted that not a single one of them working unassisted would have had a prayer of getting her, but neither were they about to attempt an assault without first manipulating the odds and insuring the outcome. Permutations and combinations, said Richard Longstreet, who was a very bright and ugly boy from Palm Beach, Florida, the frat genius, peering through his black-rimmed spectacles and grinning at his brothers who listened attentively as he outlined his plan.

The assault, as Longstreet explained it, had to be slow and patient because first of all she wouldn't be eighteen until May and they didn't want to take any chances with jail bait (hear, hear, the brothers chanted) and secondly because it just wouldn't work unless they played it cool and easy. She had to believe that each of the seven hand-picked frat brothers were independently competing for her favors, and she had to believe that they did not exchange notes and, as a point of honor, never *never* discussed a girl they were simultaneously dating. (They established this without question in the third week of the campaign, when four of the frat boys separately called to ask for a Saturday night date, seemingly ignorant of the fact that she had already made a date with another of their brothers.) To further allay any of her suspicions, Longstreet said, they would evolve a system of staggered advances that could not possibly seem like the result of collusion, but would seem instead random and erratic. Paul would be the first to touch her breast, for example, but Mitch would only *later* soul-kiss her, a seeming regression, and David would then try to get his hand under her skirt. We will even, Longstreet said, make provision for a villain in the group of seven, an expendable man who will try to go too far with her, unclasping her bra and going for her naked breasts, *knowing* the move is premature and hoping Chickie will stop dating him. He will subsequently be replaced by a more civilized fellow, selected right now, who will participate up to the time of the final assault. Paul, until then, and as part of the overall scheme, will never try to get further with her than his first grab.

Longstreet admitted that this would all be very unfair to poor Chickie because what they were going to do was drive her out of her mind (hear, hear, the brothers chanted) without her ever once realizing she was being led down the garden. What we're going to do, Longstreet said, is manipulate and control her psychological and emotional responses so that by a process of gradual conditioning she will be ready for

whatever we choose to put before her next. Her responses
will all be calculated beforehand, *we* will decide when to give
her a surfeit of affection and understanding, *we* will decide
when to deprive her or when to resume the attack. In short,
we will destroy her defenses one by one, creating a permissive
climate that will make it simpler for the next man to take her
yet a step further in persuasion, until she is conditioned to
expect a certain amount of stimulation, until she is indeed
looking *forward* to it. And by the time we have brought her
to the point of highest expectation, why then we'll see who's
gonna pluck her. After that, Longstreet said, it's anybody's.

The plan in practice worked almost the way Longstreet
outlined it, not because it was foolproof, but only because
Chickie contributed a certain amount of confused eagerness
to its execution. Whatever she told herself later, whatever
eventual surprise she professed to the boys when they explained to her in a very friendly and open manner how the
plan had worked, she *really* suspected something from the
very beginning, and her suspicions were all but confirmed by
the end of the second month. To begin with, she knew
without doubt that all girls exchanged notes, and it must
have entered her mind almost at once (whatever protesta-
tions they made to the contrary) that seven boys from the
same frat might just conceivably say a word or two about her
in passing. So she never really bought the "independent
dating" routine or the "point of honor" nonsense, nor did
she believe it accidental that she was being rushed by the
seven best-looking and most popular boys in the frat. She was
somewhat thrown off stride when Freddie Holtz took off her
bra and began fumbling around with her breasts, big clumsy
football player, especially when all the others were so tiptoey
apologetic if they for God's sake accidentally brushed against
her or anything. But even then she had the feeling she was
supposed to stop dating him, which was exactly what she did.
And, of course, he was immediately replaced by another of
the frat boys, so that there were always seven of them (in the
final week they were dating her every night, dating her in
sequence and getting her so completely confused and excited

that she was ready for anything) but hadn't she been aware from the very beginning? Frightened, yes, when Mitch thrust his tongue into her mouth and tightened his arms around her; surprised, yes, when she found her own tongue eagerly searching the soft inner lining of his mouth; surprised, too, when she felt so suddenly wet, and idiotically thought her period had come, and then pulled away from him breathlessly, terrified, yes, but aware, aware. And later when David provisionally touched her leg, and immediately pulled back his hand, she knew without question that one or another of them would go further the next time, and was not at all surprised when Mark worked his hand up under her bra and onto her naked breast the following Saturday. She had begun to detect a pattern by then, however erratic and hidden it was, and she was aware of a steady progression, a series of escalating liberties that were infallibly calculated to lead to greater liberties. She knew. But she permitted it.

She permitted it with a feeling of rising suspense, curious to discover what they had planned for her next, gradually more and more anxious to participate. She did not think beyond the ultimate and inevitable act, knowing only that by the time it finally happened, two weeks after her eighteenth birthday, she was eagerly seeking the relief it brought. Beyond it, she vaguely visualized a continuing though certainly unpromiscuous sort of girlish sexual activity. She did not know that nothing but complete and utter subjugation would satisfy her captors.

She was finally made to understand this on the weekend the frat boys rented a Philadelphia hotel room and repeatedly used her, all twenty-six of them, one after the other throughout the night and the next long day. They had prepared for the event by purchasing condoms at the drugstore owned by Chickie's father (a brilliant touch thought up by Richard Longstreet) and then had come to Chickie with a ready-made alibi. She was to say a girl from Penn had invited her up for the weekend. They even supplied her with the girl's name, Alice Malloy. Chickie had no doubt she was a real girl the boys knew. She was too frightened to refuse the invitation, and besides she didn't know what was in store for her, or perhaps she did, it was all very confusing. All through the night, they kept saying, "You love it, don't you, Chickie?" to which she kept answering, "No, I don't, no," the next boy asking the same question, "You love it, don't you, Chickie?" and always she answered no, and thought of escape, and was terrified, and finally on the afternoon of the second day, she shrieked, "Yes, I love it, I love it, I *love* it!" and began giggling uncontrollably, and knew at last she was only what they said she was, a townie piece of twat.

In later years, when these nice fraternity boys got married to girls from Radcliffe and Smith and Sarah Lawrence and Vassar, and settled down to raise families, and went to work in business suits, they separately felt a pang of guilt when they recalled what they had done to Chickie in the winter and spring of 1957. But their guilt was dissipated by memory of the strange excitement they had known at the time, the knowledge that they (or rather Richard Longstreet, the frat genius) had inadvertently stumbled upon the key to Chickie Brown: she was a terrified little girl waiting to be victimized. This was exactly what they did to her, repeatedly, until finally their own lust seemed inspired by Chickie's appetite, and they could absolve themselves of any blame they may have felt at the time; they were obviously in the company of an insatiable nymphomaniac with masochistic tendencies, or so she was described by Richard Longstreet, who was a genius.

And in later years, when Chickie thought back upon that winter and spring, as she was doing now in her office while the snow swirled against the plate-glass window, she felt again the same surge of excitement, the same flushed embarrassment, the same tremor of fear she had known then and ever since with a variety of men including the Indian who had beat her until she ached and had given her a Persian cat in remorse. So Sidney Brackman, the dear silly man, wanted to marry her. She thought again of Italy and Greece, and the warm sand beneath her. She would be wearing a bikini, they would stare at her breasts and her legs, she would experience that familiar feeling of terrified lust engorging her, rising into her throat and her head until she wanted to scream aloud, or giggle, or die.

Will you win your stupid case, Sidney Brackman? she wondered.

If I were only sure you would.

Samuel Genitori, the chief counsel for API, was a rotund little man with a balding head and mild blue eyes. He was wearing a blue pinstripe suit with a light blue shirt and a dark blue tie. He carried a pair of eyeglasses in his hand as he approached the stand, but he did not put them on. To the court clerk, he said, "Plaintiff's Exhibit Number 8, please," and when he received the chart he put on the glasses briefly, studied the chart for a moment, took the glasses off again, and looked up at Arthur.

"Mr. Constantine," he said, "yesterday afternoon a chart was submitted to this court, and marked Plaintiff's Exhibit Number 8. It listed the alleged similarities between the movie *The Paper Dragon* and your play *Catchpole*. I show this to you now, and ask if this list was prepared by you."

"By me and my attorneys, yes."

"And it purports to show, does it not, the alleged similarities that were not present in Mr. Driscoll's book?"

"Yes, it does."

"It contains *only* those that appear in the play and in the film, is that correct?"

"That is correct."

"In your examination before trial, Mr. Constantine, you testified to some other alleged similarities between the play and the film, did you not?"

"That was a long time ago," Arthur said.

"Please answer the question."

"I don't remember whether I did or not."

"Perhaps I can refresh your memory."

"Please do," Arthur said.

"Did you not testify that there is a scene in the movie where a man is shown with his foot wrapped in bandages?

Did you not claim that this man with his foot wrapped in bandages was stolen directly from your play?"

"I don't remember making that claim."

"Then let's try to be a bit more precise, shall we? This is the transcript of your pretrial examination, and I'm going to read now from page 198, this is you talking, Mr. Constantine: 'In the motion picture, there's a scene between the lieutenant and his commanding officer, and in the background we can see a line of men returning from the front. One of these men has his foot wrapped in bandages. This man was not described anywhere in the novel, but there's a scene in my play where a group of men are waiting for a stretcher, and one of the men has his foot wrapped in bandages.' Did you say that, Mr. Constantine?"

"If it's there, I said it."

"Then I take it you also said, because it's here on page 199, you also said, 'This man is a minor character, and his appearance in the movie can only be explained as an unconscious copying from the play.' Did you say that?"

"I did."

"Do you still feel this similarity indicates copying?"

"It's a minor point," Arthur said, "and I believe it was later withdrawn. That's why it doesn't appear on the chart."

"You no longer claim the man with his foot in bandages as a similarity?"

"That's right."

"Did you also testify during your pretrial examination that marksmanship was discussed in both your play and in the movie?"

"Possibly."

"Well, let's—"

"Probably, as a matter of fact."

"As a matter of fact, Mr. Constantine, I would like to read now from page 211 of the transcript, so that we can see whether it was *possibly* or *probably* or just *what* it was, shall we do that?"

"I'm willing to concede that . . ."

"On page 211, and I'm quoting from the transcript now, we have the following exchange:

> *Question:* Please explain the 'marksmanship' references.
> *Answer:* In the movie, the sergeant says, 'You're a regular Annie Oakley.'
> *Question:* And what is the reference in your play?
> *Answer:* In my play, there's a dialogue between the psychopathic colonel and the nurse. I'd like to read it if I may.

> ### COLONEL PETERSON
> Because I'm an old man, sister, a very old man, practically decrepit.

> ### DIANE
> Your records show you're only fifty-two, sir.

> ### COLONEL PETERSON
> That's old, sister. I'm shot. I'm as shot as some of those poor bastards out there. Listen to those guns, sister, listen to those guns.

> *Question:* Do the words 'You're a regular Annie Oakley' appear in your play?
> *Answer:* Not specifically.

"That's the end of the testimony, Mr. Constantine. Do you remember it now?"

"I remember it."

"Do you still feel a similarity exists here?"

"No, I do not, and again I must say that this claim has already been withdrawn, which is why it does not appear on the chart. If the evidence were all as flimsy as these two examples, the entire case would be absurd. You've picked on two points which have already—"

"These two points are flimsy and absurd?"

"That's why they were withdrawn."

"Mr. Constantine, didn't you also say that another similarity between the play and the movie was the fact that both Private Colman and Corporal Janus wear eyeglasses?"

"I did."

"And that this is another malevolent example of—"

"Did I say malevolent?"

"No, that's my word, Mr. Constantine. But you *do* feel this similarity indicates copying by Ralph Knowles, who wrote the screenplay based on the novel."

"My character Corporal Janus wears eyeglasses. Driscoll's character Private Colman does not wear eyeglasses. Yet in the movie, we have Private Colman wearing eyeglasses. Now if that doesn't indicate . . ."

"Do you still claim . . ."

"The similarity exists."

"It's not one of the flimsy and absurd ones?"

"It is an indication of either deliberate or unconscious copying. Alone, it might not be significant. But when we look at the other similarities, the fact that both men are troublemakers, and the homosexual references, and when we add the eyeglasses to that . . ."

"You're not suggesting that Private Colman is homosexual."

"In the book he is."

"But not in the film?"

"The film has taken my homosexual colonel and used him instead. I believe I've already explained the blending of two characters to form one in the book, and the subsequent separation in the film."

"And you still wish to claim this matter of the eyeglasses as a similarity?"

"I wish it to remain, yes."

"Remain *where,* Mr. Constantine? It does *not* appear on your chart, which you said earlier was a complete list. Do you now wish to add it to that list?"

"Yes."

"Very well. Would you like to add any others, Mr. Constantine. We'd like to be perfectly clear as to what you've alleged."

"No, that's all."

"You do not wish to add any other similarities to this list?"

"I do not."

"I wonder if I might now ask you, Mr. Constantine, why you chose to include in your list several similarities which you regarded as flimsy and absurd?"

"I don't know why. The examination had been going on for a long time. I was tired and . . ."

"Mr. Constantine, do you remember asking for time to go over your charts and lists in an attempt to determine whether or not you had covered everything?"

"When do you mean?"

"During the pretrial examination."

"I don't remember."

"And after you had studied your charts and lists—I believe you were gone for close to an hour, Mr. Constantine—you came back and said, and these are your exact words which I'm reading from the transcript, 'There are several other similarities I'd like to mention.' One of those similarities was the man in bandages, isn't that so?"

"Perhaps. You and Mr. Willow seemed determined at that point to get me to say this was a complete list, so I . . ."

"Yes, you said you wanted a chance to study it. Which you did, Mr. Constantine. For close to an hour, isn't that correct?"

"I suppose so, but . . ."

"Without any pressure from Mr. Willow, or me, or anyone. Isn't that so?"

"It was a very hot day, and everyone seemed to be—"

"Please, Mr. Constantine, I will have my question answered. Were you under any pressure when you reviewed your charts and came back to add the man in the bandages?"

"I've already answered the question."

"You've answered it by saying it was hot and you were tired and Mr. Willow and I were pressuring you."

"I said you seemed determined to have me say it was a complete list. I did not mention anything about being pressured."

"*Were* you being pressured?"

"I was being interrogated."

"Mr. Constantine, I am suggesting that you were *not* being

interrogated when you left the room and spent an hour alone with your charts."

"That was merely an extension of the interrogation. I knew the interrogation would be waiting for me when I returned, and you and Mr. Willow had made it clear that if I didn't list each and every similarity at that time, the opportunity—"

"Can you tell me, Mr. Constantine, who decided to withdraw these similarities which you now consider flimsy and absurd?"

"Your Honor," Brackman said, rising, "I fail to see the purpose of this line of questioning. These similarities have been withdrawn. Does Mr. Genitori wish them to be claimed again? The witness has testified that he no longer considers them valid. Why, then, does Mr. Genitori—"

"He is examining as to the witness's credibility," McIntyre said. "I will allow it."

"If your Honor please," Genitori said. "Mr. Constantine, I repeat my question. Who decided to withdraw these similarities which you now consider flimsy and absurd?"

"Your Honor," Brackman said, "those were not the witness's words. He said something about . . ."

"I said if all the evidence were as flimsy as those two examples—"

"Yes, you did say the examples were flimsy," Genitori interrupted, "*and* absurd."

"I said the *case* would be absurd, the *case*."

"*If* all the examples were as flimsy as these two which have now been withdrawn," Brackman said. "*That* is what the witness said."

"The record will show exactly what he said, Mr. Brackman."

"In any case," Arthur said, "Mr. Brackman and I decided after deliberation to withdraw these specific claims. I think that answers your question."

"Yes, it does," Genitori said. "Now, if I understand this correctly, Mr. Constantine, there are five alleged similarities on Plaintiff's Exhibit Number 8, to which you now wish to add Private Colman and his eyeglasses, which makes a total of six alleged similarities between your play and the movie."

"Yes. Plus those that appear in the book as well, of course."

"We are talking now only of those that were *not* in the book, but which you claim are only in the movie and the play."

"That's right, there are six."

"And do you base your claim upon these six similarities alone?"

"I don't think I understand your question."

"It's perfectly clear, Mr. Constantine. Do you base your claim upon these six similarities alone?"

"No, sir."

"You do not?"

"My claim is based on all the similarities that appear in the play, the book, *and* the film."

"It is our contention, your Honor," Brackman said, "that both James Driscoll *and* API copied freely from the plaintiff's play. Mr. Genitori's concern at the moment would seem to be API's right to counterclaim should—"

"Mr. Brackman," McIntyre said, "I do not see where API's right to counterclaim is a matter for discussion right now."

"The plaintiff is suing for an accounting. API's right to counterclaim later is most certainly before your Honor, if we are to be realistic."

"Your Honor," Genitori said, "my question does not go to the matter of counterclaim, though I would agree this is a consideration. It deals instead with the specific allegations against API."

"You will answer the question, Mr. Constantine."

"What is the question?"

"Do you base your claim against API on these six similarities alone?" Genitori said.

"I base it on *all* the similarities," Arthur answered.

"That concludes my cross-examination, your Honor."

"I have no redirect," Brackman said.

"Very well. Thank you, Mr. Constantine, you may—"

"Your Honor, I have one further question."

"Forgive me, Mr. Willow."

Willow walked to the witness chair and, without looking at Arthur, said, "Mr. Constantine, you said yesterday morning that you worked on a film titled *Area Seven,* is that correct?"

"That's correct."

"In what capacity did you work on that film?"

"I worked on the screenplay."

"You wrote the screenplay?"

"I worked on it together with Matthew Jackson."

Willow suddenly looked up. "Mr. Constantine," he said, "did you receive screen credit for *Area Seven?*"

"I did."

"As co-author of the screenplay?"

"We worked on it together."

"Did the screen credit state 'Screenplay by Matthew Jackson and Arthur Nelson Constantine'?"

"Screen credits are determined by the Writers Guild. They very often—"

"Please answer the question."

"No, that's not what the credit stated."

"Did it not, in fact, state 'Adaptation by Arthur Nelson Constantine, Screenplay by Matthew Jackson'?"

"Yes, that's what it stated. But 'adaptation' is a word—"

"Thank you, Mr. Constantine."

"Mr. Brackman?" McIntyre asked.

"That is the plaintiff's case, if your Honor please."

"You may step down, Mr. Constantine."

"Thank you," Arthur said. Bewildered for a moment, he began walking toward the jury box on the left of the courtroom, saw James Driscoll and his wife sitting there, started for the benches at the rear, and then responded to Brackman's signal to join him at the plaintiff's table.

Willow was still standing before the bench.

He took off his glasses, pressed his fingers into his eyes, head bent for a moment, and then put the glasses on again, and looked up at the judge.

"May I at this time," he said, "move to dismiss the action

on the ground that this court has no jurisdiction with respect to the play *Catchpole*."

He delivered the words calmly and emotionlessly, startling even Genitori, who looked up in surprise. Arthur immediately turned to Brackman, puzzled, but Brackman rested a reassuring hand on his arm, leaned forward, his attention focused on Willow, and then patted Arthur's arm twice in further reassurance. Arthur did not know why Willow was suggesting that a federal court had no jurisdiction in a copyright case. He sensed intuitively, though, that the motion had been conceived as a result of the trap Willow had set and sprung in his earlier circuitous questioning. Apprehensively, he leaned forward and waited for Willow to continue. The courtroom was silent.

"Section 13 of the Copyright Law," Willow said, "clearly states that no action for infringement may be maintained if copies of the work in question have not been deposited with the Library of Congress."

Brackman was on his feet instantly. "Mr. Willow knows very well that the play *Catchpole* was copyrighted in August of 1947," he said. "Point of fact, he conceded before trial that it would not be necessary to produce a certificate of copyright, and that . . ."

"That's on the record, Mr. Willow," McIntyre said. "I'm not sure I understand your motion."

"Your Honor," Willow said, "I believe it was proved today that this work was published a full seven months *before* any copyright protection was sought."

"May I ask . . ." Brackman started.

"Publication, your Honor," Willow interrupted, "may be defined as the earliest date of unrestricted sale or distribution of copies. In this case, the first authorized edition of *Catchpole* was the play Arthur Constantine had mimeographed in December of 1946."

"Your Honor . . ."

"He distributed copies of that play starting in January of 1947, and continuing through May of that year, when the play was optioned. This mimeographed version was *not* copyrighted, nor was the play registered with the Copyright Office until August of 1947, seven months *after* the general distribution."

"Your Honor," Brackman said, "we are engaged in a matter of semantics here. The distribution made by Mr. Constantine was not a *general* distribution, as my learned friend claims, but rather a *limited* one to theatrical producers and investors, for the sole purpose of securing production of the play."

"The fact remains, your Honor, that one hundred and twenty copies were, in the witness's own words, 'floating all over the city,' distributed without copyright notice, placing them in the public domain. I cite Section 10 of the Code, which specifies that publication or distribution without the statutory copyright notice constitutes dedication to the public."

"This was neither a publication *nor* a general distribution," Brackman said. "Under Section 12 of the Code, the common-law protection of a work is perpetual so long as the work remains unpublished. *Catchpole,* which was a dramatic composition, was 'published,' if you will, on the night the play opened in New York City to paid performances. Until that time . . ."

"A hundred and twenty copies were printed, your Honor."

"Were *mimeographed*," Brackman said.

"And generally distributed."

"It was a *limited* distribution."

"We can argue this forever," McIntyre said. "I will reserve judgment on the motion, Mr. Willow."

"May I then, your Honor, for the defendants Mitchell-Campbell Books and Camelot Books move for dismissal of the complaint under Rule 41, on the ground that on the facts and on the law the plaintiff has not made out a cause for action."

"I will deny that motion," McIntyre said.

"If your Honor please," Willow said, "I have no desire to waste the Court's time, but may I point out that our grounds are set forth in our main brief and in our reply brief?"

"I know that."

"Thank you, your Honor," Willow said.

Genitori rose from behind the API table and walked toward the bench. "May it please your Honor," he said, "Mr. Willow has made a motion to dismiss under Rule 41, and I would now like to join that motion as it refers to the first claim against API. But in addition, I would like to make another motion directed to the second cause of action, which charges independent infringement by API.

"For the purpose of this motion, your Honor, I must assume *arguendo* that Ralph Knowles, the man who wrote the screenplay and directed the film, had access to the play *Catchpole,* and that the five similarities listed in Plaintiff's Exhibit Number 8, together with the 'eyeglasses' incident which was added today—these six items were copied by Mr. Knowles directly from the play. I submit to your Honor that even *assuming* access and copying—and access alone means nothing, as your Honor well knows—even assuming *both,* these six incidents alone do not form the basis for copyright infringement.

"Let us examine them for a moment, if we may, your Honor. They are all as flimsy and as absurd as the man with his foot in bandages, or the far-fetched allusion to marksmanship, both of which claims have already been withdrawn. They are as meaningless, your Honor, as the incident of the eyeglasses, which was added to the list in this courtroom today.

"We are asked to accept as a unique idea, for example, the use of a bayonet as a weapon, your Honor—the use of a *bayonet* as a *weapon*—merely because the plaintiff's psychopathic colonel uses one. Never mind the fact that bayonet charges were prevalent during the Korean conflict, and that whereas none were mentioned in the novel, Mr. Knowles made pictorial use of them in the film. Or for example, your Honor, the plaintiff insists that because some soldiers are drinking coffee at one point in his play, and some soldiers in the film *also* drink coffee, this is another indication of access and direct copying from the play. I don't think I need bring up the other three points which are just as meaningless, and upon which the plaintiff bases his charge of independent infringement by API.

"I submit that the plaintiff's case is lacking in *any* evidence of infringement of copyrightable material. I call your attention to one of the more prominent plagiarism cases—*Morris versus Wilson,* cited on page 24 of our brief—in which Judge Weinfeld said, 'In order to suppose that these authors should have found in the plaintiff's play cues for the farfetched similarities which she discovers, one must be obsessed—as apparently unsuccessful playwrights are commonly obsessed—with the inalterable conviction that no situation, no character, no detail of construction in their own plays can find even a remote analogue except as the result of piracy.' The judge later quoted, poetically, 'Trifles light as air are to the jealous confirmations strong as proof of holy writ.'

"Your Honor, that's exactly what these six isolated incidents are, trifles light as air. Let us examine the rest of them a moment, if your Honor will allow. There is an enemy soldier being shot at and falling out of a tree, a supposedly *unique* event in time of war. There is an American soldier bursting into tears when his buddy is killed. And finally, there is a nurse putting on lipstick and using the back of a mess kit for a mirror. Your Honor, I submit that the first two of these alleged similarities are stock incidents to be found in *any* war film ever made, and that the incident with the nurse and her lipstick is noncopyrightable.

"If you will refer to page 31 of our brief—the case of *Rush versus Oursler*—Judge Thacher of this court observed, 'When two authors portray the same occurrence in the same setting; presupposing the presence of the same people in the same environment; similarities of incident unaccompanied by similarities in *plot* are not persuasive evidence of copying. The authors having worked with the same material to construct the environment or setting in which the action is laid, such similarities are inevitable; and the products of such labor are comparable to the paintings of the same scene made by different artists.'

"And a little later on, your Honor, he remarked, 'It may usually be said that such material is so unimportant and so trivial that its appropriation by copying, even if shown, would not be a substantial taking of copyrighted material.' Your Honor, the six incidents upon which plaintiff bases his second cause of action—the enemy shot from a tree, the eyeglasses, and so forth—are likewise not susceptible of copyright.

"I now respectfully submit that there is no evidence at all to support this second claim against API, and I beg your Honor to dismiss it from the case."

"Mr. Brackman?"

"I did not realize, your Honor, that Mr. Genitori was going to read us his entire brief," Brackman said dryly. He rose and walked slowly toward the bench. "Needless to say, I do not agree with him concerning the basis of our complaint, which he seems to have completely misunderstood. We are *not* claiming that these six incidents alone constitute our claim of infringement. Our complaint is quite clear on that. Our action against API is based on these six incidents *plus* all of the other similarities of theme, plot, and character which Mr. Constantine enumerated yesterday. It is a simple matter, of course, to label these similarities 'flimsy and absurd,' as Mr. Genitori has done, it is certainly much simpler than trying to explain them. But, your Honor, I feel defendant *should* and *must* explain them, especially when we consider Mr. Constantine's testimony, which indicates that in 1952 he worked with a man named Matthew Jackson, to whom he submitted a copy of his play *Catchpole*. This man Jackson . . ."

"Your Honor," Genitori said, "I only assumed access for the purpose of my motion."

"Yes, we understand that."

"API *had* access," Brackman said firmly. "There is no question about that. The play was submitted to five people at the studio in 1952, *including* Mr. Matthew Jackson, who later worked with Ralph Knowles on *The Paper Dragon*. Carl, may I see that brief a moment, please?" he said, turning to his partner. Arthur, watching him, saw that he was getting angry, and he immediately thought, Good, it's about time. Give it to the bastards.

"I don't like to waste this Court's time reading from cases. There are hundreds and hundreds of cases, as your Honor well knows, and it seems we have already heard a goodly percentage of them from my learned friend." Arthur saw Genitori smile, in spite of the withering glance Brackman directed at him. "But our brief is not exactly destitute of examples, your Honor, and if I may I would like to quote from it at this time."

"Please," McIntyre said.

"I thank your Honor for his indulgence," Brackman said. "In the case of *West Publishing Company versus Edward Thompson Company,* it was pointed out, and I quote, 'To constitute an invasion of copyright it is not necessary that the whole of a work should be copied, nor even a large portion of it in form or substance, but that, if so much is taken that the value of the original is sensibly diminished, or the labors of the original author are substantially, to an injurious extent, appropriated by another, that is sufficient to constitute an infringement.'

"So you see, your Honor, it does not matter whether we are dealing here with six incidents, or ten incidents, or twelve, or *twenty*—so long as these similarities have indeed sensibly diminished the value of the original. I'm sure your Honor is familiar with the now famous *Teton versus Caddo* case, this circuit, Judge Madison presiding, wherein it was claimed—as both Mr. Willow and Mr. Genitori are claiming—that the similarities were insignificant, even though there were a great many of them, a substantial number of seemingly unimportant similarities. There was, however, in the midst of these so-called insignificant similarities, one that was *indeed* significant, your Honor. I refer, and I'm sure you're ahead of me, to the misspelling of a place name in the original work, and the identical misspelling of that place name in the alleged piracy. This was, your Honor, the misspelling of a town in Michigan, Chippewa, which was spelled with an H at the end of it in both books, C-H-I-P-P-E-W-A-H, Chippewah—the identical error in both books, your Honor. The thief had left behind his fingerprints."

Brackman turned to look at the empty jury box where Driscoll and his wife sat, and then turned to the judge again.

"Your Honor, the thief has left behind his fingerprints in this case as well. I refer now to the numerical designation of the 105th Division, which is identical in both the play *Catchpole* and the novel *The Paper Dragon,* and which has been carried over to the film produced by—"

"Your Honor, this does not pertain to my motion," Genitori said. "I made no reference to the 105th Division."

"I appreciate that, Mr. Genitori," McIntyre said, "but if I understand Mr. Brackman correctly, he's saying there *is* a cause of action and that it goes beyond the six incidents and includes *all* of the other similarities as well."

"That's *exactly* what I'm saying."

"I'll continue to hear argument on the point."

"I was saying, your Honor, that the thief's fingerprints are clearly visible without the need of a magnifying glass, they are able to be seen with the naked eye, the 105th Division. If I may, your Honor, I would like to point out once again that there were only sixty-seven actual infantry divisions in existence during the time of the Eniwetok campaign, and that when we come to the divisions beyond the designation '100' we have the 101st, 102nd, 103rd, 104th, and *106th.* There is no 105th division. Nor was there a 105th division in 1950. There were only seven actual infantry divisions at that time, the 1st, 2nd, 3rd, 7th, 24th, 25th, and the 1st Cavalry. Today, there are twelve infantry divisions and, needless to say, none of *them* is the 105th, either.

"Perhaps Mr. Driscoll can adequately explain to this Court how he happened to hit upon those three digits in sequence. Until he can do that, I will continue to be amazed by the remarkable use of this designation, appearing again and again and again, first in the play, then in the novel, and again in the motion picture. Out of all the possible numbers Mr. Driscoll could have used to label his infantry division, he chose the identical number that appears in Mr. Constantine's work. This is an amazing coincidence, your Honor, it is almost an impossible coincidence.

"Now, your Honor, in much the same way that there are laws governing our society, there are also laws governing chance, and these are called the laws of probability, and it is against these that we must examine this use of an identical division number. If we were to take all the digits from zero to nine and try to figure out all the possible different combinations for any *three* of those digits, we would have to raise ten to the third power, which means we would have to multiply ten times ten times ten, and that would give us an answer of one thousand possible combinations. In other words, the odds would be a thousand to one that any man would choose a specific combination over any other possible combination. A thousand to one, your Honor. And those odds, as impressive as they may sound, are only the odds for a *single* event. When we come to two mutually independent events, the odds are overwhelming.

"What exactly is the probability that both these men, given the same ten digits, would then arrange three of them in identical order? I will tell you, your Honor. The laws of probability state that in the case of two mutually independent events, we must multiply the odds against Event One happening by the odds against Event Two happening. In other words, we must multiply a thousand-to-one by a thousand-to-one, and we then discover that the odds against Driscoll hitting on this same combination were a *million* to one. He had one chance in a million, your Honor, a deplorable cliché to use in a case dealing with literary matters, but those are the true odds nonetheless, a *million* to one, the figures do not lie. And even if we wish to give both men the benefit of the doubt, and say that neither of them would have designated an Army division with the number zero-zero-zero—although stranger things *have* happened in fiction, as we well know—even if we were to exclude this possibility, the odds for both men would be 999 to one, and when we multiply that by itself, the odds against Driscoll hitting on the same combination would be 998,001 to one. A million-to-one is a neater figure, your Honor, and will serve our purposes here, I believe.

"And I believe, too, that with odds such as these, we are justified in demanding an explanation, beyond the labeling of such similarities as flimsy and absurd. Thank you, your Honor."

"Do you now wish to reply, Mr. Genitori?"

"Only to say, your Honor, that my motion did not concern the 105th Division or any other similarities common to both the novel and the film."

"Yes, I understand that. Well, I want to reserve decision on your motion, and on Mr. Willow's as well."

"Your Honor?"

"Yes, Mr. Willow?"

"I understood you earlier to say you were *denying* my motion."

"If that's what I indicated . . . no, Mr. Willow, I meant that I'm reserving judgment on it."

"Thank you, your Honor."

McIntyre looked up at the wall clock. "It seems to be the end of another day," he said. "So unless there's anything further, we'll recess until tomorrow morning at ten o'clock."

7

THICK WHITE SNOWFLAKES were swirling in the air when Sam Genitori and his assistant came out of the courtroom. A cover of white clung to rooftop and pavement, hushing the city, and snow shovels scraped on courthouse steps and sidewalk, a rasping steady counterpoint to the metallic jingle of skid chains on distant streets. Genitori put on his hat, ducked his head against the fierce wind, and stepped into the vortex of flying flakes. Beside him, Michael Kahn sucked in a draught of cold air and shouted over the wind, "I love snow, I *love* snow." Sam lost his footing on the slippery steps at that moment and would have gone tumbling to the sidewalk below were it not for Kahn's suddenly supporting arm. The assistance annoyed Sam more than Kahn's redundant confession had—"I love snow, I *love* snow"—an emotional involvement Sam could neither share nor understand. Sam detested snow. It was cold and wet and damned uncomfortable, and besides it caused accidents and traffic jams. Leo Kessler was waiting for him uptown, and he didn't need a snowstorm to delay his arrival. He looked up, squinting into the wind, and saw the chauffeured limousine across the street, on Duane. "There it is," he said to Kahn, and walked swiftly toward the big car, its roof and hood covered with snow, its sides a wet shining black. The chauffeur was reading a copy of *Mad Magazine;* he barely looked up when Sam opened the back door. Kahn climbed in, and the chauffeur reluctantly put aside the magazine. Then, with the unerring instinct of all servants everywhere, he lunged straight for the jugular.

"This snow'll make us late," he said.

"Just get there as fast as you can."

"580 Fifth?" the chauffeur asked.

"No, Malibu Beach," Sam said dryly.

"By way of Santa Monica or the freeway?" the chauffeur asked, deadpan.

"580 Fifth," Sam answered, demolished by superior wit. He stretched his legs, took off his hat, patted his thinning hair into place, and then tilted his head back against the cushioned seat.

"Were you impressed?" Kahn asked.

"By whom?"

"The witness."

The car was in motion. Sam always felt a bit queasy in a moving vehicle, a reaction he attributed to his ulcer, or perhaps only to his proximity to Kahn, who seemed to be occupying a great many moving vehicles with him of late. He was constantly amazed by the fact that Kahn was not related to someone in the company. He could not imagine how anyone as imbecilic as this young man had ever managed to get through law school, no less become an employee of the firm, all without being someone's nephew. "The witness left me cold," he said, and belched.

"Excuse *me*," Kahn supplied.

"Do me a favor," Sam said. "When we get to Leo's office, shut up."

"What do you mean?"

"I mean shut up. Don't talk about the witness, don't talk about the case, just shut up and listen. You'll learn a great deal about law and high finance and tits."

"I know all about those already," Kahn said, offended.

"You can *never* know all about tits," Sam answered. "There's always something new to learn. The subject is inexhaustible.

"And I don't happen to like that expression," Kahn said. "I *don't* happen to like that expression," he repeated.

"Tits?"

"Yes, that."

"Did the witness impress *you?*" Sam asked, shrugging.

"Yes."

"In what manner?"

"I think he was telling the truth," Kahn said. "I think Driscoll *did* steal the play. Why else would Willow have moved for dismissal on a jurisdictional technicality? I'll tell you why. He knows his man stole the play, and he's afraid to put him on the stand."

"That's ridiculous," Sam said. "Willow was only trying to save time, energy, and money. If he could have got the case kicked out of court today, that would have been the end of it forever."

"I still think Driscoll's guilty. And I wouldn't be surprised if Ralph Knowles dipped into the company files, too, when he was writing the movie."

"My young friend," Sam said, "have you ever been thrown out of a seventh-floor window?"

"What?"

"All you have to do in the presence of Leo Kessler is suggest—*suggest,* mind you—that API was in any way a party to this plagiarism, and I can guarantee he will hurl you seven stories to the street below, where you will be crushed by oncoming traffic."

"Then you do think it was plagiarism?"

"Who said so?"

"You just called it plagiarism, didn't you?"

"I should have said *alleged* plagiarism," Sam amended, and then shrugged again.

"Well, what *is* your position?" Kahn asked.

"My position is the position Artists-Producers-International pays me to maintain. There was no plagiarism involved here, neither on the part of James Driscoll nor on the part of any person or persons employed by API. That is my position."

"That's your *official* position."

"That's my *only* position."

"But how do you feel personally?"

"I feel fine, thanks, except for my ulcer."

"You know what I mean."

"Sure, I know what you mean."

"Well?"

"There was no plagiarism," Sam said flatly.

They had come uptown past Canal Street, where the big black limousine had nosed its way silently through the truck traffic heading for the bridge, making a sharp left turn onto Third Avenue. The Chinese banks and groceries had given way to the wholesale clothing and lighting fixture stores, the fleabag hotels and flophouses only sparsely represented until just now, when they suddenly appeared like dim gray specters in the blinding snow. Derelicts shuffled along the sidewalks here and lay in gutters and doorways, making Sam sick just to look at them. His most vicious nightmare was one in which he suddenly woke up divested of his law degree and his position with API, his house in Massapequa gone, his boat scuttled, everything he had fought for in the past twenty years vanished with the night to leave only a trembling immigrant Italian struggling with the language, selling chestnuts on a Bronx street corner for five cents a bag. He awoke from this dream each time in a cold sweat, the smell of roasting chestnuts in his nostrils, and each time he held his hands out in front of his face, peering at them in the dark, certain that the fingers would be stained brown from the juice of the nuts. His wife would say, "Go to sleep, Sam, you had a bad dream," but he would lie awake trembling in the dark, terrified by his near miss—they had almost taken it all away from him, they had almost closed the jaws of the trap before he'd had a chance to scurry out of it. He could not account for the basis of this dream, since he had never in his life sold chestnuts in the Bronx. Nor, for that matter, had he ever even *lived* in the Bronx. Moreover, neither of his parents were immigrants, and they had never been really poor. The dream-trap was more like a race memory that could be traced back to a grandfather he had never known—and yet his grandfather hadn't sold chestnuts, either, so what the hell could it be? His grandfather had come to this country when he was twenty-one years old, after studying economics at the university in Milan. When he arrived here, he had been given a job immediately in a bank on the Bowery, where he dealt mostly with Italian-speaking immigrants. The job paid a good salary each week, and he had managed to save enough for the purchase of the house in Massapequa, which had since been passed down to Sam's father and recently to Sam himself. So what was this business with the chestnuts? And why did the sight of all these ragged bums all over the sidewalk trouble Sam so badly?

He was grateful when Cooper Union appeared on the left of the limousine. In the small park outside the school, a coed in a black hooded parka, her legs crossed, leaned forward eagerly to divulge some secret of the universe to a budding young artist or engineer, and another girl, wearing a paint-smeared smock and lighting a cigarette, came through the glass-paneled doors of the building, looked up at the sky, and sniffed the snow, ahh, to be young again.

Sam took in a deep breath. The Bowery and its dregs were falling behind the car, the hock shops appeared now like glittering toadstools. Beside him, he could smell the always-present slightly sour smell of Michael Kahn, as though someone had recently burped him but neglected to wipe his lips afterwards. Sam closed his eyes, and remained silent for the rest of the trip uptown.

There were wags in the industry, as there will be wags in any industry, who were of the opinion that the initials API did not really stand for Artists-Producers-International but stood instead for Asses, Pricks, and Imbeciles. If such was truly the case, the façade of the organization revealed neither ineptitude nor villainy, but seemed instead to echo a benign and somewhat informal attitude toward crass commercialism. The New York API offices covered the entire sixth, seventh, and eighth floors of the Longines-Wittnauer Building at 580 Fifth Avenue, just next door to Brentano's. The decorating scheme of the offices had been carefully calculated to disarm by none other than Mrs. Leo Kessler herself, better known in the industry as Katie Kessler, whose credit card—SET DRESSER: KATRINA L. KESSLER—had flashed from a hundred or more silver screens in the past two decades. To her further credit, the offices seemed to relax all visitors immediately, setting the tone for businesslike discussions in an atmosphere as informal as the living room of a Bel Air ranch. There were some who preferred the mid-Victorian decor of MCA's offices, with its old English prints in the elevators, and its green leather furniture, but Sam Genitori never failed to experience a slight lessening of tension the moment he stepped off the elevators here, and he silently thanked Katie each time.

"He's waiting for you," the seventh-floor receptionist said.

"What time is it?" Sam asked.

"Almost five. He said to send you right in."

"Is he alone?"

"Myrna's taking dictation."

"You'd better buzz him," Sam said.

The receptionist made no comment. She lifted the phone at her elbow, dialed a number, and waited. "Mr. Genitori is here," she said, and paused. "Yes, sir, right away." She hung up, nodded, and said, "You can go right in."

"Thank you."

"How's the trial going?" she asked.

"Nicely," Kahn replied.

"Mr. Genitori?" she asked, ignoring Kahn.

"Nicely," Genitori said, and walked immediately down the long corridor, followed by Kahn, who was beginning to sulk. Halfway down the hall, they passed a harried-looking brunette with a steno pad.

"He's waiting for you," she said.

"We know, Myrna."

"How's the trial going?"

"Nicely," Sam said, and glanced at Kahn, who said nothing. Kessler's office was at the end of the hall. Sam knocked on the door before opening it, and waited for Leo to shout his customary "Enter!" to which he customarily replied, "All ye who abandon hope here," and which customarily went clear over Leo's head, as it did now.

"What the hell does *that* mean?" Kessler asked.

"It's an old Milanese adage," Sam said, and started to close the door behind him.

"Michael, get lost someplace, will you?" Kessler said.

"Me?"

"Yes, I have something to discuss with Sam personally, okay? That's a good boy."

"If this relates to the trial," Kahn said, "I think . . ."

"Go get a cup of coffee, huh?" Kessler said, and waved him out impatiently. The sulking look on Kahn's face gave way to one of crumbling petulance. Sam was certain he would begin crying before he reached the corridor. He ushered Kahn out and closed the door behind him.

"Lock it," Kessler said.

Sam locked it. "Mr. President," he said, "I wish to report that the Russians have just bombed San Francisco."

"Very funny," Kessler said. "Someday you'll learn that the motion picture business is not funny."

"What *is* the motion picture business, Leo, if not funny?"

"The motion picture business is a vast fantasy surrounded by twat," Kessler said, "but not funny, not funny at all. How's the trial going?"

"All right."

"Will we win it?"

"I hope so."

Kessler rose from his desk suddenly. He was sixty-two years old, a tall slim man who wore a black suit each and every day of the week, augmented by black shoes and socks, black tie, white shirt, and generally a vest of either red or yellow corduroy with brass buttons. He was partially bald, and his nose was either naturally hooked or had once been badly broken, so that his profile had the curvilinear beauty of a modern piece of sculpture, rounded flesh sweeping into the arc of nose and jutting jaw, fierce eyes glinting from beneath black bushy eyebrows. He paced the office with his hands tucked into his jacket pockets, the thumbs overhanging, his shoulders hunched as though he were balancing an invisible load, his step springy and disjointed. He neither looked at Sam nor acknowledged his presence, speaking as though dictating a memo to a recording machine or explaining a particularly difficult dream to an unresponsive analyst.

"Scimitar," he said, "I wish I'd never heard of it. Thirty million dollars to make, plus all the trouble later with that bastard Nasser and his filthy Arabs, they should all drop dead from constipation. Thirty million dollars, and it's playing hard-ticket in twelve American cities, and with the business we're doing we won't get back that thirty million for the next thirty years, is it any wonder the stockholders are a little nervous? A *little* nervous, who's kidding who? There's a stockholders' meeting next month, January the 18th, to be exact, and I know just what's going to be proposed at that meeting because it was proposed at last year's meeting while we were still pouring money into that lousy *Scimitar,* even before Mr. Nasser started up with us, that bastard should rot in his grave. It was proposed at last year's meeting, January the 12th, to be exact, that Leo Kessler, whose father happened to found Kessler's, Inc.—before we got so cockamamie fancy with all the tax dodges and the Artists-Producers-International—it was proposed at last year's meeting that Leo Kessler step down as head of studio operations, mind you this was *before* the movie opened, *before* it started losing money even in Los Angeles, where they'll go see *anything*.

"So this year, on January the 18th, the stockholders of this fine company are going to sit back and look at the figures and they're going to learn that *Scimitar* has earned back only ten million dollars in a six-month showing, and that's a far cry from the thirty million dollars it cost to make, and an even farther cry from the two and a half times we have to earn back because that rotten director talked me into doing it in color, seventy-five million dollars before we're even off the hook. The stockholders are going to jump on that the way Moses jumped on the water, seventy-five *million* dollars. Will anyone remind them that I've earned *ten* times seventy-five million dollars for this company since my father died, God rest his soul? Will anyone remind them of *Dust,* which earned twelve million at a time when twelve million was equal to thirty-five million today? Will anyone remind them of *The Peddlers* at ten-and-a-half million profit, or *Marcia Steele* at six million profit, or *The Paper Dragon* at fourteen million, which book we bought for thirty-five thousand dollars, and which entire picture cost us only eight-fifty to make, will anyone remind them of what Leo Kessler has *done,* or only of what Leo Kessler has failed to do?

"Oh, let me tell you they are going to remind us of *The Paper Dragon* if we lose this trial. They are going to remind us that in the past three years we have had only one film that really made any kind of money, and that film was *The Paper Dragon,* which only enabled us to get rolling on *Scimitar.* Without Driscoll's book, we'd never have got involved in that lousy desert out there with that Swedish bitch screwing everything in sight, including the Moslem camel boys, and maybe the camels, too, what a production, I wish I'd never heard of it! They are going to remind us that here was a winner, *The Paper Dragon,* a profit of fourteen million dollars, and due to Mr. Leo Kessler's expert handling of the company, it turns out that this winner, ha! was plagiarized from something that was offered to API back in 1947 and again in 1952, something that is right there in our studio files for Ralph Knowles to look at while he's doing his screenplay. And when we add that to *Scimitar* and the money that's going down the drain with *that* one, you can rest assured that Mr. Leo Kessler will be out on the street selling pencils, look what happened to Griffith."

"What happened to Griffith?" Sam asked.

"*Birth of a Nation,* the biggest movie ever to be made in the history of the business, he dies a pauper in a Hollywood fleabag. Who'll remember *Dust* when Mr. Leo Kessler is kicked out on his ass?"

"Nobody," Sam said.

"You said it."

"We'll win the case," Sam said. "Don't worry."

"That's good," Kessler said, "but that's not why I sent

young snotnose Kahn out to ogle the office girls, and it's not why I asked you to lock the door, either. If we win the case, we don't need locked doors. We'll have the stockholders down on us *anyway,* but at least I can then say 'What the hell are you yelling about? Who was it who *made* the money for us to later invest in *Scimitar,* Sam Goldwyn maybe? It was *me,* it was *me* who saw possibilities in *The Paper Dragon,* it was *me* who brought it to the screen, it was *me* who made fourteen million dollars with it, so who has a better right to be daring with a picture that could still maybe earn out the cost once we're through with two-a-days and can go into general release, the Swedish bitch is big box office, and don't forget it.' That's what I can say." He paused. *"If* we win the case."

"We'll win it," Sam said. "Willow's a good lawyer."

"Is he Jewish?"

"I don't know."

"Brackman *is,"* Kessler said. "Never sell a Jew short."

"With all due respect, Leo, he's made a few mistakes already."

"Good, he should only make a *hundred* of them. I'm not worried about what happens if we *win* this case. I'm worried about what happens if it looks like we're *losing* it."

"I don't get you," Sam said.

"You don't get me?" Kessler paused. *"Did* he steal that play or not, Sam?"

"I don't think so."

"But will the *judge* think so?"

Sam shrugged. "That's why we're having a trial, Leo."

"What do *you* think the judge will think?"

"I think the judge will decide against Constantine."

"You think we'll win?"

"Yes. I think we'll win."

"But when will we know?"

"When the judge gives his opinion."

"Which will be when?"

"He can give it immediately after our summation, or it can take as long as two months. Who knows?"

"Two months after the trial *ends,* do you mean?"

"That's right, it could take that long."

Kessler nodded. He walked to the leather chair behind his desk, slumped into it, and laced his thin fingers across his chest. "You know, of course, that Ralph Knowles is flying in from the Coast, don't you? To testify."

"Yes, I know that."

"I want protection," Kessler said.

"Against what?"

"Against being kicked out of this company, what the hell do you think I've been talking about here for the past ten minutes?"

"How can I give you that?"

"By making sure Ralph Knowles is very carefully prepared before he goes on that witness stand."

"*All* witnesses are prepared, Leo. Knowles will—"

"We had nothing to do with this," Kessler said.

"What do you mean?"

"Neither API nor Mr. Leo Kessler had anything to do with this."

"With *what?*"

"I bought a book. I paid thirty-five thousand dollars for it in good honest American money. I bought it from galleys even before it became a bestseller. It was a good book, I thought it would make a great movie. I had no way of knowing it was stolen from a play written back in 1946."

"Who says it was stolen?"

"*If* we lose," Kessler said.

"I'm having trouble following you," Sam answered.

"*If* we lose—and don't tell me this can't happen, Sam, don't tell me innocent men haven't been sent to the electric chair or the gas chamber for crimes they never committed—*if* we lose this case, I want it to be clear in the record that James Driscoll was the crook. *We* had nothing to do with it, Sam, we had no way of knowing."

"Granted. But, Leo, I think he's innocent. I think he really did write the damn book all by himself, without ever having heard of Arthur Constantine *or* his play."

"Sam," Kessler said, "I respect your opinion highly, but I must tell you that your opinion isn't worth two cents. It's the *judge's* opinion that matters. And if the judge says James Driscoll stole that play, then James Driscoll *did* steal that play, and that's all there is to it."

"Well, that's not quite *all* there is to it. We can still appeal."

"Fine, we'll appeal. And by the time we appeal, I'll be out on my ass in the street selling pencils."

"Or chestnuts," Sam said.

"Everything is funny to you," Kessler replied. *"I'm* a man gasping for breath, and *you* make jokes. When I want comedians, I'll hire Charles DeGaulle."

"Okay, what do you want?"

"Ralph Knowles is the biggest horse's ass I know, and there are some very big horse's asses in this industry. I want you to make sure he understands *exactly* what he's going to say before he testifies, and that he doesn't say a word that would lead anyone to think he even *suspected* there was a copy of *Catchpole* in our files out there on the Coast."

"Did he know there was a copy of the play in our files?"

"I don't know what he knew or didn't know. Directors are to me traffic cops, and worse than actors. The only good director I ever met was the one who dropped dead on the sound stage of a picture we were making, causing us to abandon it. He saved us a half-million dollars."

"All right, I'll see that Knowles is carefully prepared."

"See that he's more than carefully prepared. Put the words in his mouth, let him memorize them. He wrote his screenplay from Driscoll's book, he consulted only Driscoll's book, he followed Driscoll's book to the letter, making only those changes necessary to adapt it to the screen. Like everyone else at API, he had no idea Driscoll was a crook."

"Leo," Sam said, "do you want to *win* this case, or simply lose it with honor?"

"I want to keep my job," Kessler said.

"Un-huh."

"Win it, lose it, I don't give a damn—so long as API comes

out clean. And if that means throwing Driscoll to the wolves or the lions or whoever, then throw him and good riddance. I'm not married to him."

"Well," Sam said, and paused. "If it's any consolation, I think we'll win it, anyway. In fact, I don't see how we can lose."

"So win it. Am I telling you to lose the damn thing? What do you think this is, a club fight in New Jersey? I saw that picture, thank you. It was with Robert Ryan."

"Julie Garfield."

"That was another one."

The office went silent. Sam looked at his watch. "What time does Knowles get in?" he asked.

"Late tonight. He'll be ready for you tomorrow morning."

"We'll be starting with Chester Danton tomorrow morning."

"Well, when will Knowles go on the stand?"

"In the afternoon, most likely. That's up to Willow. He's running the case, we agreed to that."

"Then you've got plenty of time to talk to him."

"Yes."

"What's the matter?" Kessler asked.

"Nothing."

"What's the look on your face?"

"I was thinking of Driscoll."

"What about him?"

"All the poor bastard did was write a book."

By six-thirty that evening, the three men had each consumed four martinis, and the atmosphere at their table was convivial and relaxed, to say the least. Even James Driscoll, whom Jonah usually found rather reserved, seemed cheerful and optimistic, and it was he who suggested they have another drink before parting. Jonah was not ready to part just yet, not until he had fully discussed what was on his mind. He readily agreed to the fifth drink, and Norman Sheppard raised his arm to signal the waiter.

"What we're asking you to do," Jonah said, "is to recon-

struct the events that led to your calling your division the
105th. That's all we're really trying to do."

"The hell with it," Driscoll said.

"No, we can't say the hell with it," Jonah said.

"We're having a good time here," Driscoll said. "The hell
with it."

"We won't have such a good time if we lose this case,"
Norman said. "That's why we're asking you to try to remember, Jimmy. Try to remember how you hit upon those three
digits."

"I just did," Driscoll said.

"But how?"

"I don't remember."

"Well, think about it."

"I *am* thinking about it."

"Maybe you've got some notes on it," Norman said.
"You've supplied us with a lot of other material, so perhaps . . ."

"No, I wouldn't have kept notes on anything like that."

"All we're trying to do is trace the origin, that's all."

"It's a coincidence, plain and simple," Driscoll said.

"I think I'm getting drunk," Jonah said suddenly.

"I *know* I'm getting drunk," Driscoll said, and laughed.
"That's good. Relax from the trial."

"We can't relax," Norman said.

"*I* can relax," Driscoll answered.

"I wish *I* could relax," Jonah said, and removed his glasses
and wiped his eyes. His eyes were a pale blue. He pressed
them with thumb and forefinger and then replaced his
glasses.

"Brackman is going to harp on that 105th Division,"
Norman said, "and unless you can come up with a reasonable
explanation, I feel we're going to be in trouble. I think those
are Jonah's feelings as well, aren't they, Jonah?"

"Let me say that the coincidence unless explained will
seem extraordinary."

"Well, it *is* extraordinary," Driscoll said. "I think a great *many* of the similarities between my book and the play are extraordinary."

"On Monday afternoon, I drove up to Vassar," Jonah said. "To see a friend of mine who teaches World History there. Now, I know your novel takes place during October and November of 1950, and that the action you describe was against the Chinese—but is it possible you also ran into some North Korean troops?"

"No."

"You did not?"

"I did not."

"Is it possible you overheard talk about engagements with North Korean troops?"

"It's possible, I suppose. Most of the talk was about Chinese intervention, though. We kept wondering when it would happen—even after it *did* happen."

"Would you recall anyone mentioning the North Korean 105th?"

"No. Should I?"

"Well," Jonah said, and shrugged. "You never heard it mentioned, huh?"

"Not to my knowledge. Was it an infantry division?"

"No, it was an armored brigade."

"Then that lets it out, doesn't it?"

"Not necessarily," Norman said. "If we could show it was involved in—"

"It wasn't," Driscoll said. "The major battle in the book is against Chinese troops. And even the patrol is into territory held by the Chinese."

"Well, that's the end of *that* possibility," Norman said.

"That's what I thought on Monday," Jonah answered. "But I was hoping Jimmy would say, 'Why, yes, of course! I had a long discussion with some veterans of the June-July fighting, and they told me all about the 105th Armored Brigade and their Russian-built T-34 tanks.'"

"Why, yes, of course!" Driscoll said, grinning. "I *did* have a long discussion with some veterans of the June-July fighting, and they told me all about the 105th Armored Brigade and their Russian-built T-34 tanks."

"Chicane," Jonah said, "for which I could be disbarred." He shook his head. "You'll just have to remember where the 105th *really* came from."

"How can I? I don't *know* where it came from."

"Did you steal that play?" Jonah asked suddenly.

"I never stole anything in my life," Driscoll answered.

"Good," Jonah said.

"Do you believe me?"

"Yes."

"That's nice, because I don't give a damn whether you do or not," Driscoll said, and burst out laughing. "Here're our drinks. Let's forget the trial for a minute, can't we?"

"Brackman has already brought up this matter of the thief leaving his fingerprints," Norman said, "and I can assure you . . ."

"I'm not a thief," Driscoll said.

"Nobody said you were."

"Brackman said I was. And Constantine said I was. I didn't steal his play."

"Well, we know you didn't steal it," Norman said.

"How does it feel to be colored?" Driscoll asked.

"Fine," Norman said. "How does it feel to be white?"

"I only ask because Sergeant Morley in my book is colored, and I often wondered while I was writing it how it feels to be colored, how it *really* feels to be colored."

"Listen, Jimmy," Jonah said suddenly, "you'd better start thinking about this because I'll tell you the truth I'm very concerned about it, very very concerned."

"So am I," Norman said.

"So am I," Driscoll said.

"So start thinking about it," Jonah said.

"About what?"

"The 105th."

"Oh."

"Yes."

"I *have* been thinking about it."

"What was your serial number?"

"What?"

"Your Army serial number."

"714–5632."

"Where did you live before you went into the Army?"

"On Myrtle Avenue in Brooklyn."

"The address?"

"61 Myrtle."

"What was your telephone number?"

"Main 2–9970."

"Were you married at the time?"

"I got married two months before I was drafted."

"What was your wife's address?"

"Well, the apartment on Myrtle was hers, you see. I moved in with her after we got married."

"Where were you living before then?"

"With my parents."

"Where?"

"West End Avenue. 2426 West End."

"What floor, what apartment?"

"Apartment 12C."

"And on Myrtle Avenue?"

"Apartment 37."

"Your life seems singularly devoid of the number 105," Jonah said sourly, and lifted his drink.

"Did you have a car?" Norman asked.

"Yes."

"What was your license plate number?"

"Who the hell remembers?"

"Have you ever been to 105th Street?" Jonah asked.

"No."

"What high school did you go to?" Norman asked.

"Music and Art."

"Did you have a locker?"

"What?"

"A locker. For the gym."

"Oh. Yes, I had a locker."

"With a combination lock?"

"Yes."

"What was the combination?"

"24 right, 17 left, 14 right."

"How can you possibly remember that, but not your license plate number?"

"I didn't have to open my license plate every day of the week," Driscoll said.

"You will have to think harder," Jonah said.

"I don't have to think harder if I don't want to," Driscoll answered. "I don't have to think at *all,* if I don't want to." He picked up his glass and drank from it, and then put the glass down and stared into it, aware of the sudden silence at the table. Well, the hell with you, he thought. You sit here and throw questions at me, don't you think any of this *means* anything to me, Ebie's apartment on Myrtle Avenue, and the telephone number I called maybe ten thousand times, or the old Buick I used to drive when I first started at Pratt, and my locker at Music and Art, or the apartment on West End Avenue?

I can remember every inch of that apartment the way it used to look when Pop was still alive and before my mother sold all the furniture and brought in that Danish modern crap which my father would have thrown out of the house in a minute. But her new husband Mr. Gerald Furst is in the furniture business, so what else do you do but throw out all the old mahogany stuff and bring in a sleek new line to go with your sleek new husband? The piano, too, getting rid of that. Well, nobody played it but Pop, and he's been dead for five years, so I suppose she was right in giving it away. Christ, the way he used to sit at the piano with a tumbler of whiskey resting on the arm, banging out those Irish songs while Uncle Benny stood there singing at the top of his lungs. Pink shirts. Uncle Benny always used to wear pink shirts. And Pop would offer me a sip of booze, and I'd turn my head away, pulling a face, things sure change. Here I am getting squiffed in a bar, thirty-seven years old, things sure change. Everything changes. Even Uncle Benny finally got married and moved off to Fort Lauderdale.

He could draw like an angel, that man. I would have given my *soul* to be able to draw like him when I was a kid, or even, for that matter, after I'd had more training than he'd ever had in his life. You stuck a pencil in Uncle Benny's hand, and he would conjure a world for you, name it and Uncle Benny would draw it. It was he who first got me hooked, the sweet old pusher whispering to the innocent kid, Hey, Jimbo, want to try this? Guiding my hand along the page at first, showing me how to copy things from the newspaper comic strips, easy stuff at first like Mickey Mouse and Donald Duck, all clear sharp heavy lines, and then into the more complicated stuff from *Abby an' Slats,* or *Prince Valiant.* I did a marvelous copy of the Viking with the red beard who used to be in *Prince Valiant,* what was his name? I colored his beard the same color it was in the paper, and I also did one of Val himself swinging that mighty singing sword of his against a man with a helmet that looked something like an upended garbage pail. Uncle Benny said the perspective was off, but he praised the drawing anyway. I used to have a terrible handwriting in those days, so I would ask Uncle Benny to sign all my work for me, J. R. Driscoll, which was James Randolph Driscoll, the Randolph being in honor of my grandfather, who died when I was only four months old. Uncle Benny would sign each of my drawings in the lower right-hand corner, J. R. Driscoll, and then outline the signature with a narrow box that had a very heavy line on the bottom and on the right-hand side, so that it looked as if it were throwing a shadow on the page. I colored that guy's beard with crayon, what the hell was his name?

Pop wasn't much help in the art department, except in terms of criticism, *You made his nose too long,* or *Whoever saw a dog with a tail like that?* But he was very proud of the work I did, and always asked me to bring it out whenever any of his cronies from Gimbel's stopped by. He was an upholsterer, my father, and he used to work for Gimbel's, an uneducated man who nonetheless taught himself to play the piano and who studied the dictionary night after night, taking it a page at a time and learning new words which he would spring on all of us while we sat at dinner in the big dining room overlooking the Hudson. "Do you know what a dimissory letter is?" or "What is the meaning of equitation?" or "What is the difference between geminate and germinate?" I remember one night especially because he gave us a word which became the basis for a game we later played. He said, "Use the word caruncle in a sentence," and I said, "Caruncle Benny have some more mashed potatoes?" and Pop almost died laughing, though my mother didn't think it was funny at all. In fact, I doubt if she even got it. But Pop invented the game called Caruncle, and we used to play it two or three nights a week, the three of us sitting on the brown sofa near the old Chickering, while my mother sat in the wing chair tatting; she used to make these antimacassars which she gave to everyone at Christmas, and which always looked faded and dirty when you put them on the furniture. The game Caruncle had no real rules and we played it by ear each time, the way my father played the piano. The idea was to give a word which the next person would then define incorrectly. For example, if my father used the word "disseminate," my uncle might have defined it by saying, "When you disseminate, it means you make a distinction," and then I would say, "No, that's discriminate," and my father would say, "No, discriminate is when you burn your garbage," and Uncle Benny would say, "No, that's incinerate," and I would say, "No, incinerate is when you hint at something," and Pop would say, "No, that's insinuate," and Uncle Benny would say, "No, insinuate is meat on Friday," and we would always end up laughing. Another word game we played was called Progression and was a variation of Ghost, except that the idea here was to make a new word on each turn by adding a letter to the word we already had. Pop might start with the word "man," and Uncle Benny would add a letter and change it to "mane," and then I would make it "mange," and Pop would make it "manger" and Uncle Benny would make it "manager," and so on. Or I might start with "rid" and Pop would make it "dire," and Uncle Benny would make it "rived" and I would make it "divers" and Pop would make it "diverse," the idea being to reach ten letters which was the highest score and which hardly anyone ever got. My mother never played any of these word games with us. She had an Irish brogue and was ashamed of it.

When I was about twelve years old, I made up the comic strip called *The Cat*. It was a direct steal from *Batman*. My character was a very wealthy socialite named Jim Dirkson, which name I arrived at by transposing the letters of my own name and substituting a letter here and there. The Cat was dedicated to fighting crime and evil. He wore a black costume just like Batman's, except that his face mask had whiskers on it. Uncle Benny helped me lay out the panels, and he also did all the lettering in the balloons. It was in full color, though I used Mongol pencils instead of ink. I did forty-eight panels, which I figured was enough for about twelve days, and I asked Pop if he thought I should try sending it around to the newspapers. He said, "Sure, why not? It's an excellent comic," but I never did submit it because I didn't think it was good enough. Besides, I felt funny about Uncle Benny having done all the lettering. I didn't know at the time that a lot of comic strip artists hire people just to do their lettering for them. After I saw *Pinocchio*, I decided I would make an animated movie, even though I didn't have either a camera or the faintest understanding of single-frame photography. I created all these characters freely stolen from the film, including one called Swat Fly, who was based on Jiminy Cricket and who even carried an umbrella the way he did. But I also had a two-headed giant named Galoppo, whom Walt Disney had never even dreamt of. The two heads were constantly arguing with each other. I borrowed Pop's old Remington and began typing up the outline of the movie, starting in this tiny star-washed village (like the village in *Pinocchio*) and showing Swat Fly walking down the cobblestoned street and searching for the shop of a poor-but-honest butcher named Ham. Well, I got through six pages of it, single-spaced, but nothing seemed to be happening, so I gave it up. Uncle Benny liked the sketches I'd made of the characters, however, and only casually hinted that they were somewhat derivative. "That's when you make fun of something," I said, and Pop immediately said, "No, that's derisive," and Uncle Benny said, "No, derisive are on either side of Manhattan Island."

Uncle Benny drank a lot. My mother used to call him "a disgosting drunk." He was Pop's brother, and he slept in the end bedroom, next to my room. He worked in a pool parlor, and once he took me there and ran off a whole rack for me, and then taught me how to hold the cue and how to put English on a ball, and he taught me a trick shot with which I later won a lot of money, making bets in the Army; I never forgot that shot he taught me. He also taught me geometry when I was flunking it at Music and Art. Numbers always threw me, I never was good at arithmetic. When I started geometry, there was suddenly more than numbers to cope with; there were angles and curves and Given this, Prove that, and I got hopelessly lost in the first three weeks. Uncle Benny stepped in, telling me he had once won a medal in math, and then proceeding to drill me every night, going over each formula again and again, "There, now wasn't that easy, Jimbo?" painstakingly working through every problem until he was certain I understood completely. I used to wake up in the middle of the night sometimes and see triangles and circles floating in the air, equilateral has three sixty-degree angles and three equal sides, isosceles has two equal sides, circumference equals πr^2. I ended up with a 90 on the Regents exam, thanks to Uncle Benny's persistence. He gave me a Bulova watch when I graduated from Music and Art. Engraved on the case was the inscription "To a geometrid genus," which was an inside joke based on Caruncle, "from your loving Uncle Benny."

My best friend at Music and Art was a colored fellow named Andrew Christopher, who was an art major like myself but who also played trombone in the school band. Andy lived on Lenox Avenue and 123rd Street, and I would meet him each morning on the 125th Street platform of the Broadway-7th Avenue Line, which I took up from 96th Street, and which we rode together to 137th Street. We would walk up past City College and then to the school, talking about everything under the sun, but mostly about his girl friend whose name was Eunice and who went to Washington Irving High School where she was studying fashion design. Eunice was a light-skinned girl and her parents objected to Andy simply because he was darker than she. He told me this very openly, and neither of us felt any embarrassment talking about it. It was just one of the facts of life. I never went to Andy's house, though, and he never came to mine. My mother used to call Negroes "boogies."

Andy and I both won scholarships to the Art Students League in January of 1957, after we got out of Music and Art. We had submitted samples of our work in a city-wide competition, and I think only Andy and me, and a girl from Evander Childs and another girl from a school in Brooklyn were chosen, though I still can't figure why. We really weren't that good. The first day we went to the school, they showed us around the various classes so that we could decide which courses we wanted to take—we were allowed to take two courses—and at the front of one of the classrooms there was what we thought was a white plaster statue of a naked woman until she moved. We both signed up for that course, which was Life Drawing, and we also signed up for Oil Painting. I was lousy with oils. The thing I hated most about them was cleaning up afterwards. The girl from Brooklyn had red hair, and we called her Flatbush. She was always speculating about why a girl would take off her clothes and pose naked. Both Andy and I got the impression that Flatbush would have very much enjoyed taking off her clothes and posing naked. The scholarship ended in June, by which time Andy and I were both jaded by the sight of all those naked women draped on the posing stand, and by which time I had taken the entrance exam for Pratt Institute. I was notified in July that I had been accepted. And in that same month, when Andy insisted that I pay him the dime I'd bet him on the Yankee-White Sox game, I said, "Come on, don't be so niggardly," and he got upset and refused to believe there was such a word and that it meant stingy or cheap or miserly or parsimonious. He said to me, "I knew it would come sooner or later, Jimmy, and you're a son of a bitch." Andy said that to me. Maybe I did mean niggardly, maybe I *really* meant niggardly. Or maybe, accustomed to playing word games almost every night of the week, twisting meanings and spellings and generally slaughtering the language, maybe I was making another pun, and maybe Andy was right to get sore, I don't know.

He went to Cooper Union in September, to study art there, and I never saw him again.

"I think I smell wood burning," Jonah said.

"Yes, indeed," Norman said. "He is thinking very hard, Jonah."

"My brother always used to say he smelled wood burning," Jonah said.

"Can you remember where that 105th came from?" Norman asked.

"No," Driscoll said.

"You've *got* to remember," Jonah said.

"Why? I'm not even being sued. I think I ought to remind you gentlemen of that fact."

"Not serving you was a little gambit Mr. Brackman will come to regret," Jonah said.

"Why wasn't I served?"

"I asked that very same question in a Georgia restaurant once," Norman said, and laughed.

"What did they say?" Driscoll asked.

"They said the cook had gone home."

"*Had* he gone home?"

"Certainly not. The cook was my cousin," Norman said, and laughed again.

"My wife is a Southerner, you know," Driscoll said.

"Yes, I know."

"I don't think she's consciously prejudiced, however," he said, and finished his drink. "Would anyone care for another martini?"

"Only unconsciously?" Norman asked.

"What do you mean?"

"Prejudiced?"

"No, I don't think so. She's a very nice girl, Ebie. Yes. Do you know how she got to be named Ebie?"

"No, how?"

"Edna Belle," Driscoll said.

"Huh?"

"Edna."

"Yes?"

"Belle."

"Yes."

"E and B."

"I don't get it."

"E. B. Ebie."

"That's very clever," Norman said. "Let's have another drink."

"I think we ought to work out this 105th Division," Jonah said.

"The hell with the 105th Division," Driscoll said. "Let Brackman work it out. Why *didn't* he serve me?"

"He was hoping you'd wash your hands of the whole thing."

"I almost did."

"What made you change your mind?"

"I knew Mitchell-Campbell would have brought me in, anyway."

"It's best you joined the action voluntarily," Jonah said.

"Best for whom?"

"For all of us."

"If we win this case, you know . . ." Driscoll started, and then shook his head.

"Yes."

"No, never mind."

"What were you about to say?"

"Nothing. Let's have another drink."

"That's a good idea," Norman said.

"Don't you have to get home?" Jonah asked.

"What's the hurry? You think the rats'll get lonely?"

"Have you got rats?" Driscoll asked.

"Very *large* rats."

"What are their names?" Driscoll asked, and Norman burst out laughing.

"Have you really got rats?" Jonah asked.

"Absolutely."

"You ought to get out of Harlem."

"I can't."

"Why not? You make enough money."

"My mother likes it there."

"*My* mother likes it on West End Avenue," Driscoll said.

"West End Avenue ain't Lenox Avenue," Norman said.

"That's for sure. Hey, waiter, we want another round."

"Listen, we've got to get back to this," Jonah said. "The 105th Division appears in *The Catchpole*, and it also . . ."

"*Catchpole*," Norman corrected. "There is no article. You have been told that several times already, Mr. Willow, and I'll thank you to refer to the play by its proper name."

"Yes, but nonetheless," Jonah said, laughing, "if we can discover how you hit upon that number when you were contemplating your novel, we could—"

"When I was contemplating my *navel*, you mean," Driscoll said.

"That's very clever," Norman said, laughing. "Have you ever tried writing?"

"Too serious a business," Driscoll said.

"Law is a very serious business, too," Norman said. "Let's open a whore house."

"I wish you gentlemen would try to be properly serious," Jonah said. "There's a great deal of stakes here. *At* stakes. *Stake.*"

"Jonah is drunk," Norman said.

"I will concede that, your Honor," Jonah said.

"Thank you," Driscoll said to the waiter, and then lifted his glass. "Gentlemen, I give you the play named *Maypole* and the novel named *The Paper Asshole,* and I defy you—I defy you, gentlemen—to find any real difference between these two *oeuvres,* which is French for eggs. In the play we have a degenerate leper who writes to Dr. Schweitzer, asking how he can cure his vile leching after twelve-year-olds. This same pervert is present in the novel, only this time he writes to Graham Greene for advice, and Greene being an expert only on leprosy advises him to write to Vladimir Nabokov, who is an expert on lechery. The similarity stands. In the novel, on page seventy-four, the girl enters, and she has two breasts—*two* breasts, gentlemen—exactly as in the play. I submit that a girl with two breasts is a unique invention, and I defy you to explain this remarkable coincidence, these footprints left in the sand by the thief. Now, I am not an expert on such matters, but I am willing to bet that the possibility of finding *two* young girls in the same room, both of whom have *two* breasts—gentlemen, this staggers the imagination. That is the plaintiff's case, your Honor, and I drink to it."

"All right, what about this 105th Precinct?" Jonah asked briskly.

"Division."

"Yes, what about it?"

"It's there," Driscoll said.

"Where?"

"In my book."

"It's also in the play," Jonah said. "So how about it?"

"How about it? *It's* there, and *we're* here, so the hell with it."

"I wish you could explain it," Jonah said. "I seriously wish you could explain it."

"I won't."

"What?"

"I said I can't."

"You said you won't."

"I meant I can't."

"Jimmy," Norman said, "do you *know* why you labeled your division the 105th?"

Driscoll looked across the table and said, "No, I do not. And that's the God's honest truth."

As the big jet orbited Kennedy in a holding pattern, Ralph Knowles wondered if the field were still open, and once again conjured an image of the giant airliner skidding around on the runway as it braked to a stop. The forecasters early that afternoon had reported heavy snowstorms all along the Eastern seaboard, and he had called Kessler collect from the Coast to ask whether it was still imperative that he come east today.

"Can't it wait till tomorrow?" he had asked. "I don't want to die in a goddamn airplane skidding around in the snow."

"That's not funny, either," Kessler had said. "Do me a Knowles hadn't been trying to make a joke. "You will probably be called to testify tomorrow afternoon, so you get on that plane and come east like a good boy, and stop worrying about a little snow."

"It's a *lot* of snow, from what I hear," Ralph said.

"They always exaggerate out there," Kessler answered. "It's to make you appreciate California."

"But is it still snowing?"

"Just a little."

"Well then maybe . . ."

"Ralph, this trial is important," Kessler said. "Now you just get on that plane—what plane are you getting on?"

"The four-thirty flight."

"You just get on it, and let me worry about the snow."

"I knew you could move mountains," Ralph said, "but I didn't know you could also stop snow."

"That's not funny, either," Kessler had said. "Do me a favor, and don't ever direct a comedy for us."

He could see lights below. It was never like Los Angeles, where the approach to the city was beautiful, truly beautiful, reds and greens and whites spilled across the landscape, he sometimes felt like weeping as the plane banked in over the airport, not the same here at all. He had never liked New York City, too damn big and dirty, noisy people rushing around all the time, business deals over breakfast and lunch and cocktails and dinner, no nice backyard barbecues, never any sunshine, rotten place New York, he hated it.

He shouldn't be coming here now, either, should be going in the opposite direction to meet Matt Jackson in Japan where they'd be shooting the new picture, not coming east to testify at a stupid trial, as if the trial meant anything anyway. Specious case according to what he'd heard at the studio, absolutely groundless, should have kicked it out of court, bring a man all the way east for something as dumb as this, waste of time. Only reason he was bothering was because Kessler seemed to be making an important thing of it, couldn't antagonize Kessler, not now, not when the Samurai picture was going to cost so much. Had to hold hands with the old man, six million dollars wasn't cornflakes.

The stewardess was walking up the aisle checking seatbelts, nice knockers on her, Ralph thought, how would you like me to film those beauties, honey, in wide-screen Technicolor, she doesn't even know who I am. It disturbed him that nobody ever knew who the hell he was. He always got the choice seat on a plane only because API's transportation department made sure of it, but every time he boarded the plane he could see the disappointed look on the face of the stewardess. Since API had reserved the seat, the airlines people always expected a movie star or a director they could recognize, like Hitchcock or Huston or Preminger. He knew he was a better director than any of them, but who ever recognized his face, nobody. Or, for that matter, did anyone outside the industry even recognize his *name*, seventeen movies to his credit, all of them hits, well, most of them. Anyway, ten of them. Ten resounding box-office successes, shattering spectacle *Variety* had called one of them, and this Samurai thing would undoubtedly be another big blockbuster, provided Kessler didn't balk at the six million price tag, well why should he? He wanted a hit, didn't he? Everybody in America, everybody in the world wanted a hit, I know how to deliver hits, Ralph thought, ten of them in a row, twelve if you count the critical but not box-office bonanzas, you have to spend money to make money, Kessler knows that, he'll be very sweet about the whole thing, he's a sweet old Jew bastard. God, this trial is a pain in the ass, should be heading for Tokyo, wonder if Matt has set everything up, those Japanese do good work, even Kurosawa has his face in the magazines more than I do. Open any magazine, there's *Huston* grinning up at you, it makes me want to puke. Hitchcock? don't even mention him. Supposed to begin shooting next week, can't be wasting all this time in New York, still I'll talk to Kessler about the money, getting the money is important.

"Why aren't we landing?" he asked the stewardess. "Is there snow on the field?"

"No, sir."

"There's snow on the field, isn't there?" he whispered. "You can tell me."

"No, sir, there are just several airplanes ahead of us, that's all."

"That's all, huh?"

"Yes, sir."

"How old are you?"

"Twenty-two, sir."

"That's a good age."

"For what?"

"For anything."

"Are you going to put me in pictures?" she asked, and then smiled and went up the aisle to talk to the other stewardess.

Bet she knows who I am, Ralph thought. What the hell, I'm not *that* anonymous. Maybe she saw the article they did on me in the *Saturday Evening Post,* the one that had that good shot of me when we were on location down there near Juarez, man it gets hot as hell down there in Mexico, those mules, what a stink. Must have seen that piece on me, the shot wearing the white ducks, bare-chested, all brown, the gray hair, that was a good picture of me. Have to ask her what her name is, look her up maybe, show her a good time. Must know who I am, otherwise why the crack about putting her in pictures, I'll put you someplace all right, baby.

They were coming down.

Ralph caught his breath, certain the field would be

covered with snow, no matter what anybody said. The descent seemed very rapid, they never did it this way in Los Angeles. The stewardess was hurrying down the aisle again, he wondered what her name was, too fast, this damn plane was coming down too fast.

"Miss?" he said.

"I'm sorry, sir, I have to take a seat now," the stewardess answered.

"Aren't we coming down too fast?"

"No, sir."

"What's your name?"

"I have to take a seat now."

"I'll talk to you when we land."

"All right."

"You've got great knockers," he whispered.

"I know," she whispered back, and then walked forward to take a seat in the lounge.

This was the worst part of any flight, it scared him senseless. Closer and closer to the ground, he could see buildings capped with thick snow now, were they sure none of it was on the field, everything blurring as the plane leveled, the bump of the wheels, and then the noise of the jets as the engines were reversed, the sudden lurch of the plane slowing, "We have landed at Kennedy International Airport," the stewardess said, "please remain seated until we have taxied to the terminal building and all engines are stopped. The temperature in New York is thirty-seven degrees, and the local time is twelve-seventeen A.M. Thank you for flying with us. We hope to serve you again in the future."

I hope to serve *you* in the *very* near future, Ralph thought, and kept watching her as the plane taxied. Before he left the aircraft, he asked her what her name was and where she stayed in New York. She told him her name was Sylvia Mott, and she was engaged to a boy in Pasadena, and she never dated anyone else, but it had been a pleasure flying with him, nonetheless, and she really hoped she *could* serve him again in the future.

"Thanks a lot," Ralph said, and went down the steps and walked to the baggage pickup area.

Sam Genitori was waiting there for him, small consolation.

By one o'clock that morning, the snow had stopped completely, and Hester Miers took off her shoes and went walking barefoot in the plaza outside the Seagram Building, parading past the pools and the small lighted Christmas trees. Arthur was not terribly surprised.

He was not surprised because she had been exhibiting all through supper this same phony *joie de vivre,* the single identifying characteristic of any actress he had ever met. The quality was deceptive at first. He had recognized it only belatedly in Eileen Curtis, the young lady who had played Lieutenant Diane Foster in *Catchpole.* There had been a curiosity about Eileen, a vitality, an intense concern that was contagious and inspiring. He could never be in her presence without feeling a pang of envy—God, if only *he* could be as concerned with life and living, if only *he* could bring such minute scrutiny to matters large and small, finding everyone interesting and alive, glowing with excitement at each suggested idea or phrase or isolated word, taking up the banner for any worthy cause, burning with energy, searching and working and learning and living, secure in the knowledge that this was the chosen profession, humbly grateful for the opportunity to be allowed to carry on this illuminating, sacrificing, enriching, and dedicated work.

He learned later on the Coast—where he was surrounded day and night by an intolerable army of actors and actresses— that Eileen Curtis's seeming love affair with life had merely been a love affair with herself. The same enormous ego and delicately executed phoniness were evident in Hester Miers, who squealed in delight over the crispness of the seeded rolls and smacked her lips over the "summer sweetness" of the butter, and then secretly asked him to observe the magnificent topaz brooch on the old lady at the next table, and then flirted with the waitress (the *waitress!*), using her humble and ingratiating Famous Actress smile, and then cooed over the marvelous glowing green of the Heineken bottle, and then asked Arthur if he believed in astrology, and then put five lumps of sugar in her coffee ("I *adore* it sweet, but I never stir it") and then asked the doorman outside whether it was still snowing, and to his respectful, "It stopped a half-hour ago, miss," replied in mystic meaningfulness, "Good, because it's only fair, you know," and then of course took off her shoes and hiked up her skirts and went running barefoot in the snow, "Oh, Arthur, it's deliciously cold."

This is the girl, he thought, who is supposed to play Carol, the simple daughter of an honest Bronx mailman. This is the girl.

He would have said good night to her then and there—oh, perhaps he would have helped her dry her feet, he was after all a gentleman—were it not for the fact that the presence of Hester Miers in his play would insure the capitalization. Had not Oscar Stern himself, cigar compressed between his lips, shivering in the alley of the Helen Hayes, replied only yesterday in answer to a foolish question, "Because if we can get Hester Miers to take this part, we'll raise all the money for the play immediately," had not the unquestionable Oscar said those very words only yesterday?

Yesterday was yesterday, of course, dead and gone. Yesterday the trial had begun, and by Thursday or Friday it would be concluded—but who knew when the judge would give his decision? If the judge said, "Why, yes, my son, you have been wronged, good Arthur Constantine," then he could tell Selig and Stern and even Hester Miers—who was romping in the snow now with her skirts up, fully aware that her legs were long and excellently shaped but trying to give the impression nonetheless of a six-year-old abandoning herself to her first wintry experience—he could tell all of them to go straight to hell because he would be in actual possession of, or at least in loan-acquiring promise of, ten million dollars or more. His hands began trembling.

Don't think about it, he told himself. You may *lose* this damn trial, stranger things have happened, don't even think about it. If you get Hester Miers, you get the money for the play, the play goes on, that's all you have to know. Don't think about the other, there's no fairness in this world, you learned that the night the critics killed *Catchpole* and Freddie Gerard began crying like a baby, "Why can't I bring in a winner, Arthur, why can't I ever bring in a winner?" Don't think about winning the trial, think only about getting Hester for the part. Think only about getting Hester.

She had admitted to being twenty-five years old, but Arthur suspected she was something closer to thirty. She was a tall, slender girl (she claimed she ate only one meal a day) with blond hair cut very close to her head in a haphazard coiffure, deliberately unkempt, and lending a look of overall unpredictability to her face. She was not a beautiful girl, nor could he even find anything terribly attractive about her, except perhaps her coltish legs. Her face was an elongated oval, her eyes brown and highlighted with black liner, her lipstick a pale orange on a mouth too generous for the rest of her features. A nose job had apparently been performed on her some time ago, but it was beginning to fall out of shape, and it gave her face a faintly lopsided look. She was definitely not pretty, and he was disappointed by her looks, but he kept reminding himself that she possessed a vibrant, almost luminous quality on stage, even though she looked like some kind of a jackass now, galloping around in the snow that way.

When she finally came over to him again, out of breath and flushed, he said, "What seems to be troubling you about the part?"

"Oh, I don't know."

"Well, *something* is."

"Oh, sure, something is."

"Well, what?"

"I don't know." Hester sat on the edge of the pool. The lighted Christmas trees behind her put a high gloss on her blond hair. She took a small lace-edged handkerchief from her bag, crossed her legs, and ineffectually began drying them.

"I think it's a perfect part for you," Arthur said.

"You do?"

"Certainly."

"I don't know."

"Really, Hester."

"Well, I don't know. You still haven't explained it to me. I wish you'd explain it to me," she said, and in the same breath added, "How tall are you?"

"Five-ten," Arthur said. "Seriously, Hester, I don't think Lincoln Center would object to your leaving. Not for a part like this one."

"I'm not sure about that," she answered. "Do you have a handkerchief?"

"Yes." He took a handkerchief from his breast pocket, unfolded it, and handed it to her.

"Thank you," she said. "I don't think Kazan liked me very much, but things are different now. I'm not sure they'd let me go just like that."

"It's a matter of how much you want the part, I guess," Arthur ventured.

"Yes, of course."

"So if there are any problems about it, I wish you'd tell me what they are."

"Oh, I don't know," Hester said, and rose suddenly, picking up her shoes in one hand, returning Arthur's handkerchief with the other, and then walking down the steps and onto Park Avenue barefooted, the shoes swinging at the end of her arm. Arthur took a deep breath, hesitated alongside the pool for a moment, and then followed her.

"This is the greatest street in the world," Hester said. "Tell me about Carol."

"Where do you want me to begin?"

"Where is she from?"

"The Bronx. That's pretty clear in the—"

"Do you know where I'm from?"

"No."

"Originally?"

"No, where?"

"You won't believe it."

"Try me," he said.

"Seattle, Washington. How about that?"

"Really?"

"Yes. My father was a lumberjack. Do you know you can get mugged on this street at this hour of the night, and your body dumped in the river?"

"No, I didn't know that. Carol . . ."

"A boy I know got mugged on Fifth Avenue, would you believe it?"

". . . is a girl who feels—"

"He was one of the gypsies in *Hello, Dolly*. This was after the show broke. He lived, I don't know, on 48th Street, I guess, and he was walking down Fifth Avenue, and these hoods jumped him. This city . . ."

"The Bronx is different, you know. Carol grew up in a neighborhood . . ."

"It's not *too* different really. You read about Bronx muggings all the time, don't you just love these reminders, 'Just a Drop in the Basket,' they really gas me."

The hell with it, Arthur thought, the goddamn rotten hell with it.

"You know what?" he said.

"What?"

"Actresses give me a severe pain in the ass," he said.

"Oh, really?" Hester said, and shrugged, and ran up the street to the corner, her arms raised winglike, the shoes dangling from one hand. "Oh, it's *marrr*-velous!" she shrieked. "Snow is *marrrrvelous!*"

Arthur walked slowly to the corner. There were lighted Christmas trees on the islands dividing the avenue, lighted trees perched on the marquee of the Sheraton-East, enormous wreaths hanging from the buildings, blues and greens reflecting on the snow. There was no wind, and the city was hushed. He felt like weeping.

"Would you like to know why actresses give me a severe pain?" he said angrily.

"In the ass," Hester amended. "You forgot in the ass."

"A severe pain in the ass, thank you. Would you like to know why?"

"No," Hester said. "I'll bet you always got the prettiest girl in the class, didn't you?"

"What?"

"You. Did you always get the prettiest girl?"

"What the hell are you talking about?"

"In your class."

"No, I always got the ugliest one," Arthur said.

"Do you think *I'm* pretty?"

"Not particularly."

"I have beautiful legs."

"Hester, do you want this goddamn part or not?"

"I *know* I have beautiful legs."

"Who *cares* about your legs?"

"You're not telling me anything I don't already know. In fact, you're boring me. Do you want to discuss your play, or do you want to go home?"

"I want to go home," Arthur said.

"Good night," she answered, and turned left on 52nd Street.

"No, wait a minute," he said.

"No, go home," she said. "Really, I'm bored to death. I was offered a part in a play by William Inge, did you know that? Just two weeks ago."

"No, I didn't know that."

"I could have had *After the Fall*, too, in spite of Kazan. I just didn't think it was right for me. But I could have had it."

"You'd have been terrible," Arthur said.

"That's beside the point. I could have had it if I wanted it. They think very highly of me at the Rep."

"I think very highly of you right here."

"Cut it out," she said.

"Cut *what* out?"

"When I was a struggling young actress, longer ago than I care to remember, a wise old lady said to me, 'Hester baby, don't ever ball a writer, a director, or a producer. It won't get you the part.' I followed her advice, and now I don't *have* to ball writers, directors, or producers."

"Who do you have to ball *now?*" Arthur asked.

"Don't get smart."

"I'm sorry, but I think I'm missing your point."

"My point is don't come on with me."

"I didn't know I was."

"You were," Hester said, "and the answer is no. Give me your arm, I want to put on my shoes." She caught his arm at the elbow and, leaning against him, put on first one shoe and then the other. "What are you smiling about?" she asked.

"Nothing."

"I don't like people who get dumb smiles on their face. How tall did you say you were?"

"Five-ten."

"That's short."

"It's not so short."

"It's short. I'm five-eight."

"Where do you live, Hester?"

"Over there someplace," she said, and gestured vaguely uptown. "In my stocking feet. I'm a very tall girl."

"I live on Fifty-fourth and Third," Arthur said.

"So?"

"Why don't we go there?"

"What for?"

"I'm cold."

"I'm not."

"We can discuss the play there."

"We can discuss it right here."

"Anyway, I'd like a drink."

"I know what you'd like."

"What would I like?"

"You'd like to jump right into bed with me."

"No, I only . . ."

"Forget it."

". . . want to discuss the play someplace where it's warm."

"If you want to discuss it, discuss it here."

"Okay."

"And stop smiling like that."

"Okay."

"Do you want me to play the part?"

"Yes."

"I don't believe you. I don't believe your character, and I don't believe you, either."

"Okay."

"Stop smiling. I don't even know if it's such a good play."

"It's a good play, believe me."

"Sure, you wrote it."

"It's still a good play, no matter who wrote it."

"I think it's a confusing play."

"It's real."

"My part is confusing."

"Your part?"

"The girl. Carol."

"She's honest."

"That's what's confusing."

"That's what's real."

"I don't know anybody like her."

"I do."

"She's impossible to play. I don't even *understand* her."

"I understand everything about her."

"Then *you* play her."

"No, you play her, Hester."

"I wouldn't know where to begin. Besides, why should I? Your last play was a flop."

"So was yours."

"That was before Lincoln Center."

"It was still a flop."

"I got rave notices."

"The critics hated the play."

"That doesn't mean it was bad."

"It closed, didn't it?"

"That wasn't my fault."

"Of course not, Hester. In New York, it's never the actor's fault."

"You're talking like a writer."

"What *should* I talk like?"

"You're being defensive and hostile . . ."

"But honest."

"Besides, the critics loved me."

"The hell with the critics."

"Oh, sure, the hell with them, I agree. But they loved me. Did you see the play?"

"Yes."

"Didn't *you* love me?"

"I loved you."

"You're lying."

"No, I'm being honest."

"Whenever I meet anybody who claims he's honest, I run and hide the family jewels. You just want me in your play, that's all."

"Is that all?"

"What else?"

"You're right, Hester."

"What?"

"About what else I want."

"I'm always right about what men want."

"I'd like to . . ."

"Stop working so hard," she said. She looked at him steadily. "You turned me on at least ten minutes ago."

. . . knew then I wanted to be an actress, and that nothing else would ever satisfy me, no wait here, I want to check. I have a woman sleeping in, you know, I think it's all right, yes, her door is closed. I put a television set in her room, one of those little GE's, do you know them? If she's awake I can hear the set going. I'll put the light on when we get upstairs, watch the flowerpot on the bottom step. Do you really like my legs, you never *did* say you liked them, you know. My bedroom is at the other end of the hall, there's a little wrought iron balcony that overlooks the backyard, there are dozens of daffodils in bloom in the spring, I go out every morning to say hello to them. I put them in myself last year, the bulbs. A boy dying of leukemia sent them to me, he wrote the nicest letter. His parents had taken him to see me downtown, knowing he was going to die and all, they own a seed order business upstate. He sent me the daffodil bulbs later, with this marvelous letter telling me what a dazzling actress he thought I was, and how beautiful, do you think I'm beautiful? I planted them myself last fall. I bought one of those tools, it's a hollow circle you press into the earth, it makes the hole just the right depth, and I planted them all one afternoon, there were four dozen of them. They came in a specially protected bag, you should see them now, they're gorgeous. I go out to look at them each morning in the spring, and I feel the world is coming alive, even though that poor lovely little boy is probably dead by now, leukemia, what a terrible thing. I wrote him a nice thank-you note, I hope he died happy, give me your hand, it's this way.

I don't want to put the light on, do you mind? Let's just sit here by the window. I bought this loveseat in London at the Portobello market, do you like it, it's red velvet, you can't see the color in the dark, I know, but it's the most brilliant red, and really in excellent condition. It's a genuine antique, you know, the man gave me papers for it and everything, sit here, are you comfortable? I sometimes sit here by the window and look out at the city and try to superimpose London on it, those marvelous little slate roofs, and the chimney pots, and the London sounds. I try to transport them here. I knew a very wonderful man in London, he was a correspondent for the B.B.C., they came to interview the cast one day. This was two summers ago, the weather was so marvelously sunny and bright, so rare for London, so rare. I was there with *The Alchemist*, which was like carrying coals to Newcastle, I suppose, but they seemed to love it. The critics said I was radiant, I adore the English, don't you adore the English? He had a mustache, this man in London, a big bristling cavalry mustache, and very blue English eyes, and that florid complexion all Englishmen seem to have, that fine aquiline nose, very much like your nose, Arthur, you're not English, are you? We had tea at the Stafford, and I told him all about myself, I am Hester Miers, I said, I've been acting since the time I was sixteen and won a high school contest sponsored by KJR in Seattle, well not quite *all* about myself, I've never told anyone everything about myself, do you mind the dark? I love to make the room dark. When the drapes are closed, the blackness, try to see my eyes in the dark, Arthur. Put your face very close to mine, can you see my eyes? Kiss me.

In Clovelly, you can walk miles down to the sea, a cobbled path goes down the side of the cliff, it's teeming with Englishmen on holiday.

He took me there one weekend and bought me a dish of ice cream from an old man in one of the shops, Bed and Breakfast the signs all say. He got stung by a bee while we lay in the grass on the side of the hill, the weather still so beautifully mild and bright, we lay in the high grass, and the bee flew into his open collar and stung him on the back of his neck. Oh, you should have seen him fuss, the big baby, ranting and shouting, you'd think he was about to die, I couldn't stop laughing, Arthur, it was *so* funny. On the way to Dorset, we drove up Porlock Hill, do you know what heather looks like? The hill was covered with heather, and sheep grazing, and we got out of the car and looked out over the sea, with the wind howling, I hugged my sweater around me. I was wearing a blue cashmere I'd bought in Birmingham in the Ring, have you ever been there, it's a science-fiction city, you must touch me, Arthur. George Bernard Shaw had one of his plays done there for the first time, at the Birmingham Rep, that was before the bombings, touch me everywhere.

Is it really a good part, Arthur? I read a play nowadays, and I can't tell anymore, it used to be so easy. When I was hungry, *every* part was a good part, and I wanted them all, I wanted to play every woman ever invented. And now I can't tell anymore, do you know how old I am? I'm twenty-five years old, did I tell you that? How old is Carol supposed to be, she's younger than that, isn't she? Are you really sure you want me to take the part? Arthur, I hope you don't think, Oh God, you're so warm, I hope you don't think there's a connection, I hope you haven't got it in your mind that this has anything to do with whether I play the part or not, because it doesn't. It wouldn't matter, it *doesn't* matter, oooh, what are you doing, I *love* it, there's no connection between this and the play, don't you see, this is something *else*. She's so young, how could I play a girl so young, is she supposed to be a virgin? He said I had no breasts, in Ohio this was, do you like my breasts? I was playing summer stock there, I was only seventeen. The moment he said it my nipples began to show through my sweater, and he knew, oh *boy* did he know, he was a very wise old bastard, he knew from the first day the summer began. He made love to me on the floor of the theater, upstairs where we used to paint the flats, we could hear them rehearsing down below, they were doing *Winterset,* the girl playing Mariamne was having trouble with her lines, she kept repeating them over and over again while he made love to me, oh God I was *so* excited, I was only a *girl,* Arthur, I was only seventeen. I really *don't* know about this play of yours or the confused girl in it, it's driving me crazy, I *mean* it, she is *really* a very confused person. Oh, I admit it would be a challenge, don't misunderstand me, the smell of the paint and Mariamne's lines, *And I came back because I must see you again. And we danced together and my heart hurt me,* I learned the part that afternoon, what a *long* afternoon, but I can't remember his name, isn't that funny? I'd just hate to accept your play and then disappoint you, I couldn't bear that, Arthur, disappointing anyone. I can't bear failing anyone. If I thought my note to that poor lovely boy, do I excite you, that poor lovely boy with leukemia, do I excite you very much, had failed him, well I just couldn't bear the thought, give me your cock. You have a big beautiful cock.

WEDNESDAY

8

IT WAS A CAST-IRON DAY, bitter and brooding, with fierce winds lashing the streets, and dark clouds menacing the city. Sometime during the night the temperature had plummeted to six above zero, and the freshly fallen snow had hardened to form a thick, impenetrable crust. By morning, the situation had scarcely improved, the temperature hovering in the teens, the wind keening over ice-covered streets, solemn clouds above threatening further snow.

The courtroom was sunless and dim. Gusts of wind shuddered along the length of each long high window, rattling the panes. A cold hard light streamed through the windows, draining the wood-paneled walls of their luster, tinting the room and its occupants a solemn gray. Even Chester Danton, pink-faced and pink-pated, seemed to lose some of his high flushed color as his name was called and he walked from the jury box to the witness chair. Jonah watched him as he moved into the aura of harsh light spilling through the windows. He was a rotund little man with fierce black eyebrows and a hooked nose. He wore a brown suit, and he walked with a rolling gait, pausing and then pulling up his trouser leg to preserve the crease as he climbed onto the stand and turned to face the clerk. Jonah's wrist was hurting him. Tiny darts of pain radiated from the bones into his arm, triggering memories of the accident, and then of Sally, and

then of the little Egyptian and his flaring anger against the
man, his murderous anger. In the jury box, James Driscoll sat
with his wife, both of them intently watching Danton as he
raised his hand preparatory to taking the oath.

". . . whole truth and nothing but the truth, so help you
God?"

"I do," Danton said.

Jonah massaged his right wrist, and then rose from behind
the defense table to walk toward Danton, who sat expectantly, his bushy brows lowered, his dark eyes glowering
beneath them.

"What do you do for a living, Mr. Danton?" he asked.

"I work for Mitchell-Campbell Books."

"What do you do there?"

"I'm an editor."

"And your title?"

"Executive vice-president."

"Did you work for Mitchell-Campbell in July of 1962?"

"I did."

"In the same capacity?"

"Yes, sir."

"Had you ever heard of James Driscoll before July of
1962?"

"No, sir."

"Or seen any of his work?"

"No, sir."

"When was the first time you saw anything written by
James Driscoll?"

"In July of 1962."

"What was this writing?"

"A hundred pages of a novel in progress, together with an
outline of the remainder of the novel."

"And the title?"

"*The Enemy.*"

Jonah nodded and walked back to the defense table. Norman handed him a sheet of paper which he carried back to
the witness chair with him. "Mr. Danton, would you look at
this, please?" he said, and offered the sheet to Danton, who

glanced at it summarily, and then looked up at Jonah again.

"Would you please tell the Court what this is," Jonah said.

"It's an editorial report form used by Mitchell-Campbell Books."

"Was it in use in 1962?"

"Yes, and still is."

"In this identical style and shape?"

"Yes, identical."

"What is its purpose?"

"There are a great many people at Mitchell-Campbell who read manuscripts. Each person so doing is required to record his or her reaction to the manuscript on a form such as this one."

"Does this particular form refer to a specific manuscript?"

"Yes, it refers to James Driscoll's partial novel *The Enemy*, and it is dated July 12, 1962. The novel came in over the transom and was sent directly to me, and this is my first report on it."

"By 'over the transom' you mean . . ."

"I mean it was simply mailed to Mitchell-Campbell Books, without being addressed to any specific person in the company."

"Is it usual for a manuscript to come immediately to the attention of an executive vice-president?"

"No, the first readings are usually made by others in the company. But I had edited several war novels for the firm, and it was assumed I would have special interest in a novel of this sort. I imagine that's why it was directed to me."

"You said a hundred pages . . ."

"I see the number of pages is listed in the report. It was ninety-eight pages."

"Of a novel titled *The Enemy*."

"Yes."

"Did this later become *The Paper Dragon?*"

"Yes, sir."

"I would like to offer this in evidence," Jonah said, and handed a copy of the report to Brackman.

Brackman glanced at it, and then said, "I do not see its relevance, your Honor."

"If your Honor please—"

"We already know that it's a report on Mr. Driscoll's novel. I don't see—"

"The plaintiff has claimed, your Honor, that *The Paper Dragon* was pirated from the play *Catchpole*. By tracing the development of the book, I intend to show that there was independent creation."

"Is this offer being made . . ." McIntyre began.

"This offer, your Honor, is being made to show that there were no special or mysterious circumstances surrounding the submission, the editing, or the subsequent development of the novel written by James Driscoll. We have already heard that the book came in 'over the transom,' addressed to no specific person in the company, and that it was treated as any other submission might have been, in accordance with the normal business procedure at Mitchell-Campbell Books."

"Mr. Brackman may wish you to explore this 'normal business procedure,' " McIntyre said.

"No, that won't be necessary," Brackman said. "I am ready to concede that editorial reports are the normal business of a publishing firm."

"Very well," McIntyre said.

"I am not objecting to whether or not this was normal procedure."

"What is your objection, Mr. Brackman?"

"Only that it is irrelevant, your Honor."

"Well, I will admit the report," McIntyre said. "Is it dated, Mr. Willow?"

"It is, your Honor. The date on it is July 12, 1962, but the content of the report states that the manuscript was received on July ninth."

"Mark it 'Defendants' Exhibit C,' " the clerk said.

"You have stated that you wrote this report," Jonah said.

"Yes," Danton replied.

"What did you do with the manuscript after you wrote this report?"

"I sent it to Miss Anita Lang."

"Who is Miss Lang?"

"She's an editor at Mitchell-Campbell Books."

"You sent it to her for her opinion?"

"Yes, and for subsequent transmittal to Mr. Campbell for a final decision."

"What was your own opinion?"

"I felt we should publish the book."

"Did Miss Lang make a report on the book?"

"She did."

"I ask you to look at this, Mr. Danton, and tell me what it is."

Danton took the extended sheet of paper, glanced at it, and said, "This is Miss Lang's report on the book, and I see that Mr. Campbell has indicated on it that he is to see the manuscript at once. The report is dated July 16th."

"You are familiar with Mr. Campbell's handwriting?"

"I am. That's his handwriting."

"And is this paper the actual editorial report made by Miss Lang?"

"It is."

"A report which, similar to yours, was part of the normal business procedure at Mitchell-Campbell Books."

"Yes, sir. We regularly get several opinions on any book thought to be a publishing possibility."

"I offer it in evidence," Jonah said.

"I object as before," Brackman said.

"Overruled," McIntyre answered.

"Mark it 'Defendants' Exhibit D in evidence' " the clerk said.

"Was the manuscript eventually sent on to Mr. Campbell, together with the reports by yourself and Miss Lang?"

"That's right."

"Did Mr. Campbell subsequently comment on the novel?"

"He did."

"Incidentally, is this 'Mr. Campbell' the president of Mitchell-Campbell Books—Leonard Campbell?"

"Yes."

"I ask you to look at this, Mr. Danton, and tell me what it is."

"It's the memorandum Mr. Campbell sent to me after he read the Driscoll novel."

"I offer it in evidence."

"Objection."

"Overruled."

"Mark it 'Defendants' Exhibit E in evidence.' "

"Now, Mr. Danton, I would like you to refer to Miss Lang's report on the novel. There's a paragraph in it that's marked with a pencil and then with the words 'Good suggestion.' Do you see that paragraph?"

"Just a moment," Danton said. He reached into his jacket pocket, took out a pair of eyeglasses, and settled them on the bridge of his nose. Then he studied the report and said, "Yes, I have it now."

"Can you identify the handwriting in the margin?"

"I can. It's my handwriting."

"Would you read that paragraph to the court, and explain what you meant by your penciled comment?"

Danton cleared his throat and then began reading. " 'However, one thing that does not seem well-motivated (in this initial segment, at least) is Colman's instantaneous dislike of the hero, which triggers the squad's subsequent resistance to his attempts at reaching them. Since the novel gathers its impetus from the Colman-Cooper conflict, I found it implausible that these men would be so immediately antagonistic to each other. Can't there be a stronger motivation for their hatred? It seems to me this certainly requires deeper thought from Driscoll.' " Danton looked up. "That's the second paragraph of her report," he said. "And in the margin, as you pointed out, I scribbled the words 'Good suggestion,' and of course initialed it 'CD' for Chester Danton."

"You agreed with Miss Lang that there was not sufficient motivation for hating the lieutenant?"

"Yes, I agreed with her, as I indicated in my marginal note."

"The novel did *not* contain this motivation?"

"Not when we first received it."

"Does it now?"

"Yes, it does."

"Was it Miss Lang's suggestion that this motivation be added?"

"Yes."

"And was it added?"

"Yes."

"In what way?"

"I suggested to Mr. Driscoll that perhaps the squad's attachment to their previous commanding officer made them unable to accept his replacement."

"When did you make this suggestion?"

"I don't remember the exact date. It was certainly during our first meeting about the book."

"*Whose* first meeting?"

"The first editorial meeting I had with Mr. Driscoll."

"Did you enlarge upon the suggestion in any way?"

"Yes. I proposed the idea that the former commanding officer be a major who'd been killed by a sniper."

"This was your suggestion?"

"Yes."

"Did this major exist in the novel when it was first delivered to you?"

"No, sir, he was not in the novel."

"He was added after you met Mr. Driscoll?"

"Yes, sir."

"Are you aware that the plaintiff claims as a specific similarity the fact that a man is killed by a sniper in his play, and a man is killed by a sniper in Mr. Driscoll's novel?"

"Yes, I am aware of that."

"But you have just testified that the man being killed by a sniper was your idea and not Mrs. Driscoll's."

"That is correct."

"Did you ever see the play *Catchpole* when it was produced in New York?"

"I did not."

"It was produced in October of 1947, opening on the 14th,

and closing on the 25th. Can you tell us where you were at that time?"

"Yes, sir. I was in England."

"Doing what?"

"I was handling subsidiary rights for Mitchell-Campbell at that time, and part of my duties involved arranging for the foreign publication of titles on our list. I went to England at the beginning of October that year, and I did not return until November 28th."

"You were out of the United States from October 1st to November 28th, is that correct?"

"October 3rd, I believe it was."

"And did not see the production of Mr. Constantine's play?"

"I did not see Mr. Constantine's play."

"Prior to the beginning of this action, had you ever read *Catchpole?*"

"No, sir."

"Had you ever met or heard of the plaintiff, Arthur Constantine?"

"No, sir."

"Did anyone other than yourself have anything to do with the editing of James Driscoll's book?"

"Outside of these several memorandums from Miss Lang and Mr. Campbell, the editor-author relationship was solely between Mr. Driscoll and me."

"And so it was you alone who suggested that the major be killed by a sniper, and that the squad's attachment to him form the basis of their subsequent hatred of Lieutenant Alex Cooper."

"Yes, sir, the suggestion was mine alone."

"Did you have any other editorial suggestions to make?"

"Well, the remarkable thing about the book was that it was so good and so fully realized that there were very few suggestions an editor *could* make."

"Your Honor," Brackman said, "the answer is unresponsive."

"Mr. Danton . . ."

"I made very few editorial comments, except for suggesting a new title."

"What was the title on the manuscript as it was submitted?"

"*The Enemy.*"

"Were any other titles subsequently considered?"

"Yes. One suggestion was *The Other Enemy,* but this was discarded."

"Who suggested that the title be changed to *The Paper Dragon?*"

"I did."

"You made this suggestion directly to Mr. Driscoll?"

"I did."

"When was that?"

"I don't recall the exact date. We'd been trying for a new title all along, and I believe the idea for this one came to me while Jimmy was still working on the book. I called him, and we discussed it on the telephone."

"What was the nature of the discussion?"

"The discussion concerned the theme of the book. It has since been universally accepted as an indictment of the United States Army, a bitter treatise against war. It seemed to me, however, that this was not Mr. Driscoll's intention. I thought he was attempting to show that—"

"Your Honor, Mr. Willow earlier objected to the relevancy of what a writer was *attempting* to show as opposed to what he actually *did* show. I make the same objection now."

"Mr. Danton is repeating a discussion he had with Mr. Driscoll. I believe the title of the book pertains to the theme, your Honor, and as such is relevant."

"Overruled. Proceed, Mr. Willow."

"You were saying, Mr. Danton?"

"That Jimmy . . . Mr. Driscoll did not perhaps realize what the *real* theme of his book was. This very often happens with writers. It seemed to me, though, that this was a book about, well, I deplore clichés, but it was certainly a book about man's inhumanity to man. When I suggested this to Jimmy, he seemed surprised. But it was then that I suggested

The Other Enemy, meaning not the *enemy* enemy, but the enemy that is in all men, do you see?"

"How did the idea for the present title come to you?"

"*The Paper Dragon?*"

"Yes."

"The term 'paper dragon' is familiar to most writers and editors. It's used to denote a story problem that is really nonexistent."

"Would you explain further?"

"Well, let's assume a man comes home reeking of perfume. His wife immediately suspects that he has been seeing another woman, and this creates the conflict, which in turn provokes a series of plot complications, and at last a resolution. The explanation, of course, is that the man had been buying perfume for his wife, and the salesgirl sprayed a little on him—in short, a paper dragon, a nonexistent problem. If the wife had come right out and asked her husband about it, and if he had explained, there would be no conflict, and of course no story."

"A paper dragon is, then, a nonexistent problem or conflict."

"Yes. But this doesn't prevent a lot of people from becoming energetically involved in the series of events it triggers. It's a specious literary device."

"Why did you suggest this title for Mr. Driscoll's novel?"

"I suggested it on various levels. To begin with, his novel deals with that period of time when the Chinese were coming into Korea in force, and I thought the title would indicate that the book was, after all, about war with the Chinese. Secondly, using it in an allusive sense, I thought it would indicate that the Chinese army was only a paper dragon, whereas the *real* enemy, the *real* dragon was man's innate cruelty. And lastly, I thought it would clearly label Colman's fake and private war against our hero, the conflict he constructs out of whole cloth, the way he turns the other men against Cooper, the whole chain of events based on a problem that need not have existed in the first place, a paper dragon."

"And what happened when you suggested this title to Mr. Driscoll?"

"He liked it."

"And it was decided that this title would be used on the published novel?"

"Yes."

"To get back for a moment, after your first talk with Mr. Driscoll—you said it was in July of 1962—did you then offer him a contract for the publication of his novel?"

"Yes."

"Is this the contract you sent to him?"

"It is."

"I offer the contract in evidence, your Honor."

"For what purpose, Mr. Willow?"

"To show that the book was only partially completed when submitted to Mitchell-Campbell. The contract clearly states that the company is in receipt of only ninety-eight pages and an outline, and it further specifies that the completed novel is to be delivered by January 1, 1963, and will consist of some eighty-thousand words."

"Mr. Brackman?"

"No objection."

"Received."

"Defendants' Exhibit F received in evidence," the clerk said.

"Mr. Danton, did you in November of 1962 send Mr. Driscoll a company questionnaire?"

"I did."

"Did he return the questionnaire to you, and is this the questionnaire?"

"Yes, this is what he filled out in November of '62."

"Is it signed by him?"

"No, we don't require a signature on these questionnaires. They're used only to get information which we'll need later for promotion and publicity. Most books, as you know, carry biographical information about the author, either on the jacket flap or on the last page of the book, or both. These questionnaires are helpful to the person preparing the copy.

And, too, we need information for newspaper publicity, anecdotes about the writer, his educational background, honors he may have received, and so forth."

"Are these questionnaires sent to every author on Mitchell-Campbell's list?"

"They are."

"As a part of the normal business procedure?"

"As a part of the normal business procedure."

"I offer it in evidence, your Honor."

"No objection."

"Mark it 'Defendants' Exhibit G in evidence.' "

"Mr. Danton, I ask you to recall now any further editorial suggestions you may have made concerning Mr. Driscoll's novel. Did you, for example, make any suggestion about the use of profanity?"

"Yes, I did. There was a scene in which Lieutenant Cooper met his fellow officers, and it seemed to me the profanity in that scene was excessive."

"I show you a second editorial memorandum with the initials 'CD' and I ask you now to describe it to the Court."

"Well, this is my comment . . . the report I wrote after the completed novel was delivered to me. It's dated February 4, 1963, and it mentions the fact that my earlier editorial suggestions had been successfully incorporated into the novel."

"Does it make any comments about further changes?"

"Yes, it does."

"Would you tell us what those comments are?"

"I'll simply read the last two paragraphs of the report, which are the only parts pertaining to your question. 'If anything, Driscoll has delivered a better novel than the portion and outline promised. His enlargement upon the slain major, for example, with the subsequent homosexual development of Private Colman is inventive and fresh, and completely satisfies our request for stronger motivation. I am, to be truthful, overwhelmed by the depth and scope of this novel, and it's only because the book is so good, in fact, that I bring up what might seem a carping point. I refer to the profanity.

This is a realistic war novel, of course, and the combat setting and soldier-characters make the inevitable Anglo-Saxonisms essential to the tone and the very structure. But it seems to me they can be softened somewhat in the scenes where they are used arbitrarily—as in the officers' mess scene—if only to mollify some of the more militant censors. Elsewhere, I'm afraid we can't do very much about the language because excising the four-letter words would damage the authentic sound of the entire work. One excellent scene, for example, where the men are ostensibly involved in the field-stripping of a rifle, would lose all of its sexual connotations if the language were even slightly changed.' And here, penciled in the margin alongside that paragraph, is a note dated February fifteenth, and stating that these points had been taken care of. Do you want me to go on with the next paragraph of the report?"

"Please."

"Again, I'm quoting: 'In my opinion, the last chapter is anticlimactic especially when placed in juxtaposition to the enormously effective penultimate chapter. The book needs a coda more than it does anything else, perhaps a short scene between Colman and the nurse. I have no doubt that Driscoll can come up with something to fill the bill. He has up to now delivered beyond our highest expectations. We have a fine novel here, and it's by a writer who is only thirty-three years old and who will, I am certain, go on writing many more excellent books. I feel we've made a true discovery.' That's the end of the report."

"Was the final chapter changed after you wrote your report?"

"Yes."

"And were there also subsequent changes?"

"I would guess so. Every book we publish goes through a subtle process of evolution during the copy editing and styling. Small changes are inevitable."

"I offer this report in evidence, your Honor."

"Is it dated?"

"It is dated February 4, 1963, and a note at the bottom of

the report states, 'All revisions completed March 6, 1963.' "

"My objection as before, your Honor," Brackman said.

"Overruled."

"Mark it 'Defendants' Exhibit H in evidence,' " the clerk said.

"Now Mr. Danton, you had by March 6, 1963, a completed manuscript of James Driscoll's book, had you not?"

"Yes, I had a finished manuscript by that date."

"Did you show it to anyone else working for Mitchell-Campbell?"

"I passed it on to Anita Lang."

"Did she subsequently make a report on it?"

"Yes."

"Is this the report?"

Danton took the extended sheet of paper, glanced at it, and said, "This is Anita's report."

"I offer in evidence Miss Lang's second report."

"Objection as before."

"Overruled."

"Mark it 'Defendants' Exhibit I in evidence.' "

"Would you please look at the next to last paragraph of the report where Miss Lang writes, 'It seems to me that the two flashbacks revealing segments of Private Colman's civilian life are extraneous. They advance neither theme nor plot and seem particularly obvious since we do not have similar civilian flashbacks for any of the other soldiers.' When *The Paper Dragon* was published, were these two flashbacks still in the book?"

"No, sir, they were not."

"They were deleted after Miss Lang made her report?"

"Yes, sir, they were."

"Who transmitted the request to Mr. Driscoll?"

"I did."

"In the last paragraph of her report, Miss Lang writes, 'Don't you feel we need another scene between Coop and the nurse to show how the squad's pressure on him is beginning to affect his behavior elsewhere?' In the margin, we have the penciled words, 'Fine, will do,' and the initials 'CD.' Did you write that in the margin?"

"I did."

"Was another scene between Coop and the nurse added to the book?"

"I don't remember, but I would imagine so. If Miss Lang made the suggestion, and I indicated it would be taken care of, then I'm sure I passed the request on to Jimmy. He was very receptive to most editorial suggestions, so I would say it was likely he added this scene as well."

"Before the book was finally published—what was its publication date, by the way, Mr. Danton?"

"October of 1963."

"When would you estimate you had a manuscript ready to go to the printers?"

"I would imagine some six months before then. That would be . . ."

"That would be . . ."

"In May, I would . . ."

"April, wouldn't it?"

"April or May, yes. We like at least six months' time for our salesmen to get on the road with a book."

"When did API see the book, would you know that?"

"Well, Mr. Driscoll took on an agent shortly after we contracted for the book, and I think his agent began showing it to the motion picture companies when it was still in galleys."

"Did API buy it from the galley proofs?"

"Yes."

"Would you know how much they paid for the motion picture rights?"

"Thirty-five thousand dollars."

"How much of that went to Mr. Driscoll's agent?"

"Ten per cent. Thirty-five hundred dollars."

"And how much went to Mitchell-Campbell Books?"

"Our contract called for twenty-five per cent of all subsidiary rights."

"You received twenty-five per cent of what was left after Mr. Driscoll's agent took his commission?"

"No. Our twenty-five per cent came off the top."

"In other words, you received a quarter of thirty-five thousand dollars?"

"That's right."

"You received eight thousand, seven hundred and fifty dollars?"

"That's correct."

"And Mr. Driscoll's agent received thirty-five hundred dollars, which means that Mr. Driscoll was left with twenty-two thousand, seven hundred and fifty dollars."

"If your addition is correct."

"I think it is."

"I'll accept it."

"That was his share of the sale of motion picture rights to his novel."

"Yes."

"The novel that later earned millions of dollars for API."

"Objection, your Honor. I do not see . . ."

"Sustained. Where are you going, Mr. Willow?"

"I am merely trying to show, your Honor, that Mr. Driscoll's alleged 'theft' hardly seemed to be worth all the trouble. The only ones who made any real money out of this supposed plagiarism were the people who made the movie."

"Your Honor," Brackman said, "I think a sum in excess of twenty-two thousand dollars can be considered 'real money.' Men have robbed banks for less."

"I quite agree, Mr. Brackman," McIntyre said. "I think we've had enough of this, Mr. Willow, and I see no point in pursuing it further."

"Getting back then," Jonah said with a sigh, "before publication, did you talk to Mr. Driscoll about anything in the book that might later prove troublesome?"

"Yes, we always do, as a matter of routine."

"Can you explain what you mean?"

"We're always concerned about the possibility of lawsuits. Invasion of privacy, usually. Or libel. In any work of fiction, there's the danger that someone will identify with a fictitious character and bring suit. We try to make sure that the names of the characters, for example, are not the names of any real people."

"What about telephone numbers?"

"We check those out to make sure they do not correspond to any real numbers in service."

"Did you take such care with Mr. Driscoll's book?"

"Well, there were no telephone numbers involved since the book is set in Korea, as you know. But we did ask Jimmy whether any of the names he used were the actual names of men he may have known during his Army service. He assured us they were not."

"Were any other precautions taken?"

"Yes. At one point in the book, Jimmy mentioned the lieutenant's serial number. The actual numeral appeared in the book, you see."

"Yes?"

"So we wrote to the Army and had them give us a non-existent serial number we could use."

"I seem to recall a case involving another publisher in which a telephone number in a novel—the number for a house of prostitution—turned out to be a real number for a respectable woman living in New York."

"Yes, that's a well-known story in the trade. We try to be careful of such occurrences."

"So the serial number finally used was nonexistent?"

"Yes. A dummy number supplied by the Army."

"Did you have any similar qualms regarding the use of the digits one-oh-five to label Mr. Driscoll's division?"

"No."

"Why not?"

"We had no reason to believe the 105th was anything but an actual Army division."

"You thought the 105th was a *real* division?"

"We did."

"Didn't this trouble you?"

"It did not. An Army division consists roughly of eighteen

thousand men. Worrying about the designation of such a large unit would be similar to worrying about the designation of a city the size of Scarsdale."

"Then you never brought up the division number in any of your discussions with Mr. Driscoll?"

"Never. We thought it was one of the real divisions involved in the Ch'ongch'on River fighting, and it never occurred to us that we should try to change history."

"Did Mr. *Driscoll* ever say it was a real division?"

"He never mentioned it at all."

"Not at any time during any of your discussions?"

"Never."

"Thank you. Mr. Danton, how long have you been an editor?"

"I've been with Mitchell-Campbell Books since my discharge from the Navy in 1946. I was hired to handle subsidiary rights for the firm, but I began doing editorial work in, oh, it must have been '48 or '49. I've been an editor since that time."

"As part of your job, are you called upon to pass literary judgment on manuscripts submitted to the company?"

"I am."

"Mr. Danton, have you in this past week read the play *Catchpole?*"

"I have read it, yes."

"Mr. Willow," Brackman said, "I haven't objected until now to these leading questions—but I can't remain silent when you first supply your witness with a date, and only afterwards ask him if he read the play."

"Forgive me," Jonah said. "*Have* you read the play *Catchpole*, Mr. Danton?"

"I have."

"When did you first read it?"

"I read it last week. Last Tuesday night."

"Where did you obtain a copy of the play?"

"You gave it to me."

"Did I ask you to read it?"

"You did."

"Do you have any editorial opinion on it?"

"Objection. Mr. Danton's opinion of the play is immaterial."

"Your Honor," Jonah said, "the testimony of an expert on such matters, a man who has been an editor for more than twenty years, would certainly seem relevant to me. As with my earlier offer, I am merely attempting to ascertain whether or not anyone would *want* to steal this play."

"Your Honor . . ."

"Please," McIntyre said. "What earlier offer do you mean, Mr. Willow? The newspaper reviews of *Catchpole?*"

"If your Honor please."

"Mr. Brackman?"

"The quality of this play does not go to the question of plagiarism, your Honor. On Monday, Mr. Willow remarked that many well-known works have been plagiarized in the past, and he cited *Abie's Irish Rose* as a prime example. I'm sure his reversal of the facts was inadvertent, but nevertheless the plagiarism was charged *against Abie's Irish Rose,* which was purported to have been stolen from an unknown property. Point of fact, I think we all must realize that no one in his right mind would try to steal from a *famous* book or play—unless he was intent on being exposed and brought to justice. Moreover, with all due respect to Mr. Danton's abilities, I hardly think he is the man to pass judgment on Mr. Constantine's play."

"If he has a qualified editorial opinion . . ."

"I do not see where his opinion, qualified or otherwise—"

"I will exclude it, Mr. Willow," McIntyre said.

"In that case, your Honor, I have no further questions."

"Very well."

Brackman rose from behind his table, consulted a list of notes he had made, put the notes on the table again, and walked slowly toward the witness chair.

"We know each other, don't we, Mr. Danton?" he asked conversationally.

"We met at the pretrial examination, yes."

"How are you?"

"I'm fine, thank you."

Brackman nodded, and smiled. "Mr. Danton," he said, "I'd like to go over these editorial changes you just told us about. Would that be all right with you?"

"Yes, certainly."

"To begin with, you suggested the title *The Paper Dragon*, is that right?"

"Not to *begin* with. That came much later."

"I didn't mean chronologically, Mr. Danton."

"What did you mean?"

"Was it or was it not one of your editorial suggestions?"

"It was."

"And another of your suggestions was that the squad be provided with a stronger motivation for its dislike of Lieutenant Cooper?"

"I suggested that a major—"

"Please answer the question."

"Yes, that was another of my suggestions."

"And yet another concerned the use of profanity in the officers' mess scene?"

"Correct."

"And the deletion of flashbacks showing the civilian background of Private Colman?"

"Yes."

"You also suggested that a final chapter be written . . ."

"Yes."

". . . between Lieutenant Cooper and the nurse Jan Reardon."

"No. Not between—"

"I quote from your own Exhibit I, where Miss Lang said, 'Don't you feel we need another scene between Coop and the nurse . . .'"

"Yes, but—"

"'. . . to show how the squad's pressure on him is beginning—'"

"Yes, but that was not a suggestion for the final chapter. That was earlier on in the book, a scene set in the hospital."

"But you agreed with her comment?"

"Yes, I did."

"And suggested the change to Mr. Driscoll?"

"Yes. As well as suggesting a better last chapter."

"These were two *separate* changes, is that it?"

"Yes, I thought I'd made that clear."

"It's clear now, thank you. Do you consider these changes important?"

"Which changes?"

"All of them."

"They were important to the full realization of Mr. Driscoll's book, yes."

"What do you mean by that?"

"The book was potentially excellent. I believe the changes helped Mr. Driscoll to realize that potential. Yes, the changes were important."

"During your pretrial examination, Mr. Danton, you mentioned only *two* editorial suggestions which you considered important: the change of title and the profanity. You weren't trying to mislead me, were you?"

"I certainly was not!"

"You just didn't remember these three or four other suggestions, is that it?"

"Yes, of course that's . . ."

"Which you now consider as important as the others? Important to the *full* realization of Mr. Driscoll's book?"

"I've had a chance to reread *The Paper Dragon* since then, and to remember . . ."

"Yes, but at the pretrial, you did not recall these other suggestions when we asked you about them, did you?"

"No, not at the time."

"Your Honor," Jonah said, rising, "I do not see . . ."

"He is examining the witness as to credibility, Mr. Willow, and I will allow it," McIntyre said.

"I call your attention now to the following question in your pretrial examination: 'Mr. Danton, would you say that the editing—' "

"Excuse me, Mr. Brackman," Jonah said.

"This is page 21," Brackman said over his shoulder.

"Thank you."

"And the question was, 'Mr. Danton, would you say that the editing of a book is a process of offering the suggestions and opinions of others to an author for possible assimilation into the work?' and your answer was, 'Basically, yes.' And further down on that same page, Mr. Danton, you were asked, 'Did suggestions concerning *The Paper Dragon* originate entirely with you?' and your answer was, 'No, some of the suggestions originated elsewhere in the company.' I ask you now, Mr. Danton, where else in the company these suggestions originated?"

"They came from Miss Anita Lang, as I testified earlier."

"You also testified earlier, Mr. Danton, that—and I quote— 'the editor-author relationship was solely between Mr. Driscoll and me.' Do you recall that?"

"I said it was between Jimmy and me except for the memorandums . . ."

"Solely between Mr. Driscoll and yourself."

"I also mentioned the memorandums," Danton said.

"Your Honor," Jonah said, rising, "I believe Mr. Brackman is attempting to fuse two separate answers . . ."

"I repeat his answer," Brackman said. " 'The editor-author relationship was solely between—' "

"Yes, the personal relationship," Jonah said.

"Was it or was it not an exclusive relationship?"

"Should I answer that?" Danton asked.

"Please," McIntyre said.

"It was the only personal relationship."

"What do you mean by that?"

"I mean that I was the only editor at Mitchell-Campbell who transmitted suggestions for change to Mr. Driscoll."

"Including suggestions for change that might have originated elsewhere?"

"Yes."

"Do you know for a fact, Mr. Danton, that no one at Mitchell-Campbell Books saw or read the play *Catchpole* before the publication of *The Paper Dragon?*"

Danton hesitated.

"Mr. Danton?"

"No, I do not know that for a fact."

"Do you know for a fact that Miss Anita Lang did *not* see or read the play?"

"No, I do not know that for a fact, either. But Miss Lang is only—"

"You have answered the question."

"I would like to explain . . ."

"Your Honor . . ."

"I will hear the witness," McIntyre said.

"I would like to explain that Anita Lang is a very young woman. In fact, she couldn't have been more than twenty-two or three when *The Paper Dragon* first came to us. She must have been seven or eight years old when *Catchpole* was produced in New York, so I hardly think she could have seen the play, unless her mother took her to it in a baby carriage."

"Do you know for a fact that she did not *read* the play?"

"No, I don't."

"Mr. Danton, I call your attention to a report of your own, Defendants' Exhibit H, in which you said, and I quote: 'We have a fine novel here, and it's by a writer who is only thirty-three years old and who will, I am certain, go on writing many more excellent books. I feel we've made a true discovery.' This was dated February 4th, and the notation that all the points were cleared up is dated March 6, 1963. I ask you now, Mr. Danton, whether James Driscoll has delivered any other manuscript to you since that time?"

"He has not."

"To your knowledge, Mr. Danton, is he presently at work on another book?"

"Not to my knowledge."

"To your knowledge, Mr. Danton, had he ever written anything prior to the novel called *The Paper Dragon?*"

"I believe it was his first novel."

"Was it in fact his first published work of fiction?"

"I don't know."

"I call your attention to Defendants' Exhibit G, the questionnaire sent by Mitchell-Campbell Books to James Driscoll, and I refer you to the section asking the author to list his previous works. Would you please read Mr. Driscoll's answer to the Court?"

"He says, 'I have never had anything published before.' "

"Do you accept the statement in this questionnaire?"

"I do."

"He would have had no reason to falsify an answer to that question?"

"Mr. Driscoll is not a man who falsifies anything."

"Then Mitchell-Campbell Books accepted his statement that *The Paper Dragon* was the first work of fiction he had ever had published."

"Yes, Mitchell-Campbell Books accepted the statement."

"In other words, Mr. Danton, *The Paper Dragon* in addition to being the *first* thing Mr. Driscoll ever had published, is also the *only* thing he has ever had published."

"That's correct."

"Thank you, Mr. Danton."

"Is that all?"

"That's all, thank you."

"Are you through, Mr. Brackman?"

"Yes, your Honor."

"Mr. Genitori? Any further questions?"

"No, sir."

"Thank you, Mr. Danton. I'd like to recess for lunch now."

"This Court will reconvene at two P.M.," the clerk said.

"Mom?"

"Yes?"

"This is Arthur."

"Oh, hello, son, where are you?"

"Downtown, in the courthouse. I'm in the hall here. In a phone booth."

"What is it?"

"What do you mean?"

"Did you lose?"

"It's not over yet, Mom."

"When *will* it be over?"

"Tomorrow, I guess. Or Friday."

"So soon?"

"Yes. Well, you know, it's a pretty simple case."

"Did you tell them?"

"Oh, sure."

"That he stole from you?"

"Sure."

"What did they say?"

"Well, they don't say anything, Mom. I mean, there's only the judge and the people who're involved, you know. So we present our side, and then they present theirs, and that's it."

"Did they ask you questions?"

"Oh, sure."

"And it was all right?"

"Yes, it was fine."

"How's the play?"

"Well, we're still casting it."

"When will it be?"

"When will it go *on,* do you mean?"

"Yes."

"I don't know."

"Because I want to tell my sister."

"Oh, sure. I'll let you know in plenty of time."

"Good."

"How's Papa?"

"He's in the sun porch, working on his clocks. Shall I call him?"

"No, that's okay."

"You don't want to talk to him?"

"Well, I want to get some lunch, Mom . . ."

"Anyway, he's busy. You know how he gets when he's taking one of those things apart."

"Sure. Well, give him my love, anyway."

"I will."

"Have you heard from Julie, Mom?"

"Last week. I told you. I got a letter last week."

"I meant *since.*"

"No."

"I'll have to write to her. I owe her a letter."

"Do you know who died?"

"Who?"

"Do you remember Mr. Danucci, he was a housepainter?
He always used to chase you kids off the stoop?"

"Sure, I remember him."

"He died Monday."

"What of?"

"In his bed."

"Oh."

"Well, he was an old man. You remember him, don't
you?"

"Sure, I remember him."

"Well, he died."

"That's too bad. Well, listen, Mom, I'd better go get some
lunch."

"Yes, call me when the trial is over."

"I will."

"Good."

"Give my love to Papa."

"Yes. Goodbye, son."

"Goodbye, Mom."

"Goodbye."

"Hello, Amy?"

"Daddy? Is that you?"

"Yes, sweetheart, how are you?"

"Fine. Why didn't you call Monday night?"

"I got in too late."

"The reason I didn't say to call Tuesday was because we
were going on a trip to Philadelphia, to see all that indepen-
dence craparoo, and I didn't know what time we'd be getting
back. So I figured Wednesday would be safe around noon
when we have our lunch period."

"Why'd you call, Amy?"

"Did you see the paper?"

"No. Which paper? What do you mean?"

"About Mother."

"No."

"It said she caused another disturbance in a night club."

"Oh?"

"Daddy?"

"Yes?"

"It didn't come right out and say she was drunk, but it made it pretty clear."

"Where'd you get a New York paper?"

"A girl in tenth showed it to me. A friend of mine."

"Some friend."

"She didn't mean any harm."

"Well."

"Daddy?"

"Yes?"

"Will you call her?"

"Why should I?"

"If she's going around getting drunk . . ."

"No, Amy."

"Please? For me?"

"I'm sorry."

"Daddy, I'll be home Friday, the Christmas vacation starts Friday, that's the sixteenth, and I don't even know if she's picking me up. She hasn't written in weeks. Could you call and ask her?"

"Ask her what?"

"If she'll be at the station. She *is* my mother, you know."

"I know that, Amy."

"And I'm worried."

"About what? She's perfectly capable—"

"About her falling down drunk in some damn night club, if you want to know. *Can't* you call her, Daddy?"

"I'm sorry, Amy."

"I tried to reach her three times last week, but I couldn't get an answer. Nobody even *answers*. Daddy, *please* call, won't you?"

"Amy . . ."

"Please."

"Amy?"

"What?"

"Amy . . . don't cry."

"I'm not crying."

"Please, honey."

"I'm . . . not, Daddy."

"I'll call her. Only please don't . . ."

"Daddy, you don't have to. I know you really . . ."

"Now stop crying, Amy. Please."

"I'm sorry, Daddy."

"Amy?"

"Yes. Yes, I'm fine."

"I'll call her."

"Thank you."

"How's . . . how's everything there at the school?"

"Fine."

"Everything okay?"

"Yes. I got an eight on a Latin test—that's eighty, you know. And we . . ."

"Yes, I know."

". . . won a soccer game against St. Agnes."

"Honey, what time will you be coming in? On Friday, I mean."

"Well, we usually get to Penn Station at about six."

"Would you like me to meet you?"

"Oh, *could* you, Daddy? I'd love it. Hey, I bought something very nice for you in New Hope."

"I'll be there. Six o'clock Friday, Penn Station."

"Daddy, if the train's late . . ."

"I'll wait, don't worry. I miss you, Amy."

"Yes."

"Well . . ."

"You'll call Mother, too, won't you?"

"Sure, honey."

"Thank you."

"I'd better say goodbye now. I've got some people waiting."

"Daddy?"

"Yes?"

"I love you."

"Who's this?"

"Sidney."

"Who?"

"Sidney. Your son."

"Oh, Sidney, *Sidney!* I thought you said *Shirley.*"

"No, I said Sidney."

"I was wondering how a Shirley could have such a deep voice."

"Yes, well, it's me, Pop."

"What's the matter? You're not coming?"

"No, I'll be there."

"Good. I found some nice things for you, Sidney."

"Oh. Fine."

"I'll show you tomorrow, when I see you."

"Okay. Fine."

"You're coming, aren't you?"

"Yes, certainly. I said I was. Have I ever missed a Thursday?"

"Well, I know you have a trial."

"No, I'll be there, don't worry."

"Six o'clock?"

"Six o'clock."

"Some nice things, Sidney."

"What is it? I have a headache."

"I just talked to Amy, and—"

"What does she want this time?"

"Apparently she saw an item about you in—"

"That's true, I was drunk."

"Christie . . .

"Anything else?"

"Nothing except she was concerned enough to call you three times last week . . ."

"I haven't been home."

". . . and then finally call me in desperation. Now look, Christie, your life is your life . . ."

"Here it comes."

". . . and I don't give a damn *what* you do with it . . ."

"But *our* daughter is *our* daughter."

"Yes."

"I am fully aware of my responsibility to Amy."

"Then why haven't you written to her?"

"I wrote to her last Tuesday."

"She said she hasn't heard from you in weeks."

"She's lying."

"Amy doesn't lie."

"That's true, I forgot that Amy is a paragon who doesn't lie, cheat, steal, swear, smoke, screw, or—"

"Christie . . ."

"Christie . . ."

"Christie, you've . . ."

"Christie, you've . . ."

"Christie, you've got a twelve-year-old . . ."

". . . twelve-year-old . . ."

". . . daughter two hundred miles away from home . . ."

". . . away from . . ."

"Damn you, Christie, *cut it out!*"

"Jonah?"

"What?"

"Go to hell, Jonah."

"Did you know she'll be coming home Friday?"

"Yes, I knew."

"I told her I'd pick her up at the station. Is that all right?"

"That's fine."

"In the meantime, you might call to let her know you're alive."

"All right, I will. Is that all?"

"That's all."

"Goodbye."

Dris is right, Ebie thought. Nothing in that courtroom is real, it can't be. All of them have their own ideas, the truth is only what they *want* to believe. Even the judge, even *he* doesn't know what's real, and he's the one who's supposed to decide. How can he? Does *he* know what the book is about? None of them do. So how can any of it be real, the court-room, the conversation here at this table, how can any of it be the slightest bit real?

"I don't think I get you," Jonah said.

"There's no reality in that courtroom," Driscoll answered. "There can't be."

"It seems real enough to me each day," Jonah said. "What do you think, Mrs. Driscoll?"

"I think it's real enough," Ebie answered.

"Anyway, the reality is that you didn't steal his play," Jonah said. "And the further reality is that it's a bad play, and no one would have *wanted* to steal it."

"Who says it's bad?"

"Jimmy, there's no question about it."

"You mean the critics said it was bad, and the movie companies, and the editorial expert, Chester Danton, right?"

"That's right."

"So that makes it a bad play."

"I would say so."

"Constantine doesn't think so."

"Constantine is mistaken."

"Yes, and the man who produced it was mistaken, too, because *he* obviously thought it was a good play. And the actors who agreed to play it, *they* were mistaken as well because *they* thought it was good. Everyone involved in it was apparently mistaken because the critics came to see it and said it was bad. Tell me something, Jonah. If the Honorable Frank H. McIntyre decides I stole Constantine's play, will that suddenly make it *good?*"

"You didn't steal it."

"You didn't answer my question."

"Constantine is a bad writer who wrote a bad play. What-ever McIntyre decides, it will still be a bad play. There's your reality, Jimmy."

Reality, she thought.

My first year in New York was real, the school and the small apartment I took on Myrtle Avenue, the elevated trains roaring past the window. And after that, and before I knew James Driscoll existed, reality was a boy named Donald Forbes, who limped. I'm a cripple, he said, okay? You're not a cripple, I insisted. No? Then what? I drag my leg, I limp, I'm a cripple, don't lie to me, Ebie, I'm a goddamn cripple. Holding him in my arms while he wept. He was not a good-looking boy, he reminded me of Phillip Armstrong whose nose had been too long ("I used to have this little turned-up button nose, but I had an operation done to make it long and ugly") and who was always coming down with a cold or something. Donald was that way, thin and looking like one of the hundred neediest, with large pleading Keane eyes. He took to carrying a cane in January because there was such a heavy snow that year, he said. That was just before I began sleeping with him.

". . . real or otherwise, that's my point."

"You may be giving him more credit than he's due. I'm still not sure he really thinks you stole it."

"Then why did he bring suit?"

"There's a lot of money involved here, Jimmy."

"There's more than just money involved here. Constantine thinks I stole something that is very valuable to him, no matter *what* anyone else says about it. He wants credit for his work."

"No. He wants credit for *your* work."

"What makes *my* work any better than his?"

"Jimmy, this is a foolish argument. You know *The Paper Dragon* is far superior to *Catchpole*. Now why . . . ?"

"We're not in that courtroom to judge the value of the two works, are we?" Driscoll said. "That's why I don't approve of what you were trying to do."

"What was I trying to do?"

"Make him ashamed."

"No," Jonah said.

She had never been ashamed of what she'd done, though of course she lied in her letters home, even in her letters to Miss

Benson. And yet she always felt a pang of regret at not having told her the truth, because she was certain Miss Benson would have been the only one to understand. Wasn't this what she and Miss Benson had *really* discussed on that waning afternoon, wasn't this what Miss Benson had meant by a capacity for giving? In February, when Donald stopped using the cane, she thought she must have known how that Negro lawyer in Atlanta felt when he began sleeping with Miss Benson. If a nigger in the South (and she stopped calling them niggers the moment she realized Donald disapproved of the expression) if a *Negro* in the South could just once in his life stand up and be counted as a man, be accepted as a man by a woman like Miss Benson, why then maybe he could think of himself as a man from that day forward. And maybe, if they had let him alone, if they had allowed him to give this woman love and to accept it from her in return, if they had not been so desperately threatened by the notion, then maybe he'd have walked proud the rest of his life, without dragging his leg, without limping. But of course they couldn't allow that to happen. No, you see, we can't allow that to happen, Missie, standing in the driveway and talking in low voices to the schoolgirl in her cotton pajamas and robe, we cannot allow it, Missie, you had better get the hell out of Atlanta. Maybe that's what Donald was all about, because she knew without question that she did not love him, and yet she gave him love. And in February he threw away the cane, said the streets weren't as slippery, but she knew. She would watch him combing his hair in the morning, whistling as he studied his own face in the mirror over the sink, and she knew. And she would nod silently, a small smile on her mouth, and think of Miss Benson, and think she should write to her and tell her, thank her, say something to her. But she never did. It would have been too difficult to explain, the way it was impossible to explain later on. Oh not *Donald,* you could always explain the lovers of your past, especially if they were not really lovers. Though even then, there'd been a scene, my young James Driscoll laying down the law, you will not do this, you will not do that, yes my darling, yes my darling, yes, I love you.

". . . that the work is *unworthy* of piracy, that's all."

"How do you know it is?"

"What are you talking about, Jimmy?"

"Let's suppose for the moment that I did steal his play, okay?"

"I would rather not suppose that."

"It's entirely possible."

"It is not possible," Jonah said firmly.

"I could have seen it in 1947 when they gave out those free tickets to Pratt . . ."

"I don't believe they gave any free tickets to Pratt."

"Constantine testified to it under oath."

"Better men than Constantine have lied under oath."

He's lying now, Ebie thought. He doesn't believe a word of this, he's teasing you, Jonah, playing a game and enjoying every minute of it, the way he enjoyed that first afternoon in Bertie's on DeKalb Avenue, teasing the little Southern girl who had just cut her hair, the way he teased the world with his book, *I* know what that book is about, James Driscoll.

"Even if I didn't see it at any of those preview performances, why couldn't I have caught it on Broadway? I was eighteen years old in '47, why couldn't I have seen the play? I started going to the theater when I was twelve, you know, used to go every Saturday with my father. Isn't it plausible that a play about the Army might have appealed to me?"

"Not a flop play."

"Maybe I've got a mind of my own, Jonah."

"I'm sure you have."

"Maybe I wanted to form my own opinion, despite what the critics had to say."

"That isn't the way it works, and you know it."

"Or maybe I read the reviews and decided there was the kernel of something good there. Maybe I went to the theater with a notebook, intent on stealing whatever—"

"And then waited fifteen years to write your book, is that

it? You're really an arch-criminal who entered Pratt Institute under the guise of studying art, though really wanting to be a writer all along. You searched the daily reviews to see what you could steal, and your imagination was captured by what you read about *Catchpole*. So you went there to copy it, realizing you would have to wait fifteen years before you could use the material. Is that it?"

"It's a possibility."

"Dris," Ebie said, "I wish you wouldn't talk this way. Even in jest."

"Ebie thinks I *did* steal it, you see," Driscoll said, and grinned.

"I think nothing of the sort."

"It's what she thinks, Jonah."

"Not at all."

"Tell the truth, Ebie. You think I stole that play, don't you?"

"You know I don't."

"Come on, Edna Belle, 'fess up."

"Stop it, Dris."

My name is Jimmy Driscoll, he had said. The tables in Bertie's were long and scarred, and she could remember looking away from him, down at the table top, initials in hearts, a group of engineering students singing at the other end of the room, November light filtering through the stained glass behind the tables, the room smelling of beer and steam heat, wet garments hanging on wooden pegs, his eyes were blue, she dared to look up into them. He teased her about her short hair and about her age. He imitated her Southern drawl, and then bought her a second glass of beer, the last of the big spenders, he said, and asked her out for Saturday night. She promptly refused.

You'll be sorry, he said. I'm going to be a famous artist.

Yes, I'm sure.

Come out with me.

No.

"There are good things in that play," Driscoll said. "It's

not a good play—but there are things worth stealing in it."

"I wouldn't advise you to say that on the witness stand," Jonah said.

"Why not? I'll be swearing to tell the truth, won't I?'

"Yes, but . . ."

"You wouldn't want me to lie under oath, would you? Even though better men than Constantine have lied under oath?"

"I'm not enjoying this, Jimmy," Jonah said.

"That's too bad," Driscoll answered. "What am I supposed to do, pretend Constantine is an ogre? Well, I can't. I feel closer to him than I do to you or anyone else in that court-room. He made something with his hands, he pulled it out of his head and his heart, that play of his, that terrible play, oh yes, unanimously panned and reviled—well, that play is Arthur Constantine, and not just words for lawyers to argue over and judges to decide about. He thinks he was wronged, Jonah, first by all the critics who sat in exalted superiority the way McIntyre is sitting, completely on the outside, the external critics who could find nothing good to say about his ugly little child. And next by me, who took his miserable bastard and combed its hair and shined its shoes and made a million dollars on it. That's what he thinks and believes, Jonah, and I can understand him better than I can this cold contest between professional assassins, or this almighty judge who may murder him yet another time. I weep for him, Jonah. Don't try to shame him again."

"Do you want to lose this case?" Jonah asked flatly.

"It might matter more to Constantine than to me," Driscoll said.

"Why?"

"Because I'll never write another book as long as I live."

"That's nonsense, Dris," Ebie said.

"And don't repeat it on the witness stand," Jonah warned.

"Why not?"

"Because this case can go either way, and I don't need any more headaches—not if we're to win."

"Is that so important to you? Winning?"

"Yes," Jonah answered.

It's important to Dris, too, Ebie thought, don't think it isn't. He may *say* it's unimportant, Mr. Willow, he may *say* he'll never write another book as long as he lives, but I know him better than that, I know him better than any human being on earth. He knows he'll lose, you see. He knows that, and he's hoping against hope that he'll come out of it with honor somehow, without having to speak; that somehow a miracle will come to pass, he'll win without having to say what he tried to say in his novel and only failed to say. He'd give his *life* to be free of that Vermont rock garden where he pretends to grow his meager crops, living on royalties that still come in from the foreign editions and the paperback, constantly dwindling. He'd give his *soul* to be able to come back to New York, which is his home, his *only* home, come back and look this city in the eye again, be able to feel like a man in this city that's his, maybe not even to write again, though I know that's what he wants, I know, I know. I know this man so well, I know this fierce proud stupid stubborn man, I love this man so much.

He could do it. He could do it all, he could be free at last, if only . . . we could win this case so easily, we could do it so simply, if only he would . . .

We'll lose, Ebie thought.

He'll never tell them.

9

GRAY HAIR RISING in waves from a high forehead, combed straight back without a part so that it seemed to extend the flowing line of his profile, gray eyes intelligently alert beneath black beetling brows, Ralph Knowles took the oath, and then sat, crossed his long legs, and waited for Genitori to begin.

The lawyers had decided between them that Genitori, as chief counsel for API, would conduct the direct examination. Their decision puzzled Ralph, who had never found Genitori impressive either in looks or in bearing, and who wondered now what empathy this dumpy little man could possibly evoke from the judge. He watched critically as Genitori walked slowly and ponderously toward the witness stand, and his feelings were somewhat like those of a star in the hands of a bad director. Genitori cleared his throat, sniffed, looked once at the gray sky beyond the courtroom windows, nodded to the judge, smiled, and then turned again to Ralph.

"Mr. Knowles," he said, "what do you do for a living?"

"I'm a motion picture writer and director," Ralph said.

"Have you always been a motion picture writer and director?"

"No, sir."

"What did you do before you began working in motion pictures?"

"I was a freelance writer of magazine pieces, and after that I did a great deal of dramatic work for radio. This was before the war, during the late thirties and early forties. Before television."

"What radio programs did you write for?"

"*Lux Radio Theater, Suspense, Mister District Attorney, The Green Hornet, The Shadow* . . . most of the shows that were around, I would say. One of my radio plays for *Suspense* was later made into a movie called *Armitus*. That was when I first became involved with motion pictures. I went to the Coast for story conferences on it, you see, and while I was there someone asked me if I would like to do a screenplay for him—not on my own property—and I said yes. I began doing screenplays after that, and a while later I began directing."

"How many motion pictures have you written, Mr. Knowles?"

"Since 1954, I've written seventeen screenplays, and directed nine of them myself."

"Did you write and direct *The Paper Dragon?*"

"Yes, sir."

"Alone?"

"Sir?"

"Were you the only writer of the screenplay for the motion picture titled *The Paper Dragon?*"

"I was."

"In what year was that screenplay written?"

"1963, I think it was. Yes, it must have been the latter part of '63."

"Until that time, had you ever heard of the plaintiff, Arthur Constantine?"

"No, sir."

"Or the play *Catchpole?*"

"No."

"Had you ever seen a synopsis of *Catchpole?*"

"I had not. I try to avoid synopses whenever possible. It seems unnatural, to me, for anyone to condense a five-hundred-page novel into a fifty-page report on it. If you did that with *Hamlet,* you'd end up with what sounded like a ghost story. I can remember the synopsis I read on my own radio play, the one they were filming, and I was appalled by what they'd done, eliminating all the nuances, all the depth, all the range of character, leaving only the bare bones—terrible. I made up my mind right then and there that I'd have nothing to do with synopses ever again. I've pretty much hewed to that line since."

"You did *not,* then, read a synopsis of *Catchpole?*"

"No, sir."

"Did you ever see it performed?"

"Performed?"

"Yes. At the Fulton Theatre in New York?"

"No."

"Or anyplace else?"

"No, sir."

"Have you ever served with the United States armed forces?"

"I have."

"When?"

"May I ask where this is going, your Honor?" Brackman said.

"You'll see in a minute, Mr. Brackman," Genitori replied. "When were you in the armed forces, Mr. Knowles?"

"From July of 1943 to January of 1948."

"In what branch did you serve?"

"I was a fighter pilot in the Army Air Corps."

"Did you ever serve overseas?"

"Yes, sir. I left the United States in January of 1945, and was assigned to the Pacific Theater of Operations, where I remained until the time of my discharge."

"Where were you stationed in October of 1947, when Mr. Constantine's play was showing in New York?"

"I was stationed in Tokyo. Japan."

"When did you begin working for API?"

"In August of 1954."

"As what?"

"A writer at first. And later on, a director."

"During your initial period of employment there, was material ever submitted to you for consideration?"

"Material?"

"Plays, novels, television scripts?"

"Do you mean as possibilities for motion pictures?"

"Yes."

"Well, no. No one ever asked my opinion on whether or not a story should be purchased, if that's what you mean. In the beginning, I was simply handed a novel or a play, or whatever, and told it was my next assignment."

"To write a screenplay on it?"

"Yes. And when I first began directing, it worked much the same way. I would be assigned to direct a film, and I would direct it. Later on, of course, I was *asked* to direct, a producer would *come* to me with the material and ask if I would like to direct it or not."

"Material that had already been purchased?"

"Yes. And now, of course, *I* can ask the studio to buy a property that I think is interesting, and if they agree it'll make a good movie, they'll usually go along with me and buy the property for me to make."

"Did you see synopses of any material you did not later translate to the screen?"

"No, sir. I told you, I avoid synopses like the plague."

"Now, you said earlier that you wrote the screenplay for *The Paper Dragon* . . ."

"Yes, sir, and directed it as well."

"How did you go about writing this screenplay?"

"I don't think I understand you."

"What did you use as source material?"

"Oh. Well, the *book*, of course. It had been submitted to the studio in galleys, and a producer there liked it—Jules Fairchild—and asked me to take a look at it, and I thought it was something I'd like to do. I think I saw the magazine serialization, too, which was pretty close to the book, *McCall's* published it, I think, or *Redbook*, I'm not sure which, a two-part serial."

"The book was your basic source, would you say?"

"Yes. Although I did do additional research on my own. A book, you understand—even a fine book like *The Paper Dragon,* for which I have only the greatest respect—it's still only a book, you see, and there's a great deal involved in turning it into a motion picture . . . well, I don't know if I should go into all of this."

"Please do," McIntyre said.

"I was introduced to Mr. Driscoll for the first time this morning," Ralph said, "but I suppose he must have been a little puzzled by the changes made in bringing his book to the screen—so perhaps this will be instructive to him as well." Ralph turned and smiled at Driscoll, who was watching and listening attentively from the jury box. "There are some people who feel that the novel and the motion picture are similar in technique and in scope, but I disagree with them. They argue that a novelist can immediately turn from a minute examination of a woman's mouth, let us say, to a battlefield with hundreds of men in an infantry charge, that sort of thing—in other words, from a closeup to a full shot, and all without any transition, in much the same way that a camera would handle it. But we must remember that the novelist is dealing with the written word, and he must describe that woman's mouth in words, he must describe that infantry charge in words, which means that those words must first be registered on the reader's eye, and then carried to the reader's brain where, depending on how good or bad the writer is, there will be an intellectual response that will hopefully trigger an emotional response.

"Well, we have a situation completely diametrical to this in the motion picture, because we go directly for the emotional response; there is no need for a middleman, there is no need for a brain that will translate words into images that may or may not stimulate the tears or laughter we are going for. We *start* with the images, you see. That is our job, putting images on the screen in sequence, arranging and editing and putting in order these images that are designed to evoke a *direct* emotional response. I can tell you that if I come at that screen with a blood-stained knife, you are going to rear back in fright and I don't need any words to accompany it, that knife is its own motivation and its own explanation. Or if I fill that screen with a beautiful woman's face, and I show her eyes lidded and her lips parting, I don't have to accompany it with any interior monologues, I don't *need* poetry to describe her, we *know* she wants to be kissed, and we *want* to kiss her because the appeal is direct and emotional, the response is immediate.

"So, in beginning my work on a screenplay, I look upon the novel or the stage play or whatever it is I'm translating only as an outline of something that will become larger and grander than the printed word allowed. Even an excellent book like *The Paper Dragon,* for which I have nothing but the deepest veneration, becomes a detailed study for what will be my film. I sift through it and sort through it, trying to cut through the maze of words, trying to get through to the emotion hidden there, distilling what the author meant, translating his *words* directly into *images* so that the audience reaction will be immediate and overwhelming. In short, I eliminate the intellectual response in favor of the emotional. *Then*, if we're lucky, when these images have registered, when they have evoked the proper *emotional* response, why then the audience, if we are lucky, will experience an *intellectual* response as well. That's the difference between a novel and a motion picture, and it is this very difference that makes the film a much more difficult form in which to work and, in my estimation, a much higher art form."

"I see," Genitori said.

"Yes," Ralph said, and glanced toward the jury box to smile at Driscoll.

"You said you did some additional research . . ."

"Yes."

". . . before you began work on your screenplay?"

"Yes."

"Can you tell us what this research was?"

"Yes, certainly. As I indicated earlier, I spent a great deal of time in the Pacific during and after World War II, and I think it was the setting of Mr. Driscoll's fine novel that first attracted me to it—the possibility of shooting in Korea, a beautiful country, we got some really excellent footage of the countryside, you know. But in addition to that, I was interested in the book as a study of war, as an extension really of my own attempts to understand war in my early radio plays and also in one or two other films I had made before *The Paper Dragon*. War and its impact on man, what it does to men, what it causes them to become, this was what interested me. I discovered that a lot of material had been written on the subject, not only fiction, and not only the elongated minute-by-minute battle breakdowns, but serious studies that appeared in a great many of the magazines—*Life, Look,* the *Saturday Evening Post, The New York Times Magazine*— learned and informative articles about the behavior of our soldiers during the Korean conflict, the Korean *war,* I should say.

"These articles, and books as well, were written by military analysts, and psychiatrists, and historians, all of whom were probing the behavior of our men during that small war—I thought at one point of changing the title of the picture to *The Small War,* by the way, which I thought would be more emotionally effective than *The Paper Dragon,* but the studio objected because they didn't like the use of the word 'small' in any title. Where was I?"

"Books and magazine articles . . ."

"Yes, about the behavior of our men in Korea, the betrayal of comrades, the informing, the brainwashing, all of it. I studied these books and articles very carefully, using Mr. Driscoll's novel, of course, as my primary source because it was an excellent book and, let's face it, the only one we owned the rights to. We didn't own any of these other books or articles I studied for background material, you see, and besides Mr. Driscoll's novel was very exciting in itself and a firm basis upon which to build a movie. But before I began translating it into images, I also went to several Army bases to get a feeling of what the situation was like *today* as opposed to what I experienced during World War II. I visited Fort Bragg in North Carolina, and Fort Dix in New

Jersey, and also the infantry school at Fort Benning. That was the extent of the research I did before I began writing my screenplay."

"Would it then be fair to say that a screenwriter must perforce make certain changes in translating a novel into a film?"

"Absolutely."

"I ask this because I would like to explore some of the *specific* changes you made, Mr. Knowles, and perhaps find an explanation for them. For example, in Mr. Driscoll's novel, the character named Private Colman does *not* wear eyeglasses. Yet when you brought this character to the screen, you chose to show him *wearing* eyeglasses. Now why did you do that?"

"For the actor," Ralph said.

"What do you mean?"

"Not entirely, but at least that was a major consideration. The actor who portrayed Private Colman was a man named Olin Quincy, and he wears eyeglasses. I mean, off the screen, as a part of his normal life. There was a part of the screenplay that called for him to read from a map, and he asked me if it would be all right for him to wear his glasses throughout, so that he could actually do the reading as called for. I said it would be all right. So that was one consideration. But also, if you remember, there's another soldier in the book who wears eyeglasses—Kenworthy, the fellow who swears a lot—and in one scene there's a mortar attack and his glasses are lifted from his face by the concussion. It seemed to me that if he were the only one in the movie wearing eyeglasses, it would look like a put-up job, as if we had him wearing glasses only so they could be later knocked off, do you understand? So to take the curse off this, I decided to put glasses on another soldier as well, and the logical choice was Private Colman."

"Why was he the logical choice?"

"I like to avoid the obvious in my films. It would have been obvious to present Colman as a sneering sort of person, the way he is in the book—though you can get away with that in a book because there are also interior monologues and thought passages revealing various aspects of a character; however, you can't do that in a film. And rather than present Colman as a stereotyped villain, I thought it would add to his menace if he seemed to have a scholarly look about him, a rather meek look. In other words, if he wore eyeglasses. Which is not unusual, anyway. Many men in the Army, even in combat, wear eyeglasses."

"Now do you remember a scene in your film where you have a group of soldiers drinking coffee together?"

"Yes, sir, I do."

"This scene is not in the novel, is it?"

"No, sir, I don't believe it is."

"Why did you put it in your film?"

"For a very good reason. It is in this scene that I have Private Colman suggest they murder the lieutenant. Now, if you'll remember this same sequence in the novel—and this is what I was trying to illustrate earlier about intellectual as opposed to emotional response—Colman's decision to murder the lieutenant takes place entirely in his mind. Mr. Driscoll handled this static scene very well, to be sure, but the appeal was intellectual, and I was searching for an emotional approach to put across this very important plot point. All right, I decided to have these men doing something very commonplace, something almost homey, very cozy, you know. All of them sipping steaming coffee—the way we shot it, you could see the vapor rising from the cups—a break in the battle and these grizzled combat veterans have their hands wrapped around these steaming coffee cups, not even discussing the lieutenant, just enjoying the coffee, and bam! out of the blue, Private Colman says, 'Let's kill him.' Now that's an emotional shock, for the audience to hear those words, and the shock is heightened by the very mundane act in which the men are engaged, the drinking of coffee. That's why I put that scene in my film. I took something that was introspective and static, with all due respect to the excellent writing in that particular passage, and created instead an image that would shock and startle."

"You also put a bayonet charge in your movie, and this was not in the novel either."

"Correct."

"Can you explain why you did this?"

"Yes. To foreshadow the death of Lieutenant Cooper."

"But he isn't killed by bayonet, is he?"

"Correct."

"He is not?"

"No, sir, he is not. The lieutenant is killed by Chinese guns. I chose to foreshadow this by showing a vicious, almost bestial bayonet charge by our own soldiers, Americans. Also, I use the bayonet charge as a visual symbol. These men have been knifing the lieutenant in the back all through the movie, and now we see a visual representation of how cruel men can be to each other, bayonets being plunged, men dying just as the lieutenant later dies when he sacrifices himself to save Morley."

"Now, there's also in the movie you made a scene depicting an enemy soldier being shot at and falling out of a tree. Can you tell us the origin of this?"

"I don't know the origin."

"It was not in the book, was it?"

"Not to my recollection."

"Do you remember how you came to put it into your screenplay?"

"It was a vignette, part of a montage of scenes showing the horrors of war. Certainly a man being shot at and falling from a high place is almost a cinema cliché. I have seen it before in many movies, both war pictures and Westerns, too. I don't claim to have originated that particular image, though I must say we used an extraordinary camera angle on it, pointing directly up at the tree, and when the soldier is shot, he falls directly toward the camera, getting bigger and bigger until he fills the entire screen. That was a really fine piece of camera work, and I credit my cameraman Andy Burstadter for it."

"In this same montage of scenes, you show an American

soldier bursting into tears when his buddy is killed. This, too, is not in the novel, and I wonder if you can tell me where it originated."

"Your Honor," Brackman said, "in a case without a jury, I would as a matter of course refrain from objecting to a question containing a description, such as the one Mr. Genitori just put to the witness. But I think you will agree that the witness was being led, and that this was a blatant violation of the rules of evidence."

"Sustained. Please rephrase it, Mr. Genitori."

"Is there a scene in your film where an American soldier bursts into tears?"

"There is."

"What was the basis of this scene? Where did it originate, can you tell us?"

"Yes, I can. It originated, the idea for it came from a book of photographs called *The Family of Man*. Since motion pictures are really a series of still photographs arranged in sequence, I will very often leaf through books of photographs, and this happened to be an extremely fine collection. I believe the actual photos had hung in exhibit at the Museum of Modern Art here in New York, and this was an artful presentation of most, if not all, of them. The idea for that particular scene came to me in one of the photographs. I don't remember who the photographer was, a war photographer for *Life*, I believe, and it showed two soldiers, and one of them is comforting his buddy who is crying. That's the origin of that particular vignette."

"What about the nurse putting on her lipstick?"

"What do you mean?"

"You have a scene, not part of this montage, but an actual scene in the film, where the nurse is putting on lipstick and she uses the back of a mess kit as a mirror. This was not in the novel, but there is a similar scene, or at least a stage direction to that effect, in Mr. Constantine's play. Now where did you get the idea for this scene?"

"It happened during the shooting."

"Of the film?"

"Yes. The screenplay called for the girl to put on her lipstick, and when she began to do so—with the camera rolling—she discovered that the prop man hadn't put a mirror in her bag. So she picked up a mess kit that was on the table, and she turned it over and discovered it was shiny, and she used that. She was a very inventive actress, Miss Shirley Tucker, and she sensed the scene was going very well, this was the first take, and rather than risking another take where we might not get the same dramatic qualities, she ad-libbed with the mess kit, and we left it in."

"You left it in the completed film?"

"Yes, sir."

"But it was *not* in the screenplay?"

"No, sir."

"Thank you, Mr. Knowles."

"Is that it?" Brackman asked, surprised.

"I'm finished, Mr. Brackman," Genitori answered.

Brackman nodded, consulted his notes, and then walked toward the witness chair. Ralph watched him as he approached. If anything, he was even less impressive than Genitori, a short, unattractive man whose clothes looked rumpled, whose hair stood up ridiculously at the back of his head, whose tie was the wrong color for his suit.

"Mr. Knowles," Brackman said suddenly, "would you say that a screenplay is similar to a stage play?"

"No, sir."

"They both deal with the spoken word, do they not?"

"Yes, sir."

"And with a visual arrangement of scenes?"

"Yes, sir."

"With actors portraying parts created for them?"

"Yes, sir."

"Then you would agree that there is at least *some* similarity between a screenplay and a stage play? At least the similarities we have just enumerated?"

"Yes, but they are really very different. I've adapted several Broadway plays to the screen, and it's an enormously difficult job. If they were as similar as you seem to think they are, the job wouldn't have been nearly so difficult."

"You have adapted plays to the screen?"

"Yes."

"Stage plays?"

"Yes."

"In addition to adapting novels?"

"Yes. I've also adapted short stories and television plays. If the material is good, it doesn't matter what form it's originally written in. It must all be translated to the screen, anyway."

"So I understand. But before you begin these screen translations, do you always engage in additional research?"

"I do."

"As you did with *The Paper Dragon?*"

"As I do with every project."

"We're concerned here with *The Paper Dragon.*"

"My career did not suddenly begin with *The Paper Dragon,* you know. I had written and directed a great many successful movies before that one."

"And for each of these you engaged in thorough research?"

"Correct."

"Such as visiting Army bases?"

"For *The Paper Dragon,* yes."

"You said you went to Fort Bragg, and Fort Benning, and Fort Dix."

"Yes."

"Did you visit any Army bases in Korea?"

"No, sir."

"Even though the novel was set in Korea?"

"Correct."

"Why did you go to these bases in the United States?"

"To catch up on the language of the men, the slang, their conversation, little things they might be doing, little things that caught my eye and remained in my memory during the shooting of the film."

"At any of these Army bases, Mr. Knowles, did you witness a man being shot out of a tree?"

"No, sir."

"Did you witness an American soldier crying because his buddy had been killed?"

"No, sir."

"Did you see a nurse using a mess kit as a mirror?"

"No, sir."

"You certainly didn't see a bayonet charge?"

"No, sir."

"Or a man killed by a bayonet?"

"No, sir."

"Mr. Knowles, you said you were a fighter pilot during World War II."

"Yes, sir."

"What kind of plane did you fly?"

"I flew most of the aircraft in use during World War II, sir. Fighter planes, that is."

"Like what?"

"I flew the P-51 Mustang, and the P-38 Lightning and P-39 Airacobra. On one occasion, I even flew a Navy fighter plane, the Hellcat, sir, the F6F."

"You had very little opportunity then, while you were flying, I mean, to witness ground troops in action."

"I witnessed them from the air."

"But never on the ground. You were never on the ground during combat?"

"I flew forty-three combat missions, sir."

"On any of these combat missions, did you ever witness a man being shot out of a tree?"

"No, sir."

"Did you ever witness a bayonet charge?"

"No, sir."

"Then these 'little things that caught your eye and remained in your memory'—I think I'm quoting accurately—were things you saw neither during your time in the Air Corps nor during your subsequent visits to Army bases in the United States. They must have come from somewhere else, isn't that so, Mr. Knowles?"

"I've already told the Court where they came from."

"What does a story editor do, Mr. Knowles?"

"At a motion picture studio, do you mean?"

"Yes."

"I'm not sure I know."

"Well, there must be story editors at API."

"Yes."

"Do you know what they do?"

"I think they look over material that's published or produced and then make recommendations to the front office."

"What sort of recommendations?"

"As to whether the material should be considered for
purchase."

"Do you think *The Paper Dragon* was seen by story
editors?"

"The novel? I would guess so."

"Story editors employed by API, I mean."

"I'm not too sure of their function, so I can't say whether
this would be a routine thing or not. I simply can't answer
that question."

"Do you know a man named Joseph Edelson?"

"He's dead."

"Did you know him when he was alive?"

"Yes, I did. He was the head of API's story department."

"Did he work in any capacity on *The Paper Dragon?*"

"No, he did not. I wrote the screenplay without any assistance, and I directed—"

"I want to know if he worked in *any* capacity on the film."

"Not to my knowledge."

"Do you know Miss Iris Blake?"

"Not personally."

"Have you ever heard of her?"

"Yes. She's in API's story department too."

"Did she work in any capacity on *The Paper Dragon?*"

"No, sir."

"You said you began working at API in—when was it?"

"In August of 1954."

"Were Joseph Edelson and Iris Blake working there at
the time?"

"Joe was because that's when I met him. I don't know Miss Blake, so I couldn't tell you about her."

"Had you ever been to the studio before August of 1954?"

"Yes, I had been there for consultations on a property of mine—the radio play—which they were turning into a movie."

"Were you ever at the studio before April of 1954?"

"Yes, I believe so."

"Did you ever meet Mr. Constantine on any of your visits to the studio?"

"Never."

"He was working for API until April of 1954. Is it conceivable that you may have met him and perhaps forgotten . . ."

"I remember everyone I've ever met in my life," Ralph said flatly.

"But you *did* know two of the people to whom Mr. Constantine showed his play in the time he was working for the studio."

"Which two people would they be?" Ralph asked.

"Mr. Edelson and Miss Blake."

"I knew Mr. Edelson. I have never met Miss Blake, though I understand she is a charming and a beautiful woman."

"And you insist they had nothing to do with the filming of *The Paper Dragon?*"

"That's correct."

"Do you know Mr. Andrew B. Langford?"

"I do not."

"He is the secretary of Artists-Producers-International."

"I can't be expected to know every secretary at—"

"You misunderstand me, Mr. Knowles. He is *the* secretary of API."

"Whatever he is, I don't know him."

"You've never met?"

"Never."

"We asked Mr. Langford, on May 16th, to supply us with a list of anyone who had worked on *The Paper Dragon* either before or during its production. As Script Writer and Director he listed 'Ralph Knowles, under employment to the studio.' You are that same Ralph Knowles, are you not?"

"I am."

"As Story Editors he listed 'Joseph Edelson and Iris Blake, under employment to the studio.' Mr. Langford swore to the truth of his responses, so we have good reason to believe they were accurate. Yet you seem to disagree with him."

"In what way?"

"You have told this Court that neither Mr. Edelson nor Miss Blake had anything to do with your production of *The Paper Dragon*."

"Correct."

"Yet Mr. Langford swears they were employed by the studio . . ."

"That may be so, but—"

". . . as story editors on *The Paper Dragon*."

"I'm telling you they had nothing to do with my film."

"Were they or were they not story editors?"

"I don't know what they were. This is the first time I'm hearing of this credit. Was it in the titles?"

"What?"

"Of the film. Did this credit show in the titles? I never heard of it before today."

"Mr. Langford swears . . ."

"Well, he ought to know who was hired or who was not hired by the studio. But even if they *were* story editors, would you mind telling me what that has to do with my movie?"

"That's what I'd like *you* to tell *me*, Mr. Knowles."

"I've already told you. Neither of them had anything to do with *The Paper Dragon*."

"Yet you knew Mr. Edelson personally?"

"Yes, I did."

"If I told you that Mr. Constantine knew both Mr. Edelson and Miss Blake, would you take my word for it?"

"Why not?"

"But you yourself never heard of Mr. Constantine before this action began?"

"The only Constantine I'd ever heard of was the Roman emperor," Ralph said, and smiled.

"But not Arthur Constantine?"

"No. *Not* Arthur Constantine."

"Are you familiar with a film called *Area Seven?*"

"I am."

"In what way?"

"I saw the film, and I know the man who wrote the screenplay."

"Which man are you referring to?"

"Matthew Jackson."

"Was it a good film?"

"It was nominated for an Academy Award. Whether that makes it a good film or not is open to debate."

"Has Mr. Jackson ever mentioned Arthur Constantine to you?"

"Never."

"Were you aware of the fact that Arthur Constantine worked on that film?"

"I was not."

"Yes. He adapted it."

"I didn't know that."

"Will you take my word for it?"

"Certainly."

"Do you know a man named Rudy Herdt?"

"No, sir."

"A woman named Betty Alweiss?"

"No, sir."

"They are both presently employed by API, and have been working there since 1949. Are you sure you do not know them?"

"I am positive."

"You don't seem to know too many people at the studio, do you, Mr. Knowles?"

"I'm not gregarious," Ralph answered.

"How about Mr. Silverberg?"

"Who?"

"Mr. A. Silverberg. Or it may be *Miss* A. Silverberg, I can't tell from this. Mr. Genitori, would you know . . .?"

"It's *Mr.* Silverberg," Genitori said. "Abraham Silverberg."

"I don't know him," Ralph said.

"Have you ever read any synopses prepared by Mr. Silverberg?"

"I do not read synopses."

"And therefore you have not read the synopsis Mr. Silverberg prepared on *Catchpole?*"

"No, I have not."

"Have you ever read *any* synopsis of the play *Catchpole?*"

"Never."

"But you *have* read the play itself."

"No, I have not."

"No one at API gave you a copy of the play to read?"

"That's correct."

"I am referring now to the period of time since this action began."

"I have never read *Catchpole,* nor do I intend ever to read it."

"Didn't your attorneys suggest that you read it before coming here to testify?"

"They did."

"But you chose not to read it?"

"I am too busy to read anything that does not personally interest me."

"And I take it that *Catchpole* does not personally interest you?"

"Correct."

"How can you tell this without reading it?"

"I've read transcripts, or depositions, or whatever they were, and I knew from those that the play would not interest me."

"Do you mean transcripts of the pretrial examinations?"

"Correct."

"And I take it you were not overly impressed with Mr. Constantine's work?"

"I was not."

"Are you ever impressed with anyone's work other than your own?"

"Objection, your Honor."

"Sustained. Let's leave off with this, shall we, Mr. Brack-man?"

"Mr. Knowles, did Matthew Jackson work with you on the filming of the motion picture *The Paper Dragon?*"

"He did."

"In what capacity?"

"As assistant director."

"What does an assistant director do, can you tell us?"

"Certainly. It's his job to see that everything is functioning properly, actors have their scripts and know their lines, props are ready, extras are in place, quiet and order are maintained on the set. An A.D. is an invaluable person on a film, and Matthew Jackson is a good one."

"Does an assistant director ever *direct?*"

"Sometimes."

"Did Matthew Jackson direct any of the scenes in *The Paper Dragon?*"

"He may have."

"Which scenes?"

"Second-unit stuff, I would imagine."

"Was the bayonet charge second-unit stuff?"

"It may have been."

"Who directed the bayonet charge?"

"I'm sure I directed the sequences involving the prin-cipals."

"And the other sequences?"

"Matt might have. Mr. Jackson."

"Was the montage second-unit stuff?"

"Which montage?"

"The one containing vignettes of the soldier being shot out of a tree, and the soldier crying . . ."

"I directed all of that."

"Mr. Jackson did not help with it?"

"Only as A.D. on the sound stage, that's all, his normal function."

"Let's talk about Private Colman for a moment, shall we?"

"Certainly."

"You portrayed him as wearing eyeglasses . . ."

"Yes."

". . . and you testified that you did this because the actor playing the part, Mr. Olin Quincy, wore glasses in real life?"

"Correct."

"And would not be able to *see* unless—"

"No, I didn't say that. He's as blind as a bat, that's true, but I wouldn't have given him glasses if the part didn't call for him to *read* something. There was a very complicated scene in the film where the positions on a map are being traced, just preparatory to heading into enemy territory, the same as in the book, and Olin thought it would be a good idea if he could *see* all these Oriental place names and actually *read* them from the map, rather than trying to memorize them."

"Do you remember the character of Colman well?"

"Yes, sir."

"As presented in the book?"

"Yes, sir, I do."

"Was he wearing eyeglasses in the book?"

"No, sir."

"Was there a character named Corporal Finlay in the book?"

"No, sir."

"Was there a Corporal Finlay in the movie?"

"Yes, sir."

"Would you say that he possessed some of Private Colman's characteristics?"

"What do you mean?"

"Colman's characteristics from the book."

"Yes, sir, I would say so."

"Would you say that Private Colman and Corporal Finlay in the movie were *both* derived from the single character of Private Colman in the book?"

"I would say so, yes."

"You would say that both these characters were derived from the single character of Colman?"

"Well," Ralph said, and hesitated. "Finlay was a composite."

"Of whom?"

"Of Colman and several other characters in the book."

"Which other characters?"

"Characters who were dropped from the film."

"Which?"

"Well, I would have to think for a moment."

"Yes, please do."

"There were a lot of soldiers in the platoon . . ."

"Yes . . ."

". . . and we obviously couldn't use all of them in the film, or we'd have had a picture that ran for six hours."

"Yes, I understand that."

"But many of these were minor characters, and I sort of bunched them together to create the single character called Corporal Finlay."

"Yes, but from which characters *besides* Colman was this character derived?"

"I don't recall their names offhand."

"Can you remember their characteristics?"

"Not offhand."

"Would you say that Corporal Finlay was derived primarily from Colman as he appeared in the novel?"

"Yes, primarily, I suppose."

"In that Colman in the novel became *two* characters in the film: Colman and Finlay."

"Correct."

"Are you familiar with the character named Colonel Peterson in *Catchpole?*"

"No, sir."

"The character description of him states that he is a tall, slender, frail-looking man. Would you say that the man who played Corporal Finlay in your film—what was his name?"

"John Rafferty played the part."

"Would you say that he is a tall, slender, frail-looking man?"

"I don't know what you might consider tall," Ralph said.

"Well, *I'm* a short man, Mr. Knowles, and *you're* a tall man. Is John Rafferty more your size or more mine?"

"He's about as tall as I am, six feet give or take an inch."

"Is he slender?"

"I would say so."

"And he does, does he not, give an impression of frailty?"

"Well, I don't know about that."

"We have all seen the film, Mr. Knowles, and I think you will have to agree that John Rafferty gives an impression of frailty on the screen."

"All right, all right."

"In *Catchpole*, Peterson is a psychopath. Would you say that Corporal Finlay is a psychopath?"

"No, sir."

"Would you say he is a neurotic?"

"I don't know the distinction."

"Would you describe Finlay as being disturbed?"

"He is disturbed, yes. But you're forgetting that the character in the book was disturbed, too."

"Which character? Private Colman, do you mean?"

"Yes."

"Yes, and you've testified that Private Colman was divided to form two *separate* characters in the film."

"Correct."

"One who was still called Private Colman, and the other who became Corporal Finlay. I'm a little puzzled by this, Mr. Knowles, because it was my impression that in writing a screenplay the idea was to *eliminate* extraneous characters, tighten the action, generally bring a novel—which can be loose and sprawling—into sharper focus. Why then did you choose to make two characters out of what was a *single* character in Mr. Driscoll's novel?"

"I must have had reasons, though I'm not sure what they were right now. This may have been a suggestion from Olin, who played the part of the troublemaker, I'm not sure. Actors do have a say, you know."

"Yes, of course. Can you remember what it was he might have objected to in the character Colman as presented in the novel?"

"No."

"But whatever it was, it caused you to invent another character, the one you called Finlay."

"I would suppose so."

"Mr. Knowles, do you remember a scene in which you have Lieutenant Cooper requesting Corporal Finlay to assist him with some paperwork, and Finlay replies, 'I can't, sir. Paperwork is for sissies,' and the other soldiers burst out laughing, do you remember that scene?"

"Yes, I do."

"If you'll look at this . . ."

"What is that?"

". . . in reel 3, page 4 . . ."

"Oh, yes. What page was that?"

"Page 4."

"Thank you. Yes, I have it."

"Would you look at the dialogue there, please?"

"Yes?"

"Where, right after the speech I just quoted to you, Private Colman says, 'Why don't you give him a hand, sweetie?' And then Kenworthy says, 'You could work in his tent, honey,' and Colman shouts, 'You'll enjoy it!' Do you see those speeches?"

"I do."

"What do they mean?"

"They mean, Oh boy, here comes the lieutenant with some more paperwork, everything according to the book. These men are joking, they're trying to make a fool of the lieutenant."

"How about the words 'You could work in his tent, honey'? What do those words mean? These are *men* talking, you understand."

"Of course. That simply means they consider paperwork to be sissy work."

"Is Corporal Finlay a sissy?"

"No, but he feels the way the others do, that paperwork is sissy work. And the men pick this up and make a big thing out of it, the way they do with everything throughout the film, badgering the lieutenant and trying to make him feel ridiculous, the idea that paperwork could be even remotely enjoyable to this soldier . . ."

"Enjoyable?"

"Yes."

"In what way?"

"Just the suggestion that it could be enjoyable, the suggestion Colman makes, you'll enjoy it."

"*Enjoy* it?"

"All right, I see where you're going, why don't we put it right on the table?"

"Sir?"

"Homosexuality."

"Yes, what about it?"

"That's what you're driving at, isn't it? You're trying to say there was a homosexual implication in this scene."

"Was there?"

"Certainly not."

"The words 'sweetie' and 'honey' used between men do not suggest homosexuality to you?"

"No, sir, they do not. Lieutenant Cooper is not supposed to be a fairy."

"Is Corporal Finlay supposed to be a fairy?"

"No, sir."

"And yet, he is based on Private Colman in the book, isn't that what you said?"

"That's what I said."

"Isn't Private Colman a homosexual?"

"No, sir."

"Not in your movie, I realize that. But how about the book?"

"I don't know what he is in the book."

"Surely you read the book?"

"Yes, of course I read the book."

"Then surely you are aware of the stream of consciousness passage—it is seven pages long, Mr. Knowles—wherein Private Colman clearly remembers and alludes to a homosexual episode with the dead major. Surely you remember reading that?"

"If I read it, I automatically discarded it as possible movie material. There is no homosexuality in any of my films, or even suggestions of homosexuality."

"But we do have a disturbed corporal whom the men rib about doing sissy work."

"Yes."

"Calling him names like 'honey' and 'sweetie' . . ."

"Yes."

"And suggesting that going into the lieutenant's tent might prove enjoyable."

"I didn't say that. *Nobody* says that. They only say he might enjoy the *paperwork*."

"Is that what they actually mean? Paperwork?"

"Yes. They're kidding the lieutenant about the paperwork, about how he thinks it's enjoyable, they're belittling his idea of enjoyment."

"I see. And you intended no homosexual reference, either concerning the lieutenant *or* the corporal."

"Absolutely not."

"Let's get to the girl in your movie, shall we, Mr. Knowles?"

"Fine."

"You said that she invented the business with the mess kit while you were shooting the film, that it did not appear in your screenplay. Miss Tucker ad-libbed it on the set because your property man had neglected to include a mirror in her handbag."

"That's right."

"When you noticed the missing mirror, why didn't you stop the shooting?"

"Because the scene was going very well."

"Yes, but it was only a first take, wasn't it?"

"Of a very difficult shot."

"Well, surely you could have stopped the camera, and then given Miss Tucker a mirror, and continued shooting. Movies are a matter of splicing together scenes, anyway, aren't they?"

"That would have been impossible with this particular shot. If I had stopped the action, we would have had to go again from the top. Besides, as I told you, I didn't *want* to stop the action. The scene was going very well, and when I saw what Shirley was up to, I just let her go right ahead."

"Why would it have been impossible to stop this particular scene without starting again from the beginning of it?"

"The camera was on a boom and a dolly both. There was continuous action, the dolly moving in . . ."

"The dolly?"

"It's a . . . well, I guess you can call it a cart or a wagon on tracks, and the camera is mounted on it. As the scene progressed, the dolly was coming in closer and closer to Miss Tucker, and then as she picked up the lipstick we began to move up on the boom . . ."

"I'm afraid you'll have to tell me what a boom is also."

"It's a mechanical—well . . . a *lift,* I guess would describe it—that moves the camera up and down, vertically. When we were in close on her, we went for the boom shot, all without breaking the action. In other words, I wanted this scene to have a complete flow, without any cutting, and it was necessary to shoot it from top to bottom without stopping. That's why I let her use the mess kit. As it turned out, we got the scene in one take and were delighted with it. It's one of the best scenes in the movie, in fact."

"An ad-libbed scene?"

"Well, the part with the mess kit was ad-libbed."

"It was not in your screenplay?"

"No, sir."

"Would you turn to reel 5, page 2 of this, Mr. Knowles?"

"What?"

"Please. Reel 5, page 2."

"Yes?"

"Do you see the numeral 176, right after the lieutenant says, 'Colman's the one who's responsible for their anger and their hatred.' Read on after that, would you, from DS—which I assume means 'downstage.' "

"No, it means 'dolly shot.' It says, 'DS—JAN—AND INTO BOOM SHOT: She takes lipstick from her purse and then, finding no mirror, picks up a mess kit from the table, discovers that its back is shiny, and uses it as she applies her lipstick.' "

"Now you testified that this scene was ad-libbed. Yet right here in your screenplay . . ."

"This is *not* my screenplay," Ralph said.

"It has your name on it."

"It's the cutting continuity of the film."

"Isn't that the same as . . . ?"

"No, sir. This is the *cutting* continuity, reel by reel. It's a record of all the action and dialogue in the film as it was shot. The cutter put this together."

"From the shooting script?"

"No, sir, from the completed *film*."

"Exactly as it was shot?"

"Exactly. But this is not a screenplay. This was not in existence until the film was finally completed."

"It is nonetheless a script, no matter what you choose to call—"

"No, sir, it is the continuity of the actual *film*. It is not a script in any sense of the word."

"But it nonetheless shows exactly what happened on the screen?"

"Yes."

"And what happened on the screen was that the girl used a mess kit for a mirror."

"Yes."

"That's all, thank you."

"Have you concluded your cross, Mr. Brackman?"

"I have, your Honor."

"Any further questions?"

"None, your Honor," Genitori said.

"None," Willow said.

"Thank you, Mr. Knowles," McIntyre said.

"Thank *you*, sir," Ralph said.

"Your Honor, Mr. Knowles is on his way to the Orient where he is beginning a new film. Would it be possible to release him at this point?"

"Certainly."

"Thank you," Ralph said, and rose and began walking toward the jury box. Behind him, he could hear the judge telling everyone that it was now ten minutes to four, and then asking Willow whether he wanted to begin his direct examination of James Driscoll now or would he prefer waiting until morning. Willow replied that he would rather wait until morning, and McIntyre commented that this was probably best since he thought they were all a bit weary, and then the clerk said something about the court reconvening at ten in the morning, and Ralph kept walking toward the jury box and then realized that everyone was rising to leave the courtroom and turned instead to head for the bronze-studded doors. He was very pleased with himself, and he nodded and smiled at Driscoll, who was rising and moving out of the jury box, and then he glanced over his shoulder to see Genitori rising from behind the defense table and moving very quickly toward him, and he continued smiling as he opened the door because he knew without doubt that he had performed beautifully and perhaps saved this miserable little trial from total obscurity.

"You're a son of a bitch," Genitori said.
"What?" Ralph said. "What?"
"You heard me, you prick!"
"What? What?"
He had wedged Ralph into a corner of the corridor, and now he leaned toward him in fury, his fists bunched at his sides, his arms straight, his face turned up, eyes glaring, as though he were restraining himself only with the greatest of effort. He is very comical, Ralph thought, this little butterball of a man with his balding head and pale blue eyes, hurling epithets, I could flatten him with one punch— But he did not raise his hands because there was something terrifying about Genitori's anger, and Ralph knew without question that the lawyer could commit murder here in this sunless corridor, and he had no intention of provoking his own demise.

"What's the matter with you?" he said. "Now calm down, will you? What's the matter with you?"

"You son of a bitch," Genitori said.

"Look, now let's watch the language, do you mind? You're . . ."

"What do you think we're doing here? You think we're playing *games* here, you son of a bitch?"

"Now look . . ."

"Shut up!"

"Look, Sam . . ."

"Shut up, you egocentric asshole!"

The juxtaposition of adjective and noun amused Ralph, but he did not laugh. The anger emanating from Genitori was monumental, it was awesome, it was classic. He knew that a laugh, a smile, even a mere upturning of his lips might trigger mayhem, so he tried to ease his way out of the cul-de-sac into which Genitori had wedged him, but the walls on either side of him were immovable and Genitori blocked his path like a small raging bull about to lower his horns and charge.

"Now take it easy," Ralph said.

"What did we discuss last night, you miserable bastard?" Genitori said. "Why did I drive all the way to Idlewild . . ."

"Kennedy."

"You son of a bitch, don't correct me, you miserable jackass! All the way in from Massapequa, you think I *enjoy* midnight rides?"

"Now look, Sam . . ."

"Don't look *me,* you moron! There's a man's career at stake in that courtroom, we're not kidding around here! We lose this case, and James Driscoll goes down the drain!"

"What did I *do,* would you mind . . ."

"What *didn't* you do? You gave them everything they wanted!"

"How? All I . . ."

"*Is* there a homosexual colonel in that goddamn play?"

"What?"

"I said—"

"How do *I* know? I didn't say there was a—"

"Well, there *isn't*. But you were so busy denying even the *suggestion* of one in your movie . . ."

"How was I supposed to know . . ."

"Is even the *suggestion* threatening to you?"

"Now look here, Sam, nothing about homosexuality threatens *me*, so let's not . . ."

"Then why did you insist a clearly homosexual scene *wasn't* one?"

"I told the truth as I saw it!"

"Yes, and made it sound as if you were hiding a *theft*."

"I didn't intend . . ."

"Were you also telling the truth about dividing Colman into two characters?"

"Of course. What's wrong with that? I was explaining . . ."

"It's exactly what they *claimed* was done."

"Huh?"

"Huh, huh? They said Driscoll changed it when he copied the play, and you changed it right back again. *Huh?*"

"I did?"

"That's what you *admitted* doing, isn't it, you stupid ass!"

"I was under oath. I had to explain how I wrote the screenplay. That's what he asked me, and that's what I had to tell him."

"Do you even *remember* how you wrote it?"

"Yes. Just the way I said I did."

"I don't believe you. I think if Brackman said you'd made *fifteen* characters out of Colman, you'd have agreed."

"Now why would I do anything like that, Sam?"

"To show that your movie was an original act of creation, something that just happened to pop into your head, the hell with Driscoll and his book, you practically ad-libbed the whole movie on the set!"

"I never said that! The only scene we ad-libbed was the one with the mess kit. How was I to know all this other stuff was so—"

"Why didn't you read the play, the way we asked you to?"

"I have better things to do with my time."

"Like what? Destroying the reputation of a better writer than you'll ever be?"

"Now that's enough, Sam. You can't—"

"Don't get me sore, you . . . you *porco fetente*," Genitori said, apparently having run out of English expletives. "You've done more toward killing this case . . ."

"Look, Sam . . ."

". . . than any witness the *plaintiff* might have called!"

"Look, Sam, I don't have to listen to this," Ralph said, having already listened to it.

"No, you don't, that's true. All you have to listen to is that tiny little voice inside your head that keeps repeating, 'Ralph Knowles, you are wonderful, Ralph Knowles, you are marvelous.' That's all you have to listen to. Are you flying?"

"What? Yes."

"Good. I hope your goddamn plane crashes," Genitori said, and then turned on his heel and went raging down the corridor.

Boy, Ralph thought.

10

HE SAW HER for the first time in Bertie's on DeKalb
Avenue, a girl with short blond hair, wearing sweater and
skirt, scuffed loafers, her elbow on the table, her wrist bent,
a cigarette idly hanging in two curled fingers. Unaware of
him, she laughed at something someone at her table said,
and then dragged on the cigarette, and laughed again, and
picked up her beer mug, still not looking at him while he
continued to stare at her from the door. He took off his
parka and hung it on a peg, and then went to join some of the
art-student crowd jammed elbow to elbow at the bar. Some
engineering students at the other end of the long, narrow
room were beerily singing one of the popular sentimental
ballads. He watched her for a moment longer, until he was
sure she would not return his glance, and then wedged
himself in against the bar with his back to her, and ordered
a beer. The place smelled of youthful exuberant sweat, and
sawdust, and soap, and booze, and of something he would
have given his soul to capture on canvas in oil, a dank
November scent that seemed to seep from the windswept
Brooklyn street outside and into the bar.

He knew all at once that she had turned to look at him.

He could not have said how he knew, but he sensed
without doubt that she had discovered him and was staring at
him, and he suddenly felt more confident than he ever had in

his life. Without hesitating to verify his certain knowledge, he turned from the bar with the beer mug in his hand and walked directly across the room toward her table—she was no longer looking at him—and pulled out the chair confidently without even glancing at any of the other boys or girls sitting there, nor caring whether they thought he was nuts or whatever, but simply sat and put down his beer mug, and then looked directly at her as she turned to face him.

"My name is Jimmy Driscoll," he said.

"Hello, Jimmy Driscoll," she answered.

"What's *your* name?"

"Goodbye, Jimmy Driscoll," one of the boys at the table said.

"Ebie Dearborn," she said.

"Hello, Ebie. You're from Virginia, right?"

"Wrong."

"Georgia?"

"Nope."

"Where?"

"Alabama."

"It figures."

"What do you mean?"

"Honey chile, that's *some* accent you-all got there."

"Don't make fun of it," she said, and then turned toward her friends as laughter erupted from the other end of the table. "What was it?" she asked them, smiling in anticipation. "I *missed* it, what was it?"

"Ah-ha, you just try and find out," one of the boys said, and they all burst out laughing again.

"Would you like a beer?" he asked.

"All right," she said.

"Waiter, two beers," he said over his shoulder.

"Who'd you just order from?" she asked, and laughed.

"I don't know. Isn't there a waiter back there someplace? Two beers!" he yelled again, without looking behind him.

"Come and get them!" the bartender yelled back.

"You think you'll miss me?"

"Huh?"

"When I go for the beers."

"I doubt it. There's lots of company here."

"You may be surprised."

"I may be," she said.

He went to the bar and returned with two mugs of beer. She was in conversation with her friends when he approached, but she immediately turned away from them and pulled out a chair for him.

"How'd it work out?" he asked.

"I missed you, sure enough."

"I knew you would."

"Here's to your modest ways," she said, and raised her glass.

"Here's to your cornflower eyes."

"Mmm."

"How's the beer?"

"Fine."

"Would you like another one?"

"I've just barely sipped on this one."

"So what? Let me get another one for you."

"Not yet."

"Do you always wear your hair so short?"

"I cut it yesterday. Why? What's the matter with it?"

"You look shaggy."

"Say, thanks."

"I meant that as a compliment. I should have . . ."

"What *else* don't you like about me?"

". . . said windblown."

"What?"

"Your hair. Windblown."

"Oh," she said, and brushed a strand of it away from her cheek.

"That's nice."

"What is?"

"What you just did. How old are you?"

"Nineteen."

"That's good."

"Why?"

"Older women appeal to me."

"What do you mean? How old are *you?*"

"Eighteen."

"Oh? Really?"

"I'm a first-year student."

"Oh?"

"But very advanced for my age."

"Yes, I can see that."

"You think this'll work out?"

"What do you mean?"

"I don't know, the age difference, the language barrier . . ."
He smiled hopefully, and let the sentence trail.

"Frankly, I don't think it has a chance," she said, and did
not return his smile.

"Let me get you another beer."

"I'm not ready for one yet."

"I'll get one, anyway."

"I'm really not that thirsty."

"It doesn't matter. I'm the last of the big spenders," he
said, and smiled again, but she only glanced toward her
friends, who had begun a lively discussion about Mies. "Well,
I'll get one for you."

"Suit yourself," she said, and shrugged.

He rose and went for the beer, half afraid she would leave
the table while he was gone, aware that he was losing her,
desperately searching in his mind for something to say that
would salvage the situation, wondering where he had made
his mistake, should he not have told her he was eighteen? or
kidded her about the accent? if only he could think of a joke
or an anecdote, something that would make her laugh. "One
beer," the bartender said, and he picked it up and walked
back to the table with it.

"Drink it quick before the foam disappears," he said, but
she did not pick up the mug, and they sat in silence as the
bubbles of foam rapidly dissipated, leaving a flat smooth
amber surface an inch below the rim of the mug.

"Tell me about yourself," he said.

"My hair is shaggy," she said, "and I have a thick Southern accent, and . . ."

"Well, I know all that," he said, and realized at once he was pursuing the same stupid line, the wrong line, and yet seemed unable to stop himself. "Isn't there anything *interesting* you can add?"

"Oh, shut up," she said.

"What?"

"Just shut up."

"Okay," he said, but he could not remain silent for long. "We're having our first argument," he said, and smiled.

"Yes, and our last," she answered, and began to turn away from him. He caught her hand immediately.

"Come out with me this Saturday night," he said.

"I'm busy."

"Next Saturday."

"I'm busy then, too."

"The Saturday after . . ."

"I'm busy every Saturday until the Fourth of July. Let go of my hand, please."

"You'll be sorry," he said. "I'm going to be a famous artist."

"I'm sure."

"Come out with me."

"No."

"Okay," he said, and released her hand, and rose, and walked back to the bar.

He knew then perhaps, or should have known then, that it was finished, that there was no sense in a pursuit that would only lead to the identical conclusion, postponed. But he found himself searching for her on the small windswept campus, Ryerson and Emerson, the malls and the parking lots, Steuben Walk in front of the Engineering Building, and then in the halls and classrooms themselves, and even on the Clinton-Washington subway station. In his notebook, he wrote:

She never happened. I am sure she never did. In Bertie's yesterday where I went to look for her, a girl walked over to me — blue smock, brown eyes, black hair hanging loose over one eye, that type — and said, "Who broke your nose?" And when I said, "No one," she answered, "You're a liar," and walked away laughing. I don't know who she was or is, had never seen her before that minute, and haven't seen her on campus since. Was she real? Or did she exist only in my imagination, like Ebie Dearborn?

I sometimes think I'm crazy.

The notebook, which he had begun in October, and which he would continue to keep through the next several years, was a curious combination of haphazard scholarship, personal jottings, disjointed ideas and notions, doodlings, line drawings, and secret messages written in a code he thought only he could decipher. He had learned from his uncle a drawing technique that served him well all through high school, though it was later challenged by his instructor at the League. Revitalized provisionally at Pratt, it was an instant form of representation that sometimes veered dangerously close to cartoon exposition. But it nonetheless enabled him to record quickly and without hesitation anything that came into his line of vision. The technique, however, candid and loose, did not work too well without a model, and as his memory of the girl he'd met only once began to fade, he found himself relying more and more upon language to describe her and his feelings about her. A struggle for expression seemed to leap from the pages of the notebook, paragraphs of art history trailing into a personal monologue, or a memorandum, or a query, and then a sketch, and now a poem or an unabashed cartoon, and then again into desperate prose, until the pages at last were overwhelmed with words:

as those artists who populated the 15ᵗʰ
century Burgundian court of the Duc
de Berry.

<u>Pol de Limbourg</u> (Tres Riches Heures
du Duc de Berry)
1— Prayers, calendar, psalms, lessons
   for layman's devotions.
2— Vivid, realistic landscapes.
3— Free from ecclesiastical.
4— Wealth of detail, no crowding or
   confusion.
5— Tremendous influence on Hubert
   and Jan Van Eyck.

<u>Jan Van Eyck</u> (Adam and Eve, Ghent
                Altarpiece, St Bavon
                       Ghent)
1— Designed to fit specific space (as
   opposed to later <u>Arnolfini and Wife</u>,
   where space becomes ELEMENT OF DESIGN).
2— Harsh, almost photograph (as opposed
   to A & W's humanity).
3— Ecclesiastical symbol.

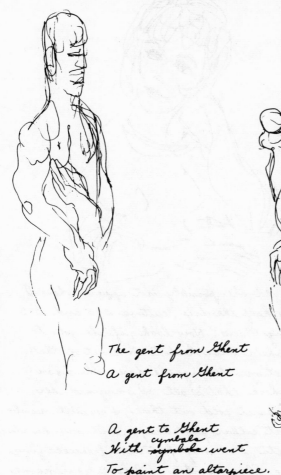

The gent from Ghent

A gent from Ghent

A gent to Ghent
With ~~symbols~~ cymbals went
To paint an altarpiece.
And all ecclesiastical
~~Had paint~~ Depicted Cain as set to kill
Upon the altarpiece.
And yet ecclesiastical
Set Eve and Adam deshabille
Upon the altarpiece.
If Evie's ass elastic'll
Entice our Adam, jump he will
Upon the altar piece.

How could she possibly not appear when I sat out there half the day, cutting 2-D and 3-D both, watching Main? Now look, if she goes to school here, she'd have had to come out of that building sometime during the day. She doesn't go to school here, that's all. I imagined her.

Boy, was it cold out there, I'm still numb. I had my coat collar pulled up, and my hands in my pockets, but my feet were freeeeeezing, and I blame Ebie Dearborn (I love your name Ebie Dearborn). I blame _you_ for my discomfort of feet and also my discomfort of heart. You are breaking my heart by appearing as the Mysterious Vanishing Lady, for the First Time in America, Folks, watch her as she captivates the hearts and feet of helpless young men, subjugates them with a cornflower glance, enslaves them forever, now listen, Ebie, where the hell are you?

There was once today when I thought I saw her, and I got up off the bench, feet freezing, slapping my hands against my sides, and ran after this blonde girl in a peacoat, guess what, it wasn't Ebie; surprise!

Listen, Ebie Dearborn, we are standing here on the threshold of what may turn out to be the Romance of the Century, you hear me? So stop this idiotic game of hide and seek and come rush into my loving arms because there are a multitude of things I desire to say to you, and I can't say them alone on a bench in the goddamn cold November, shaking. You hear?

help!

My Ebie's hair is like a golden helmet
Poured molten, sitting on her head.

My Ebie's hair is like a golden helmet
Poured molten, shaped to fit her head
Haphazardly.

My Ebie's head

My Ebie's hair is like a golden helmet
Poured molten, shaped to fit
Haphazardly.
And yet despite

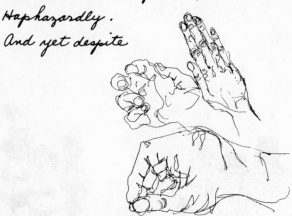

Due Tuesday 11/8
Finish Chapter XXI - Painting of late
Middle Ages
Answer all questions at end chapter,
pp 511-512

<u>Jerome Bosch</u> (1450 – 1516)

1 – Recorder of horror, reflection of terror
of Middle Ages.

2 – Illustrated man's depravity with
creatures, monsters, psychos, etc.

3 – Master of graphic invention.

4 – Keen observer of human behavior.

5 – <u>Christ Before Pilate</u> (Museum of Historic
Art, Princeton)

   A – Painted 1502.

   B – Christ subordinate figure to
soldiers, Pharisees, and Pilate.

   C – Modern day lynch mob (similar)

   D – Helpless man in grip of un-
reasoning mob — hatred
dominates picture.

   E – Sacrifice for man's inhumanity.

Nineteen years old would mean she was born in 1928, a good year for the Chateau Mouton Rothschild, monsieur. Thank you very much, this wine tastes of cork. Nineteen, which means she's been at the school a year, and is practically halfway toward graduation. Why would she want to waste time with me, the lowest of the low, the bottom of the social order? Balls.

McCarthy had a party

The thing to do is to find out specifically whether or not she goes to Pratt, and the only way to do that is to track down some of those people who were in Bertie's with her. Only thing is I can't remember what any of them look like. Great.

I'm beginning to forget what she looks like.

umber and ochre,
          palette knife

Eyes cobalt,
          touch of white

Frankie Laine —
Mamselle

Ebie Dearborn
Or does she spell it Ebey
Or Ebee?
Ebee Dearborn

Ebie Dearborn

Mrs. Ebie Driscoll
Mrs. James Randolph Driscoll
Mr. and Mrs. James Randolph Driscoll

Mr. and Mrs. Blank Dearborn
of Blank, Alabama
announces the imminent eminent marriage
of their daughter
Ebie Ebey Ebee Dearborn
to
James Randolph Jose Hans Fritz Henri
Sven Running Deer Driscoll
Come one Come All Come all 03 h2 2lly Yeah!

Due Monday 11/15
Chapter XXII, XXIII Greek Sculpture, Hellenistic
Sculpture
Sketch: Three Fates, Lapis Battling a Centaur,
Victory of Samothrace, Laocoon and
his Sons.

On Friday, November 12th, he hit upon the idea (and dutifully recorded it verbatim in his notebook) of perhaps asking a second-year art student about Ebie. Outside an illustration class, he stopped a girl with her arm in a cast, her hair pulled back into a pony tail, and asked her if she knew Ebie Dearborn.

Who?
Ebie Dearborn.
The little Southern girl?
Well, she's not so little.
But the one from Alabama.
That's the one.
Sure, I know her.
Have you seen her around lately?
No.
Do you know where she is?
She's sick, I think.
With what?
I don't know.
Well, where does she live?
On Myrtle Avenue.
Where on Myrtle?
I don't know. Near the school.
But where?
Why don't you look it up in the phone book?

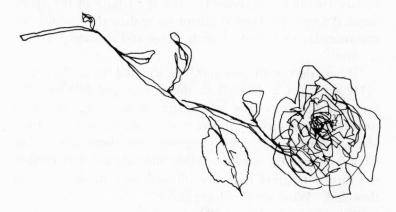

Late that afternoon, he spent the last of his week's allowance on a dozen red roses, and went up to her apartment without calling first. The building she lived in on Myrtle was a crumbling red brick structure with enormous bosses on either corner, a simulated keystone arch over the front doorway. The elevated trains roared past the building, but he scarcely heard them over the pounding of his heart, or so he wrote faithfully in his notebook that night:

> She lives in the third floor front apartment.
> I framed the stairwell in wintry afternoon
> light, building my secret rectangle around
> the scene, choosing my pigments for the
> hand worn banister, and the chipped
> white tiles on the floor, and the smudged
> hallway window (a blue-gray light bathes
> the door.) the numerals 3 and 7, with the
> 7 hanging slightly crooked on one screw, the
> brass gleaming dully in the pale light, my
> heart beating wildly. I knocked on the door.

"Come in," she said.

He tried the door, found it unlocked, and stepped into a narrow corridor that seemed to run the length of the apartment. An ornately framed mirror hung directly opposite the entrance. He looked at his own image and shouted, "Where are you?"

"Where do you think I am?" she shouted back. "In here."

He shrugged at himself in the mirror and followed the sound of her voice. She was sitting up in a large bed in a small bedroom facing the street and the elevated structure. She was wearing a blue nightgown, and there was a blue ribbon in her hair. She looked thin and pale and very tired as she turned to greet him. She blinked once in surprise and then said, "What are *you* doing here?"

"Who'd you think it was?" he asked.

"Peter."

"Who's Peter?"

"The boy who lives upstairs. He's been bringing me chicken soup and such." She paused. "How'd you know where I lived?"

"I've been searching for you."

"What are those?"

"Roses."

"For me?"

"Yes."

Ebie nodded, and then stared at him and continued nodding. At last she said, "I'm sick."

"Yes, I know."

"Who told you?"

"A girl with a broken arm."

"Cathy?"

"I don't know her name."

"With a pony tail?"

"Yes."

"That's Cathy Ascot. She's accident prone."

"She told me you were sick and that you lived on Myrtle Avenue. Why are you listed in the book as Dearborn, E.B.?"

"So everyone'll think it's a man living here and I won't get calls from all the nuts in Brooklyn."

"I know one nut who's going to be calling you a lot."

"Who? Oh. You mean you?"

"That's right."

"Well, I don't guess I can stop you from calling."

"No, I don't guess you can."

"Are you going to just stand there with those roses in your hand?"

"I should put them in something, huh?"

"I think there's a vase in the kitchen. The cabinet over the stove."

"You won't disappear, will you?"

"What?"

"When I go for the vase."

"I don't usually disappear," Ebie said. "I just happened to get sick the day after I met you, that's all."

"What've you got?"

"Oh, it's so clichéd it makes me want to puke."

"What is it?"

"Mononucleosis."

"I never heard of it."

"Peter didn't know what it was, either. Hey, can you see through this gown?" she asked suddenly, peering down at her breasts.

"No."

"I wasn't expecting anyone but him," she said, and shrugged.

"You mean Peter?"

"Yes. He usually stops by in the afternoon."

"I don't think I like Peter."

"He's very sweet."

"What's his last name?"

"Malcom. Peter Malcom. He's an actor."

"Mmm?"

"Yes. He works mostly in television. Usually, he plays heavies. He's blond and has sort of a curling lip. He can look very sinister when he wants to."

"I'll bet."

"But you didn't come up here to talk about Peter," she said, and looked down at the bed covers. "Did you?" she said.

"No."

"I didn't think so."

"I don't even know Peter, you see," he said. He was beginning to get very angry. He stood at the foot of the bed, foolishly holding the goddamn roses, and wishing he had not bought them, and wondering what mononucleosis was, and wondering if it was contagious; it sounded like something you sprinkled on meat to tenderize it. "Look, uh . . . where'd you say the vase was?"

"In the kitchen. Over the stove."

"I'll just put these in water for you, and then I'll take off."

"Why?"

"Well, you're expecting Peter, and I really . . ."

"Well, he may not come. He doesn't always come."

"I see."

"And . . ." She shook her head.

"And what?"

"Nothing."

"Okay." He walked out of the bedroom and down the corridor and into the kitchen where he found a cut glass vase in the cabinet over the stove. He filled the vase with water, put the roses into it, and carried them back to the bedroom.

"Where shall I put these?" he asked.

"On the dresser yonder, I guess."

"Yonder," he said.

"Yes. Please."

He put the roses down. When he glanced up into the mirror, he saw that she was staring at his back. His eyes met hers, and she quickly looked away. He turned and leaned against the dresser. Without looking at him, and in a very small voice, she said, "What *did* you come up here to talk about?"

"You," he said.

"What about me?"

"I came up here to tell you I love you."

"Oh."

"Yes."

"Oh, I see," she said.

"Yes." He shrugged. "And so, having said it, I will clear the premises so that Peter can come down with his chicken soup and such, and look through your nightgown."

"You *can* see through it, can't you?"

"No."

"Tell me the truth."

"That's the truth."

"Is it true what you said before?"

"What did I say before?"

"That you love me?"

"Yes, it's true."

"I think that's very sweet."

"Yes."

"Really," she said.

"Mmm."

"Gee," she said, and grinned, and heaved her shoulders in a massive sighing shrug. "I've never had anyone fall in love with me just like that. I really think it's so sweet I can't tell you."

"Well, I think it's pretty sweet too," he said.

"Oh, it is," she said, "it *is*."

"Well."

"Mmm."

They stared at each other silently. He decided he would kiss her. He leaned against the dresser gathering courage, turning to touch one of the roses, plotting. He would cross the room swiftly, cup her face in his hands, taste her mouth, risk all, *now*, do it now, go ahead, go, man. The outer door to the apartment opened. It opened with the speed of familiarity, banging back against the doorstop, no knock, nothing, bang went the door, and heavy footsteps pounded surely through the apartment toward the bedroom. "Ebie!" a man's voice shouted, and he knew with certainty that this was Peter, enter Peter, would he be carrying chicken soup? and hated him at once and intensely, even before he laid eyes on him.

He was a tall blond man of about twenty-two, handsome, with the curling lip Ebie had described, blond eyebrows thick over pale gray eyes, a clean profile, even white teeth that looked as though they had been capped. He was smiling when he came into the bedroom, but he saw immediately that Ebie was not alone, and the smile dropped from his face.

"Oh, hi," he said. "I didn't know you had company."

"Peter, this is . . . what's your name again?"

"Jimmy Driscoll."

"This is Peter Malcom."

"Hi," Peter said.

"Hi."

They looked each other over. Unexpectedly, almost unconsciously, Peter reached into his jacket pocket and took out a pair of eyeglasses. Perching them on his nose, he turned to study Driscoll with deliberate scrutiny.

"You go to Pratt?" he asked.

"Yes."

"That where you know Ebie from?"

"Yes."

He nodded, took off the glasses, replaced them in his jacket pocket, and then turned toward the bed, completely dismissing Driscoll. "How do you feel?" he asked Ebie.

"Much better," she said.

"Good."

"She's got mononucleosis," Driscoll said.

"Yes, I know."

"It's what you put on meat to tenderize it," Driscoll ventured cautiously, and was immediately relieved when Ebie burst out laughing.

"That's very comical," Peter said dryly.

The room went silent.

"Well," Ebie said.

"Well, here we are alone at last," Driscoll said, and

grinned, and felt a new surge of confidence when Ebie laughed again.

"Listen, I sure as hell hope I'm not interrupting anything," Peter said, scowling.

"Well, yes, as a matter of fact you are," Driscoll said. "I came to bring her some notes."

"Notes? What do you mean?"

"For one of her courses."

"What course?" Peter asked.

"Sculpture," Ebie said.

"Really?" Peter said.

"Mmm."

"Well, in that case . . ."

"Maybe you can drop by later," Ebie said.

"Yes, well, it won't be till after dinner, Ebie. I've got to see my agent."

"That's all right," Ebie said. To Driscoll, she said, "He's an actor."

"Yes, I know. You told me."

"He's a very good actor."

"I'll bet you play a lot of heavies," Driscoll said.

"Yes, I do." Peter looked surprised. "How'd you know?"

Driscoll shrugged. "Intuition."

"Well," Peter said, "I'll see you later, Ebie." He glanced at Driscoll. "Nice meeting you."

"Pleasure," Driscoll said.

"So long now, Ebie."

" 'Bye, Peter."

"Yeah," he said, and scowled again at Driscoll, and then turned abruptly and went stamping through the apartment. The front door slammed shut behind him.

"He makes a lot of noise," Driscoll said.

"But he's very nice," Ebie said. "He really does bring me chicken soup."

"Mmm." He cleared his throat.

"Yes?"

"Nothing."

"I feel as if . . ."

"Yes?"

"Nothing."

"Listen, I . . . ."

"Yes?"

"I think I'd better be going."

"You just got here."

"Well, still. He'll be back, and . . . ."

"Not until after dinner."

"Still . . ."

"Well, if you have to go . . ."

"Yes, I think I'd better."

"All right."

"Fine," he said. He started for the door, turned, and said, "Well, I hope you get better."

"I feel better already," she said.

"Well, I'll see you around," he said.

"Listen . . ." she said.

"Yes?"

"Wouldn't you like to . . ."

"Yes?"

"Kiss me goodbye or something?"

"Well, yes, I would," he said.

"I would," she answered. "I would too."

"But what about . . ."

"Well, why don't you?" she said.

"What about Peter?"

"I mean, don't you want to?"

"Yes, but you've got mononucleosis, and . . ."

"Oh, boy," she said.

"It's just . . . who'll take care of you? If I get sick too."

"Peter can bring us *both* soup. Come on over here and kiss me."

"You really think I should?" he said, grinning.

"I really think so. As you yourself pointed out, I'm much older than you . . ."

"Hey, I'm sorry I said that. I didn't mean to . . ."

". . . and it's my mature opinion that you should come

here and kiss me because you can't just go saying sweet things like I love you and then not even kiss a girl goodbye."

"I do love you, Ebie," he whispered.

"Then kiss me."

"I love you."

"Kiss me."

"I love you."

"Kiss me, kiss me, kiss me."

Her mouth then in that small bedroom on Myrtle Avenue, the elevated train rushing past outside as he took her face in his hands and covered her lips with his own, the softness of her mouth. Her mouth now in the hotel room as he lay full length on the bed and looked across the room to where she sat before the dresser putting on lipstick, the same mouth, deeper lines radiating now from the flaps of her nose to the edges of her lips, but the same mouth, nothing could change her mouth, she could live to be a hundred and that perfectly formed mouth would sit upon her withered face like a rose blooming in the desert. The smell of roses wafting across the room from the dresser top, and her lips parting to accept his kiss while the train rushed past in a roaring clamor that rattled the windows of her bedroom. His hands touched her naked breasts beneath the blue nylon gown, he could feel her blossoming nipples and the warmth of her body, the low fever burning inside her. Everything seemed in that moment to take on a truer scent and color, a deeper intensity—the roses, the lowering dusk, the aroma of soap in her hair, the blue ribbon loosening and the golden strands falling free and whisper-light upon his cradling hands—as though her mouth demanded a fuller response, a keener awareness. He held her against him and felt rather than heard her murmur deeply, the sound moving into her lips to hum secretly against his own, trembling with vibration that deepened as she moaned against him, mouth locked to mouth. The sound of the elevated express engulfed the room, and suddenly there was only a whirling vortex the center of which was her mouth. He thought he would lose consciousness, struggled to catch his breath, felt certain he would come against the bedclothes covering her, her mouth persisted, there was nothing in the world but Ebie Dearborn's mouth.

They came up over the brow of the hill from beyond the river that cold November day, he could remember hearing only the bugles at first, could remember wiping his hand across his mouth, and thinking immediately of Ebie, and thinking he might never kiss her again, might never be able to kiss her again, and then he saw them in the distance. Stumbling out of the hole, he reached for his rifle and saw them silhouetted against the misty November sky, the bugles bleating, the terrifying shrill whistles, the shouts in Chinese. They were wearing strange fur hats that gave their faces a foxlike look, pointed, with sharp erect ears. The bugles kept sounding over and over again, like angry screams on the early morning air. There was rifle fire now as his men sleepily stumbled into the mist and tried to halt the charge. The letter, he thought, and touched the pocket of his combat jacket, and then began shooting angrily and randomly into the horde of advancing Chinese, shouting obscenities at them, firing with a wild glee.

"Dris?"

"Yes."

"Are you all right?" she asked.

"I'm fine, Ebie."

"Shouldn't you get ready for dinner? We ought to go down soon."

"I'll shave in a minute," he said.

"What were you thinking about?" she asked.

"I was thinking about November," he answered.

11

HESTER MIERS CAME INTO SARDI'S accompanied by fat Mitzi Starke who, despite her mink coat, looked as though the bitter cold outside had penetrated to her marrow and frozen her solid. Her face was red and her eyes were tearing, and she took off her gloves immediately and began kneading her hands as she scanned the tables just inside the entrance, her glasses fogging. Oscar Stern rose from the table where he was sitting alongside Arthur, and waved at the door, mouthing Mitzi's name. Mitzi did not see him because of the fogging glasses, but Hester took her elbow and began leading her toward where the three men were sitting. Mitzi took off her glasses as they walked, wiping the lenses on a tiny lace-edged handkerchief which she took from the pocket of the mink. She had replaced them on the bridge of her nose by the time they reached the table, and she smiled amiably in recognition, shaking hands all around, kissing Stuart Selig—whom she had known for many years—and telling Arthur she had heard a lot about him and thought he had written a wonderful play. Arthur thanked her, and then held out a chair for Hester, who sat directly alongside him, so that he was between Oscar and Hester, with Mitzi and Stuart on the other side of the table. Stuart asked if the ladies would care for a drink, We've had a head start already, and Mitzi said, Yes, she certainly would like a drink, it was too cold out there even for the brass monkeys. Hester pretended not to know which brass monkeys her agent was referring to. She pressed her knee against Arthur's under the table and said she would like a very dry martini.

"How did the opening in Philly go?" Oscar asked.

"Very well," Mitzi said. "Well, Boris is a marvelous actor, marvelous. He could read the telephone book and make it exciting, you know that."

"Certainly," Stuart said, and glanced at Arthur.

"But the play is a very good one, and that helps," Mitzi said, and smiled graciously at everyone, and then glanced over her shoulder to see what was keeping the drinks. When they came, she downed hers almost at once, and asked the waiter to bring another, a double this time. Hester sipped demurely at her martini, her knee pressed against Arthur's. The table was silent for several moments, and then Oscar said, "I can only remember once when it was this cold. That was four years ago, I'll never forget that winter."

"Yes, it's very cold," Mitzi said.

"I'm sure Arthur wants to hear about his play," Hester said.

"Well, that's why we're here," Stuart said, and smiled at her. "Mitzi tells me you'd like to do it, is that right?"

"Well, she has certain reservations," Mitzi said, and then said "Ahhhh" as the waiter brought her second drink. "Here's to your fine play, Mr. Constantine," she said, and Arthur nodded acknowledgment and raised his own glass.

"It *is* a lovely play, Arthur," Hester said.

"Thank you."

"Though, of course, it *does* need a few minor things done to it," Mitzi said.

"Well, any play needs changes," Stuart said. "A play isn't *written*, it's *rewritten*."

"That's right."

"But nothing serious," Hester said. "Nothing basic to the structure."

"*Or* the theme, for that matter," Mitzi said.

"No, we wouldn't want to touch any of that. You can ruin a play by tampering too much with it," Stuart said.

"Oh, don't I know it," Mitzi said. "The changes we have in mind are really minor and transitional. If they were anything more than that, I assure you Hester wouldn't be interested in the part at all."

"Of course not," Stuart said.

"That's right," Oscar said.

"But Hester very definitely *is* interested in doing the play, and I'm fairly certain we can spring her from Lincoln Center. At least I'm hoping we can, I haven't discussed it with them yet. I wanted to get Mr. Constantine's reaction to the changes we had in mind before I contacted anyone."

"Arthur's been very reasonable about any suggestions thus far," Stuart said, "so I can't imagine . . ."

"That's right," Oscar said.

". . . him refusing to make a few minor changes now, when we're so close to getting the play on at last."

"That's right."

"We're dealing with a professional writer here," Stuart said, and smiled at Arthur.

"Well, thank you," Arthur said. He started to put his hand on Hester's knee, and then changed his mind. She looked very lovely, with her blond hair still arranged in its careless coiffure, and wearing a blue sheath scooped low in the front, a string of pearls around her throat. She smiled at Arthur assuringly, and he lifted his glass and sipped at it and began to feel a warmth spreading through him, a genuine feeling of fondness for all the people at the table, including fat Mitzi, who had put down her drink and was blowing her nose into a tiny handkerchief. She had still not removed the mink coat, and she still seemed to be suffering from exposure.

"Well now," she said, giving her nose a final wipe and putting the handkerchief back into her pocket, "I think we should start with the age of the girl, don't you think so, Hester?"

"Yes," Hester said, "I think that's important."

"Important, but minor. Hester's twenty-five, you know, and whereas she comes off a bit younger onstage, we think we'd be asking for trouble if she tried to pass for nineteen."

"Well . . ." Arthur said.

"That's right, we don't want the critics to start picking on stupid little things," Oscar said. "They'll find enough anyway, without any help from us."

"So we thought the girl's age might be raised to twenty-two or twenty-three," Mitzi said. "That would be more reasonable, in terms of Hester playing the part."

"Well, there's a lot of stuff in the play about her nineteenth birthday coming up," Arthur said. "I'd have to . . ."

"So it'll be her twenty-third birthday coming up," Oscar said. "That's no problem."

"No, but she's supposed to be leaving for college in the fall."

"Yes, we—"

"In fact, the conflict, you know, is between this girl who wants to go to college and . . ."

"Yes, that's a problem, admittedly."

". . . her uneducated father, a Bronx mailman who, you know, wants her to marry this guy and settle down. That's the conflict."

"Yes, we know."

"So she'd have to be a college girl, you see."

"Well, she can be a college girl at twenty-two," Stuart said.

"That's right."

"She can just be *graduating* college maybe," Stuart said, "and she wants to go to graduate school or something, and her father objects. That could be exactly the same."

"Well . . ." Arthur said.

"Of course, Hester played a college girl in the last thing she did at the Rep," Mitzi said.

"Mmm," Stuart said.

"If she keeps playing college girls . . ." Mitzi said, and shrugged.

"Well, Carol *is* a college girl," Arthur said. "That's the part. I mean, that's the part."

"The way it is now, yes," Mitzi said.

"But we'd have to make her older," Hester said. "Don't you think so, Arthur?"

"I don't know. I think you could pass for nineteen," he said, and decided to squeeze her knee after all, which he did.

"That's very sweet of you, Arthur," she said, and smiled, "but I think the girl *has* to be older."

"She's supposed to be a virgin," Arthur said. "Do you know any twenty-two-year-old virgins?"

"I don't even know any *seven*-year-old virgins," Oscar said, and laughed.

Mitzi laughed too, and then said, "Actually, she doesn't *have* to be a virgin, does she? That really doesn't add anything to the play."

"Well, there's an entire scene where . . ."

"Yes, with the boy . . ."

"Yes, the one her father wants her to marry . . ."

"That's right."

"And he tries to, well, to lay her, you know, and this is another thing that adds to the conflict of this girl trying to lead her own life without interference from her father or from the people her father has chosen for her."

"The boy, you mean?"

"Yes. So the scene has meaning only if she's a virgin, you know, and is, well, saving herself for . . . for the person *she* chooses."

"Well, do you think girls actually *save* themselves anymore, Arthur?" Mitzi asked, and smiled.

"I don't know, but Carol is supposed to be . . ."

"I mean, you said yourself not three minutes ago that you didn't know any twenty-two-year-old virgins."

"Carol's only eighteen, going on nineteen. I think . . ."

"There's a difference, certainly," Stuart said. "But, Arthur, is it really *that* important that she be a virgin?"

"Or even a college girl?" Hester asked.

"What?"

"Is it important that she plans to leave for college in the fall?"

"Sure it is."

"Why?"

"Because that's the conflict."

"Yes, but the conflict can be *any* conflict, isn't that true? So long as it's between the girl and her father."

"I think we all need another drink," Oscar said, and signaled to the waiter. "Mitzi? Hester?"

"Yes, I'm still cold," Mitzi said.

"I'd love another," Hester said, and smiled at Arthur.

"The same all around," Oscar said to the waiter.

"Double for the lady?"

"Yes, a double," Mitzi said.

"We ought to think about ordering," Stuart said.

"Oh, we've got plenty of time. Let's thrash this out, shall we?" Mitzi said. "I know Mr. Constantine is anxious to hear our views, and we're certainly anxious to know his reactions to them. I can't make a move with the Rep, you know, until . . ."

"Certainly," Stuart said. "What do you think, Arthur?"

"Well . . . about changing Carol's age, do you mean?"

"About having her a little more experienced," Stuart said.

"A nice girl," Mitzi said, "but a little more experienced."

"So she's been to bed with one or two guys already," Oscar said. "That doesn't make her a slut."

"A *dozen* guys wouldn't make her a slut," Stuart said.

"A dozen?" Arthur asked.

"Well, I don't think that's exactly the image we want for Hester," Mitzi said. "Arthur's right in that respect. We want Carol to be a sweet and confused young girl. If we have her sleeping around with half the men in the city . . ."

"I was only trying to indicate . . ."

"I think she may have had one affair," Hester said. "She *is* twenty-two, you know, going on twenty-three. It would seem implausible otherwise."

"One affair sounds reasonable," Stuart said. "What do you think, Arthur?"

"I'm trying to think of the whole," Arthur said. "We've got to think of what any revisions would do to the whole of the play. I really feel it's important that she be a virgin."

"Here're the drinks," Stuart said.

The waiter put their glasses on the table, and they all drank silently for a moment. Mitzi blew her nose again, and then said, "It's just that a girl like Carol who has, after all, been around a little . . ."

"But she hasn't," Arthur said. "Her father's kept her cooped up in—"

"Well, a social worker would get to meet a great many people," Mitzi said. "Isn't that so?"

"A great many people," Hester said.

"What do you mean?"

"A social worker."

"I still don't get you."

"If Carol were a social worker," Mitzi said.

"Instead of a college girl," Hester said. "Working for a state agency, you see. Or even a private agency."

"And her father objects to her wanting a life of her own, and insists that she marry this boy he has chosen for her. And the boy tries to lay her, just the way you've got it now, which only strengthens her resolve to lead her own life, choose her own friends, her own lovers, and this leads to the showdown in the third act, just the way you've got it now, between her and her father."

"A social worker," Arthur said blankly.

"Yes, instead of a college girl," Hester said.

"She played a college girl in that last thing at the Rep, you know," Mitzi said to Stuart.

"Yes, she was very good," Stuart said.

"Did you see it?" Hester asked.

"Yes, you were marvelous."

"But, of course, she's done the college girl bit," Mitzi said, "and there has to be a challenge, otherwise what's the sense?"

"That's right," Oscar said. "There has to be a challenge."

"I don't know anything about social work," Arthur said.

"What do you know about mailmen, for that matter?" Oscar said.

"My father was a mailman."

"Well . . ."

"Do you think the father in the play *ought* to be a mailman?" Mitzi asked.

"If his daughter is a social worker?" Hester said.

"Do you know anything about social work?" Arthur asked her.

"No, but we can find out anything we need to know. For any scenes showing the girl in her office."

"What office?"

"Where she works."

"Where she does her social work," Mitzi said.

"She could have a colored family she's working with," Hester said, "and maybe her father objects to that, too. Maybe he's a bigot."

"But he *isn't*," Arthur said. "He's just narrow and . . . and oriented to . . . to . . . to the way things were in the old country. And in the old country, a girl didn't go running off to school, she . . . she got married and had children and . . ."

"Do you think that's a universal problem these days, Mr. Constantine?" Mitzi asked.

"What do you mean?"

"An immigrant father and a daughter who rebels . . ."

"I think the conflict between a father and a daughter *is* universal, yes. We're dealing with Electra here, what difference does it make whether the father is an immigrant or—"

"That's just my point. If we're dealing with something as universal as the Electra bit, why does the father have to be an immigrant mailman who can hardly speak English?"

"He speaks English fine," Arthur said.

"Well, you know what I mean."

"No, I don't. He's been in this country for thirty-five years. He's a man who's fifty-eight years of age, he speaks English fine. But he still clings to the old traditions, he's got a background of traditions . . ."

"That's *Fiddler*, isn't it?"

"What?"

"Fiddler on the Roof. That's Tevye's character, isn't it?"

"That's a different thing entirely," Arthur said. "I *lived* through this with my father and my sister, and I can tell you . . ."

"When was that, Arthur?"

"I don't know, she's married now and has three children, it must have been ten, twelve years ago. But I can tell you that the showdown between those two shook our house from the roof to the—"

"Very often, though," Oscar said, "something can seem very dramatic in life, but not when it's put on the stage."

"I think he's presented it *very* dramatically," Hester said, and smiled.

"Yes, no one has any objections to the dramatic structure," Mitzi said.

"It's just these few character changes."

"Why can't the father work in an office someplace? Or why can't he have his own business? If you insist on his being Italian, why can't he be a building contractor?"

"There are a great many Italian building contractors," Hester said.

"I don't see why he can't be a mailman," Arthur said. "The way I wrote it."

"We're trying to understand him in terms of the modern theatergoer."

"Besides, there was a mailman in the Schisgal play."

"Which Schisgal play?"

"The Tiger."

"Write me a play like *Luv*," Mitzi said, "and I wouldn't ask for a single change."

"Brilliant," Stuart said.

"Penetrating," Oscar said.

"Can't I be a social worker, Arthur?" Hester asked. "I'm *so* tired of playing college girls."

"If this man were educated . . ." Stuart said.

"Which man?"

"The father. If he were educated, we could offer the part to somebody like Fonda, you know."

"In fact, I hear Fredric March is looking for a play," Oscar said.

"They'd be great with Hester."

"I'd love to work with either one of them," Hester said.

"Don't think they wouldn't love to work with *you*, baby," Mitzi said, and finished her drink.

"You're a marvelous actress," Stuart said.

"Thank you. I see the social worker as a very dedicated person, don't you?" Hester said, turning to Arthur.

"I don't know anything about social workers," Arthur said. "My sister was a simple girl living in a house she wanted to get out of. That's what this play is about. The fight between her and my father. She wins the fight, Carol wins the fight and goes off to school. All this other stuff . . ."

"That's not your sister's real name, is it?" Mitzi asked.

"Carol? No."

"What's her name?" Oscar asked.

"Jule. Why?"

"I just wanted to know."

"I didn't know this play was based on an actual experience of yours, Arthur," Stuart said.

"Well, most fiction comes out of a man's life, doesn't it?" Mitzi said.

"I guess so."

"We're not asking you to change the *reality* of the situation," Hester said.

"We're just asking for a few revisions that would make the story more understandable to a modern audience."

"You talk as if I wrote it back in the Middle Ages," Arthur said, and Oscar immediately laughed. Everyone at the table laughed with him.

"Well, you understand what we mean," Mitzi said, drying her eyes.

"Yes."

"What do you say, Arthur?" Stuart said.

"I don't know. I'll have to think about it."

"Certainly," Mitzi said. "We don't expect a man to make a snap decision. Not when he's worked on something for such a long time."

"That's right," Oscar said.

"You think about it," Hester said.

"Can you let us know by Friday?" Mitzi asked.

"That's only the day after tomorrow," Arthur said.

"Yes."

"Well, I thought . . . I'm in the middle of a trial, you see, and . . . I thought I'd read the play over the weekend and see if your suggestions . . ."

"Well, the only reason I'm suggesting Friday," Mitzi said, "is because they're bringing the new Osborne play over from London, and they've asked Hester to play the part."

"Osborne," Arthur said.

"Yes."

"His new play."

"Yes. And I promised I'd give them an answer before the weekend. And then, of course, I'd still have to go to the people at the Rep and work all that out, so I think you can understand the reason for speed."

"Well, I . . ."

"The changes seem reasonable, Arthur."

"Well . . ."

"I think a social worker could be very exciting," Hester said.

"Fonda would be great for the father," Oscar said.

"Think it over, and let us know by Friday, will you?" Mitzi said.

"I'll think it over."

"He'll let you know by Friday," Stuart promised.

He had been watching the office from the drugstore counter across the street on Madison Avenue, drinking three cups of coffee, and then wandering over to browse the paperback racks near the plate glass window (*The Paper Dragon*, he noticed, was still in print) and then going back to the counter for a fourth, and finally nauseating, cup of coffee. He

was heading for the paperback racks again when he saw the
lights go off across the street. He quickly paid his check and
went to stand just inside the entrance to the drugstore.
Chickie came out onto the sidewalk first, wearing a black
cloth coat with a black fox collar, and Ruth came out of the
office immediately afterwards, pulling the door shut behind
her, locking it, and then trying the knob once again before
stepping out of the doorway. She looped her arm through
Chickie's, and the two women started up Madison Avenue,
their heads ducked against the wind. Sidney opened the door
immediately and went outside. The sidewalks had been
shoveled almost clear of snow, but the footing was treacherous, and the wind was brutally sharp. His eyes began to tear
at once. He was wearing gloves, but he thrust his hands into
his pockets nonetheless, looking up immediately to make sure
the girls were still in sight, and then wondering again why he
was behaving so foolishly, following them home from work
this way, ridiculous, a man his age.

Ruth lived four blocks from the office, and he supposed
they were heading there, though he didn't much care *where*
they were heading so long as they *got* there quick. His feet
were freezing, and his ears throbbed. He lowered his head as
a fierce gust of wind knifed the avenue, took one hand from
his pocket to clutch his homburg tightly onto his head,
holding it there as the wind raged. His coat flapped wildly
about his knees, his trousers were flattened against his legs, he
coughed bitterly and hung on to his hat, pushing against the
wind, trying to keep his footing on the slippery pavement.
The wind died momentarily, and he took a deep breath and
raised his head and then stopped dead in his tracks because
the girls were directly ahead of him on the corner, not fifty
feet away.

A tan Cadillac was parked at the curb, its engine running,
white fumes billowing from its exhaust. The driver of the car
had leaned over on the front seat toward the window closest
to the curb, which was open. Both Ruth and Chickie, vapor
pluming from their mouths, were slightly bent as they talked
to the man in the car, snatches of sound rising, carrying

unintelligibly on the wind to where Sidney stood rooted to the sidewalk. He watched a moment longer, and then realized how vulnerable his position was. Ducking into a doorway, he stared at the Cadillac from his new vantage point, watching as Ruth opened the front door and got onto the seat beside the man driving. She reached behind her almost immediately to unlock the back door, and Chickie opened the door and climbed in. Sidney blinked. The car idled at the curb a moment longer, and then gunned away in a burst of power, skid chains clanging.

Sidney emerged from the doorway and watched the car as it went up the avenue and out of sight.

In a moment, the wind rose again.

Leo Kessler was wearing an overlarge red robe, belted loosely at the waist. Beneath the robe, he wore a ribbed undershirt with shoulder straps, and red-and-white check undershorts with black piping on either leg. He had taken off his shoes and replaced them with fleece-lined slippers, but he was still wearing black socks supported by yellow and black garters. Every now and again, he dipped his nose into the brandy snifter in his hands, and then looked up at Sam Genitori, who was outlining what had happened that day in court. "Mmm-hmmm," Leo said, "mmm-hmmm," and then dipped his nose into the brandy snifter again, and looked up at Sam, and rose and walked to the windows and then walked back to his easy chair angled before the marble fireplace in his apartment on East 57th Street, and made himself comfortable, looking down at his long hairy legs and flashy garters, and nodding, and saying "Mmmm-mmm, mmm-hmmm," and then sipping a little brandy again.

"So I told him just where he could go," Sam said. "You got any more of that brandy?"

"Help yourself," Leo said.

"Damn egotistical jackass," Sam said, and poured some brandy into a shot glass.

"I think you were a little too rough with him," Leo said. "Don't you want a snifter for that?"

"I don't know where they are."

"Under the bar. Near the wine glasses."

"Too much trouble," Sam said. "*Salute,*" he said, raising the shot glass, and then downing the brandy in one swallow. "Ahhhhhhhh," he said. "What do you mean too rough on him?"

"*He* seems to think he did a good job today."

"Knowles, you mean?"

"Mmm-hmmm."

"How do you know?"

"He told me."

"You saw him today?"

"Yes."

"Where?"

"At the office."

"He came to the office?"

"Mmm-hmmm."

"Why?"

"To ask for six million dollars."

"Did you give it to him?"

"I gave it to him."

"You gave him six million dollars?"

"I authorized six million dollars for his new picture, yes."

"You gave that idiot six million dollars?"

"Someday, Sam, when I have a little time, I'll explain the motion picture business to you."

"Don't bother," Sam said. "All I know is that after his performance in court today, I wouldn't even trust him to walk my dog around the block. So you give him . . ."

"I don't have a dog," Leo said.

"Even if I *didn't* have a dog," Sam said, "I wouldn't trust Knowles to walk it around the block."

"He's a good director."

"He's a lousy witness."

"He makes good pictures."

"That's debatable."

"I'm not talking about *artistic* pictures, Sam. Artistic pictures can get you in the subway if you also happen to have a fifteen-cent token. Ralph Knowles is a good director because his pictures make money."

"Some of them."

"Most of them."

"He *still* almost wrecked our case today."

Leo shrugged. "I'm not so sure he did, Sam. I heard him telling it this afternoon, and I've just now heard you tell it again, and I'm not so sure he wrecked our case at all."

"Leo, take my word for it . . ."

"Driscoll, maybe. Maybe he wrecked *Driscoll*. But not the case, and not API."

"He told them—"

"He told them he used the book."

"Yes, but he also—"

"He also told them there are no fairies in his pictures. What's so bad about that?"

"Leo, the point—"

"You want a man to go around saying there are fairies in his pictures? Come on now, Sam."

"Leo, by saying what he said—"

"It made it seem like Driscoll wrote a dirty book."

"No! It made it seem—"

"Which Knowles made into a clean picture."

"Leo, I think you're missing something important."

"What's more important than making clean pictures the whole family can go see? Is Walt Disney doing so bad with it?"

"Leo . . ."

"He also said he made two characters out of one character, right?"

"Yeah, did he tell you about *that?*"

"He told me. But *they* claimed one of those characters was a fairy, and *that's* where he had them, Sam. Because it wasn't."

"What wasn't?"

"A fairy."

"Leo, he walked into a trap, don't you see that?"

"It would have been worse the other way."

"What other way?"

"If he denied something he actually did. If he told them he *didn't* make two characters out of one."

"Leo, the truth is he doesn't *remember* what he did."

"Oh, certainly he does. He wrote the picture, didn't he? He directed it, didn't he?"

"All right, suppose he *did* make two characters out of one?"

"That's exactly what he did."

"Then where did he get the idea?"

"What do you mean?" Leo asked.

"For the other character? The *second* character."

"Where?"

"From the play, Leo."

"What play?"

"*Catchpole.*"

"What?"

"In our files, Leo."

"What?"

"At the studio, Leo."

"He never said that."

"He didn't have to say it."

"Why would anyone think . . ."

"Because first he said, Yes that's what I did, I made two characters out of one, but then he couldn't remember which characters he'd put together to form the second character, and then he said the villain in the book wasn't a queer, or even the guy in the picture, and Leo I am telling you he made a holy mess of the whole damn thing."

"Well, he may be a horse's ass," Leo said, "but he is a *bright* horse's ass. I cannot believe . . ."

"It's what he did, Leo."

"He's too smart for that."

"He's a jerk, Leo."

"A whole lot smarter than most directors around."

"A moron, Leo."

"And certainly smarter than a tinhorn shyster like Brackman."

"Leo, he may have wrecked our case beyond repair."

"The stupid bastard," Leo said.

If Christie were here, Jonah thought, she would pour some boric acid into hot water (it must be *scalding* hot, darling, she would say) and then insist that I soak my wrist in it, changing the water whenever it got lukewarm, that's what Christie Dunseath Willow would do. And I would allow her to do it while marveling at how adequately she ministered to my needs, and delighting in the sight of her, and simultaneously knowing that we did not have a marriage at all. Oh how surprised they all were, our friends, oh how shocked, stunned, disbelieving when they learned that Christie and I were going to part (but they're such a *darling* couple) that we were going to take up separate residence and live separate lives (so marvelously alert, so much *fun* to be with) that finally we were going to end this ridiculous, sham exercise, recognize it for what it really was, and chalk it off as a total failure (both so bright and talented, so very much alive).

Talented, yes, the very talented Jonah Willow who defended a pair of Communist adolescents trying to change the world by blowing up Gracie Mansion, and then found himself defending similar unpopular clients and causes in the years that followed. Talented, yes, and bright enough to recognize the public need for a champion, clever enough to set out to fill that need. A man loses his innocence once and for all time when he makes a calculation he knows is even slightly dishonest, makes it (he will tell himself) for the sake of Survival, or Ambition, or Health or Sanity, or for the sake of Honesty to Oneself (the most dishonest reason) but makes it coldly and shrewdly and with malice aforethought. Jonah was bright enough and clever enough to recognize that he had successfully defended two rather unsavory individuals (because their Rights Were Being Violated, he told himself, and perhaps was being Honest to Himself) and that his less than brilliant courtroom display had put his name before the public eye, where he intended to keep it. It was no accident that the firm of Gauthier and Willow defended in the next several years a succession of individuals accused of murder, rape, pornography, spying, draft evasion, government manipulation of contracts, obscenity, and other such exotic and lofty activities executed by believers, fanatics, followers and fools of every persuasion.

But if a man loses his innocence only once, a woman surely loses it twice, and neither time has anything to do with her defloration. Christie lost her innocence for the first time when she realized her father wasn't God, and she lost it for the second time when she realized Jonah wasn't God, either. She realized this in the early years of her marriage and was not bright enough to find any solace in historical precedent. She only knew that she had married someone who pretended to be what he was not. What she expected Jonah to be was never clearly defined to him, although she repeatedly told him he was a fraud and a fake, even *before* the succession of unpopular wrongdoers began parading to his office door. He quite naturally regarded this condemnation as unfair and a trifle hostile, even though he suspected it had nothing to do with professional ethics or personal ambitions, but only with Christie's image of him as a man, an image he was somehow destroying. He once asked her, "*Why* am I a fake and a fraud?" and she answered, "Because you *are*," which was considerably enlightening and which helped to ease tensions between them that week, especially since she was in her sixth month of pregnancy by that time, and had begun denying him connubial rights in her fourth month. "You're insensitive," she told him. "You don't know what a woman feels."

Amy came on the seventh of May, 1954, and the birth was every bit as painful and as horrible as Christie knew it would be, an ordeal for which she never fully forgave Jonah. She made it clear the day she came home from the hospital that this was to be their one and only venture into parenthood, and that if he so much as looked at her before she was properly prepared for "having sex," she would strangle him without remorse. Her preparations for "having sex," as she invariably referred to it ("Do you want to have sex?" she would ask, not without a wicked glint in her eye) assumed ritual proportions in the months that followed. She would spend what seemed like hours in the bathroom before coming to him. Once he fell asleep waiting for her, and once he sent her a memo on a Tuesday, actually mailed it from his office to the house, reading: "Thursday night! Get ready!" But despite these rigorous preparations, they "had sex" often and with apparent satisfaction, and the only time he ever thought of getting himself another woman was in the year just before the divorce, by which time things had become really impossible.

Christie was a beautiful woman, and most beautiful women can say or do anything they wish, as long as they perform with a certain amount of style. She possessed style in abundance, from the tips of her Bendel shoes to the top of her Victor Vito coiffure. Her eyes snapped with whiplash certainty whenever she delivered another of her absurd banalities. She would stand with hands on narrow hips, flat-chested but sinuous and sexy as hell, splendid legs widespread as though she were trying to maintain balance on the deck of a lurching yawl, head tossed back, tiny beauty spot penciled near her lips, a spirited laugh (her mother's) erupting after each of her own half-witticisms. "Craparoo," of course, was her identifying theme, and was repeated with the regularity of the NBC chimes. But she knew other devastatingly funny catch phrases, too, and she used them with similar frequency, to the amusement of all their new friends.

Nor was her comic virtuosity limited to verbal thrusts alone. She began drinking too much, and told Jonah to go to hell whenever he brought this failing to her attention. He once found her in the bedroom with a young actor whose nose he punched, her skirt up over her knees, oblivious to what the son of a bitch was attempting. (On the night they decided to end it, she kept sipping a glass of sherry which she finally left on the dresser, and which the next morning had its surface covered with a scum of floating dead fruit flies.) Figuratively, Christie rode her mother's horse into every living room, theater, restaurant, concert hall, and night club in New York—and because she had a good seat and remarkable hands, everyone applauded her performance. Except Jonah. Jonah wondered what had happened to the little girl who used to pick her delicate way through the forsythia bushes.

Maybe she grew up too soon, or maybe she never grew up at all, or maybe they both grew up simultaneously but in opposite directions. This too shall pass, she assured him, but of course it did not. By the tenth year of their marriage he was ready to agree with her that it was all craparoo. The odd thing about it, he thought now as he struggled with his pajama top, his wrist throbbing, the odd thing about it was that he had loved her all that time, and probably had still loved her when they decided there was no use going any further with it. He could remember watching her undress one night, here in this bedroom, taking her time with her underthings, and then floating a nylon gown down over her slender body while he watched from the bed, delighting in her presence, could remember the sidelong glance she gave him as she turned out the light, could remember his intense excitement, and her cold "Put that away, buster. We're calling it quits, remember?" Yes, he could remember.

And remembering, could not understand. Or perhaps understood all.

He pulled back the covers and climbed into bed.

On impulse, he reached for the telephone, lifted the receiver, and began dialing Christie's number. No, he thought, and hung up. He sat staring at the phone for a moment. Then he lifted the receiver, waited for a dial tone, and called Sally Kirsch.

Her phone rang six times before it was answered. Sally's voice, edged with sleep, started to say "Hello," but the receiver must have slipped from her grasp. He heard a clatter as it tumbled onto a hard surface, and then heard her mutter, "Oh, god*damn*," and then heard her recovering the receiver, and then her voice again, hardly more awake this time, "Hello?"

"Sally?"

"Who's this?" she said flatly, and suspiciously, and somewhat angrily.

"Jonah."

"*Who?*"

"Jonah." He paused. "Willow."

"Oh."

There was a silence.

"What time is it?" she asked, and yawned.

"Two o'clock, something like that."

"Mmm?"

"Were you asleep?" he asked.

"Mmm."

"Are you awake now?"

"Mmm."

"Would you like to have lunch with me tomorrow?"

"*What* time did you say it was?"

"Two o'clock."

"In the *morning,* do you mean?"

"That's right."

"Mmm," Sally said, and again was silent.

"How's your lip?" he said.

"Haven't you got court tomorrow?"

"Yes, I have."

"Don't you think you ought to go to bed or something?"

"I *am* in bed."

"To sleep, I mean."

"I wanted to ask you to lunch first."

"It's two o'clock in the morning," she said.

"I know. *Will* you have lunch with me?"

"Yes, I'll have lunch with you."

"Good. How about dinner?"

"When?"

"Tomorrow night."

"Tomorrow night," she repeated.

"Yes."

"What is all this, Jonah?"

"I want to have lunch with you tomorrow and dinner with you tomorrow night."

"All of a sudden."

"Yes. All of a sudden."

"All right," she said, and he was sure she shrugged.

"Can you meet me at Gasner's?"

"What time?"

"Twelve, twelve-thirty, give me a chance to get from the courthouse."

"Listen . . ." Sally said.

"Yes?"

"Aren't you married or something?"

"No."

"Somebody told me you were married."

"Who told you that?"

"A friend of mine. The night we met. At that party."

"Said I was married?"

"Yes."

"No, I *used* to be married," Jonah said. "That was a long time ago."

"How long ago?"

"Why?"

"Because I don't kid around," Sally said.

"I was divorced in 1962."

They were silent.

"You mean you thought I was married when you went up to Vassar with me?" Jonah asked.

"Yes."

"Do you usually go out with married men?"

"No. Well, once before I did."

They were silent again.

"Well," he said.

"Well," she said.

"They turn off the heat in this building at eleven o'clock," he said.

"Here, too."

"It's like an icebox."

"Yes, here too."

"Well," he said.

"Well," she said.

"Well, I'll see you tomorrow."

"I'm looking forward to it," she said.

"Good night," he said.

"Good night," she said.

Chickie did not come into the apartment until two-thirty A.M., using the key he had given her. He was asleep in an armchair near the bookcase, and he was startled into wakefulness by the sound of the key being turned in the lock, the tumblers falling. He opened his eyes and looked toward the door just as it opened. Chickie stood there for a moment, silhouetted by the light burning in the hallway. With one hand on the doorknob for support, she lifted first one foot and then the other to remove her shoes. Holding the shoes in one hand, she closed the door behind her and tiptoed into the room.

"Hello, Chickie," he said.

"Ooooo," she answered, "you scared me."

"Put on a light."

"I thought you were asleep."

"I was."

"Did I wake you?"

"Yes."

"You poor dear man."

"I thought you'd be here before midnight."

"What?"

"You said you'd be here before midnight."

"Oh, yes, I know, but we got all hung up. I'm terribly sorry, Sidney."

"I've got to get some sleep, you know," Sidney said. "Driscoll goes on the stand tomorrow morning."

"I know. Sidney, do you have any milk in the fridge? I'm dying for a glass of milk."

"I think so. What's today?"

"Wednesday."

"I think they deliver on Wednesday."

"Don't go away, you dear man," she said, and she padded out of the room and into the kitchen.

"What time did you leave the office?" he called.

"What, dear?"

"What time did you leave the office?"

"Oh, I don't know. It must have been six or six-thirty. Why?"

"I just wondered."

Chickie appeared in the doorway to the kitchen, holding a glass of milk in one hand and a cookie in the other. She took a bite of the cookie and then drained half the glass of milk. "Mmmm," she said, "that's good. Would you like some milk?"

"No, thanks. Where'd you go from the office?"

"We went out to eat."

"Where?"

"Oh my, listen to the lawyer," Chickie said. "How's the rial going?"

"Pretty well, I think. Where'd you eat?"

"Pavillon, where else?"

"Come on, Chickie."

"Chambord."

"Chickie . . ."

"The Four Seasons."

"I'm trying . . ."

"The Forum."

"I want to know where you and Ruth went."

"We went to eat at a restaurant on Madison, a few blocks from the office. I don't even know the name of it. It's a tiny little dump."

"And then where did you go?"

"Up to Ruth's, where we worked on the trip."

"What trip?"

"The trip I was telling you about."

"The one you said might materialize?"

"That's right. Only now it looks as if it might very *well* materialize. How's the trial going, Sidney?"

"I told you. Pretty well."

"Does that mean you'll win?"

"I don't know."

"Well, you must have some indication, Sidney."

"I think it's going our way. They put on a witness today who was a real *shmuck,* he did them a lot of harm."

"Who was that?"

"Ralph Knowles."

"I never heard of him."

"He's a movie director."

"What did he direct?"

"What difference does it make?"

"I'm only trying to understand what happened, Sidney. Do you mind if I take off my dress?"

"I've got to get some sleep," Sidney said.

"Are you afraid I won't let you sleep?" Chickie asked, and smiled.

"No, but . . ."

"I'm very tired myself, darling," she said. "Unzip me, will you?" She walked to where he was sitting, and then turned her back to him. He lowered the zipper. "Thank you," she said, and walked away from him into the bedroom. "It's very smoky in here," she said. "Were you smoking in here, Sidney?"

"What?"

"In the bedroom here."

"Yes, I had a cigar when I got home."

"What time did you get home?"

"About eight," he said. He paused. "I got a lift." He paused again. "In a Cadillac." He could hear her rustling around in the bedroom.

"I'm just exhausted," she said.

"Those Cadillacs are very nice."

"They're the only kind to have, Sidney," she said.

"What time is it?"

"It's a little past twelve. Come to bed, Sidney."

He rose and went into the bedroom. She had put on one of his robes, and was standing by the mirror brushing out her long red hair. "Have you ever been in a Cadillac?" he asked.

"Of course."

"Recently?"

"Sidney," she said, without turning from the mirror, "what is this?"

"What is what?"

"What is all this business about Cadillacs? Are you thinking of buying one, is that it?"

"Well, if I w-w-win this case . . ."

"Yes, you'll be very wealthy."

"I c-c-could . . ."

"You could buy three or four Cadillacs, Sidney, all in different colors."

"You don't believe me, d-do you?" Sidney said.

"Believe you about what, dear? That you're going to win your case?"

"I *am* going to win," he said.

"Well, don't get so fierce about it, Sidney. I believe you."

"I *am*," he said.

"Mmm-huh."

"If you were to m-m-marry me . . ."

"Sidney, let's not go into that right now."

"I'm only saying."

"Yes, but not now." She put the brush down on the dresser top, and then turned and leaned against the dresser and folded her arms across her breasts and smiled thinly and said, "Would you like to do Eddie Cantor?"

"No," he said.

"I thought you might like to."

"No."

"The way you did at Harvard."

"No."

"What was it called, the group? Hasty Pudding?"

"No, it was just the Dramatic Club."

"Anyway, I thought you might like to."

"No."

"Well," she said, and shrugged. "I can't force you, I guess." She shrugged again and then took off the robe. Naked, she walked to the bed, pulled back the blanket, and propped herself against the pillows.

"Chickie," he said, "there's something we've got to talk about."

"It's a shame, though," she said, "because you know how much I love it."

"I get the feeling that something's going on and I don't know what."

"The way you roll your eyes, and wave your hands around, I just love that, Sidney."

"What's going on, Chickie?"

"What's going on where, baby?"

"With . . . with you and Ruth."

Chickie looked down at her breast, took it in one hand and idly examined the skin around the nipple. Without looking at him, she said, "Did you see us get into the Cadillac tonight, Sidney? Is that it?"

"Well . . . yes."

"Were you following us, Sidney?"

"Yes."

"What, Sidney?"

"Yes. I was."

"Following us?"

"Yes."

"To see where we were going, Sidney?"

"Yes."

"Because something's bothering you?"

"Yes."

"If I were to marry you, Sidney, would you still follow me around?"

"I . . . I don't know. I get the feeling . . ."

"Would you, Sidney?"

". . . that you're lying to me all the time, that something . . ." He shook his head. "I don't know wh-what, I j-j-just don't know."

"Don't stammer, Sidney," she said, and looked up at him.

"I j-j-just . . ."

"The man in the Cadillac was a man named Jerome Courtlandt . . ."

"I didn't ask you."

"Shut up, Sidney, and listen. He's the man we're arranging the European trip for, and he was heading for the office when he happened to spot us, and he asked Ruth if he could drop us off someplace, because it was so bitter cold, and she said, Yes certainly, and he drove us to the restaurant. Now that's what happened with Mr. Jerome Courtlandt."

"I didn't ask."

"No, you just sneaked around and followed me from work."

"Because . . ."

"Because you don't trust me."

"I t-trust you, Chickie. It's just . . ."

"Oh my," Chickie said, "how could I possibly marry a man who doesn't trust me?"

"I trust you, I do."

"Who doesn't care about me at all . . ."

"I care about you."

"Who follows me around . . ."

"I'm sorry, Chickie."

"Do Eddie Cantor," she said.

"No, I . . ."

"Do it."

"It's . . . undignified," he mumbled.

"Do it."

". . . and silly."

"Do it."

He hesitated. "If . . ." he started, and then stopped.

"That's it," she said.

"If you knew . . ."

"Go on, honey."

"If you knew Susie . . ."

"Go on, baby, go on."

"I can't. I feel . . ."

"Do it, Sidney."

"If you knew Susie," he sang, "like I know Susie . . . oh, oh, oh, what a girl . . ."

"Roll your eyes. You're not rolling your eyes."

"There's none so classy," he sang, and then raised his hands, the elbows bent, and began hopping from one foot to the other in a sliding sideward motion, rolling his eyes, his voice suddenly going higher in imitation of Cantor, "as this fair lassie," rolling his eyes and hopping back and forth, mouth pouting, eyes rolling, "oh, oh, holy Moses, what a chassis . . ."

"That's it, baby," Chickie said, and began giggling.

"If you knew Susie," he sang, his voice stronger now, "like I . . ."

"Yes, yes," she said, giggling louder.

". . . know Susie . . ."

"You're marvelous," she said, "wonderful!"

". . . oh, oh, oh, what a girl!" he sang, and then abruptly turned toward the bed, and dropped to his knees and wrapped his arms around her waist and fiercely pressed his face to her naked belly.

"Yes," Chickie whispered. "Yes, baby, that's it."

THURSDAY

12

EVERY THURSDAY, Driscoll's mother would fuss and fret in the bedroom before coming out to breakfast. When she finally appeared, shawl draped over her shoulders even on the hottest summer days, she would complain bitterly about the simple fact of Thursday, letting everyone in the house know that she felt it was a mistake to get out of bed on Thursday, that the safest place to be on that hoodoo jinx of a day was under the covers with the blinds drawn and the windows closed and the doors locked. He wondered if she still complained about Thursdays to her new husband the Danish furniture man Mr. Gerald Furst. He could remember his mother making a joke only once in his life. His father had been playing the piano, and his mother was listening with her head cocked to one side, a slightly pained expression on her face. "In the old days," she said at last, "when your father played piano, the ladies used to stay home in droves." Uncle Benny immediately topped her by looking up from his drink and saying, "Even worse, Irene, the ladies often drove home in stays." He never learned why his mother so detested Thursdays. His father died on a Wednesday.

Now, as he stepped into the courtroom, he knew something of his mother's superstitious fear, and wished he were being called to testify on any day but this. He had hoped for sunshine, had listened to the forecast the night before with rising anticipation: warmer temperatures, they had said, the possibility of clear skies. The temperature had indeed climbed into the low forties during the night, and the thermometer reading had been forty-eight when he and Ebie left the Astor that morning. But the sky was heavily overcast, and he was afraid now that it would begin raining sometime during the day, turning the snow underfoot to slush, casting a pall over the city—Thursday, a hoodoo jinx of a day.

The courtroom was hardly less cheerless than the street outside. The same dull light streamed through the windows, giving the room a curiously one-dimensional appearance, negating perspective, dulling all reflecting surfaces. He led Ebie to the empty jury box, and then went to sit beside Willow at the defense table, shaking hands with him, and listening to his words of encouragement while his eyes roamed the courtroom. Brackman was in whispered consultation with his partner at the plaintiff's table. Constantine sat at the far end of the table, reading the paperback edition of *Lord of the Flies*. The court clerk was waiting near the door to the judge's chambers, watching the big wall clock over the bench. The spectators' benches were empty. Even the Columbia student had abandoned the proceedings.

At ten o'clock sharp, the clerk called "All rise!" and the judge entered and went directly to the bench and then gave a peremptory nod, the signal for everyone in the courtroom to sit again. Driscoll heard Willow call his name, and then rose with the dread of Thursday looming huge within him, and walked slowly and self-consciously toward the witness stand. He felt suddenly that he had dressed wrongly, that his dark blue suit looked too much like a confirmation garment, that his simple blue tie was not bright enough, that he gave an impression of someone drab and hardly inventive, barely intelligent, certainly uncreative, "truth and nothing but the truth, so help you God?" the clerk said.

"I do," he answered, and sat.

Willow rose from the defense table in sections, unfolding his length, walking loosely and easily toward the witness chair, and then smiling up briefly at Driscoll, and very quietly and calmly asking, "Are you the author of *The Paper Dragon?*" as if that were not the prime issue before this court.

"I am," Driscoll answered.

"Did you write it independently and of your own creation, without reference to any other work of fiction?"

"I did."

"What is the date of your birth?"

"March 12, 1929."

"How old were you in October of 1947, when the play *Catchpole* was produced?"

"Eighteen."

"Were you a theatergoer at that time?"

"Yes, sir. I began going regularly to the theater when I was twelve years old."

"Did you attend any performances of the play *Catchpole?*"

"No, sir."

"Had you, before this action began, ever read the play *Catchpole?*"

"Never."

"Or heard of the plaintiff, Arthur Constantine?"

"No."

"What high school did you attend?"

"The High School of Music and Art."

"Which is where?"

"It's on 135th Street and Convent Avenue."

"Where were you living at that time?"

"In Manhattan. On West End Avenue."

"Did you go to Music and Art for the full four years?"

"No, sir. I began as a sophomore, coming directly from a junior high school, and I remained until graduation. Three years."

"When was this?"

"From 1944 to 1947."

"Were you graduated from Music and Art in 1947?"

"Yes, sir. January of 1947."

"Did you then continue your schooling elsewhere?"

"I won an art scholarship to the Art Students League, and I went there for approximately six months, I forget the exact length of time, the duration of the scholarship."

"To study art?"

"Yes, sir. I was studying drawing and painting—oil painting."

"Were you an art major in high school?"

"Yes, sir."

"What happened after you left the Art Students League?"

"I began studying art at Pratt Institute in the fall of that year, 1947."

"For how long?"

"Until June of 1950."

"What happened then?"

"I graduated and was drafted into the Army."

"Until you were drafted into the Army, would it be correct to say that you were training to become an artist?"

"A painter, yes, sir."

"In 1947, did you receive complimentary tickets to a preview performance of the play *Catchpole?*"

"I did not."

"Do you remember a distribution of free tickets?"

"I do not."

"Were you advised of such a distribution?"

"I was not."

"Did you see the play in any preview performance?"

"I never saw the play in *any* performance."

"You were graduated from Pratt in June of 1950?"

"That's right."

"And went directly into the Army?"

"Yes, sir, almost immediately after graduation."

"Which would be?"

"I went into the Army on June 21, 1950."

"And when were you discharged?"

"August 11, 1953."

"Honorably?"

"What?"

"Were you honorably discharged?"

"Yes, sir."

"What did you do after your discharge?"

"In September of 1953 I began attending New York University."

"To study art?"

"No, sir. I was an English major."

"Why did you choose this major?"

"While I was in the Army, I decided that I would like to try writing."

"Did you receive a degree from N.Y.U.?"

"Yes, sir, I did. A Bachelor of Arts in June of 1957."

"And after you were graduated, did you begin writing?"

"No, sir."

"What *did* you do?"

"I held a series of jobs."

"Like what? Would you list them, please?"

"I worked for the telephone company, and I worked for an import-export firm, and an advertising agency for a little while. Things like that."

"Did any of these jobs entail writing?"

"No, sir."

"Art work?"

"No, sir. For the most part, they were stopgap jobs."

"When did you begin writing *The Paper Dragon?*"

"In 1961."

"Do you remember exactly when in 1961?"

"October."

"In other words, you began writing *The Paper Dragon* eleven years after the actual events it portrays."

"Yes, sir."

"The Chinese offensive across the Ch'ongch'on River was in November of 1950, isn't that correct?"

"That's correct."

"Why did you wait eleven years?"

"I wasn't sure I would write it at all."

"Why did you write it?"

"I had to."

"Why?"

"For my own peace of mind."

"You felt you had to put the events on paper for your own peace of mind?"

"Yes."

"Your Honor," Brackman said, "I do not see where these questions . . ."

"Yes, Mr. Willow, where are you heading?"

"Your Honor, I am attempting to trace the creative process."

"Very well, go ahead."

"Mr. Driscoll, how tall are you?"

"I'm six feet tall."

"What color are your eyes?"

"Blue."

"Would you say that your hair is light or dark?"

"Dark."

"How old were you in 1950 when you were drafted into the Army?"

"I was just twenty-one."

"And you went into the Army directly from Pratt Institute?"

"I did."

"Did you go into basic training?"

"Yes, sir, at Fort Dix."

"Did you then go to Officer Candidate School?"

"I did. At Fort Benning."

"And were you then sent to Korea?"

"I was."

"Would you consider this a fair description of Lieutenant Cooper in your novel: he is twenty-one years old, six feet tall, with blue eyes and dark hair. He is drafted into the Army from Pratt Institute, is sent to O.C.S. and then shipped to Korea?"

"I would consider that a fair description."

"Did you once live on West End Avenue?"

"I did."

"Did your fictitious character Lieutenant Cooper live on West End Avenue?"

"Yes."

"Did he attend Music and Art High School, as you did?"

"Yes, sir."

"Was he an art major, as you were?"

"Yes, sir."

"Did he later receive a scholarship to the Art Students League, as you did?"

"Yes, sir."

"And then went on to Pratt Institute, as you did?"

"Yes, sir."

"I probably need not even ask this question, Mr. Driscoll, but would you please tell the court upon whom you based the character Lieutenant Alex Cooper?"

"On myself, sir."

"Was he based on Lieutenant Roger Mason in *Catchpole?*"

"I had never heard of Lieutenant Roger Mason until last month when you showed me the play."

"Then your character was *not* based on him?"

"Definitely not."

"Mr. Driscoll, I show you these pages and ask you what they are."

Driscoll took the pages and studied them briefly. "They're a preliminary outline for the first several chapters of *The Paper Dragon.*"

"I offer the outline in evidence," Willow said, and handed the pages to Brackman.

"Any objection?" the clerk asked.

"None," Brackman said.

"Mr. Genitori?"

"No."

"Defendants' Exhibit J received in evidence," the clerk said.

"Please," Willow said to the clerk, "I'd like to refer to it." He took the extended outline, glanced at it, and then turned to Driscoll again. "Is this a detailed outline, Mr. Driscoll?"

"It is."

"Does that mean you followed it precisely when you were writing the first hundred pages of your book?"

"The first ninety-eight pages," Driscoll said. "But no, I didn't follow it precisely."

"You made changes as you worked?"

"Yes."

"As you went along?"

"Yes."

"Why?"

"Well, I didn't want to feel too tightly restricted by the outline. I wanted to leave some surprises for myself."

"Did you expand upon this outline at any time?"

"Yes. This covers only the first portion of the book. When I sent the completed portion to Mitchell-Campbell, it was accompanied by a longer outline, a less detailed outline, but one covering the remainder of the book, the full book as I hoped to complete it."

"And you sent your completed portion together with an expanded outline to Mitchell-Campbell?"

"Yes, sir."

"Did you know anyone working at Mitchell-Campbell?"

"No, sir."

"Why did you send the book to them, rather than to another publisher?"

"They seemed like good publishers."

"Upon what did you base this judgment?"

"They seemed to do a lot of advertising for the books on their list," Driscoll said, and McIntyre burst out laughing.

"I believe this is the standard writer's gauge, your Honor," Willow said, laughing with him. "Did you address the book to anyone's attention, Mr. Driscoll?"

"No, I simply sent it to the Editorial Department."

"With a return envelope?"

"Well, no, I sent the book in a box. But I accompanied it with a money order for the return postage. If it was rejected."

"Did you expect a rejection?"

"It was my first novel, I don't know what I expected."

"What happened next?"

"I received a letter from Mr. Danton, asking if I would come in to discuss the book."

"When was this?"

"I don't remember exactly. Either July or August."

"Of 1962?"

"Yes, sir."

"Did you in fact meet with Mr. Danton?"

"Yes, I went up to his office."

"Can you tell us what happened at this first meeting?"

"Chester wanted to know what my plans were for finishing the book, and I expanded verbally upon the outline I'd submitted. He then told me that the feelings of himself and another editor at Mitchell-Campbell were that the squad, and particularly Colman, should be given a stronger motivation for their hatred of Lieutenant Cooper. He suggested that I use the idea of a previous commanding officer being killed in action and my hero replacing him."

"Did he suggest how this officer might have been killed?"

"Yes, he suggested that a sniper kill him from ambush."

"Did he make any other suggestions?"

"Yes, I believe he was concerned about the book's profanity even then, and he suggested that it be toned down during the writing of the remainder. He also thought we should begin thinking about another title."

"Was that the substance of your conversation at this first meeting?"

"Yes, sir."

"What did you do then?"

"I went home to finish the book."

"What procedure did you follow?"

"Well, first I outlined the next four or five chapters in greater detail. And then I began writing them."

"Was this your standard working procedure?"

"Yes. I would outline several chapters at a time and then begin work on those chapters—the actual writing of them. When I'd finished those, or was close to finishing them, I would outline the next several chapters, and so on."

"Until you completed the novel?"

"Yes."

"You used your general outline as the basis . . ."

"Yes . . ."

". . . and then outlined in closer detail as you went along?"

"Yes, that's exactly what I did."

"Now here are some pages, Mr. Driscoll, with the words 'Chapter 7,' on the first page, and on the last page here, we have 'Chapter 15.' Are these pages part of your actual working outline?"

"Yes, sir, they are."

"The detailed outline?"

"Yes, sir."

"Now page 5 is torn, do you see that?"

"I see it."

"Only part of the page is here in the outline."

"That's right."

"Is this exactly how you found this page in your files?"

"It is."

"Do you know why a portion of the page is torn off?"

"I have no idea. The page following it is marked 5A so I imagine I didn't like what I had outlined and simply tore it off and put in another page called 5A. Yes, I probably tore off the bottom of this page, and then replaced it with a '5A.' "

"I offer the outline in evidence," Willow said.

"Have we seen this before, Mr. Willow?" Brackman asked.

"No, sir, you have not."

"I'm not objecting, but I would like to know why this was not previously shown to us."

"Because we only received it just before the trial began."

"Nevertheless, withholding it was in violation of the court order directing—"

"Your Honor, we have assiduously respected the court order, and have turned over to the plaintiff any papers received from Mr. Driscoll. He did not locate these until just before the trial began, and I did not have the opportunity to turn them over. May I say, however—"

"I think you might have *found* the opportunity, Mr. Willow," Brackman said.

"May I say that my friend has fallen prey to his own

gambit. Had he chosen to serve Mr. Driscoll as a party to this case, he could have examined him before trial. He chose not to, in the hope—"

"I don't think we need go into Mr. Brackman's tactics," McIntyre said. "Are you objecting to this going into evidence?"

"No, your Honor," Brackman said. "Nor did I dream of offending Mr. Willow."

"You haven't offended me," Willow said.

"This action has been going on for a long time now," Brackman said, "and I don't think we've once raised our voices to each other, either outside the courtroom or since this trial began. I only meant to say that I wish you'd have let me see these papers before now. Perhaps you'll allow me to study them at greater length later."

"Of course."

"Mark it 'Defendants' Exhibit K in evidence,' " the clerk said.

"Now, if you will look at this outline, Mr. Driscoll, you will see certain notations on it, such as '60,000 words, 10/12' and immediately following that, '58,500, 10/12.' On the second page here, in ink, '63,000 words, 10/19' and following it in pencil, '62,300 10/20' and it goes on in this manner throughout. Did you write these notations?"

"I did."

"What do they mean?"

"The numbers in ink, '60,000 words,' for example, '10/12' represent a goal and a target date. I hoped to have completed 60,000 words of the book by October 12th, that was probably a Friday. The penciled indication on the right shows the actual number of words I had written by that date—58,500 words."

"You fell short of the target that week."

"Yes. But that's what these notes indicate throughout."

"The number of words you hoped to have written by a certain date?"

"Yes, sir. There was a deadline, you see. The contract called for delivery of the book by January, I think it was, and

I tried to adhere to a schedule that would enable me to meet that deadline."

"And you felt it necessary to indicate what you *had* accomplished in addition to what you'd hoped to accomplish."

"Yes, as a guide to completion. I had to know that I would finish it one day, you see."

"What do you mean?"

"A book takes a long time to write."

"Yes?"

"Well, I can only speak for myself."

"Yes, go on."

"I'm not a professional, this was my only book. I can only tell you what I experienced when I was writing it."

"Which was what, Mr. Driscoll?"

"I thought it would never end."

"And is that why you kept your record?"

"Yes. I had started the book in October of 1961, and I . . . I wasn't even sure I'd *ever* start it, you see, but finally I did and it went very slowly. It took me eight months to finish those ninety-eight pages and the outline, and it was very difficult all the way, writing does not come easily to me. It began going a bit more smoothly after Mitchell-Campbell contracted for the book. I suppose Chester's enthusiasm for it, and his . . . his faith that I could complete it, this was an enormous shot in the arm. I found I was working much more quickly, that I could count on from three to five thousand words a week, that was a lot for me. But at the same time, I had to know that I wasn't writing into a void, that one day the thing would be *finished*. I could take the last page out of the typewriter and it would be done. That's why I kept a timetable. So that I'd know I was getting there."

"And, of course, eventually you *did* get there. You completed your book."

"Yes. Eventually."

"Before that time, before the book was actually finished, did you acquire an agent?"

"Yes, sir, Mr. Hollis Marks. He's still my agent."

"Here are some letters to Mr. Hollis, dated November 5th and November 9th . . ."

"Mr. *Marks.*"

"Mr. Marks, excuse me, and addressed 'Dear Hollis.' "

"Yes."

"November 15th, November 20th, November 23rd, December 3rd, December 7th, December 11th, December 12th, December 14th, December 20th, and December 28th. Did you send these letters to Mr. Marks?"

"I did."

"Reporting on your progress on *The Paper Dragon?*"

"That's right."

"If your Honor please, we can call Mr. Marks as a witness, but I know what he will tell the Court concerning these letters."

"What would that be, Mr. Willow?"

"That they were taken from his files and written by Mr. Driscoll on the dates indicated. I offer all of them in evidence as one exhibit."

"For what purpose are these being offered?" Brackman asked.

"Again, to show the creative process. Your Honor, if a book is being pirated, the thief would hardly send progress reports to his—"

"No objection," Brackman said.

"Defendants' Exhibit L received in evidence," the clerk said.

"Mr. Driscoll, when you were writing your book, did you contact anyone for information you needed?"

"Yes, sir."

"Whom did you contact?"

"Colonel Lewis Hamilton."

"He was your commanding officer . . ."

"The company commander, yes . . ."

". . . in Korea?"

"Yes, sir. He was a captain at the time."

"What was your initial contact with him?"

"I wrote a letter to him, explaining that I was working on

a book, and asking for his help. I suggested that we meet one afternoon for lunch or after working hours—he was working in this area at the time, at the Army Recruiting Office on Whitehall. He called me when he received my letter, and we met later that week, on a Friday I believe it was. At the beginning of November."

"Where is Colonel Hamilton today?"

"He was called back to active duty in Vietnam. I'm sorry to say he's dead."

"I show you this, and ask you to describe it to the Court."

"It's a carbon copy of the letter I wrote to Colonel Hamilton."

"I offer it in evidence."

"Your Honor," Brackman said, rising, "as I understand it, Colonel Hamilton is dead. Now Mr. Driscoll states that this is a copy of a letter he sent to the colonel, but I know of no way of ascertaining that. I cannot question a dead man."

"Your Honor . . ."

"I object to it as irrelevant, and I submit that it would be impossible for me to ascertain whether it is authentic."

"Is this letter necessary to your case?" McIntyre asked.

"To my mind, your Honor, anything that clearly shows the step-by-step development of Mr. Driscoll's novel is not only necessary but essential to the case. This letter shows beyond doubt that in addition to personal experience, Mr. Driscoll sought the advice of an expert on matters that were beyond his ken. If he were copying . . ."

"Yes, but won't Mr. Driscoll be testifying anyway about his meeting with the colonel?"

"Yes, your Honor, but his testimony will be more persuasive when supported by this letter."

"Is this letter being offered for the truth of what it contains, or simply to establish a working procedure for Mr. Driscoll?"

"I think it even goes beyond these matters, your Honor, to clearly indicate the kind of man Mr. Driscoll is. In his letter to the colonel, for example, he modestly, almost shyly, reintroduces himself . . ."

"Mr. Willow, it's my opinion that this letter is not the same as those from Mr. Driscoll to his agent, sent as part of a daily working routine. I will sustain your objection, Mr. Brackman. The letter will not be admitted."

"May I offer it for identification?" Willow asked.

"Of course."

"Mark it 'Defendants' Exhibit M for identification,' " the clerk said.

"You said earlier, Mr. Driscoll, that you met with Colonel Hamilton . . ."

"Yes."

". . . sometime after you wrote to him. Where did you meet?"

"In a restaurant down here someplace. I don't remember the name of it."

"Can you tell us what happened at this meeting?"

"I asked Colonel Hamilton a great many questions, and he answered them for me."

"I show you these four sheets of paper, and ask you if they are the notes you took at the meeting you just described."

"They are the notes I jotted down during the meeting."

"I offer the notes in evidence."

"Well, I must object to that, Mr. Willow," Brackman said, rising again. "You're showing here a collection of answers the witness supposedly got from a dead man. There is no possible way of questioning the dead man as to whether he really did give those answers."

"Is this being offered to show the truth of what it contains?" McIntyre asked.

"No, your Honor."

"I will admit it if its limited purpose is to show the witness's working procedure on his novel."

"To show the evolution of the book, your Honor."

"I will admit it."

"Mark it 'Defendants' Exhibit N in evidence.' "

"Mr. Driscoll, I show you another sheet of paper that lists the steps in the disassembly of an M-1. Did you use this information in your book?"

"Yes, sir. I had the lieutenant ask the men to strip their rifles, as an exercise."

"I am referring now to the so-called 'female rifle' scene."

"Yes, sir, I'm familiar with that scene."

"Was it based upon information you received from the colonel?"

"Well . . . yes and no. I did receive the information from the colonel, but what actually happened was that I told him what I needed when I spoke to him on the phone, and he brought a book called *Military Science and Tactics* with him, in which he had marked the section on stripping the M-1. I copied the information directly from the book."

"Onto this sheet of paper?"

"Yes, sir."

"I offer it in evidence."

"I object," Brackman said.

"On what grounds, Mr. Brackman?"

"The witness has testified that his scene was based on information in a book and not on what is now before this Court. I do not see the relevance."

"He has testified," Willow said, "that his notes were taken from a book given to him by the colonel . . ."

"I did not hear him say the colonel *gave* him the book."

"Mr. Driscoll, could you . . ."

"He didn't actually *give* me the book. He brought it with him to the meeting, and I copied these notes from it."

"We have only the witness's word, your Honor, that the colonel brought the book with him. The alleged exchange involves a dead man who purportedly—"

"Section 4519 does not apply here," Willow said. "In no way can this be considered a transaction with a deceased . . ."

"I understand that," Brackman said, "and this is not my objection."

"Now just a minute, just a minute," McIntyre said. "It seems to me that the offer is being made only to show that Mr. Driscoll had in his possession material which could have formed the basis of the scene in his novel. Isn't that so, Mr. Willow?"

"Yes, your Honor."

"I will admit it. I think your objection is unfounded, Mr. Brackman."

"Mark it 'Defendants' Exhibit O in evidence.' "

"Mr. Driscoll, when you were writing your book, did you prepare a map upon which were written certain numbers and notes?"

"Your Honor, it pains me to have to object so continuously, especially when I know how interested we all are in having this trial proceed smoothly and rapidly," Brackman said. "But during the pretrial examinations, I can clearly remember Mr. Willow objecting at one point because the witness was my own and I was leading him."

"I'm sure you can also clearly remember, Mr. Brackman, that at the time I also stated I was not objecting to ninety per cent of your questions because we had agreed to be informal about the entire matter."

"That was the pretrial, Mr. Willow, and this is the trial, and I must object now to these leading questions."

"Mr. Driscoll, I show you a drawing of a map, and on this drawing there are certain numbers and notes. Who prepared this map?"

"I did."

"You drew the map?"

"Yes, sir."

"Is this the original drawing?"

"Yes, sir."

"What is it a map of?"

"It's a map of Korea, an enlargement of the Ch'ongch'on River area."

"Do you recognize the handwriting on it?"

"Yes, sir. It is my own."

"What do these notes and numbers signify?"

"They purport to be a patrol route and a timetable."

"Was this map used in your novel?"

"Yes, sir. That's the map that was reproduced in the book.

It depicts the area between the Ch'ongch'on and the Yalu, and the map was put there for the reader's convenience so that he could follow what was happening, the trap being set for Lieutenant Cooper."

"The path of the patrol is indicated on this map, is it not?"

"It is."

"And the times at which the squad expects to reach certain marked areas on the map?"

"Yes, sir, the checkpoints."

"In other words, the notations on this map indicate goals and expected times of arrival, do they not?"

"They do."

"Similar to the goals and target dates you made for the writing of your book."

"Objection," Brackman said.

"Sustained. Really, Mr. Willow."

"Is this patrol an important incident in your book?"

"It is."

"A climactic incident?"

"It is."

"I offer the map in evidence."

"No objection."

"I'm grateful Mr. Brackman has no objection," McIntyre said, "but I must admit, Mr. Willow, that my own curiosity is somewhat piqued. For what purpose is this map being offered?"

"Again, your Honor, to show the evolutionary development of this novel. To show how it was written and re-written, to show the research that went into each scene, to show the devotion to detail, the combination of personal knowledge and imagination that resulted in a unique creation which could not conceivably have been plagiarized from any existing work. This scene in particular, your Honor, this patrol, is one that plaintiff claims is based on the escape of his psychopathic officer and the subsequent accidental killing of a sergeant. When we see how carefully this patrol was conceived and detailed, when we recognize how everything in Mr. Driscoll's novel leads to this patrol and to the subsequent sacrifice his lieutenant makes, we can clearly see . . ."

"But doesn't this map appear in the novel?"

"A reproduction does, yes, your Honor."

"And has not the novel itself already been admitted in evidence?"

"It has, your Honor."

"Then why on earth do we need the original drawing?"

"Only to call attention to the fact that Mr. Driscoll thought the patrol important enough to make his own drawing illustrating it. That is all, your Honor."

"I do feel, Mr. Willow, that it might have been a simpler matter to have shown him the reproduction in an exhibit already admitted, and then asked whether or not he had drawn the original."

"If your Honor please," Brackman said, "I quite agree with you, even though I have been exceedingly reluctant to interrupt Mr. Willow. I remind him again that there was a court order we may be violating here, the one stating that all documents be delivered to us. I assume Mr. Willow is not deliberately sidestepping that order, and that several of these documents which I'm hearing of for the first time today were truly received just before the trial began. Nonetheless, the offer of so many of them is cluttering the record unnecessarily."

"How many more will there be, Mr. Willow?" McIntyre asked.

"I've tried to limit them, your Honor . . ."

"Yes, but how many more will there be?"

". . . to those concerning specific alleged similarities. But we will be brief."

"How many more?"

"Two or three, your Honor."

"I hope so, Mr. Willow. I will admit the map."

"Mark it 'Defendants' Exhibit P in evidence,' " the clerk said.

"Mr. Driscoll, when did you complete the first draft of your novel?"

"In January of 1963."

"Do you remember the exact date?"

"Yes, it was January 26, 1963."

"How do you happen to remember this date?"

"I remember it because I wrote a note to Hollis the next day, just before I delivered the book."

"I show you this and ask if it is the note to which you just now referred."

"It is," Driscoll said.

"I offer it in evidence, your Honor."

"No objection," Brackman said wearily.

"Mark it 'Defendants' Exhibit Q,' " the clerk said.

"What did you do with this note, Mr. Driscoll?"

"I put it in the box containing the completed manuscript, and I delivered the note and the manuscript to Hollis Marks."

"When?"

"That Monday. January 28th."

"May I ask how you happen to recall this date?"

"I marked it on my desk calendar."

"I show you this page torn from a desk calendar for January 1963, and ask if this is the notation to which you just now referred."

"It is."

"I offer the calendar page in evidence, your Honor."

"No objection," Brackman said.

"Mark it 'Defendants' Exhibit R in evidence.' "

"Mr. Driscoll, would you please read the notation to the Court?"

"It just says 'Deliver PD,' that's all. And the date is circled, January 28th."

"Is this your handwriting?"

"It is."

"And by PD, did you mean *The Paper Dragon?*"

"Yes, that's what it was called by that time. That was the new title."

"Mr. Driscoll, when did you receive galley proofs of your book?"

"At the end of May sometime."

"What did you do with them?"

"I corrected them and sent them back to Mitchell-Campbell."

"Did you request a set of corrected galleys from them?"

"I did."

"For what purpose?"

"I wanted my uncle to read the book before it was published."

"Did you subsequently send those corrected galleys to your uncle?"

"I did."

"I show you this and ask you to describe it," Willow said.

"It's the carbon copy of a letter I wrote to my uncle in June of 1963, telling him the galleys were on their way, and asking him for his opinion of the book."

"I offer it in evidence," Willow said.

"Your Honor, I cannot see its relevance."

"If a man has stolen another man's work, your Honor, he does not send galley proofs to his uncle for an opinion. I am merely trying to establish a logical order of events, culminating in the finished product which Mr. Driscoll showed to his uncle, a man he loved and respected, for his approval."

"I will admit the letter," McIntyre said.

"Mark it 'Defendants' Exhibit S in evidence.' "

"Your Honor," Brackman said, "we had Mr. Willow's promise to watch his P's and Q's, but we have come beyond those and now seem to be up to our S's in documents."

McIntyre burst out laughing. Brackman chuckled quietly, pleased by his own wit. Even Willow and his assistant began laughing. The laughter continued for perhaps a minute. Driscoll, observing the others, did not crack a smile. He noticed that Arthur Constantine, sitting at the plaintiff's table, was not smiling either.

At last Willow said, "There will be no further documents, your Honor."

"I guess that answers your doubts, Mr. Brackman," Mc-Intyre said.

"Yes, and I'm greatly relieved, your Honor."

"Mr. Driscoll," Willow said, still smiling, "when your book was completed and delivered to Mitchell-Campbell, did your agent request a second copy of the manuscript?"

"He did."

"For what purpose?"

"For serial rights submission."

"Do you mean for submission to the magazines?"

"Yes."

"Did you sell first serial rights to the book?"

"Yes, sir."

"Which magazine bought the rights?"

"The *Saturday Evening Post*—and not *McCall's* or *Redbook*, as Mr. Knowles surmised yesterday."

"When did it appear in the *Post?*"

"In September of '63."

"And when was it published as a book?"

"In October of '63."

"Was the book successful?"

"I suppose so."

"Well, would you know how many copies it sold in its hard-cover edition?"

"Chester Danton would be able to tell you that more accurately. I believe it was something like fifty or sixty."

"Fifty or sixty?" McIntyre asked.

"Thousand, I mean."

"Fifty or sixty thousand copies of a first novel, your Honor —and the figure may be a shade higher than that—is considered phenomenal. And this was exclusive of the book club edition, was it not, Mr. Driscoll?"

"Yes."

"It *was* a book club selection?"

"Your Honor, what is the purpose of all this?" Brackman asked.

"Mr. Willow?"

"If your Honor please, I wish to demonstrate for Mr.

Driscoll only what Mr. Brackman earlier attempted to demonstrate regarding the plaintiff: that he is a man of recognized talents."

"How would this be any more relevant than plaintiff's—"

"If your Honor please, the Court permitted Mr. Constantine to go on and on about his screenplays, most of which were obscure and frankly mediocre works. It would seem to me that Mr. Driscoll should in all fairness be permitted to enumerate the very real honors bestowed upon his novel."

"Your Honor, I don't see how playing the numbers game, telling us how many copies were sold and all that, is going to indicate anything about Mr. Driscoll's talents."

"We *did* permit Mr. Constantine, however, to list his credits. All right, I will allow it. Go ahead, Mr. Driscoll."

"May I answer the question?"

"Yes, go on."

"It was a book club section. Book-of-the-Month took it."

"Was a paperback edition sold?" Willow asked.

"Yes, to Camelot Books."

"Would you happen to know how many copies were sold in that edition?"

"We sold a quarter of a million copies in the first eight days of sale."

"And afterwards?"

"It went on to sell something more than two and a half million copies."

"May I say, your Honor, that this constitutes a wildly successful sale in paperback."

"What time is it?" McIntyre asked the clerk.

"Eleven-fifteen, your Honor."

"Let's take a ten-minute recess."

The little Egyptian had obviously dressed for the occasion, and looked considerably more formal than he had on the night of the accident. Uncomfortable and a trifle embarrassed, he informed Sally that his name was Ibrahim Hadad, and then took a cigarette tin from his pocket and nervously opened it. He was wearing a rumpled brown suit and white shirt, a striped brown and yellow tie hanging down the shirt front and tucked into the waistband of his trousers. He wore yellow socks and brown shoes, and his heavy brown overcoat and brown fedora rested on his lap as he fumbled inside the tin, spilling a half dozen cigarettes onto his lap, retrieving them with fingers caked with the grime of his trade, impregnated in every wrinkle and pore. He smiled up at her palely, white teeth appearing in a sickly grin below his long hooked nose, his face the color of dust, the thin smile doing little to add a semblance of cheer to the solemn purpose of his visit. He put one of the cigarettes between his lips and then belatedly offered the tin to Sally, who shook her head.

"Very good cigarettes," he said. "Turkish."

"Thank you, I don't smoke," she said.

Hadad shrugged, closed the tin with a suggestion of finality, adjusted his coat and hat on his lap, put a lighted match to the cigarette tip, shook out the match, exhaled a giant cloud of smoke, and then nervously smiled again at Sally, who tented her fingers and waited for him to resume.

"Criminal assault," he said. "That is what." He shrugged. He puffed again on the cigarette. "When was it, the accident? Monday night?"

"Yes."

"The hospital, everything, I go home to my wife and children, she almost breaks my head for me all over again." He smiled. Sally kept watching him. He had a fascinating way of holding his cigarette between thumb and forefinger, the wrist bent outwards, so that he seemed rather effete as he puffed on it, rather like Peter Lorre playing a spy on the Orient Express, completely unlike a bricklayer.

"Tuesday is okay," he said. "Yesterday all day is okay too," he said, "but last *night,* ah! Six o'clock, yes? I come home from work, and who is waiting there? A detective."

"A police detective?"

"Correct," he said, and gave a small nod of his bullet-shaped head, and then cupped the cigarette in his reversed manner, and took a long obviously satisfying drag on it, and again exhaled a cloud of sweet-smelling smoke. My mother should be here, Sally thought, she would die from the smell alone. What is he smoking, Sally darling—pot? Mother, I'm sure it's not pot, what do you know about pot? I read the *New York Post*, Gertie would reply.

"Is it bothering you, the cigarette?" Hadad asked.

"No," she lied. "What about this detective?"

"It comes around that your friend, the lawyer, he has called *his* friend, the judge. His name is Santesson, the circus judge."

"Circuit," Sally said.

"Correct," Hadad said, and puffed again on his cigarette. "This detective, he comes from the judge's suggestion, he is investigating the *big* accident!" Hadad waved the hand with the cigarette in a grand sweeping gesture, smoke trailing behind it. "Criminal assault, he says."

"Who?"

"*Me,* who else?"

"This detective was investigating a charge of criminal assault against you?"

"Correct."

"Yes, go on."

"A year in prison, he says. Is this true?"

"I'm not sure."

"Or pay five hundred dollars?" Hadad said, looking at her expectantly, as though hoping she would deny it.

"Perhaps," Sally said.

"I can't afford neither," Hadad said, and sighed deeply. He looked at the cigarette in his cupped palm, sighed again when he discovered it had almost burned down, and then took the tin from his inside jacket pocket again and began going through the same complicated and fumbling maneuver of extricating a fresh cigarette from the sliding, tumbling, willful cigarettes in the box, the task made more difficult because he was now holding a lighted cigarette in one trembling hand. Watching him, Sally felt a sudden empathy, as though this shoddy, nervous man in his Sunday clothes accurately reflected the shabbiness of her Fourteenth Street walkup legal firm, sidewalk law at discount prices. He sat before the huge plate-glass window overlooking the street, the goldleaf letters S. KIRSCH, ATTORNEY AT LAW inverted so that they read correctly from the street, and below that the word ABOGADO, and in the corner of the window, also backwards so that the street trade could read it and perhaps be tempted by it, NOTARY PUBLIC, and the red seal below that, and further down the word translated into Spanish for the benefit of the myriad Puerto Ricans in the city who were constantly being asked to have legal documents of all sorts notarized. She sat behind an old wooden desk which she had bought at one of the secondhand furniture places on 23rd Street, in a revolving chair her mother jokingly said had once belonged to Oliver Wendell Holmes or Sherlock Holmes, she forgot which one, and looked across as Hadad finally extricated a cigarette from the tin and then shakingly began plucking loose cigarettes from his lap as though they were scattered daisy petals, the dark green filing cabinets behind him, the ancient inoperative air conditioner built into one window panel, the sky beyond as gray as death. This is what I have, she thought. I'm thirty-three years old, and I was graduated from N.Y.U. Law in the summer of 1963 (a late bloomer, Gertie called me) and here I am in a shabby office on a shabby street, watching an Arab pluck cigarettes from his lap. Sally Kirsch, Attorney at Law.

Sally Kirsch, attorney at law, had moved out of her mother's apartment the week after she passed the bar exams. Her mother Gertrude, a stout blond lady of dubious German-Austrian-Serbian extraction, when informed that Sally's new apartment was in the Village, immediately asked, "What will you do now? Start sleeping with all those beatniks down there?" Sally informed her that she had not yet slept with anyone (a lie), beatnik or otherwise, although the opportunity had certainly presented itself on many an occasion even while living here in the sanctified atmosphere of this fine home on Third Avenue and 85th Street. She did not expect to begin now, she said (another lie necessitated by the first lie), unless she chose to, which is exactly what she would have done no matter where she lived. "A fine girl," Gertie said. "You wouldn't be so smart if your father was alive."

Unfortunately, her father was not alive, had in fact been dead since Sally was six, at which time he was struck down by a bus on Second Avenue while crossing the street from his dry goods store. Sally had always suspected he was drunk at the time. Her sharpest memory of her father was of a tall, thin man with her identical green eyes and sandy hair, stooping to kiss her on the cheek, his breath smelling of something she only later could identify as wine. She was *sure* he'd been drunk. A man didn't get hit by something as big as a bus unless he was too drunk to see the damn thing. Her mother (significantly, she felt) never drank. She sometimes wondered if her mother had ever made love, evidence of conception and birth to the contrary.

In some of her more lurid fantasies, Sally reconstructed an image of her own first bed partner, an N.Y.U. undergraduate, now married and teaching English somewhere in Schenectady, unable to forget that hot sophomore maniac who had almost eaten him alive. In soberer moments, she thought of herself as essentially healthy, but hardly very passionate, a girl who understood the biological needs of her body and periodically set out to gratify them. Her three affairs had been of short duration, the most recent having been with an internal revenue agent, of all things, and having ended in April when he asked her (after a particularly passionate session) whether she had remembered to file her W-2. He also happened to be married, which may have partially accounted for her sudden decision, although she did not normally consider this an excluding factor. She did not, in fact, know what specific rules governed her morality or lack of it, except a basic rule of survival which advised her never to get pregnant.

Getting pregnant, according to Gertie, was one of the most horrible misfortunes that could ever befall a woman. "You were such a cranky baby, Sally darling, kept me up half the night, my milk wouldn't flow, my breasts were always hurting, and besides your father wanted a boy"—which translated from the dubious German-Austrian-Serbian meant "I, *Gertie*, wanted a boy." In any case, the advice had stuck. It was bad to get pregnant under the best of circumstances, but tragic to get pregnant if you did not happen to have a husband. Since Sally did not happen to have a husband, nor particularly want one, she had immediately after her encounter with the budding Schenectady English teacher, and without any fuss or bother, rushed off to buy herself a diaphragm. (In later years, upon reading Mary McCarthy's precious "peccary" anecdote, she had said aloud, "Oh, how cutesy-cute!") Seven months ago, when she first took up with the internal revenue agent recently dispossessed, she abandoned the diaphragm in favor of birth control tablets, which she still religiously swallowed each morning. In one of her customary fishing expeditions, Gertie had asked what she thought of these new birth control pills, and Sally had replied, lying with a gracious blush, that she possessed no knowledge whatever of them. Her mother stuffed a dried apricot into her mouth, nodded her head sagely, and said, "They grow beards on women," and Sally almost brought her hand unconsciously to her chin.

She suddenly remembered, there was a time, she remembered, she could see, there was, it was the basement of a department store somewhere in Manhattan, a twelve-year-old girl trying on coats while her mother sat and watched, Gertrude Kirsch with her hands folded over her pocketbook, Sally trying on garment after garment for her approval. There was a time, it overlapped this silent shabby Fourteenth Street office, the pink coat suddenly and magically appearing on the rack, how had she missed it before? She touched the cloth, she lifted the coat from its hanger and held it tentatively for just a moment before putting it on. Gertrude Kirsch sat in silent expectation, her hands folded on her pocketbook. Sally came toward her hesitantly and executed a brief model's turn, elbows against her sides, arms up, fingers spread in delicate supplication. Quietly, she asked, "How do I look, Mama? Make believe I'm a person."

Hadad lighted the fresh cigarette from the butt of the old

one, and then looked for an ash tray. Sally pushed one across the desk.

"Why?" Hadad asked.

"Why what?" she said, but of course she knew what he meant and had wondered the same thing the moment he came into the office and began telling his tale.

"Why does he pick on me, your boy friend?"

"He's not my boy friend," Sally said, and then wondered about that, too.

"He is a big man."

"Yes."

"A big lawyer."

"Yes."

"Why me, a bricklayer? Was someone killed in this *big* accident, *no*," he said, and again waved the skywriting cigarette. "Was someone serious injured, *no*. Is there enormous damage to the vehicles, *no*. Anyhow, I have insurance. the insurance will pay."

"Yes, Mr. Hadad, but . . ."

"Why does he make a stink?"

"I have no idea."

"Your own boy friend, you have no idea?"

"I only know Mr. Willow casually," Sally said, and felt immediately foolish. "I really don't know why he's . . . he's bringing this pressure to bear."

"Persecution," Hadad said. "Is he a Jew?"

"No," Sally answered.

Hadad shrugged. "You will help me?"

"How?"

"You will talk to him?"

"About what?"

"About he will leave me alone," Hadad said. "I do not wish to go to prison. I do not wish to pay five hundred dollars. I do not wish trouble of any kind. It was a dark night, it was anyone could have an accident, why does he pick on me? I am small beans. What does he want? My license, my living, my life? What does he *want* from me, this man?"

"I don't know," Sally said.

"Is there even a case?" Hadad asked. "Can there be criminal business here? Is it possible I can go to prison?"

"I don't know that, either. I'd have to read the law."

"I will pay you."

"For what?"

"For help, for advice, for salvation."

"I don't want your money, Mr. Hadad," Sally said.

"I am not a rich man, but I have some aside. I can pay."

"There's nothing to pay me for."

"You will talk to him?"

"I'll try."

"Ask him to stop," Hadad said, and then curiously added, "This is America."

They came back into the courtroom, both sides, plaintiff and defendants, considerably refreshed by their brief recess. They had exchanged words of reassurance, each to each, the plaintiff certain that Jonah Willow had extended himself beyond reasonable limits, introducing a plethora of documents that had only confused and bored the judge; the defendants convinced that Sidney Brackman had objected far too often and far too strenuously, irritating McIntyre and jeopardizing the case for the plaintiff. Brackman had told his client that he could read with fair accuracy the reactions of any judge, and he was certain McIntyre was beginning to lean more and more in their favor. Willow, on the other hand, assured his witness that he was coming over with dignity and calm, impressing the judge with his quiet integrity and his innate honesty.

So they all came back ready to engage each other in combat once again, seemingly forgetting that the real battle had been fought a long time ago, fought when Constantine committed his play to paper, fought when Driscoll later wrote his book. There was the scent of victory in the air, and both sides sniffed of it, and confidently surmised it was intended for their nostrils alone. Driscoll, after Jonah's peptalk in the corridor outside, felt certain that the trial was going their way, and that if no one involved in the defense brought up the matter of the 105th Division, why then no one on the plaintiff's side would mention it either. There was a curious holiday air in that courtroom when the trial resumed at 11:25 A.M. It belied the lowering clouds outside the long windows, it belied the fact that for every victor there is a loser, it belied the possibility that perhaps for every loser there is yet another loser or even a score of losers.

"Mr. Driscoll," Willow said, "before our recess, I was about to go into certain specific alleged similarities as listed on Plaintiff's Exhibit 6, which is titled Character Similarities. For the time being, I am going to bypass the character of Lieutenant Alex Cooper, who you have already testified is based on yourself. Instead, I am going to ask you about Private Colman, the troublemaker, who is certainly the second most important character in the novel, would you agree?"

"I would."

"Is Private Colman a homosexual?"

"He has had homosexual experiences."

"With whom?"

"With the major who had been commanding officer of the platoon."

"The plaintiff alleges, Mr. Driscoll, that your Private Colman is based on *two* characters in the play *Catchpole*. One of these characters is Corporal Janus, who is depicted as a troublemaker, and the other is Colonel Peterson, who is said to be a homosexual. Have you read Mr. Constantine's play?"

"I have."

"When did you read it?"

"Last month, when you gave it to me."

"Where was this, Mr. Driscoll?"

"You gave me the manuscript at your office in New York, and I took it home with me and read it there. In Vermont."

"Did you read it carefully?"

"I spent an entire weekend with it."

"Are you familiar with these two characters in the play? Corporal Janus and Colonel Peterson?"

"I am."

"Well now, wouldn't you consider it a remarkable coincidence that there are a troublemaker and a homosexual in Mr. Constantine's play, and there is a homosexual troublemaker in your book?"

"No, sir."

"Why not?"

"Because whereas Corporal Janus *is* a troublemaker, I could find no indication in the play that Colonel Peterson is a homosexual."

"He is *not,* in your estimation, a homosexual?"

"I do not think he could be considered homosexual in *anyone's* estimation."

"Has he not had homosexual experiences?"

"He has not."

"Does he not make homosexual references and allusions?"

"He does not."

"Does he not use endearing terms when talking to other men?"

"He does not."

"Did you find *any* character in the play who could be considered homosexual?"

"I did not."

"Your Honor," Brackman said, rising, "I am fully aware of Mr. Driscoll's reputation as a novelist, but I was *not* aware that he holds a degree in psychology. May I point out that what *he* considers homosexual or heterosexual may *not,* in the opinion of experts, actually be the case."

"If your Honor please," Willow said, "I believe Mr. Driscoll's testimony can be considered as competent as was Mr. Constantine's."

"Not when we are dealing with psychological matters, your Honor," Brackman insisted.

"Your Honor, we have allowed Mr. Constantine to testify that his colonel *was* a homosexual. I do not see the difference . . ."

"He *created* the character," Brackman said. "He ought to know whether or not he intended a homosexual."

"We have already agreed, Mr. Brackman, that *intent* is not on trial here," Willow said.

"I will allow the testimony," McIntyre said. "Mr. Driscoll is not offering a psychological analysis, nor does the Court consider it such. He is discussing a literary matter in literary terms. I believe even a layman can discern the difference between a homosexual and a heterosexual in a work of fiction, and I must certainly accept Mr. Driscoll as being someone considerably more advised than a layman. I will admit the testimony. Please go on."

"In other words, Mr. Driscoll, your character Colman could not have been based in part upon a homosexual colo-nel in *Catchpole* because no such homosexual colonel exists."

"That is correct."

"And the charge that Mr. Knowles later reverted to the original . . ."

"There was no original to which he could have reverted."

"While we are on Private Colman, we have had a great deal of testimony here about his wearing eyeglasses in the motion picture whereas he does not wear eyeglasses in your book. Corporal Janus in the play *does* wear glasses, of course, as I'm sure you noticed in your reading of *Catchpole*."

"Yes."

"How do you explain this appearance and disappearance of eyeglasses?"

"There's nothing to explain. Private Colman *does* wear glasses in my book."

"He does?" Willow asked, and turned to look at Brackman in mock surprise. "Where do you find any evidence of this, Mr. Driscoll?"

"There's a scene in which Lieutenant Cooper pulls up in a jeep, and just before he steps out, Colman takes a pair of glasses from the pocket of his blouse and puts them on to get a better look at him."

"What page does this occur on, Mr. Driscoll?"

"Page 37."

"May I add, your Honor, that there are eleven people in this courtroom at the moment, and five of us are wearing eyeglasses—almost half of the people present. In fact, Mr. Brackman's partner is one of those people."

"I wear glasses myself when I'm reading," McIntyre said, "so we can raise that number to six."

"Out of eleven, your Honor."

"I assume this is privileged, is it, Mr. Willow?" Brackman asked, and smiled.

"Merely an observation, Mr. Brackman, merely an observation."

"I do not see its relevancy."

"All right, all right, let's continue," McIntyre said.

"We have heard testimony here, Mr. Driscoll, to the effect that you named your private Peter Colman after Colonel Peterson in *Catchpole*. Is this in fact so?"

"It is not."

"How did you in fact come upon the name Peter Colman?"

"Peter is a phallic reference."

"Why would you use a phallic reference for a character who is clearly homosexual?"

"As a personal joke."

"And Colman? What is the significance of this surname?"

"It's a literary pun."

"In what way?"

"It refers to *The Iceman Cometh*."

"How?"

"The iceman in Mr. O'Neill's play means death. The character Colman in my book also means death—for the lieutenant."

"I still do not see either the connection or the pun."

"When I was a child, my mother used to tell me stories about buying ice for the icebox. She would take a wagon each morning and walk over to 96th Street, where there was a coal station. She used to buy the cake of ice there and then wheel it home. In my mind, 'iceman' and 'coal man' are identical and interchangeable. The name Colman is simply an elision of 'coal man,' which is in turn a pun on 'iceman.'"

"That's a rather complicated reference, isn't it?"

"All fictional references are complicated."

"Did you intend to—"

"Objection," Brackman said immediately.

"Sustained."

"Was this written for the reader to grasp?"

"No, sir. It was entirely personal. I did it for my own amusement."

"It was not, then, a reversal of Colonel Peterson's name."

"I had never heard of Colonel Peterson until last month when I read the play."

"You were present in this courtroom yesterday, were you not, when Chester Danton testified concerning several editorial reports made at Mitchell-Campbell?"

"I was."

"Do you recall the report made by Miss Anita Lang, the one containing suggestions about Private Colman's civilian life?"

"I do."

"And the flashbacks about his civilian life?"

"I do."

"She suggested, did she not, that there was too much emphasis on his civilian background?"

"Yes, she did."

"Did you change Colman's character in accordance with Miss Lang's suggestions?"

"I only met Miss Lang once before the book was published. I didn't know at the time that the suggestions were hers. I thought they came from Chester Danton, who was my editor at Mitchell-Campbell."

"But you did make the changes?"

"Yes, I deleted the flashbacks. There were two scenes showing his civilian life. I can recall them both very clearly, if you want me to take the Court's time to describe them."

"Very briefly, if you will."

"One of the scenes finally discarded from the novel described Colman's experience in a television studio during a rehearsal—all the hectic background, the setting of lights and cameras, the cueing-in of music, makeup men, costume people—Colman had been an actor in civilian life, you see, and this was supposed to be a rehearsal for a live drama series."

"Was this scene based on an actual experience of your own?"

"A friend of mine from Music and Art later became a set designer for television, and I once attended such a rehearsal with him, yes."

"And the other scene?"

"The second scene was between Colman and his mother, and tried to show the beginnings of his homosexuality. He's appearing in a high school play, and his mother is attending the performance, and after the play there is a short and very bitter . . . well . . . anti-mother scene, I guess you'd call it, while Colman is taking off his makeup in the dressing room. It was a good scene, and I'm sorry they asked me to cut it."

"But you did cut it."

"Yes, for the sake of the narrative flow."

"Were there any changes made in Colman's character aside from the deletion of these two scenes?"

"No. Once I hit upon the concept of him as a homosexual, the character remained more or less constant. And even after I cut those two flashbacks, his motivation was clearly understood by me, because the scenes were still there at the back of my mind."

"In other words, the flashbacks that were cut remained as a sort of underpainting?"

"Exactly."

"Referring again to Plaintiff's Exhibit 6, there is said to be a similarity between Sergeant Morley in your novel and Sergeant D'Agostino in *Catchpole*. Is Morley, in fact, based upon D'Agostino?"

"No, sir. Morley is an original creation."

"Is he based upon any real person?"

"Yes, he is based on a boy I knew at school."

"What was his name?"

"Andrew Christopher."

"Does this real name in any way account for the fictitious name you used?"

"Yes. Christopher Morley was a favorite author of mine.

The name Christopher automatically suggested Morley, and so I named the sergeant in my book Morley."

"Is Andrew Christopher still alive?"

"I don't know. I haven't seen him since we were in school together."

"Is Andrew Christopher a Negro?"

"Yes."

"Is the character Morley a Negro?"

"Yes."

"And a sergeant?"

"Yes."

"D'Agostino is also a sergeant, and a member of a minority group. How do you explain this similarity?"

"Sergeant D'Agostino is only *accidentally* a member of a minority group. Sergeant Morley is *deliberately* a Negro, for valid plot and character purposes."

"What are these valid plot and character purposes?"

"To further the conflict between the squad and the lieutenant."

"In what way?"

"By having Morley suspect the lieutenant of bigotry."

"Mr. Constantine has testified that there is a recurring thread of suspected prejudice in his play as well. Did you find this to be so?"

"No, sir."

"You did *not* find a recurring thread of suspected prejudice?"

"I did not."

"But there are references to D'Agostino being Italian, the lieutenant being white Protestant?"

"Yes, there are. But these are oblique and tangential and could not have been intended as development in a—"

"Objection, your Honor."

"Mr. Brackman?"

"We are getting into intent here, are we not?"

"Well, I won't know until I've heard the rest of his sentence," McIntyre said.

"If your Honor please, the witness has *already* used the word 'intended.'"

"Well, let's hear the rest of the sentence."

"I was only going to say that Mr. Constantine knows how to write a play, and there is ample evidence throughout that he knows how to sustain a thought and build it to a dramatic payoff. But he has not done this with D'Agostino's Italian background. The oblique references there seem intended only as incidental information."

"That's what I mean, your Honor," Brackman said. "I do not see how Mr. Driscoll can possibly know or even surmise what Mr. Constantine's intentions were."

"Yes," McIntyre said. "Well." He was silent for a moment. Then he said, "I think we will have to strike both the question and the answer, Mr. Willow."

Willow sighed and then said, "Mr. Driscoll, it has been alleged that the character called Kenworthy in your novel is based upon the character called Franklin in *Catchpole?* Is this in fact so?"

"No, sir."

"Both these men are addicted to the use of obscene language, are they not?"

"No. Again, we come to intent." Driscoll paused. "I really don't know how I can explain this without talking about *why* these characters are in the separate works."

"Your Honor?"

"Yes, Mr. Willow."

"May the witness proceed?"

"I have heard no objection."

"I most strenuously *will* object, your Honor, if he plans to analyze the thought processes of another man."

"He only plans to compare the characters, your Honor."

"That's not what he said."

"Mr. Driscoll?"

"I would have to go into intent."

"In that case, I would object," Brackman said.

"Well now," McIntyre said, and again was silent. "Will

this take the same form as the testimony you just gave concerning bigotry and so on?"

"I would imagine so."

"It does seem to me, Mr. Brackman, that we allowed your witness a similar latitude in his testimony."

"We did not permit him to testify as to intent, your Honor."

"Not in the strictest meaning of the word, perhaps. But was he not, for example, when discussing the reversal of Colonel Peterson's name to form Peter Colman's name, was he not then *really* analyzing Mr. Driscoll's intent?"

"He was basing his analysis on the actual works, your Honor, and not on what was intended."

"He may not have used the word 'intent,' but surely he was telling us that Mr. Driscoll *intended* an anagram."

"If your Honor please, I feel we are beginning to confuse execution with intent. We are here to compare the two works. In that manner alone can we determine whether or not an act of piracy was committed."

"But wouldn't it be helpful if we knew the intent as well?"

"Your Honor, it seems to me that a man can state in print that white is white, and then later claim he really intended to state that *black* is white, and the intent and the execution would be in direct contradiction."

"But isn't it important for us to know what both these men were *trying* to accomplish?"

"Not in a court of law, if your Honor please. We are not, after all, professional book or play reviewers."

"I think we *are* reviewing these works, nonetheless, Mr. Brackman."

"Only in an attempt to prove or disprove similarities. I know your Honor recognizes the gravity of this contest, and I'm certain the Court would not wish to compare these proceedings to something as trivial as the reviewing of books and plays."

"On the contrary, Mr. Brackman, we may be getting very close to the heart of the matter here."

"Which is what, if your Honor please?"

"What both these men were *trying* to do."

"It is our contention, your Honor, that James Driscoll was trying to do nothing more nor less than steal Mr. Constantine's play."

"And what was Mr. Constantine trying to do?"

"He was trying to write a wholly original work. Your Honor, in all frankness, I must say that anyone's comments—mine included—concerning this matter can only confuse the issue beyond understanding."

"You mean the matter of author's intent?"

"Yes, your Honor. It seems to me that it is the author's burden to make his intent clear in the execution."

"And it is the *judge's* burden to try for an understanding of both execution *and* intent."

"If that is your ruling . . ."

"That is my ruling."

"Will the record note my exception?"

"It will be noted. Proceed, Mr. Driscoll."

"I've forgotten the question," Driscoll said.

"Are both Franklin in the play and Kenworthy in your novel addicted to the use of obscene language?"

"No, sir, they are not."

"Do you accept the use of the word *bug* or its variations as a substitute for an obscenity?"

"I do."

"And you still maintain that Franklin in the play does not use obscenity?"

"He *does* use obscenity, but not excessively."

"On what do you base this?"

"On an actual count of the number of times the words *bug* or *bugging* are used in the play."

"How many times are they used?"

"The play runs one hundred and twenty pages, and is divided into three acts. Throughout the length of the play, Private Franklin uses this word a total of seven times. Compare this to *The Eve of Saint Mark,* where the word *ruttin'* is used a total of twenty-eight times during the course of the play . . ."

"Objection, your Honor," Brackman said. "We are not here to compare *Catchpole* with *The Eve of Saint Mark*."

"Overruled, Mr. Brackman. The comparison is being made only to clarify this matter of excessive obscenity."

"How often does your character Kenworthy use obscene language in *The Paper Dragon?*"

"Every time he speaks."

"Did you count the times?"

"No."

"Moving to Plaintiff's Exhibit 5, Plot Similarities, it is alleged that in both your novel and the play the lieutenant falls in love with an Army nurse. Is this so?"

"Yes, it is."

"How do you explain the similarity?"

"I wanted to tell a love story. In order to tell a love story, I needed a woman. In a combat situation, the only possible female characters would be either a native woman or a woman connected with the services. I chose a nurse."

"Why couldn't you just as naturally have chosen a Korean girl?"

"Because this would have brought up the racial matter again, and I wanted to explore that in terms of Sergeant Morley."

"Does the nurse in *Catchpole* outrank the lieutenant?"

"Yes."

"Does the nurse in your book outrank Lieutenant Cooper?"

"Yes."

"How do you explain this?"

"The nurses in Korea were in a combat situation, and most of them were experienced officers."

"Did you meet any nurses in Korea who had been recently commissioned?"

"No."

"What was the lowest rank you came across?"

"A nurse's rank, do you mean? In Korea?"

"Yes."

"First lieutenant."

"What rank does Jan Reardon in your novel hold?"

"First lieutenant."

"Has she been in the service longer than Lieutenant Cooper?"

"Yes, a full year longer."

"And does this explain her higher rank?"

"Yes."

"It has been alleged in this same Exhibit 5 that the men in the respective squads hate their new commanding officer because someone they liked and respected had been killed by a sniper. Is this so?"

"Yes, but the sniper wasn't my idea. It was Chester Danton's."

"What was the plot development in your original version?"

"The struggle originated with Private Colman. It was strictly a personal struggle between Colman and the lieutenant. Only later did it assume larger proportions that led to the lieutenant's death."

"There had been no previous commanding officer killed by a sniper?"

"No. Besides, in the play the lieutenant is *really* responsible for the death of one of his men, and the squad's resentment is somewhat justified. In my novel, the major is killed a full month before Cooper even arrives in Korea. The resentment is solely Colman's, the struggle is strictly between the two."

"A struggle for what?"

"For . . ." Driscoll hesitated. "Survival," he said.

"Which the lieutenant loses?"

"Yes. The lieutenant is killed. What Colman finally does to kill the lieutenant."

"Is this his plan?"

"Unconsciously, yes."

"Is this not also the plan of Corporal Janus in the play?"

"Yes."

"To murder the lieutenant?"

"Yes."

"How do they differ?"

"One is a melodrama."

"Which one?"

"The play. It is really a play about a murder conspiracy, and the events leading up to that murder and the eventual foiling of it through a series of further related events."

"Do you agree that the theme of *Catchpole* is 'The Idiocy and Foolish Waste of War'?"

"No, sir."

"What *is* the theme of *Catchpole?*"

" 'Crime Does Not Pay.' "

"And what is the theme of *The Paper Dragon?*"

"It would be difficult to express simply."

"How *would* you express it?"

"I suppose the theme is that people are capable of . . . of hurting each other beyond endurance by . . . by thoughtless and . . . ill-conceived actions."

"Like war, do you mean?"

"The war is inconsequential, it's only the background. I tried to . . . you see . . . the lieutenant knows a deep and very real love for this woman . . . the nurse . . . and this is wrecked . . . their love is destroyed by a single thoughtless act."

"But isn't it true that more than just their love is destroyed?"

"Yes, the . . . the future they might have had together."

"I'm referring, though, to the actual death of the lieutenant."

"Oh. Yes. But I saw that as symbolic."

"You did not see the nurse's deprivation as symbolic, did you?"

"No, that's real enough. She's lost him."

"Forever," Willow said.

"Yes." Driscoll paused. "Forever."

"But then, there *are* no winners in your novel, Mr. Driscoll, isn't that so?"

"Yes."

"The whole series of events, in fact, seem pointless by the end of the book."

"Yes."

"Everyone has been involved in a bitter struggle that solves nothing, a paper dragon. Moving on to Plaintiff's Exhibit 7, we are told that the 'female rifle' scene in your novel is based on the pig scene in Mr. Constantine's play. *Is it?*"

"No, it's not."

"It is alleged that these scenes are similar."

"I don't see how."

"They are both said to be sexual."

"Mr. Constantine's scene is about capturing a pig. My scene is about a woman."

"It's about stripping a rifle, isn't it?"

"No, it's about stripping a woman and taking her to bed."

"It purports to be about a rifle."

"The scene is transparently about a woman, whereas Mr. Constantine's pig scene is clearly a scene about *food*. There are no sexual allusions in it at all."

"Thank you, Mr. Driscoll," Willow said. "That is all for this witness, your Honor."

He nodded at Driscoll, smiled briefly, turned his back and walked to the defense table. Brackman took his time assembling his notes. Driscoll watched him warily. Constantine whispered something to him just before he rose from the table, and Brackman nodded and then walked toward the front of the courtroom. He pursed his lips, swallowed, looked up at Driscoll, and said, "Mr. Driscoll, if I understood your earlier testimony correctly, you said that you were an art major at the Art Students League and Pratt Institute. When did you enter Pratt?"

"In September of 1947."

"And you went into the Army in June of 1950?"

"Yes."

"Still intending to be an artist?"

"I'm sorry, what?"

"Did you plan on continuing with your art work when you got out of the service?"

"Yes."

"When did you change your mind?"

"I don't know when. I suppose it was a gradual process."

"Starting when?"

"Starting when I was at Pratt, I would imagine."

"And you entered Pratt in September of 1947?"

"Yes."

"A month before Mr. Constantine's play opened on Broadway."

"Yes."

"And that was when you began changing your mind about becoming an artist?"

"Not exactly then."

"Exactly *when?*"

"I said it was a gradual process."

"Starting in September of 1947?"

"It was a matter of beginning to gauge my own talents. There were a lot of talented people at Pratt. I began looking at my own work in terms of theirs."

"And decided to become a writer?"

"Not until much later."

"Not until *when?*"

"Sometime before I was discharged from the Army."

"So that when you returned to civilian life, you abandoned your study of art, and decided instead to take courses in writing?"

"Yes."

"You became an English major at N.Y.U.?"

"Yes."

"And I assume you took whatever creative writing courses the school had to offer."

"Yes."

"And that's where you learned to write."

"I don't know where a person learns to write."

"That is, nonetheless, where you had your formal training as a writer?"

"Yes."

"Did you begin writing for gain or profit immediately after you were graduated from N.Y.U.?"

"No."

"When did you begin writing?"

"Not until 1961."

"Four years after you were graduated."

"Yes."

"Even though you had been so splendidly prepared for a career in writing?"

"I don't know how splendidly I was prepared. I certainly didn't expect to step out of college and be acclaimed a new Hemingway."

"So you postponed writing your novel, is that correct?"

"Yes."

"Until you felt certain you *would* be acclaimed a Hemingway?"

"No, until I felt I could write the book I *wanted* to write. My *own* book. Not a Hemingway book, or anyone else's book."

"Had you written anything before you started your novel?"

"In college, yes."

"Was any work of yours published?"

"No."

"What sort of writing did you do in college?"

"Short stories mostly."

"Never a novel?"

"No."

"*The Paper Dragon* was your first novel."

"Yes."

"Your only novel."

"Yes."

"Did you submit any of your stories for publication while you were in college?"

"No."

"Why not?"

"They weren't good enough."

"Did you feel *The Paper Dragon* was good enough for publication?"

"Obviously, I did. I wouldn't have sent it out if I hadn't."

"Suddenly, out of the blue, you wrote a novel—never having written one before—and it was good enough for publication. In fact, according to Chester Danton's testimony yesterday, 'the remarkable thing about the book was that it was so good and so fully realized that there were very few suggestions an editor *could* make.' Do you agree with Mr. Danton?"

"In what way?"

"That the book was remarkable in its quality and in its realization."

"I would have no way of judging my own work."

"You seem perfectly capable of judging Mr. Constantine's work."

"But not my own."

"Do you think many first novels come to a publisher 'so good and so fully realized'?"

"I don't know."

"What would you guess?"

"Your Honor, the witness has already stated that he does not know."

"Sustained."

"Did you take any courses at N.Y.U. on the writing of a novel?"

"No."

"You just sat down to write one."

"Most novels are written by people who just sit down to write them."

"And they come out of the typewriter 'so good and so fully realized,' is that correct?"

"I don't know how anyone else's novel comes out of the typewriter."

"Were you satisfied with the way *yours* came out of the typewriter?"

"Not wholly. But it was the best I could do at the time."

"Can you do better now?"

"I don't know."

"The fact is, you haven't written anything since *The Paper Dragon*, have you?"

"No, I haven't."

"No other novels, no short stories?"

"Nothing," Driscoll said.

"Do you *plan* to write anything else?"

"No."

"But you're a writer, aren't you?"

"I'm a Vermont farmer."

"I thought you were a writer."

"You've been misinformed."

"Apparently," Brackman said, and smiled. "Mr. Driscoll, you have testified that Lieutenant Alex Driscoll . . ."

"Lieutenant Alex *Cooper*."

"Yes, forgive me, Lieutenant *Cooper* is an idealized version of yourself, is that true?"

"Yes."

"He is not entirely yourself?"

"Not entirely."

"Because, for example, Lieutenant Cooper is killed in the next to last chapter of your novel, and you, sir, are obviously not dead."

"Obviously not."

"So he is only partially based on yourself?"

"Yes."

"Would it be fair to say that somewhere along the line he ceases to be you?"

"Yes, it would be fair to say that."

"Mr. Brackman, I'm sorry I must interrupt you at this point," McIntyre said, "but it's exactly noon, and I think we should recess for lunch."

13

THE TWO MEN had hot dogs and orange drinks at the Nedick's on Duane, and then walked up Centre Street, past the County Court House and the Criminal Courts Building, and then onto Baxter and Bayard and into Chinatown. The weather was not mild—there was in fact a strong wind blowing—but it seemed almost balmy in contrast to yesterday's bitter fierceness. As they turned into Mott Street, Arthur felt for the moment as though he were entering an actual Chinese street in a Chinese city—Shanghai or Tientsin, Canton or Soochow—the undecipherable Chinese calligraphs, the quiet watchful men in doorways, hands tucked into their armpits, exotic women rushing by in abbreviated coats and slit skirts, pushing shopping carts or carrying baskets, the snug, tight, intimate landscape of winter in a foreign place, where the language is strange and the faces are alien and the only link with past experience is the weather. The sudden appearance of a grinning cardboard Santa Claus in a window brimming with ivory and jade shattered the illusion, brought once more into focus the strictly Anglo-Saxon proceedings downtown and the presence of Kent Mercer at his side, walking briskly and prattling on about the horror of the ghetto and these poor underprivileged Orientals. Did Arthur know there was no juvenile delinquency among the Chinese? The women pushed their shopping carts. Somewhere, he could smell roasting pork. He thought suddenly of Lamb's *Dissertation,* and then heard Kent's voice again, the slightly lilting monotony of it, the strident note that told Arthur he was about to get to the point, at last.

". . . in the middle of a *trial* and everything, but I thought I *should* see you before this thing came to a head. That's why I called you this morning, Arthur."

"Um-huh," Arthur said.

"I understand they've made some suggestions concerning the play," Kent said.

"That's right."

"At least, that's what Oscar told me."

"Yes, they made some suggestions."

"What do you plan to do?" Kent asked.

"I don't know."

"Will you make the changes?"

"I don't know."

"Well, I don't like to *press* this, Arthur, nor do I wish to risk that *terrible* look you get in your eyes whenever . . ."

"I don't get a terrible look, Kent."

". . . whenever you're angry," Kent said, and smiled. "Oh, you *know* you do, Arthur. You're a completely menacing person when you're crossed."

"Well," Arthur said, and sighed.

"But I *would* like to know what your plans are because—I might as well be frank, Arthur—I've *got* to know where we're going with this play."

"Why?"

"I've got to know whether it's going to be done."

"It'll be done," Arthur said.

"Do you mean you've decided to make the changes?"

"Well, no, not yet."

"Did the changes sound reasonable to you?"

"No."

"Not at *all?*"

"Well, some of them maybe."

"Which ones?"

"I don't remember."

"Arthur, I'm going to be frank with you," Kent said, and stopped in front of a candy store, and turned to face Arthur, and put one hand on his arm. "I've always been frank with you, you've got to admit that."

"Yes, you have."

"Arthur, you *must* make those changes."

"Why?"

"Because Hester won't take the part unless you do. And if Hester doesn't take the part, the play will *not* be produced. I'm being frank with you."

"All right."

"All right what?"

"All right, you're being frank with me."

"*Will* you make the changes?"

"Was this Oscar's idea?" Arthur asked suddenly.

"What?"

"This. Your calling me, this little talk."

Inside the candy store, an old Chinese woman with her hair pulled back tightly into a knot, was handing a coin across the counter and smiling at the proprietor. Again, the feeling of strangeness came over Arthur; he had never seen a woman like this one before, her clothes had been stitched in Singapore, her hair had been greased with hummingbird fat by a hairdresser who traveled from province to province, he knew she had just consumed a rare exotic drink and was now paying for it in foreign coin. Probably an egg cream, he thought, and smiled, and saw that Kent thought the smile was directed at him and was offended by it.

"You needn't look so smugly superior," Kent said, "because this was definitely *not* Oscar's idea. This was my own idea. I've got to think of myself, too, Arthur, I can't *continually* think of everyone *else* involved in this project."

"I understand that."

"I've been offered certain other things and, I'm being frank, some of them look very attractive to me. I've got to give people a yes or no answer, Arthur, I'm sure you can understand that."

"Of course."

"And this has nothing to do with your play, believe me. I love your play, you know that. But I've got my own career to think of, you know how it is with these things. If you don't say yes or no, people think you're not interested and begin looking elsewhere. There are only so many jobs, Arthur, and I don't have to tell you how many directors."

"I see."

"So what do you plan to do?"

"I don't know."

"How well do you know Hester Miers?"

"Only casually," Arthur said.

"You mean she hasn't yet made a grab for your jewels?" Kent said, and laughed. "I'm surprised, really."

"What about her?" Arthur said.

"I'm told she's very good in bed," Kent went on, unmindful of Arthur's tone. "She gives magnificent head," he said, and laughed again.

Arthur stared at Kent for a moment, and then abruptly began walking away from him. Kent stood rooted to the sidewalk. The door behind him opened, and the Chinese woman came out, shuffling past Kent, who rolled his eyes heavenward in a gesture of despair that Arthur missed, and then quickened his pace to catch up with him.

"She's a very *good* actress, Arthur," he said solemnly.

"I know."

"And I think she could be right for Carol."

"Sure, if we make her twenty-three instead of nineteen, and change her to a social worker instead of a college girl, and make her father the head of General Motors, and . . ."

"Well, I think you're exaggerating . . ."

". . . make her a whore besides."

"What?"

"Instead of a virgin."

"No one suggested she be made a whore."

"No, not exactly."

"Not in *any* respect, Arthur."

"Okay, not in *any* respect."

"I love the faces on these Chinese children, don't you?"

"Yeah."

"*One* affair was what they suggested, actually," Kent said.

"I know."

"*Every*body's had at least one affair," Kent said, and shrugged.

"But not Carol."

"Art need not imitate life quite so closely, need it?" Kent asked.

"I see they told you she's based on my sister."

"Yes. There's nothing wrong with that."

"I should hope not."

"But at the same time . . ."

"At the same time, let's make all the changes."

"I'm being frank with you, Arthur."

"Sure you are. You want a job."

"Not *any* job, Arthur. I want *this* job. But I'll tell you frankly, if I thought *this* job was in danger of evaporating, I would most *certainly* take another one."

"If I win this case . . ."

"What?"

"Nothing."

"Let's not talk about personal matters right now, Arthur."

"My play *is* a personal matter. To me."

"I'm sure it is. And to *me,* too. Which is why I hate to see it scuttled."

"There are other actresses."

Kent sighed. The sigh encompassed a lifetime of talking to writers and producers and actors, the sigh was one of sorrow and wisdom, sorrow because he had to give this same speech again to a writer intent on suicide, wisdom because he knew without doubt that what he was going to say was incontrovertible and stark and absolutely valid. The sigh was a tired one; Arthur heard something in it that compelled him to listen to Kent for perhaps the first time during their walk.

"Arthur, I know a little more about this business than you do," Kent said. "I've been in it for close to forty years now, as actor and director both, and I can tell you frankly that there's a time to stop *thinking* about a project, and a time to begin *moving* on it. At this moment, your play and the people involved in it are ready to *move,* the whole project has a *feel* to it, a sense of growing *power,* a certainty that all the planets are finally in conjunction and that we are about to *move,* Arthur, we are about to get *moving.* All you have to do is make those changes, agree to make those changes, and the thing will start humming and ticking, they'll spring Hester out of that actor's graveyard, she'll sign a contract, the backers will be fighting to get a piece of the action, and your play will be *done.* That's the feeling I get, that's what forty years of theater experience is telling me right now. It's telling me to *move,* Arthur, to get this thing on its feet and *moving.* Because if we don't, Arthur, if we allow Hester to get away, your play will *not* be produced by Selig and Stern. They've exhausted their people, Arthur, they cannot raise the money, they will let the option expire."

"There are other producers."

"Arthur, I've been in this business too long, really. Oh, yes, there are the success stories about the plays that have made the rounds of four *hundred* producers, and lo and behold the four-hundred-and-*first* snaps it up and it becomes a smash hit and runs for fourteen years and makes everyone involved a millionaire. I have heard all those stories, Arthur, because I've been around a long long time, I was born in the proverbial trunk. But I can tell you that if you don't move when everything is right for moving, things may *never* be right again, things may *never* come to that exact spot in time and space again."

"Maybe I'm willing to take that chance."

"You'd be smarter to compromise a little, Arthur."

"I've been compromising a little all my life," Arthur said.

"Then do it one more time. Make the changes. There'll be God knows how many revisions during rehearsal, anyway. The thing may get changed right back to what it was originally."

"Come on, Kent."

"All right, it won't, but will that be such a great loss? No one's trying to *corrupt* your play, Arthur. They're only trying to *improve* it."

"They're trying to change it, Kent."

"But only to improve it."

"No, only to change it. Only to make it theirs and not mine. Goddamn it, Kent, this is *still my play.*"

"I've got news for you, Arthur. Without an actress, it isn't a play at all, yours or anybody's."

"No? Then what is it?"

"A manuscript."

"There are plenty of actresses around. We can always get—"

"No, Arthur."

They stopped on the sidewalk and silently turned to face each other. In the window behind Kent, a plaster statue of the Virgin Mary knelt beside a cradle bearing the infant Jesus. To the left of the manger, a large Chinese calendar hung, a slant-eyed girl in a bathing suit looking back over her left shoulder. To the right of the manger, alternating green and red cardboard letters spelled out the words MERRY XMAS, dangling from a string.

"This is the time," Kent said. *"Now!* Either *make* the changes, Arthur, or resign yourself to the fact that your play will never be *done.*"

"I don't know," Arthur said.

"I'm being frank with you."

It's because I'm a Negro from Harlem, Norman Sheppard thought, and looked again at Ebie Driscoll and could not shake his feeling of discomfort. It's because I know the lady is from the Deep South, suh, and I am merely projecting her own discomfort onto myself. She is not used to dining with Nigras, suh, and this is why she constantly brushes that strand of blond hair away from her cheek, a gesture I have seen her perform a hundred times since this trial began, a nervous mannerism, that's all. And quite naturally, her nervousness has leaped across the table and I, being a sensitive person with a lot of natural rhythm, am reacting to it. I'll have to

report this to Dr. Maloney on Monday, he'll find it very
interesting. "What do you think about it, Mr. Sheppard?" he
will ask, and I will then try to separate this extraordinary
feeling of *déjà vu* from the very ordinary complicated feelings surrounding it, such as why I might feel uncomfortable
in the presence of any beautiful, blond, white woman from
Alabama even if I didn't think we'd met someplace before (a
likely possibility, to be sure) even if I didn't think I knew
her. Or, to be more exact, since Dr. Maloney insists on
exactitude, not only do I feel I know Mrs. James Driscoll, but
I further feel I know her exceptionally well. Or to be precise,
Dr. Maloney, I feel the young lady and I have been intimate,
yes, how about that for a clue to the Negro Revolution? I
will bet you any amount of money, Dr. Maloney, that she has
a small crescent-shaped scar on her thigh, and that she got it
from a piece of broken glass at the base of a statue or something in her home town, what do you make of that, Dr.
Maloney? "Well," he will reply, "what do *you* make of it, Mr.
Sheppard?"

"You came over very well," he said to Driscoll. "I think
McIntyre was impressed."

"I hope so," Driscoll answered.

Now how would I know about a crescent-shaped scar on
the lady's thigh when I have never *seen* the lady's thigh? How
did I know she was going to be left-handed even before I saw
her pick up her utensils at lunch the other day, tell me that,
Dr. Maloney. It *is* true, yes, Doctor, that I myself am left-
handed and therefore am constantly on the alert for members
of the race, human, who are similarly endowed, they being
acknowledged leaders whatever their color or religion.
Michelangelo was left-handed, did you know that? Kim
Novak, as it happens, is left-handed. Mrs. James Driscoll is
also left-handed, which fact I knew *before* I knew it, that's
exactly what I mean about this *déjà vu* phenomenon, doctor.
Am I making myself clear, or is it possible that all I want to
do is lay Ebie Driscoll? "Well, let's examine that, Mr. Sheppard," he will say.

Ebie Driscoll brushed the same strand of hair away from her cheek. There it is again, Norman thought, and I knew she would do it even before she did it the first time we met, felt I had seen her do it a thousand times before that. Or the way she tilts her head, look, just before she's going to say something, look, telegraphing her words, here it comes, she is about to speak, "May I have the salt, please?" Ebie asked. Norman handed her the salt and pepper shakers together, and intuitively knew she would say exactly what she said next, "No, just the salt, please." He frowned and turned his attention back to Driscoll, convinced that he was possessed of extrasensory powers and determined to put them to better use, like perhaps opening his own numbers bank in Harlem and taking bets only on numbers he knew would lose, not a bad thought.

"I think Jonah's approach was the proper one," he said. "Tracing the creative process."

"Mmmm," Driscoll said.

"That's really his forte, you know, hitting on the right approach. That's not as easy as it may sound. A lot of lawyers commit themselves to the wrong strategy from the beginning. Jonah's never done that to my recollection, and he's certainly had some difficult cases over the years."

"Has he?"

"Oh, sure," Norman said. "I didn't join the firm until after the San Quentin case, of course, but even since . . ."

"What San Quentin case?"

"The one with the guard. Didn't you follow it?"

"No."

"It was in all the papers."

"I must have missed it somehow."

"Well," Norman said, plunging on despite a detected note of sarcasm in Driscoll's voice, "a prisoner there was serving a life term—an ax murderer no less, you can imagine the kind of sympathy he aroused—and one of the guards kept bothering him, so he picked up a fork in the dining room one day and stuck it in the guard's throat."

"He killed him?" Ebie asked.

"Yes."

"Illlfffff," she said, and pulled a face, and the expression and the grimace were both familiar, he knew them from somewhere, but where? How come I pay you thirty dollars an hour, Dr. Maloney, and all you can tell me is that I must adjust as a Negro in a hostile society? Why can't you explain all these inscrutable things that keep happening to me?

"It was a mess," Norman said, "horrible case, but Jonah took it on. He's had a lot of tough ones. Listen, this one isn't such a cream puff, either." On impulse, he turned to Ebie and said, "Have you ever been up to Harlem, Mrs. Driscoll?"

"Never," she replied.

"Well," he said, and cocked his head to one side, and thought She's never been to Harlem, Dr. Maloney, so it isn't even possible we met in Small's Paradise or any of those other quaint places. "You ought to take her up to Harlem sometime, Jimmy," he said, and smiled.

"Invite us," Ebie said.

"I will."

"Do."

"If you mean it, I *will* invite you."

"I mean it," Ebie said.

"Ebie always means what she says, isn't that true?" Driscoll said.

His wife did not answer. She busied herself with her plate instead, cutting another piece of steak, and then meticulously and carefully placed her knife at the rear of the plate, as if this simple act required all her concentration.

"She's straightforward and honest," Driscoll said, staring at her with a cold, pained smile on his face. "It would hurt Ebie to lie, wouldn't it, Ebie?"

"Shut up, Dris," she said flatly, without looking at him, and the table went silent. Norman saw the anger that flared in Driscoll's eyes, and suddenly wondered whether he had misinterpreted the Harlem invitation. Here we are at the crux again, Dr. Maloney, here we are getting right down to

the heart of the old matter, which is: Can a Negro Boy from
Harlem Find Happiness with a White Woman in a Small
Mining Town? And the answer is No, not if Whitey thinks
you are eventually going to corral *all* of his women, leaving
him nary a soul to set his table or warm his bed. Understand,
Jimmy, understand Mr. Driscoll, suh, that I did not intend
my invitation for your wife alone, I intended it to include
yourself, suh. "Well, let us examine that," Dr. Maloney will
say, "especially in the light of your feeling that you and this
woman have been intimate. Tell me again about this small
scar on her thigh, crescent-shaped, did you say?"

Casually, and without looking at either Driscoll or his wife,
Norman said, "In any case, Jonah's approach is the right
one, and it's plain to both of us that you're holding your own
with Brackman."

"It didn't feel that way," Driscoll said. He addressed the
words to Norman, but he was still staring at his wife.

"Don't let him scare you," Norman said. "All you have to
remember is that McIntyre isn't an idiot. He'll see this as
clearly as the rest of us do."

"Mmm," Driscoll said.

"I'll tell you how *I* know you didn't steal that play."

"How?"

"The patterns."

"Meaning?"

"The play and the book have entirely different patterns,"
Norman said, completely aware that neither of them were the
least bit interested in what he was saying, but convinced he
had to say *something*, anything, to avert a homicide right
here at the table, and then perversely deciding he would ask
Mrs. Driscoll whether she still had that cute little crescent-
shaped scar on her thigh, and then deciding against it. I
know, Dr. Maloney, I'm chicken, I'm afraid of the white
man. Has it ever occured to you, Dr. Maloney, that *you* are a
white man and that I am paying you for the privilege of
informing you about how a Negro feels about white men like
yourself? I know, I know, I'm paying you because I'm afraid

of you too, man, you can't win. He sighed and said, "The patterns are obvious to anyone who's read both works carefully."

"Have *you* read them carefully, Mr. Sheppard?" Ebie asked.

"I read them both twice."

"And they're both about war, aren't they?" she asked, and looked up at her husband.

"Yes," Norman said, "but that's only the superficial pattern. I'm talking about something else. Look, there's a pattern to a bullfight, too. It never changes, it's always the same, it's timeless. But the *bulls* are different, and the *men* are different, and what happens each time is different from what happened the time before, even though the sequence of events may be identical. Or take a trial, for that matter, take any court case. Nothing changes there, does it? All rise, and the judge comes in, and the clerk tells us who the plaintiff is and who's defending, and the witnesses come up, and are sworn in and examined and cross-examined, all prescribed and tight, all according to strict rules and regulations—a pattern conceived and executed by men. It's my personal theory that *all* the civilized structures men create *have* to be patterned because life itself is so formless."

"I don't agree with that," Driscoll said.

"You don't think life is formless? Coincidental? Even inconclusive?"

"It's certainly not inconclusive. It ends."

"Who says an *end* is a *conclusion?*"

"Webster."

"What the hell did *he* know? All he did was give us a formal pattern for our language, which is exactly what I'm talking about. We *have* to have these patterns. Life would be unendurable otherwise. Look, the logical conclusion for life *is* death, isn't it—formless, mysterious, inexplicable? But do we accept it? No. We invent another pattern, an *after*life, a complex of heaven and hell, thereby extending life, and creating a concept we can hope to understand. We set up rules and regulations for everything, the same way *you* did when you were writing your novel, the same way Constantine did when he was writing his play. A pattern. A logical structure. You even went a step further by laying out a timetable for yourself, target dates and word goals, superimposing a *second* pattern upon the pattern already established for your novel. You had to know that at least the task would be conclusive."

"What do you mean?"

"The pattern you'd established for your book was inconclusive, Jimmy. You know that. The novel simply ends."

"It's conclusive, all right," Ebie said. "Perhaps you didn't understand it."

"I think I understood it."

"Perhaps not," she said. "In many respects, you see, *The Paper Dragon* is a mystery."

"What do you mean?"

"Just that it's a mystery," she said, and shrugged, and glanced at her husband.

"*Any* good novel is a mystery," Norman said.

"I don't mean a mystery *story*," Ebie answered.

"What *do* you mean?" Driscoll asked sharply.

"A book with a key."

"Like a diary?" Norman asked, and smiled.

"Yes," Ebie answered unsmilingly. "Like a diary."

"I wish *my* diary could earn as much money for me," Norman said.

"I think my wife is trying to say that all fiction is personalized fantasy. In that respect . . ."

"No, that's *not* what I'm trying to say."

"But that's it precisely," Norman said, leaning forward. "That's why the two works are so very different, because one is exclusively *Constantine's* fantasy, and the other is exclusively *yours*. The patterns are as different as your fingerprints."

"What about the 105th?" Ebie asked, and the table went silent again.

"Patterns are created by humans," Norman said at last. "The 105th is a human coincidence, pure and simple."

Ebie's eyes met her husband's, but she said nothing.

Sidney Brackman ate quickly and alone, and then went out into the street to rehearse his plan, deciding again to go ahead with it, and then deciding almost immediately that he was behaving foolishly again and in a manner that could only incur Chickie's wrath. She had said it last night, of course, and she'd been absolutely right, was he going to distrust her even after they were married? What kind of foundation was that, how could two people live and grow together if they did not trust each other?

He supposed there was a Jerome Courtlandt, and he supposed the agency really was planning a trip for him, but it seemed very coincidental to him, well, what the hell, life was full of coincidences, still it seemed very coincidental to him that Jerome Courtlandt in his tan Cadillac just happened to be on the way to the agency at closing time, just happened to pick up the two girls and, according to Chickie's testimony, drop them off at a restaurant. Well, why not? It had been a bitter night, thank God the temperature was a little milder today, it looked like rain, and how was Courtlandt to know what time the agency closed? Still, it was rather late to be heading there, well no, not if he thought the agency was open. And she had, after all, *told* Sidney about this Courtlandt fellow, she wouldn't have mentioned his name if there were anything funny about it, would she? Of course not. So why had he conceived his ridiculous plan, and why was he intent now on putting it into action? He either believed the girl or he didn't, trusted her or didn't. And why would she jeopardize their very good relationship, a relationship that could only get better once he won the case, once he came into his share of what the Court awarded Arthur, once they were married, he would have to call.

No, don't, he thought. Don't ask for trouble. Leave well enough alone. You're going to marry this girl, leave well enough alone.

He found a telephone booth in the drugstore on the next corner. He lingered outside the booth while a woman chattered interminably with someone she kept calling "*Boon*dy," and then went to the Manhattan directory only after the woman had vacated the booth. He hesitated before opening the book, turned to the C's and hesitated again, closed the book and walked directly out of the drugstore and into the street, it still looked like rain.

I'm doing the best thing, he thought. Why would I want to check up on her, for God's sake, she told me what it was all about, didn't she, she even told me the man's name, Jerome Courtlandt, would she have given me his name if there'd been anything to hide? He spotted a bar in the middle of Murray Street, quickly turned right, and went into it. There were a lot of colored girls scattered at the tables, eating lunch and drinking beer, girls who worked in the various municipal offices in the area, he supposed—what would New York City do without its colored civil service employees, sink into the ocean, that's what. The juke box was playing a lovely melody, he could not place it, one of the new things. He had stopped remembering the tunes or words to songs when he was eighteen, and had always considered it a loss. The phone booth was at the end of the bar. A lighted sign above it advertised Miller's High Life. By the light of the sign, he searched the Manhattan directory and found a listing for Courtlandt, Jerome, on East 36th Street, well, he exists, he thought, and closed the book. He stood undecided for a moment. The bartender was watching him. He opened the book again, found the listing again, memorized the number, and went into the booth to dial it.

He dialed the first two numbers, and then hung up.

His dime clattered into the return chute.

He retrieved the coin, put it into his pocket, sat in the booth a moment longer, rose, opened the door, closed the door again, sat, took the dime from his pocket, lifted the receiver from its cradle, inserted the dime into the coin slot, heard the dial tone humming against his ear, and quickly dialed the number. He could hear the phone on the other end ringing once, twice, three times . . .

"Hello?" a man's voice said.

"May I speak to Mr. Courtlandt, please?" Sidney asked.

"This is he."

"Mr. Courtlandt, this is Mr. Simmons of Trans World Airlines."

"Yes?"

"About your European trip," Sidney said. His heart was pounding. He was certain his lie had already been detected, certain Courtlandt would instantly call his bluff.

"Yes?" Courtlandt said. There was a pause. "Trans *World* Airlines, did you say?"

"Yes."

"I don't understand. I thought we were flying Pan Am."

"Well, there seems to be some confusion about the booking," Sidney said.

"Why don't you call the agency?" Courtlandt suggested. "I'm sure they can straighten it out."

"What agency would that be?"

"Travel Time on Madison Avenue."

"Thank you, sir."

"I'm sure they said Pan Am. How'd this happen, anyway?"

"Probably a duplicate booking. We'll straighten it out, sir, don't worry about it."

"Okay."

"Thank you, sir."

"Thank you for calling," Courtlandt said, and hung up.

Sidney immediately replaced the receiver on its cradle and sat with his eyes squeezed shut, trying to catch his breath. All right, it was true. He was their client, he was taking a trip, it was true, it was true. He would call Chickie and apologize immediately, tell her he loved her, tell her he trusted her. Well, he couldn't apologize, he didn't want her to know he'd called Courtlandt. But he'd tell her he loved her and trusted her, that was what he'd do. He found another dime in his pocket, put it into the slot, and quickly dialed the agency. Ruth McCutcheon answered the phone.

"Travel Time," she said, "good afternoon."

"Good afternoon," he said, "may I speak to Miss Brown, please?"

"She's out to lunch right now," Ruth said. "May I help you?"

"Well, no, I don't think so," he said, and was about to hang up.

"Would you like to leave a message?" she asked. "May I say who called?"

"Yes, this is . . ." He hesitated. She had not recognized his voice; she did not know who he was. In the three seconds it took him to make up his mind, he did not even consider the fact that he was intuitively behaving like a lawyer, putting to practical use the years of experience he had had in court-rooms, covering ground already covered, stating and restating the same point, examining and re-examining, driving for the complete truth where only the partial truth was known. He knew only that he possessed information now, he had re-ceived information from Mr. Jerome Courtlandt, and that he could use this information to learn the whole truth, three seconds to make a decision, nothing but the truth, three seconds in which to conceive a strategy.

"This is Pan American Airlines," he said.

"Yes, well, this is Miss Brown's partner," Ruth said, accept-ing the lie.

"I see." He hesitated again. Let it go, he thought. Leave well enough alone. "I'm calling to verify a flight," he said.

"Yes?"

"For Mr. Jerome Courtlandt."

"That's been verified already," Ruth said.

"Not according to my information."

"I handled it myself," Ruth said.

"I'm sorry, but there's obviously been an error."

Ruth sighed. "I don't know why everything always has to be done six times," she said. "All right, let's get it over with."

"Which flight *is* that?" Sidney asked.

"Saturday morning. I haven't got the number right before me. Don't *you* have the number?"

"To London, is that?" Sidney said.

"No, to Rome. Oh, *boy*," Ruth said. "It's four seats to Rome on Saturday morning, the nine forty-five flight. Just a minute, I'll get the flight number for you. Oh, boy."

He heard the clatter of the receiver on the desk, heard the clicking of high heels across a hard floor, heard another phone ringing somewhere in the distance, "Travel Time, good afternoon." He waited a moment longer. He could hear her indistinctly in the background. He did not know what further information he needed or required. Courtlandt was obviously leaving for Italy, they were obviously handling the trip for him, there was nothing more to know.

He hung up abruptly and came out of the booth, oddly unsatisfied.

They talked about Christmas gifts during lunch, exchanging ideas about the people on their lists, but she had the feeling Jonah's mind was elsewhere, and her own thoughts were about the little Egyptian who had come to her office that morning. They walked up Broadway afterwards, stopping now and then to inspect the wares displayed in each holiday window. There were decorated Christmas trees everywhere, and on each corner a Santa Claus despondently shook his bell at the passing crowd. On Park Place, a Salvation Army band was playing "Adeste Fidelis." The snow underfoot had turned to slush, and the weather was milder than it had been all week. It did not seem as though Christmas was only ten days away.

They walked back toward the courthouse slowly. It was only one-thirty and the trial would not resume until two. They discussed the change in the weather, and the possibility of more snow in time for Christmas—had she ever seen that movie with Bing Crosby and Fred Astaire, yes, *Holiday Inn*, wasn't it, yes, who was the girl in that film? They sat on a bench facing Centre Street on the smallest of the Foley Square islands. A sharp wind swept around the corner of Duane off the river beyond. Gray pigeons echoed the gray slush on the curb, nibbling for peanuts around the benches.

Jonah was quiet, hands thrust deep into his coat pockets, legs stretched, head bent, dark hair moving with each fresh gust of river wind. His glasses reflected the gray pavement and the parading pigeons, hiding his eyes from view. She wondered suddenly if anyone had ever looked directly into the eyes of Jonah Willow, and just as suddenly wondered what he looked like in bed, without his glasses. There were no more Christmas gifts to discuss, and all the talk about the weather had been exhausted. They had both seen *Holiday Inn* and could not remember the name of the girl in it, and now they sat in silence while he thought God knew what, and she thought of the Egyptian. She took a deep breath.

"Hadad came to see me this morning," she said.

"Who?"

"Ibrahim Hadad. The man we ran into Monday night."

"The man who ran into *us*," Jonah corrected, and then suddenly sat erect and turned to face her. "What do you *mean* he came to see you? Hadad?"

"That's right."

"What'd he want?"

"He told me he'd been visited by a detective. He said you'd called Santesson of the Circuit Court . . ."

"Yes, so . . . ?"

". . . and that Santesson assigned a detective to investigate."

"Yes, that's what I asked him to do."

"Investigate what, Jonah?"

"Third-degree assault."

"You're kidding."

"No, I'm not."

"Are we talking about the same accident?"

"I think so."

"There was no assault, and you know it."

"Sally, with all due respect, I hardly think you're familiar enough with the penal law to give an opinion on . . ."

"I read Section 244 this morning, after Hadad left. How do you figure there was culpable negligence?"

"He went through a full-stop sign."

"He didn't."

"Sally, you were asleep. I saw him."

"I was *not* asleep. He stopped the car just before he came onto the highway."

"He may have hesitated, but he didn't come to a full stop."

"Jonah, the district attorney would still have to prove disregard of the consequences and an indifference to—"

"Please don't throw precedent at me. Hadad went through a stop sign on a very dark night, driving his vehicle in a culpably negligent manner, and causing bodily injury to two other people. That's third-degree assault."

In the silence, she heard the wind sweeping around the corner of the courthouse. Crossing over from Centre Street, two obvious prostitutes ducked their heads against the sudden gust, one taking the other's arm as they stepped gingerly over the slush against the curb and then ran across Duane, probably on their way to the Criminal Courts Building. Behind them, a sailor looked up as he lighted his cigarette, decided to follow them, then decided against it, and turned and headed downtown toward City Hall. Sally put her hands in her pockets and looked at the tips of her shoes.

"Jonah, I don't see why you're doing this," she said.

"He violated the law."

"He's a poor slob who was coming home late from a—"

"I don't care what he is. He could have killed us both on that goddamn highway."

"But he didn't."

"He could have. He's guilty, Sally."

"I thought people were innocent until . . ."

"Now cut it out, will you!"

"Jonah, there's something behind this."

"There's nothing . . ."

"There's more than just . . ."

"There's *nothing*, I said!"

They fell silent again. The pigeons cooed around the bench. In the distance, they could hear the sound of heavy trucks rumbling toward the Brooklyn Bridge.

"We don't know each other well enough for this," Jonah said.

"No, we don't."

He rose suddenly, startling the pigeons into frantic flapping flight. He stood before the bench for a moment, as though about to say something, staring down at her, his glasses reflecting the pavement—you can never see his eyes, she thought again—and then abruptly seemed to change his mind. He held out his hand. "Come," he said.

"Where?"

"I've got to get back."

They crossed over to the courthouse in silence.

"Will I still see you tonight?" he asked.

"Do you want to?"

"I want to."

"All right."

They stood on the courthouse steps without speaking. At last Jonah said, "He's guilty, Sally."

"The Egyptian?"

"No. James Driscoll."

He turned and walked up the steps.

"Mr. Driscoll," Brackman asked, "would it be fair to say that Lieutenant Alex Cooper is an idealistic officer?"

"It would be."

"Were *you* an idealistic officer?"

"No, I was not."

"So on that score at least, Alex Cooper is *not* James Driscoll."

"That's right."

"Alex Cooper is single, is he not?"

"Yes."

"Were you single when you went into the Army?"

"No, I was married."

"Mr. Driscoll, did you have a love affair with an Army nurse while you were in Korea?"

"No, sir, I did not."

"But Lieutenant Cooper did?"

"Yes."

"You're familiar with *Catchpole,* I know, and I'd like to ask you now if you recall that Lieutenant Mason in that play is an idealistic officer. Do you recall that?"

"Yes."

"That he is an idealist? The same as your Lieutenant Cooper."

"He is an idealist, yes. He is *not* the same as Cooper."

"In what respect do they differ?"

"In many respects."

"They physically resemble each other, do they not?"

"Yes."

"They're both single."

"Yes."

"They both have an affair with a nurse."

"Yes."

"And they are both targets in a murder plot."

"Yes."

"In those respects they are similar, are they not?"

"Yes."

"Point of fact, in those respects they are *identical.*"

"No. They are not identical. They are two separate men. I don't know who Constantine's hero is based on, but Lieutenant Cooper is based on *me.*"

"Even though you possess none of these characteristics which can be attributed to him?"

"I possess *most* of the characteristics that can be attributed to Lieutenant Cooper."

"Like his idealism?"

"No, not that."

"Or his single state?"

"No."

"Or his love affair with an Army nurse?"

"Those are three isolated aspects of his character. For the most part, Cooper's mental processes are identical to my own, and he behaves as I might have behaved in the circumstances."

"But you were in identical circumstances, were you not?"

"I was in Korea, if that's what you mean."

"In a combat situation."

"Yes."

"As the officer in charge of an infantry platoon."

"Yes."

"Just as Lieutenant Cooper is in your book."

"Yes."

"And as Lieutenant Mason is in the play *Catchpole*."

"Is that a question?"

"It is a question."

"Lieutenant Mason is an officer on Eniwetok during World War II."

"But similar in all other respects."

"If you mean that he's in command of a combat infantry platoon, yes."

"A great many things happen to Lieutenant Cooper in the course of your novel. Did all of these things happen to you while you were in Korea?"

"No."

"You invented some of them, is that it?"

"Yes."

"Which of the events *did* happen to you, Mr. Driscoll?"

"Many of them."

"Well, let's just go over them one at a time, shall we? Let's try to find out which were based on your own experience and which were invented. To begin with, you've testified that you did *not* have an affair with an Army nurse, so I think we can safely conclude you invented that particular character and that particular event. Did you invent Private Colman as well?"

"Partly."

"You mean there *was* someone like Colman in your platoon?"

"No. But I'd met people like him before I went into the Army."

"But not in Korea, not in a combat situation?"

"No."

"Was there a troublemaker in your platoon?"

"No."

"Was there a homosexual?"

"No."

"Yet Colman is a homosexual troublemaker."

"Yes."

"You testified earlier that Sergeant Morley was based on a Negro who did in fact exist."

"Yes."

"A boy you knew in school . . ."

"Yes."

". . . and whom you have not seen since."

"Yes."

"Did this real person ever fall under the influence of someone like Colman, as Morley does in your book?"

"No."

"Then this situation was invented?"

"Yes."

"Did this real man ever become instrumental in a murder scheme?"

"No."

"This, too, was invented?"

"Yes."

"Were you ever the target in a planned murder, Mr. Driscoll?"

"No."

"You *do* agree that the men in your novel actively plot the murder of Lieutenant Cooper?"

"His death."

"They plan to lead him into a trap, do they not?"

"They deliberately lead him into a concentration of Chinese troops."

"Which they know exists."

"Yes."

"This would be cold-blooded murder, wouldn't it?"

"Yes, I suppose so."

"But your men never planned such a murder, did they?"

"No."

"Nor did they ever lead *you* toward a strong concentration of Chinese soldiers . . ."

"No."

". . . as the men in the book do?"

"That's right."

"You invented this."

"Yes, I invented it."

"Did you similarly invent the 'female rifle' scene, as it has been called?"

"No, that actually happened to me."

"The men made sexual allusions to a rifle while they were disassembling it?"

"Yes, sir. I changed the emphasis in the book, though. This really happened at Fort Dix, and it was a very comical thing. In the book, I've made it a malicious episode inspired by Private Colman."

"Who is named after your mother's iceman, is that correct?"

"I never said that."

"Perhaps I misunderstood you."

"I'm sure you did."

"I thought you said your mother's iceman was named Colman."

"No, I didn't."

"Well, the record will show what you said."

"Yes, shall we go back over it right this minute?" Driscoll asked.

"I'm sure there's no need for that, Mr. Driscoll."

"Just to clarify exactly what I *did* say."

"It was a pun, isn't that what you said?"

"Yes. But I didn't say he was named after my mother's iceman."

"Forgive me. You mentioned *The Iceman Cometh,* though, didn't you?"

"Yes, I did."

"You said this was some form of literary joke, isn't that right?"

"Yes."

"Are you fond of puns and jokes?"

"Yes."

"And of course you're familiar with plays? You said you've been a theatergoer since you were twelve."

"That's right."

"Did you see *The Iceman Cometh?*"

"I did."

"And felt it was perfectly all right to make a literary allusion to it?"

"Yes."

"Saw nothing wrong with that?"

"*Is* there something wrong with it?"

"I'm asking *you,* Mr. Driscoll."

"No, there was nothing wrong with the allusion."

"Did you see the play *The Eve of Saint Mark?*"

"No."

"Did you see the movie?"

"Yes."

"And you read the play, of course."

"Yes."

"Before this trial began?"

"Yes, I read it many years ago, and again recently."

"Therefore, you were familiar with Sergeant Ruby long before you began writing your book."

"That's right."

"And before you created your character Kenworthy, the one who swears a lot."

"That's right."

"By the way, was *he* based on any actual person? Kenworthy?"

"He was a composite."

"An invention?"

"In that he was not any one person."

"Was his similarity to Sergeant Ruby another literary joke?"

"He is not similar to Sergeant Ruby."

"They both swear a lot, don't they? By actual count, the

word *ruttin'* is used a total of twenty-eight times in *The Eve of Saint Mark*, isn't that what you said?"

"That's right."

"Did you make the count recently?"

"Yes, last week."

"You didn't count all those *ruttin's* before you began writing your book, did you?"

"No."

"And you see no similarity between Ruby and your character?"

"They both swear a lot. That's the only similarity."

"Yet you do not feel that Private Franklin in *Catchpole* swears a lot?"

"He does not."

"You have heard the old adage, have you not, to the effect that if a man takes one drink on the stage, he's a social drinker; two drinks, he's an imbiber; three drinks, he's an alcoholic."

"I've heard something similar to that."

"Expressive of the shorthand used in the theater."

"Yes."

"Do you think the same shorthand might apply to a character who swears?"

"It might."

"So that if Franklin swore once, he might be considered normally agitated, whereas twice would make him somewhat salty, and *seven* times would indicate he was addicted to the use of obscenity."

"Absolutely not."

"You do not feel this would apply to Franklin, who swears seven times during the course of *Catchpole?*"

"Certainly not. Especially when much stronger swear words are used by other characters in the play. Words like 'bastard' and 'whore' and—"

"I don't think we need catalogue them, Mr. Driscoll, though you do seem very familiar with the play."

"I am."

"You read it one weekend a month or so ago, is that right?"

"That's right."

"You must have read it very carefully."

"I did."

"Did you intend Colman to be a homosexual?"

"Obviously."

"This idea did not come from Chester Danton, did it?"

"No."

"The dead major came from him, however?"

"Yes."

"But not the idea of Colman as a homosexual. You invented that all by yourself."

"Yes."

"You testified earlier that you did not believe Colonel Peterson in the play *Catchpole* is a homosexual."

"That's right."

"Do you know a great many homosexuals, Mr. Driscoll?"

"I know some."

"Personally."

"Yes, personally."

"Would you say that homosexuals are as different one from the other as are heterosexuals?"

"I would say so."

"Would you also agree that it is sometimes difficult to tell whether or not a man is a homosexual?"

"Sometimes."

"Do you think it would be possible to know whether or not a man were a homosexual, for example, if he did not utter a word, if he never spoke?"

"It might be difficult."

"Might it be similarly difficult to determine homosexuality in a letter written from one person to another? The words themselves, the words in the letter, might seem absolutely noncommittal, might they not?"

"I'm not sure I know what you mean."

"I'm asking, Mr. Driscoll, whether words in a letter written from one person to another might not seem entirely heterosexual in character when unaccompanied by either mannerisms of gesture or voice. That is what I am asking."

"A letter from a homosexual, do you mean?"

"If you will."

"I suppose."

"Do you also agree that the words in a *play*, the words in a mimeographed copy of a play, such as the one you perused one weekend last month, could seem equally noncommittal?"

"If a writer intended a homosexual character . . ."

"Let us not for the moment go into Mr. Constantine's intent. He has already testified that he *did* intend a homosexual. I'm asking whether—"

"If that's what he intended, it did not come across in the play I read."

"Did it come across in the play you *saw?*"

"Objection!" Willow shouted.

"Sustained. I'll have no more of that, Mr. Brackman."

"Will you accept my word, Mr. Driscoll, if I tell you that Colonel Peterson as played on the New York stage *definitely* came across as a man with homosexual tendencies?"

"I found no evidence of that in the mimeographed play."

"If I tell you it was in the play as staged, will you accept it?"

"Not unless you also tell me the part was played by a homosexual actor."

"You would not accept it otherwise?"

"I would not."

"Because you found no lines or scenes in the play that indicated Peterson was homosexual."

"I found none."

"Would you take this please, Mr. Driscoll, and turn to page 2–6, the middle of the page, Colonel Peterson speaking. Do you have the place?"

"Yes."

"The colonel is in the field, he is standing in the midst of carnage left by a Japanese counterattack, and he is with Corporal Janus and Sergeant D'Agostino, two of our principal characters. Are we clear as to the background?"

"Yes."

"May I read this to the Court then? And would you please follow it in the copy I've given you."

Brackman cleared his throat. The courtroom was silent. From the corner of his eye, Driscoll could see his wife sitting erect and attentive in the otherwise empty jury box. At the defense table, Jonah Willow was idly toying with a pencil.

"This is the scene," Brackman said, and began reading:

PETERSON

Look at them.

D'AGOSTINO

Easy, sir.

JANUS

Try to get a hold of yourself, sir.

PETERSON

Who's this man?
    (He kneels, rolls over one of the dead men.)
Sergeant, who is this man?

D'AGOSTINO

That's Kirby, sir. Sir . . .

PETERSON

    (Clasping his hands together)
He has blood all over his hair, sergeant.

D'AGOSTINO

Sir, let's get out of here. Let's get back to . . .

PETERSON

All over his hair.
    (He touches Kirby's hair.)
Kirby? Kirby, are you all right?

D'AGOSTINO

He's dead, sir.

PETERSON

Open your eyes, Kirby.

JANUS

Colonel, the man's . . .

PETERSON

(*Shrieking it*)

No!

(*He lifts the dead Kirby into his arms, slowly rocks him as he would a child.*)

"That's the end of the scene," Brackman said. "Were you able to follow it, Mr. Driscoll?"

"I was."

"Since you seem to be an expert on matters homosexual . . ."

"I never said I was an expert."

". . . perhaps you can tell me what this scene is all about, if not homosexuality?"

"This scene is all about a man on the edge of a mental breakdown."

"And nothing more?"

"On the next page, they take him to the field hospital, and he's raving about death and blood and—"

"We're concerned with *this* scene, Mr. Driscoll, and not with what follows it or precedes it."

"You're taking it out of context," Driscoll said flatly.

"I have read nothing in this particular scene out of context, and I would like to address my questions to *this* scene and to what is *in* this scene. Does the colonel touch the dead boy's hair in this scene?"

"He does."

"Do you consider that normal?"

"I've just told you that the colonel is about to crack up. Whatever he does—"

"Please answer the question."

"In the context of what is about to happen, this is a natural gesture."

"Do either of the other men touch the boy's hair?"

"No. But neither of them are about to suffer a mental breakdown."

"You find nothing homosexual about one man touching the hair of another man?"

"Not in this scene. The colonel is obviously losing control, he's just noticed blood in the dead man's hair . . ."

"Losing control in what way?"

"Losing control of his mental faculties."

"Not of his inhibitions?"

"Certainly not."

"Do you feel it is natural to touch hair that is covered with blood?"

"In this scene, in a combat situation, where a man suffering from battle fatigue . . ."

"Please answer the question."

"Yes, I think it's a natural gesture."

"What about rocking him in his arms?"

"I accept it in this scene."

"You do not feel there is anything homosexual about one man rocking another man in his arms?"

"The author did not indicate anything homosexual."

"He says in the stage direction that Peterson takes the dead boy in his arms and slowly rocks him."

"Read the rest of the sentence," Driscoll said.

"What?"

"Read the rest of the sentence. It says 'slowly rocks him as he would a child.' "

"Yes, well?"

"What's homosexual about that?"

"About a man rocking another man in his arms? That would seem clearly homosexual to me."

"It would seem only paternal to me, especially when the author indicates he's rocking him as he would a child. He does not say as he would a *woman*, or as he would a *lover*, he specifically says a *child*."

"And you find nothing homosexual in that?"

"Nothing."

"I will accept your answer."

"What?"

"I said I will accept your answer. Do you recall the rank of your nurse, Jan Reardon, in *The Paper Dragon?*"

"She is a first lieutenant."

"Do you recall the rank of Mr. Constantine's nurse, Diane Foster, in *Catchpole?*"

"I think she's a first lieutenant."

"She is in fact so. How do you explain this similarity, Mr. Driscoll?"

"I've already said that the only nurses I met in Korea were—"

"Did you meet any nurses who were captains?"

"I did."

"Or majors?"

"Yes."

"Yet you chose to make your nurse a first lieutenant. Why?"

"A first lieutenant sounds more feminine somehow than either a captain or a major. Besides, she has only been in the service a year longer than Cooper, and a higher rank than first lieutanant would have sounded implausible."

"Mr. Driscoll, *you* wrote the book, did you not?"

"Yes."

"Therefore her length of time in the service was not proscribed. You *chose* the exact amount of time, you chose *one* year rather than two or three or four."

"Yes."

"And it was this length of time that determined her rank?"

"Yes."

"Are you sure it was not her *rank* that determined the length of her service? Which came first, Mr. Driscoll?"

"Her being a year . . . her being in the service a year longer."

"Are you certain?"

"I'm certain."

"And this is the only explanation you have of their identical ranks, the two nurses?"

"It's the only explanation."

"Or the identical line 'I outrank you'?"

"This line is not in Mr. Constantine's play."

"But his nurse *does* joke with the lieutenant about rank."

"Only superficially. A point is not made of it."

"I see. Mr. Driscoll, what do Alex Cooper's fellow officers call him?"

"Coop."

"What do Roger Mason's fellow officers call him?"

"Mase."

"You have stated that the character Alex Cooper is based upon yourself."

"Yes."

"What does Jonah Willow call you?"

"What do you mean?"

"Familiarly."

"He calls me Jimmy."

"What does Chester Danton call you?"

"Jimmy."

"What does your agent, Hollis Marks, call you?"

"Jimmy."

"Do any of your friends call you anything but Jimmy?"

"No."

"In *Catchpole,* Lieutenant Mason is called 'Mase,' and in *The Paper Dragon,* Lieutenant Cooper is called 'Coop.' Was your name ever shortened to 'Dris' while you were in the service?"

"No, it was not."

"Mr. Driscoll, in your novel there is a long discussion between the enlisted men about big-name bands, and especially about Glenn Miller. Do you recall the scene to which I'm referring?"

"Yes, but it was not especially about Glenn Miller."

"Glenn Miller is mentioned prominently in that scene, is he not?"

"Only in conjunction with the names of other band leaders. The men are playing a sort of guessing game, trying to remember the theme songs of the big-name bands."

"Yes, and isn't it true that an argument develops between two of the men as to whether Glenn Miller's theme song was 'Moonlight Serenade' or 'Sunrise Serenade,' and it is Sergeant Morley who correctly identifies the theme."

"That's true."

"A scene which was later carried over into the film. Your novel is set in Korea during the months of October and November in the year 1950, isn't that right?"

"Yes."

"The soldiers in this scene are all young men, aren't they?"

"Yes."

"Some in their late teens, some in their early twenties, is that right?"

"Yes, that's right."

"Do you know when Glenn Miller is presumed to have died?"

"Yes, I do."

"When was it?" Brackman asked.

"It was December of 1944."

"December 15th, to be exact," Brackman said. "Now, do you think it likely that people—especially very young people —would in 1950 still be discussing a band leader who reached the height of his popularity in the late thirties and early forties?"

"I grew up with the music of Glenn Miller and all the other big-name bands mentioned in that scene. When he was reported missing, I must have been fifteen years old, and I can remember being deeply affected."

"And you find nothing odd about men discussing him in the middle of Korea six years after his death?"

"I do not."

"Are you aware that in *Catchpole*, there is a scene where a group of men are discussing the death of Glenn Miller?"

"I am aware of that."

"How do you explain the similarity?"

"There is no similarity. The men in *Catchpole* are discussing Glenn Miller's death. The men in *The Paper Dragon* are discussing the theme songs of the big-name bands, and Glenn Miller's name is only incidentally mentioned."

"Is there not an argument about his theme song?"

"A difference of opinion, not an argument."

"And doesn't this difference of opinion, as you call it, focus attention on his name?"

"Momentarily."

"In much the same way that attention is focused on it in *Catchpole*."

"We seem to be speaking two different languages," Driscoll said.

"I think we are speaking the same language, Mr. Driscoll, and I would like an answer to my question."

"I have already answered your question. I have already told you that the scenes are about two different things. One is about the death of Glenn Miller and the other is about the theme songs of the big-name bands. So when you ask me if attention is focused on the name in the same way, I can't add anything to what I've already said, which is that attention is focused in entirely *different* ways."

"And you find nothing unusual or odd about the similarity?"

"I've already testified that there *is* no similarity. But I did find something odd, yes."

"Are you now saying . . ."

"In *Catchpole*."

"Yes, are you now reversing . . ."

"I found it odd that in February of 1944 those men were discussing the death of Glenn Miller, which did not take place until *December* of 1944. Don't *you* find that odd?"

"I'm not b-b-being examined, Mr. Driscoll."

"I just thought you might find it odd."

"I w-w-would imagine that was nothing more than d-d-dramatic license."

Hearing the stammer, seeing the sudden pink color rising in Brackman's cheeks, Driscoll realized with a feeling bordering on wild exultation that he had flustered him, and knew in the same instant that he was cleverer and brighter and infinitely more agile than the lawyer was. He glanced toward the defense table to see if Willow had noticed and appreciated his entangling maneuver, and saw only that Willow was frowning. Willow's displeasure, however, did nothing to quell the rising sense of triumph, the reckless knowledge that he could parry anything Brackman put to him, and then thrust with deadly accuracy to leave the inept little lawyer helpless and forlorn, bereft of any weapon. Come on, he thought. Let's go, Mr. Brackman. Come on.

"This m-m . . ." Brackman started, and then cleared his throat and consulted his notes, and Driscoll had all he could do to keep from laughing out loud. "This matter of the eyeglasses," Brackman finally managed to say. "When you say that Private Colman *does* wear glasses in your book, are you referring to this passage on page . . ." He turned to his partner. "What page is that, C-C-Carl?" he asked.

"37," his partner replied.

"Page 37," Brackman said. "Is this the p-p-p-passage you mean?"

"Which passage is that?" Driscoll asked, knowing full well which passage Brackman meant.

"I am about to read it to you," Brackman said.

"I'm waiting," Driscoll answered, and again glanced at Willow to find that he was still frowning. Imperceptibly, Willow shook his head. Brackman had already begun reading, but Driscoll missed the first few words of the paragraph, so startled was he by Willow's unmistakable warning.

" '. . . mud spattering from the wheels, as the jeep swerved into the compound and ground to a stop. Colman saw two officers on the front seat of the jeep, one of whom he recognized as Captain Benjamin. The other man was tall and lean, wearing his hair cropped close to his head in a boyish crewcut. Colman reached into his blouse and took out his glasses, which he perched on his nose. Peering through them owlishly, he studied the new officer with deliberate scrutiny.' And following that," Brackman said, "there's a detailed description of Lieutenant Cooper. Is that the passage?"

"That's the passage," Driscoll said.

"What sort of glasses does Colman take out of his pocket?"

"I don't think I understand you," Driscoll said.

"Are they the sort of glasses, for example, that Mr. Willow has been wearing in this courtroom every day this week?"

"No."

"Are they reading glasses?"

"I never specifically labeled them. If anything, they would be reading glasses, yes. Colman only wears them occasionally."

"Does he in fact wear them anywhere else in the book?"

"I don't think so."

"This is the only place in the book where you specifically describe Colman as wearing eyeglasses?"

"Yes."

"In just this one paragraph which is . . . . let me see . . . eight lines long. That's the only mention in the entire book."

"Yes."

"Mr. Driscoll, do you recall a character in your book called Major Catharine Astor?"

"I do."

"And who is also called Major Catastrophe by Lieutenant Cooper and Jan Reardon?"

"Yes."

"Is this another of your literary puns?"

"Yes, an affectionate one."

"How would you describe Major Astor, or Major Catastrophe as she is affectionately called?"

"She's a woman in her late fifties, and she's been a nurse for perhaps fifteen years or so. Irish background, rather tall and big-boned, ample-breasted, and . . . big feet, she has big feet. She's constantly predicting doom, which is how she earns her nickname. She carries a note from the lieutenant to Jan in one scene."

"I ask you now if you remember a character in *Catchpole* called Captain Sykes?"

"I do."

"Do you remember that she is an Army nurse?"

"Yes."

"Do you remember how old she is supposed to be?"

"No."

"Will you turn to the page immediately following the title page of Mr. Constantine's play, the page titled 'Cast in Order of Appearance,' and will you look down that page to the description of Captain Sykes? Have you got it?"

"Yes, I have."

"Do you see her age there?"

"I do."

"What is the age?"

"Fifty-two."

"Do you recall why Captain Sykes has joined the Medical Corps?"

"Yes."

"Would you tell us, please?"

"She enlists after the death of her husband."

"Let's get back to your character, shall we? Major Catastrophe. How does she happen to be in Korea?"

"She is sent there."

"Is it not true that she becomes a nurse after her husband dies?"

"Oh, boy," Driscoll said.

"I beg your pardon?"

"Are you going to claim . . ."

"Please answer the question, Mr. Driscoll."

"Yes, I'll be very happy to answer the question," Driscoll said angrily, "if I may be permitted briefly to go into the backgrounds of these two characters."

"Briefly, but not with as much volume, I hope," McIntyre said.

"I'm sorry."

"We're none of us deaf," McIntyre said. "Go on, go on."

"The senior nurse in my book, Major Astor, has been in the Army since 1935. She joins several years after her husband passes away, of natural causes, in his own bed. There is no indication that she enlists for patriotic reasons or for any reason other than to give herself a worthwhile occupation. The nurse in the play *Catchpole* is a woman who left nursing to get married. Her husband is a doctor who is killed in action in a bombing attack on a London airfield. To avenge his death, she joins the Medical Corps and is ironically sent to the Pacific where the enemy are the Japanese rather than the Germans. She is pictured as a rather bitter woman who strongly resents the developing love affair between Mr. Constantine's principal characters. I don't see any similarity between these two women, aside from the fact that they are both nurses in the same general age bracket."

"Is it not true," Brackman asked, "that Captain Sykes in *Catchpole* helps Diane Foster to arrange a rendezvous with Lieutenant Mason?"

"No, it is not true. She makes it extremely difficult for the pair to meet."

"Does she not deliberately leave them alone together one night?"

"She does not do it deliberately. One of Mason's friends gets her drunk and puts her to sleep in a weapons carrier. It's a comic scene in the play."

"Where is this scene, Mr. Driscoll?"

"In the second act someplace."

"Do you recall whether or not Captain Sykes has a nickname?"

"Yes, I think she does. They call her 'Big Red.'"

"Why do they call her that?"

"Because she has flaming-red hair."

"Is this fact ever mentioned?"

"Yes, when Mason's friend dumps her into the weapons carrier, he puts his Eisenhower jacket over her head because he's afraid someone will spot the red hair."

"What color hair does *your* nurse have?"

"Brown."

"You're talking about Major Astor now?"

"Yes."

"Does Major Astor deliver a note to Jan Reardon in your novel?"

"Yes, she does. Arranging a meeting with the lieutenant."

"Doesn't Captain Sykes in *Catchpole* also deliver a note to someone?"

"No."

"Isn't there a scene with the colonel where . . ."

"That isn't a note."

"What is it?"

"She shows him his medical record."

"Your Honor," Willow said, rising, "I do not see where this is going."

There was a peculiar note of warning in his voice, and whereas he had addressed the words to McIntyre, Driscoll had the certain feeling he was trying to communicate something, was objecting not to Brackman's questions but rather to his own answers. Confused, aware of the warning but unable to ascertain what he was doing wrong, he stared at Willow in puzzlement, and suddenly his hands began to shake.

"We are attempting to explore the similarities, your Honor," Brackman said. "That is all."

Brackman's explanation sounded reasonable enough, and yet Driscoll detected a note of confidence that had not been there several moments ago when he could barely stutter his way through a sentence. He tried to understand what had happened between then and now, but he could find no clue, and McIntyre's next words left him with a curiously unsettled feeling, as though he were on treacherous ground that was giving away beneath his feet, inch by crumbling inch.

"I find this all to the point," McIntyre said. "Proceed, Mr. Brackman."

"Mr. Driscoll, you have testified that you met with your erstwhile commanding officer, Colonel Hamilton, in order to get some information from him about specific scenes in your book."

"Yes."

"Some of this information was about disassembling a rifle, is that right?"

"Yes, I wanted the exact language describing the operation."

"You did not possess any books that might have given you this information?"

"No."

"Weren't you issued any such books when you were in the service?"

"Yes."

"Did you later discard them?"

"I must have."

"So you had to go to Colonel Hamilton for the information."

"I went to the library first, but I couldn't find it there. Nor could I find a breakdown of the Chinese troop concentrations, or some of the other information I needed."

"Like what?"

"Like some of the actual code names used in the Ch'on-gch'on River operations."

"Which Colonel Hamilton supplied."

"Yes. This was no longer classified material."

"I understand that, nor am I intending to impugn a dead man's loyalty. In Officer Candidate School, Mr. Driscoll, you took a great many courses, did you not?"

"I did."

"And I assume you took notes in these courses."

"In most of them. In some courses, for security reasons, we were not permitted—"

"Yes, I understand that. But you *did* take notes in most of the courses?"

"Yes."

"Do you still have those notes?"

"No, of course not."

"When you were released from the Army, Mr. Driscoll, you attended N.Y.U., I believe you said, and you took some courses in creative writing."

"I took most of the writing courses the school had to offer."

"Did you take notes in those courses?"

"Yes."

"Do you still have those notes?"

"No."

"Your Honor," Willow said, "again I must ask . . ."

"It will become clear, Mr. Willow," Brackman answered.

"I hope so," McIntyre said.

"You have testified that you wrote several short stories while you were a student at N.Y.U. Did you make carbon copies of those stories?"

"Yes."

"Do you still have those carbons?"

"No."

"Do you generally save things?"

"Important things."

"You did not save any of your Army notes, or your college notes, or carbon copies of your short-story attempts."

"I did not think they were good enough."

"The stories?"

"Yes."

"So you discarded the carbons?"

"*And* the stories, too."

"So it would seem that there are some things you do *not* consider important enough to save."

"Yes."

"Yet you did feel it important to save every bit of material, every letter, every note you ever made concerning the novel *The Paper Dragon.*"

"Not *all* the material."

"The last document this court admitted was marked 'Exhibit S in evidence,' which means nineteen documents were submitted to this Court—letters to your agent, and letters to Mitchell-Campbell, and a letter to Colonel Hamilton, and notes you took at your meeting with him, and outlines, and the original drawing of your map, you saved all these things pertaining to *The Paper Dragon,* all of these things that purport to show the independent creation of the novel, isn't that so, Mr. Driscoll?"

"That was my working procedure."

"*What* was your working procedure?"

"I had a box full of typing paper. I took the cover off that box and put it on one side of my typewriter, and whenever I pulled a completed page out of the machine, I put it into the empty lid of the box."

"What does this have to do with your letters and notes?"

"When the book was completed, I put all the research material and information in the same box containing the carbon copy."

"Your letters as well?"

"No, I kept those in a separate file."

"Do you keep carbon copies of all your letters?"

"Yes. Would you like me to bring them in?"

"I don't think that will be necessary. Do you have a good memory, Mr. Driscoll?"

"I think so."

"Why did you meet with Colonel Hamilton?"

"To check certain factual aspects of the novel."

"Such as the disassembling of a rifle?"

"Yes."

"How many times, offhand, would you say you stripped a rifle while you were in the Army?"

"I don't recall."

"Did you perform the operation many times, or just a few times?"

"Many, I would say."

"Yet you could not remember the steps, and you had to—"

"I didn't say I couldn't remember them. I wanted the exact language because the success of the scene depended on the language in it."

"You would not trust your memory."

"That's right."

"So you went to Colonel Hamilton for the sake of authenticity."

"Yes."

"Even though you have a very good memory."

"I think I do. But I could not be expected to remember the technical language describing—"

"Yes, yes, I understand that. How many times would you say you stripped a rifle? Ten times perhaps?"

"Perhaps."

"Twenty?"

"Perhaps."

"More than twenty?"

"Yes, many times more."

"You stripped a rifle more than twenty times, *many* times more, but you could not remember the steps in detail when it came time to write about them."

"I could not remember the *language*."

"Yet you read the play *Catchpole* only once last month, and you can remember in detail and with absolute accuracy some of the more obscure aspects of the play."

"I read the play more than once."

"How many times did you read it?"

"Five or six times."

"Not more than twenty times?"

"No."

"You could not remember an operation you performed more than twenty times, but you could remember details of a play you read only five or six times."

"I could not remember the *language*. How many times must I repeat that?"

"You thought this rifle scene was important enough to seek information about, didn't you?"

"Yes."

"And you thought it important enough to *keep* the notes you made on it."

"Yes. But only as part of all the other material I kept. Material pertaining to the book."

"Why did you keep this material?"

"I don't know. I save some things, and others I throw away."

"What else have you saved?"

"Scraps of everything."

"What kind of scraps?"

"Anything I think is important."

"Did you save your notebooks from your student days at Pratt Institute?"

"Some of them."

"Why? Were they important?"

"Yes. Some of them."

"And obviously the complicated process of writing your novel was also important, so important that we have a detailed step-by-step record of its creation. Do you have any notes concerning the 105th Division, Mr. Driscoll?"

"No."

"Did you ask Colonel Hamilton about the 105th Division?"

"No."

"You asked him about the *Chinese* divisions involved in the Ch'ongch'on River offensive, did you not?"

"Yes."

"Why?"

"For the sake of accuracy."

"You wanted the exact designations for those divisions?"

"Yes."

"Yet you designated your American division the 105th, and did not think of checking its authenticity with the colonel."

"There was no need to do that. I knew the division was fictitious."

"How did you know?"

"Because I knew which American divisions were involved in the battle."

"You trusted your memory concerning those divisions?"

"Yes."

"But you did not trust your memory concerning the stripping of a rifle."

"For the last time, the scene was built on a juxtaposition of sexual allusions to absolutely technical language. Its effectiveness was based on the accuracy of the technical detail. Which is why I consulted Colonel Hamilton."

"And the battle scenes? Was their effectiveness based on accuracy of detail?"

"Yes."

"So that it was essential to give the Chinese armies their proper designations?"

"And their strength. The climactic chapter in the book is the one in which the patrol moves up on an overwhelming force of Chinese."

"Did you use an actual division number for the Chinese force in that scene?"

"Yes, I did."

"And you checked this number with Colonel Hamilton?"

"He gave me the division designation, and also its estimated strength."

"Information from Army files?"

"Yes."

"You did not check the 105th Division with him?"

"No."

"Why not?"

"I told you. I knew it was fictitious. I knew I had invented it."

"*How* did you invent it?"

"I don't know."

"Well now, Mr. Driscoll, you seem to have a detailed record of every other piece of information that went into your novel, you have chapter-by-chapter breakdowns, and you have expanded outlines, and you have target dates and notes to yourself, and yet you can't remember how you happened to invent the 105th Division. Did it simply come to you out of the blue?"

"I don't know."

"Try to remember, Mr. Driscoll. Was the 105th a sudden inspiration?"

"Nothing about the book was a sudden inspiration."

"In that case, you must have pondered the designation for a long time before you decided on its use."

"No."

"Did you ponder it for a short time?"

"I didn't ponder it at all. I simply used it."

"But where did it come from?"

"It did *not* come from Mr. Constantine's play."

"I am not asking you where it did *not* come from. I am asking you exactly where it *did* come from, Mr. Driscoll, and I would like an answer."

"I don't know."

"Is that your answer?"

"That is my answer."

"I have no further questions, your Honor."

"Mr. Willow?"

"No questions."

"Thank you, Mr. Driscoll."

"Thank you," Driscoll said, and rose from the stand. He looked out over the courtroom for a moment, and then went to take a seat in the jury box alongside his wife.

"Is there any further evidence?" McIntyre asked.

"No, your Honor," Willow said. "That is all for the defendant Mitchell-Campbell."

"Your Honor," Genitori said, rising, "the contract between API and James Driscoll, dated August 16, 1963, contains the indemnity clause favoring API, and is annexed as Exhibit A to our answer and crossclaim. May it be deemed to have been submitted in evidence?"

"No objection," Willow said.

"Fine," McIntyre said. "Is there any further evidence to be offered by either side?"

"The plaintiff rests," Brackman said.

"Your Honor, may I at this time renew our motion to dismiss on the ground that no cause has been made?"

"I assume, Mr. Willow, that you will want to argue this motion as well as the merits of the alleged similarities, won't you?"

"Yes, your Honor."

"I hope, too, that both sides will be submitting proposed findings of fact and conclusions of law."

"Yes, sir."

"We will, sir."

"Well, it's almost four o'clock now, gentlemen, but perhaps we can be ready to do that tomorrow morning. In the meantime, I'll reserve any further comments and rulings until then."

"May we consider the case closed for all other purposes, your Honor?" Brackman asked.

"Yes," McIntyre said. "The case is closed for all purposes other than the submission of conclusions of law, findings of fact, and argument."

14

THEY TAKE YOU BACK, Driscoll thought, they force you
to go back to a time and place forgotten or at least deliberately obscured. It is instant therapy, it is crash analysis, this
confrontation with yourself, an odd meeting with a seeming
stranger who moves steadily closer until you recognize him
with a start—he is you, but he is no longer you. Comparisons
are odious, the man said, I forget which man. But what were
they doing to me today if not forcing me to resurrect my
youth (upon whom was Sergeant Morley based?) and then
moving by logical if tedious progression into my so-called
maturity (when exactly did you begin writing your book, Mr.
Driscoll?) until they had brought the biography to date, into
my dotage, my slow if clinging expiration (you are a novelist,
are you not, Mr. Driscoll? No, I am a Vermont farmer).

The farm in Vermont is the here and now, the present. It
was purchased for eight thousand dollars, a portion of my
share of the movie money on *The Paper Dragon*. The farmhouse is red, you approach it over a rutted, ice-covered road
in the winter; in the spring, the road is running and wet,
soggy and mired. There is a falling stone wall bordering the
property, said to have been built by colonial settlers, which
theory I personally buy since there are still enough boulders
firmly embedded in the two acres of arable land to construct

yet another wall from there to Boston and back. I pretend to grow forage crops there, alfalfa and hay and oats.

It is interesting, don't you think, that were I a novelist, were I truly a working novelist, my daily routine would be concerned primarily with seeking truth in terms of fabrication, the enlargement of fantasy, the exercise of imagination, a pretense hardly less energetic than that of being a Vermont farmer, which I am not, but which I purport to be.

I do not know what I am.

I have not known what or who I am for a very long time now, I thank *you* for that, darling.

We go to bed early in Vermont because a farmer, I am informed, must rise to take care of this and that, sowing, reaping, harvesting, breathing deep of clear Vermont air, ahhh, the outdoor life, rise and shine at five-thirty A.M., walk with springing step to the barn where Ebie begins her chores with the chickens. Yes, we have chickens, did I neglect to tell you that, Mr. Brackman? We have seventy-two chickens. We bought those with the movie money, too. So it is early to bed in Vermont, and since the bed part is never very good or very interesting anyway, it's really not too terribly difficult to throw back the covers before dawn and touch the cold wooden floor, scarcely colder than the bed in which Mr. and Mrs. James Driscoll lie, though we do sometimes make love. We lie in love, so to speak.

Stay, she used to say, why must you go home? But go I would. I still don't know why. Perhaps there was in me, at eighteen, more of my mother than I imagined there was, the humorless woman wearing her black shawl. How could I explain to her that I was deliriously in love with a girl in Brooklyn and that all I wanted to do was hold her and touch her and look at her and love her day and night? How could I explain with the sound of Holy Mary, Mother of God coming from her bedroom each night, as if she were doing penance for God knew what mortal sin, every night, Holy Mary, Mother of God. While I thought of Ebie lying alone in that large bed on Myrtle Avenue, waiting for the next afternoon when I would taste her once again—that is the distant past, that is the far distant past. The present is Vermont, and a love-making that is only necessary, a biological release for both of us. We have not spoken the words "I love you" in so long I think if I heard them said or uttered them myself, I would begin to weep. We perform mechanically, we lie in love, my Southern flower and myself, remembering a past when all was fire and death, "the little death" the ancients called it, was that Hemingway? Did you feel the earth move? Yes, *guapa*. Truly? Yes, truly. You old bewitcher, you seduced a generation.

The distant past. Long before the red Vermont farmhouse I insisted on buying, half hoping she would refuse to come with me, half hoping she would pull out at last, abandon the marriage, end the loveless grappling, but no. Not Ebie, not that determined Southern flower. She had made the vows, oh my yes, and she would honor them, come crumbling wall or overflowing spring, rutted roads or bone-chilling winter. And how are you today, Mrs. Driscoll? the Vermont ladies all say, and she answers with a pert nod of her head and tells them about the pies she has baked, or asks their opinion on how to rid the house of flies. There are a dreadful number of flies in the house all the time, she says to Mrs. Dimmity, who is our next-door neighbor in the gray farmhouse across the road. Mrs. Dimmity does part-time housework for the skiers who rent the old Kruger place. They are a noisy lot, college boys and girls who speed along the black road at midnight every winter Friday, racing over the dangerous ice. I visualize them booming mountains in the daytime, shagging themselves into exhaustion each night. They bring the past into our fake present. I saw one of them one cold forbidding morning, she was blond and tall, so young, she wore a black parka and black stretch pants, she raised her mittened hand to greet me in the frosty dawn as I came out of the barn. I returned the wave, my heart was pounding.

The exterminator has visited us some five times already, but he cannot rid the house of mice. I cannot bear the thought of them scurrying in the night, scarcely secret sharers of our roof. They are the final insult, the final invasion of a marriage that certainly needs no further intruders. I visualize them nibbling at the wallboard, or licking the wallpaper paste, undermining the rotting original timbers of the old house until one day it will fall down upon our ears and a great cloud of mouse dirt will rise on the air, and they will run, they will scatter away from the crumbling ruin, chattering and squeaking in triumph, having destroyed it at last, having destroyed even the meager shaky structure that has managed to survive until now.

It seemed so strong, it seemed so indestructible.

In the past, the distant past—and this goes back, my child, to a time when ships were made of wood and men were made of iron, all the way back at least to 1948, do you remember the blizzard that January? It was centuries ago. It was the time of the Great Brooklyn Renaissance, perhaps you may recall the legend of the Uncertain Knight who rode out of West End Avenue carrying a black tin watercolor box under his arm, coming into the Valley of Pratt where he met the Lady Edna Belle. My Ebie's hair is like a golden helmet/Poured molten, shaped to fit/Haphazardly/And yet despite—the ode ended there, because there were no words. Not then. Not as yet. No words to express what I felt for Ebie, the incredible awakening I knew in her arms and, yes, between her legs. Yes, that was a very real part of it, it *had* to be, I had known only one other girl before Ebie—Liz McPherson, known to every young and budding Studs Lonigan along 96th Street. She lived near Lexington Avenue, but the crosstown walk never fazed any of us, through the park's transverse path and over the hill to grandmother's house we went, grandmother being Liz who shared a room with her baby sister. The infant would lie asleep in her crib beside Liz's narrow bed where we made fitfully inexperienced love, with sometimes two or more other young bucks waiting outside the closed door in the tenement kitchen. Poor Liz, I wonder what ever became of her; Liz the Whore, we ungallantly called her.

When Ebie told me about the boy who limped, I was furious at first. I conjured the image of a Brooklyn Liz, far removed from 96th Street, but sisters under the skin, a long line of cock-in-hand suitors outside her apartment door. Donald was his name, *had* been his name; apparently the affair had run its course several months before we met in Bertie's, *l'affaire de sa jeunesse:* emblazon the motto on a field argent, two bronze balls pendant beneath a sinister hand couped at the wrist, holding erect a cane. I went to church the day she told me, I had not been inside a confessional since I was fifteen, and I was there to confess not my own sin, but the sin of a girl I deeply loved, or thought I loved, a girl who had become in six short months—this was May of 1948, I can still remember the day, bright with spring sunshine, a bird chirping incessantly in the budding tree just outside the stained glass window above the confession box, *Bless me, Father, for I have sinned*—a girl who had become in half a year my only reason for existence.

The priest spoke with a faint Italian accent, there was in his voice the echo of an ancient race, but in his words there was no wisdom. I left the church unsatisfied, the bird still chirping its inane song, the sun bright in an opaque sky, I could not understand why she had not waited for me to come along, why she had foolishly given herself to this boy who limped. I tried to tell Uncle Benny about it that night, the telephone beckoning, knowing that Ebie was waiting for my call in her Myrtle Avenue apartment, or at least *hoping* she was waiting. But I couldn't tell him. I sat there in the living room with him, we were both sitting on the piano bench, side by side, our hands separately clasped and hanging between our respective knees, like two old men in the park, staring solemnly at pigeons. But I could not tell him that the girl I loved had been living with some goddamn cripple for five months, how could I tell this to Uncle Benny or to *anyone,* for that matter? So we talked about my studies, Uncle Benny was always fascinated by the *theory* of art, and I told him I was having trouble with one of my instructors, I was sure the man disliked me, and Uncle Benny told me there would be instructors all through my life who took a dim view of me, or vice versa, and the thing to do with them was simply face the fact that it would be difficult, but to do my best, do my work the best way I knew how, and get through it somehow, that was the important thing. And we sat there on the piano bench with the question of Ebie hanging on the air, unresolved, unspoken. I nodded and said, Yeah, but Uncle Benny this guy is a real son of a bitch, and Uncle Benny said, That only means you've got to work harder, Jimbo, you've got to get what you can out of the course, *despite* the way he feels about you, you've got to rely on what's inside *yourself*, Jimbo, there's lots of good stuff inside you. Yeah, I said, and nodded. Sure, Uncle Benny said, and nodded. After a while, I got up and thanked him, and went into my room. I could hear my mother in her bedroom next door, already beginning the litany of Hello Mary, Mother of God. I threw myself down on the bed, and tried to figure out what I should do. I decided two things. First, I decided I could never let go of Ebie Dearborn because I loved her too much, and second, I decided I would extract from her a promise that Donald Who Limped was to be the last of her little adventures, that James Randolph Driscoll was now on the scene having ridden long and hard from West End Avenue, and he was on the scene to *stay,* and she had better get that through her golden-helmet head. I was still furious when I told it to her in the curtain-rustling stillness of her bedroom later that night. She sat in a straight-backed chair near the window, the curtains stirring behind her with each fresh spring breeze, unsmiling, sitting as straight-backed as the chair. When I was through, she started to say something but the goddamn elevated express roared by and we were caught in a moment of mechanical suspense, waiting for the train to pass, waiting for the room to be still again.

In a sense, that day in 1948 was the beginning. Oh yes, Norman Sheppard said only this afternoon that there are no endings in life, and perhaps he was right, perhaps there are no beginnings as well—but for me, it was a beginning, and I think it was for Ebie, too. For me, for us, it was the start of a gradual loss of identity. If the love we made was a little death, then the love we knew was a littler death still, this loss of self, this certain overlapping of person upon person, blending,

merging, no longer Ebie and no longer me, a single unit
responding and reacting in rare empathy, osmotically perhaps, or perhaps symbiotically because, yes, we surely fed
upon each other and sustained each other and became each
other, inseparable, indistinguishable, one.

Who can remember, can *I* remember, any of my own
responses as apart from Ebie's? Reconstruct all of the events
that led to our marriage in 1950, arrange them in sequence
and what can I remember that does not include Ebie? Once I
walked alone in the shadow of the Queensborough Bridge
and wrote in my head a suspense story for Alfred Hitchcock,
spies chasing counterspies over wet cobblestones and under
dripping metal cross-supports, but the heroine of that movie
(running through the rain, blond hair stringy and wet, head
snapping back over her shoulder to steal a quick glance at
God knew what awful pursuer) was Ebie Dearborn, all was
Ebie Dearborn. And once I sat alone in the living room of
the West End Avenue apartment, the winter afternoon waning, and tapped out a melody on the old Chickering, note by
faltering note, using only one hand, but the symphony was
Ebie Dearborn, all was Ebie Dearborn. You are wrong,
Norman Sheppard; there are beginnings, and there are endings as well, and I have known them both. I can remember
the day our Fainting in Coils instructor (Lewis Carroll's
chapter was big with the students at Pratt, who quite right-
fully thought of themselves as very *inside* concerning art and
the art world and things artistic) took us to see the bona fide
studio of a bona fide artist named Bernardo Casamorte,
whose name we later learned meant "house of the dead,"
hilariously inappropriate after what we had seen. Casamorte
lived on West 18th Street in a skylighted loft that had once
been a hat factory. Hat molds, some of which he had decorated with grinning faces, most of which he had left un-
adorned, still rested on every flat surface in the place, cluttering the room. In order to stand or sit, the class—there were
thirty of us—had to move molds, or easels, or finished and
unfinished canvases, or palettes, or pots of paint and glue, or
soiled clothing draped or tossed or hanging, or the remains of

breakfast. There were seven cats in the place, and a large boxer who had dipped his snout in vermilion, and who gave the appearance of a comic strip drunk with illuminated nose. There was also a mistress-model who slunk around the loft in an electric-blue silk dressing gown while Casamorte gave us his lecture on what it was like to earn a living as a painter, a premise we seriously doubted on the evidence presented. We kept hoping the mistress-model would do a little posing for him while we were there; she was a dark brunette with enormous breasts swelling the gown; she held the gown closed with her folded arms, its sash having been misplaced in the general disorder of the joint. We decided afterwards, Ebie and I, that the loft was in reality a stage set designed and built by Pratt, and that Casamorte, his busty model-mistress, his seven cats, and his drunken boxer were all actors hired by the school for this special outing each year. This was the only class Ebie and I shared together, by dispensation, since she was a full year ahead of me. She was much better in oils than I was, I never could get the hang of oils. She had a fine sure touch with pigment, she really might have become a good artist if she'd stuck with it. In Vermont now, even in Vermont where she has all the time in the world, she never paints anymore. Never. It is as if everything in *her* has gone dead as well.

Casamorte was alive though, and real I suppose, certainly more genuine an artist than I was at the time. Oh, I loved the *role* of being an artist, I played the role a bit more amateurishly perhaps than Casamorte, but I played it nonetheless. I would sit on subway trains or buses, incessantly sketching, not because I really itched to draw—or perhaps I did, who the hell knows anymore?—but only because I wanted everyone sitting opposite me to see that I was an artist, to understand that I was an extremely talented and serious person who was sketching, sketching, sketching all the time, oh boy, was I serious! Sometimes I would walk into a luncheonette still wearing my paint-smeared workshirt, knowing that everyone at the counter would turn and stare at me and think again Oh lookie, there's an artist, especially if Ebie was with me in her dirty green smock, her cheek smeared with pigment, she was a good painter but a sloppy one. Or I would sometimes stop dead in the middle of the sidewalk, and raise both hands in front of my face, palms flat, thumbs touching, to form a fleshy picture frame around a tree or a bench or a building in the distance, once again courting appreciation from the people in the street, the onlookers, the outsiders, those poor, untalented, uncreative souls. I think I knew even then I would never become a painter. I have since seen music students practicing scales on subway trains, their fingers running over imaginary keyboards in their laps; I have watched architectural students describe with soaring hands the engineering feat of the Guggenheim; I have overheard playwrights discussing the interminable and incomplete second acts of their works in progress; and I have learned without question that those who *play* the part never *live* it. I was only playing at being an artist. *I* knew it, and *Ebie* knew it, but neither of us ever mentioned it.

And yet there were times when, visual evidence to the contrary, talented people surrounding me day and night, doing work I could see, work I could compare against my own, there were nonetheless times when I felt I really had it in me. Laboring late into the night in Ebie's apartment (stay, she would constantly plead, *must* you go?), I would feel a solitary isolation (never truly solitary because I knew she was there across the room) a total absorption with the drawing pad before me, the charcoal or pencil moving in my hand as though directed by someone, something, other than myself, the line clean and sure and unfaltering. That was real. *That*, at least, was real. That, and Ebie.

Ebie was everything; everything paled beside her.

I can recall the first time we saw El Greco's *Cardinal* at the Metropolitan, standing before the painting—silken scarlet robes stiffly parted over intricately detailed lace, beringed left hand tensely gripping the arm of the chair, eyes covertly regarding something beyond the frame—my own eyes were on Ebie alone, watching her reaction, thrilling to her response. She caught her breath in wonder, a radiant awestruck look crossed her face, and I watched her in soaring delight; El Greco, for all his magnificance, could have been for me that day a Greenwich Village hack exhibiting seascapes on a Sixth Avenue sidewalk.

I loved her so much.

So very much.

There were daffodils blooming in the courtyard of the church on the day we were married. A stone baptismal font, fallen into neglectful disrepair, stood lopsidedly in one corner of the garden against a stone wall covered with English ivy. Beyond the wall and behind it, the city's buildings rose against an April sky stretched in taut blue brilliance. We stopped in the garden after the ceremony. The wedding party was on the sidewalk in front of the church, the photographer wondering how he had managed to lose us in the blizzard of tossed confetti and rice, the rented limousines at the curb, relatives and friends shaking hands in greeting, exclaiming no doubt on the beauty of the bride and the nervousness of the groom, anxious to get on with the reception, all waiting for the newly married Mr. and Mrs. James Driscoll to join them. But we had seen the garden earlier, separately, and now we were drawn to it together, neither of us uttering a word, as we ran down the church steps through the flying rice and paper, Ebie's hand in mine, and then raced along the stone wall to the low iron entrance gate. The gate was painted green, chipped in spots to reveal the rusting iron beneath. I opened it, it squeaked into the silence. We went into the small cloistered garden, treading softly over the slate walk to where the daffodils ringed the fallen stone font.

The ceremony had already taken place, but it was there in the garden that we were really wed.

With her hand in mine and her eyes wet, Ebie looked up at me and said, "Forever."

And I whispered "Forever" to her.

Louis Brackman lived in a garden apartment in Queens, a complex of six buildings set around a grassy court in which there were concrete benches and a lily pond. In the summertime, the benches were invariably occupied by young housewives taking a late afternoon breather before the dinner hour, which was just about when Sidney arrived each time. In the winter, as now, the benches were empty, the lily pond was a dark amoeba reflecting the starless sky above. It was six o'clock. The lights in the buildings surrounding the court were aglow and cooking smells wafted on the evening air. Sidney quickened his step and moved along the shoveled concrete walk to his father's ground-floor apartment. Through the kitchen window, he could see Louis wrapping something at the table, why did he always *wrap* the stuff, Sidney wondered. Why not simply say "Here, Sidney, here's some worthless crap for you" instead of going through this idiotic ritual each time? Sidney sighed and rang the bell.

His father did not ask who it was because he knew this was Thursday, and he knew that Sidney arrived every Thursday at close to six o'clock. Sidney did not expect him to call out, nor did he expect anything less than a five-minute wait on the doorstep since that was usually how long it took his father to get from the kitchen to the front hallway, give or take a few thousand years. He did not ring the bell again, nor did he exhibit any signs of impatience. He leaned against the brick wall of the building instead and looked up at the sky, wishing there were stars, and smelling rain in the air, and beneath that the aroma of borscht, his father was cooking borscht again. When Louis finally opened the door, the two men embraced silently, and then walked slowly into the kitchen, where Sidney would spend most of the visit. Sidney supported his father as they walked, one arm around the old man's waist, deploring his smell and the smell of the beets boiling in the kitchen, permeating the entire apartment until Sidney thought he would suffocate.

Louis was eighty-two years old, and Sidney could not remember a time when the old man had not been a burden, even when his mother was still alive. Dimly, only dimly, he perceived in this shell of a man someone who had once punched a Bowery wino, who was strong, who had black hair and dark shining eyes. That person was a stranger to Sidney, as was the old man he helped down the hallway and into the kitchen.

"I'm making borscht," Louis said.

"That's good."

"You like borscht, don't you?"

"Mmm."

"Your mother, may she rest in peace, made the best borscht."

"Mmm."

"Look what's on the table, Sidney," he said.

"Sit down, Pop."

"I can stand, I'm not a cripple, thank God. Look what I found for you."

There were three packages on the kitchen table, each wrapped in brown paper and tied with white string. "Well, sit down, Pop," Sidney said, and looked wearily at the packages and thought, Here we go again. His father took a seat at the table, and then put his hands before him on the table top, palms down, and smiled and looked at the packages. Sidney nodded and looked at the packages too.

"Your cousin Marvin called this morning," Louis said. "Don't you want to open the packages, Sidney?"

"Sure, Pop. What'd he want?"

"Who? Oh, Marvin. Nothing, nothing, he was complaining about his wife again, who knows?" Louis waved the problem aside with his bony hand and again looked at the packages. Sidney lifted one of them, shook it, and said, "This isn't a time bomb, is it, Pop?"

"Sure, sure, a time bomb. Open it."

"It won't blow up the whole apartment, will it?"

"Sure, blow up the apartment," Louis said, watching as Sidney fumbled with the knots on the package. Sidney loosened the string, and then pulled back the folds of wrapping paper. He recognized the bank at once, a small wooden box made of bamboo, with sliding panels that were pushed back one at a time and in sequence to reveal the keyhole. His father had given it to him as a present when he was ten years old. He had never kept more than a few dollars in coins in it at any time, but the knowledge that he was the only one who knew the secret of the sliding panels was a source of comfort and security at a time when he needed assurance most.

"Do you remember it?" his father asked.

"Yes, I do. Where'd you find it?"

"Oh, with the stuff in the closet. There's lots of stuff in the closet."

"Mmm," Sidney said. Automatically, his fingers moved to the first sliding panel, and then the second. He could not remember the sequence after that. He put the bamboo box down on the table, a faint pained smile on his face.

"Will you take it with you?" his father asked.

"Sure." He would take it with him and then throw it in the garbage when he got home, the same as he did with almost everything his father gave him.

"Open the others," Louis said, pleased.

The second package was long and flat. Sidney knew it was a book even before he loosened the string. He nodded as he pulled back the brown wrapping paper.

"From Harvard," his father said.

"Yes, I see."

It was a notebook he had kept for an Ethics class at Harvard when he was still an undergraduate. He had no interest whatever in it, but his father was watching him, so he leafed through some of the pages and pretended amazement at what he had written.

"I thought you could use it," Louis said.

"Yes," Sidney said, and nodded.

"Can you use it?"

"I'll find some use for it," Sidney said.

"I found it in the closet," his father said, and seemed to want to say more, but let the sentence trail instead.

"All this stuff," Sidney said, and let his sentence trail as well. He broke the string on the third package. The brown wrapping paper rattled open to reveal a wooden inkstand he had made in a shop class in elementary school. There were two holes for ink bottles, drilled into a solid block of wood that was affixed to a larger, flatter piece of wood. A scalloped bar in front of the inkwells was designed to hold pens. The inkstand was stained walnut. Sidney turned it upside down to its raw, unstained bottom where he had gouged out his name with a knife, s. BRACKMAN, and then filled in the letters with black ink. The date beneath his name was 2/7/25. February 7, 1925. He tried to remember the boy who had made this inkstand, but the image was vague. He turned the stand over in his hands again. Something else to throw in the garbage, he thought.

"You brought that home to your mother," Louis said.

"Yes, I remember."

"It was in the closet."

"I'll take it home with me."

"Sure, I have no use for it," Louis said. "I thought you might like it."

"Sure, I'll take it home."

"Well, how is the trial going?" Louis asked.

"Fine."

"I told all my friends you're in a new trial."

"That's good."

"Is it a murder case?"

"No. Plagiarism."

"What's that?"

"When somebody steals from something that's copyrighted."

"Books?"

"Yes. Or plays. Pop, do you have anything to drink in the house?"

"In the living room, there's something," Louis said. "Don't drink too much."

"No, I won't," Sidney said, and went out of the kitchen and into the darkness of the living room. He snapped on the light and searched in the low cabinet for his father's whiskey supply. There was a partially filled bottle of scotch, and a bottle of banana cordial someone had brought to Louis from Puerto Rico. Eventually, Louis would wrap the cordial in brown paper and present it to Sidney, who would throw it in the garbage the moment he got home. He poured two fingers of scotch into one of the glasses, and then turned off the light and went back into the kitchen.

"You ought to get some bourbon," he said, and went to the refrigerator.

"Isn't there bourbon?"

"No, you've only got a little scotch."

"Well," Louis said, and tilted his head.

Sidney put two ice cubes into his glass, sat at the table with his father, and sipped at the whiskey.

"So what's new?" Louis said.

"I'm getting married," Sidney said. "I think I'm getting married."

"Oh?"

"It's about time, huh?" Sidney said, and smiled at his father, and then took another sip of his scotch. "Forty-eight years old, that's a long time to be single."

"Sure, it's about time," his father said. "Who is the girl?"

"Her name is Charlotte Brown."

"Is she Jewish?"

"No."

His father was silent for a moment. Sidney sipped his drink.

"What is she, then?" his father asked.

"Irish, I think. Or English."

"You don't know?"

"I think she's Irish."

"Charlotte Brown?" his father said. "This doesn't sound Irish to me."

"I think it is."

"She's a nice girl?"

"Yes."

"An older woman?

"Well, she's twenty-seven."

"That's very young, Sidney."

"I know."

"She's pretty?"

"Yes."

"Well," Louis said, and again tilted his head skeptically.

"I'll bring her around someday."

"Yes," his father said, and nodded.

The men were silent. On the stove, the beets were boiling. Sidney finished his drink and went back into the living room for a refill. His father said, "Don't drink too much, Sidney."

"I won't," he answered, and came back into the kitchen. He would take home his father's presents and dump them in the garbage, the inkstand he had made when he was seven, the Chinese bank he had received as a gift when he was ten, and the Harvard notebook from his undergraduate days. He would dump them in the garbage.

"Pop," he said, "why haven't you ever . . ." and stopped.

"Yes?" his father said.

". . . gone back to that doctor on Park Avenue?" Sidney improvised.

"I went."

"You did?"

"Sure. He says it's nothing to worry. It's arthritis, I'll keep taking the cortisone, it isn't God forbid anything worse."

"Well, I'm glad to hear that," Sidney said. "Does the cortisone help?"

"A little."

"Well, that's good."

"Sure."

"Her nickname is Ch-Chickie," Sidney said suddenly.

"What?"

"My f-f-fiancée. Her nickname is Chickie."

"That's a funny name," his father said, and smiled. "Chickie."

"Yeah."

"Your mother, when she was a girl, they used to call her Sarale."

"I know."

"May she rest in peace."

"Mmm," Sidney said. He had finished the second scotch, and he wanted another drink, but he knew his father would frown upon a third. He sat at the kitchen table, jiggling his foot and looking up at the wall clock. It was only six-thirty.

"Do you remember your Aunt Hannah?" Louis asked.

"Yes." He was always asking Sidney if he remembered people he couldn't possibly ever forget. His Aunt Hannah had lived in the apartment next door on Houston Street when he was a boy. He'd spent half his childhood in her kitchen, and now his father asked if he remembered her. How the hell could he possibly ever forget Aunt Hannah?

"Her daughter is going to have a baby," Louis said.

"Another one."

"This is only three."

"I guess it is."

"You should go see your Aunt Hannah every now and then."

"I always mean to."

"Your mother, may she rest in peace, would have liked it."

"Maybe when the trial is finished," Sidney said. "Maybe I'll stop by one day."

"Well, I know you're busy. What did you call it? The trial?"

"Plagiarism."

"That's important?"

"I guess so."

"I'll have to tell my friends."

Yes, you tell them, he thought. Tell them your very important lawyer son is arguing a very important plagiarism case downtown. "There's ten million dollars involved," Sidney said.

Louis whistled softly.

"If we win the case, Carl and I will share four million dollars."

"That's plenty," Louis said.

"Tell your friends," Sidney answered.

He sat in his father's beet-smelling kitchen, and he longed to tell him about Chickie, about the love he felt for her, longed desperately to discuss something *important* with his father for once in his life, not cousin Marvin's idiotic troubles, or Aunt Hannah's third grandchild, but something important to *him,* to Sidney, to your *son,* Pop, to *me.* And he knew in that moment that winning the case would mean nothing to him if he did not also win Chickie. He almost made a bargain with God on the spot. Look, he thought, visualizing himself once again as a sunset-stained rabbi raising his eyes to heaven, Look, God, let me *lose* the case even, I don't *care,* really *I don't care,* just so long as you permit me to win Chickie. The offer startled him, and he revoked it at once because he didn't want God to take him too seriously. And yet, what difference would it make, win or lose, except for the money involved? And was even that important if he could not share the future with Chickie? Would it really matter, win or lose, if . . .

If there was no one there to . . .

Without realizing why, he suddenly said, "Why don't you ever . . ." and hesitated.

"Why don't I ever what?"

"I thought you might like . . ."

"Yes, what?"

Ask him, Sidney thought. At least give him the opportunity.

"Would you like to come down?"

"What?"

"Downtown."

"What do you mean, downtown?"

"The courthouse. The court. Tomorrow."

"What's tomorrow?"

"Friday. I'll be giving my summation. I thought . . ."

"I have to be home to light the *shabiss* candles."

"That's not until sundown. I'll get you home by then."

"How would I get there?"

"By cab. Or I can pick you up, if you like."

"Where is this?"

"Foley Square. Downtown."

"In New York?"

"Yes. I could pick you up in the morning, if you like."

"I have my medicine here," his father said.

"Well, you can take—"

"What time does it start?"

"Ten in the morning."

"The super's coming in tomorrow. To fix the radiator there in the bedroom. It leaks all over the floor."

"I just thought you might like to see . . ."

"Yes?"

". . . a . . . a court case," Sidney said. "Me," he said.

"I saw a court case when Harry Bergner was sued that time."

"I just thought . . ."

"They're all the same, no?"

"Yes, they're all the same," Sidney said. He paused. "I'd like another drink."

"Don't drink too much, Sidney," his father said.

It began raining at half-past seven, and the pressure call to Arthur came not ten minutes after the storm started. He knew at once that it was going to be a pressure call because when he answered, two voices came back at him with "Hello, Arthur," one from Stuart Selig and the other from Oscar Stern on the extension.

"Some storm, huh?" Stuart said.

"Yeah," Arthur said.

"We aren't interrupting anything, are we?" Oscar asked.

"No, I was reading."

"Anything good?" Stuart asked.

"Anything that might make a play?" Oscar asked.

"I don't think so. What's on your mind?"

"We might as well come straight to the point," Stuart said.

"That's right," Oscar said.

"Kent Mercer was up here just a little while ago. He told us he met you for lunch today."

"Yes, we had a long talk," Arthur said.

"According to Kent, you've got some doubts about making these changes Hester wants."

"I'm still thinking it over."

"Well, when do you think you'll know, Arthur? This is Thursday night."

"I know what it is."

"Tomorrow's Friday, Arthur."

"We promised Mitzi we'd let her know by Friday, Arthur."

"We don't want to pressure you . . ."

"That's right."

". . . but you haven't got all the time in the world to make your decision, you know. Maybe you don't have a clear picture of the situation."

"I think Kent gave me a pretty clear picture."

"Did he tell you he's dropping out if you don't make the changes?"

"He hinted it."

"Well, he did more than *hint* it when he was up here. He's the man for your play, Arthur, you realize that, don't you?"

"Yes, but if we have to lose him . . ."

"We *don't* have to lose him," Stuart said.

"That's right," Oscar said.

"We don't have to lose *anybody*. If you agree to make the changes, we'll have one of the best directors in the business and one of the brightest young actresses around, and we'll also get our financing—which is the most important thing."

"You know how much money I'll get if I win this case?" Arthur asked.

"Meantime," Oscar said, "you haven't won it."

"I could produce the play myself, six times over. A *hundred* times over."

"I don't bet on horse races or on trials," Stuart said. "Will you make the changes, or won't you?"

"The Dramatists Guild contract . . ."

"Screw the Dramatists Guild *and* their contract," Stuart said. "Nobody can force you to make the changes, that's true, you're protected. But is the Dramatists Guild going to raise the money for your play?"

"Are *you?*"

"If we sign Hester, yes."

"Guaranteed?"

"Guaranteed. I've been on the phone all day. I've got more than enough promises already."

"That's right."

"Promises aren't cash," Arthur said.

"I can guarantee these promises, Arthur. I'm not exactly new in this business, these are people who've invested with me before. They'll come in if we get Hester."

"She's very hot, Arthur."

"Arthur, we have to know what you plan to do."

"I don't know yet."

"Will you call me later tonight?"

"I may have to sleep on it."

"Do me a favor, don't sleep on it. I want to be able to call Mitzi first thing in the morning and tell her you're eager to get to work on the revisions."

"I'm not."

"*Fake* a little enthusiasm."

"Stuart, I don't like this kind of pressure. I really don't."

"That's right, this is pressure," Oscar said. "We're all under pressure, Arthur, not just you."

"I don't like to make important decisions under pressure."

"Nobody does. But that's the way most important decisions are made."

"We may know about the trial early next week. Can't we—"

"And you may not know for six months."

"It never takes that long."

"It could."

"Anyway, even next week is too late. Arthur, maybe you still don't understand the situation. Hester's going to sign for that Osborne play unless you go along with these changes. Now which is it going to be? Everybody rich and happy, or everybody behaving in a highly unprofessional manner?"

"What's unprofessional about wanting to preserve what I wrote?"

"This is the theater, Arthur. Don't talk like a hick."

"Any play is a collaborative effort, you know that," Oscar said.

"I don't like collaborating with pants pressers."

"What are you talking about?"

"Mitzi Starke is a pants presser. What the hell does she know about playwriting?"

"She doesn't have to know *anything* about playwriting," Stuart said, "as long as she's got clients like Hester Miers."

"If you'd raised the goddamn money, we wouldn't be in this situation," Arthur said angrily.

"We tried our best. And we can still raise it, if you'll compromise a little."

"A little, sure," Arthur said.

"A little, yes. Will you call me later tonight?"

"If I've decided."

"Decide, Arthur," Stuart said.

"Good night, Arthur," Oscar said.

Arthur almost slammed the receiver onto the cradle, but something restrained him. He put it down gently, and then turned from the phone and walked to the rain-streaked window and looked down at the gleaming wet street outside. He went to the closet then, and put on his raincoat and an old rain hat, a battered corduroy he had bought six years ago and perhaps worn as many times since. He looked at the room unseeingly for a moment before turning off the lights, and then went out of the apartment and into the street.

The rain was cold. It fell from the sky in slanting sheets that swept sidewalk and gutter, driven by a sharp wind. He almost changed his mind, and then decided the hell with it and kept walking, the collar of his coat high on the back of his neck, his hat pulled down over his forehead, his hands thrust into his pockets. He did not know where he was going, or why he felt he could think better in the rain than in his apartment, but he continued walking nonetheless, heading west toward Lexington Avenue, and then continuing westward, turning downtown whenever he was stopped by a corner traffic light.

It seemed to him that his decision hinged entirely on the outcome of the trial. If he knew he were positively going to win the case, he could tell them all to go to hell, he would not need anyone's money to produce the play, he could produce the damn thing himself. On the other hand, if he knew for certain that the case was lost, there would be no hope for production unless he were willing to make the changes. Yes, he could take the play around again, but he knew Kent was right on that score, too, a dead duck was a dead duck. He had circulated the play for six months before Selig and Stern optioned it, showing it to most of the theatrical producers in town. It was highly unlikely that anyone would suddenly become interested in it again, not after word went around that they'd had trouble raising the money. Word had a way of getting around in this town, faster than the speed of light. He was willing to bet that Lincoln Center already knew Hester was planning to leave, and exactly why—to star in Arthur Constantine's new play.

If he made the changes.

All you have to do, he thought, is make the changes. It'll be easy to make the changes, God knows you made enough changes when you were working for the Hollywood pants pressers. Out there, anyone was entitled to a suggestion, including the studio typists. He would never forget the day Charlie Mandell asked the *barber* what he thought of a scene they were discussing, right there in Charlie's office, Charlie sitting in his big stuffed green leather chair with the barber's cloth around his neck. And the barber very seriously offered his advice on what he thought would be a better approach to the scene, and Charlie took the suggestion and said, "I think we ought to work it out along those lines. After all, Arthur, these are the people who go to *see* the movies. I'll never sell the little man short." If he made the changes now, he would indeed be selling the little man short because his play was *about* the little man, not about a barber of course, nor even about the little man Charlie Mandell had in mind perhaps, but certainly about a simple ordinary man who happened to be his father. It was an honest play. It was the first honest thing he'd written in a long long while, and now they were asking him to change it, make changes that might not damage its honesty but, yes, he thought, yes. The changes *will* damage the honesty. It will not be the play I wrote anymore.

He had let Freddie Gerard do that to *Catchpole,* well, wait a minute, it wasn't fair to turn on Freddie, if it hadn't been for Freddie the play would never have been produced at all. And yet he *had* allowed Freddie and the director, a man named Fielder Crowell, to turn the play upside down, to rearrange scenes, to emphasize here and to excise there, "This isn't working, Arthur, can you change it to . . . ?" Of course, you can change it to. You can change it to anything. You can bring six hundred pink elephants on stage at any given point, and if you are a skillful enough writer, you can make those elephants seem plausible and reasonable and in fact necessary to plot and theme and character. Yes, you can change it to. You can change a whore to a nun, and a doctor to an Indian chief, you can put this scene at the beginning and that scene at the end, you can change words and lines and speeches, you can rewrite the entire second act in New Haven, and after you've changed everything to, you can change it *back* to again. You can juggle all these bits and pieces in the air like a circus performer and forget exactly what you intended in the first place. You can allow them to march right through the play with mud on their feet, tracking it up while you scurry along behind them trying to wipe up the footprints. Yes, I can change Carol to a social worker who has had one affair, I can change the father to a small business man or a minor executive, I can change the play, I can make it their play, the way I made *Catchpole* their play and therefore nobody's play. And then, maybe years from now, a James Driscoll will step in and *really* finish the job, just the way he did with *Catchpole,* step in and make it not my play, and not their play, but *his* play, steal it right from under my nose, and it'll serve me right because I didn't have the guts to stand behind what I'd written. You want to change it? Fine. Go write your own play. This is my play, and it's going to stay my play.

It's going to stay your *manuscript,* you mean.

Oh sure, very clever, Kent. Go to work on the frightened writer, give me a few good ones right now while I'm up against the ropes. I'm worried about this trial, you see, I really am. I don't know what's happening down there, I haven't heard anyone in these past four days mention the fact that *Catchpole* is worthless so long as *The Paper Dragon* is credited to James Driscoll; that anyone reading my play will say, "Why this was stolen from that novel, what was the name of it, it's a direct steal," instead of the other way around. I've heard a lot of arguments in these past four days about diminishing the value and so on, and I've learned all about Driscoll's creative process, but no one has brought up *my* creative process, the months of hard work I put into that play, the pain each time they asked me for another change, the gradual metamorphosis to what the play became, and the hope, the constant hope that someday someone would recognize what I'd done, but no, not even there, not even in that court of law. It's been Driscoll, Driscoll, Driscoll, *The Paper Dragon* is the glittering success, and *Catchpole* is the shabby little beggar hanging around the fringes of the trial. So get in here, Kent. Get in here with your faggot wrist hanging and tighten your hand into a fist for just a few good ones, a few short sharp ones to the gut. This is a good time to take Constantine. He doesn't know whether he's coming or going, he doesn't know whether to dig one grave or two, let's finish him off once and for all, pow, pow, it's going to stay your *manuscript*, kid, pow, that's the way, it's now or never, kid, wham, again, again, we can't force you to make the changes, zap, whack, bam, but you can't force *us* to produce it, either, you get it, kid? wise up, kid, make the changes, kid, pow.

I don't know, he thought. I just don't know.

If I could climb inside McIntyre's head for just a minute, listen to his thoughts and get some sort of inkling, just a clue is all I need, how can I plan on anything if nothing's sure, if it all depends on the opinion of one man?

Ten million dollars.

Look, Oscar, ten million dollars.

Look, Stuart, the book really *was* stolen from me.

Look, everybody! Look!

He was suddenly chilled to the bone. His face was cold and wet, and his shoes squished water with each step he took. He ran across Sixth Avenue, hurdled the slush against the curb, and spotted a bar in the middle of the block. He walked toward it hastily, glanced through the plate-glass window, and then went inside. Taking a booth near the juke box, he pumped a handful of coins into the machine, and ordered a double scotch.

The city's buildings thrust their broken illumination upward into a sky black with rainclouds, reflected themselves downward again against shining black asphalt. Each brilliant red and green traffic light, each glowing amber street lamp, each twisted tube of orange neon found its echo on the sleek wet surface of the street, so that the city seemed to reverberate with light, seemed to shimmer with light pierced by slanting silver needles of rain. The rain fell remorselessly. It beat noisily upon rooftops and skylights, rattled in gutters and drains, raged in windswept fury across the avenues, hurled its light-smashed slivers against pavement and street. Crumbling pieces of snow splashed away from the banked slush, twisted and whirled like paper boats in the dark curbside torrent, tumbled toward sewer grates, plunged underground in cascades of paper scraps and broken sticks.

They stood in the teeming rain under Jonah's big black umbrella, trying to get a taxi, listening to the irregular beat of the falling drops. There was an insular quality to their corner haven, the secrecy of an attic hiding place. Sally leaned against him, her arm looped through his as they watched the oncoming traffic, Jonah signaling now and again to cabs he thought were free, only to discover they were either carrying passengers or showing their Off Duty signs. But there was no sense of urgency to Jonah's attempts, and Sally exhibited no impatience when, after ten minutes, he still had not succeeded in getting a cab. They began walking idly up Sixth Avenue, looking at the rows of diamond rings in lighted pawnshop windows, stopping to study an old gold locket in one of the smaller antique places, window-shopping cameras and books and phonographs and hardware and records and sewing machines and paint and practical jokes, pausing to study menus taped to restaurant windows, strolling up the avenue as though it were springtime and they were visiting a bazaar.

He had told her at dinner that he'd contacted Santesson late that afternoon and asked him to call off the dogs. He had no doubt now that this was what accounted for the success of the evening, the pleased and somehow flattered smile Sally wore all during the meal, the way she held his arm in easy intimacy now as they walked up the avenue. He could remember walking through the rain with Christie, her hands thrust into the pockets of her white raincoat, a yellow kerchief on her head, the black bangs fringing her brow, her eyes dancing with delight. They had gone to see four movies that day, one at the Roxy, another at the Capitol, a third at the Strand, and the last in a fleabag on 42nd Street, necking furiously in each one. And then they were out in the rain again, and he held her elbow and helped her to pick her delicate way through the puddles, and she said to him quite suddenly, "Jonah, I will never love anyone but you."

And then, one thought linked to the other, one image repeating the other the way the Dunseath looks repeated themselves generation after generation, fading, he thought of Amy. Last week, he had seen a ring in a jewelry shop window on East 61st, a beautiful tiny cameo set with a single diamond. He had known immediately that it would make a perfect Christmas gift for Amy, and would have purchased it on the spot had the shop been open. He had written down the name of the place, and then tucked the card into his wallet, intending to return at the earliest opportunity. But something had always intruded, the ring (he *hoped*) still sat in the jeweler's window, and Amy would be home tomorrow. He wanted to present it to her when he picked her up at the station, a harbinger of the holidays, welcome home, Amy, Merry Christmas, my darling. He would have to pick it up tomorrow, after court broke, there'd still be time. If only life weren't so goddamn cluttered, he thought, if only everything didn't scream at you from a hundred different directions, all the cheap merchandise in these store windows, a thousand shabby Santa Clauses shaking their bells, a million late shoppers rushing past, a lifetime rushing past. He would have to pick up the ring tomorrow, yes, after court broke. They would undoubtedly be out early; the summations would not take that long.

"There's one!" Sally said suddenly.

"Where?"

"There! Quick!"

He saw the cab, and began running for it just as a little man in a dark green trenchcoat leaped off the curb and began signaling wildly to the driver. There was no doubt in Jonah's mind that Sally had seen it first, but even if there had been a question of priority, he did not intend losing the cab. He ran past the little man just as the cab pulled to a stop. Clamping his fingers around the door handle, he said "Sorry," without looking at the man, and then signaled to Sally, who immediately came off the curb to join him.

"This is my taxi," the man said.

"It's my taxi," Jonah said flatly, and held open the door for Sally. The man, he now saw, was perhaps sixty-five years old, and he was drenched to the skin. He stared up at Jonah without rancor, a pleading, frightened look on his wet, red face. He wore rimless glasses, and they were speckled with raindrops. The brim of his hat kept dripping water.

"My wife is waiting there on the sidewalk," the man said lamely.

Jonah did not answer. He hurried Sally into the taxi, slammed the door shut as soon as he was inside, and then gave the driver Sally's address.

"Did you see a woman on the sidewalk?" he asked her.

"No."

"I didn't either."

"I did," the driver said.

"What?" Jonah said.

"Forgive me for living," the driver said, "but there *was* a little old lady huddled in the doorway there near Stern's, that was probably the guy's wife."

"Well, I didn't see her," Jonah said.

"It's none of my business," the driver said, "and I don't

like to get into arguments with passengers, but by rights, this was that guy's cab. If a man signals to you, that's his cab. He gives you a signal, and you give him a signal back. You either wave your hand out the window, or dip your lights, anything to let him know you seen him. That's your contract, mister, that means you ain't gonna pick nobody else up, and he ain't gonna jump in no other cab before you get to him. That's the way it works in this city. You from New York?"

"I'm from New York," Jonah said.

"Then you should know that's the way it works here."

"A new slant on contract law," Jonah said to Sally.

"What was that?" the driver said, glancing over his shoulder.

"Don't you think you ought to watch the road?" Jonah said.

"I'm watching the road fine, thanks. I been driving a taxi for seventeen years, and I never had an accident yet, thank God. Don't worry about my watching the road. That guy signaled to me, and I signaled back, and by rights this was his cab, not that it's any of my business. Also, there *was* a little old lady huddled in the doorway there near Stern's, dripping wet, no matter what you say."

"Look, just drive, will you?" Jonah said, annoyed.

"Forgive me for breathing," the driver said.

Sally cleared her throat.

"But if you think it's fun driving a cab on a rainy night, you ought to try it sometime."

Jonah did not answer. Sally squeezed his hand, and he nodded to her in the darkness of the back seat. The driver was silent for the remainder of the trip downtown. When they reached Sally's building, the fare on the meter was a dollar and ten cents. Jonah tipped the driver a quarter, and got out of the cab to follow Sally, who had taken the umbrella.

"Hey, just a minute, buddy," the driver said.

Jonah hesitated. He ran back to the taxi, stooped to peer through the open front window, and said, "What is it?" The rain was beating down on his head and back. It splashed noisily in the curbside puddles, drummed on the roof of the taxi.

The driver had his hand extended, the dollar bill resting under the dime and the quarter. "You sure you don't need this more than I do?" he asked.

Jonah looked at him steadily.

"Yes, I do," he answered and gingerly picked the quarter from his palm. "Good night," he said politely. He turned away from the cab, and ran through the rain and up the steps to where Sally was wrestling with the umbrella, simultaneously trying to unlock the vestibule door. Behind him, the driver shouted, "What're you, a *wise* guy?" and gunned the taxi away from the curb.

They climbed the four flights to her apartment. Jonah's trouser legs were sticking to him. The shoulders of his raincoat were soaked through to his suit jacket. Sally quickly unlocked the door and said, "You must be drenched," which he acknowledged with a surly nod as they entered the apartment. He took off the dripping raincoat at once, and then removed his jacket and draped it over the living room radiator. His shirt was wet too, clinging to his shoulders and chest. He took off his glasses and dried them briefly on his handkerchief.

"Here," Sally said, "try some of this."

"What is it?"

"Spanish brandy."

Jonah took the extended glass. "Let's drink to the little old lady huddled in the doorway of Stern's," he said.

"It bothers you, doesn't it?" Sally said.

"Yes."

"Then admit it."

"I admit it."

"No, you're joking about it."

"All right, I won't joke about it. It bothers me. It bothers the hell out of me. I don't like the idea of having beat an old lady out of a taxicab. All right? I may be a son of a bitch, but I'm not that ruthless."

"Who says you're a son of a bitch, Jonah?"

"I don't know," he said. He could hear a radio playing somewhere in the building. In the bathroom, the rain drummed noisily on the skylight. "Listen," he said.

"I hear it."

Her head was studiously bent as she poured brandy into her own glass, her light brown hair hanging over one cheek, her eyes intent on the glass and the lip of the bottle. Watching her, he felt curiously relaxed, as though this tiny apartment, the sound of the rain and the distant radio, the feeling of contained heat, this tall and slender girl gracefully putting the cork back into the bottle, all evoked a memory for him that was both comforting and secure. And then, as she turned from the coffee table, head rising, soft brown hair settling gently into place beside the curve of her cheek as though in slow motion, her eyes meeting his, her mouth slowly widening into a smile, everything so slow and easy and tirelessly simple, he remembered the alcohol ring on the bedroom dresser, where Christie's glass of sherry had rested through the night, and the morning had dawned bleakly on the dead and floating fruit flies of their marriage. Without realizing he was about to say it, without recognizing his need to tell her about it, he said "Have you ever been to San Francisco?"

"No," she said. "Whatever made you think of San Francisco?"

"It rained the whole weekend we were there," he said, and shrugged.

She waited. She looked at him expectantly, and waited.

"My partner," he said.

"What?"

"We went to San Francisco together. Have you ever been inside a prison?"

"No."

"You wouldn't like it."

"I guess not."

Silence again, the rain unceasing, the distant radio carrying snatches of melody on the night air, unrecognizable, and still she waited and he thought, What the hell do you want from me? and realized, of course, that she had asked for nothing.

"What is it?" she said.

"What?"

"A . . . a strange look just came over your face."

"No," he said. "Nothing."

"Tell me."

"Nothing," he said.

She nodded, a curious nod that was more like a shrug, and then she sat and crossed her legs, still waiting, knowing he would tell her when he was ready, and wondering if she wanted him to tell her, and remembering the way Hadad had kept referring to him as her boy friend. The internal revenue agent's name had been Ronny, and she'd been very fond of him. Even Gertie had liked him, but of course Gertie didn't know he was married and lived in Scarsdale with his wife and small son. She had not been to bed with a man since she and Ronny ended it in April. She felt no desire now, and yet she knew without question that she would go to bed with Jonah Willow tonight, and she wondered why.

"We were asked to defend a prisoner out there, that's all," Jonah said. "At San Quentin."

"I see."

"He'd killed one of the guards. Said the man had been harassing him."

"Had he?" she asked.

"Who knows? The guard was dead, so we certainly couldn't ask him. Smith maintained—that was his name, Orville Smith—said the guard had made things impossible for him from the moment he arrived. He was serving a life term, you see. He'd murdered his wife and daughter. Killed them with an ax." Jonah paused. "A California firm was handling the case, they called us in to see if we'd be interested. We . . . our firm . . . Raymond's and mine . . . had built a reputation by then and . . . there was a mandatory death penalty involved, you see, if Smith got convicted, that was the law."

"Did you take the case?"

"Well . . . it seemed to me, it seemed to me there *had* been provocation. After all, Smith was pretty much at this fellow's mercy, you know, and had to take his abuse and listen to his remarks. What finally caused him to crack, in fact, was a simple remark, that's all. Smith said the guard called him 'Lizzie' one day, after Lizzie Borden, and that was it. They were in the dining hall, and Smith grabbed his fork and went for the guard's throat and didn't quit until the man was dead. It took four other guards to pull him away, he was a powerful man, six-four, with arms like this."

"Did you take the case, Jonah?"

"I didn't even like the man, I couldn't possibly bring myself to like him and yet . . . I . . . I did feel he had been abused. I tried to explain this to Raymond, why I thought we should take the case. We were sitting on the porch of the guest cottage, Raymond and I, looking out at the rain and the high illuminated walls of the prison, and Raymond very quietly suggested that maybe I was confusing my private life with my professional life. When I asked him what he meant, he said maybe I was equating the *actual* murder of a wife and child with what was only the *symbolic* murder of a wife and child. Now what's *that* supposed to mean, I said, and he said I'm talking about the divorce, Jonah, and I said, *What* divorce? and he said, *Your* divorce. I'd been divorced that August, you see. Just two months before Raymond and I went to San Quentin together."

"I see."

"He'd always been very fond of Christie. My wife. My former wife."

"I see."

"So . . . so I could understand why he was disturbed about the divorce, and . . . and about Christie drinking and . . . and the things she was doing. He'd known her from . . . from when we were first married you see, when things were very different. But I couldn't understand what any of this had to do with defending Smith, so I . . . I tried to be very calm because Raymond was my closest friend and my partner. . . . I . . . I very calmly explained that I didn't feel any guilt about the failure of my marriage, that Christie had made it virtually impossible to go on living with her, and that we'd both agreed divorce would be best for all parties concerned, including Amy. My daughter. I have a twelve-year-old daughter."

Sally nodded.

"Raymond just said, Sure, Jonah, sure, and then, all of a sudden, he said, I don't want to defend this man. So I . . . I asked him why he didn't want to defend him and he said because Smith is repulsive and rotten and obviously guilty, and I said, Wait a minute, and he said, No, you wait a minute, Jonah, defending that bastard would be contrary to everything I believe about law and justice.

"The rain was coming down, we sat on the porch in those big wicker chairs painted white by the prisoners, and I said, Raymond, you know this man's rights are in danger of being violated, and he said, Don't give me any more of *that* shit, Jonah, all you want is another newspaper headline. And . . . and then he . . . he told me I . . . was nothing but a self-seeking son of a bitch who had never really understood Christie, who had forced her to become what she was by totally ignoring her needs in my ruthless . . . he used that word, ruthless, he said . . . in my ruthless ambition to become the biggest and best-known lawyer in the history of the goddamn profession, that . . . that I was responsible for the divorce and for . . . for ruining a . . . a damn sweet lady."

Jonah's glass was empty.

He put it to his lips, discovered the brandy was gone, and then put the glass down on the table.

"I guess Smith was guilty, Sally, but . . . even if he *had* stabbed that officer in full view of God knows how many men, the thing wasn't premeditated, it wasn't malicious, it *couldn't* have been, it was a spur-of-the-moment act provoked by the guard. Raymond had . . . Raymond had no right to . . . to say the things he said to me.

"But they were said. They were out. And when people pass that certain line, wherever it may be . . ." His voice trailed. "There . . . there are things people say to each other that can never be retracted. Christie and I had said those things, we had hurled all the goddamn filthy words we

could think of, we had accused, we had condemned, and it
ended." He closed his eyes and sighed. "And then Raymond
and I said all there was to say. And there was no going back."
He looked up suddenly. "I keep losing partners."

"Maybe you don't need a partner, Jonah."

"Maybe not."

"Did you take the case?"

"Yes. I argued it with everything that was in me, just to
prove, just to show Raymond that he was wrong, just to *win*
it, and to show him. Mitigating circumstances, I said, provocation, your Honor, here was a man in bondage being tor-
mented by his jailer. We could say, your Honor, we could
almost say this security officer was a man seeking his own
death, tormenting a convicted murderer. We could in a
sense, your Honor, say this man was intent on committing
suicide, your Honor, we could say he took his own life. And
must we now take yet another life to justify the vagaries of
this troubled mind, the labyrinthine motivation of a man
intent on suicide? Must we do that, your Honor, to satisfy
whatever primitive clamor for blood we recognize within
ourselves? When it was all over, they sent him to the gas
chamber. Period. I lost."

She suddenly knew why she would allow him to make love
to her, knew it even before he said what he said next.

"I'm going to lose this one too, Sally."

"How do you know?"

"Driscoll is guilty."

"That doesn't mean you'll lose."

"Maybe I *want* to lose."

"Will that help?"

"He's guilty," Jonah said. "He sat in that courtroom today
and constructed a totally plausible network of deceit, attempting to trace the workings of the mind, something
Brackman couldn't *hope* to contradict. Iceman is coal man,
and coal man is Colman, and Colman is death, and death is
the iceman in *The Iceman Cometh,* expecting us to swallow a
literary association test delivered with a straight face. Peter is

a phallic reference, and Morley is a Negro he knew as a boy, renamed Christopher in honor of the novelist, and Major Catharine Astor is definitely *not* Constantine's major, and yet Driscoll knew the color of her hair and the minor incident of showing the colonel his medical record, but no this is not the basis for the letter-carrying scene. Nor was the 105th Division based on Constantine's. Then where *did* it come from? How in hell could he have hit upon those identical three digits, and why didn't he have a psychological explanation for *them*, too, the way he had for every other alleged similarity? He slipped the other day when we were having drinks together, he said, 'I won't explain that number,' and then he changed it to 'I can't explain it,' but he meant 'I *won't*,' goddamn it. And the reason he wouldn't is because the number stuck in his head, it remained in his head after he saw Constantine's play—he's been a theatergoer from the time he was twelve, he's probably seen every piece of garbage ever presented on the Broadway stage, he practically admitted as much to me in private. So how *could* he tell us where he got that number, when telling us would have sent the case straight up the chimney?

"He's a lying bastard, and a thief, and I'm defending him."

Sally put down her glass, rose, and walked to where he was standing. Very gently, she put her hands on his shoulders and lifted her face to be kissed. She thought how odd it was that men could talk about losing partners and losing cases and even losing wives, and never once realize what they had really lost. She kissed him and hoped that when he lost this case as well (because he was defending a guilty man he thought was James Driscoll and not himself) perhaps he would remember he had been to bed with her, the way the English teacher in Schenectady would always remember he had been to bed with her.

She knew suddenly that she would not be seeing much of Jonah Willow once the trial ended.

She knew this with certainty, and with sadness, and relief. There were far too many things he was still trying to forget, far too many ghosts in his life; she had no desire to become yet another one of them. She hoped only that he would remember her.

Once she had asked her mother to make believe she was a person, and her mother had said, No, Sally, that coat isn't right for you, take it off.

The rain stopped at midnight, just as they came out of the movie theater and into the street. They walked up Broadway together, Ebie's arm through his, watching the after-theater crowd, relishing the noise and the clamor of New York City, so unlike what they knew in Vermont. Under the marquee of the Astor, a crowd of people in formal wear stood laughing and chatting, trying to get taxis, boisterous and loud, obviously enjoying themselves. The women wore mink coats over flowing gowns of pale blue and lucid pink, corsages pinned to bodice or waist or—as with one pretty brunette in a lustrous dark fur—pinned to her hair, just above the ear. There was a holiday mood outside the hotel and in the lobby as well, where men in dinner jackets told dirty jokes to each other and women laughed raucously with them, and then remembered to blush. A man dressed as Santa Claus, drunk as a lord, came staggering toward the revolving doors, snapping his fingers in time to the music that came from some hidden ballroom. Ebie's face suddenly broke into a grin.

"Listen," she said.

"What is it?"

"Listen."

He could not place the tune. Violins carried it on the noisy lobby air, evoking a mood, frustratingly elusive.

"Come," she said, and suddenly took his hand.

They went through the lobby, searching out the source of the music, following the strains of the orchestra until at last they stood just outside the Rose Room, and nodded to each other like conspirators. She raised her arms, and Driscoll automatically took her hand and cradled her waist, and they began dancing silently in the corridor outside the ballroom.

He felt again the way he'd felt when they were young together, in love together, possessed of a confidence that was now alien to him. She was light in his arms, her feet skimmed over the polished floor. They danced past two old ladies in gloves and hats, who looked at them in wonder. The old ladies delighted him, their looks of astonishment, the way the one in the purple hat opened her eyes wide to express shock, outrage, surprise, wonder, bemusement, even a little touch of wickedness. He wanted to scoop up both old ladies, catch them both in his arms along with Ebie, and dance them down the corridor and out the side door and onto 44th Street and over to Sardi's and maybe clear to the Hudson River and across to Jersey and points west, all the way back to their homes in Albuquerque or Des Moines, and then on past California and across the Pacific to exotic Oriental places that would cause the lady in the purple hat to open her eyes wide again and drop her jaw in shock, outrage, surprise, wonder, bemusement, and wicked glee. He felt, when things were right, as they were now, the same happiness he had known in those years before he left for the Army.

Their feet no longer touched the ground, they seemed to float on air an inch above the floor of the corridor. One of the old ladies was laughing now, all the world loves a lover, a bellhop carrying a wreath of flowers danced out of their way as though he were part of a consuming ballet, the world would soon be dancing with them, people would come out into the streets dancing and singing and shouting their fool heads off because James Randolph Driscoll and Edna Belle Dearborn were in love.

Had been in love, he thought.

As suddenly as they had begun dancing, they stopped.

October, he thought.

Out of breath, Ebie laughed and squeezed his hand.

1950, he thought.

He looked down at her and tried to remember what it had been like before then, and wondered how it could ever be that way again. They walked to the elevators in silence.

I got a medal in October of 1950, he thought, it was pinned right between my eyes, I've been wearing it ever since.

"Oh, my, that was fun," Ebie said.

They entered the waiting car. The doors closed. The elevator streaked up the shaft, cables whining and groaning.

I got my medal for being a nice guy and a fool, he thought, that's what they gave medals for back in those days.

I wrote all about my medal in a book called *The Paper Dragon*, perhaps you've read it, madam. It's about the Korean War, yes, and about this nice young man who is victimized by these horrible people who eventually cause his death, a symbolic death, madam, Oh yes, an *actual* death in the book, but really symbolic—I testified to that effect before the learned and honorable judge today. It is now a matter of record that the death of Lieutenant Alex Cooper, according to his creator (although such status is still in serious doubt), was intended as a symbolic death. If you're ever haggling over that one at a literary tea, just look up the trial record and you'll know the death was supposed to be symbolic. Yes, madam, my medal was delivered in the crisp October, it was a nice medal to receive. I wore it into battle when they came charging across the river, it gave me courage because I didn't give a damn anymore, you see. That's why medals are awarded, to give you courage.

They are all looking for medals in that courtroom, all except me. I got my medal, and I described my medal, and it took every ounce of strength I had, and there's nothing more inside me, nothing left to say or do. I wanted only to die quietly on that farm I bought in Vermont, so why did you have to come along, Mr. Constantine? Why did you have to start this ridiculous suit, opening all the old wounds again, why did you have to do this, Mr. Constantine?

Oh, sure, I can understand. You want a chestful of medals, right? You want all those millions API made on the film, and you want credit for the book as well because you think the book was the medal when it was really only the catalogue description of the medal. The real medal is pinned right here between my eyes, and I'm sure you wouldn't want that, Mr. Constantine, because it has hurt like hell ever since 1950, can't you see the scars, yes, quite painful when it rains. What'll they do if you win this case? Will they have to tell everybody you really wrote *The Paper Dragon?* Will they pull back all the copies and cross out my name, so sorry, put yours in its place? Is that what they do when someone has made a terrible mistake, oh my goodness, we've credited the wrong man with authorship. We gave the medal to the right man, however, and if *The Paper Dragon* is a fairly accurate description of the events leading up to that singular decoration, how then is it possible that the chronicle was stolen? Strange, passing strange indeed.

Do you know what I managed to do in court today?

Under oath?

I managed to tell the truth, and yet *not* tell the truth.

It was quite simple. I could do it with a completely straight face and hardly any increase in my pulse rate. I wouldn't be surprised if I could beat a lie detector test, I'm getting very expert at telling only partial truth. Maybe I'll suggest to his Honorable McIntyre that they give me a lie detector test and ask me if I wrote *The Paper Dragon,* and I will say, Yes, I wrote it, and then they'll ask me if I stole it from Constantine's play, and I'll say, No, I did not steal it from anybody's play, I stole it from in *here,* and in *here,* that's where I stole it. It's a secret I stole from a dying man who has been suffering from a rare incurable malady since October of 1950, that is who I stole it from, whom.

Then how do you account for *this,* sir, and how do you account for *that,* sir, and how do you account for the *fact,* sir, and *tell* us, sir, *tell* us, and I'll partial-truth that infernal machine until it short circuits itself and goes completely out of business, I can beat any machine in the house.

I've already told you once, I told the *world* once, isn't once enough? You know about my medal, what the hell more do you need? Shall I spell it out for you syllable by painful syllable, go over it one more time for the slow ones, cater to the lip readers, spare me, please. Make what you will of it, it's over and done with, the trial is over, the case is closed. I don't even want credit for the book, give the damn book to Constantine, let him go tell his mother *he* wrote it, I don't care.

The elevator doors opened. They stepped out into the corridor and walked to their room. At the door, she hesitated and put her hand on his arm.

"Dris," she said, "there's still a chance."

"For what? The case is closed. Tomorrow they'll make their set speeches, and that'll be that."

"There's something to save," she whispered.

"What's there to save, Ebie?"

"Us."

"Don't make me laugh."

"You thought so once."

"I never thought so."

"When you were discharged, when you came home, you tried to understand."

"I tried to understand for eleven goddamn years. I never could, Ebie. So forget it. I have."

"You haven't forgotten it, you've only exorcised it."

"That's the same thing."

"No. You can't erase something by writing a book about it."

"I wrote a book about the Army in Korea."

"Dris, if you won't tell them the truth, I will." She looked up at him, and he saw that there were tears in her eyes. "I'll tell them about the 105th," she said.

He did not answer her. He stared at her and tried to fathom whether or not there was substance to her threat, but he did not speak.

"I know," she said. "I know it's not a hundred and five."

He kept staring at her.

"I know it's two numbers, Dris. I know it's a ten and a five, and I know *why* and I'll *tell* them why."

"And kill me twice," he said.

"No. And save you once."

He turned away from her and unlocked the door. He hesitated in the doorway, seemed about to say something, and then went into the room instead.

Ebie followed him in soundlessly.

FRIDAY

15

THE DAY WAS COLD and clear.

A brilliant blue sky swept from horizon to horizon beyond the tall courtroom windows, cloudless, reflecting a cold light that caused tabletops and walls, benches and chairs, even pencils lying in repose to leap toward the eye in startling clarity. Each line of the American flag beside the judge's bench seemed inked with a thick pen, its alternating red and white stripes folded in bold black shadows. Driscoll's trained eye followed each wavering dark line, dipped to the point of the flag hanging low, retraced itself upward through crossing draped and overlapping patterns toward the creased blue field and crumpled white stars. He walked behind Ebie to the empty jury box, sat beside her, glanced at Willow, and then turned toward the plaintiff's table, where his eyes met Constantine's.

For a moment, the men almost nodded to each other, almost acknowledged each other's presence. Constantine seemed ready to lift his hand from the table in a short gesture of greeting, Driscoll seemed about to smile in recognition. And then one or another of them, or perhaps both by mutual, silent, and simultaneous consent, snapped the slender thread that hung invisibly in the air between them, severed all communication, and turned once more to the business at hand.

"All rise!" the clerk called, and McIntyre swept from his

chambers, took his seat behind the bench, and signaled for everyone to sit. He was carrying with him the documents submitted to him earlier that morning by both plaintiff and defendants, in which they hoped to show findings of fact and conclusions of law to support their respective cases. He had gone through these briefly in his chambers, and he spread them on the bench top now and looked out over the courtroom, locating Willow and asking, "Are you ready with your argument, Mr. Willow?"

"If your Honor please," Willow said.

"You may proceed."

Willow rose from behind the defense table, a tall and impressive figure in a dignified blue suit, holding his prepared text in his left hand, putting on his glasses as he approached the bench. He glanced at the text for just a moment, and then lowered it, as though he had already committed it to memory and would not have to refer to it again during the course of his summation. He looked up at McIntyre and very softly, so softly that Driscoll could barely hear him from the jury box, said, "If your Honor please, the matter before us these past several days concerns itself solely with whether or not a theft has been committed. The plaintiff has alleged that James Driscoll freely copied from the play *Catchpole* when he was writing his novel *The Paper Dragon*. But the plaintiff has testified that he has no proof, his allegations to the contrary, that Driscoll actually possessed the manuscript or even that he saw the play before writing his book. The entire case, therefore, rests on the alleged similarities between the two works. Now, I know your Honor is familiar with and has certainly studied the record of other cases where plagiarism was claimed. I know, too, that your Honor is aware of the great number of similarities brought before the courts in those other cases, a hundred similarities, two hundred, and in one case something more than four hundred supposed similarities. In most of those cases, however, despite the overwhelming weight of similarities, the courts found *against* a claim of plagiarism. I mention this, your Honor, because the plaintiff's case before us rests on only a very slender body of supposed similarities, all of which are insignificant.

"I do not intend to ask the Court's indulgence while I go over each and every one of these supposedly matching points, your Honor. The plaintiff has put a necessary stress upon them because, lacking any other proof, they are his sole hope of showing theft. But, your Honor, I think we have neglected the fact that most of these similarities—even if they *were* copied—would not form the basis for a plagiarism suit. They are not even copy*right*able, your Honor. An idea is not copyrightable. A theme is not copyrightable. A plot is not copyrightable. Nor is a character copyrightable. The only thing an author may hope to copyright is his manner of expression. Judge Learned Hand has made this abundantly clear in the prevailing cases in this jurisdiction. *Only* the manner of expression can be copyrighted, and *nothing else.*

"Well, your Honor, you have read both play and novel, and you have seen the motion picture—which does not concern us at the moment, but which I believe, by the way, was written and filmed using only the book and related research as sources, and without reference to the play. You have also gone over the charts submitted by the plaintiff, and you have studied the trial transcript and I'm sure you have noted that any of these so-called similarities are due to the fact that both men were dealing with the same subject matter and the same background—the United States Army in time of combat. It would be impossible, your Honor, to present this topic without having similar conflicts springing from the very situation both writers independently chose. One cannot describe a seascape without mentioning the shore or the waves or the sky beyond, and the fact that two authors write of green waves or white foam or wet sand does not indicate one author copied from the other. Such similarities are inevitable.

"The astonishing thing about the plaintiff's claim, of course, is that there is a paucity of even these *non*copyrightable similarities. I can only attribute this to the playwright's poverty of wit, language, insight, and imagination. Your Honor knows that *Catchpole* was badly received by the critics in 1947, and I believe I intimated that the reviews were really devastating, that the play was all but laughed off the stage. The only remarkable thing about this play, in fact, is that it was produced at *all,* and that it managed to sell tickets even for twelve days. I would like to say, incidentally, that Mr. Constantine's testimony concerning the distribution of *free* tickets to Pratt Institute is one area where I can be critical of Mr. Brackman."

"Where does this testimony appear in the record?" McIntyre asked.

"It's in Mr. Constantine's direct, your Honor. I'll find it for you."

Willow walked back to the defense table and leafed through the transcript. Turning toward the bench, he said, "It's on page 11, your Honor." He picked up the bulky transcript and carried it to the bench with him. "He says, 'Yes, sir. There were a series of previews held while we were still rehearsing the play in a loft on Second Avenue.' And when asked which colleges received tickets to these previews, he says, 'C.C.N.Y., Hunter, Brooklyn College, L.I.U., Pratt Institute, and several others.'

"As your Honor knows, the plaintiff was examined at great length before trial by both Mr. Genitori and myself. Never once, your Honor, not once during all those pretrial examinations did he mention preview performances, *or* free tickets, *or* Pratt Institute. And yet, suddenly, we are presented with this startling testimony. And *why* was Pratt Institute so singled out? The answer is simple, your Honor. On the biographical questionnaire Mr. Driscoll sent to Mitchell-Campbell Books, and which was submitted to Mr. Brackman only *after* the pretrial examinations, he mentions that he was a student at Pratt Institute in 1947. So all at once Mr. Constantine remembers that free tickets were distributed to a number of colleges, including Pratt, thereby hoping to establish that Mr. Driscoll at least *could* have seen a performance of the play. I'm surprised, your Honor, I really am surprised that Mr. Brackman permitted his client to testify in such a manner. I'm sure Mr. Brackman did not create this testimony himself, but it was clearly an afterthought and might have been considered more circumspectly by him.

"In the long run, of course, it would not have mattered if a bushel of free tickets went to Pratt, because the play in rehearsal was performed without scenery and would not have afforded Mr. Driscoll the opportunity to see the magic number 105, upon which the plaintiff places such enormous stress—the fingerprints of the thief, Mr. Brackman has repeatedly said. Well, your Honor, we have Mr. Driscoll's testimony that he does not know where the number came from, and that is about as honest an answer as any man can give. He simply does not know. He has also testified that he did not see a performance of that play in 1947 when he was an art student and not at all interested in writing, and he has testified that he did not see a copy of the manuscript until I gave him one several weeks ago. Moreover, the only man who worked with him in an editorial capacity on that book, Mr. Chester Danton, testified that he was abroad in 1947 when the play was produced.

"In his findings of fact, of course, Mr. Brackman emphasizes that there is no claim against Mr. Danton's contributions to the novel. If your Honor please, one of the specific similarities claimed, one of the specific similarities *stressed* by Mr. Constantine in his direct testimony, was the incident of a sniper killing an American soldier. This was supposedly one of the most amazing similarities between the play and the novel. I could understand Mr. Brackman's consternation at discovering the sniper was Mr. *Danton's* idea, a suggestion *he* transmitted to Mr. Driscoll, and *not* Mr. Driscoll's invention at all. I can understand why Mr. Brackman asked during his cross whether Mr. Danton had been trying to mislead him. I can understand all this, your Honor, but the fact remains that the sniper did not appear in the novel as originally submitted to Mitchell-Campbell Books.

"Let us examine that novel for a moment, if we may. I personally, your Honor, have always been fascinated by the creative process, the way in which a writer, a painter, or a composer goes about producing his work. When we strip it of the mystique surrounding it, when we pause to look upon the artist as a man rather than a vague symbol, when we accept the fact that there are no muses involved in honest creation, we must then also see, your Honor, that the true professional is as systematic as an engineer. Richard Strauss, for example, filled dozens of filing cabinets with outlines and ideas, developments of themes, partial scores, all recorded in a unique and personal manner. In much the same way, James Driscoll has provided us with a unique and personal record of the development of his novel, from inception to completion. We have seen his rough outlines and his detailed outlines, we have seen his schedules and his progress reports, his letters to his editor and his agent, as well as reminders to himself, questions he asked, answers he received. We have learned that he would not even write about an operation he had performed a great many times—the disassembly of a rifle—until he had first painstakingly checked on the exact technical language. We have learned that he would not write about the Chinese armies in Korea before learning which of them were in the battle area and in what strength. We have seen the care with which he drew his own map of the patrol route his fictitious squad took into enemy territory. As we go through all this material, your Honor, it becomes crystal clear that here is a man creating his own work, relying upon his own knowledge and background, and supplementing this with meticulous research. This is not the work of a copyist, a plagiarist, a thief. There is no question here, your Honor, but that James Driscoll created *The Paper Dragon* alone, independently, and without reference to any existing work of fiction. In fact, your Honor, I think that even a casual reading of both works clearly indicates that one was not copied from the other.

"Why, then, did I spend so much time during the course of this trial discussing these alleged similarities, some of which the plaintiff himself has labeled 'flimsy and absurd,' when a mere reading shows that there was no plagiarism? Why did I dignify each of these separate charges by examining them with such scrutiny? Why did I amass proof to show Mr.

Driscoll's creative process? I would like to explain, your Honor, lest these co-called similarities seem to take on a significance they do not truly possess.

"There are large sums of money involved here, your Honor. We can suppose without a detailed accounting that the motion picture grossed upwards of ten million dollars, and we have heard testimony to the effect that the novel in its paperback edition alone sold more than two and a half million copies. And whereas it was not mentioned during the trial, I know that the book went into eleven foreign editions, each of which sold extraordinarily well because of the impetus provided by the film. So there is unquestionably a great deal of money involved. But there is more than money, and it is this further consideration that prompted my detailed probing of the similarities, your Honor. I speak now of the reputation of an extremely talented, diligent, and earnest writer, James Driscoll."

He turned to look at the jury box, and Driscoll read his face and his eyes, read them swiftly and in the brief instant it took Willow to glance at him and then turn back toward the judge. But he knew in that single sharp exchange that Willow did not believe a word of what he had just said. The knowledge startled him. He glanced at Ebie and saw that she was sitting with her hands clasped tightly over the pocketbook in her lap, her eyes intent on Willow.

"Now, your Honor, I could easily stress the legal argument, I could easily repeat that even if Mr. Driscoll *had* taken this material he is alleged to have copied, why none of it is copyrightable, the only thing a man may copyright is his manner of expression. And were I to stress the legal argument, and were I to win on that point alone, this would undoubtedly be a victory for Mitchell-Campbell and for Camelot Books, but what about this man James Driscoll? What about this man whose career lies ahead of him, who has written a brilliant first novel, this man who, in Chester Danton's words, 'will go on writing many more excellent books'? What about James Driscoll? Your Honor, we have been asked to believe, for example, that the use of the word

'Loot' when addressing a lieutenant in the United States Army is indicative of copying by this man, James Driscoll. Well, your Honor, I think that this sort of specious reasoning is indicative only of the groundless claim we have before us. We have cited, in our brief, one of Judge Hand's opinions in which he describes an obsessive sort of paranoia that attacks some authors, and I think we have exactly that syndrome here. *Catchpole* was a totally unsuccessful play on a theme which was later successfully explored by James Driscoll in *The Paper Dragon*. It is not difficult to understand how Mr. Constantine, unable to accept the failure of his work, attributed the success of Mr. Driscoll's work to copying. We have this throughout, your Honor. We have Mr. Constantine testifying, for example, that the use of obscenity is common in the armed forces, and then insisting nonetheless that the soldier in his play is a unique creation who must have been stolen by Mr. Driscoll. My friend Mr. Brackman looks troubled, so if your Honor wishes, I'll find the exact place in the transcript . . ."

"I'm not troubled, Mr. Willow. I'm merely very interested in what you're saying."

"Very what?" McIntyre asked.

"Interested, your Honor."

"Well, you looked extremely troubled there for a moment," Willow said. "I'll be happy to find the testimony if . . ."

"He doesn't look at all troubled to me, Mr. Willow," McIntyre said, "but I would like the exact page in the transcript if you have it."

Willow accepted the transcript from his assistant, leafed through it, and said, "It's on page 89, your Honor. This is Mr. Constantine's testimony. 'Question: Do you think they were rarities? Answer: No. Question: They were commonplace? Answer: They were to be found everywhere in the Army.'" Willow looked up from the transcript and said, "You understand, your Honor, that these questions and answers are referring to men using obscene language."

"Yes, I understand that."

"And later, on page 92, I asked Mr. Constantine, 'Yet you still maintain that your character's use of obscenity is unique?' and he replied, 'It is unique, yes.' That's an indication of what we're being asked to accept in this courtroom, your Honor. These clear admissions that the so-called similarities between the two works are really based on common material, and then the stubborn insistence that one work was nonetheless copied from the other. Well, your Honor, that soldier is *not* unique, and we *know* he is not unique. We know, in fact, that a soldier such as this is undoubtedly a commonplace, and it would be very easy to find against the plaintiff on the grounds that the material he claims was copied is not copyrightable material. That would be a perfectly reasonable finding, your Honor, except that it would leave a stain on Mr. Driscoll's character, it would leave a stigma on his career. Such a finding would indicate that he *did* copy from another man, but only material that was in the public domain. And that would be a terrible injustice, your Honor. I ask you, therefore, to consider this in your decision, because I believe with all my heart that James Driscoll has done nothing to warrant this charge of plagiarism. James Driscoll is an artist, your Honor, who wrote a fine book in his own manner and using his own resources. For this, your Honor, we owe him only respect and gratitude."

The courtroom was silent. In the silence, Driscoll looked at Willow, and again knew without doubt that the lawyer had been mouthing words he did not believe. Willow returned the look, and then walked slowly back toward the defense table. Genitori, dressed in his customary pinstriped suit, had already risen, prepared text in hand, and was walking toward the bench. He smiled briefly at no one, cleared his throat, and said, "If your Honor please, concerning the first cause of action against Artists-Producers-International, I can say nothing that Mr. Willow has not already said, and I ask that his argument be adopted as my own. With respect to the cause of action claiming independent infringement, however, I would like to call your Honor's attention to page 127 of the

transcript, where I moved for dismissal and assumed arguendo . . ."

Driscoll stopped listening. He was disturbed by what he
had detected in Willow's manner, but Ebie's sudden agita-
tion concerned him even more. He knew that she too had
sensed the hollowness of Willow's praise—there had never
been a time when they both did not react identically and
simultaneously to any given stimulus—and he was now
troubled to see her fingers working nervously on her handbag, fastening and unfastening the clasp, a small deadly click
punctuating Genitori's words, "spend this Court's time in
repeating it now," click, "later called Ralph Knowles to the
stand," click, "respected and honored director," click, "in-
conceivable to imagine he had the slightest need for copying
any of the plaintiff's paltry work," click.

He did not know what Ebie would do, or even what she
could do now that the case was officially closed and the
arguments begun. He knew only that she was unpredictable,
had always been unpredictable, and that she had openly
threatened him only the night before. He knew, moreover,
and this was what troubled him most, that she was the kind of
woman who moved swiftly and directly once she had decided
on a course of action. He had learned that in 1950, had
learned it once and for all time, and he watched her nervous
hands now as they worked the clasp, knowing that her mind
was churning with possibilities, listening to each small click
with rising anticipation, ". . . the defendant API quite
properly replied, Yes, Mr. Edelson and Miss Blake had indeed worked as story editors on those dates," click, "but for
the *studio,* you understand," click, "and not in connection
with *The Paper Dragon,* which possibility Mr. Knowles put
to rout forever when he testified in simple, forceful English
that neither Mr. Edelson nor Miss Blake had anything *whatever* to do with the production of his movie," click.

Genitori nodded, and then consulted his text once again,
and then said to McIntyre, "I therefore ask you to find, your
Honor, that Mr. Ralph Knowles did not see or read the play
Catchpole before writing his movie, that the motion picture

The Paper Dragon was written and produced independently of that play, and that the claim against Artists-Producers-International should be dismissed. Thank you, your Honor."

Sidney Brackman took a long while getting up from his chair and then moving past Constantine and around the plaintiff's table and into the aisle, where he walked slowly to the front of the courtroom. He turned to look first at Willow, and then at Genitori, and then he looked up at McIntyre and said, "Your Honor, I have been practicing law for twenty-two years now, but there's always something new to learn, I guess. Mr. Willow pointed out to me today, just a few minutes ago, that it was my duty as a lawyer to prevent a witness from giving testimony while he was on the stand under oath. Mr. Willow seems to feel that I permitted testimony which was at best questionable, but I would like to say that Mr. Constantine was *never* asked about preview performances at any time during the pretrial examinations. I can assure Mr. Willow that had the question been asked, it would have been answered honestly, the same way Mr. Constantine has answered every question put to him since this suit began. If Mr. Willow did not think to ask about any performances other than those on Broadway, I do not see why his oversight should then become a reflection on my integrity."

"I assure you, Mr. Brackman, that your integrity is unquestioned," McIntyre said.

"Thank you, your Honor. Thank you, and forgive me for taking the Court's time to clear up this seemingly insignificant matter, but it *was* important to me."

"I understand."

"Thank you. Mr. Willow has also commented on the scarcity of claimed similarities between *Catchpole* and *The Paper Dragon,* pointing out to your Honor that most plagiarism cases will have two hundred, or three hundred, or even four hundred claimed similarities. He also stated that most of these cases were lost by the plaintiff, and I would like to suggest that it was the very weight of the similarities that helped to defeat these claims. When there are so many, your Honor, when every word and every comma becomes a matter for debate, well, obviously the plaintiff is stretching the truth, obviously he is predicating much of his case on sheer imagination. We have not done that here, your Honor. We have claimed only similarities that are plain for all to see. Some of them are less important than others, yes, but they are all pertinent. They are all pertinent because they show that there was copying, and without copying there can be no charge of plagiarism."

"Excuse me one moment, Mr. Brackman," McIntyre said, "but is it your belief that Mr. Driscoll *saw* this play?"

"Your Honor, I know that Mr. Driscoll is now a highly respected writer, and I know that he has been acclaimed as a literary phenomenon, and I know that his novel is still being dissected in the literary journals and, for all I know, being taught in colleges and universities all across these United States of ours. But, your Honor, he was *not* highly respected before he wrote *The Paper Dragon,* he was *not* being lionized, he was in fact totally unknown. By his own admission, he had written only a few unpublished short stories before writing the novel, and he has written *nothing* since. The only reason for his reputation now, in fact, is that he stole another man's work."

"Mr. Brackman, do you think he saw the play?"

"I think he was in possession of it."

"Of what? The play?"

"I think he was in possession of the plaintiff's play, yes."

"Before he wrote his novel?"

"Before he wrote his novel, and perhaps while he was writing his novel."

"I see."

"Your Honor, the evidence cannot show otherwise. Mr. Willow took the time and trouble to amass a great deluge of trivia, a landslide of outlines and letters and maps and what-have-you, but what do these prove? If we believe Mr. Driscoll, then indeed all these collected scraps of paper were the result of personal work habits, and show that he was a diligent man with perhaps an eye on future historians, keeping as it were his own personal time capsule for posterity. But if we do *not* believe Mr. Driscoll, then he was only a clever thief seeking to hide his plagiarism by constructing a supporting body of evidence to substantiate a claim of independent creation."

"I don't wish to interrupt your argument further," McIntyre said, "but I would still like to know whether it is your belief that Mr. Driscoll actually *saw* this play. A minute ago—"

"I don't understand, your Honor."

"Well, you said you thought he possessed a copy of it."

"Yes."

"Do you think he *saw* it as well?"

"Do you mean in performance?"

"Yes," McIntyre said. "Do you think he saw the play on the stage?"

"I don't know."

"Very well."

"He says he did not, your Honor, he has testified to that. He has also testified that he never saw a copy of this play until, when was it, several weeks ago, when Mr. Willow gave him one to read. How then can we explain these similarities—and there are, if your Honor please, exactly twenty-six of them, plus of course the six that were found to exist only between the play and the movie. How do we explain twenty-six concrete and specific similarities between the play *Catchpole* and the novel *The Paper Dragon* unless Mr. Driscoll had access to this play, unless—"

"Mr. Brackman," McIntyre interrupted, "you said earlier that some of these similarities were less important than others. I would—"

"But all pertinent, your Honor. We've set them forth in our brief, and I think we've covered them extensively over the past several days. I certainly don't want to weary you with them again, unless you wish me to do so."

"I merely wanted to know which ones you consider important."

"They are *all* important, your Honor, they are *all* pertinent, including those we concede to be minor. For example, your Honor, we claim that there is a similarity of plot, and then we go on to show exactly how and where the plots are similar, even *identical* in some places. Well, Mr. Willow in his summation said that a plot cannot be copyrighted, and yet one of the cases Mr. Genitori cites in his brief—"

"Yes, Mr. Brackman, I don't think we need belabor the point. If two works have identical plots, even though 'plot' per se is not copyrightable, this would certainly be evidence of copying. Don't you agree, Mr. Willow?"

"Yes, your Honor, *if* the plots were identical."

"Or significantly similar," McIntyre said, and then paused. "Or inexplicably so."

"Yes, your Honor," Willow said.

"So let's not belabor the point."

"By the same token, your Honor," Brackman said, "my opponent has gone to great lengths to show that many of the incidents and events and characters, much of the language, the settings and so forth used in the novel are there only because it happens to be a novel about the United States Army. He says, in effect, that *any* novel about the United States Army, *any* play about the United States Army would necessarily have sergeants in it, or obscenity, or barracks, or what have you. All right, we concede this. Where there's an army, there are necessarily men in uniform, and there are rifles, and battlefields, and enemy soldiers, and wounded men, and nurses, all right, let us say *all* of these things are in the public domain. Nonetheless, your Honor, even material in the public domain may be so combined or compiled as to be copyrightable."

"Yes, I know that, Mr. Brackman. But while we're on this point, I'd like to ask another question. Neither you nor Mr. Willow have said a word about the *differences* between the play and the book, but it strikes me that there are tremendous dissimilarities, and I wonder now whether we shouldn't concern ourselves with these as well. I wonder, in fact, whether we are not *dutybound* to study these dissimilarities in trying to determine whether there was indeed any copying here."

"If your Honor please," Brackman said, "the plaintiff's b-b-b-burden would be to prove th-that the similarities, and not the *dis*similarities, are so overwhelming that, your Honor, that there are enough of them to support a claim of plagiarism."

"Yes, but Mr. Willow admitted for the purposes of argument that even if all these alleged similarities were indeed copied, they would still add up to something too insignificant to be called plagiarism. Wasn't that his point?"

"I believe that was his point," Brackman said.

"Isn't that the point you made, Mr. Willow?"

"It was one of my points, yes, your Honor."

"Your Honor," Brackman said, "I do not believe *any* of these similarities are insignificant, nor do I believe someone can be guilty of just a little plagiarism, in much the same way a woman cannot possibly be just a little pregnant. How many of these similarities need we show before we recognize they cannot all be accidental? How else can we hope to prove plagiarism except by putting the works side by side and saying this corresponds to this, and that corresponds to that? Will the thief oblige us by admitting his theft? Of course not. So how else can we prove this theft, your Honor, except by comparing the works, by locating these seemingly unimportant and insignificant similarities, these so-called coincidences scattered throughout the work, and appearing far too often to be called coincidental? How else, your Honor? By inspecting what is *dissimilar,* as you have suggested? Would this support our claim? No, your Honor. It would only indicate that the work was not copied in its entirety, and that is *not* what we have claimed, nor is it what we have proved here in this Court. We have only proved that *enough* of it was copied to significantly deprive the plaintiff of his rights.

"Mr. Driscoll has claimed, your Honor has heard him testify, that the character Lieutenant Alex Cooper in *The*

Paper Dragon is based upon himself, and yet when asked which specific incidents or events happened to him, James Driscoll, he was hard put to find any such events that were not common to both the book and the play. Lieutenant Cooper was idealistic, yes, but James Driscoll was not. Lieutenant Cooper was single, James Driscoll was not. Lieutenant Cooper had an affair with a nurse, James Driscoll did not. And all down the line, your Honor, we see this same disparity between what *actually* happened to James Driscoll and what happened to the officer supposedly based on himself. Did Mr. Driscoll ever have a man like Colman in his platoon? No. Was there a troublemaker in his platoon? No. Was there a homosexual? No. Was there a murder scheme? No. Was he ever the target of a planned murder? No. He claims first that the book is autobiographical, and then when pressed to tell us just *how* it is autobiographical, he can tell us only that he *invented* most of the incidents.

"I do not think I have to comment on the preposterousness of his Colman-iceman story, or the farfetched allusion to Eugene O'Neill's play, or Mr. Driscoll's insistence that an obviously homosexual character in *Catchpole* was not at all homosexual and was not indeed the basis for the homosexual character in his book. We have Mr. Ralph Knowles's expert testimony—and was it not Mr. Genitori who said he was a highly respected and honored director?—we have his expert testimony that he *did,* in fact, combine two characters in the novel to form the single character of Colman in his film. And *this,* your Honor, is why James Driscoll insisted Colonel Peterson was not a homosexual, only because he knew very well that he *had* taken Peterson and Janus and combined them to form Colman, which process Knowles reversed in making his picture.

"And then, your Honor, we come to what I earlier called the thief's fingerprints and which I still maintain are the fingerprints of a thief, and I refer now to the labeling of the 105th Division."

A silence fell over the courtroom. In the silence, Driscoll heard the click of Ebie's handbag once again, and he turned to look at her and saw that she was straining forward in her seat now, leaning over at a sharp angle, her eyes on Brackman, her mouth drawn into a tight, narrow line.

"The 105th Division," Brackman repeated. "Here, your Honor, I do not think there can be any question whatever of coincidence. No one in this room would be willing to bet even fifty cents on correctly picking the same three digits in sequence, and yet that's exactly what Mr. Driscoll did, he picked three digits at random, one, oh, five, and they just happened to correspond with those same three digits in the play, even though the odds against this happening, as we saw, were a million to one. Now your Honor, that is *too* much to believe, and Mr. Driscoll *knows* it is too much to believe, and so he tells us he does not know how he hit upon those three digits, he *honestly* does not know how they happened to come to him, perhaps on the wings of a muse. Or more likely, your Honor, perhaps as the result of an error, the single error this thief made in his painstaking robbery. After the meticulous compilation of all his covering outlines and plots and maps, after the careful disguising of each and every character and event, here was the one mistake, here was the identifiable—"

Ebie rose.

She rose silently, with both hands tightly clutching her pocketbook, the knuckles white. It seemed for a moment as though she were simply going to leave the courtroom, as though she were unable to listen a moment longer to Brackman's accusations. But she did not move from where she stood in the jury box. She looked up at the judge. Brackman, seeing McIntyre's puzzled frown, stopped speaking and turned to face her.

"Your Honor," she said softly, "may I talk to Mr. Willow?"

Driscoll suddenly put his hand on her shoulder. She looked at him curiously, as though unable to read the gesture, and then turned again to the judge and plaintively inquired, "Your Honor?"

There was, for perhaps thirty seconds, total silence in the courtroom. Brackman did not object, although he was in the middle of his summation and any such interruption was forbidden and in fact unthinkable. Willow made no motion to recess, even though his client's wife had just asked if she could talk to him. The silence was complete, a stunned silence that stifled all action. Like children turning to their father for guidance when one of their peers has unforgivably transgressed, the lawyers looked toward the bench at the front of the courtroom, where McIntyre squinted in consternation, silent himself.

At last he said, "This Court will recess for ten minutes."

They returned to the courtroom at four minutes past eleven. McIntyre called the three attorneys to the bench, where they stood ranged before him, Willow in the center, Brackman and Genitori on either side of him. He fussed about in his chair, making himself comfortable. Then he folded his arms flat on the bench top, leaned forward, and brusquely said, "All right, Mr. Willow, what's this all about?"

"Your Honor," Willow said, "I would like to make application to reopen the case."

"For what purpose?"

"To submit additional testimony."

"Mr. Brackman?"

"Your Honor," Brackman said, "any additional testimony from the defendant at this point, after I've almost completed my summation, could only be injurious to my case. I respectfully submit . . ."

"That may be so, Mr. Brackman. I must say, Mr. Willow, that I have never had anything like this happen to me before."

"I believe we could find precedent for it, your Honor ."

"Yes, I'm sure we could, Mr. Willow," McIntyre said, "especially if we looked at Section 31.45 of the *Cyclopedia of Federal Procedure*."

"Your Honor, I'm not familiar with that section."

"I *am,* Mr. Willow."

"Forgive me."

"The section states, Mr. Willow—and next time you might wish to consult it before asking that a case be reopened—the section states that even after testimony has been entirely closed, the Court may receive additional evidence in its own discretion."

"Your Honor," Brackman said, "if this were a case before a jury . . ."

"It is not a jury case," McIntyre said, "but even if it were, Mr. Brackman, the Court could in its discretion permit additional testimony."

"I'm sorry, your Honor, I was not aware of that."

"I would like to remind Mr. Willow, however, that such additional testimony cannot be allowed for light reasons, such as to let in cumulative or immaterial evidence."

"Your Honor," Willow said, "I believe this testimony to be exceedingly important, and I know the record would be incomplete without it."

"If your Honor please," Genitori said, "I do not see how in good conscience we can exclude any testimony that may shed light on the matter before us."

"Mr. Brackman?"

"Your Honor, my summation was predicated on what the record already shows. If additional testimony . . ."

"I would have no objection," Willow said, "to Mr. Brackman making a second summation after the new testimony is given."

"Your Honor, I know you can in your discretion—you have just informed me that you can in your discretion reopen the case, but . . ."

"Don't you feel the record should be complete, Mr. Brackman?"

"Indeed, I do, your Honor. But I also feel Mr. Willow should have called all his witnesses when it was time for him to do so, and not—"

"Your Honor, this was unforeseen, and as much a surprise to me as it was to the Court."

"Well," McIntyre said flatly, "I will reopen the case."

"Thank you, your Honor."

"Let the record so indicate. Mr. Brackman, I will allow you to make a new summation later if you so desire."

"Thank you," Brackman said.

"Call your witness, Mr. Willow."

"Edna Belle Driscoll," Willow said.

"Edna Belle Driscoll, please take the stand," the clerk said.

Ebie rose hesitantly, and looked inquiringly at Willow, who nodded. She put her bag down on the bench in the jury box, looked plaintively at her husband, and then walked to where the clerk was waiting with the Bible.

"Edna Belle Driscoll, you do solemnly swear that the testimony you are about to give to the Court in this issue shall be the truth, the whole truth, and nothing but the truth, so help you God?"

"I do," Ebie said.

Her voice was very low. She looked puzzled for a moment as she tried to find the steps leading to the witness stand. When she located them, she moved rapidly to the chair, and then hesitated again before sitting. She looked up at the judge once, and then turned away as Willow approached her.

"Mrs. Driscoll," he said, "are you familiar with the novel *The Paper Dragon?*"

"I am."

"How many times have you read it?"

"Many times. I don't remember the exact number of times."

"Would you say you've read it more than twenty times?"

"Yes."

"From cover to cover?"

"Yes, from cover to cover."

"Then surely you are familiar with the nurse in the book, the woman called Lieutenant Jan Reardon."

"Yes, I'm familiar with her."

"What color hair does Jan Reardon have?"

"Blond."

"Will the record show, your Honor, that Mrs. Driscoll's hair is blond. What color eyes does Jan Reardon have?"

"Blue."

"Will the record show, your Honor, that Mrs. Driscoll's eyes are blue. Where is Jan Reardon from originally, what part of the country?"

"The South."

"Where in the South?"

"Alabama."

"Where are *you* from, Mrs. Driscoll?"

"Alabama."

"Mrs. Driscoll, is Jan Reardon left-handed?"

"Yes."

"Are you left-handed?"

"Yes."

"Does Jan Reardon have a crescent-shaped scar on her thigh?"

"Yes."

"Do you have a similar scar on your thigh?"

"Yes. Yes, I have."

"What was your maiden name?"

"Dearborn."

"Your Honor, may I point out to the Court that the name Reardon with the single exception of the letter *b* contains the exact same letters as are in the name Dearborn, transposed."

"What was that again?" McIntyre said. He picked up a pencil and moved a pad into place before him.

"The name Reardon, your Honor, can be formed by dropping the *b* from Dearborn, and then transposing the letters."

McIntyre wrote silently for a moment, and then studied the pad. "Yes, I see that," he said. "Proceed, Mr. Willow."

"Mrs. Driscoll, can you tell us when and where you first met your husband?"

"At Pratt Institute in 1947."

"Were you a student there at the time?"

"I was."

"How long had you been at the school?"

"A year."

"How long had Mr. Driscoll been there?"

"He had just entered. He was a first-year student."

"And you were an upper classman?"

"Yes, I was in my second year. It was a three-year non-accredited course. The course I was taking."

"So that the relationship between you and your husband, in terms of seniority at least, was similar to the relationship between Lieutenant Alex Cooper and Jan Reardon in the novel *The Paper Dragon?*"

"Yes, it was."

"Was it similar in any other respects?"

"Yes."

"In which respects, Mrs. Driscoll?"

"All of them. Everything."

"Would you explain, please?"

"It was our story."

"Whose story, Mrs. Driscoll?"

"Ours. Dris and me."

"Dris?"

"Yes, my husband."

"Is that what you normally call him?"

"It is what I've always called him."

"What does the nurse call Cooper in *The Paper Dragon?*"

"Coop."

"Your Honor," Brackman said, "I have remained silent until now because I wanted to see where Mr. Willow was heading. It seems to me now that he is introducing Mrs. Driscoll's testimony as that of an expert on the novel *The Paper Dragon,* and I must object to this."

"Your Honor," Willow said, "I am introducing her testimony as that of an expert on what actually happened between her and her husband beginning in the year 1947 and ending in October of 1950. I don't think, your Honor, that I'm going to have to elicit too many responses in order to show what *The Paper Dragon* was all about."

"Overruled. Go on, Mr. Willow."

"If I understand you correctly, Mrs. Driscoll, you are saying that the events in *The Paper Dragon* parallel certain *real* events, is that correct?"

"Yes."

"Can you give us any examples of this?"

"Well . . . for . . . for example when Dris and I first met, we had a fight, not a fight, a sort of an argument. He asked me out and I . . . I thought he was just a fresh kid, he was younger than I, you know, and a first-year student, so I tried to discourage him, but he kept insisting, said he was going to be a famous artist one day, all that sort of thing. And the . . . the same thing happens in the book. When the lieutenant first gets to Korea, he's sort of a . . . a brash person and he tries to get friendly with this nurse, who just refuses his advances. They have this terrible argument, and he tells her she'll be sorry because he's going to be a war hero with the Medal of Honor, you know, he goes on about how he's going to win the Korean war singlehanded, but she still refuses. Then . . . she's sent to Tokyo for a week's leave, and he tries to find her, but he can't until a senior nurse in the book—"

"What's her name?"

"The nurse's? Major Astor. Catharine Astor."

"Is she based on any real person?"

"Yes."

"Who?"

"An older girl at Pratt. Her name was Cathy Ascot, and she told Dris where he could find me. You see, I was sick in bed for a week or so after we met, and Dris didn't know where I lived or anything."

"And in the book?"

"In the book, Coop can't find her because she's in Japan, of course, on leave, and he makes contact with the major who tells him the whole story. Then he gives her a note to pass on to Jan when she gets back. So she's . . . she's instrumental in getting them together, you see. In starting their . . . their romance."

"Is there anything else you can tell us about Cathy Ascot?"

"Yes. She had a broken arm that November. She was always breaking something. She was accident prone."

"Is Major Astor accident prone in the novel?"

"No, but she's always predicting dire happenings and such."

"Are you familiar with the character Peter Colman?"

"I am."

"Is he based on anyone you or your husband knew?"

"He is based on someone we both knew."

"Upon whom is he based?"

"He is based upon a boy who used to live upstairs from us on Myrtle Avenue."

"What was his name?"

"Peter Malcom."

"Your Honor," Willow said, "may I again call the Court's attention to this same device of transposition, where a real name becomes a fictitious name. The letters in both names are almost identical, with the exception of substituting a final *n* for what would have been a final *m*."

"Yes, I see that," McIntyre said. "Please go on."

"Wasn't the fictitious Peter Colman an actor before going into the Army?"

"Yes."

"What was Peter Malcom's profession?"

"He was an actor."

"Now you said that you and your husband lived in the same building with this man . . ."

"Yes. Well, when we got married, Dris moved into my apartment. Peter had always lived upstairs, you see. So Dris knew him, too."

"Was Peter Malcom a homosexual?"

"No, he was not."

"The character Peter Colman in your husband's book is a homosexual. How do you explain this discrepancy?"

"Your Honor," Brackman said, rising, "I don't know what we're doing here, but earlier we allowed Mr. Driscoll to testify concerning the *plaintiff's* intent, and now it seems we are calling upon Mrs. Driscoll to speculate on her *husband's* intent. I don't see how she can possibly explain why or how her husband happened to conceive a character . . ."

"I can tell you *exactly* how," Ebie said.

"Your Honor, I have made an objection," Brackman said.

"Yes, Mr. Brackman. The objection is overruled."

"Mrs. Driscoll?"

"I was going to say . . . I was only going to say that Dris was very jealous of Peter and so he . . . he . . ." Ebie stopped.

"Yes?"

"He first conceived of the character as just a . . . a man, you know, and then later when Mr. Danton suggested the business about the major having been killed, well then it . . . it . . . he decided to make the character less of a man, a homosexual. Because, as I say, he was very jealous of him."

"Does the physical description of Colman in *The Paper Dragon* match the description of Malcom in real life?"

"Exactly."

"In other words, Mrs. Driscoll, is it correct to say that *The Paper Dragon* is based on your husband's courtship of you, and subsequent marriage to you, and his jealousy of a real person you both knew?"

"Yes, and other things as well. His childhood background and the people he knew and thoughts he's had, and expressions he uses, and mannerisms . . . and . . . it's *his* book. It's him."

"Thank you, Mrs. Driscoll."

"Is that all?" Brackman said.

"That's all," Willow said.

Brackman walked slowly toward the witness stand. Ebie was suddenly frightened. Apprehensively, she watched as he moved closer to her, and then turned to look fleetingly at her husband, who was staring straight ahead, looking through the tall windows at the sky beyond.

"Mrs. Driscoll, when did you decide to reveal this information to the Court?" Brackman asked.

"Last night."

"What prompted your decision?"

"I felt that my husband might lose the case unless I spoke up."

"Did you discuss this with Mr. Willow?"

"No."

"You did *not* tell him you wanted to testify?"

"Not until just now. When he asked for the recess."

"I see. Mr. Willow, then, knew nothing of your plans until you surprised us all this morning."

"Yes."

"You did discuss this with your husband, however?"

"Yes."

"What did you say to him?"

"That I would tell."

"Tell what?"

"About . . . the book. Everything."

"And what did he say?"

"He asked me not to."

"Why would he do that?"

"He said the case was closed."

"As indeed it was," Brackman said dryly. "But why would he have objected to you giving testimony that would help him?"

"It was finished in his mind."

"What was finished?"

"The case. It was closed."

"You do feel this testimony will help your husband, don't you?"

"I hope so."

"It certainly won't injure his case, will it?"

"No."

"Then why would he have objected to it?"

"I don't know."

"Perhaps because it makes some of the testimony he gave earlier sound a bit suspect, could that be the reason?"

"Objection, your Honor."

"Sustained."

"Are you aware, Mrs. Driscoll, that your husband earlier

claimed 'Peter' was a phallic reference and that the name 'Colman' was a literary pun on iceman, his mother's iceman, are you aware of that?"

"Yes."

"You were sitting in this courtroom when he gave that testimony, so I'm sure you are aware of it."

"I said I was aware of it."

"Yet your testimony seems in direct contradiction to what your husband swore to. You have just told us that there was a *real* person named Peter Malcom and that your husband based his fictitious character upon this individual."

"Yes."

"Well, Mrs. Driscoll, which of you are we to believe?"

"There *was* a real Peter Malcom. There *is* a real Peter Malcom."

"Then why didn't your husband mention him? Surely the existence of a real man who is so similar to the fictitious character would have been a stronger argument for independent creation than a story about an iceman. You do agree with that, don't you, Mrs. Driscoll?"

"Yes, I do."

"Then why would your husband have—I hesitate to use the word, Mrs. Driscoll, because perjury is a serious charge and a charge that can be prosecuted by the district attorney—why would your husband have *sounded* as though he were trying to, shall I say, *mislead* this Court? Do you think he simply *forgot* about Peter Malcom, the man who lived upstairs?"

"No, but . . ."

"You just testified that he was jealous of him. So how could he have forgotten him?"

"I didn't say he forgot him."

"You *did* say he was jealous of him."

"Yes."

"Why?"

"Because Peter and I were good friends. He was a very troubled person, you see, he was having difficulty getting the kind of acting roles he wanted and . . . we would discuss all this, he would tell me what his ambitions were and . . . and the problems he was having and . . . I would offer encouragement to him . . . I would listen to him."

"So your husband became jealous of him?"

"Yes."

"I see. And that's why he forgot all about him when he was testifying here earlier. Because he was jealous."

"No, he didn't forget all about him. I think it was *both*. I think he really was making a literary pun, in addition to the play on Peter's real name."

"The pun on *The Iceman Cometh*, you mean?"

"Yes."

"The 'Iceman' signifying Death."

"Yes."

"Did Peter Malcom ever try to kill your husband?"

"No."

"Or ever conceive a murder plot against him?"

"No, of course not."

"Yet Peter Colman in the novel does exactly that. In fact, he succeeds in causing the lieutenant's death."

"I know that. I'm quite familiar with the book."

"Since you're so familiar with it, how do you explain it, Mrs. Driscoll?"

"The lieutenant kills *himself*. He sacrifices himself."

"Yes, we all know that. But only because he recognizes Colman's plot."

"Yes."

"But you've just testified that Peter Malcom, the man who is supposedly the source for . . ."

"He *is*."

"Yes, we have your word for that, Mrs. Driscoll, although it does seem to contradict your husband's word on several points. But nonetheless, we *do* have your testimony that this real man Peter Malcom never plotted against your husband's life. Was there ever any trouble between them?"

"Trouble?"

"Yes. Did he and your husband ever fight, or . . ."

"No."

"Or exchange harsh words?"

"No. Dris didn't like him and . . . he . . . he wouldn't have him in the house."

"Did they speak to each other?"

"I don't know. I don't think so."

"Did *you* speak to him?"

"Peter? Yes, of course."

"I see. Even though your husband disliked him?"

"Yes. Peter was . . . I told you. He was a very troubled person. You can't just turn your back on someone, you can't just let them . . . let them get lost or . . . or hurt. You can't just let people die."

"I see." Brackman sighed, walked back to the plaintiff's table, picked up a pencil there, walked to the witness stand again, pursed his lips, looked down at the pencil in his hand, and very quietly said, "Mrs. Driscoll, was there anything in your husband's past to suggest the 105th Division?"

"No," Ebie answered quickly, and then felt she had answered too quickly because Brackman looked up at her sharply, and then smiled.

"Nothing at all?"

"Nothing."

"None of his courses were numbered a hundred and five, were they? Design 105, or Illustration 105, or whatever your husband was studying?"

"No, the courses weren't numbered that way at Pratt."

"Did your husband ever make any reference to having seen a play called *Catchpole?*"

"Certainly not."

"Or to the division insignia in that play?"

"No."

"An insignia with the number 105 in yellow on a black field?"

"No."

"No reference to a hundred and five?"

"No."

"Then where did it come from, Mrs. Driscoll? Was it perhaps the apartment number on Peter Malcom's door?"

"No, he lived in apartment 47."

"Was it *your* apartment number?"

"No."

"Was it your husband's APO number perhaps? When he was overseas?"

"No, it was none of those things."

"Well now, I was really hoping, Mrs. Driscoll, that you could clear up the mystery for us, since you seem to have cleared up so many of the other troubling points. It seems, however, that the thief's fingerprints are still very much in—"

"Don't say that," Ebie warned.

"I beg your pardon, Mrs. Driscoll. But since the theft of another man's work is the matter before this—"

"My husband didn't steal anyone else's work!"

"Then perhaps he may have mentioned to you how he hit upon that number, Mrs. Driscoll, if not by seeing it on the stage?"

"He did not see the play."

"How do you know?"

"He told me."

"Where *did* he get the number, then?"

Ebie hesitated.

"Do you *know,* Mrs. Driscoll?"

"Yes, I know," she whispered.

"What?" the clerk asked. "I'm sorry, I . . ."

"She said, 'Yes, I know,' " Brackman said.

"What?" the clerk said again.

"Yes, she *knows,*" McIntyre said.

"If you indeed know, Mrs. Driscoll," Brackman said wearily, "will you tell us?"

"Yes."

"Please."

"Yes," she repeated, and looked at Driscoll. He was still staring directly ahead of him. "The . . . the number isn't a . . . it isn't a hundred and five."

"Oh? What is it then?"

"Its . . . it's two numbers. It's a ten and . . . and a five."

"I see. It's a ten and a five," Brackman said, and smiled up at the judge. "But not a hundred and five."

"No."

"Mrs. Driscoll, perhaps you'd like to tell us the difference between a ten and a five in sequence, and the number a hundred and five."

"Yes."

"Please."

"The ten and the five are a date."

"What?" Brackman said.

"A date. It's ten slant five."

"I'm not sure I understand you, Mrs. Driscoll," McIntyre said. "By 'ten slant five,' do you mean 'ten *virgule* five?' "

"I don't know what 'virgule' means," Ebie said.

"Well . . ." McIntyre said, and rapidly scribbled onto the pad in front of him. "Is this it?" he asked, and held up the pad for her to see:

$$10/5$$

"Yes," Ebie said, "that's it. October 5th."

"October 5th," Brackman said musingly. "Of any particular year, Mrs. Driscoll, or just any year picked at random?"

"1950," Ebie said. She kept watching her husband, but he would not turn to meet her glance.

"October of 1950, I see," Brackman said. "October 5th in the year 1950. And what does that date commemorate? An anniversary, perhaps? Were you married on October 5th?"

"No."

"Did your husband go into the service on October 5th?"

"No."

"Was it your birthday?"

"No."

"Or *his?*"

"No."

"Or Peter's?"

"No."

"Or *anyone's?*"

"No."

"Then *what* was it, Mrs. Driscoll? Why did your husband attach such importance to this number, which you are now telling us is a date, ten virgule five, and not *really* a hundred and five? Perhaps you can tell us."

"October 5th was the date on a . . . a letter."

"What letter?"

"A letter I . . . a letter I wrote to my husband in Korea."

"I see."

"Yes," she said.

"Did you write your husband many letters while he was in Korea?"

"Yes."

"But he took the date from this one letter, is that it?"

"October 5th."

"Yes, that's quite clear. Did you also write to him on October 2nd, perhaps, or October 4th . . ."

"Every day."

"But this particular letter was the one he . . ."

"You . . . you asked if it was an anniversary."

"What?"

"Yes."

"What?"

"It was."

"Oh, it *was* an anniversary, I see. You remember now that it—"

"It was the anniversary of the . . . the death of our marriage," Ebie said, "the death he wrote about in his novel. He . . . he labeled his division the 105th as . . . as another one of his little jokes, a reminder that I had written my letter on the . . . the 5th of October . . . the letter that . . . that told what . . . what . . ."

"I think you have answered the question," Brackman said. He seemed suddenly alarmed. He turned from her swiftly and said, "Your Honor, I have no further—"

"I would like to hear the witness," McIntyre said.

"Your Honor . . ."

"You interrupted the witness before she had concluded her answer, and I would like to hear the rest of that answer now," McIntyre said. "Go on, Mrs. Driscoll."

"Yes," she said and nodded, but remained silent. She kept watching Driscoll, who would not turn to meet her gaze. The courtroom was silent.

"Mrs. Driscoll?"

"I wrote the letter because I loved him," she said. "I wrote it to explain."

She fell silent again. Driscoll did not look at her.

"I wrote and asked him to understand that I was . . . that I was telling him only because I loved him and . . . didn't want a lie between us for the rest of our lives. I asked him to understand."

Her hands were working nervously in her lap now, where only McIntyre could see them. She kept staring intently at her husband, but still he would not look at her. She shook her head as though sorry she had come this far, and then gave a small weary shrug, as though knowing she was committed and would have to go further. Her eyes were suddenly wet. She closed them immediately, and then lowered her head so that the judge would not see her tears. She did not raise her head again until she began speaking once more, and then she did so only to look at her husband. She cried soundlessly while she talked. The tears streamed down her face, but she did not wipe at them. She talked quietly and steadily, and she did not take her eyes from her husband, who never looked at her once during her long unbroken speech.

"I wrote to him because I had to tell him. We had been married that April, you see, and this was only September, the end of September. The truth was terrible, I know that now, I knew it then, I *knew* it was terrible but . . . in his book he described it as a plot to murder him, a theft of his life, his manhood, and it was never any of those things, never anything planned or schemed, only something that . . . one night . . . happened. He might have been able to understand, Dris might have, if only . . . but we had said 'forever' just that April, you see, and then he was gone in June, and this was . . . So how *could* it seem any less awful than it was, how *could* he believe I hadn't wanted it or expected it? I don't know, I don't know. We . . . were, I was upstairs in his apartment, I shouldn't have been there, I know it, I shouldn't have gone up when he asked me to. But I was lonely, Dris was gone, and he seemed so troubled, so in need. We talked, we . . . no, nothing explains it, nothing *can* explain it. It happened. Maybe I wanted it to happen, maybe Dris was right about that, I don't know. But it happened. I was twenty-two years old, and my husband was fighting a war in Korea, and I . . . I went to bed with Peter Malcom.

"I didn't love him, but I went to bed with him. So simple. So very simple. At first I thought I could live with the idea, forget what I'd done, forget I'd given myself to him. I'd always believed, you see, I'd been taught to believe it wasn't shameful to . . . to love someone. But this wasn't love, no. I couldn't deceive myself into thinking this was anything like love, the only man I ever loved was in Korea. I . . . I continued to write to him, I had to keep writing, my letters to him were the same for almost a week, lie after lie after lie, and then . . . then I couldn't bear it any longer, I knew I had to tell him the truth or allow the lies to destroy our marriage. Instead it was the truth that destroyed it.

"So . . . so you see the ten and the five are the date on that letter, October 5th was when I wrote it, and the man in my husband's book is Peter Malcolm who . . . who made love to me . . . and . . . and . . . and I . . . the nurse in the book is only me, and the . . . the lieutenant is my husband, who . . . who testified in this courtroom yesterday that their love and their future are lost because of a single thoughtless act—isn't that what he said here yesterday?—their love is ruined because of a deception that . . . that causes a man to get killed. That's . . . I don't think that's Mr. Constantine's play. I don't think even Mr. Constantine can believe that's his play. My husband's book, you see, is about . . . about *us,* you see. That's what his book is about. And . . . I . . . I don't think I have anything else to say."

The courtroom was silent.

"Mr. Brackman, do you have any further questions?"

"No questions, your Honor," Brackman said.

Again, there was silence.

"Very well, thank you, Mrs. Driscoll."

Ebie rose, and wiped at her eyes. She looked down when she approached the steps, and then swiftly walked to the jury box. Her husband did not turn toward her as she sat.

"Mr. Brackman," McIntyre said, "I'll allow you to change or add to your summation now if you wish. Or, if you feel you need time for preparation in light of this additional testimony, we can set a date and hear your final argument then."

"I have nothing to add to what I have already said, your Honor."

"Very well. Does *anyone* have anything further to say?"

"If your Honor please," Willow said, "my opponent has suggested that Mr. Driscoll was attempting to mislead this Court. I have no comment to make on that except that I hope in the light of this subsequent testimony, you will take into consideration the personal elements involved. Thank you, your Honor."

"Anything else, gentlemen?" McIntyre asked. "Very well. I'd like to congratulate you on a good trial and argument. I want you to know that despite whatever moments of levity there were during the trial and in some of our discussions, I nonetheless consider this a most serious matter, and not only because of the large sums of money involved. So it's my intention now to reserve decision on the motions and on the entire case until such time as I can render the opinion a case of such gravity warrants. Thank you, gentlemen. I enjoyed it."

The judge rose.

Everyone in the courtroom rose when he did, and then watched in silence as he came from behind the bench. He walked to the door on his right, nodded briefly as it was opened for him, and then went into his chambers.

The door closed gently behind him.

The courtroom was silent.

There was—Arthur and Driscoll felt it simultaneously and with the same intensity—a sense of incompleteness. They both knew, and had known all along, that there would be no decision on the day the trial ended, and perhaps not for weeks afterward. But whereas this sense of an ending delayed, a final result postponed, was something both men had experienced before and knew intimately, they could not accept it *here*, not in the context of an apparatus as structured and as well ordered as the law. They sat in pained silence as though willing the judge to reappear, refusing to accept the knowledge that there would be no decision this day, there would be no victor and no vanquished. Instead, there would be only the same interminable wait that accompanied the production of a play or the publication of a book, the same frustrating delay between completion and inalterable exposure.

The judge did not return.

The door to his chambers remained sealed.

The writers stared at the closed door, each slowly yielding to a rising sense of doubt. No matter *what* Driscoll's wife had been induced to say, Arthur still knew without question that his play had been stolen; and Driscoll knew with equal certainty that he had not stolen it. But what were their respective opinions worth without the corroborating opinion of the judge? In spiraling anxiety, Arthur realized that if the judge decreed his play had not been copied, then the time and energy put into it had been lost, the play was valueless, the play was nothing. And Driscoll similarly realized that if the judge decided against *him*, then whatever he had said in his novel would mean nothing, he would be stripped of ownership, the book might just as well never have been written.

They each knew despair in that moment, a despair that seemed more real to them than anything they had felt during the course of the trial. In near panic, they wondered what they had left unsaid, what they had forgotten to declare, how they could prove to this impartial judge that there was merit to their work, that they were honest men who had honestly delivered, that they could not be summarily dismissed, nor obliterated by decree.

And then despair led inexorably to reason, and they recognized with sudden clarity that the judge's decision would really change nothing. The truth was there in the record to be appreciated or ignored, but it was there nonetheless, and no one's opinion could ever change it. If there was any satisfaction for them that day, it came with the relief this knowledge brought, a relief that was terribly short-lived because it was followed by the cold understanding that even the trial itself had changed nothing. Whatever paper dragons they had fought in this courtroom, the real dragons still waited for them in the street outside, snarling and clawing and spitting fire, fangs sharpened, breath foul, dragons who would devour if they were not ultimately slain.

The two men sat in silence.

Around them, there was not even a semblance of ceremony or ritual consistent with what had gone before. The attorneys were whispering and laughing among themselves, packing their briefcases, the paid mercenaries taking off their armor and putting away their weapons, and hoping to go home to a hot bowl of soup before hiring on again to fight yet another man's battle on yet another day. Genitori shook hands with Willow, and then Kahn shook hands with Willow, and Sheppard shook hands with both attorneys for API, and then Brackman and his partner walked over to where the defense lawyers stood in a shallow circle and offered his hand first to Willow and then to Genitori, and then introduced all the men to his partner, who beamed in the presence of someone as important as Willow, and then each of the men congratulated each other on how well and nobly the case had been fought, and Brackman said something to Willow off the record, and Willow laughed, and then Genitori tòld Brackman how wise he was not to have made a second summation, and Brackman in turn complimented Genitori on how expertly he had handled a conceited ass like Ralph Knowles, and they all agreed Knowles had been a very poor witness indeed.

Arthur and Driscoll, apart, watched and said nothing.

Briefcases packed, amenities exchanged, the lawyers again shook hands to show there were no hard feelings between any of them, to assure themselves once again that whatever vile accusations had been hurled in calculated anger within these four walls, they could still express an appreciation of courage and skill, they could still part in the hope that one day they might meet again as battle veterans to reminisce about that terrible week in December when they were fighting a ferocious plagiarism case. And then, because their clients were waiting for the reassuring words that would tide them over through the weeks or perhaps months before the decision came, they moved away from each other cordially and filed out of the courtroom, forming again into two tight, separate groups in the corridor outside, where they talked in low whispers.

They talked only about the trial.

It was easiest to talk about the trial because, for the most part, it had been orderly and serene, moving within the confines of a described pattern toward a conclusion, however delayed. They talked about the trial, and seemed reluctant to leave the corridor, letting several elevators pass them by while they continued to chat, unwilling to make the decisive move that would take them into the next car and then to the street below. Jonah told Genitori and Sheppard that he was positive they had won, positive, and his eyes were glowing even when he sincerely apologized to Driscoll for ever having thought he was guilty. Is that all you have to apologize for? Driscoll asked, and for a moment the corridor went silent, for a moment a pall was cast upon the abounding good fellowship, but only for a moment, only until Jonah grinned and clapped Driscoll on the shoulder and said, Come on, Jimmy, it's all over now, we can all relax. Sheppard grinned too, and chastised himself for having been so stupid, he should have known all along that Mrs. Driscoll was the girl in the book.

He saw the pained expression that crossed Driscoll's face, and fell silent. Genitori swiftly said he too was confident they had won, and then speculated aloud on how much the judge would award them for counsel fees.

Near one of the other elevators, Sidney told Arthur that Mrs. Driscoll's testimony had sounded very phony to him, and probably would not affect the trial in the slightest, the case was still airtight, he was certain the judge would decide in their favor. Arthur nodded, seemingly preoccupied, and when Sidney's partner commented on the fact that he didn't seem terribly elated, Arthur said, Well, I've got my new play to think about, you know. Sidney's partner nodded and said, Of course, of course, and then suddenly remembered he had not called his wife to tell her how the trial had ended. He asked Sidney if he had a dime and while Sidney was fishing in his pocket for one, he said, Isn't there someone you have to call, Sidney? Sidney was silent until he located the coin. Then he handed it to his partner and, with a secret smile, said, Why, no, Carl, there's no one I have to call.

And then all the talking was done, there seemed to be nothing more to say to each other. The afterglow of the trial could no longer warm them, no longer generate a sustaining energy among people who were essentially strangers to each other. They shook hands again, and—still reluctant to get into the elevator that would take them down to the street— broke into smaller groups, lingering in the hallway, Genitori saying he wanted to talk to the clerk before he left, clerks were always infallible indicators of how a trial had gone, and Jonah saying he wanted to go to the men's room, and Sidney telling Arthur to run along, he knew how busy Arthur must be, he would wait for Carl to finish his call. The groups dispersed soundlessly, Driscoll and his wife avoiding Arthur, who took a separate elevator down.

The corridor was empty.

When Genitori came out of the courtroom he told Kahn that the clerk thought McIntyre would find in their favor. Kahn seemed extremely pleased. He confided to Genitori that he had known the plaintiff's case was groundless all along, but that he never ceased to marvel at how the American system worked, a man being able to have his day in court, and to settle his problems there.

God bless America, Genitori said.

16

HE SPENT the afternoon alone.

He was in excellent spirits, walking along Fifth Avenue for a while, his coat open, his muffler loose around his throat, simply walking, and watching everyone, and enjoying himself. Then he sat on one of the benches in Rockefeller Plaza, still watching the people who went by, comparing all the pretty girls to Chickie and deciding, as he had a hundred times before, that he was the luckiest man in the world. He watched the skaters for ten minutes or so, and then crossed over to Saks to listen to the Salvation Army band outside the store, all the while feeling a sense of impending joy, as though his present good mood were only the prelude to something inconceivably better.

He attributed part of his mood to the fact that Christmas was almost here. As a Jew, he had never fully appreciated the religious aspects of the holiday, but he could not deny the excitment that swept over New York at this time each year, nor could he attribute it entirely to the increased activity in the business community, as his father did. Well, his father attributed everything to either good business or bad business, his father was an old *pisher,* and that was all that could be said for him. So he listened to the tinkling of the bells everywhere around him, and the voices singing, and the trumpets and tubas, and the high-heeled rushing click along the sidewalks, and he savored the bite in the air, and knew it was the joyous holiday spirit that accounted for some of his own happiness.

Another part of his happiness, though, had to do with the fact that the trial was over. There was pure relief attached to the completion of any trial, but expecially this one where his opponent had been someone like Jonah Willow; he had to hand it to the bastard, he certainly knew his stuff. As he walked, Sidney still wondered whether Mrs. Driscoll's testimony had really been a surprise. He couldn't believe it hadn't all been carefully planned beforehand by Willow, but my God, what a chance to take, suppose McIntyre had refused to reopen the case? Well, it was finished now, there was nothing to do now but wait for McIntyre's decision which would be God knew when, especially with Christmas just around the corner, and then New Year's, they'd be lucky if they heard before March. In the meantime, he didn't have to worry about preparations, and he didn't have to worry about catching every word Willow said lest he miss an important point that could later trip him up, he didn't have to worry about anything but one thing, and that wasn't bothering him at all. That, in fact, was what accounted for the major part of his joy on this fine December afternoon.

He had put off calling Chickie because he wanted to give her time enough to make her decision, but he knew now, he sensed intuitively that she would marry him. He could not have said how he knew, just a feeling, just a tiny little something inside that told him nothing could go wrong today, everything was being done for the benefit of Sidney Brackman. The beautiful weather, the music in the streets, the city all dressed up in her holiday clothes, this was all for Sidney Brackman who had handled himself pretty well throughout the course of a grueling trial, even if he had to say so himself, right, Sidney? Right, he thought, and looked at his watch, and smiled.

It was close to five o'clock, which meant Chickie would be leaving the office soon, and which meant he should start uptown. He wanted to catch her shortly after she got home, wanted to ask her for her decision, certain he knew what the decision would be—after all, if a girl *isn't* going to marry you, she doesn't say she'll think it over, does she? She just says No, I'm sorry, go peddle your papers. He would kiss her. Very gently. No sex, just a gentle kiss, and he would say Well, darling, now that it's all settled, put on your coat, sweetheart, and we'll stroll right over to Tiffany's and pick out a diamond for you, I'm sure they're open late every night of this wonderful holiday season. And then he would take her to dinner in one of the best restaurants in New York, he'd pick a real fancy one, something very nice and suitable to the occasion, and they would drink champagne and talk quietly about their future plans.

The lights were on in her apartment when he reached the building. He glanced up, smiled, and then went into the foyer and rang the doorbell. Chickie answered his ring immediately, he *knew* it, nothing could go wrong today, everything was perfect and fine and right. He was beginning to think he might even win his cockamamie case, *despite* Mrs. Driscoll's sob story, McIntyre would certainly see through a bleeding heart gambit like that one. He climbed the stairs rapidly, his step light, feeling very young, feeling the way he had in Boston with Rebecca Strauss, wanting to sing, sliding his hand along the banister, tipping his head jauntily, actually humming a little tune inside his head, if you knew Susie, like I know Susie, oh, oh . . .

He knocked on her door.

"Ruth?" she said.

"No," he said. He smiled. "It's me. Sidney."

"Oh. Just a minute, Sidney."

She opened the door immediately. She was wearing black slacks and a black sweater. The sleeves of the sweater were pushed up to her elbows. Her hair was pulled to the back of her neck, tied there with a green ribbon. She was wearing no makeup. She looked beautiful, but she did not look as if she had just got home from the office.

"Come in, Sidney," she said.

There was a curious disorder to the apartment, shoe boxes dumped on the living room floor, pieces of tissue paper trailing through the foyer, jackets and dresses draped over chairs and on the sofa, skirts hanging from doorknobs, blouses laid out in rows on table tops, bras and panties piled in stacks everywhere.

"Some mess, huh?" Chickie said, and smiled.

"Yes," Sidney said, amused. "What are you doing, cleaning out your closets?"

Chickie pecked him on the cheek and said, "Would you like a drink, Sidney?"

"All right," he said. "Where does a man sit in all this . . . this . . ." He gestured helplessly with his open hands, still amused, and feeling that he looked boyish and cute, putting a slightly exaggerated puzzled look on his face and hoping she would kiss him again.

"What can I get you?" she said. "I'm all out of bourbon, but I've got scotch and rye. Choose your poison."

"Well, you certainly sound cheerful," he said, smiling.

"Oh, I *am* very cheerful," she said.

"In that case, I think I'll have one of each, how's that?" he said.

"All right, Mr. Brackman, one of each it is. You asked for it."

"I asked for it, right," Sidney said, and laughed, and watched her as she walked to the bar. "Well, the trial's over," he said, and impulsively clapped his hands together.

"Did you win?"

"Who knows, who cares?" Sidney said. "It's over, and the hell with it."

"That's a good attitude," Chickie said. She was busy at the bar, her back to him.

"Have you made up your mind yet?" he asked, smiling. He knew for certain that her happiness, her cheerfulness, her busy puttering little female motions at the bar were all due to the fact that she had decided to marry him. So he smiled as he asked his question, asked it a trifle coyly and in the same boyish manner he had used when opening his hands wide at the mess in the room, even though she couldn't see him.

"Made up my mind about what?" Chickie said.

"You know," he said, still coyly, still confidently, feeling more and more confident all the time. He took off his hat and sat down on the arm of the big easy chair, avoiding her stacked underwear spread on the chair's seat, certain that Chickie was playing her usual teasing game with him, the game they always played together, and loving her for it. She turned from the bar, carrying a small tray just below her breasts, smiling as she came across the room to him. She offered the tray. There were two glasses on it.

"Scotch and rye," she said, and smiled, and curtsied.

"Thank you, miss," he said, "I think I'll try the scotch first." He lifted the glass and sniffed it. "Ahhh, excellent," he said, and drank. "And now the rye."

"You're going to get sick, Sidney," she warned.

"No, no, this is nothing for an old sailor, nothing at all." He sniffed at the second glass. "Is this any good?" he asked. "How's your rye, miss?"

"How's *your* eye?" Chickie said, and burst out laughing.

"You still haven't answered my question," he said.

"My eye is fine, thank you. Hey, get your hand off there, you fresh thing."

"Oh, excuse me, m'dear," he said, using a W. C. Fields voice, "excuse me, m'little chickadee, wandering hands, bad failing, here we are, let me taste this fine rye whiskey of yours."

He swallowed the second shot, feeling the whiskey burning all the way down to his stomach. "About my question," he said.

"What question?"

"You know."

"Oh," she said. "Yes."

"And, m'dear?"

"Sidney," she said, "I've decided to take a trip to Europe."

"Oh, really?" he said, smiling. "Well, now *that's* an interesting development, m'little chickadee, that's truly a very interesting . . ."

"Really, Sidney," she said.

"What?"

"*Really,*" she said, and she stressed the word so strongly that he knew all at once she was serious. The smiled dropped from his face.

"Wh . . . what do you mean?" he said.

"I'm going to Europe, Sidney. Ruth and I are going to Europe."

"What did you say?"

"I said we're going to Europe. Ruth and I."

"What?"

"*Yes,* Sidney."

"Europe?"

"*Yes,* Sidney. Italy and Greece. We're leaving for Rome tomorrow morning, the nine forty-five A.M. flight."

"You're . . . you're joking," he said, knowing she was not, and not at all surprised when she did not answer. "Chickie?"

"Yes?"

"You're joking," he said again.

"No."

"But . . . I thought . . ."

"What did you think, Sidney?"

"That . . . that . . . I don't know."

"You poor dear man," she said, "I'm going to Europe."

"Ch-Ch-Chickie?"

"I'm going to Europe, Sidney."

"But . . ."

"I'm going, Sidney. Really."

"You d-d-didn't tell me."

"I wasn't sure. I had to decide. Now I've decided."

"Wh-wh-what about me?" he asked. "What about me?"

"You poor dear man," she said. "Sidney, I must rush you out now, because you see I've got a million things to do before tomorrow morning."

She caught both his hands in her own, and pulled him gently off the arm of the chair.

"Now put on your hat like a dear man," she said, "and let me get all this packing done. I hate to pack. Don't you hate to pack, Sidney?" She had led him to the door, she was reaching for the doorknob, she was twisting the knob, she was opening the door.

"Chickie, *wait!*" he said sharply.

"Yes, Sidney?"

"I have to . . . Chickie, it's . . . it's im . . . p-p-p-por-tant to me to . . . Chickie, you've *got* to . . ."

"Sidney, dear," she said, opening the door wide, "what can I say? It's all arranged. Really, Sidney, I'm terribly sorry, but it's all arranged."

"Chickie, I love you," he said.

"Yes."

"I love you."

"Yes, Sidney." She stood silently just inside the open door. "Goodbye, Sidney," she said, easing him into the hallway.

"Chickie . . . what about me?" he asked. "What about me?"

"I hope you win your case," she said, and blew a kiss at him.

The door closed. He heard the lock turning, the tumblers falling.

"What about me?" he said again.

Behind the door, he heard her giggle.

It was 6:10 when Jonah got to Pennsylvania Station.

He did not expect the terminal to be so crowded because by all reasonable standards *next* Friday was to be the start of the Christmas weekend. But he had not counted on the scheduling vagaries of colleges and prep schools; the station was thronged with milling students and excited, waiting parents. There seemed to be an overabundance of servicemen as well, sailors carrying seabags, soldiers lugging duffles, everyone hurrying and intent, worlds colliding, separating, touching, dispersing, touching again, everyone in frantic, busy motion. He asked the man behind the information counter what track the train from Trenton would be on, and was told the train had been in for fifteen minutes already. Shouldering his way through the crowd, he hurried toward the gate.

She was waiting at the entrance.

She was wearing a plaid skirt and a black ski parka. A kookie leather Ringo hat rested lopsidedly on her dark head. She stood with her legs slightly spread, the Dunseath posture, but there was a spring-tight tension in her body, and her eyes flashed searchingly at each passing face. A small suitcase rested near her feet. She was wearing black boots her mother had bought for her at Bendel. He walked up to her swiftly, and she turned to him immediately and mouthed the word "Daddy" soundlessly, and threw herself into his arms. He held her close to him, and closed his eyes, and kissed her cheek and said, "Hello, darling," and she said, "Oh, Daddy, how good to see you," and threw her arms around him again, and kissed him again, and hugged him to her and said, "Do you like my hat?"

"It's lovely," he said, "where'd you get it?"

"It's my roommate's, Yolanda's, did I tell you about Yolanda?"

"I think so. Is this all you have?" he asked, picking up her bag.

"I always travel light," she said, and wiggled her eyebrows, and then laughed, her mother's laugh, her grandmother's laugh, head thrown back, blue eyes flashing. He took her hand in his own, and they hurried through the station. He was tremendously proud of her, aware of her trim good looks, pleased when young college boys turned to look at her, their eyes traveling down over her youthful backside and to her legs. She walked with her mother's loping gait, hips thrust forward, wearing her nutty hat with all the authority of a *Vogue* model, talking to him animatedly as they came out onto Eighth Avenue and tried to find a taxi.

". . . boy had a guitar, he got on at Philadelphia, and we just sang songs and were drinking . . ."

"Drinking? What do you mean?"

"Oh, just a little beer, Daddy, one of the senior boys had a six-pack."

"Honey, you're a little young, don't you think, to be . . ."

"Daddy, he was a senior boy, he must have been seventeen at least."

"I know, honey, but you're only twelve."

"I'll be thirteen in May."

"I know, but still . . ."

"Anyway, I only had a sip. What we did mostly was sing. It was such fun, Daddy, and we got here so *faaaast,* it seemed like no time at all. Have you ever seen such crowds, did you call Mother?"

"Yes, I called her. She's expecting you."

"I know, I spoke to her last night."

"Good."

"Are you going to come up?"

"I don't think so, Amy."

"All right," she said.

In the taxi, she said, "What are you working on now, Daddy?"

"We just concluded a trial today," he said.

"Something good?"

"A plagiarism case."

"Did you win?"

"I think so. We won't know for a while."

"How can you bear waiting?" she said.

"Well, there are always other things coming up. In fact, when I got back to the office today, there was a new case already waiting."

"What kind of a case?"

"An exciting one, I think. A man's been charged with income tax evasion, but he claims he's not *evading* anything, he's simply refusing to pay. He says he will not give money to support an undeclared war, and that unless Congress is allowed to decide whether we should or should not be at war, why then he's being deprived of representation. And without representation . . ."

"No taxation," Amy said, and nodded. "But doesn't *every-one* have to pay income tax?"

"Certainly, honey."

"Then he's guilty. I mean, if he won't pay . . ."

"Well, there are principles involved," Jonah said.

"Will you take the case?"

"I think so. Yes, I think so, honey." He clasped her hand and squeezed it.

"Oh my God, I almost forgot!" Amy said, pulling her hand away and reaching for her suitcase. She unclasped it quickly, burrowed beneath a sweater and a blouse and produced a small slim package wrapped in red and green paper, tied with a bright green bow. He remembered in that instant that he had not yet bought her the ring.

"I got this in New Hope," she said. "Merry Christmas, Daddy."

"Christmas isn't until next week, honey," he said.

"I know, but I wish you'd open it now."

"Shouldn't I wait?"

"Open it, Daddy. Please."

He nodded. Carefully, he slid the bow off the package, and then unwrapped it. It was an address book, black leather, his initials in gold on the cover, J.W.

"It's beautiful," he said.

"Do you like it?"

"Yes, very much."

He knew he should have had the ring to give to her now, knew that this was a very private and personal moment to Amy, this offering of her gift in a taxi speeding to her mother's apartment. He had nothing to offer her in return. He had forgotten to buy the ring, and so he sat and stared at the leather address book with his initials on the cover, J.W., and wondered what he could say, wondered how he could begin to make her understand that he had really intended to have a present for her, to meet her with it at the station, but instead had become involved the moment he got back to the office. Surely she would understand. Surely she would realize that Christmas was still more than a week away, there was still time, wasn't there? Wasn't there still time?

"There's something nice I plan on getting you," he said, and patted her hand.

"Oh, sure, it can wait," Amy said.

"I'll get it to you before Christmas," he said, "don't you worry.

"Oh, sure," Amy said, and was silent. Then, unexpectedly, she shrugged and said, "Christmas is all craparoo, anyway."

He did not call his uncle until eleven o'clock.

He did not know why he was calling, unless it was because he and Ebie were leaving for Vermont in the morning, and Vermont was more distant from Fort Lauderdale than New York City. His uncle's voice was just as he remembered it, gravelly, with a hint of a brogue; he recalled in a rush the living room on West End Avenue, the Chickering piano, his uncle's pink shirts.

"Hello, Uncle Benny," he said, "this is Jimmy."

"Jimmy? Jimbo? Where are you, Jimbo? Are you in Florida?"

"No, no, I'm in New York."

"Hey, Vera, it's my nephew," Uncle Benny shouted. "Hey, how are you, Jimbo?"

"I'm fine, Uncle Benny."

"Good, good. *Vera*," he shouted, "it's my *nephew!*" To Driscoll, he said, "She's upstairs in bed, Jimbo, hasn't been feeling too well."

"Oh, I'm sorry to hear that."

"Well, it's nothing serious, just a little cold."

"A little cold is what we have in Fort Knox," Driscoll said, and smiled.

"No, that's a little gold," Uncle Benny answered. "What you're thinking of, lad, is a tiny creature in a monster movie."

"No, that's a little ghoul," Driscoll said. "I hate to correct you, Uncle Benny, but I think you mean a small measure of unmitigated nerve."

"Unmitigated nerve?"

"That's right."

"A little *gall!*" Uncle Benny shouted, and burst out laughing. "Ahhh, Jimmy, Jimmy, it's good to hear your voice. How are you, boy? How *are* you?"

"I'm fine."

"And Ebie?"

"Fine. Fine."

"When does the trial start? Is that why you're in New York?"

"Well, yes, but it *ended* today, Uncle Benny."

"It *did?* Did you win?"

"I think so. Yes, I think so."

There was a silence on the line.

"What's the matter, Jimmy?" his uncle asked.

"What do you mean?"

"Why are you calling me at eleven o'clock at night?"

"I just wanted to talk to you, Uncle Benny."

"What about?"

"I just wanted to talk to you."

"Is something wrong?"

"No, no, I just felt I had to talk to someone I . . . someone who . . ."

"Isn't Ebie there?"

"Yes, she's upstairs. In the room. Upstairs."

"I see," Uncle Benny said, and was silent.

Wise old Uncle Benny, he thought, and listened to the crackling silence on the line, the seconds ticking away.

"Uncle Benny," he said at last.

"Yes, Jimmy?"

"I don't know what to do."

"About what?"

"Uncle Benny?"

"Yes?"

"Uncle Benny?"

"Yes, boy, what is it? What is it, Jimbo?"

"Help me."

"How?"

"Help me, Uncle Benny."

"Is it Ebie?"

He nodded, and then realized his uncle could not see him. Very quietly, he said, "Yes, it's Ebie."

"What about her?"

He could not tell him. He sat in the phone booth in the lobby of the hotel, and looked at the receiver clutched tightly in his hand, and could not tell his uncle. The silence lengthened.

"Jimmy?" his uncle said.

"Yes, Uncle Benny."

"Jimmy, whatever it is . . ."

"Yes?"

"Face it. Face it, and it'll vanish."

"Vanish is when you kick somebody out of the kingdom," Driscoll said, and tried a smile.

"No, that's banish," Uncle Benny said automatically, but there was no humor in his voice.

"No, banish are guys who wear masks and go around stealing," Driscoll answered.

"Jim," his uncle said, "don't play games."

"What?" Driscoll said.

"I think you heard me, Jim."

"Yes, but . . ."

"Do you understand me?"

"Uncle Benny, I called because . . ."

"Yes, I know why you called, Jim, now you listen to me, Jim. Where are you?"

"I'm down here. I'm in the lobby. Near the drugstore. Uncle Benny . . ."

"Now you listen to me, Jim, and don't play games, do you hear me? You go right upstairs, do you hear? You go right upstairs and you face whatever it is that's waiting for you there, you face it, Jim, now that's what I'm telling you."

"Yes."

"Do you hear me?"

"Yes."

"All right, that's what you do."

"Yes."

"Good. I've got to go up to Vera now, I think I hear her calling me. Do you understand me, Jim?"

"Yes, Uncle Benny."

"Good. You keep in touch with me."

"Uncle Benny?"

"Yes?"

"Give my regards to Vera."

"I will."

"Uncle Benny?"

"Yes?"

"I . . . I hope she feels better."

"I'm sure she will. Good night, Jim."

"Good night, Uncle Benny."

There was a click on the line.

He stood holding the dead receiver, and then he looked at it in disbelief and slowly replaced it on the hook. Well, that was very helpful, he thought, who the hell called you to play games, Uncle Benny, would you mind telling me? That was really quite helpful, thank you very much, Uncle Benny, I'm certainly glad I called you all the way in Florida to listen to your homespun philosophy. Thank you very much, Uncle Benny, you've certainly set everything right with your words of wisdom, and as a matter of fact I happened to think the banish definition was very good indeed. The phone rang. He lifted the receiver.

"Yes?" he said.

"One moment for additional charges, sir," the operator said.

"Thanks," he said. Additional charges, he thought. That's exactly what I need for a call that I was crazy to make in the first place.

"That'll be thirty-five cents, sir," the operator said.

"Thank you," he said. He dug into his pocket, found a quarter and a dime, and deposited them in the box.

"Thank you, sir," the operator said.

"Sure," he said, and again hung up. He went out of the booth. Tomorrow morning they would leave for Vermont, back to the old hay, alfalfa, and oats, back to the farm he hated, the most insistent crop on which was rocks. What the hell was a city boy doing in Vermont, anyway, how far can you run? Face it, Uncle Benny had said, face it. Thank you, Uncle Benny. Thank you for all the good things if I seem ungrateful now for this singular piece of worthless advice.

She was asleep when he got back to the room, snoring very lightly, his charming wife. He undressed quietly in the dark, and then got under the covers and lay there silently with the green neon Sardi sign illuminating the black windowpane across the room, and Ebie snoring lightly beside him, her body warm, his hand lying close to the curving flank of her naked flesh. She never slept with a stitch on, his sweet Southern flower, never when he first met her and not now either. He wondered if she had slept naked with Peter Malcom, wondered, lightly snoring, and wondered why he did not leave her. Face it. The bed was strange, he did not like hotel rooms. In Vermont, you could hear the mice rattling away the night in the attic. They slept in separate beds in Vermont, twin beds are for Englishmen and other people with severe cramps Uncle Benny had said one night dis*gost*ingly drunk. Face it. He listened to her even breathing, the snoring had stopped now, felt the warmth of her close to him and wondered again why he James Driscoll the Cat did not leave her, sleeping side by side in the Vermont twin beds with the mice racing in the attic, face it, tickytackyticky *tack* their little feet on the ceiling, face it, and then wondered why *she* did not leave him, why Ebie did not leave him.

He touched her shoulder.

She did not stir. He touched her again, more insistently this time. She murmured something in her sleep, and then turned toward him. She sat up. He could not see her face in the darkness.

"Ebie," he whispered.

"What is it?" she said. "What's the matter?"

"Ebie," he said, "do you love me?"

"Yes," she said.

"I'll never understand," he said. "Ebie," he said, "I love you."

"I know."

"I love you very much, Ebie."

"I know."

"But, Ebie, I'll never understand. As long as I live, I will never understand."

"Do you have to?" she asked.

He closed his eyes. "Never understand," he said, "never understand," and was suddenly exhausted. He sighed heavily. As he drifted off into folds of unconsciousness, he thought *Ebie, let's try,* and then was not certain whether he had thought it or said it, and said aloud, certain that he was saying it this time, "Ebie, let's try, Ebie," and sighed again, and said, "I love you, Ebie," and fell into a deep sleep.

He could not seem to get drunk.

He had begun drinking shortly after dinner, sitting in his apartment alone, refusing to answer the telephone because he knew each time it rang that Stuart Selig or Oscar Stern would be on the other end, and he did not know what he wanted to tell them. The bottle of scotch was half empty now, and he still did not know what to do, except sit here alone in his apartment, the way he had been sitting alone in his life from the time he was eighteen and went into the Army, the result of which was *Catchpole.* He could not believe that Driscoll's wife hadn't been coached, could not believe her testimony had not been carefully prepared beforehand, and then sprung by Willow at precisely the right moment, the courtroom magician pulling a rabbit from his tophat, a cuddly Southern bunny with large wet eyes, he could not believe his play had not been stolen.

Well, he thought, it's because I let them do it to me in the first place, I let Freddie and Fielder talk me into making all those changes, I wrecked my own play, and Driscoll stepped in and made a success of it, it's all my own fault when you get right down to it. Which is why I should tell Selig and Stern to go screw, along with Hester Miers and Mitzi Starke, and Walter Kerr thrown in for good measure. Tell them all to go screw, I will not make the changes in my play, I'm going to *win* this damn case and produce the play myself, maybe buy the Helen Hayes, no, not the Helen Hayes, not that jinx Fulton of a theater, I'll buy something nice and cozy and lucky, and maybe I'll buy the *New York Times* as well, how much do you want for your little paper, Mr. Sulzberger?

He was tempted to call Julie in Minnesota, because what they were asking him to do, really, was obliterate his past by obliterating his family, his sister, and by rights she should have something to say about her own demise. He wondered what time it was in Minnesota, and he lifted the telephone receiver from its cradle and when the operator came onto the line, he said, "Operator, I'm thinking of making a long-distance call to Minnesota, can you please tell me what time it is there?"

"Well," the operator said, and hesitated. "Just a moment, sir."

He waited. He owed it to Julie to consult her on her own eradication. Too many things in life got eradicated without consent, what had ever happened to the Sunday feasts at his grandfather's house, who had ever decided *that* issue without a vote?

"Sir?" the operator said.

"Yes?"

"Sir, Minnesota is on Central Standard."

"What does that mean?"

"They're an hour behind us, sir."

"Well, what time is it there?"

"It's almost midnight here, sir, so I would imagine it's almost eleven there."

"I see. Thank you."

"Did you wish to place your call, sir?"

"Well, I don't know yet," he said. "Thank you."

He hung up. Eleven o'clock, he thought. That wasn't

really so late, but Julie probably went to bed early, houseful of kids to get off to school, besides *everybody* probably went to bed early in Minnesota. I really should call her, though, he thought, how can I change her without first getting her permission? They want me to make you a social worker, Julie, he thought, I know you'll get a laugh out of that, it's really pretty comical when you think of it. A social worker who practices the flute in her bedroom next door with the pink curtains on the window and the BEWARE VICIOUS DOG sign tacked crookedly on the white-painted wood, I don't know, Julie.

They told me nothing, Julie.

I thought they'd tell me something in that courtroom.

They told me nothing.

Julie, do you remember once, do you remember when we were walking to the library together one night? and you asked me not to walk quite so fast, my legs aren't as long as *yours,* do you remember that? and I said I'm in a hurry, do you remember? I was in a hurry to get there, Julie, to get where the words were, all the words.

Julie, honey, I never got there.

Julie, they told me nothing, I was hoping they'd tell me something.

Look, we've got to discuss this. Look, what's the sense, we've just got to discuss this.

He reached for the telephone.

What's the sense? he thought.

He waited, his head bent, his hand resting on the telephone. He sighed and lifted the receiver. Rapidly, he dialed. He heard the ringing on the other end, once, twice, and quickly he hung up. He stared at the phone a moment longer, his heart beating wildly, and then he reached for the bottle of scotch and poured himself another drink.

He placed his call at one-thirty A.M. He was very drunk by that time. "Hello!" he shouted into the mouthpiece.

"What? Who's this?"

"Well, I've been sleeping on it," he said.

"What? Who's this?"

"This is Edward Albee. Don't you recognize my voice?"

"Listen, who *is* this?"

"Every writer has a voice, didn't you know that?"

"Arthur?"

"Yes, very good, this is Arthur Miller."

"What is it, Arthur? Are you drunk, Arthur?"

"Why, Stuart, what a thing to say to a man of my talents and respect, what a thing to say. Would you say such a thing to Tenafly New Jersey?"

"I've been trying to get you all day," Stuart said. "Have you decided, Arthur? Is that it?"

"I have decided."

"What have you decided?"

"I have decided to sell out," Arthur said.

"What do you mean?"

"Again," Arthur said.

"I still don't know what you mean."

"I have decided, Stuart, to sell out again. I have decided to sell out because I'm afraid."

"Arthur, that's no attitude to . . ."

"I'm afraid I'll lose the case, Stuart, and I'm afraid if I don't grab Hester then Osborne'll get her, and I'm afraid my sweet little play'll die, Stuart, it'll curl up and die stillborn, never see the light of day, never have a chance to breathe at all. So I'm selling out, I'll do whatever the pants pressers want me to do, make any revisions they want, change little Julie to a whore with a line of sailors waiting outside her bedroom . . ."

"Julie?"

"*Carol*, whatever the hell her name is, who cares?"

"Look, Arthur . . ."

"Tell Mitzi Starke she just bought herself a writer."

"Arthur . . ."

"Tell Hester I'll fit the part to her like a tailored suit from wherever it is fine actresses like Hester Miers buy their tailored suits, tell them they got themselves a tailor, and when I finish the garment they can press it. Tell them."

"Arthur?"

"What?"

"Arthur, are you crying?"

"No," he said.

UNITED STATES DISTRICT COURT
SOUTHERN DISTRICT OF NEW YORK

-- X

ARTHUR NELSON CONSTANTINE,

                              Plaintiff,

                         -against-

JAMES DRISCOLL, MITCHELL-CAMPBELL BOOKS, INC.,
CAMELOT BOOKS, INC., AND ARTISTS-PRODUCERS-
INTERNATIONAL,

                              Defendants.

-- X

BRACKMAN & HARTUNG, of New York, N.Y.
Attorneys for the Plaintiff

SIDNEY BRACKMAN, ESQ., and
CARL HARTUNG, ESQ., of Counsel.

SAMUEL GENITORI, ESQ., and
MICHAEL KAHN, ESQ.,
Attorneys for Defendant Artists-
Producers-International

LORRIMER, WILLOW, LEVINE & MAGUIRE, ESQS.,
of New York, N.Y.
Attorneys for Defendants James Driscoll,
Mitchell-Campbell Books, Inc., and
Camelot Books, Inc.

JONAH WILLOW, ESQ., and
NORMAN SHEPPARD, ESQ., of Counsel

MC INTYRE, FRANK HARLAN

    The plaintiff in this action is Arthur Nelson Constantine, a citizen of New York.[1] He is the author of a play titled "Catchpole," a copy of which was deposited in the Copyright Office in 1947, Certificate of Registration under 17 U.S.C. § 12 issued on August 3, 1947. The play was subsequently produced in New York City and ran for twelve days in October of 1947 at the Fulton Theatre.

    James Driscoll,[2] a citizen of New

---

[1]
Jurisdictional findings such as this relate to time of action.

[2] Plaintiff did not bring suit against Driscoll. Cross claims against Driscoll, however, have been asserted by Mitchell-Campbell and API should plaintiff recover against them. A cross claim has also been asserted by API against Mitchell-Campbell. All cross claims were deferred by order of this Court, pursuant to Rule 42(b) Fed. Rules Civ. Proc., 29 U.S.C., until defendants' liability has been decided.

York, is the author of a novel titled "The
Paper Dragon," published in 1963 by Mitchell-
Campbell Books, Inc., a New York corporation.
The novel was subsequently filmed by Artists-
Producers-International, a Delaware corpor-
ation, and put into general release in 1964.
At that time, a paperback edition of the book
was published by Camelot Books, Inc., a New
York corporation.

It is the plaintiff's claim that the
novel by James Driscoll and the motion picture
written and directed by Ralph Knowles for API
were copied from "Catchpole," thereby depriving
plaintiff of his rights in the copyrighted
composition. An accounting of profits,
damages, injunction, and attorneys' fees[3] are
sought by the plaintiff.

---

[3]Attorneys' fees under 17 U.S.C. § 116 are
sought by defendants inter alia, and consideration was reserved until main issues have
been settled.

I

The defendants contend that the
plaintiff Constantine forfeited both statutory
and common-law copyright by making a "general
distribution" of his play prior to its Broadway opening. Since the plaintiff's case is
based entirely on copyright law and since such
a contention, if valid, would be cause for
dismissal, I will consider it before coming to
the merits.

Constantine has testified[4] that one
hundred and twenty mimeographed copies of his
play were distributed to "producers, agents,
investors, and anyone interested in the
theatre" between January and May of 1947.
Earlier findings of this Court with regard to

---

[4]Tr. p. 78

a similar distribution,[5] where a hundred
copies of an uncopyrighted work were given
"to certain theatrical producers free of
charge in an effort to induce them to produce the work," was that such distribution
"was not a publication within the meaning of
the act." Similarly, in a case[6] where two
thousand copies of an unpublished song "were
distributed to broadcasting stations and
professional musicians for 'plugging' purposes," the Court of Appeals for the District
of Columbia would not hold that there had been
"such general publication as to vitiate
appellant's copyright."

    The defendants have cited
Judge Palmer's holding, and the affirmation

---

[5]Ilvin v. Avon Publications, 144 F. Supp. 368,
373 (S.D.N.Y. 1956)

[6]Hirshon v. United Artists Corp., 243 F. 2d
640 (D.C. Cir. 1957)

of it by the Court of Appeals for this Circuit,[7] that a distribution of one hundred copies, not limited "as to persons or as to purpose"[8] constitutes a forfeitable publication. But there is every indication in this case that Constantine's distribution of the play "Catchpole" was limited and selective. He sent his play only to theatrical people, and for the sole purpose of generating interest in its possible production. Whether the work was copyrighted under 17 U.S.C. § 12, or uncopyrighted, such restricted distribution would work no forfeiture of the plaintiff's rights.

I therefore find against the defendants' argument.

---

[7] Continental Casualty Co. v. Beardsley, 151 F. Supp. 28 (S.D.N.Y. 1957) modified and affirmed 253 F. 2d 702 (2 Cir. 1958) cert. denied, 358 U.S. 816 (1958).

[8] Ibid., 253 F. 2d at 707.

II

Whereas the plaintiff's first cause of action alleges that Driscoll either possessed a copy of the play or saw it in performance, there is no evidence to support either supposition. Driscoll has denied ever seeing a copy of the play or a performance of it before this action began. When the play was produced on Broadway, he was eighteen years old and studying art at Pratt Institute. His ambition was to become a painter, and although he testified that he later studied writing at New York University, one cannot assume that he had in 1947 already decided on a career in letters.

Lacking forceful evidence of access, therefore, the merits of this case must be decided on the strength of the similarities said to exist between the works.

To support his claim of plagiarism
against Driscoll, the plaintiff has prepared
and presented to this Court three charts outlining in detail the specific Plot, Character,
and Language similarities between the play and
the novel. I have studied these charts
closely, and I have read both the play and the
novel many times, always keeping in mind the
alleged similarities. I have also carefully
observed and listened to all of the witnesses
presented by both sides.

In <u>Holmes</u> v. <u>Hurst</u>, 174 U.S. 82, 86
(1899), it was established that "ideas" per se
are not copyrightable, and that "expression"
is the only matter susceptible of protection.
Whereas it is often extremely difficult to
categorize material as either copyrightable
or non-copyrightable, there is nonetheless a
formidable background of law against which to
evaluate the plaintiff's allegation.

- 8 -

I quote Judge Learned Hand:

"...Upon any work, and especially
upon a play, a great number of patterns of
increasing generality will fit equally well,
as more and more of the incident is left out.
The last may perhaps be no more than the most
general statement of what the play is about,
and at times might consist only of its title;
but there is a point in this series of
abstractions where they are no longer protected, since otherwise the playwright could
prevent the use of his 'ideas,' to which,
apart from their expression, his property is
never extended... Nobody has ever been able
to fix that boundary, and nobody ever can...

"...But we do not doubt that two
plays may correspond in plot closely enough
for infringement. How far that correspondence
must go is another matter. Nor need we hold
that the same may not be true as to characters,

quite independently of the 'plot' proper,
though, as far as we know, such a case has
never arisen. If 'Twelfth Night' were copyrighted, it is quite possible that a second
comer might so closely imitate Sir Toby Belch
or Malvolio as to infringe, but it would not
be enough that for one of his characters he
cast a riotous knight who kept wassail to the
discomfort of his household, or a vain and
foppish steward who became amorous of his
mistress. These would be no more than
Shakespeare's 'ideas' in the play, as little
capable of monopoly as Einstein's Doctrine of
Relativity, or Darwin's theory of the Origin
of Species. It follows that the less developed
the characters, the less they can be copyrighted;
that is the penalty an author must bear for
marking them too indistinctly."[9]

---

[9]Nichols v. Universal Pictures Corp., 45 F. 2d
119, 121 (2 Cir.), cert. denied, 282 U.S. 902
(1930)

The Court also remarked:[10]

"A comedy based upon conflicts

between Irish and Jews, into which the marriage

of their children enters, is no more suscep-

tible of copyright than the outline of 'Romeo

and Juliet.'"

Nor have the following plot ideas

been held to be protectible:

The anti-Semitic behavior of German

students during Hitler's regime.[11]

A new bride brought by her husband

to live in the house he once shared with his

first wife.[12]

A murder committed in a theatre while

a performance of a play was being given.[13]

---

[10]Ibid., 45 F. 2d at 122

[11]Rosen v. Loew's, Inc. 162 F.2d 785, 788
(2 Cir. 1947)

[12]MacDonald v. DuMaurier, 75 F. Supp. 655, 660
(S.D.N.Y. 1948)

[13]Rush v. Oursler, 39 F.2d 468 (S.D.N.Y. 1930)

The plaintiff's alleged similarities were studied against this and other pertinent precedent, in order to determine which were copyrightable "expressions" and which were unprotectible "ideas."

III

The plaintiff's second cause of action alleges that API independently copied from the play "Catchpole." The claim of access gains credibility through API's concession that the play was submitted to them in 1947 before it was produced, and again by the plaintiff when he was an employee of the studio. Infringement, however, cannot be found on the basis of access alone.[14] The motion picture rights to "The Paper Dragon" were purchased

---

[14]Arc Music Corp. v. Lee, 296 F. 2d 186 (2 Cir. 1961)

- 12 -

by API in 1963, and the film version of the
novel was written and directed by Ralph Knowles
under employment to the studio. He has testified that he used the novel as his primary
source, expanding upon it or deleting from it
to meet the exigencies of the screen, translating it, in effect, to an entirely different
medium. He has also testified that he did
additional research on his own, such as reading
related articles and books, and visiting various
Army bases to refresh his memory on the language
and behavior of United States soldiers. He
testified that he never read plaintiff's play,
either in its full length or in synopsis, and
that he never saw a performance of it.

     To support the claim against API,
plaintiff has supplied the Court with a fourth
chart purporting to show additional similarities
existing only between the play and the motion
picture. I have closely studied this fourth

- 13 -

chart, in conjunction with all the others,
and I have read the cutting continuity of
the film, and I have seen the motion picture
at a private screening.

IV

Upon reviewing all of the evidence
presented in this case; upon careful study of
the play, the novel, and the motion picture;
upon close observation of the various witnesses
and evaluation of their credibility; upon
reference to findings of fact; it is my judgment that the allegations of plagiarism are
groundless, and that the claimed similarities
are the result of the plaintiff's misled
enthusiasm and diligency, "that obsessive
conviction, so frequent among authors and
composers, that all similarities between their
works and any others which appear later

must inevitably be ascribed to plagiarism."[15]

Concerning the claim against defendants
JAMES DRISCOLL, MITCHELL-CAMPBELL BOOKS, INC. and
CAMELOT BOOKS, INC., it is my finding that:

James Driscoll is the sole author of
"The Paper Dragon."

"The Paper Dragon" was not copied in
whole or in part or in any manner or form from
"Catchpole" and does not infringe on the play.

The theme, plot, and characters of
"The Paper Dragon" are not similar to the theme,
plot, and characters of "Catchpole."

The claimed similarities between the
play and the book are either totally absent,
non-copyrightable, or the result of a natural
and independent development of different works
set against a similar background.

---

[15]Deller v. Samuel Goldwyn, Inc., 150 F. 2d
612, 613 (2 Cir.), cert. denied, 327 U.S.
790 (1945)

<u>I further find that</u>:

The character Alex Cooper in "The Paper Dragon" is based upon James Driscoll.

The character Jan Reardon in "The Paper Dragon" is based upon James Driscoll's wife.

Many other major and minor characters in "The Paper Dragon" are based upon actual individuals James Driscoll has met or known.

The use of the number 105 to designate an Army division in "The Paper Dragon" has as its basis a highly personal event in James Driscoll's life, and was not copied from the plaintiff's play.

<u>Concerning the claim against defendant ARTISTS-PRODUCERS-INTERNATIONAL, it is my finding that</u>:

Neither Ralph Knowles nor API copied

from the plaintiff's play in the preparation,
writing, filming, or editing of the motion
picture "The Paper Dragon."

The motion picture "The Paper Dragon"
does not contain any copyrightable matter that
was present in the plaintiff's play.

The motion picture "The Paper Dragon"
is adapted solely from Driscoll's novel of the
same name.

V

It is therefore my conclusion that
there was no plagiarism, that none of the
defendants copied from the play "Catchpole,"
that the plaintiff was not deprived of his
rights, and that the defendants are entitled
to a judgment dismissing the complaint on the
merits. The foregoing shall constitute the
Court's findings of fact and conclusion of

- 17 -

law in accordance with Fed. Rules Civ.

Proc. 52(a), 28 U.S.C.   A decree, in accord-

ance with these findings, may be settled on

notice.

Frank Harlan McIntyre

U.S.D.J.

THIS BOOK WAS SET IN

BASKERVILLE AND AIRPORT DISPLAY TYPES

AND BOUND BY

AMERICAN BOOK—STRATFORD PRESS, INC.

IT WAS PRINTED BY

MAHONY & ROESE, INC.

TYPOGRAPHY AND DESIGN ARE BY

LARRY KAMP